Brethren

Other books by the author

Blood Is Thicker Than Water
Love & Benjamins

Brethren
Raised By Wolves
Volume One

W.A. Hoffman

ALIEN
PERSPECTIVE

Aurora, Colorado

This book is a work of fiction written for the purposes of entertainment. Though some personages mentioned herein were actual people, their personification in this story is purely of the author's fabrication and not meant to reflect in any way upon the original individuals. Readers interested in separating relative truth from fiction in regard to the historical people, events, or social structures portrayed in this novel are invited to read the resource material listed in the bibliography and make their own determinations.

Brethren: Raised By Wolves, Volume One
First Trade Edition - Published 2006
Printed in the United States and United Kingdom by Lightning Source

Published by:
Alien Perspective
4255 S. Buckley Rd., #127
Aurora, CO, 80013
www.alienperspective.com
info@alienperspective.com
1-866-GOALIEN

ISBN13 - 978-0-9721098-2-6
ISBN10 - 0-9721098-2-X
Library of Congress Control Number: 2006920249

Dedication

This book and its brothers have been labors of love and faith, made possible by the following people. I dearly wish to thank:

My husband, John, for being my matelot through thick and thin, artistic despair and ecstasy, and for richer or poorer. Thank you for loving me. I could not do it without you.

Barb, my editor and bestest writing buddy ever, for her unflagging optimism and encouragement, loving critiques, and eagle eye. Thank you for helping me look good.

My mother, for teaching me how to dream and always reach for what I want. My brother, for being my biggest fan. My sister, for her love and support. My father, for teaching me to think and judge for myself. I am very grateful I was not raised by, or with, wolves or sheep.

Jim, for his enthusiasm and faith in this project. Maggie, Adam, and Bryan, for reading every revision I threw at them, and still continuing to give me feedback. And all of the other people who have read my work, either this piece or others, and offered their support and encouragement. Thank you all.

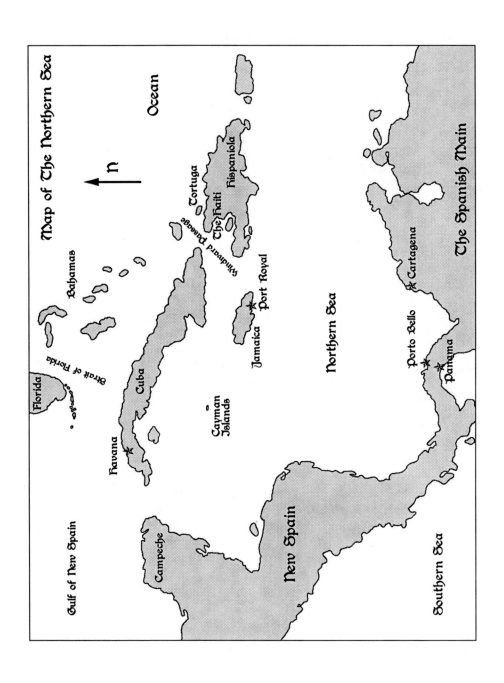

Map of The Northern Sea

Ocean

Bahamas

n

Tortuga

Hispaniola

The Haiti

Windward Passage

Florida

Strait of Florida

Port Royal

Gulf of New Spain

Havana

Cuba

Jamaica

Cayman Islands

Northern Sea

Cartagena

Porto Bello

The Spanish Main

Campeche

Panama

New Spain

Southern Sea

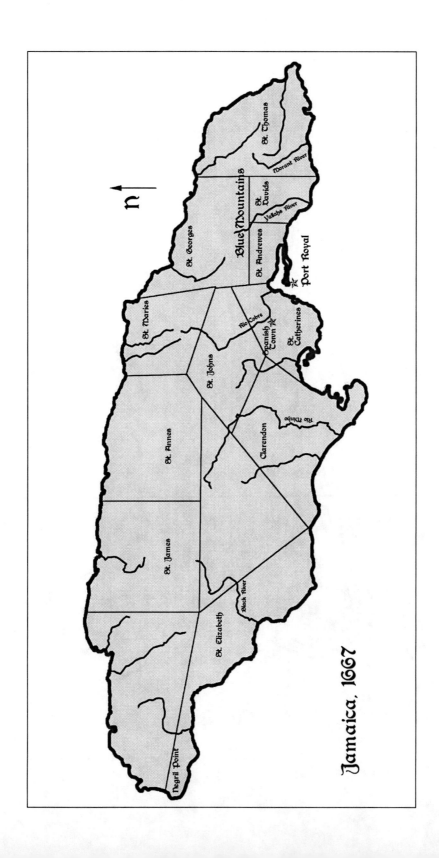

Jamaica, 1667

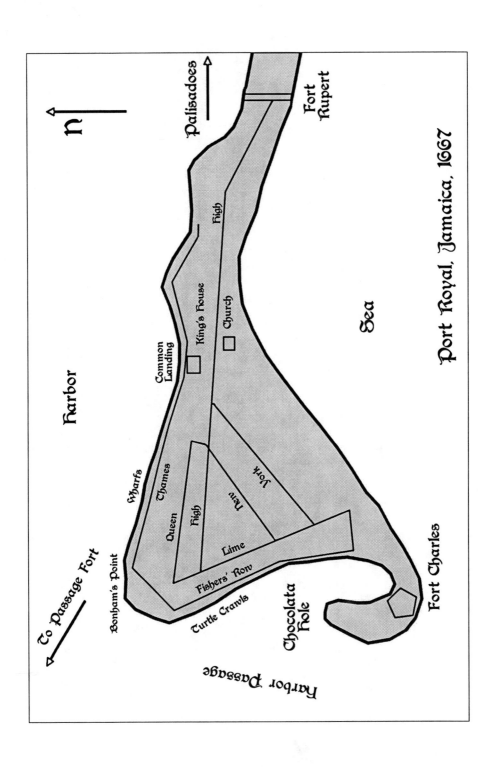

Port Royal, Jamaica, 1667

Table of Contents

Florence

September
1666

I

One

Wherein I Take My Leave
of Florence and Love

"Ulysses, are you prepared?" Alonso asked as he joined me.

"How do I appear?" I asked, turning from the wall mirror with a flourish. "Do I look the part of an English barbarian fool who some beleaguered and cultured denizen of Florence has attempted to dress?" I knew well that I did, and that it was less an act and more a truth than I often wish to own.

Alonso chuckled. "Perfectly. I could not envision a better representation of such a thing than you embody now. Your attire is expensive, though a trifle plain."

I shrugged. I have never been one to cater to the fashion of the day. I suppose it has much to do with being raised during the Reformation. Though I am not a Protestant, my constant exposure to stolid black and brown during my youth left me ever ill-prepared for the colorful and ostentatious attire worn by all other men of means in Christendom. Though the cut of my clothing was as it should be for a wealthy denizen of Florence, I had chosen not to have my garments embellished with all the bows and feathers Alonso wore.

He was, as always, far more resplendent than I; though this would be true even if he stood there naked. His mahogany mane was naturally wavy, and curled quite obediently in the humid air. The feathers in his hat did not even droop, but sat at just the correct jaunty angle. I felt like some poor, pale, and bony relation from the distant north. It was worse when we shared a bed.

He crossed his arms and put two fingers to his lips as he perused me. He gestured with them as he spoke. "That blue silk does truly match your eyes."

I looked down at my silk jerkin and breeches. They were a vibrant azure. I had been quite taken with the color when our tailor showed me the fabric. And though I knew my eyes were blue, and had occasionally seen them clearly in particularly fine mirrors, I still found it difficult to believe they were the shade of my attire.

"And the servants have done wonders with your hair," Alonso continued. "I did not think that straw you carry about on your head could be made to curl."

I had not either, and I was well pleased with the result. I fingered my curling tresses and snorted. "Caterina has expressed an interest in my locks precisely because they are the color of straw and not dark. Or as she said, they glow like spun gold in candlelight. Of course, she was a bit drunk at the time." I shrugged. "All my wigs are dark. I am thankful I have not been tempted to cut my hair of late. If I had, Gregorio would not have had so much to work upon. Still, you should applaud me for suffering hours of his ministrations in the name of tonight's business."

Alonso smiled and awarded me a polite clap. "You suffer so for the cause. I am sure Caterina will be truly dazzled by your golden locks. That is, if she is not blinded by that sword. Good God, Uly, could you find a gaudier weapon? It is irony at its finest. It is so appallingly encrusted with jewels and filigree as to appear unusable."

I drew the sword and handed it to him. He tested the weight of the blade.

"This is actually a fine weapon," he remarked. "Well balanced indeed. It is a damn shame it is so pretty."

I rolled my eyes. The hilt of his sword was well worked in gold, with rubies set in the pommel. It matched the buckles on his shoes and the pendant nestled in the ornate lace of his collar. He was calling the kettle black indeed.

"It will serve me well, and I do not mind drawing attention to it," I said of the sword. "Or losing it, as I will surely do this night. If your plan comes to pass, and I am actually perceived as a lovestruck barbarian swain, then it is fitting that I should be such a fool as to have spent all of my money on a gaudy and unusable sword. Though after three years here, much of it so obviously in the company of our fair patroness, I am sure I am well enough known that the ruse you have concocted should be nigh impossible for any but the naïve to swallow. So, if my reputation precedes me, as it often does, at least with this weapon they will not think I have come to duel this night."

He returned the sword with a bow and a smile. "Forgive me, my fair Ulysses, for assuming you had not put much thought into the matter."

I snorted. "Si, it is a rare thing indeed, my thinking." Though he thought all philosophy the purview of fools and sophists, Alonso was ever chiding me and calling me a simpleton for the lack of thought I give much of my life. I prefer to live in the day at hand, and leap into opportunities as they present themselves. Alonso is more the careful sort, ever mindful of consequences.

I returned the blade to its equally ornate scabbard and stepped in to kiss him. As always, when we were not in our rooms, his dark eyes darted about to see if anyone had observed my demonstration of affection. As if anyone in Teresina's house did not know we were lovers.

With an annoyed sigh, I went to the parlor's sidebar and poured us wine. He joined me; his arm stole around my waist.

"I worry when you do that," he whispered.

I stifled another sigh and said gently, "Alonso, I am not naïve, or blind. I know you are anxious of it. I am sorry I troubled you." The last was a trifle more acerbic than I intended.

"Consider it flattery," I added quickly in a milder tone. "Occasionally I am not content to merely gaze upon your beauty."

He rolled his eyes and awarded me a kiss to savor.

"I am sorry; I simply do not understand how you can be so free about it," he whispered when at last our lips parted.

"Why not? I have nothing to lose. And do you truly feel everything you do here will be reported to Madrid? You are working for a courtesan. I should think that would carry more familial reprisal than taking a man into your bed."

He dissembled like a boy with a hand in the sweets tin. "I do not see us as working for her."

"Si, she merely provides us with a house for some philanthropic purpose of her own." I clinked my glass to his and drank. I grinned. "Something of a wayfarer's shelter for the rogue sons of noblemen."

"What is this about rogues?" Teresina asked in Latin as she swept across the room. Her Castilian was not excellent, but proficient enough for her to hear or comprehend what she wished or needed. This had proven an embarrassment on occasion, as Alonso and I usually spoke Castilian with one another so as not to be understood.

She was resplendent in a gown of patterned silk, with enough jewels in her intricately-piled chestnut hair and around her long white throat to ransom a prince, which I suppose in some way they may have. She was far more beautiful than her accoutrements, though. Venus had truly smiled upon Teresina.

She gave me a warm kiss and then had another for Alonso. I watched them together with desire. In an unusual turn of events, her only business at the ball was to escort us, so perhaps she could be enticed to welcome us into her boudoir this night. It had been months since the three of us cavorted together. It had been weeks since I had been alone with her, though I did not oft expect it. Her time was taken with men who brought her baubles, land, and power. I was thankful she took the services I rendered her as coin enough to spare me her attention on occasion. I did not begrudge her this. It was the way of her livelihood.

She took Alonso's right hand and my left, and stepped back to the length of our arms to regard us critically. She smiled approval and then raised an eyebrow.

"Uly, that sword is... truly... ornate. For you," she added quickly after glancing at Alonso's.

I chuckled and went to sprawl across an overstuffed brocade chair. "The tragedy is it is actually a fine blade. I asked the smith why he designed it so, and he told me he had made it unadorned, but then some rake had asked for one with this type of working and he had not had another blade ready. So he did this, much to his chagrin. The miracle is that he was still able to balance it. Then the damned rake did not return to purchase it, despite having given a retainer for its completion. Our thought was that the fool lost his life dueling with another ostentatious piece of work that was not really a sword underneath. So I found it perfect for my purposes, and he was relieved to be rid of it. Who am I to refuse a gift from the Gods?"

"Ahhh," Alonso moaned, and pinched the bridge of his nose as he always did when annoyed. I had taken to imagining him tightening some little lock there to keep the anger in. "Ulysses, do not blaspheme."

Teresina threw her head back and laughed.

"Alonso," I chided. "We have discussed this many times. I do not believe in the Gods of the Romans. Like many a cynical Roman and Greek, I merely ascribe their names to the whimsy of fate and providence."

"Most would assign the name of God to His work," Alonso replied with a stern demeanor. He truly did worry about such things.

"However trivial..." I sighed. "I would not imagine He spares much time for me. He has kings and popes to advise, does He not?"

"Uly, I fear you will suffer eternal damnation," Alonso said.

"And you with me. Unless, of course, you Papists are correct, and you can truly be shriven of all your sins on your death bed. I cannot see how any God that created leprosy would be so magnanimous."

His stolid stance and glare were nicely juxtaposed by the cascade of Teresina's laughter. I gave him my best smile, which many call boyish. He did not return it.

"Oh, Alonso," Teresina said. "He only says such things to rile you."

"That is true. While I do believe such things, I only speak of them to rile you. If you were not so amusing when angry, I would not bother." I laughed.

He relented with a languid roll of his eyes. "I do not wish to speak on the matter again, or hear it spoken of." This was not the first time our discussion of this topic, jesting or otherwise, had ended with that pronouncement. And I would respect his wishes on the matter, until the next time I felt compelled to needle him.

Two of Teresina's girls joined us, and we were now fully assembled. Alonso and I would ride, and they would take the carriage. It was unlikely that if everything went as planned we would be leaving with the ladies. I gave the livery boy a coin, and Hercules, my black Moorish stallion, a kind word and a treat. Alonso mounted his grey gelding without comment. I was not sure if he was still angry with me, or whether he was annoyed that I was doting upon my horse again.

We rode ahead. Even though the streets of Florence have been paved for centuries and are not prone to dust, I despise riding behind a carriage. I do not like having my pace constrained by the decisions of the driver and exigencies of the road. I wished I had time to take Hercules on a pleasant run through the countryside to soothe our spirits.

As we crossed the Ponte Vecchio, the setting September sun bathed the Arno red beneath us. The bloody river flowing into the coming night beckoned to my soul, and I steered aside and stopped to allow Teresina's baroccio to pass.

"Is something amiss?" the footman asked as they went by.

"No, no, it is just..." I sighed. Were they blind? The scene before us was spectacular. I could not look away and ride on without savoring it for a moment. "Go along, I will be with you shortly," I called above the clatter of hooves on brick.

Alonso was beside me a moment later. "Why do you do this?"

"Watch sunsets?" I queried without turning.

"Worry me."

"My dear Alonso, I was engaging in this night's activities for years before I was graced with knowledge of your existence. Why do you fret so?"

"There is much at stake."

I chuckled. "All the more reason to watch the sunset then, is there not?"

He sighed and settled into his saddle. "What are your thoughts?"

"Amusing things you do not wish to discuss. I am gripped by this scene of unfathomable beauty before us, and I find myself wondering whether it is a thing without meaning that would occur with or without my observance of it. Or whether it is a thing the ancients would have deemed a portent sent by the Gods, or God. What does a blood-red river flowing into the west mean to one such as me? There are the obvious associations, to be sure. However, I do not believe that the gods and goddesses potentially involved in the delivery of omens would be so simple, much less direct, in their message. Gods are supposed to be mysterious and fickle entities."

He sighed heavily.

I echoed it. "And I am not saying this to rile you. You asked my thoughts."

He turned his handsome countenance skyward. I knew many a sculptor in Florence would find God's blessing in being able to recreate the planes of his face in that pose of heavenly supplication. I knew, because occasionally I suffered from delusions of having an artistic bent and wished to portray Alonso in marble or on canvas myself. At the moment I was less interested in him, though, and wished to embarrass myself with paints in an attempt to capture the sunset before us for posterity. I turned back to the river. The sun had sunk farther, and the Arno was no longer red. The spell was broken. I urged Hercules forward, and he eagerly complied. Alonso quickly came alongside.

The sunset image continued to burn in my mind.

"You came as I did to a city renowned for its art," I teased, "and yet you seem to care not for beauty when God visits it upon you." Alonso had not come to Florence for its art, though I had.

"I do not possess your artistic soul," he said quietly. The words were almost lost in the clatter of hooves as we trotted to catch Teresina's carriage. I heard them, though, and recognized them for what they were, which was as much of an apology as I would receive. "I do not understand you," he added with vigor and volume.

"No, and I am pleased. If you did, you would cast me off, as you do all things you grow bored with."

My words apparently gave him pause, as he reined his horse in. We had closed on the baroccio, and as the vehicle pulled away again I saw the footman reward us with the exasperated look servants always adopt when their masters are behaving oddly. I grinned and waved at him before I turned to rejoin Alonso, who sat staunchly in the middle of the road. He was soon to be run over by the next carriage. I motioned for him to move aside, and we cleared the way. Once we were somewhat safe, I glanced about to see what else might have caught his attention; but there was nothing. His gaze remained steadfast on my person. I gave him a quizzical look.

"You drive me to abstraction," he muttered.

"I am even more pleased." I grinned. "As you are often so anchored in the firmament."

"Uly, please be serious."

Teresina's baroccio was pulling into the palace gates well ahead of us; but I waited and regarded Alonso in somewhat patient silence. He was watching the other guests pass us by. When he did not speak, I asked pleasantly, "Alonso, what am I to be serious about?"

"Do you truly feel I would cast you aside so easily?"

"Alonso, do not behave like a bleeding twit if you wish me to be serious about the night's endeavor."

His shoulders stiffened, but his face was calm. "I am concerned."

"Have you been visited by dire portents?"

"No, I was... realizing how much I would miss you if..." He looked away.

I dearly wanted to embrace him. I had not expected such words. Yet I forced myself to merely smile lightly and say, "Let us get this night's work behind us, then retire to the house with a bottle."

He nodded and urged his horse between a set of carriages. I quickly followed him. We stayed clear of the baroccios and their alighting passengers at the steps, riding further into the courtyard to dismount and hand our horses to the livery boys. I passed a coin to the lad who took Hercules' reins, and bade him care well for the animal. The boy smiled and bowed with sincerity; Alonso rewarded me with a frown and an annoyed shake of his head. I grinned as I followed him through the battleground of arriving vehicles. He never understood my generosity with servants; he was a true wolf, and viewed all things created by God as existing for his convenience and little more. It was a sad philosophy, and I often tried to relieve him of its constraints.

In surveying the arrivals, I decided that anyone of any import in Florence was in attendance tonight. I remarked for Alonso alone, "You know, all who live here have told me that their beloved Florence is well past her prime, that she saw the flower of her glory a good century ago. However, I find it difficult to give credence to such dour pronouncements on nights such as this, when her entire populace seems to have arrived rolled in gold and splendor."

Alonso shrugged. "I wonder how it seemed when she was in her prime."

Teresina waited for us on the steps. She, of course, did not appear to be awaiting us. Teresina is a creature of appearances, and waiting upon men is not an image her reputation could bear. So she was deeply engaged in conversation with a wealthy widow, the Baronessa di Pantaglia, who was of sufficient status not to fear being seen conversing with a courtesan. This stratagem worked well for all of the parties involved. It gave the widow the opportunity to eye Alonso and myself appreciatively, Teresina the leisure to wait upon us without appearing to do so, and we tardy boys the chance to escape a scolding from our patroness. Of the utmost importance, though, we gained the additional piece on the board I had been hoping for: an unescorted woman who would be announced upon entry.

Raven-sharp eyes were everywhere, hungry for gossip and any scrap of drama. We had stepped onto the stage the moment we entered the palace courtyard. I maneuvered beside the Baronessa and commented, "It is indeed a regrettable situation when a woman of your grace, beauty, and stature should arrive at such a fête unescorted."

She was amused by my overture, and not at all naïve. "I would be delighted to have a fine young gentleman as escort. I have not danced in..." She paused and smiled demurely. "Let us say it has been far longer than I am willing to own."

"I will be honored to escort you and share the floor with a lady who has practiced more than once or twice," I said.

She laughed and took my arm. And so I entered the soiree with a woman of sufficient status to be announced as we entered the hall. The moment her name was called out, several hundred eyes were upon us. I was assured the individuals I had business with tonight were aware of my presence, without my having to seek them out or do more to attract their attention.

Alonso followed with Teresina on his arm. It would have been exceedingly unacceptable for Teresina to be announced, but of course she did not require it. A ripple of eye flicks and whispers spread through the ballroom as she made her entrance.

The Baronessa led us through the crowd, greeting this person and that. She was gracious in her introductions, treating me as if I were what I actually am, a nobleman's legitimate son and heir, and not what she thought me to be: an English noble's bastard turned rogue. Though I must admit the rogue appellation would be correct in either opinion of my person. She was a handsome woman who carried her years gracefully, as they had not been harsh to her in the slightest. I found I enjoyed her company, and I was almost loathe to go about my business. As we parted, I vowed to call on her, and she seemed pleased with my offer and all it might imply.

I had sighted my quarry, Caterina Garibaldi, shortly after my arrival an hour ago. She had maneuvered to stay within sight, and appeared relieved when I broke away from the widow. I went to make casual greeting, and found us under the watchful gaze of her cousins. This was as planned. I enjoy predictable people almost as much as I enjoy unpredictable ones. I made a clumsy go of surreptitiously suggesting that Caterina meet me in the gardens. She nervously agreed, her darting eyes ringing in her intent like the bells of a cathedral heralding mass. I was pleased with her.

Venus had not smiled upon Caterina, merely smirked. The young lady possessed all the features of an attractive woman, but they did not work in concert to provide her with beauty in form, body, or air. If matters were not as they were, I would not have given the girl a second glance. Yet, as matters were as they were, I had paid her great heed at all of our prior encounters. I had even gone so far as to intimate she was the beauty of any given soiree. My lingering glances, dancing, courteousness, and attentiveness had taken their toll. I was sure she would meet me in the gardens in an hour as I wished, even though she was betrothed to Giancarlo Damazza, the nephew of one of Florence's wealthiest and most influential citizens.

While awaiting the appointed time, I sought out Alonso and the other young men of our acquaintance, where they were smoking on the balcony. I pretended to consume far more alcohol than many would consider prudent. Alonso pulled me aside to discuss the matter, and made a show of removing the bottle from my hand.

"Oh, stop, I am not drunk," I complained loudly, as if I were indeed intoxicated.

He towed me farther from the others, making a greater show of trying to quiet me. Once we were far enough removed to be able to speak in private, he grinned slyly. "And?"

"She is well hooked," I said quietly in Castilian. "We will meet at the clock's strike in the gardens." I grinned.

The tension left his shoulders, and he took a long pull of wine.

"I think I will pay the Baronessa a call," I said.

He rolled his eyes. "Uly, why?"

"She is a most pleasant lady, and I feel she has been too long without a good tumble. It is the least I can do in repayment of her unwitting assistance this night."

He shook his head and grinned. "You are an incorrigible philanthropist."

"You say that as if it reflects poorly on my character," I teased. I moved closer and pulled the bottle away in an unsteady manner, so that I lost my balance and leaned into him. Pretending embarrassment, I stepped back too quickly, and was forced to grab his arm to steady myself. He gave me a warning glare. I smirked and drained the bottle.

"Uly, you are so convincing at playing the fool you often sway me." His eyes were filled with admiration, and I laughed at his compliment, even though I bridled a little at the actual meaning. I knew his words to be true; he did often fall for my acts, though not always the ones he was aware of. However, after two and a half years, I felt he should know me well enough not to fall for the masks I showed the world.

I was almost distracted into sobriety by the arrival of Giancarlo Damazza on the balcony. He was with his older cousin, Vincente, who was the son of the wealthiest man in Florence. Even though the ball was not in his honor, Vincente was the reason of all of my night's activities. For Alonso and me, he was the focal point of several months' worth of work.

Vincente noticed my gaze. The guilt he may have seen in my eyes was sincere. I made little attempt to hide it. Then I made a show of nervously glancing at his cousin and slipping away.

Caterina met me in the gardens. We walked among roses, and flirted around the marble pillars of the galleria. I played the gallant swain who was too intoxicated with both wine and love to resist my infatuation. She played, with all sincerity, the blushing maiden who was too excited by the prospect of dallying with one of Teresina's boys to recall she was betrothed.

On the pretext of showing me a flower she plucked, she darted in and pecked my check quite sweetly. As we were still surprisingly alone, I decided to amuse myself by teaching the girl to kiss; and I swept her into my arms and claimed her mouth. Her initial modest protest smothered, she surrendered to passion, and the lesson proceeded smoothly enough to garner the heretofore missing interest on the part of my manhood.

This pleasantness was interrupted by a great deal of commotion, as Giancarlo and his companions finally found us. I looked over Caterina's head and past the apoplectic rage of her betrothed, to find Alonso playing the part of the placating friend and attempting to make excuses on my behalf to Vincente. The stage was set and the cast had arrived.

I feigned drunken shock and surprise at Giancarlo's presence and rage.

"Good sir," I sputtered in English, and then switched to Latin. "Good sir, this is not as it appears," I avowed loudly, with the appropriate slurring, while still clutching the horrified girl.

"Release her! Release her at once!" Giancarlo bellowed. He was a boy of slight build and a braying voice, and it was rather like being confronted by a belligerent goat. I let Caterina go; she slumped to her knees between us, sobbing and clutching at Giancarlo's breeches. Everyone ignored her, except for one of her brothers, who quickly pulled her to her feet and out of the way.

"I fear I..." I began.

"Fear, yes, you have much to fear, sir. I demand satisfaction," Giancarlo brayed. Vincente stepped forward and placed a restraining hand on Giancarlo's sword arm; but the boy would have none of it, and shook him off with vigor.

"I understand, good sir," I said with as much dignity as a supposedly intoxicated Englishmen should have been able to muster. "Please name a time and place."

"Now!" the lad yelled.

It was as I had hoped.

"I s-s-s-ee, with what weapon...?" I stammered and checked to ensure I was wearing a sword with a fumbling hand. His hand was already on his hilt. I watched in amazement as he drew.

He was truly enraged beyond reason, and had no intention of following any of the proper etiquette for a duel. This was better than I had hoped. The other men stepped back. Alonso was giving me a worried look, and I gave him the subtlest of shrugs. I was not truly concerned. I had seen the boy practice with the sword, and he had of course never seen me do the same. This was better than pistols; once a bullet was involved, there was at least the remote possibility that the idiot would injure me. With swords, there was little probability of my suffering a wound at all, unless I wished it or the Gods took a sudden disinterest in my person.

I pulled as quickly as I dared without revealing that I was not intoxicated, and blocked his first rush, making sure I stumbled back. The fight continued on this way, with me swinging as badly as he, and both of us gaining and retreating in a seemingly haphazard manner around the pillars of the galleria, until I marked the position of everyone present and developed a plan. I began to drive him in the desired direction.

When he tripped on a broken tile, I pressed on with a drunken rush that brought us toward Vincente and Alonso. My excellent fortune held out, and Giancarlo tripped again, toward his cousin, who felt obliged to catch him. A sober man in a serious duel would have stopped and allowed his opponent and a non-combatant to recover. I kept charging; and a moment later I ran Vincente through, seemingly by drunken accident in the heat of combat. It was nearly perfect. Unfortunately, Giancarlo was not aware of this, and was still flailing about with his weapon. I was forced to block with my arm, getting myself badly cut in the process.

Then all was silence as everyone, including the now-cognizant Giancarlo, watched Vincente slump to the ground with my sword in his chest. Giancarlo dropped his weapon and stepped away, as another of their cousins checked Vincente's condition. Alonso rushed to my aid and wrapped a kerchief around my wound. Caterina's wails were smothered by one of her brothers. The man kneeling next to Vincente raised his eyes to Giancarlo, and shook his head sadly. I gasped in feigned horror, and stumbled forward to check the body myself. Vincente was quite dead. Our job here was done. It was time to leave.

"Oh my God, please forgive me," I said quietly and stood.

Giancarlo would not meet my gaze; but the man who had checked the body regarded me with sympathy and whispered, "It was an accident. All here saw that."

I looked around, and found myself regarding Federico, Vincente's younger brother and the man who would now inherit their father's fortune. Federico was tractable and manageable in all the ways his brother Vincente had not been. Once their father passed, his power would be in the hands of Federico; and the boy would be in the hands of the individuals who had asked Teresina to task Alonso and myself with this little drama. Federico's eyes were filled with rage and sorrow. He had been quite fond of his brother, and was not at all aware of the plot he was now in questionable benefit of.

"I am sorry," I breathed.

"I cannot accept that," Federico whispered. I wanted to laugh at the irony.

The other man stepped between us. "It was an accident." He looked over his shoulder at me. "You should leave."

I nodded mutely, and allowed Alonso to help me retreat. We quickly skirted the building and made the courtyard to retrieve our horses. Within the hour, we were at the house Teresina had loaned us for the last two years. A surgeon had been summoned to see to my arm; and I had retired to my room to shed clothing and boots and drink in earnest while awaiting his arrival.

Vincente was not the first man I had killed for purposes other than my own. I was relatively sure he would not be the last. Since I had left my father's house, I had learned to forgive myself a good many things. Still, the initial guilt was strong, and I wanted nothing more than to drown it before it pulled me into the murky depths of melancholy.

Teresina and Alonso joined me. She was still in her gown and dripping jewels, but he had shed his jerkin. She gave me a deep kiss filled with promise, as all her kisses were. It did not drive the darkness away.

"Alonso said you were magnificent as always." She smiled beautifically as she sat on the footstool and arranged her skirts.

I had planned and executed the deaths of three men at her request. I had not done it because of her exquisite bone structure, or the bewitching conformation of the curves of her breast and hip. I did not do it because she occasionally granted me the privilege of her bed, or because she had taught me things I had not dreamed were knowable in the pleasing of myself or others. I did not do it because she provided me with a house, servants, horses, weapons, clothing, and anything else I might fancy in order to live at the level of comfort I was born to. I did not do it because she was one of the more formidable powers in Florence, and crossing her meant certain death or destruction. No, I did it because I loved her. Even though I well knew that loving her was lunacy of a high order.

Teresina did not love. She doted, nurtured, befriended, and adored on occasion, but she did not love. Yet any man in her presence understood why a man would dash himself against the rocks of her fortitude for even the hope of entrance into her heart – even while any wise man knew that it was probably a barren place to obtain, and the journey was worth far more than the arrival. I am the sort of man who enjoys journeys and romantic notions and idealistic foolishness, and so I loved her.

Gazing upon her now did not make Vincente's death taste any better, but it did make it easier to swallow.

She leaned forward and took my hand. "Uly, my love." She paused and sighed. There was such sadness in her eyes.

My breath held in my chest, and fear clutched at my bowels.

"What is wrong?" I whispered.

"You need to leave Florence now. All are saying Vincente's death was an accident. Yet you are still responsible. If you stay, I will be forced to deliver you up to appease the father's anger. I would rather miss you than lose you."

My heart thudded painfully, as it understood her words far more readily than my flailing mind did. I was unable to speak or move, except for my eyes. I looked to Alonso, hoping he would make a lie of her words. I wished to see him grinning as if this were some grand jest they had concocted. Alonso did not appear surprised, and his eyes were sympathetic. He had known.

"Ulysses, you knew this day would come," Teresina said softly.

This was true. I forced myself to breathe and smile.

"Lady, I know death will come but I avoid it because I can rationally foresee the devastation it will wreak upon my life. Yet after death, I will be beyond this mortal coil, and either in eternal pleasure or damnation. This thing that you do is worse than death, as it will leave me alive and in a perpetual state of agony. You may as well cast me into Hell."

She shook her head with a sad smile. "Uly, if you feel this is Heaven... well, then, how very little you expect of perfection."

I chuckled. "I strive to ask little of life in order to avoid disappointment." I studied her. "There is truly no other way?"

She shook her head again.

"You knew this was the outcome." I was not asking; I was merely stating what all in the room now knew, now that I had achieved some degree of understanding. I felt betrayed. Yet I wondered what I would have done differently, if I had known; perhaps devised a strategy that would have accomplished the objective without our involvement being known. Why had no one suggested that very thing?

In answer to my statement and the questions she must have guessed at, she squeezed my hand. "Please do not hate me."

She wanted me to leave. She was through with me. I managed to say, "At the moment I do not feel that is possible. I cannot offer guarantee as to my future feelings, though."

Now I wanted her to go. I did not want her to witness my pain and anger. She had suddenly and inexplicably become the enemy. I marveled that her eyes still seemed sincere.

"Go home, Uly. Regain your father's good grace, marry, have children, and then make some courtesan a very happy woman." Her features settled into resignation, and she stood with a tired sigh. "You are free to do anything your heart desires. Make yourself happy." She leaned down to kiss my cheek. I did not try to touch her, even though her words had squashed my anger.

"You can leave here," I said as she walked to the door.

She turned to regard me sadly. "No, I cannot." She held up a hand to stifle my protest. "I do not wish to leave," she added.

Without doubt, I knew she lied. I wanted to know who I had to kill to release her, what walls I had to tear down to set her free. There was so much sincerity in her lie, though, that I could not battle it. I was overcome with helplessness, and I did not feel I could battle that, either.

"I will miss you."

She appeared relieved at my words. "I have brought money to provide for your journey."

"I do not..."

"I know."

I sighed. "There is one thing I would have of you."

"If I am able," she said.

"That." I pointed at the portrait of her on the wall. It was one of the last paintings my beloved Joseph had done. It was as tall as I, and I did not know how I would transport it if we were on the road. "Please keep it safe until I can send for it."

She nodded and smiled. She gave Alonso a parting look, and I realized they had already said their farewells. Then she was gone.

I sat watching the door where she had stood. I did not want to think. I did not want to converse with Alonso. I did not want to exist in this moment in time. I wanted to be far away, and all of this only a passing memory.

The surgeon arrived. Alonso handed me a goblet as the man examined the wound. After a night of pretending to be intoxicated, I wanted desperately to drink myself blind. I gasped in pain at the man's prodding, and realized I would not manage to become inebriated enough to dull the wound or my heart before I would be forced to experience their agony. I could still make the attempt, though.

So I drank wine and let Alonso hold my arm, while the surgeon pronounced the wound a clean slice and stitched it closed. I could not look at it myself, as I am quite squeamish when it comes to my own blood. The damned man added that there was always the possibility it might become noxious and feverish, and I could lose the arm in the end.

Finally the surgeon left, and we were alone. Alonso found another bottle on the sideboard and opened it.

"I did not expect it all to end so soon," he said in Castilian.

At first I thought he meant the bottle in my hand. I was pleased I had already managed such stupefaction. Then I knew what he truly meant, and I felt he was lying. He had obviously thought it would end much sooner than I had. I was not drunk enough to escape just yet.

"I am beginning to feel a trifle bitter," I said carefully. "I am sure it will become a raging torrent of righteous indignation all too soon. How long have you known?"

"Since she asked us to perform the task," he said with an apologetic shrug.

I glared at him.

"Uly, you are truly brilliant when it comes to strategy, but you never consider the consequences past the problem at hand. You are always living in the day, and never thinking about the future. I have been thinking about the future a great deal lately."

There he was, saying it again. And there he was, being ever so correct yet again. He would never understand that tonight's events were why I do not think about the future. If I did, I would fear things such as had transpired.

"I am proud of you," I muttered.

"Uly, please, we need to talk now."

"Alonso, I feel betrayed, and used, and discarded."

"We are the tools, not the tool users."

"I do not wish to be either, but I suppose the only other alternative within the human milieu is to become a sheep."

He raised a curious eyebrow.

"We are wolves," I said, happy to ramble about something and nothing in an effort to think nothing or something. "We were raised by wolves to be wolves. We are members of the aristocracy, despite whatever condition we may find ourselves in over the course of our lives. It is in our blood, and etched upon our minds and probably even our souls. We are destined and designed for lives of power and privilege. We rule over sheep."

"So noblemen are wolves and peasants sheep?" he asked.

I frowned. "No, nobility does not make a wolf, but wolves are most often nobles and peasants are most often sheep. A wolf will seize power if he is not granted it by birth, and fight like a demon to keep it. They can see no other way to live. Sometimes one finds wolves in sheep's clothing, acting timid and allowing themselves to be herded.

But in their hearts, they are wolves and expect to be allowed to act like sheep. On the other side of the fence, sheep do not believe they have the right to expect any such thing, such as being allowed to act like a wolf. Occasionally you get a very bully sheep who does think like a wolf, in which case a wolf they become; and they are no longer a sheep, no matter what skin they may don."

He was grinning at me mischievously. "So, a sheep can become a wolf, but a wolf cannot become a sheep."

"Correct, it would be akin to stuffing the chick back into the egg."

"So you feel the natural order is for sheep to become wolves."

"Si, if they are able. Everyone wants to be a wolf, if they are intelligent enough to understand what being a wolf means. Many sheep think the thing that separates them from the wolves is gold, or blood, but they are wrong. Sheep and wolves are different because wolves have big teeth and fangs and eat sheep and they know it. Sheep do not eat wolves. It is a state of mind. It is a thing of assigning primacy to one's own well-being above all other things, including the lives of others."

"So you cannot become a sheep by your own admission."

"True. I am a wolf without a pack."

"Are you sure you have no pack?" he asked kindly.

"I do not know. It has been ten years now since I departed. Perhaps."

"I did not mean in England."

I regarded him with a twinge of guilt as I grasped his meaning. "No, I am not sure I have no pack. Yet, I am not sure I have one, either. One I counted amongst its number walked out that door not long ago."

He moved closer, and his fingers traced my cheek. "Abandoning you is not my intent."

"What, then? Where shall we go? If you have known, you, who think about the future, must have some plan in mind. So where? Will Venice or Rome be safe? Genoa? I have only been away from Vienna these three years, and I feel that is not sufficient time for tempers to have cooled there. Paris, perhaps? How is your French?"

His big brown eyes managed to convey both guilt and hope. My gut clenched even tighter.

"What?" I prompted quietly.

"I have been corresponding with my family."

That was interesting. He had often told me he communicated less with them than I did with mine. And since my communication with my family was limited to an annual set of letters to my Uncle Cedric and my former tutor, Rucker, Alonso's frequency and depth of discourse should have been very small indeed; but apparently not.

He sighed. "Uly, we are getting too old for this life. I will have thirty years soon, and you have what, twenty-seven?"

"Twenty-six," I said flatly. I was visited by the impression that he had rehearsed this speech many times.

"You are the eldest son and heir of the Earl of ..." he frowned.

"Dorshire." I did not fault him on not remembering; I spoke little of it and thought on it less. "I am John Williams, Viscount of Marsdale, and heir to the Earl of Dorshire." I had not felt myself to be my father's heir since I left his house in the middle of the night; but while I lived, I surely was. Unless I had been disinherited, of course.

Alonso nodded. "Unlike you, I am not the eldest son; yet I believe I have duties to my family, and to myself. I have given it great thought, and recently come to the conclusion that it is time to put aside boyish adventures and return home to the life that is expected of me."

Oddly, his words came as no surprise. Perhaps it was the wine, or perhaps I had known he would say such a thing someday.

"You said you were not abandoning me."

His eyes conveyed hope again. "I want you to accompany me."

I blinked, as he had grown foggy in my vision for a moment. "To Madrid?"

He nodded.

"Are you mad? Our nations are at war."

"I do not think so," he said with a perplexed frown.

"Perhaps not at the moment, but they are always on the brink, and nonetheless they like each other little."

"Your Castilian is excellent."

"For an Englishman. Alonso, I am blond, pale, and skinny. You are robust and swarthy."

"We have skinny and blond Spaniards."

"Do tell? Who speak Castilian like Englishmen?"

He sighed and rolled his eyes.

"I would look like a scarecrow left in the sun too long," I added.

"I did not think you would pretend to be Spanish. You have several personas, with documents."

"Si, I do." In truth I was already considering various means of enacting his plan. "I could assume an Austrian identity, unless I ran afoul of someone with an ear for languages."

He warmed to my seeming acquiescence. "We would not remain in Spain long."

"Truly? Then what?"

"My family wishes for me to join my brother in the New World and assist with our interests there. We have a plantation in Panama."

I was vaguely aware of Panama's location. I believed it to be on the Main itself and not in the West Indies. I was curious about the New World, yet there were many things troubling me. I took a long breath, relieved him of the bottle he held, and finished it.

"That is wonderful. Perhaps I shall pay you a visit, if my travels ever lead me there."

He stood with annoyance and went to the window to peer into the night, presenting me with his back.

"I thought that," he said carefully. "I knew that you would not want to leave here until forced. That is why I did not discuss it with you. I harbored the hope that you would wish to accompany me because... at least you would still have me."

I was seeing things in a truly harsh light, as I recognized his tone and gesture as one of calculation and practice. But all that really meant was that he truly wanted me to go and he was willing to play everything in his hand to achieve it.

I loved Teresina with a boyish romantic fancy. Alonso, however, had been my companion for more than two years. He was not an unreachable destination, but a fellow traveler on the journey. I studied the lines of his back and wondered how I would live without him. Alonso had been gifted by many a god: Adonis, Mars, Apollo, and even Jupiter when one considered his birthright as the son of a Spanish count. Alonso was all any man should want to be, and as such he was attractive to me in every facet. I loved Alonso in a manner that I would never love Teresina, or be loved by Teresina, or any woman for that matter. And I was not merely thinking of carnal delights. Alonso was a man, and I am one of those men blessed or cursed to favor men. I prefer their company, and their bodies, but mostly their company. Alonso and I had shared plans, schemes, homes, beds, weapons, jokes, friends, women, and wine. He was my lover, and brother in all but name and blood.

So there were two questions hanging betwixt us. How could I let him go without at least trying? And how could he have been so close and yet know me so little?

"And what would we do there?" I asked. "Who would I be?" My thoughts floated along in the wine, and I did not like where the river was leading. "Would I be posing as your manservant?"

He turned back to me and eagerly closed the distance between us. "It would not be like that." He did not seem convinced by his own words.

"Then how would it be, Alonso? You say I do not think things through; you are correct. Let me rectify that now. What would we do? What is this plantation like? What does it grow? Would we while away our days hunting and drinking?" Something else tickled at my mind. "What else does your family expect of you? Marriage?"

He nodded glumly. "They have already found me a wife." He threw up his hands. "But it is nothing. You know women. I will need to bed her until she gets with child, and then leave her alone until well after she births it. If I am lucky, I will only share her bed a few times a year."

"Will you be able to share mine the rest of it?" I asked.

Alonso grimaced. "Uly... You know... We would need to be discreet, even more so than here. And you do not like me to share your bed every night."

"And you would not want me chasing boys; so if I am your servant, what does that leave me, your maids?" I asked.

He was taken aback by this. I realized he had not thought everything through.

"Alonso, I have seen men like myself living lives of that nature. Always... outside... watching and waiting for their lover to come to them, when it is safe, or convenient. I do not want that."

"It will not be that way," he said doggedly; but I knew he could see what I spoke of. He knelt beside me, his face earnest. "Uly, I want you. I care for you more deeply than I ever imagined I would. And these last weeks have been very hard on me, knowing we would come to this discussion. I do not want to be without you. I am willing to do everything I can to keep us together." His eyes were pleading, moist and bright in the dim candlelight.

The wine had finally truly dulled my senses and my heart. My arm even throbbed less. I was in a distant place, observing him through a lens that brought him closer yet kept him out of reach.

"Alonso, I love you, and I will miss you terribly. Yet, I could no more live in your shadow for the rest of my existence than you could live in mine."

His shoulders tightened. Then he sighed before regarding me with a new resolve. "Maybe we could travel elsewhere, then?"

Those words pushed through the fog of wine and grasped at my heart. I found myself nodding, yet there were reservations in my soul. I could feel them rustling about, though I could not name them. It did not matter: we were beyond further discourse. He closed the final distance between us, and his lips covered mine. I returned the kiss and urged him to deepen it. When we pulled apart a breathless minute later, I whispered, "Your room."

He smiled and shrugged. I still disliked sharing a bed with anyone in the aftermath of passion, even him. I stood on shaky legs and let him lead me down the hall.

We took turns pleasuring one another for hours, until what remained of the night was spent and we along with it. He performed every trick he knew to convince me that I could not live without him. My body surrendered to his ministrations time and again, until he had verily wrung me dry more times than I could remember. I even allowed him to do that which he always most desired and I usually refused. With my ankles on his shoulders, I watched him through the haze of pain, both real and remembered. I knew he loved me, but I felt little of that lofty emotion, and it was not solely due to the wine.

At last we lay in the grey before dawn, he sleeping and I watching him, wondering how deeply asleep he truly was. I was not sure when I reached the decision, but reached it I had. It must have been the carnality; it always makes me think. He was correct. We had played the fools too long. It was time we made amends with our birthrights and accepted the yoke of duty. I would go home. I did not know what awaited me there, and perhaps I would not stay; but I would at least make the attempt.

And more important than concerns of familial honor and the like, I could not run from Shane forever. There was much to resolve. I was no longer the boy who had run away in the night. I owed it to myself to exorcise that demon.

It had taken Alonso months of patience and persistence to induce me to yield to our mutual desires and overcome the fear that haunted me. Yet finding peace in his arms had not healed me; it had only made me aware of how very wounded I still was. In some utopian version of the world that only existed in my dreams, I would return to England with Alonso, confront Shane and say, "Here, this is what it can be." But that was the stuff of fantasy, and fantasies are like brightly painted eggs. They are beautiful to consider, but if you grasp one it shatters, and you are left with a most unholy stench.

I pushed a strand of hair from Alonso's brow and told myself that it was better this way, as I would never see his beautiful body sag and turn to fat. I would not be forced to watch him wed. Or worse yet, and even more probable, watch him slip away from me in the manner of people everywhere as they grow and age. He would always be perfect in my mind as he was at this moment. Except that was not true. At the moment he was no more perfect than Teresina had been in that last conversation. I was angry, and as a result my memories of them now held a taint. I hoped that would pass.

Love, so far, had not proven to be an invincible gem of beauty, but rather an ephemeral ray of color in the morning mist, something easily seen until one turned one's head. It had not been a thing that could easily be lifted and transported in all its glory to another place or time. This wispy, momentary quality of love had permeated every relationship I dared label as love. I wondered at the words of poets and philosophers who professed of loves that transcended all earthly concerns and bound the participants with unbreakable chains of the heart. Perhaps they had only been dreaming, too.

I slipped from his bed and padded on bare feet back to my room. I almost tripped on a small bag at his door. There was another at mine, which I hefted with surprise. Teresina had been generous in funding our travel. My bag contained a fortune in florins. I was thankful, as I had little else to call my own, save my weapons and horse. I had lived ten years through the beneficence of friends and the misfortune of adversaries. Now, I supposed, I would throw myself upon my father's goodwill, as was my birthright.

I began to pack. The growing loneliness did not burn so much as it froze. I grew numb. Even though it was Alonso I was deserting, it felt as it had with many of the women I had taken as lovers. It was morning and I wanted to be away with the changing of the heavenly watch. I wanted Florence behind me, since there was nothing in it to hold me anymore. I left everything except the money, my weapons, and a few changes of warm clothing.

Many would think me mad to consider crossing Europe alone on horseback carrying a small fortune, especially while riding a fine horse. I may be rash, but I am not naïve. I would avoid the inns and well-traveled roads. The hardships of the journey would serve to buff the mettle of my soul. This would serve me well, as I would need to know what I was made of before entering my father's house again.

Less than an hour later, I sat upon Hercules and chewed the remains of my hurriedly-snatched repast. I rode to a bridge over the Arno and watched the sun rise. The angle was wrong, due to the difference in direction from the night before. The river did not glow gold as it had burned red. I rode west anyway.

Perhaps the Gods had been trying to tell me something, after all.

England

November, 1666
~ January, 1667

II

Two

Wherein I Return To England

To my dismay, I was apprised in a little market in Turin that France was at war with England. I abandoned my identity as Ulysses, adopted Austrian papers and accent, and headed for Paris anyway, as I had little recourse.

Once in that fair city, in which I had spent several years after first leaving England, I located a fine horseman I had known and made him a gift of my Moorish stallion. He was pleased to have so beautiful a horse for breeding, and I was content to know that Hercules would spend the rest of his days frolicking in green pastures and mounting mares.

I, on the other hand, was forced to make a choice between a long barge ride down the Seine to the sea, where I would have to place myself at the mercy of smugglers or pirates to reach England – or a miserable coach ride north to Antwerp to book legitimate passage across the Channel. As I knew smugglers would have little incentive not to slit my throat, even if I gave them all of my money upon boarding, I chose the least comfortable route. I bought a pillow to give some comfort to my arse, and a bottle to make the conversation and odors of my fellow passengers somewhat palatable.

I finally arrived on English soil at London in the last week of November, 1666, per the Julian calendar: which, now that I had returned to my native soil, I was forced to adopt once again. A storm had harried the crossing and it had been quite violent, remarked upon by even the sailors. The following ride up the Thames had been exceedingly wet and cold, as the storm had delivered copious amounts

of sleet. I hoped fervently I would never have to board another vessel,
but I knew that to be folly. I could not imagine staying in England for
the rest of my life, and since she was an island, some amount of sea
travel would be required to escape her yet again.

Though it was amusing and comfortable to hear and speak English
again, England was much as I had remembered: cold and wet. The sight
of London sank my spirits even further. As I traveled, I had heard that
much of London burned on September second: which had been a mere
week before I departed Florence, even with the difference in calendars.
Hearing and seeing are two very different things, though; and I was
absolutely stunned at the devastation still in evidence when I arrived
almost three months after the event.

Acres and acres of the city were missing, the buildings reduced
to heaps of rubble. I almost expected them to be still smoldering; but
no, we were well past that. Despite the missing buildings, or perhaps
because of them, the streets were filled with activity. Wagons rumbled
by, loaded with debris to be removed, while others arrived with building
supplies. Not everything was being replaced immediately, but the sound
of saws and hammers was an omnipresent din muffled by the low
clouds.

I wondered how the people who had lost everything were getting on.
I doubted the King had opened the treasury to feed and house them all.
Thankfully fewer had been displaced than might have been, due to the
plague having paid England a visit this year. The wealthy had escaped
the city to avoid the Black Death, and the poor had been decimated by
the reaper well before the fire.

All in all, I saw little of the Restoration flowering of London that
others had told me of. It was as drab and dreary as I had left it during
the Reformation.

I had known this great city. Though I had still been little more than
a youth, I had frequented London prior to my departure from England,
as our family kept a house there and Shane and I had been bored boys
with money and arrogance in abundance. We had bemoaned Cromwell's
refusal to allow truly amusing pursuits in the city, such as theater and
galleries. Well, at least I had. Shane could not have cared less for those
things. He enjoyed gambling and whoring far more than art. Still, even
without advertised sources for boyish amusements, we had oft managed
to find enough trouble and debauchery to keep ourselves entertained.

I bought a bay mare of a pleasant disposition and, after wandering a
bit, managed to locate the place where I believed our family's townhouse
had stood. Without any remembered landmarks, it took me a good deal
of time to locate the street and block. The three-story building was gone,
leaving nothing but a rectangle of bricks and foundation stones and
the bases of the chimneys. Apparently my father had not yet chosen to
rebuild.

I wondered at that. I could not remember when the House of Lords
met and when he would need to stay in town. I could not remember a

good many things of that nature. I had never been interested enough in them to commit them to memory.

I wondered if they were well, my father, mother, and two sisters. Had they fallen to the plague? I had written my uncle on occasion, and four times his letters had found me during my travels. The last one had been over a year ago. He had said they were well then, but regarding the devastation I rode through now, I realized how very long ago that was.

The long road across the Alps and France had awarded me ample time to wonder what I would find here, and what my reception might be. My sisters would be nineteen and seventeen years of age. I was not sure of my father's exact date of birth, but I thought he might be fifty-two. I recalled that he had remarked once that he had been twenty-six, the age I was now, when I was born. That in itself was a disturbing thought. In my mind, he was an old man now, yet what did that make me? I felt I had not aged much at all, even though I knew ten years had passed.

My second cousin, Jacob Shane, would be twenty-seven now. I could not envision him as such. To me, he was still the lad of seventeen I had last seen. And in truth, though I had thickened across the shoulders a little, I still saw myself as the scrawny boy I had been. Some of that was due to my never growing as much as I expected. My father was a large man, wide of shoulder and deep of chest, yet I took after my mother's family. They were lean and not necessarily tall.

Deep in thought, I began to ride to my uncle's house at Dunfield, a good day's journey to the north. It was late afternoon; and as I set out, the chill was already biting through my cloak and breeches. As dusk approached, I decided warmth might trump caution and I might wish to consider a room at an inn. I was no longer riding an expensive mount and my clothes were quite road-worn. I did not look wealthy in the slightest. Unfortunately, I was already following my usual habits of avoiding swashbucklers, by not traveling on the highway that ran more directly from London. The little road I was on wound through the Hertfordshire countryside, and there was not an inn in sight.

Thus, I considered myself lucky when I spied a dilapidated barn well off the road. The surrounding field was not cultivated, and I saw no houses nearby. I rode down the overgrown path cautiously and saw no one. However, I heard the rustle of movement inside the aged building after I dismounted to investigate the door. I thought it an animal, until I heard a furtive whisper. I drew both pistols and held my ground. If they wished to shoot me, they could have already done so. It seemed an unlikely place for highwaymen, anyway.

"Hello?" I queried. "I do not mean to trespass. I am merely seeking shelter for the night."

"Do not shoot," a voice said, with the awkward catch and squeak of a boy on the verge of manhood. There was a snicker and a muffled curse, followed by the unmistakable sound of flesh hitting flesh and then a squawked "ow!" A youth emerged from the canted opening between the sagging doors. He shot a glare back over his shoulder. I guessed he was the speaker, as he seemed caught somewhere betwixt boy and man.

I pointed both pistols skyward and said, "Greetings," in my friendliest voice.

"What da ya want?" the boy asked, doing his utmost to keep his voice steady.

"I am just on the road and in search of a place to spend the night. I will move on if this structure is occupied, which apparently it is."

He regarded me as if I were daft. "Where ya be headed?"

"Dunfield."

"Are ya lost? The highway be o'er yonder."

"If I were on the highway, you would be older and armed."

He considered my words and nodded thoughtfully. "Tisn't much 'ere abouts, lest ya 'ave ta hide from farmers real careful."

"Well, that is a pity," I sighed and returned the pistols to my belt. The moon was well waned, not that it would have shown through the damn clouds anyway. Riding on once night fell would be difficult. And finding a place to hide from farmers, as he suggested, would be even more so. Not that I felt great need to hide from farmers. Providing them explanation for my presence could prove tedious, though.

The boy seemed to work his courage up as the weapons were taken out of play. "Do ya 'ave food? Ta share? You can stay if'n ya 'ave victuals."

He was eyeing my horse and few bags. By the looks of his arms, which were almost skeletal, I gathered he would just as soon eat my mount as ride it.

I nodded. "I bought more provisions than I need for such a short trip. I would be happy to share in exchange for a safe place to sleep."

He understood my meaning. "We'll cause ya no trouble."

"Then we have an agreement." I eyed the building. "Is there an opening large enough for my horse?"

He shrugged and grinned. "Aye, 'alf the back wall be missin'."

With a chuckle, I led my horse round, and entered to find a band of eight boys lurking in the shadows and straw. The one I had been speaking with, Big John they called him, was the leader and the oldest. The youngest could not have been more than six or so. They were thin and barefoot, with tattered clothes. I wondered why they were not begging on a city street instead of hiding in a barn in the countryside. Then I remembered most of the city was missing, and there had been the plague.

We huddled around a small and carefully maintained fire, and supped on a pair of rabbits the boys had, and the sausage, cheese, and bread I was carrying. To pass the time, I asked why they were there. They told me a number of tales. All had been thrown out by their families, or orphaned outright by the plague or other misfortune. They huddled in this barn due to everything from the fear of press gangs to the threat of gaol or death.

I knew well enough there was no place for them. I guessed they had

brethren all over England. Times were difficult. There was little honest
employment to be had, even for those who were skilled, and people were
starving as a result. Unless a family worked the land and had need of an
extra pair of hands, young boys they could not apprentice off were not
worth feeding for many families.

I looked at the little ring of soot-smeared faces in the flicker of
firelight, and wondered what would become of them. I pondered what I
could do to aid their cause. They trusted no one, and I knew of no one I
would trust with their welfare. I was also sure they would resent, if not
rebel against, any attempt to tame them now that they had gone feral.

I dozed cautiously that night, because I knew if they were truly
cunning they would rob me in my sleep. And indeed, I found myself
being observed for a lapse in vigilance several times. Even though I was
weary to the bone, I grudgingly applauded them.

Between naps, I recalled many a thing my tutor, Rucker, had said
concerning social classes and the duties and responsibilities of nobility.
My father would have been absolutely appalled if he had ever heard
much of what Rucker imparted to my impressionable ears. I had learned
that setting wolves to guard sheep is never good for the sheep. That
lesson had been reinforced by observing and listening to my father when
he held discourse with his peers. Wolves all, they cared not for those
they governed. They made policies to suit themselves, and complained
bitterly when any attempted to defy them. Even under Cromwell, when
they had not quite maintained the power they had before, they had still
been wolves; and the structure of the government mattered little.

I had seen the workings of the nobility throughout my travels, as
I had lived amongst the courts and those that would be my peers by
station of birth. I had avoided the poor, as I had not wished to see the
effects of noble machinations. I had not wanted to see because, as with
these boys, there was nothing I could do but toss them a coin. I could
not give them all work. I could not educate them. I could not free them
from the bondage of poverty or peasantry.

In the deep hours of the night just before dawn, I was distracted
from further attempts at slumber by quiet rustling in the straw. The
noise was sustained and rhythmic, and I guessed the activity involved.
As I continued to listen, my suspicion was confirmed by a series of small
grunts followed by a cessation of all sound, except for a series of very
quiet wet kisses and a few whispered words. I knew from the location,
and his age, that one of the participants was Big John. I assumed the
other to be the next oldest boy, as they had been very close and caring
with one another throughout the meal and conversation that followed.

For a moment, the knowledge of their union filled me with aching
loneliness tinged with a bit of nostalgia. I was pleased that in their
dismal lives they at least had someone to hold and rub against in the
cold and dark. Then old memories rose from the grave, and it was all I
could do not to flee as fear clutched at my bowels and my heart raced.
My first explorations with sex and love, and Shane, had occurred in

a barn much like this one, only one in better repair. I was overcome
with the smell of hay and horses, and the memory of giggles and furtive
touches that quickly turned to passionate murmurs and caresses. That
had been the first step on the road to ruin. In the end it had not gone
well, not well at all.

Yet the beginning had not been unpleasant; it had been wonderful,
in fact. I marveled at the workings of my mind. Why had it latched onto
that first time in the straw and decided to braid it in with all the horror
that came later? Was it because of Goliath's death? Was it because the
stable had often been our private trysting place? Surely that first time
had not been evil in and of itself. That time, and the year that followed,
had been filled with love and promise. Before Shane decided what we
did was wrong. Before he decided I should be punished for leading him
astray. Before he decided that it was less morally repugnant to take by
force what I offered freely than to accept it in the spirit it was given.

And now I was returning. Could I kill him this time? Would I?

I did not sleep again. I held still and cursed a demon of my own
making.

We woke at dawn, or at least rose to move about with the sun, as I
had not truly slept. The boys were quick to douse the flames so as to
avoid alerting anyone to their presence. We ate the rest of the bread and
cheese. Knowing I could buy more, I left them with my spare clothing.
Knowing it would probably result in someone's death, probably his, I left
Big John with a pistol, shot, and powder. He stammered and regarded
me with awe as we went a good way from their shelter, and I taught
him how to load and shoot the piece. Then I gave him some of the silver
coin I had. It was a good amount; used sparingly, it could keep them fed
through the winter. It was the best I could do.

I was touched by reverent hands as I mounted the mare. I wished
them well and rode on. For a while I felt I was deserving of praise, and
my heart was light. Then the truth of the whole matter and the probable
outcome of their short lives engulfed me once again. With that, and the
omnipresent knowledge that Shane lay at the end of my journey, I was
in a fine fit of melancholy by the time I reached Dunfield late in the day.

My uncle had a modest estate and a fine comfortable house with a
lovely garden. He was not a man given to ostentation or airs. Being my
father's younger brother, and with my being my father's eldest son and
presumed heir, my uncle would never inherit a title. He always seemed
relieved by this, as it left him free to travel and hunt at his whim. He
had married once, but she had died in childbirth; and since he had been
very much in love with her, he had never bothered to make the attempt
again.

As luck would have it, my uncle was not at home. However, his
housekeeper recognized my name, became flustered, and seemed on
the verge of a fit of vapors at the sight of me. My uncle's manservant
had to help her to a chair. As I stood in the foyer and watched her pant,
I wondered what had been said of me in my absence. Then I realized I

knew her. She had been in my uncle's employ before I left England.

When the woman recovered, she seemed happy to bid me enter; and they showed me a guest room posthaste, so that I could rest from my travels. My uncle would not return for several days; but they assured me he would be very happy to find me there upon his arrival, and most vexed if they did not offer me every hospitality. I ate from a plate and bathed for the first time since Florence. I thanked them for all their work, and then asked them to leave me be for as long as I might sleep. Finally in a comfortable place of safety after nearly three months of hardship, I slept through the night and most of the next day. And then only hunger and the need to relieve myself pulled me from the deep feather bed.

I ate in the kitchen, and happily submitted to the doting of the cook and the other five members of the staff. Apparently my uncle had told them lavish tales of my adventures as related from my letters. As he was something of an adventurous man himself, and also dearly in love with a good yarn, he had embellished what little I told him a great deal. I was amused to learn I had seduced a princess in Austria and fought a duke in France. I hoped I did not disappoint them, as I was sure my uncle had told tales of a far taller and handsomer man while he was at it.

By the time the meal and tale-telling were finished, it was dark yet again. I returned to bed with a snifter of brandy and a book from the library, only to find I did not wish to read or sleep. I watched the lamplight flicker on the ceiling and sipped from my glass. I felt warm and comfortable and well sheltered from the rain pattering on the roof. Yet it did little to calm the unease in my soul.

Nothing seemed to have changed since the last time I visited here. That would have been a month or two before I departed. I felt the imposter in this happy place that stood safe from the ravages of time. I had surely changed; yet they treated me, despite the stories, as if I had not, as if I were still that boy. And thus I felt I was still that boy, and I found it alarming in the extreme. That boy I had once been knew so very little of the world.

He would not have realized that it was odd that they had not spoken of my family or asked why I had left and then returned. They had wanted to hear stories of my travels, yet they had given me little back. With this thought, I understood that I had indeed changed in their eyes. They knew all too well that I was no longer the boy. This eased my worries some, and with the brandy warm in my belly, I turned down the lamp and settled in to sleep again. I only checked for the pistol and dirk under my pillow once.

My uncle arrived during the evening of the next day, and his embrace nearly brought a tear to my eye: not out of heartfelt emotion, but from the reverent force of it. He was as big a man as my father; and as I had the night before, I felt small and young again. When he let me breathe, we retired to the study to eat by the fire and drink and talk. He studied me with a critical eye, and I returned it. He was older, and it showed about his blue eyes and wide mouth. His hair was grey now. He was still well-muscled, though, and seemingly in robust health.

"You look well," I commented.

He smiled. "As do you, my boy." His eyes narrowed. "You have grown into yourself. I daresay traveling and adventure has suited you."

"Some would say so, but there are times when I wonder what I would have become if I had stayed."

His eyes narrowed ever so slightly, and he looked away. "You would be miserable." He grinned widely and adopted an enthusiastic tone. "Married and bored and hoping for any chance to see a tenth of what you have seen now."

"Aye, aye, but there have been times I wished for..." I had planned to say the safety of home, but that would have been absurd. That was a fantasy I had concocted, the history of a character I had played in many drawing rooms. I had not come from a loving or safe home, which was why I had left. I watched the brandy swirl in my glass and started again. "There have been times when the situations I found myself in were fraught with danger or irritation, and I have wished for a quiet place to retreat to."

My uncle smiled. "A den to hide in is a fine thing indeed, but one cannot stay in it long without it becoming cramped and even more irritating. I have been here too long now. I have not traveled in over a year. I had planned a trip to the north to hunt this fall; and then London burned and I had matters to attend to. But I have discovered something even better now." His eyes twinkled with an inner light that far outshone the flames reflected in them.

"And what would that be?"

"The New World. The colonies."

"Do tell? You plan to travel there?"

"Aye, I have become involved in some business with a man who owns land in the Massachusetts colony. They say the forests there stretch uninterrupted for as many square miles as there is in the whole of Christendom, with mountains and rivers and game you can scarcely believe. And so I am going to see it for myself. You should come with me."

Even if it was a fairytale, it did sound intriguing. "Should I?"

"Aye, before you settle down or whatever it is you returned here to do." His voice had grown distant again, and I looked up to find him frowning at the fire. "Why did you return?"

I frowned and shrugged. "Was it ill-advised?"

"Nay, aye, damnit all, that is not as I meant it to sound. I was wondering at your motivation. Where were you last, Florence, I believe? Did something occur there to bring you back to us?"

I had thought on this question; not on the truth of it, but on what I would tell others. There were a good many people I would easily dissemble to, and then there was my uncle: one of only two people I had wanted to reassure that I was alive and thus remained in contact with.

"I was involved in an endeavor with certain political and legal consequences. Instead of traveling even farther..." I caught myself; I should have said instead of running. I sighed. "My closest friend gave me a lecture on accepting the yoke of responsibility, and how he would be off to do that very thing and not accompanying me on further adventures and... I cannot run anymore. There are matters that must be dealt with."

His smile was sad. "Your father will do everything in his power to keep your cousin and you from each other's throats. Which is not for the best in my opinion; I think you two should settle matters. But you are not my son."

I had expected that. I had not thought my uncle would be so quick in the relaying of it, though.

"Has he gone and adopted Shane yet?"

"Nay, nay," my uncle sighed. "And he never... should. You are his heir while you live. He..." He studied the fire and considered his words. When he spoke, his smile was reassuring.

"When I get enough wine in him, he talks of how he wishes you would return. When he is sober, he is afraid you will. All the while, he tells any who ask that you are doing well and studying this or that artistic pursuit. He makes a fuss over how unfortunate he is to have a son who will not come home and behave properly. Yet... He always implies in those discussions that despite being an aggravation to him, you at least have interests beyond whoring, drinking, and hunting foxes, which is what his friends' sons do."

I was mystified. I could barely remember what I had written my uncle over the years, and I doubted he had told the same tales to my father that he had told his servants. Why had my father decided I was pursuing artistic endeavors? Granted, I had from time to time; but I had found I had no talent for it. It intrigued me that he would choose that as the lie. My father seemed to have little use for art. I could not imagine him pretending to have pride in a son who practiced it; yet perhaps that was a kinder thing than what he did think I pursued across Christendom.

I had never told my uncle precisely why I left, though he knew that I fought with Shane and he understood there was much to settle. Battered or despondent, I had occasionally taken refuge at his house. Once, when asked at a weak moment, I had admitted to the nature of my relationship with my cousin. My uncle had not seemed surprised. I was now curious as to what had been said to whom after my departure.

I did not believe my father was fond of me. The more I thought on what my uncle said, the more I was able to place it in the proper context. My father was an Earl. Noblemen need heirs, thus his wishing for my return. Wolves are exceedingly competitive and like to brag, thus his lies to his peers. My father still loved Shane far more than he loved me, thus his fear that we would fight if I returned. There was no true caring, only his needs. I was a disappointment to him in so many ways.

He was not a disappointment to me; I expected so little of him there was no pedestal for him to fall from.

"How are... they...?" I asked. "Your letters have said all is well, but it has been some time since I received one so..."

"Your mother is ailing."

"How so? The plague?" I was not distraught; I was not close to the woman. When I pictured her, the only expression I could ever remember her having was one of utter disapproval at something I had said or done on the rare occasion I was allowed in her presence.

He sighed and shrugged. "Nay, nay. We were all spared that, out here in the country. Nay, no one will say precisely, to me anyway, but I have gathered it is a matter of her female organs. There is no answer for it and your father's physician merely prescribes increasing amounts of laudanum. Apparently there is great pain."

"So she is dying?"

My uncle nodded. I did not have to hide my lack of emotion at this revelation from him. He knew my feelings on the matter. He was not fond of her, either. Her marriage to my father had been well arranged. I do not remember my parents ever behaving with any fondness for one another. As I had aged and come to know how children were created, I had oft wondered how it was that I was conceived and had two sisters. I had decided my father was a very dutiful man.

"And the others? My father?" I asked.

"He is well."

"Nothing was disrupted by the Restoration, or the fire, or plague, or war with France?"

He shook his head. "Your father has a keen mind for matters of money and politics, and he has kept himself well-insulated from things that would harm him. He engages in calculated risks and often reaps rewards."

I wondered if he still taxed the peasants more than they could spare.

"He is a good wolf," I muttered. My uncle frowned and I sighed. "A good nobleman."

He smiled. "That he is. Born and bred for it, just as you and I are."

"I do not forget that," I said with a trace of guilt. "And my sisters?"

"Elizabeth is quite the twit. She will marry next June. Making a match has been the sole aim of her existence; and now that she has achieved it, I wonder what she will do with herself. Probably drive the poor fellow to drink or a mistress."

I chuckled. Elizabeth took after my mother; except, by all accounts my mother was an intelligent and shrewd woman, and her oldest daughter was not.

"Sarah?" I had been reasonably fond of Sarah, even though she had been only six years of age when I left.

"Now," he smiled. "She is the one you would do yourself well to make the acquaintance of. I have taught her how to shoot, and she rides like the wind. She has your penchant for books. It is a shame she did not have your tutor; but perhaps that is for the best, too, as I seem to remember he filled your head with an odd notion or two."

I chuckled. Apparently there might be an interesting person to look forward to meeting at the house.

"I am glad to hear Sarah has grown into something of note. How is my tutor?"

My father had dismissed Rucker even before I left home, as he had blamed the poor man for many a thing related to why I was such a disappointment. Rucker had gone to live with his sister and teach at a village school. I had continued to send him letters through my uncle, on the rare occasion I chose to write.

"I am sorry, I honestly do not know. I have not seen him in years. The man I dispatched last with a letter said he received it himself."

I nodded. For all of my uncle's seeming kindness, he was not a man prone to befriend a poor scholar such as Rucker.

"I shall visit him next."

"And then? Should I tell anyone you are here?"

"I do not know. I will see them. But... What of Shane? Is he whoring and hunting foxes?"

"Aye, and assisting your father with various business matters."

"As a good son should," I muttered.

"Marsy," he chided. It was the name he had used for me in my youth. "You left."

"I was driven out."

"Your father would never permit that..."

"You are wrong!" I was as surprised as he at my sudden flash of anger. I stood and paced and attempted to explain myself, but that only made matters worse. "He was not blind or deaf. When things escalated to the level where Shane tortured my favorite horse near to death and I was forced to relieve the animal of its misery..." Unbidden, all of the sensations and emotions returned to me, and for a moment, I was standing in the stable listening to Goliath's pained breathing, watching him try to stand with his legs slashed to the bone, his trusting eyes glazed with agony and confusion. I had left him at the manor because he had come up lame before I had to travel to London. I knew now Shane was responsible for the lameness. He had wanted to buy himself time to break my hunter, the one he could not ride.

I looked away from the fire. "I gave Goliath a funeral pyre, in the main lawn, with all of my father's alcohol as fuel. My father was in his study. The windows faced the flames. The drapes were not drawn. It was night. Yet he never once asked why I emptied the sideboards of every bottle and burned a horse in front of his window. Not once! Not a word was said!" Nor had anything been said all of the times I had come to dinner with bruises about my face.

My uncle was grimacing. He sighed heavily when my eyes met his. "Marsy, you must understand, he did not understand. He thought you were just being boys. He wanted to allow you to address the matter yourselves. He felt if he interfered, then he would have to manage the situation for the rest of your lives. He regrets that. You do not know how much he…”

“Enough.” My anger transmuted to a distant horror, and I sat heavily in my chair. I poured another glass and downed it, to burn the threat of tears away.

“You must speak with your father,” my uncle said gently.

“Why? I cannot recall having a conversation with the man that did not involve the weather, the disposition of the hounds, or the state of the roads.”

My uncle rubbed his temples until they seemed as red as the flames, and then poured himself another glass. “I love my brother, dearly, but he is such a God-damned fool at times.” His arm shot out to grasp my hand painfully. “You must talk to him.”

“I hate him.” My voice sounded hollow, even to my own ear. “Almost as much as I hate Shane.” Or myself for that matter, for allowing it to go on as it had, for not putting a stop to it, no matter what the consequence. I had killed so many men since those days when I had not killed the one I most needed to.

My uncle released me and sat back. “That is obvious. And he has given you reason. But, Marsy, he does not know that. He does not understand.”

“Do you truly feel he could be made to at this late date?” My tone was far harsher than I intended.

He did not regard me. The silence hung in the room, broken only by the crackle of the flames.

“I apologize. You are not the one I am angry with. You have been… more of a father to me than he ever was. I do not mean to bring you pain.”

“Oh, Marsy. My Lord, I am honored by that, yet, it is not as it should be.”

“Aye, I know. I will speak to him, and not of the weather or the wine or things of a meaningless nature. And then I may take you up on your offer to go to this Massachusetts.”

He smiled. “You will be welcome if it comes to that; but perhaps it would be best if you stayed and… became accustomed to life here again, or allowed it to become accustomed to you.”

“You feel my father would take more interest in me if I were not a ghost.”

“Correct.” His eyes bored into mine again. “And you cannot kill Shane. As much as you may hate him, for whatever reason you may have. That road will only lead to you hanging from a gibbet or renouncing your title and running for the rest of your days.”

“I understand.” What he said was true. I was known here. If I killed Shane, even in a duel, I would be forced to run. But perhaps it would be worth it. Then at least I would be running from something more tangible, in a fashion, than my own shame. I did not share that thought

with him, though, and we discussed pleasanter things until we were
weary.

In the morning we went hunting game birds, and had an
unremarkable and peaceful time. I knew he had sent word to my family
that I was in England, but we did not speak of it. I spent close to a
week with him before riding on to find Rucker, whose residence lay in
the opposite direction from my father's lands. Thus I would pass by my
uncle's house on my return, and learn who wished to see me and where.

The sun shone, yet it was cold as I rode east. It matched my mood
well. Since the discussion with my uncle, I felt that light had been
shed on a great many things. Yet I found myself as numb and frozen
as I had felt leaving Florence. I did not know what to think or feel.
Therefore it was easier to do neither; and I had done everything I could
to avoid straying into the aegis of either of those twin pillars of human
consciousness.

Unfortunately, once on the road, I had little to do but ride and think.
I carefully kept myself on the task of composing my thoughts on my
travels into essays of a sort, much as I would do if writing them down,
so that when I told Rucker of them, he would not find me completely
empty of all the knowledge he had attempted to impart to me.

Ira Rucker had been my tutor from the time I was six until the age
of fourteen, when my father dismissed him. I had been his sole pupil –
until Shane came to live with us after his parents died, when I was eight
and he was nine.

Even though Shane had been added to our lives, when it came to
matters of books and learning, Rucker and I were in a world of our own.
Rucker had given Shane lessons and taught him everything a young
gentleman needs to know, but he had paid little attention to Shane
beyond that. He had doted on me because I possessed an inquisitive
and flexible mind. If anyone else had ignored Shane when we were
young, I would have been very vexed. Rucker ignoring Shane was
acceptable to me, because I truly did not want to share him, even with
Shane.

I had no proof, but I believed Shane was responsible for Rucker's
leaving. Matters were never clearly stated, but someone had intimated
that perhaps my relationship with my tutor was a little too much in
keeping with that of a teacher and student from the days of ancient
Greece. This was complete and utter hog-wallow. My relationship with
Rucker had been in all ways chaste, and I had in truth never harbored
any thought of that nature concerning the man.

I did recall once discussing the subject of men loving men, in
relation to some writings, and learning that Rucker did not favor men in
the least. However, he was fond of the idea of men living together away
from the distractions of women and children, that they could engage
in pure discourse for the sake of intellectual development. To Rucker,
sex was an unfortunate byproduct of our basic animal nature, and the
need for it was something to be overcome if one wished to engage in

the pursuit of knowledge. When this talk occurred, I had been in the bud of my adolescence and had just discovered the interesting things my member could do when aroused. Thus I had thought he was full of manure. My cock has always held a great deal of fascination for me, such that I could never be compelled to ignore it.

Rucker now lived with his sister and brother-in-law, in a modest house in a pleasant little shire. The brother-in-law was a pewtersmith and well respected in the village. They had five children. When last we spoke in person, Rucker had been pleased with his living arrangements, but unhappy with his employment. He was not a man prone to marriage, and despite his vocation, truly abhorred young children. He preferred older students who could engage in discourse and be taught something of use beyond manners, enunciation, letters, and basic arithmetic. Thus he had despised teaching in the local school, where any child reaching adolescence was plucked away and sent into the fields or a trade.

I had visited him often after his dismissal, and seen him a mere month before I left. Still, unlike my uncle's housekeeper, Rucker's sister did not recognize me when I arrived; not even my name. Despite the lack of knowledge of my person, she seemed keenly interested in the fact that I was a gentleman coming to call, and immediately asked if my visit was in regard to some form of employment. As I waited for the maid to fetch him, I wondered how long Rucker had been without a position.

At the sight of me, tears filled his eyes; and he embraced me as heartily as my uncle, though he was half the other man's size. I had forgotten how diminutive he was, and I realized I might have gained a few inches in height after my departure after all. When he pulled away, he looked me up and down again and said quietly, "Lord Marsdale, look at you, you are a man now. Truly. I am overwhelmed. I wondered if..."

A throat was cleared, and we turned to his sister, still standing in the doorway to the parlor. Rucker explained that I, the Viscount of Marsdale, was the Earl of Dorshire's son. She immediately ordered the maid to bring refreshments. Rucker pointedly chose that we should take our tea in his rooms. The sister seemed dismayed by this; but I was assuredly relieved, as I did not wish to converse with her.

I followed him up the stairs, to a small garret room with a window overlooking the garden – not that one could get close to the window, with the great piles of books on the table before it. Every flat surface that could be used to support paper was overflowing with some form of it. One can forget how books smell until one is surrounded by them in a stuffy space. On the whole, it appeared exactly as his quarters had in my father's house, only smaller.

He cleared a seat on a chair for me, and I sat.

"I was wondering when and if I would ever see you again," he said as he perched on the corner of the trunk at the foot of the bed, within an arm's length of me. The room was so small I thought we would have had more space if we both sat on the bed. Though it was little more than a cot, it took up much of the floor.

"You received my letters?" I asked. "I believe I wrote six."

"With great delight. I have them still. I am sorry I did not respond with more than two; however, I knew not what to say, really. You were the one seeing things, and it was not as if we corresponded regularly enough to engage in discourse."

"True. I am the one who should apologize, for both the infrequency of my writing and its relative brevity. Often months would pass, and I would find myself in another season quite to my surprise. And so many things occurred that I did not know where to begin; and I would have had to write books to describe them. And, also, much of what I was engaged in was best not written down in the event my correspondence was apprehended."

"Do you have time to talk now, or..."

I waved him off. "For the time being, I am at your disposal, good sir. And I have much I wish to tell you. I have no place I must be. My uncle knows where I am, and will send someone if a matter arises that..." I sighed. "Other than my uncle, I have not seen my family yet, and am not sure of their reception." I shrugged. "I can take a room at the inn. We are limited only by your own duties."

He smiled. "Which are none and nothing except for the tasks I choose to set upon myself, which currently involve writing and corresponding with the few friends I have." He grimaced. "I do not mean to sound maudlin."

"So you are no longer teaching?"

"I was dismissed, for... filling their minds with unnecessary hog-wallow. That was the mayor's words to my person, not the nicely worded letter they sent. Apparently I would be allowed to teach them only if I swore not to teach them to think." We chuckled.

"As you always taught me, men who think have proven to be the most dangerous of all over the course of history," I said.

"So, have you been a dangerous man?"

I laughed. "I would like to think so."

"Have you returned here to be dangerous?"

That gave me pause. "Aye, but not in the manner you mean."

He appeared saddened by this. "Why have you returned?"

We were interrupted by the arrival of our tea; and I used the distraction to consider what I should say. By the time the maid left, I had decided on the truth. So I told him of Florence, and political machinations, and Teresina, and even Alonso and all that had happened in the end, including Vincente's death and my part in it. I alluded to the intimacy of my relation with Alonso without stating it, and I sensed that he understood. And then I told him of the final discussion I had with Alonso and the decisions I reached that led to my subsequent leave-taking.

When I finished he was sitting with arms crossed, regarding the corner. I knew from times gone by that this posture was contemplative, and not indicative of negativity toward my tale.

He finally looked at me. "May I ask... several questions?"

I nodded.

"When I left your father's employ, you seemed rather taken with your cousin. I recall being dismayed that you would give so much credence to him, as it always seemed to me that he treated you with great reserve if not coldness. I wished better for you, but I assumed that was the nature of things. A lord's sons must be discreet and all. So my question is, are, were you intimately involved with him, and what occurred to make you leave?"

"Aye. I loved him. I think once he loved me as well, when we were very young. Later, he deplored his desire for me. He was ashamed. Yet this did not stop him from forcing himself upon me. I stayed at first because I harbored the hope that he would overcome these internal conflicts he seemed obsessed with. Then there was that last straw, and I felt I had no other recourse than to kill him, so I left."

I was rather proud of myself; I had managed to say all of that without bawling. He fished a bottle from a drawer in his nightstand and handed it to me. I took a long pull and found it to be brandy.

He took a drink after I did. He was contemplative again.

"My Lord, there was nothing you could do, was there? May I ask why you did not kill him? Obviously you would have faced arrest and trial and... Well, obviously you could not. Unless you ran as you did, but then you would never have been able to return. So there, I may have answered it."

"Nay, I thought none of that at the time. I was confused. On one hand, I still loved him and could not simply take his life unawares; and on the other, I did not think I was capable of winning a duel with him. All of those days I spent reading, he spent practicing more martial pursuits."

"And now?" he asked: curiously, without censure.

"Now I believe I possess far more experience than he could have gained in actual combat. I have not heard that he has been in the military; and even if he had, officers often make the worst duelists. If he had engaged in the things I have, he would have been forced to leave as many cities as myself."

"Hmmm, an excellent observation, I think, though I know nothing of combat myself. And now, what will you do?"

"I have oft fantasized about challenging him and running him through. Yet..."

"That would allow him to destroy your life completely."

I nodded, as he had just put into words the thing my mind had been dancing around for days. "It is a hateful irony. I met eight boys on the road between London and my uncle's. Orphans and castoffs, they were homeless and unwanted. I could have slaughtered the lot of them, and even if someone by some odd chance ever traced the crime to me, I would not be punished. But in truth, they would never trace the crime to me, as it would not be seen as a crime, but more as clearing vermin. Yet, my cousin could do what he did and I cannot bring charges against him, because of the nature of the offense and because of our station. And I will be hounded out of England and hanged, if caught, for taking the matter into my own hands".

He smiled sadly and handed the bottle to me again. "I am sorry."

I shook my head. "Thank you. There were those who could have... interceded, and did not, but that is another matter. You were gone before the situation became... well, before it escalated into a war. Looking back on it all, it was always intolerable after a fashion. I was just too naïve to know."

"So what will..." He stopped and thought. "What did you do with those boys you met? Did you toss them a coin and ride on?" His gaze was almost predatory, and I recognized it from the classroom. He was testing me.

"I spent the night with them in an abandoned barn, shared what food I had, and left them with some silver and a pistol. I do not know if I did them any great service by that. It was all I could conceive of at the time to ease their situation."

He chuckled ruefully. "I feel you have to arm a great number of sheep before they can save themselves."

"As do I."

"If... you are not irreconcilably estranged from your family – not Shane, but your father – then you will inherit his title, will you not?"

I took a long pull on the bottle and felt the fool, as the epiphany exploded through my mind and soul. Many would find it very hard to believe, but I had truly not perceived the situation in that light in a very long time. I remembered thinking as a child that, when I grew up and became Earl, then my father's peasants would be treated differently. But then so much had occurred to make that seem a hollow promise. Cynicism had taken hold, and I had watched men of that station get destroyed by monarchs and their own peers whenever they dared challenge the status quo. Yet, one Earl could positively affect the lives of at least his own people. If I were my father, or for that matter, even in his good graces, I could have found a place for those boys. I might not be able to make a difference in the lives of sheep everywhere, but I could save one flock. That was truly the duty and responsibility of my birth that I had forgotten.

I smiled. "I have been told that I am not irreconcilably estranged from my father unless I wish to be, that the matter is perhaps in my hands. I will not know until he says he wishes to see me and we talk. And besides, I am his oldest and only son, even were he to adopt my cousin. So I will inherit... someday, as long as I outlive him, and fail to give him geat cause to be rid of me."

Rucker smiled. "I spend my days writing essays and political tracts, a dangerous pursuit in itself. Yet you may be by far the greatest contribution I have ever made to the welfare of others." He looked stricken at his words. "I... What hubris I have."

I laughed. "You have shaped me well. I wish I could repay you in some fashion."

He shook his head. "You owe me nothing; and as we have discussed, I feel you will someday."

"Do you have any prospects?"

"Nay, I spend much of my time writing and reading. There is much afoot in the world." He sighed. "I have a small stipend from my father's estate, and it serves to pay my way here." He frowned at me, then smiled. "If you were able to gain some sort of stipend from your father and wished to donate to a worthy cause, I know of many."

"I would be delighted; but though I know he will support me, I do not know what allowances he will make for my personal expenditures. And I may not stay, depending..."

"Ah. Where will you go now if you leave?"

"I have been invited to accompany my uncle to the New World, to the colony of Massachusetts."

"Truly?" This seemed to excite him greatly. "If you go, you will have to write me detailed letters concerning the English treatment of the Indians there."

"Of course," I muttered. I had forgotten there were Indians there, and my uncle had made no mention of them.

"Aye, aye," he said and dug through papers. "I have been corresponding with a professor at Oxford and a Jesuit priest in France concerning the absolutely deplorable treatment of the Indians of the West Indies and the Spanish Main at the hands of the Spaniards. And there has been much discussion of finding some way to ameliorate the English treatment of the Indians in our new colonies. We must behave better than the Spanish." With that, he dumped a handful of tracts and pamphlets in my lap, and I knew immediately what I would be doing for the next several days.

I felt more content than I had in months. I still did not know what would occur with Shane, but I had a new sense of purpose; and I vowed I would make the attempt to reach an understanding with my father.

Perhaps the Gods had a plan for me.

Three

Wherein I Return To My Place of Birth

A letter arrived from my uncle two days later. My father was staying with a friend, as was Shane. My father wished to see me. He would return to the family estate, Rolland Hall, before the Christmas twelveday. He wished for me to join the family then. At the moment, my mother was the only member of the family in residence at the manor, as my sisters were in Hertfordshire at the home of Elizabeth's betrothed. It was now late in the first week of December. I informed Rucker I would remain with him until a week or so before the holiday. Thus I spent most of December in peace and relative tranquility, and learned a great deal about the New World and the colonies: so much so that I was determined to travel there. I urged Rucker to accompany me, and he said he would think on it.

The day finally arrived when I could wait no longer, and I knew I must make the journey to Dorshire. The day dawned bright, but a steady wind heralded another storm. I made excellent time to my uncle's. Of course, when I reached him, he insisted on accompanying me; and suddenly we were an entourage with a small wagon and several servants. I stifled my initial annoyance; and spent the much slower ride that followed, and the evening, in an inn, pleasantly discussing my uncle's pending journey to the Massachusetts colony.

After another slow day of travel, we at last reached my birthplace, just before sunset. I gazed upon Rolland Hall from the road beyond the south pasture. I quickly realized I was regarding it with the eyes of a stranger. The great house, adjoining structures, lawns, gardens, and surrounding countryside all looked the same, as if I had never left; but the entirety of it was as if I were remembering a dream. I recalled it all quite clearly, but felt nothing other than a purely rational recognition, with no emotion at all. I was thankful for this.

The servants did not make as much of a fuss over my arrival as my uncle's had. Any who would have fussed over my arrival, such as my nanny, had departed before I did.

I was informed there were other guests for the holiday: my mother's sister, the recently widowed Dowager Lady Graeland, and her son, the new Lord Graeland, who I had always known as a sallow youth named Percival. They had often visited when I was young. Percival and I had not been friends. In the days before Shane, when I had been starved for companionship, I had talked poor Percival into climbing a tree, and he had broken his arm. I had been strapped for it, and not permitted to play with him again. He was apparently now as much a grown man as I, and married. His bride, the new Lady Graeland, was with them.

To my amazement, my bedchamber was exactly as I had left it; well, a little cleaner. I shooed the maid out and immediately performed a habit I had learned in this very room: I slid a chair to the door and under the knob. Its legs settled into the grooves in the floor they had made one night when Shane had tried kicking the door open while in a drunken stupor. I was apparently home.

On a whim, I tried on several coats from the closet, and found that none of them fit me. I had indeed widened markedly across the shoulders. They were woefully out of fashion, anyway. The court of Charles II was a modern one, and the fashions were more in keeping with the rest of Christendom now. I dressed for dinner in the clothes I had purchased in London with Teresina's money.

My uncle knocked on my door. "I thought you might not wish to go down alone," he said quietly.

"I do not wish to go down at all, but I thank you for your company."

He watched me strap on a sword belt and my favorite rapier.

"Marsy, you will not need that here." The look I gave him stopped his words.

He shrugged. "Shane will remain in London."

I was equally relieved and disappointed, but I had expected as much.

"Lovely, I am sure that will cause some amount of bitterness," I said. "I care not what Shane feels about that matter, but I am concerned the others will hold ill will over it. He has, after all, been the good son."

"Would you prefer him to be here?" he asked with concern.

"Nay, nay, we will leave him there, thank you. If I am not to kill him, I would rather not see him."

We were down before many of the others, except for my mother. She sat on a settee, a skeletal figure swathed in pale pink satin that managed to be more deeply hued than her white skin. She regarded me through a haze of laudanum, while her nurse tried to explain who I was. The understanding that I was her son finally dawned; and then that look of disapproval I remembered all too well pinched her features. I paid my respects with a forced smile and the exceedingly clear enunciation I use for idiots and drunks. She managed to glare at me. She said nothing, however. I recalled being told at a very early age that the nanny whose lap I dearly loved was not my mother and this cold and hideous woman was. I had been disappointed, more so when I became old enough to understand that other mothers loved their offspring. I hoped she ran out of laudanum before she died.

My aunt wafted into the room in a cloud of blue satin, and reminded me how regal my mother had been capable of appearing once upon a time. They were very similar in countenance. Thankfully there was no commonality between them in demeanor. My aunt embraced me and bid me welcome, before asking of my journey. There was no sincere emotion in it, but she was at least cheerful and polite in paying the courtesy due a guest. As I had often been a guest in gracious homes, I felt at ease in her presence. I knew how to deal with strangers I wished to get on well with. Thus I regaled her with trivial tales and complaints of my journey from Florence, rarely touching on the truth.

My sisters arrived. They paused in the doorway, like two dogs unsure of an intruder's intent. Was I to be barked at, or licked, or both? Elizabeth had grown into quite the beauty, with all the regal air my mother had once possessed and, once she made up her mind to enter, all of my aunt's social talents. Her hair had darkened into a pleasant brown, like my mother's. Her eyes were not my mother's hazel, though, but the vivid blue of many of my father's family, a color I shared with my uncle.

Sarah was not as attractive as our sister. I assumed that, at seventeen, she had reached her full growth in both height and bosom. Both were short of Elizabeth's measure in those areas by several inches. She still shared my blond hair, but she had my father's misty grey-blue eyes. Unlike Elizabeth, she did not flow into the room in a rustle of satin to embrace me and welcome me home. She entered diffidently and kept her distance.

I did not have time to approach her, as they had been closely followed by my cousin, the new Viscount Graeland, and his bride. He was still as sallow and knock-kneed as I remembered. Thankfully, the new Lady Graeland turned out to be a sweet, red-headed girl named Constance. I was immediately informed that she was with child. I complimented Graeland, as that seems to be what new fathers expect for accomplishing a thing they would dread with anyone but their wives. The Graelands three then pestered me for tales of my travels, and I mentioned cities I had visited and lived in. They, in turn, asked banal questions that made it apparent they had little understanding of geography or politics. Thankfully, they would never travel and embarrass England.

Finally my father put in his appearance. I stood, and there was an awkward silence as we studied one another. He appeared much as I remembered; a little thicker about the middle, perhaps. I supposed his hair was a little thinner, but evidence of this was not available, as he was wigged. I had only seen him without a wig a half-dozen times, and his periwigs were as unchanging as the sheep pasture. There were dour lines about his eyes and mouth: not the crinkles of a man who laughs often, but the furrows of one who frowns a great deal. He finished perusing me and gave a small nod. "Lord Marsdale."

"Lord Dorshire." I nodded and bowed in return.

He nodded again, more to himself than anyone, and asked the butler to see to dinner being served quickly, since he had been so tardy and made us all wait.

I wanted to scream. Here we were after all these years, and all I received was a mere acknowledgement. I supposed I should be grateful he still granted me the title he had bestowed upon me when he inherited his father's.

I followed the others into the dining hall, and took a seat at the middle of the table, with Elizabeth on one side, Lady Constance Graeland on the other, and Lord Graeland across from me. I quickly seized upon asking Elizabeth about her betrothed and her pending nuptials; and though it earned me the grimaces and glares of many at the table, I was left to eat in peace while she prattled on through three courses.

At some point, my aunt smiled and said cheerily, "That is enough, dear," and there was another awkward silence.

"Will Shane be home for the holiday?" Lady Graeland asked. "I am sure he will want to see Lord Marsdale. You grew up together, did you not?"

I was thankful I did not have food in my mouth, as I surely would have spat it onto her husband's plate in surprise. I thought my father was going to choke; and only his brother's pounding him on the back seemed to alleviate his duress. I studied everyone else. My aunt seemed ill-at-ease, but Lord Graeland appeared as confused as his wife over my father's reaction. My mother was in a haze. Elizabeth looked unhappy. Sarah was the image of contained fury.

"Nay," my father gasped when he could breathe again.

"Oh, well that is unfortunate," Graeland said carefully, his eyes darting about, as if the truth of the matter were a fly he could possibly get a glimpse of.

"I am afraid I am to blame," I said pleasantly. "It is best if Shane and I do not occupy the same building."

"Why?" Lady Graeland asked with startling naïveté.

"One of us will kill the other," I replied in the same pleasant tone of voice.

"Do you think you are capable?" Sarah asked, as if she did not feel I would be.

"Aye. How many men has Shane dueled?"

She did not reply.

"Killed?" I added.

She blinked at that.

"You?" she asked, as if I should not be questioning my betters.

I counted, and remembered to add Vincente. "That I am sure of their death, and that were not merely wounded with the possibility of recovery, nineteen."

I studied her. She swallowed and would not return my gaze. I let my eyes drift to my father, and was amazed to see a smile twitch across his lips. He quickly masked it with a sip of wine. The rest were silent and appalled, except for my uncle, who was trying very hard not to laugh.

"Were you involved in... well, military action?" Graeland asked hopefully.

"Nay. Many were duels; most of the rest were cutthroats who had the appalling bad fortune to choose me as a victim." I did not add that I had murdered several of the list.

"And there have been no... repercussions?" my aunt asked.

I shrugged. "There are several cities that it would be in my best interest not to return to."

"Give me a list sometime," my father said, "so that in the event we have family business there, I do not make the mistake of sending you."

I was at a loss as to how to comprehend or respond to his words. They implied a great deal.

My uncle changed the subject soon after, and managed to get us through dessert without further incident.

After dinner, we retired to the hall, and my aunt played the piano while Elizabeth and Lady Graeland sang. They were not appallingly bad; in point of fact, my sister had a lovely voice. Still, it was not how I wished to spend the evening. My father kept his distance from me, and retired with my mother at an early hour.

That night I went to my room and contemplated the bed. I lay upon it and discovered that it did engender memories I did not wish to experience. I slept in a chair by the fire, with a pistol in my lap.

The next day, my father and sisters went to spread cheer to the peasants, by giving small coins to the children and gifts to the village families. My uncle informed me that my father was not quite ready to speak with me. I wondered how many weeks he would make me wait. That night, after a dinner in which I did not say anything untoward, we men retired to the study to drink and smoke, and left the women to needlework. As there were four of us, including Graeland, the situation would not be conducive to the kind of serious conversation I wished. I imagined it would devolve into talk of politics and business.

I looked about my father's study and found it to be much as it had been a decade before: filled with a great hearth, a great table, a great desk, and shelves of ledgers and scrolls and very few books. The only things I had ever found of interest were the ancient weapons my grandfather collected and my father's maps. I had spent many a happy hour here in my childhood perusing those maps, under Rucker's watchful eye of course.

As a servant poured brandy and prepared pipes, I crossed the room to peruse one of my favorite maps. Most of my father's maps were kept rolled, as he did not possess enough walls to display them. This one hung in an elegant frame suitable to the work of art it surely was. It was a Spanish creation, and showed the New World, or at least that portion of it the Spanish had interest in. I had marveled at it as a child, and recently struggled to remember it as I worked my way through Rucker's treatises. It was seventy years old, and the cartographer had not bothered with anything as far north as the land where the Virginia colony now resided, or far enough south to show the Portuguese holdings on the Main. But it did seem to depict with some accuracy, in comparison to a number of other maps I had seen of the region since, the entirety of the Spanish Main, Terra Firma, and the Isles of the West Indies scattered about the Northern Sea between them.

My eyes were immediately drawn to Panama: the little bridge of land connecting the Spanish Main, to the east and south, with New Spain, to the west and north. I wondered if Alonso were there yet.

To my surprise, my father led the others over to join me. He awarded me a polite nod before stepping between me and the map. He pointed enthusiastically at an island nearly exactly in the middle of it, and told Graeland, "That is Jamaica."

"Ah," Graeland said and sipped his brandy, while my uncle leaned around me to peruse the little oblong shape with interest.

I was curious, not about Jamaica per se, but as to why my father found merit in mentioning it. Jamaica had become an English colony in 1655, when Cromwell's men wrested it from the Spanish. Many thought little of it, as the Protector had sent his army to capture one of the island's nearest neighbors, Cuba or Hispaniola. Jamaica had merely been the best they could do.

However, it was many times the size of any other English holding in the West Indies. I glanced at the north-south chain of islands separating the Northern Sea from the ocean beyond. The Spanish cartographer had not assigned them names, and they were merely misshapen dots. I knew we now had five colonies there, the largest and most prosperous being Barbados. I could actually find it, as it sat the farthest east. The Spaniard had depicted Jamaica as being larger than all of the little islands put together.

Jamaica was still much smaller than Cuba and Hispaniola, though. I would have wondered how we continued to hold it, if I had not learned that the Spanish really had little use for it. Of course, they could choose to descend upon us and drive us out of the West Indies altogether; but from what Rucker said, they really lacked the fleet to do such a thing these days. On the other side of that coin, we lacked the fleet to defend our colonies if they did muster a force against us.

"So, sugarcane, is it?" Graeland asked and disturbed my reverie.

"Aye, aye," my father said. "They have found it to be a wonderful and lucrative crop on the islands."

"I thought they could grow little there," my uncle remarked. "A man gave me some tobacco from Barbados and it was truly foul."

My father scoffed. "Tobacco does not grow in the tropics, at least not in our colonies. Sugarcane, however, is another matter. A single plantation can produce molasses, and the Devil's drink, rum, and muscovado, the brown sugar that can be refined into true sugar here in England."

"And this is lucrative?" my uncle asked.

"Very." My father smiled. "And those of us with a like mind will keep it that way. It will not be taxed as tobacco is; there will be laws to prevent the colonies from refining the sugar, so that the prices can be controlled on English soil. And the King has interest in the matter, as these plantations require a great number of laborers. He has chartered an enterprise to provide Negro slaves for the islands, so that we do not have to rely on the damn Dutch."

"What about bondsmen?" my uncle asked.

"The planters cannot get enough of them, either." My father shrugged. "England has taken to shipping convicts. There are those who prefer the Negroes. They are truly slaves, thank God, and you can treat them as you will, and you need not release them. They are also easier to recover once they escape."

I found the topic sad, and retreated to sprawl in a chair and light a pipe.

"So you plan to invest in one of these sugarcane plantations?" I asked.

My father looked about, and frowned as if he were just noticing my presence. "Aye. The land is free on Jamaica. They will grant thirty acres to any man who wishes to work it, and thirty more for any family member or servant he brings with him."

I snorted. "One lord could easily be granted the entire island. But surely you do not intend to sail there."

He snorted in return. "Nay, of course not. I will send an agent to see to my interests with as many bondsmen as can be retained. I have already obtained the services of a purportedly trustworthy barrister in Jamaica, and he has hired an experienced plantation manager from Barbados." He turned back to Graeland and softened his tone somewhat. "All my agent need do is see to it that my interests are truly represented by these men, and sit about and sip rum."

Graeland eyed the map thoughtfully.

I sighed and scoffed, "It is rife with pestilence. Some say that one out of four men dies within his first months in the West Indies. It takes over a month to reach the islands by sea, and just as long to return. Ships cannot even cross the ocean during the storm season, as the great storms, the ones the Indians call hurricanes, will send any craft foolish enough to dare their wrath to the bottom. And there is no peace beyond the Line; we are ever at war there with the Spanish and other nations.

And then you have your usual rabble and pirates and freebooters. I would imagine a man lacking in experience with sword and pistol would be in imminent danger. It is not a place for the sane or timid."

The horror on Graeland's face showed that he considered himself both sane and timid. I wondered what my father had been offering him in return. My father was ill-pleased with me; but as that was ever the way of it, I did not care.

My uncle was attempting to hide his amusement. "A man familiar with sword and pistol might do well there indeed."

I chuckled. "Indeed."

I found my eyes on the map again, and my humor faded. I had no interest in plantations, sugar, or slaves, but there was appeal into going to such a place. And, ironically, it was very close to Panama, though with what I had recently learned, I knew I would never be able to pay Alonso a visit.

I felt I was under scrutiny, and turned to find my father regarding me thoughtfully. His gaze quickly left, and he began to talk of other things.

The following day was Christmas Eve. I chose to wake late and spend my day wandering about the house and grounds in some nostalgic quest. At length I found myself in the stable. Goliath's old stall was occupied by a friendly cobb. Down the row, my bay mare seemed happy to see me. I considered riding, but the day was bitter; and I could not think of any place I wished to see, for I was beginning to feel that nostalgia was as overrated as love.

There was a clatter of hooves outside, and horse ears perked all along the row of stalls. I stepped out, wondering who had been riding on such a day. One of the stable boys held the reins of a magnificent white hunter; and as I watched, the girth was loosened and the saddle removed. I peered at the diminutive boots and legs in riding breeches visible under the animal with interest. Sarah was handing the saddle to another stable boy as I came round the horse. Her wearing breeches had to be a side effect of my mother's being on laudanum.

"You have a fine mount," I commented.

Sarah awarded me a thin smile. "Thank you; I have had him since he was a colt."

"I had a black hunter when I lived here; he was only a little wider and deeper in the chest than your stallion there. I raised him from a colt."

"I remember him; Goliath." Our mother's disapproving look was settling across Sarah's nose and mouth.

I frowned. "Do you remember that he died?"

"Aye, and I was told you shot him after Shane had ridden him."

My composure shattered, and I recoiled.

"Oh, aye," I snapped. "Well, he tried to ride him. Goliath threw him several times, I am told. Shane beat the animal bloody with a whip and then slashed his legs until he could not stand and then ordered the stable hands not to touch him. I did not return from London for another day. It was a testament to Goliath's strength of will that he lived as long as he did. And I curse the time I stood in front of his stall overcome by abject horror as minutes wasted in not finding the means to end his suffering!"

This time she recoiled.

"Shane would not do that," she said, with a quavering voice, from behind her fingers.

"You do not know Shane as I do," I snarled.

Her ire returned. "Nay, not like you do at all. I daresay I know him far better. You are a sodomite and a pervert, and you feel the need to sully his name simply because you could not have him."

I was stunned, but not beyond the capacity of my rage to feed words into my mouth. "Oh, but I did. He went to great lengths to make sure I had him. Sodomy was perpetrated, to be sure; but upon me, not by me. I would warn you, nay, I would fear for you, but I realize there is no reason to. Fucking women is permissible in Shane's mind; he will not revile you for desiring you."

"How dare you speak of him in that manner? How dare you speak of me in that manner? I am to marry him!"

I could not stop the bark of laughter. "So that is his plan. He will be my father's son yet, will he not? When did he hatch this scheme? Did he wait until you had begun to bleed?"

She crossed the distance between us and slapped me. The blow stung on my cold cheek, but it surprised her far more than me. Still, it shattered my anger. She was indeed a tiny thing, barely coming to my shoulders; and I looked down on her from a place of knowledge and experience. She did not know. She had believed what he told her. No one else in the household would have ever dared speak of it all, and so she only had him to rely upon. And, I understood.

"I know how it is," I said gently. "I truly do. Love is so rare a thing in this house that we have the tendency to latch onto the first teat that seems to offer it. I know how charming he can be. I adored him, too. I would have killed any who besmirched him when we were young, before the trouble began. And even then, I kept hoping..."

I turned and walked away. I retreated to my room and a bottle, with the chair blocked under the knob. I did not dare let myself think.

Duty called that afternoon, and we were all required to attend mass. The brandy had numbed me somewhat. Though, thankfully, I did not have enough on hand to become truly drunk, as I soon found myself being greeted by and introduced to everyone in the shire. I had seen shorter reception lines at noble weddings, and I was thankful I had years of practice at smiling pleasantly and seeming sincere while inebriated and not in the mood for any such gathering. They all became a blur of faces, and I knew I would not remember a single one in the morning.

During the mass, I noticed Sarah eyeing me on occasion when she thought I was not looking. She was not glaring and did not appear disapproving, and I was still cognizant enough to wonder at that. I also wondered how formal this planned marriage was. I did not think he would have made offers to her that he did not plan to keep, merely for the purposes of seduction. He stood to gain far too much by actually marrying her. I supposed no one else had made mention of it because of the situation between Shane and me.

Once we were all home, I retired to the study with my father, my uncle, and Graeland. And so for another night, I was not granted an opportunity to broach any subject of import, much less the matter of the supposed marriage. Conversation once again turned to this or that matter of politics or business. For one jolting moment I could see the entirety of the remainder of my life spread before me, as a series of meaningless social functions and time spent smoking in studies while discussing how to rob people within the law. I could not bear it, and excused myself to retreat to my room.

I woke to a knock. It was still dark, and the embers had not fully burned down in the fire.

I took a pistol to the door. "Aye?"

"It is Sarah. Open up before I am seen," she hissed.

I removed the chair and opened the door. She rushed past me, wrapped in a robe with a small lamp in her hand. I closed the door and stopped myself from returning the chair to its place under the knob. She eyed me curiously.

"I block the door with it," I muttered and pushed it aside. "Old habit from when I lived here before."

Then I noticed her eyes were actually on the pistol and not the chair.

"Old habit from the days when I did not live here," I said sheepishly, and set the weapon on the bureau. "Though it would have served me better here."

I studied her. She seemed calm and not angry. She had a bottle hanging at her side.

"What do I owe..?"

She cut off my words. "I want to know."

"What?" Though I knew.

"Everything."

We stood whispering in a pool of lamplight. For some reason I felt safe.

"May I ask a question first?"

She nodded resolutely.

"Is there a formal betrothal?"

She sighed and shook her head. "Father would not approve."

That was indeed interesting. "Without offending, or attempting to rally you, whose idea was it?"

This was greeted by another sigh, and she turned and went to the chairs by the fire. She sat and pulled her feet under her before answering forlornly, "It was his. I have seen the other women who have caught his eye, and at one time I thought he fancied Elizabeth; but then he turned his attention to me, and I was gratified. I am too plain to attract the attention of most of the young men, and too opinionated for them if our father's title draws them in. But Shane appears to appreciate me for who I am. And then you said what you said this morning, and I... began to wonder."

It was my turn to sigh. I put wood on the fire, and curled under my blanket in the chair I had been sleeping in.

"Far be it from me to defend him, but his feelings for you may be sincere. What occurred betwixt him and me need not be indicative of..."

"It would be indicative of his character, would it not?"

I shrugged my acquiescence and pointed at the bottle. She took a pull and passed it over. I took my own drink and started at the beginning. "I was very happy when he came to live with us. Mother was heavy with you, and Elizabeth was still in the nursery. I had been alone for eight years, really, with the exception of my nanny and the other servants – whose children would not play with me, I might add. To have a playmate was a gift from God, as far as I was concerned. I did not care why he had come. I was told his parents had died, but he never spoke of them."

"He was a dour child, all dark hair and eyes and pale skin. I was this happy child for the most part. At least that is what I remember. I was lonely, but happy. I had learned to read, and I had Mister Rucker. And then I had Shane. I saw us as a pair of childhood friends who would grow up to do great things together. At that age, I tended not to dwell on how those stories often went bad."

She smiled.

"We did become the fastest of friends, and we complemented each other well," I continued. "He was always just a bit better than I at all things physical, though, with the exception of riding. He had no affinity for horses, nor they for him. I excelled at books, though he outshone me in mathematics and matters of logic on occasion. He had no mind for philosophy, history, or literature, and often fought with Mister Rucker over the need for anyone to learn any of it. Art was beyond his comprehension. I doubt any of this has changed."

She smiled and shook her head.

I nodded. "Despite our differences, all was truly well until we reached our adolescence and I discovered, though I did not understand the implications at the time, that I favored men far more than women. My adoration of Shane did indeed take a different path at that time, and I yearned for things I did not know how to ask for. I was awkward and unsure and, despite not truly understanding what a sodomite was, or what buggery actually referred to, or anything of that nature, I was leery of expressing my feelings to anyone, because Shane and all the other boys our age only spoke of their interest in women. I thought women were fine, but I wanted to touch boys. So I said and did nothing, and then there was this afternoon where we ended up in a barn during a cold rain and our attempts to warm one another led to something else."

I glanced at her, and found her blushing and studying the fire. I was not flushed. I refused to allow myself to dip below the quiet surface waters my tale was drifting on, and drop down into the murk of memory where I knew the pain and emotions lurked.

"After that afternoon, things were still well between us, for a time. We would sneak into the other's room, or steal away to the hay loft or the woods whenever we could to... ease one another's adolescent fervor. Truly, he always initiated our trysts. Outside of when we were alone and actually engaged in the activity, he would not speak of the activities or our meeting to engage in them; nor would he allow me to. He struck me on several occasions for doing so. And there was one time when he trounced me thoroughly for wiping my hand on the sheets. He had been terrified the maid would know. I had explained that I was sure the maids knew everything anyway, and I always used the bed linen. I went to breakfast with a black eye."

I shook my head. "I remember mother getting that look she has. And Shane daring me to say anything with his eyes. And Father, he did not look at me at all."

My anger was surfacing out of the murk, and I took a long pull on the bottle. Sarah looked sad and did not ask for it back.

"I think we may need another," I said.

"You finish it," she said.

I set it down. I had distracted myself sufficiently. I found the emotional distance I needed again, and went on.

"Then came the period when he began to shun me publicly, not around the family, but around the few friends and acquaintances we had. He called me sodomite and all manner of things. Then he would drink and show up at my room in the wee hours of the morning. He would apologize and explain that people were talking and one of us had to be blamed, and everyone thought I was something of a sissy, anyway. I was mortified, but he always soothed me and I always let him. Eventually it became more than even my love of him could overlook, and I told him no more and began to block my door."

I could not let myself think anymore. I simply let the words tumble out, as I had once rehearsed them in some fantasy I held about speaking of it all to someone. It was sad and amusing to me that I had fantasized about such a thing. I concentrated on that, and not the meaning of the words I spoke.

"That was when the real trouble started. That was when he began to use force to take what he wanted, and our liaisons were no longer pleasurable sessions of mutual release but increasingly violent violations upon my person. I would fight him on occasion, and he would beat me senseless and do what he wanted. Yet I still did not take up arms against him. And I knew I could tell no one, as I would somehow be held to blame in all of it. And, in some way I did feel I was to blame. It was not until he destroyed my horse that I admitted the situation was truly intolerable, and not a thing he would grow beyond or overcome. And then I left."

I was pleased with myself in the telling. I was not crying, though my eyes were moist and my throat constricted. Nor had I shouted or broken anything. I had not delved into the emotion much at all.

"I have never relayed all of that to anyone before," I said.

It was true. I had not told it all even to Alonso, as I had been too ashamed and thought he would think less of me for allowing any of it to happen more than once.

"I am sorry I asked it of you," she whispered.

"Nay, nay, it was for the best. I should have told someone years ago."

"I have seen..." She paused, and I found her eyes as teary as my own. She gave me a grim smile. "I have seen him exhibit some of the behaviors you describe. I have heard whispered things about those years. I have examined this room and seen evidence of strife. I have seen him strike servants. I... He has always displayed the utmost kindness to me. Yet, I sense violence deep in his soul. I found it intriguing. I thought of him as being like all the heroes from the stories, virile, stoic, misunderstood. And... now I feel somewhat the fool..."

"Do you know how many young women I have seduced because they found me dangerous and different?" I asked gently.

"A fair number, I would imagine," she snorted sadly. "More than the number of men you have killed?"

"Far more," I grinned.

"Now I am confused." She smiled. "I know not whether to feel less alone or less unique in my fascination."

"Why do you think I was attracted to him?"

She chuckled, and then sobered to touch my arm. "Oh, Marsdale, he has said such awful things about you. I was heart-set on you as a villain. Yet when you spoke this morning, it was as if your words lit a lamp; and I saw so many things I had hoped would stay hidden in the corners because I did not wish to see them." She took a deep breath. "I think he killed a young boy in the village."

I regarded her sharply. "One that will not be missed, I assume."

She nodded sadly. "All called the fellow a sodomite. I saw Shane with him once. Shane struck him upon seeing me, though they had not seemed to be engaged in a dispute prior to that; quite the opposite. Then he told me the boy had made advances to him. I had, of course, been appalled, and decided what I had seen had been a misunderstanding on my part.

"Some time after that, I made some comment to Shane about being careful when entering the village, lest he be stalked like a buck. It was just a jest. Yet Shane replied quite seriously that he had seen to that matter. Later I learned the boy had been missing for some time. Many thought he had run off to London, but then they found a body with his clothes in the creek the next spring. Many said it was a good riddance, and nothing was made of it."

I sighed sadly. I was not at all surprised. "Justice is only served if you have money or status. I have never known or heard of any place that was not that way. And even then, one can find one's hands tied."

"I do not wish him dead," she implored.

"It is not in my best interests to seek his death," I said with equal solemnity. "Be that as it may, I am concerned for your well-being in light of what I am interpreting as a profound change of heart on your part, which I have been a willing participant in."

She nodded sadly. "He will be quite put out."

"Do you have a... relationship, with our father? Can you speak to him of this?"

"Aye."

"Then I suggest you do so."

"Have you ever told him... anything?" she asked.

"Nay."

She frowned. "Then do I have your permission to...?"

"Aye, tell him anything you feel the need to."

Her embrace was unexpected, but I felt relief in her arms. Once she was gone, I indulged myself in tears and the rest of the bottle. Despite the chair, I slept more soundly than I had since that first night at my uncle's.

I was awakened by another knock on my door. This time, light greeted my opening eyes. I called out an inquiry without rising. The room seemed very cold, and I did not wish to emerge from the blanket. I had not barred the door, and if it was Sarah or the maid I intended to tell them to enter. It was my father's manservant. My father wished to see me.

"It is Christmas morning," I said. This meant nothing to the insistent man.

I dragged myself out of the chair and drew on my coat. I was exceedingly disheveled as I followed the man to the study. My father was in a robe, and pacing. I crossed the room to warm myself at the roaring fire. I decided the light seeping through my drapes had been something of a lie. The sun had not broken the horizon yet.

"You wished to speak with me?" I asked after his man had withdrawn.

"I have been speaking with your sister." His eyes were dark with emotion.

I raised a brow. She had made fast work of that.

"She apparently does not indulge herself in stewing upon matters," I remarked.

He smiled. "Nay, she does not." Then the smile was gone and his eyes held mine. "Do you blame him?"

"For a great many things, but which particular act are you referring to?"

His lips quirked again. "For wanting to marry into the family."

"Nay, nay, I do not blame him for that at all. Nor do I think him a fool for wanting to marry Sarah; she will be more than enough of a catch for most men, though most men would not have the spine to take her on."

"True." He nodded appreciatively. "Thus it irks me that he wished to marry her merely for her relation to me. I had feared that very thing. He asked me for Elizabeth's hand several years ago, and was quite distraught when I told him her betrothal was of some political use to me. I do not think he loved her, either. Not that I truly cared. With Sarah, I care."

I thought it must be good to be Sarah. "So, you had guessed at his design."

"Aye. I am not blind." He shrugged.

"Father, take this how you will, but you have given me great reason to believe you are blind about such things."

His breath was heavy, but his eyes held no malice. "I was not blind then, either."

I felt very cold, despite the fire reddening my hands. "Then, if you were not blind, then one might assume you condoned what occurred."

"I did."

I struck him, good and hard on the jaw, and he was thrown back to his desk. I had not known I would do it until my fist clenched. He seemed no more surprised than I had been at Sarah's slap the day before. He pulled himself up and tested his jaw a little, before retreating to the far side of the desk, where he pulled a bottle and two glasses from a cupboard. He motioned for me to take a seat across from him, and poured for both of us. I sat.

"I deserved that," he said with a rueful grin, "and probably a great deal more."

"Then why?"

"First, let me say that I did not realize events had advanced so very far. When he tortured a horse in order to anger you, I decided enough was enough. I was called away before I could confront him, and by the time I returned, you were gone."

Fury gripped me, and I very carefully set the glass down before I crushed it in my hands or hurled it at him.

"Son," he continued. "You must understand that I will regret that for the rest of my days."

"That will make two of us, then. Why? You did not intend for it to go as it did, but apparently you were not against it occurring."

"I thought it might put you off men." There was no amusement on his face. He was stating a truth.

On several occasions I have been confronted with situations in which there can only be two responses: tears or laughter. I was damned if I was going to cry in front of him, so I laughed.

"It is a damn good thing you are on the other side of this table."

"I know," he chuckled in return. "Why do you think I walked over here?"

I wanted to smash something. I held my voice steady. "Damn you to Hell, you are an utter arse, truly a bastard of the worst design."

He accepted my words with a solemn nod.

"What did I do as a child to earn your hatred?" I asked.

He shook his head thoughtfully. "I never hated you."

"Fine, your dislike then, because I can never remember you approving of me. And that far predates my favoring men."

He sat forward. "Christ, boy, you never knew when to be seen and not heard. And when you were not telling the world about every thought that ran through your head, you were doing a great number of things to insure that you were seen, heard or not. You made pictures with your food. You spoke to your mother's spaniel and every other animal you encountered, as if they would respond. We could not allow you to be seen by proper guests, after you informed the Lady Willoughby that she should have a portrait made like your mother's, because the painter would make her look prettier than she was. In that instance you were three years of age, and you had gotten the better of your nanny's dull wit and escaped the nursery."

I was incredulous. "And you hate, excuse me, dislike me for all of that?"

"You were not as I expected." He sat back, face stern again.

"What did you expect? Shane, a child with little imagination or wit?"

"Aye, I believe I did," he sighed. "I control all facets of my life, and you were this little monster who did things in a totally unexpected fashion."

And thus one of the great questions of my life had been answered; two, actually. It was an anticlimax of the worst sort.

"I was a fool," he said into the silence, his eyes suffused with guilt. But oddly, it was a distant thing, as if he were not confessing to me, as if I were not the one wounded.

"Well, I do not disagree with you," I said sadly, "but why do you feel thus?"

His eyes were back on me, and there was a trace of a smile on his lips. "You have become ten times the man I expected."

I was at a loss. "What...? How...? Damn it, why would you feel thus? What have I done to earn your favor now? Returned home? Admitted I killed a number of men? Dissuaded my sister from a marriage? Been civil to the pastor? Struck you? How can you decide such a thing when truly you know so little of me?"

The smile slowly spread across his face. "I never envisioned a day when I could speak with you in this manner, man to man. I never envisioned a day when I would wish to. And beyond that, your uncle has shared what news you gave him. You have made a man of yourself. You never asked me for anything. You never tarnished our family name. Despite the hardships you were forced to endure, you did not go mad or become a drunk. You survived."

Teresina's words echoed in my head. *Uly, if you feel this is*

Heaven... well, then, how very little you expect of perfection. My father had expected very little of me, indeed. Yet still he was attempting to compliment me, and I felt he was sincere.

"Thank you."

"I will not ask you to forgive me," he said seriously, as if it had been a negotiable matter.

"That would be best, as I am feeling quite torn at the moment, and I would not wish to offer promises I might not be able to keep."

He winced a little. "I understand."

"So, now what do we do?" I asked pleasantly.

He smirked and sighed. "A very good question. What do you wish?"

"Well, I cannot kill Shane. So that is denied me."

"Damn," he sighed. "I thought that your intent. Understand this: I cannot simply banish him, nor would I. He is integral to certain matters now, and well-accepted as my right hand. His loss would be disruptive and difficult to explain."

I shrugged. It was as I had expected, and I thought he dissembled. He would not banish Shane because he did not wish to; no excuses or reasons were necessary.

"My uncle has invited me to accompany him to the colonies. I must confess I have been intrigued by the option. I also do not feel I am ready to spend the rest of my days in studies discussing business and politics. It is probably best that I leave, until the matter of Shane has been resolved in some other fashion. If you are very lucky, someone else may kill him and save you having to make a choice. Or I may die, and then you can adopt him."

Instead of wincing or grimacing, he smiled. "Damn, boy, you are indeed my son."

I did not feel that it was a thing I should take pride in at the moment.

"I have a better idea," he said, and rifled through the papers on the side of the desk. He found one and sailed it across the table between us, so that it came to rest at an angle in front of me. It was a map of Jamaica.

I chuckled with sincere amusement. "So, you will endeavor to solve your problem by sending one of us to the other side of the world."

"You have an excellent grasp of the situation." He grinned.

"You would trust me to see to your interests?"

He chuckled. "I would trust in the fear your presence will engender in the men I have hired, such that they will see to my interests."

"Ah, and what will you expect me to do?"

"Whatever you please. I will grant you ten percent of the profits. You can drink, whore, duel, or whatever else you engaged in throughout your travels in Christendom. You could even marry and produce an heir if you have it in you."

I ignored his jibe and asked solemnly, "How long would this endeavor be expected to last?"

"A year or two; no more, I would imagine." He was growing more enthused with my interest.

"When would I be expected to sail?" I asked.

"As soon as possible in January." He at least had the good sense to grimace at that.

"Then much is in order already, I trust."

He nodded.

"Who did you plan to send if I had not arrived and proven a likely prospect? You surely knew Graeland was ill-suited."

"I thought to send Shane... but..."

"I take it Shane did not wish to go. Or is it that you did not wish to part with him?"

He chuckled and shrugged. "Shane was intrigued by the prospect."

"But you did not wish to risk him."

He met my gaze and sighed. "Nay."

I shrugged. "I will go."

Calm descended over me like a comfortable blanket. I now knew where I stood, and many a question haunting me had been answered. I could not accomplish my goal, as of yet. And I still was not sure if killing him would actually solve much of anything, so I was willing to allow Shane to live for now.

And as for Jamaica, I was actually delighted by the prospect. It would be adventure. And, oddly, it would put me in better graces with my father. Despite the ambivalence I felt toward that at the moment, Rucker's words about my being Earl some day still rang in my heart. If I survived.

Perhaps the Gods were laughing.

Four

Wherein I Obtain Sheep

I found myself on the road to Brighton in the second week of January, 1667; alone save two of my father's men, who were along to protect me from highwaymen and handle my baggage. I did not feel I needed them for the former; but was thankful they were present for the latter. I was not happy with the chests full of clothes, bedding, chamber pot, cookware and other necessaries I was told it would be difficult to obtain in Jamaica, and was pleased someone else was about to lug them around.

I did have some baggage I was pleased to bring, which included my swords and pistols, a moneybox, and two muskets from my father's house. One was a new flintlock my father had given me, and the other Shane's favorite wheellock, which I had quite frankly absconded with. The flintlock was a well-crafted and more functional weapon. The wheellock was an expensive thing of beauty over fifty years in age, its barrel and firing mechanism fabricated to exacting standards by a fine gunsmith in Amsterdam, and its stock inlaid with mother-of-pearl. It had been my grandfather's, and I was damned if I would let Shane keep it.

Another crate was filled with books I had acquired in London with Rucker, and cards, a fine chess set, and other amusements I doubted I could find in the West Indies without paying outrageous sums for their transport. As it was, I was thankful my father had given me a healthy purse with which to outfit myself.

So not all of the baggage was without merit, though it was

cumbersome and not in keeping with how I usually traveled. Conversely, though I usually journeyed alone, I was ill-pleased that on this trek but there was no one to go with me.

Rucker professed not to have the temperament to venture into the unknown. He wished for me to test the waters, as it were, and to tell him if traveling there were truly safe. Likewise, my uncle had already made definite plans concerning Massachusetts, and would be sailing a little later in the spring. I very much wished I could take Sarah with me; but that was not considered appropriate, and I was not sure what I would find in Jamaica in terms of disease or even housing. I assured her she could visit as well, and my father assured me he would be diligent in sheltering her from Shane's wrath. As he actually cared for her, I took his word.

Brighton is a busy place filled with merchants, sailors, marines, and whores. After over a month in the country, I was quite intoxicated to be around so many people. I do not favor a bucolic existence. Yet, considering the nature of the place, I was pleased my leaving would be quick.

Thankfully, the weather was good when we arrived, and it looked as if we would sail on the planned departure date one week hence. Of course, this being January, I was sure that would all change.

I took a room at a pleasant-enough inn, and left the men to handling the trunks, while I slipped away to walk unescorted down to the docks. After a few questions, I located the ship we had chartered, the *King's Hope*. She was a modest three-masted vessel of a hundred tons and four cannon. Our cargo of initial provisions, sugar-mill grinding wheels, gears, pots and trappings, and the other supplies needed to start a plantation, including bondsmen, would comprise most of her cargo. She would be carrying some other goods and passengers, though, and I would be forced to share a cabin.

The vessel was not docked, but moored in the harbor. At my current distance from her, she looked seaworthy enough to my untrained eye. However, I knew not how to judge if a ship was truly fine. To me, all seacraft seem to look something alike, once they become large enough to be ships with several masts and not merely sloops or longboats. Though I still thought of my journey with enthusiasm, the knowledge that I would spend nearly two months cooped aboard that ship damn near put me off the endeavor.

Conversely, I knew if I stood on the dock long enough, the cold wind coming off the bay would make me swim to her if necessary. The last two months spent in an English winter had made me long for my balmy days in Italy. I thought I would be well-pleased with the tropics, as they were warmer still.

A fellow about my own age stood nearby, watching me. He appeared pleasant enough, with large eyes and a drooping face. I was sure he would have jowls as he aged if he put on weight, which he looked to do imminently. Middle age would most likely make him jolly.

I sighed at my bothering to make that much of an assessment of him. The means of my travel to England, the company I kept while here, and especially being ensconced in my father's house, had left me no recourse with which to exercise my manhood. I now found myself eyeing everyone with hope of an interesting dalliance. Sadly, unless I was exceedingly discreet, I could not act on a quarry even if I found one, not while I traveled as my father's son. It did not bode well for my future, and was not a thing I had considered when I accepted his offer. I hoped my horizons would widen considerably once I reached Jamaica.

The man smiled and nodded when I looked his way. "May I offer you assistance, sir?"

"I do not know. I am merely looking over that fine vessel there."

"I see that, sir. Do you have interest in her? She sails within the week, but we still have a little room for another passenger or cargo."

"Are you with her, then? I am the Viscount of Marsdale."

He paled. "Oh, my Lord... Marsdale." He remembered to bow.

I suppressed a sigh. That was going to be another inconvenience of traveling as my father's son. I abhor bowing and scraping, the bestowing of it or the receiving.

"Who might you be?"

"Second Officer James Belfry, sir." He bowed again.

"Pleased to meet you, Mister Belfry. May we board her? I wish to look about."

"Aye, my Lord." He happily led me to a ladder on the side of the wharf, and down to a longboat with four waiting men. I surmised he had been on his way out to the ship.

The vessel thankfully appeared larger as we approached in the small craft, until I climbed the ladder to her deck and beheld its true size. She might have appeared larger from the water, but she was every bit as small as I feared. It would be a long voyage, indeed.

After a moment's indecision, seemingly concerning where to go first, Belfry led me to the hatch and down into the hold. I do not know where he thought the ship had additional space in which to stow further cargo. All of the available volume below deck seemed crammed with crates and barrels, so that there was only a small aisle to stand in, directly below the hatch.

"Mister Belfry, you do know we are to take on bondsman. Where are they to take passage?"

He frowned. "On deck, my Lord."

"And that is customary?" I thought of the biting wind whistling across the box of the hatch above us and grimaced.

"Why yes, my Lord. Is that a problem, sir?" He appeared genuinely confounded.

"It is miserably cold on deck, and I would imagine it is worse at sea."

His frown deepened. "Aye, for the first week or so, sir." Inspiration struck him, and his earnest smile returned. "Then it warms, until all will be pleased they are on deck once we cross the Tropic. We have crossed many a time, sir, with the deck full of men, and our own crew sleeps beneath the forecastle above. We do not lose any men due to cold. Most are dressed for it when they arrive... Unless you have contracted for convicts, sir. In which case we were not aware of it, and other provisions need be made as those men must be kept chained and it's..."

I cut him off with a friendly shake of my head. "Nay, we will hire them here, purportedly. And I am sure you are correct as to them already being dressed appropriately for the weather. You say you do not lose any due to the cold. What, then, are men lost to on the voyage?"

"Well, my Lord, most often to fevers and poxes they bring aboard." He shrugged as he thought on it. "If they are sickly to begin with, sir, they do not often survive the seasickness and..." He grimaced and stammered on. "Well, sir, at the end of a voyage, if we have been becalmed about the Tropic a goodly time, or some other unfortunate, um, well... If it be a difficult voyage, the victuals and water have been known to run low, and some do not survive that. But that is a rare occurrence, my Lord; and rest assured, we will always keep aside adequate food for our passengers, especially your person, sir. You will eat as well as the Captain."

I did not feel reassured and did not think I would rest well on it at all. I did not want to hire men, only to kill them upon a voyage, due to exposure to the weather, the spread of disease, and starvation.

"How much of this cargo is provisions?" I asked. "How much can be expected to spoil on so long a voyage? And how much is allotted per man per day?"

"My Lord, we were instructed to lay in enough victuals for threescore men. They are to receive a pint of beer, a bowl of broth or gruel, a salted herring, an apple, and two biscuits per day. Toward the end we have often run through the herring and apples. And everything will have worms and weevils."

It sounded as if they were in prison, though I suppose prisoners received far less. They definitely did not receive a daily pint.

"There is no meat beyond herring?"

He chuckled. "Nay, my Lord; do not be alarmed, though. There is meat for yourself, sir, and the officers and paying passengers. We will load on four barrels of salted beef and pork, and we have a coop for chickens. Our cook is a fine and skilled man, sir. True, you will not eat as you do in a manor, but I believe we provide fare to rival the local inns."

"I am sure I will be well satisfied," I assured him. "Yet... Mister Belfry, if we were to take on twoscore men instead of three, could they not be fed more?"

"Well, aye, my Lord. But sir, Mister Steins, your agent here, said you wished to reach Jamaica with twoscore men. If you do not take on three, or as many as you can get, you may not arrive with the number you need."

"My God, man, are you suggesting that a third of the men on this ship will die en route?"

He appeared as dismayed as I felt, but I knew it was not for the same reason. "My Lord... It has been known to happen, sir. There is little for it if there is some ailment running amongst them. And in God's truth, sir, though far be it... Well, sir, you may find it difficult to sign on threescore men who are healthy and willing and able to work. I daresay your agent will... well, scrounge up the number you need..."

"How so?"

"The same way the Navy does it, my Lord, and many a ship that is short a crewman or two."

"Press gangs?" I snapped, and he winced.

"Aye, sir, and well, we will take on some besides the ones you need. We can sell their contracts in Jamaica readily enough, if you do not have need of them."

I was truly appalled; and I remembered the boys I met on the road, and how they avoided the cities because of press gangs and disease. My righteous anger deserted me as I realized the men who would travel in what I considered so poor a fashion upon this vessel were actually better off than those boys had been. They would surely eat more.

This kind of thing was why I avoided the poor. Their wretchedness filled me with despair, and I was but an observer. I wished to aid them in some fashion, but there was so very much that need change in order to better their condition. And I was powerless to change the world, unless I gained power through my father. And to do that, I was forced to play the wolf and enslave men to build his wealth. But, by the Gods, I would not starve them or have them indentured against their will.

"Mister Belfry, that is unacceptable," I said sternly. His face fell, and I took pity on him. He was not responsible. "I would see Mister Steins at once."

He nodded quickly, pleased at the prospect of allowing another to deal with the mad lord.

Mister Steins proved to be an agreeable-seeming fellow, despite pinched features and beady eyes. He greeted me warmly, and was surprised at seeing me so soon upon my arrival.

"All is in order, Lord Marsdale." He smiled. "The cargo is loaded. We have had a number of inquiries and will begin signing contracts on the morrow. If God continues to grant us pleasant weather, I will have a crier on the wharf."

"Thank you, I am sure the matter is in excellent hands. There is one small detail..." I paused as Belfry cringed at my side. Steins was regarding a paper a clerk had handed him, and had not witnessed Belfry's consternation. I gave Belfry a reassuring smile, as Steins returned his attention to me.

"And that would be, my Lord?"

"I have heard rumor that, on occasion, bondsmen are pressed into service and..."

Steins frowned. "If you wish to proceed in that manner, it can easily be arranged. It will expedite the process. There are more than enough wretches in this port who have proven unable to govern themselves as good Christians, and spend what little money they have on wine and women. Seven years' labor in a new land, where they may well excel if they prove to have the proper demeanor, will surely do them a world of good."

I considered my own thoughts about the band of boys before I let my anger flare. He was very likely correct.

"I feel you speak the truth... however..." Steins and Belfry regarded me intently; even the clerk had stopped scratching his pen across a page to watch. I braced myself for their derision. "I would rather the men be willing. It has been my experience that tasks are performed better by men who agree to do them."

"And mine, my Lord." Steins smiled pleasantly. "Men who are lazy here will be just as prone to it there, and most likely require you to appoint or hire more overseers, which of course will have cost implications of its own. Please be aware that the process will be somewhat slower without augmenting the roll with pressed men. And if all does not go well, as in days pass and we still lack the necessary number of men, then we may wish to revisit pressing."

I was greatly heartened by this, and forged on. "Excellent. As to the required number of men. Am I to understand that the reason we take on many more than we may want... upon arrival, is due to assumed losses during transit?"

"Aye, my Lord. It is a regrettable part of this business." He shrugged.

He was so very reasonable; he minded me of many a man I had seen, who could order the deaths of many without a second thought. In that, I realized this business I now engaged in was much like any other I had become party to.

I nodded agreeably while choosing my words. I finally remembered Commander Kroener, a jolly mercenary I had crossed paths with. He had held me for ransom for two weeks. The situation had not been unpleasant, as I had been treated as a guest, dining every night at his table and thus learning a great deal from him.

I smiled at Steins. "I traveled extensively prior to my recent return to England. This is one of the reasons my father and I thought I would be well-suited to this endeavor."

This garnered interest from Steins; and he frowned slightly as he listened, paying more heed to my words, now that he knew I was not some lord's son with little experience beyond London and my father's estate.

"In my journeys, I was fortunate to make the acquaintance of an esteemed general. He once told me that he would take a hundred men over a thousand for a prolonged campaign, as a hundred men could move faster and more easily be provisioned. And well-fed men were able to fight better." Kroener had other reasons for this as well, mostly involving the inherent greed of mercenaries and the division of booty, but they were not salient as of yet to this discussion.

"What are you suggesting, my Lord?" Steins asked with genuine curiosity.

"That we hire the number of men we need, healthy, able, and willing men, and we feed them better on the voyage and thus keep them all alive."

He nodded thoughtfully. "Your suggestion is sound in theory. However, I must be honest with you. I do not know if we can recruit twoscore willing men in a fortnight, even with the incentive of land." He paused with pursed lips.

"What incentive of land?" My father had surely not reckoned on giving anyone any land.

"My Lord, bondsmen are indentured for seven years, in exchange for their passage and room and board and other necessities during the term of their contract. On Jamaica, land is currently available to any who petition for it. Thus, we tell the men we recruit that they can become free farmers on their own land after their term is completed."

I was pleased, but something about him indicated it was a thing offered but not guaranteed. I sighed. "But that is not truly the way of it."

"Precisely, my Lord. Their contract of indenture contains many clauses that allow for the extension of their service."

That, my father had mentioned. He had nearly crowed over it, as on Jamaica there would be few to side with the bondsmen and ameliorate excesses on the part of their masters – unlike England, where the peasants could occasionally find someone to sympathize with them.

"May I peruse a contract?"

"Certainly, my Lord." He nodded at his clerk, who produced one. "And as you are presumably aware, many a man dies who ventures to the West Indies. None are spared God's choice in that matter." He gave me a pointed look.

I nodded with a compressed smile. "I am aware of the risk to my person."

"Good, my Lord. So, in short, many of the men we sign will not survive beyond their contracts, though the worthy will live. The ones who are hale and, presumably, favored by God, survive. Truly, a good God-fearing man who is willing to work hard and respect his master has little to fear from indentured servitude or the tropics."

"I am sure you would thrive there." I smiled.

He was taken aback by my words, and struggled for a moment to divine my intent. Finally deciding I had meant him no ill will, he nodded agreeably.

"However, my Lord," he added, "if a man is truly good and God-fearing, he is presumably well-employed here in England, and has little reason to travel elsewhere to seek his fortune."

I found his statement absurd, considering the recent ravages of the plague and London's fire, much less the last forty years of chaos the Reformation and subsequent Restoration caused. There were good poor men all over England. I bit my tongue and struggled to keep the incredulity from my face.

"So you feel we will not be able to recruit men who will stand to reap the benefits of travel to a new land, because... if they were the type of man who would do well here, they would not be seeking to go elsewhere?"

"Precisely, my Lord." He smiled. "So we will do what we are able to acquire good men, and then we will do what we must per your father's instruction."

I clamped my teeth firmly on the inside of my cheek. So there it was. Though he would honor my requests, he would not truly be taking orders from me on the matter. And if my requests proved an impediment to completion of the task to my father's specifications, he would dismiss my concerns like crumbs swept from a table. I was sure I would face the same issue on Jamaica, with both the barrister and the manager my father had retained.

And so I dismissed Belfry back to his ship, and sat at a desk in Steins' office and read through a contract. It was as dreadful as I expected. A bondsman was a virtual slave. I could do anything to them I wished, short of outright murder; and as I well knew, even that could be justified if one dined regularly with the local magistrate. I vowed to ignore most of the document and write up my own. Whether or not I could bring the Jamaican barrister and the Barbadian manager into line with my plans would be another matter.

The next day dawned cold and clear. As I walked down the wharf, I heard Steins' promised crier telling of the fabulous life awaiting any soul adventurous enough to travel to balmy Jamaica. When I arrived at Steins' office, there was a sign advertising our needs outside, and his clerk was setting a small table to rights just inside the door. I was heartened when two young men entered, hats in hand, before the clerk had uncorked his inkwell. They looked to be fine healthy lads, and judging from their resemblance, brothers.

"You be wantin' men for a plantation in the West Indies, sir? And there be land in it for us at the end of the term? What be the term, sir?" the older asked.

The clerk nodded twice. "You will be able to petition for a grant of land. The term is seven years."

"For passage?" the younger asked with some incredulity.

"Passage to a land of opportunity is very expensive," the clerk replied without a trace of humor. "All food, housing, clothing, and other necessities will be provided throughout your term of service."

"What would we be doin', sir?"

"Whatever your master finds you suitable for."

"Me brother's a cooper," the younger added enthusiastically. The older promptly smacked him.

"I was an apprentice cooper, sir," the older said diffidently.

"If you truly possess that skill, it will be of use and valued," the clerk said. He pushed two contracts across the desk to them. "Make your mark there. Then wait outside. Someone will escort you to a longboat and out to the ship this evening. You will be fed then."

That appeared to please them, but they eyed the papers timidly. The older fingered one of them. Surely neither of them could read.

"Hold," I said and approached the table. The clerk and Belfry looked to me with alarm. I ignored them and smiled at the brothers. "I am the Viscount of Marsdale. We are recruiting for my father's plantation, which I shall be involved in managing." They looked to each other and sketched clumsy bows. This close to them, I judged both to be under a score of years. "May I ask why you two wish to journey to Jamaica?"

"Nothin' here, my Lord. My master died," the older said. "And Billy here has no prospects."

"Well, I am sure we will be glad to have you. I just wish for you to be aware of what you stand to lose... and gain."

Behind the table, the clerk cleared his throat nervously. I glared at him and he quieted.

"Jamaica and the West Indies are a dangerous land, but you look like two strong boys ready for adventure."

They smiled.

"There is a good amount of disease there," I added.

"Beggin' your pardon, my Lord, but there be disease here," the older said. "Our family died of the plague."

I had to admit he had a good argument there. I picked up one of the contracts. "Can you read?"

They shook their heads as one.

"Do you wish to know what this says?"

They looked at one another as if I had presented them some great puzzle.

"Is it important, my Lord?" the older asked. "Truth be told, I've never had to make my mark before."

I sighed. I was the fool, not they.

"It says that I will own you for seven years, and that I may do as I wish toward you within the laws of God and man. And if you attempt to escape, or in any way break whatever rules I may set, then your term of service will be extended."

They nodded as if that were perfectly acceptable to them. I smiled wanly and handed them each a contract. Then I retreated from the proceedings and went to a tavern to drink.

I do not understand sheep. Though I do not feel pride at being numbered amongst them, I well understand wolves. I suppose that sheep do not understand wolves, either. I had often bemoaned all of this, but it is quite another thing to witness such an example. I drank and vowed to stop worrying about the damn sheep, or rather to care for them in a responsible manner, but not waste my time attempting to treat them as wolves.

I composed a letter to Rucker in order to air my frustrations and concerns to someone, even if it was only to the silent page. I knew I would not receive a reply prior to sailing.

We, or rather Steins' clerk and Belfry, recruited twelve men that day. And so we proceeded into the next, when we gained ten more. Steins was not pleased with our progress, but he held his tongue as to other options when next we met. On the third day, we garnered fifteen. This nearly gave me the twoscore I wished for.

I decided to wait one day further and move aboard the ship. I had my father's men deliver my baggage to the wharf, and gave each several of my father's coins before dismissing them with my blessing back to Rolland Hall.

As I came aboard the *King's Hope*, men were forced to part and crowd about in little pockets, in order for me to gain the deck. My luggage further complicated matters. One would not think thirty-seven men could appear to be such a crowd, but upon the deck of the *King's Hope* they were indeed. I wondered how the Devil the Captain ever thought to pack threescore or more into the same space. Surely with them crammed so closely together, they would not be able to recline to sleep unless they took turns at it. And the sailors were stepping over men as it was.

Though much of this was because the men were not allowed to spread out beyond the prescribed area of the waist of the main deck. The sailors kept them clear of the two upper decks, those being the fore and aft castles. The forecastle contained the foremast and all manner of rigging. The aftcastle deck was the quarterdeck, which in this instance did not take up a quarter of the length of the vessel, but more a fifth. The quarterdeck contained the aftmast and the rigging for same. And it was reserved strictly for officers and invited passengers, of which Belfry assured me I was one. The bondsmen were also kept out of the shallow but sheltered space below the forecastle, as that is where the *King's Hope's* fifteen crewmen bedded and the cooking was done. Neither were the indentured men allowed under the quarterdeck, as most of this space was taken with the three cabins. The Captain's cabin ran the narrow width of the ship's stern; and the other two cabins, one for all the officers and the other for all the paying passengers, were narrow little rooms on the port and starboard of the sheltered steerage area.

So we would have more than twoscore men packed into a space only half the length of the ship, that is to say perhaps forty feet and only a score of feet wide. They might have all fit as comfortably as they would in the common room of an inn, if that same deck had not been filled with the mainmast, the hatch, the windlass, rigging, and four six-pound cannon on their carriages.

Belfry assigned the stowing of my chests to a Mister Cox, the bo'sun. He began to yell at his sailors to have them put the lot into what little space remained in the hold. I retained one bag with a few favored things and my weapons, and Belfry led me to my home for the next two months: the port-side passenger cabin.

I regarded the little room with dismay, while Belfry cheerfully informed me I would be sharing it with three other men. The cabin was only an arm's length wide and maybe ten feet long. I did not see bunks.

"How are we to sleep?" I asked Belfry, not bothering to hide my mounting horror.

He swallowed and looked apologetic. "Hammocks, my Lord. It's a thing they use in the West Indies."

He indicated two sets of knotted rope affixed to the fore and aft corners of the cabin. He took up an iron loop on one of them and pulled it to a hook in the middle of the outer wall, thus extending a web of netting diagonally across half the room. This one was chest high, and there would be another below it. Once all four were extended, there would be no room to move in the cramped space.

"You, um, crawl into it, my Lord." He demonstrated in a somewhat ungainly manner. Once he was in the bag of netting, he seemed quite comfortable. "It's quite a bit cooler on the body when we enter the tropics, and they also preserve the space of the room during the day, as they can be hung, so," Belfry added after he had managed to crawl out of it.

I noted that, with or without other nets of humanity swinging around one, it was seemingly difficult to enter or leave a hammock in a timely fashion, and it would be best to have one's weapons handy while in one. I also thought it would quickly be obvious who had been in one, as the rope netting would surely leave marks on any skin it touched. My thoughts strayed; I briefly considered the possibilities of sex in one, and found myself quite amused. Then my unrequited needs in that regard filled me with annoyance.

"The Captain would sail soon, my Lord, there's talk of a good blow descending on us in the next week. He would leave before it. He has spoken with Mister Steins."

I nodded. "I will meet with Steins this evening after we know today's count."

Belfry nodded and added cheerfully. "We've had five this morning, my Lord."

"So forty-two, that is excellent."

He left me in the little room I would be trapped in. I set my bag in the corner and contemplated indentured servitude. For a maudlin moment, I wondered if my circumstance was any different than that of the men beyond the door. Was I not granting years of my life to another's whim in exchange for the mere hope of a better future? Then I came to my senses and reminded myself I am a wolf. If I wished to sever my ties to the endeavor I would, and quickly, and God pity any who blocked my path of egress.

I set about learning of hammocks, and determined they would be far more stable if anchored in more than two places. Belfry had not made clambering into one look easy; and I was thankful for that, as it had shown me the possible points of contention before my own attempt.

Thus I did not throw myself head-first upon the floor. However, my sword became stuck in the mesh, and in attempting to free it, I almost fell out. Then I became somewhat bound in the edge, and felt a great urge to thrash about like a fly in a web.

Sometime later, I was relatively assured of being able to enter and exit one without looking the fool, and was beginning to find reclining in one quite comfortable. Upon hearing approaching steps, I quickly clambered out, as I did feel somewhat vulnerable hanging in midair.

Apparently my three roommates had arrived. I saw my own disdain and surprise mirrored in their eyes as they perused the cabin. Or maybe it was at the sight of me; but no, I was greeted with a smile by the first man in. He was an exceedingly handsome youth several years younger than myself. He possessed a slim and attractive build I found appealing, with bright blue eyes and white-gold hair.

He bowed graciously. "Lord Marsdale, I assume."

"Aye." I returned his bow. "And who might I have the honor of addressing?"

"I do not know if it be an honor, my Lord, but I am Thomas Eaton. And these are my fine companions, Mister Harold Scofield and Mister Richard Benton."

Scofield appeared to be an earnest but happy young man with dark hair and eyes and a boy's smile. Being shorter then the others, he seemed quite young in comparison. Benton was tall, lanky, and seemingly older by a year or two. He was effete in the extreme, and dressed with exceptional care. Though his clothing was not notably expensive in cloth, it fit quite well, and was nicely coordinated in both color and texture.

"Oh, this is such a small room. However shall we... manage? Where are the beds?" Benton rattled on, and then took me in and beamed. "And I have never had the pleasure of meeting an actual lord before." I thought he might give me his hand to kiss.

I was once again annoyed with my heritage, or at least with others' knowledge of it. "We will be sleeping on these hammocks, and I would greatly prefer it if you simply called me Marsdale."

"You may call me Dickey if it pleases you, my Lord, everyone else does. And they are Tom and Harry."

Eaton looked a trifle embarrassed. I smiled indulgently. "However you prefer to be called."

"I am actually used to going by Tom, and he is used to being Harry," Tom said. "Though it is boyish of us."

"If that be the case," I shrugged, "I will not stand on formality. Please refrain from the *my Lords* and other acknowledgments of my title. I am rather used to going without them." This seemed to please them.

I moved aside, and let them examine the open hammock and attempt to clamber into it. I initially offered no assistance, and was quite amused by their antics. Finally I decided to relent and offer them advice, and in time they were able to mount their respective hammocks. I made sure I maintained the upper one closest to the door.

We availed ourselves of the built-in bureaus and small shelves, and I warned them away from my weapons bag. When asked what it contained, I was quite forthright about the quantity, if not the quality, of the pieces inside. All three wore swords as any young gentleman would, but only Tom possessed a firearm; and they were quite surprised at the extent of my "arsenal" as Harry dubbed it. I also noted with interest that only Dickey's sword appeared to have any wear about it. I assumed he had inherited it from someone.

"If I may ask, why are you three gentlemen traveling to Jamaica?" I asked. "And what have you heard of it?"

This caused looks of consternation to pass amongst them, and I waited patiently until they decided who would speak. It was Tom, as I surmised. He was definitely their leader.

"There was a bit of a scandal, my Lo…" He shrugged and continued sheepishly, "I have an uncle in Jamaica, and it was decided that I should travel there along with my companions, who were somewhat involved in the incident in question. It is truly not as if we had great prospects awaiting us here in England. We are not first born. If things do not go well in Jamaica, we plan to return in several years. By then the other matter should have calmed considerably."

"I understand how scandal can befall a young man quite easily, and I would never presume to sit in judgment of such a thing," I said. This seemed to relieve them, and yet none of them mentioned the nature of the tale. I was now quite curious as to whether it involved girls or boys. I chose not to pry.

I shrugged. "But as to my second question, what know you of Jamaica?"

"Nothing," Harry said quickly.

"Does your uncle know you to be coming?" I asked Tom.

He nodded. "A set of posts were exchanged."

"So this matter has been decided for a good four months?" Since it took forty-five days to reach Jamaica, I thought this was a good estimate of the fastest a letter could be sent and returned.

"Aye," Dickey said with a wave. "Far longer, actually, as no ships traveled during the storm season or some such thing."

I suppressed a curse at my foolishness. Here I was playing the expert, and I had forgotten no ships sailed to the West Indies in autumn. Their letter would have gone last summer and the reply received late this fall.

"We spent the months with my aunt until a reply was received," Dickey continued.

"So you have been in hiding for a time?" I grinned. "One would think perhaps long enough for the scandal to have resolved itself."

Tom sighed and shrugged. "You have surmised correctly, sir. I seduced a prominent young lady and got her with child. As I had not sufficient prospects, my brother married her."

I grimaced with sympathy and grinned. "And how were your fine companions involved?"

"She was my cousin, and I am the one who arranged their trysts," Harry said dejectedly.

"I am their loyal friend, and their families have never liked me anyway. In fact my own was quite delighted to shoo me out the door," Dickey said with forced cheer.

I truly sympathized with their plight, though I had seen it many times before. I had successfully avoided it myself. It is very easy to play the rogue in a foreign country, and in truth I do not know how many bastards I have sown. I have fought duels over my seductions, but my family was never involved. And, thank the Gods, I have successfully avoided any attempts at forced matrimony. Of course, that has much to do with why I am no longer welcome in several cities.

"Well, look on the bright side," I said. "At least someone paid your passage, and you were not forced on a boat under contract or sent off to the military or navy."

"I thank God for that nightly," Harry said with comical sincerity.

Tom smiled. "As do we all. Though I do not think I would have minded the military or navy so much, as the possibility of a commission existed. One was offered to me, but Dickey and Harry would not have fared as well, and I decided to stand by them."

"That is quite commendable," I said. Harry and Dickey appeared embarrassed by his words, but I could tell there was a strong bond amongst the three of them.

"And why are you traveling to Jamaica, sir?" Tom asked.

"My father wishes to start a plantation there. I am going as his agent."

"And what do you know of Jamaica?" Harry asked.

I grinned. "You may wish to acquire your own arsenals and become proficient in their use. There is no naval or military presence in Jamaica, just militia and the buccaneers."

"Excuse me, the what?" Harry asked.

"Buccaneers. My father's associates were not forthcoming on the origin of the name. They are a group of wild men the Jamaican Governor issues Marques of Reprisal to and allows to dock at Port Royal, in order to receive their Spanish plunder. They provide protection of a sort for the colony. They are privateers and harass the Spanish no end. It is my understanding Port Royal is rife with them."

"Wild men?" Dickey asked.

I grinned. "English, French and Dutch men: purportedly deserters, dissidents, escaped bondsmen and white slaves, former convicts, and all other manner of rabble if the reports are to be believed."

"And they're protecting the colony?" Harry asked with alarm.

"Aye." I wondered what he thought the composition of the English army was, as it differed little from what I had just described.

I had read all I could find on the buccaneers with relish. They were the reason, in part, the Spanish did not drive us off Jamaica. They were truly wild men: though principally English and French, they were a polyglot of a dozen nations, and they called none master. This alarmed a great many in England. Wolves cannot abide another pack of wolves who are not harnessed into the hierarchy in some fashion. Needless to say, everything I heard about the buccaneers and Port Royal only served to intrigue me more.

"You do not appear to be concerned," Dickey noted.

"Aye, I have spent the last ten years traveling about Christendom."

This delighted them, and they pestered me for details of my travels. And thus we partook of the quarterdeck, and whiled away the day spinning tales and watching the goings-on in the port about us.

As the sun sank low, I rowed to shore with Belfry to pick up the day's recruits and speak with Steins. There were eleven more men waiting outside the office. I was both pleased and dismayed, as I thought that sufficient but doubted anyone else would.

"We appear to be at forty-eight," I said upon entering. "It is my understanding Captain Starling wishes to tarry here no longer. I am satisfied with our success in the matter of recruitment."

Steins sighed heavily. "I have never understood how these sailors predict bad weather, though I have learned they are oft correct. My Lord, I would have you wait two more days and employ other methods."

"But as we must sail," I added quickly.

He frowned and glanced at Belfry. "Would you leave us for a moment?"

Belfry nodded and left.

Steins lowered his voice. "Lord Marsdale, you may have sufficient men if all survive; but the Captain would like a few more, as any who survive above the number you require will garner him extra profit."

"I fail to see where that is my concern, and it is my understanding he is the one who wishes to sail anon."

"My Lord, he has requested I employ other methods and deliver another dozen if possible before you sail on the morning tide."

"Must I tolerate that? Is there some contractual obligation?"

"Nay, my Lord, more of an unspoken agreement." Steins shrugged. "However, you may wish for the additional men, if many of the willing ones take ill. You will still have first choice to reach forty. You only have eight to spare now."

"The devil with Captain Starling's profit. I know well how much we paid to charter his craft. I will not be party to the other."

"I thought as much," he sighed. "My Lord, be aware you will not have befriended the man."

"What will he do, have the cook spit in my soup?"

Steins recoiled in surprise. "Nay, my Lord. Captain Starling is a civilized man. He regularly plies between here and Jamaica, and it would behoove you to have a friendly Captain at your disposal. It could save you a great deal of money, and provide for much convenience when you need cargo shipped or goods from England."

"I will take my chances with another if it comes to that," I said.

"Does your father share your principles, my Lord?"

I liked not the sound of that. I imagined he would be writing my father soon, though thankfully it would not reach him prior to our sailing.

"Nay, merely my stubborn disposition. A man would do well not to cross between us. We have a tendency of maiming messengers."

He blanched and nodded quickly. "Well then, my Lord, it has been a pleasure."

"Thank you for all of your fine work on this endeavor."

We exchanged further pleasantries, and I exited and sent Belfry in. I waited outside with the men who would be in my employ; and vowed I would keep every one of them that survived, just to deny Starling his additional profit and Steins his percentage of it. Thus, more from cantankerousness than kindness, I introduced myself to the eleven waiting men, and assured them we would sail on the morrow and all would be well. Belfry appeared ill-at-ease when he joined me.

I pulled him aside as the bondsmen loaded onto the longboat. "Mister Belfry, have my principles inconvenienced you?"

He removed his hat and fidgeted with his periwig. "Well, my Lord, I am due a percentage of any bonus money we receive on each voyage."

"And with our only taking forty-eight, it is likely there will be no bonus money."

"Precisely, my Lord. May I speak frankly, sir?" At my nod, he continued earnestly. "Please understand, I agree in principle with not taking pressed men; they are generally an unruly lot, and far fewer of them survive than those that come willing. And we have trouble enough keeping the sailors on in port." He sighed. "If it were up to me in this instance, we would remain and recruit another day, and perhaps take on a few more barrels of victuals to address your other concerns. But it is not... up to me, that is. And so I am somewhat disappointed that we will sail with so few. And this is due solely to my getting married upon my return, and my anticipating the bonus money as I truly have not before. I must wrestle with my own greed, my Lord. It is not your concern."

I did not blame him in the least. "Mister Belfry, say we had ten additional men and they were sold for a common amount in Port Royal. How much would you expect to reap?"

"Ten percent, or about thirty pounds, my Lord." He flushed a little. "I realize it is not a large sum by your reckoning, but it is near my salary for a year and..."

I held up my hand to stop his justification. "Mister Belfry, I will give you thirty pounds if you will assist me on this voyage in insuring these men are cared for and well-fed with the victuals we have."

His face was suffused with wonderment, until he gathered his wits and nodded enthusiastically. "Aye, my Lord. I can do that, sir. May I say that you are an exceedingly kind and good man, sir."

"You may say that. I am not sure if it is truth, but you may say it. But Belfry, do not tell anyone of our arrangement."

"Of course not, my Lord. The Captain would have me strung up if he knew."

"Then let us avoid that." I grinned. I thought it likely my father would have me strung up for giving this man thirty pounds of his money.

That night, I was invited to dine with Captain Starling. He proved to be a tall, gaunt man of middle age, with an intense gaze and great reserve. I guessed he made few friends, as I could not imagine him smiling or enjoying much of anything in life; especially since he moved with the careful precision of a man in pain. I had seen men who looked as he did before; they always died of something within a year or two. This reminded me of my mother, and due to my earlier mood, I felt affliction had been delivered upon a person who deserved it once again.

If Starling was angry at my decision to not take pressed men for his profit, he said nothing of it. He was a proper gentleman, though not very personable; and he asked polite questions of my travels and the like, and I told him polite half-truths. I asked him of Jamaica, and he assured me that though Jamaica was fine indeed, a true jewel upon the sea, Port Royal was a wretched place much as Sodom and Gomorra must have been. He hoped God would wreak some punishment upon it someday, and advised me to stay on my plantation and well clear of it. This was mainly due to the damn buccaneers, who did not know their place amongst good Christian men, and could not be well controlled as they were all armed. I was amused.

My first night on the ship, I could not sleep. On many occasions in my travels, I have cursed being born to a life of such privilege that I never needed share my bed or even my room as a youth. The luxury of private accommodations and closed doors has left me ill-prepared for sleeping amongst others. Snoring keeps me awake; and due to Shane, the nearness of other bodies in the dark makes me quite anxious.

So I lay swaddled in a single blanket against biting cold, which the small brazier in the corner did little to dispel. My hammock swayed with the ship in the gentle waves of the harbor. I found this both lulling and disconcerting, as I was not used to moving about while sleeping, either. I listened to water lapping upon the hull and the breathing of my sleeping companions. Either all three did not snore or one of them slept no better than I this night. After much listening, I determined Dickey was the one who would be as tired as I on the morn. I considered speaking to him, but thought it might wake the others. Eventually I succumbed to exhaustion.

I woke with a start, to noise and movement which differed markedly from the gentle sounds and waves of the night before. I roused myself and found my roommates already absent. I joined them on the quarterdeck to watch our departure. Already the *King's Hope* was turned about, and a few of her sails had been raised.

It was cold enough for the rigging to be iced and the sails stiff. The sailors pressed the bondsmen into service: not out of need of the extra hands, but because they could not get around them to hoist the sails, and it was easier to have the men standing where the job needed to be done, do it, than find a way to move them.

We caught a good tailwind once we were out of port, and began to make our way south across the ocean. All ships, regardless of nationality, head south until they reach the northeast trade winds, which will blow a ship west from the coast of Africa to the West Indies. These winds lie between the Tropic of Cancer at thirty degrees North latitude and the Equator. I looked to the Captain's charts and saw that Brighton lay at almost fifty-one degrees North latitude. We would be sailing south past France, Spain, and the north of Africa. By necessity, we would stay well to sea, to avoid encountering enemy vessels.

Within hours of being under way, I began to feel a little queasy: just as I had in both of my prior seafaring experiences. In short order I excused myself to the cabin. I clambered into the hammock and lay still, hoping the feeling would pass. Harry joined me shortly; and when dinner came, we both confessed our stomachs were too unsettled to eat, and we were feeling very ill. Belfry came round and assured us we had seasickness and would not die. We would just be miserable until it passed. I had known that. I also knew with some men it never passed. The idea that I might feel this way all the way to Jamaica made me consider holding the Captain at gunpoint and forcing him to turn the damn ship around and put me safely ashore.

That night I managed to consume a little bread and water, only to find myself up on deck mere moments later heaving it over the side. I noticed that there was a great deal of this going on, as it seemed fully half the bondsmen found the sea as disagreeable as I. Not wanting to go back to the confines of our small cabin, where Harry had not cleared the room prior to heaving, I slumped on the deck in the clear place I had found to stand. I listened to the moaning and retching, while regarding what little I could see around me in the light of the sparse lanterns and moon.

It was damn cold and I was thankful my already ailing body felt no need to relieve itself in another fashion, as Belfry had clearly instructed us that any business we must attend to was done on the bow, downwind of everyone else. I did not want to imagine how cold one would be once one dropped trou and squatted on the little rails, above the waves in the wind and spray. I had been lucky to find a chamber pot in my cabin on my last crossing to England, and been able to pay a boy to empty it.

I was somewhat warm on the deck at the moment, since I had dropped down into the multitude of bodies. My elbow was in some poor man's back, and I was practically sitting on another's feet. This man was quiet and tucked into the shadows beneath the gunwale, and in my duress I had not noticed him.

"I am sorry if I trod upon you," I said.

I could see him shrug in the moonlight, though I could not clearly see his face.

"Are you feeling better?" he asked with a rich pleasant voice.

"Nay, but at least I am empty."

He chuckled at that. "Everyone seems to be ill; thankfully, I have not contracted this malady yet."

"It is seasickness, and I have been assured it will pass, though I fear it will not."

"I have never been on a boat before," he said. "I must be lucky; though it could strike on the morrow, I would guess."

"I am Marsdale, who might you be?" I extended my hand.

"Charles Fletcher," he said, and gave me a firm handshake.

"It is a pleasure to meet you, Mister Fletcher."

"Likewise."

"And why, may I ask, have you signed on for this endeavor?"

I could see his toothy smile in the moonlight. "I am a miller by trade, and I had no prospects. A fellow talked to the master miller I apprenticed with, and said they were looking for millers in Jamaica to learn to operate sugar cane mills. I don't know what this sugar cane looks like, but I have no family here, well in England, and so no reason to stay – so I decided to see something else of the world and take my chances."

"Good for you."

"And you, sir?"

I wanted no more fawning and I did not wish to scare him, so I was torn as to whether to speak the truth. Lies were not worth the trouble they could cause on such a long voyage, though. "I am the man you are indentured to; or rather my father is, and I am his agent."

"Oh... I apologize for being forward, sir."

"Pish," I snorted. "If I did not wish to speak with you, I would not be doing so, now would I?"

"I would not think so, sir."

"So, Mister Fletcher, as I cannot sleep in my present condition, and you also seem to be quite awake, tell me of milling. It is a thing I know little of, yet I eat bread on a regular basis."

He seemed quite content with this turn of topic, and lulled me into a peaceful state of mind – despite the duress of my stomach – with a very informative lecture on the proper way to grind grain and the placement of water wheels.

Later I returned to my hammock and found it quite satisfactory: the swaying it performed now, in accordance with the movement of the ship, somehow served to minimize the movement I felt overall. Despite the stench and the constant moaning and caterwauling from Harry – and now Dickey, who had also become quite ill – I stayed in my hammock most of the next day. I moved only under the duress of another bout of nausea.

In the afternoon, I found myself on deck again, next to Fletcher. In the light of day, I was pleased to see him as an honest-faced man of large proportions. He seemed concerned by my presence, and I noted Belfry watching from the quarterdeck.

"What is amiss?" I asked.

"Well, sir, the second officer said we were not to converse with the paying passengers, and... Well, sir, knowing you are our master... well, sir, does that apply?"

I glared at him and then at Belfry, who I summoned with a flick of my finger.

Poor Belfry tried to affect a manner of seriousness and gravity, and only succeeded in making himself appear constipated.

"Is there a problem, Lord Marsdale?" he asked diffidently.

"I was informed there is a rule against fraternisation between the passengers and the cargo."

He sighed and looked perplexed. "My Lord, um, well sir, usually we do not allow them to mingle with the paying passengers, as the passengers do not wish it. You are an exception of course, my Lord, in all things."

I laughed. "Thank you for that fine assessment of my character, Belfry."

"Lord, I did not..."

I waved him off. "And how are things today, Mister Belfry?"

"Fine, my Lord; we have a good wind off the starboard quarter and we're making way. How are we feeling today?"

"Not well, but thank you for your inquiry."

With that, Belfry returned to the quarterdeck; and I watched the sails for a moment as another bout of nausea gripped me. It was good to be a wolf, but my stomach cared not for the matter.

"May I ask a question of a personal nature....my Lord?" Fletcher asked quietly.

I nodded.

"You are a nobleman?"

I eyed him and the others listening to us with a heavy sigh. "I am the Viscount of Marsdale. My father is the Earl of Dorshire."

All eyes went wide.

"Oh, stop, it is a mere accident of birth."

The sailor rummaging in the nearby equipment locker chuckled at that, and I eyed him curiously. He was a powerfully-built young man with dark hair and the glint of amusement in his eye. That interested me. I did not see it in the eyes of the others around us. His gaze flicked my way, and held on mine when he saw I was watching him. There was a degree of diffidence, and he almost dropped his eyes; then defiance flared for a moment, and he held my stare. I smiled at him.

"Tell me, how do you all combat this affliction?" I asked him.

"It passes," he said kindly. "Don't return often once it does. My Lord," he added belatedly.

I snorted and waved him off. "How long?"

"I was sick a month first time I was at sea, my Lord. Course I weren't in any good health to begin with."

"Truly? Why?"

"Press gang."

"This ship?"

"Navy."

"How old were you?"

"Fourteen."

He appeared to be of an age with me; so after being kidnapped, he had spent close to half his life at sea. Once again I thought of Big John and his band of boys.

"Do you enjoy being at sea?"

He shrugged his massive shoulders. "Don't know nuthin' else, my Lord."

"What is your name?"

"Davey Moore."

"Nice to meet you, Mister Moore; I would stand, but I am somewhat incapacitated."

He chuckled. "You should lay there, sir... my Lord. An' it just be Davey. Don't trouble yourself on account o' me." He went about his business with an impish grin, and I decided I liked him.

The bondsmen in earshot were staring at me, and I sighed and slowly began to get to my feet. I regarded Fletcher when I reached my knees. He was watching me with a mixture of awe and fear.

"Mister Belfry is correct; you are quite eccentric, are you not, my Lord?" he asked.

I grinned. "Aye. And you would do well to appreciate it, and not expect me to act as if I am something I am not." I meant well by the words; but I was not sure how he interpreted them as I made my way back to my cabin. I reminded myself once again of the truth of the matter: I was the one who should heed my own advice, and not expect others to be things they were not. But I truly yearned for some of them to be wolves and not sheep. I was lonely. For now, though, I would need to learn to be happy herding the flock I had gathered. I am sure it is a lonely path for all wolves who choose it.

Thankfully, I felt I had the Gods as allies in the endeavor.

Jamaica

March
1667

III

Five

Wherein I Sail Home To Jamaica

The affliction continued for most of a fortnight before abating. Finally, as we approached the Tropic of Cancer three weeks later, I was starting to feel rather well. Except for a few poor souls, everyone had either recovered or was making great strides on the matter. Four bondsmen had died since we sailed, one of them from a sudden onset of pain to his abdomen. In the other three cases, it had not necessarily been from seasickness, but as Belfry had warned, more from the sickness taking its toll on bodies already taxed by some illness they had contracted prior to embarking. Three more men looked to be in such a state that they would not last the week. I was told there was little that could be done for them; though, true to his word, Belfry was seeing that all were well-fed and looked after.

The weather had turned quite balmy as we approached the tropics, and I quickly found my coat and hose to be too hot. So I ceased wearing a coat and took to walking the decks barefoot: much to the amusement of my cabin mates and the chagrin of the Captain and officers, who gave no ground to the heat other than to doff their periwigs. I cared not for their opinion, as I was comfortable, while they became more and more miserable as the temperature climbed. As most of the men, sailors and bondsmen alike, were also shedding layers of clothing, they seemed pleased I was one of their number in regard to the matter.

In that and other ways, I began to be known to them and they to me. As they lost their fear of my rank, they began to speak openly in my presence, and thus became men and not just sheep in my eyes. In addition to Fletcher, I met Grisholm. At thirty-six, he was the oldest man we signed; and Steins had only done so because Grisholm was skilled as a carpenter. I learned the brothers we signed first were named Jenkins. Billy was the younger and Bobby the older. Patterson had been accused of a theft he swore he had not committed. Humboldt's wife and child had died in the plague; and now he was traveling because he did not wish to marry his wife's sister, who was also widowed.

In the back of my thoughts, I could well hear Shane and my father scoffing at me, and even see the sad shake of Alonso's head. I was a piss- poor wolf. You were not supposed to befriend anything you might have to eat. Yet I continued to think of myself as a lonely shepherd, and took comfort in the image.

Truly, I embraced it. After learning that Fletcher could not read, I began to give lessons. I have never endeavored to teach another such a thing, and quickly found the process both frustrating and rewarding. Soon almost all of the men, including the sailors, sat quietly and listened to my instruction. The captain was gracious enough to allow this disruption of the daily activities, only because he thought it proper that all men be able to read the Bible.

I thought it important that all men on a ship know how to read a chart and navigate, but I did not broach this with Starling. Instead I took to having Belfry give me lessons as he was able. In exchange, I aided him in taking the log readings and kept him company on the night watches. I found I hated the shipboard schedule of watch changes every four hours. A man cannot sleep properly when he is expected to be awake for four hours, asleep for the next, and so on. Yet Belfry assured me it was the proper way of things and all ships practiced it.

My cabin mates often joined me in the endeavor of learning sailing. Soon we were all trying to guess what orders the captain or the first officer would give as the wind changed. Tom seemed to possess the most talent at this, and I often teased him that he should have taken a commission in the Navy after all. As he truly hated the watch schedule, he disagreed.

On another front, the return of my health and the increasing heat and resultant lack of clothing amongst threescore men became a source of consternation for me. My libido had returned, and I found myself confronted at every turn by something my manhood found of interest. I retreated to my cabin to handle myself as often as I dared without arousing suspicion; though my attempt to dissemble about it was a fool's errand, as everyone was thus engaged. In a week, I thrice came upon men in the act of buggery, and had to force myself to turn away and not watch. Not so much for the sake of their privacy, as for the sake of my sanity, as I would find it far too frustrating to witness without wanting some of the same.

I was aware that I could have had just about any man on the ship, if I so chose; but that seemed a wrongful use of my position of authority, and I knew I would not enjoy any conquest in that manner. In truth, I was sure any tryst I deigned to engage in would be heavily tainted by the other man's knowledge of my title, even were I not his master.

At first I decided any possible dalliance would therefore be unacceptable under the circumstances, and I would have to survive with my own good hand. Then I saw yet another pair of men fucking and decided enough was enough. I had needs, and there were people presumably available and willing to satiate them. Yet I was unwilling to approach the sailors or bondsmen who met my eye in the moonlight amongst the snoring mass. On one hand, they were sheep, and I have never harbored much interest in them unless it is for a simple tryst. And on the other hand, if my quarry were not discreet, news of the encounter would be all about the ship by morning. It has been my experience that men in authority, which I surely was as their shepherd if not their master, have a more difficult time maintaining respect and order, if all about them know what they shout when the pleasure grips them. Nay, discretion was required if I was to proceed; and therefore I must choose my target wisely.

And so I began to waste endless hours considering the men around me. I was not interested in Belfry. Fletcher, though a sheep, was an apt pupil at letters, and a fine man with a good heart in everything I saw him do or heard him say. I did not think this intrinsic goodness was due to his abiding faith in God, as I have met many an evil God-fearing man, at least within my definition of such things. Yet, his religious conviction did keep him from any act he considered sinful. The night I found him praying for the souls of two coupling sailors I abandoned all thought of him.

My roommates were of interest to me, but that situation also did not appear to be mutual or possible.

"I do not understand how any man could bear to be with another," Tom said one night after literally stumbling upon a coupling on deck.

"Have you never found another man attractive?" I asked with a teasing grin.

He raised an eyebrow at my question. "Aye, and horses on rare occasion, but I do not fuck them. That is why God made women."

"What if there were no women?" I asked.

"Tom can always find women," Harry bragged.

Dickey was in his hammock studying the ceiling. "Aye, he can."

"The sailors on this ship are not allowed ashore. And no women come aboard. What are they to do?" I asked.

"Then they should bloody well kill someone and find a way to get off," Tom said, and rolled over in his hammock to sleep.

I thought it was spoken like a wolf, and I understood his sentiment; but at the same time, it angered me. I told myself he was just a boy who had no real understanding of what he would do in many situations.

Harry nodded his agreement with Tom. He always agreed with Tom. He often followed Tom with his eyes. I was amused at that, rather than angry. I had often seen that before, too.

Dickey continued to stare at the ceiling, deep in thought. He was not the type of man who appealed to me. And though he was quite the fop, I also did not feel he favored men. However, the poor man had probably been told that being effete equaled being a sodomite so many times that he wondered, himself. On this voyage, it did not help that he seemed to blush at everything sexual.

Tom ribbed him about this continually. Despite this, and I guessed, despite many things, Dickey was devoted to Tom. To my experienced eye, it was obvious he thought of the other man as a friend, though, and did not harbor other desires. For one thing, though he blushed at any mention of sex and at the act itself, he did not ever blush upon seeing a man naked, not even Tom.

I crossed them all off my list.

So that left Davey, who was one of the men I had seen engaged in sodomy, and so knew possessed an obvious willingness about the subject. He was quite attractive, far more so than any man I had been with save Alonso, or in truth, Shane. I had been spending a good deal of time around him while learning about sailing, and I had caught him eyeing me a number of times. The stage seemed set, and I but awaited my cue to enter and say my lines.

We were sailing west of Africa now, and approaching the Tropic of Cancer. By the Captain's estimation, we would cross thirty degrees North latitude at approximately midnight, due to our good tailwind and not yet being caught in the doldrums that usually plagued ships just outside the trade winds. As the wind continued into the early afternoon, we were informed there would be a party for all aboard that night. This would include the tapping of a keg of wine. With glee I awaited the night, as this would be an obvious chance to slip away to some nook in the hold with a crew member.

The afternoon rolled around, and I sat with Fletcher and Harry in what had become Fletcher's accustomed place: next to the port gunwale and the forward wall of the passenger cabin. Davey joined us, and I eyed him happily. I think he was beginning to read my looks correctly. His face seemed to alternate between speculation and anxiety as he regarded me.

"So is there a party every time the ship crosses this line?" Harry asked.

Davey nodded and shrugged. "It's tradition. It's not as important as crossin' the Equator, though."

"I wonder why," I mused. "Though I assume it is more likely an excuse to have a party than any meaning being attributed to this or that line."

"Sometimes we're in the doldrums for days tryin' ta reach it, and then we celebrate 'cause we made it and we should hit the trades soon," Davey replied.

I had to agree with that. It was my understanding that we had been lucky so far, and we had made good time traveling south from England under benefit of fickle winds.

"What is this Tropic thing?" Harry asked.

"Thirty degrees North latitude," I replied. They all regarded me with blank expressions of confusion, and I sighed.

"It is the farthest north the sun comes in the summer. The low point is the Tropic of Capricorn."

They were still immersed in incomprehension.

"You know the sun moves, correct?" I asked. "It is high in the sky during the summer, and the days are longer; and then, in winter, it is to the south, and the days are shorter, at least from the perspective of someone in England. Around the Mediterranean they do not get so short... but I digress."

This received nods from all of them.

"All right, then, the sun comes thirty degrees north of the equator at the height of summer."

"What's a degree?" Fletcher asked.

"A degree of latitude." I explained latitude and longitude to the best of my ability, and why we could easily reckon latitude, but our lack of accurate ship's chronometers kept us from reckoning longitude at sea. Fletcher and Harry seemed to grasp the idea, at least in concept; but Davey was not comprehending at all, and growing belligerent.

"How do we know it?" Davey asked. "These things weren't here when God made the Earth, were they?"

"Nay, well, in concept. Men decided on it. We had to have a way to navigate and draw more precise maps."

"But how do we know?"

"Because the math tells us it is correct."

"How do we know math works?" he asked.

At this juncture, I was not sure if he was being contrary or if he really could not grasp the concepts of math and geometry. Either way, my ardor died; and I put aside all thoughts of him. My manhood protested loudly, but my mind was able to staunch its cries with thoughts of how damn embarrassing it would be to engage in intercourse with a man I could not converse rationally with. I have some pride.

A vast melancholy settled over my soul within the following hours. I sat on deck and looked over the men arrayed around me, and listened to Harry relay my lecture to Dickey and Tom in a somewhat inaccurate manner. At least he had learned something; but I had assumed the three of them to be far better educated, and this knowledge that they lacked knowledge was most disheartening. These were the type of men who traveled to the New World, who I would have at my disposal for conversation and more intimate pursuits in the West Indies.

I might as well have joined a monastery of morons. There were no universities, studios, libraries, galleries, courts, or gardens frequented by artists, poets, philosophers, courtesans, and learned men or women of any kind; at least, not unless you were Spanish. I would not find myself amongst the company I was used to associating with in the locales I was used to associating in. And while I had known all of this, spending time with Davey, Fletcher, and my cabin mates made the matter so evident as to be impossible to tuck into the back corners of my mind and ignore.

In truth, this was not much different from most of my life. I long ago became resigned to spending my time in the company of individuals who are not my peers in one fashion or another. Either my former associates had been intelligent but common and uneducated, or noble and educated yet stupid, or intelligent and noble yet disagreeable, or any other combination of traits that always required my making some form of sacrifice or compromise in order to appease my social or sexual desires.

I was still in such a state of mind when the festivities began for the line crossing. As I was quite depressed, I drank a copious amount of wine and hid in our cabin, leaving those who knew me to think what they would. Our tailwind gave out at dawn, and we floated using the mizzen sail to catch what little breezes we could. We were becalmed thus for three days, and I shared the frustration and melancholy of all aboard, though I had preceded them quite handily into the state.

Tempers began to flare in the still heat, and several fights broke out amongst the bondsmen. I was forced to mediate, lest the Captain make good on a threat to clap the offending men in irons and throw them below, into the narrow caverns of sweltering heat, shifting crates, and rats.

As for the crew, I saw Mister Cox, the bo'sun, lay about quite often with his starter, which was a length of knotted rope. He would strike any man he felt was shirking his duties or not moving fast enough for his liking. The sailors seemed to accept this grudgingly, and cringed whenever the man was near, like the good sheep they were.

I have had the good fortune of never being in a situation, since Shane, in which I have been struck and not able to retaliate. And even though I viewed that situation as being of my own making, and I could do nothing about it in the near future, it would not go unpunished. As a wolf, I have never been able to comprehend the equanimity with which sheep face regular beatings and other humiliations. If I am struck, I demand satisfaction, even if obtaining that satisfaction may result in my death.

So knowing Davey had that spark of defiance that had attracted me to him in the first place, I was not wholly surprised when, on the third day, he struck the bo'sun. Or so he was charged. I did not witness the event in question, and by the time I heard about the whole affair, they already had him stripped to the waist and bound to the main mast shrouds. And so I stood there and watched with everyone else, as Davey was given ten lashes on his already-scarred back. I was pleased to note he took the whole thing with anger and not submission. The only sound he made was a growled curse when they doused him with salt water afterwards. This, of course, earned him another two lashes, as the Captain disliked profanity.

In the aftermath, I experienced great consternation. I had not attempted to stop the proceedings, or even questioned the Captain's judgment. It would have been imprudent and quite arrogant, though I could have as my father's son. But that kind of thing would have reflected badly upon me, and news would have traveled about Port Royal of the incident. And unlike not wishing to sign pressed men, which would be understood by some, having reservations about a man being flogged for insubordination was not a thing another wolf would understand. Yet, as a result, I felt I had abandoned one of my flock. I was not being a good wolf, in that I was not protecting them. But I was being a good wolf in the eyes of my fellow wolves. What were my father's name and the damn title going to mean to me in the end? Was it worth my soul?

When they released Davey, I waited a while for things to die down, and then I went to the cramped space under the forecastle where the sailors slept. The old sailor who was the ship's carpenter and the closest thing she had to a surgeon was tending Davey's wounds. I dropped down next to them and waited until he finished. Davey eyed me with smoldering wrath.

"I would ask what happened, but I suppose it does not matter," I said.

He shrugged and regretted it. "I was gonna hit him, but I didn't."

I nodded and waited until the old man left. We were relatively alone, and I leaned closer to whisper, "Do you wish to stay on this ship when we reach Port Royal?"

He frowned and studied me. "What da ya mean?"

"I could aid you in getting off this ship and in finding other prospects, if you so desire."

"Why would ya?" He regarded me speculatively and I remembered where I had left off four days ago in thinking about him. He had possibly not abandoned thinking about me, and did not know I was no longer interested.

I chose not to address that particular issue unless he did. "I derive great satisfaction from acting as a benefactor."

"That why you're teachin' all to read?"

"Precisely."

"You got a plantation. Don't want field work. Rather stay here."

"That is not what I had in mind. You could learn a trade or join the privateers or what have you."

"What else you want? 'Cause if it's that, you won't have to pay."

Well, he had addressed it. "That is not what I want. I considered... that, but I do not feel it is in either of our best interests."

He raised his head and glared at me in challenge. "Why?"

I swore silently but smiled. "I often engage in casual carnal relations with women; however, I tend to engage in relationships of a longer duration with men." Though I had buggered and run on numerous occasions, he need not be aware of it. "Until I understand how such things could be perceived, I cannot afford to be seen with a man in the circles I must travel while doing my father's business. And I do not want either of us to feel beholden to each other in that way."

He frowned and I realized, as I had several times before, that in my need to speak formally I had spoken over his head.

"I do not know how they look upon sodomy in Port Royal, and I do not want to cause trouble for my father."

He nodded his understanding. "I'll feel beholden to ya."

"Would it not be worse if we were fucking?"

He nodded again. "Aye, I can see that." He was thoughtful for a moment. "I'll take yar offer."

As usual, my first reaction to the acceptance of one of my overtures of philanthropy was a feeling of grace. This was always followed by a feeling of doubt. I thought through the possible courses this act of kindness could follow, and decided I did not care. I would help those I could, how I could, and damn the consequences.

Thus I truly added Davey to my flock.

Reduced to fouler and fouler victuals, we ran due west at seventeen degrees North latitude until we saw grey smudges upon the horizon. The Captain claimed it was the English colony of Antigua. I was thankful. I thought we would anchor there and bring fresh water aboard; but nay, the Captain altered our course to the north, and we passed a number of other islands, until he turned us south and we dropped through a passage into the Northern Sea.

Belfry informed me that we did not stop until Jamaica, because additional victuals and water would cost money, and there was a chance bondsmen would slip over the side when we were in the shallow waters of a bay. Apparently this would be a concern when we reached Port Royal, as well. I had not thought of that, and I eyed my remaining forty-one bondsmen with suspicion – until I realized that none of them could swim. I surely could not. And then I wondered if I would wish to pursue them, if they so greatly wished to escape their contracts that they were willing to brave sharks and drowning to do so.

I thought that if I were not allowed to disembark soon, I might brave splashing about in a bay. I was tired of being at sea, though I had become very familiar with the motion of the vessel and the daily rhythms of life on a ship. However, I was beginning to experience disturbing dreams of sailing forever with sharks in my wake, never finding land and being alone without a soul to hear my cries.

Once past the Windward Islands, we were no longer in the ocean, and now sailed the clearer waters of the Northern Sea. It was the first week of March, 1667. We had been at sea over five weeks. Anticipation was winding its way through all our minds, and every man aboard spent time gazing to the north in hopes of sighting land. We settled back into a strictly westward course at seventeen degrees North latitude, which would take us south of Puerto Rico and Hispaniola before we reached Jamaica. All three islands were in an orderly row, and I wondered at that. Were such things truly a plan of God, or was there some more mundane explanation?

The water we sailed through became so clear I could see things of color in its depths. While relieving myself, and any other time I had occasion to be at the rail, I took amusement in studying the sharks. In this water, one could see the entirety of their bodies and not just their fins. They were sleek and handsome creatures. They resembled the porpoises that occasionally paced us. Everyone delighted in the porpoises, as they were jolly fanciful animals that seemed to make fun of life. The sharks were hated and feared, and no one was pleased they kept us constant company.

"I am thankful the sharks do not have a penchant for, or possibly the ability to, leap out of the water as the porpoises do," I observed after my morning trip to the poop deck. Fletcher, Davey, and my cabin mates were around as usual, awaiting breakfast.

"God must have made them unable to jump in order not to plague seaman more than necessary," Fletcher said. "It's bad enough they follow us everywhere."

"We keep dumping refuse over the side," I said, with a vague gesture in reference to my recent activities. "They appear to eat it or at least consider eating it. Though most I have observed have possessed better taste. However, any other matter of waste we produce, they quickly gobble down, rather like pigs or crows. If we stopped dumping things over the side, they would probably desert us."

As usual, the religious content of his comment disturbed me. I had spent a good deal of time ruminating on where I would lead my flock. Most wolves are only religious when it suits them. Sheep are usually highly religious, and I thought they could stand to lose some of that. As many have noted, I am not the most religious of men and it is very likely I will burn in Hell.

"And Fletcher, I find your theory a little farfetched," I added jovially. "Sharks have been in existence for all of recorded history, and I am fair certain far longer than that, surely before man put to sea in any kind of craft."

"God foresaw that we would do such things," Fletcher replied.

I studied him and my companions. They seemed to either not understand the overreaching philosophy of what he was saying, or more likely, did not care.

"But Fletcher," I protested. "I can put no stock in that, either. I cannot see God the Creator sitting around thinking of things such as not making a shark leap, so that future sailors could dangle their rears over the sides of ships to safely do their business."

My lack of faith, or possibly reverence, was apparently being noted by Fletcher. He awarded me a somber frown followed by a grimace of consternation.

"Lord Marsdale, then what do you suppose God thinks about?"

He was not asking as a child asks a teacher, but quite the other way around, and I realized he was seeking purchase to lecture me on the subject. On the one hand, I was proud of him for wanting to challenge me, but on the other, I was appalled at the nature of it.

Four other pairs of eyes were now staring me down, though. I sighed. "I imagine God thinking of things such as...." In truth, I was not sure I had ever thought about God as an entity thinking about anything. Whole weeks of my life passed quite happily with not a single thought of the divine in my head. "As...As, whether or not the granting of freewill was in His best interest. And possibly mathematical equations."

"Are you saying that God would doubt his own decisions?" Fletcher asked, somewhat aghast.

"Aye, we were made in his image, and we doubt; why should He not?" I replied.

Our companions' minds were now filled with the vile substance of doubt; I could see it on their faces. Well, if I had done nothing else today, even if I be branded heretic by nightfall, at least I had made my sheep think.

"God is perfect," Dickey countered hesitantly.

"Then where does the doubt come from?" I asked.

"The Devil," Tom said as if the answer should be known by all.

"The Devil, you say?" I teased. I was not sure if I remembered enough of my Sunday lessons to truly engage in the discourse at hand, but it was a discussion of sorts, philosophical even, and it had been ages since I had been granted the opportunity. "Did not God make the Devil?"

"But not in his own image." Dickey quickly countered.

"Then in what image did He make him? Is God not all things? So how could something exist beyond God that God could pattern something from? By the very definition of God's omnipresence, are not all things in God's image?"

There were frowns and grimaces all around.

"Perhaps discussing this is unwise," Harry said.

"In what way, good sir? Do you feel God will hear us from on high and judge us heretics? Did God not give us the ability to question and reason, presumably in his image?"

"Respectfully," Dickey said.

"If God feels we are being disrespectful, may he command the sharks to leap forth from the sea and bite our hairy arses," I said.

Dickey blanched. "Sir, with all due respect, yours is the hairy arse that should be bit, as you began this."

Without doffing my breeches, I hung my arse over the gunwale so that it could easily be seen by the one shark doggedly keeping pace with us on that side of the ship. It did not leap forth from the water.

"God will deal with you later, I am sure," Dickey said with a great deal of dignity.

I laughed.

"Land ho!" the lookout shouted from the crow's nest. I was almost disappointed, as this summarily dismissed the subject at hand, while we all tried to crowd to the bow or stand on something so that we could see beyond the others. I was truly disappointed when my aching eyes finally beheld another faint smudge on the northwestern horizon.

I joined Belfry and the captain on the quarterdeck.

"Hispaniola?" I asked.

The captain was reckoning our latitude, and nodded shortly. "It would be best if it were, my Lord."

"Otherwise we are lost?"

He snorted.

As we drew closer over the course of the day, the land continued to meet their expectations in general shape and supposed chart location, and we steered so that we could keep it in sight but stay well clear of it. Hispaniola is a Spanish colony, and though most of the traffic through the Northern Sea usually plied the passages between Hispaniola and Cuba to the northwest, the island did have a number of cities on her southern side. It was, of course, not in our best interests to run afoul of any ship that might be visiting them; though, oddly, it was unlikely any such ship would be Spanish.

The Captain had assured me, as I had already known, that we had little to fear of running afoul of a Spanish vessel. We were more likely to encounter smugglers, privateers, or pirates in these supposedly Spanish waters. The Spaniards had never recovered from the loss of their armada in 1588. For all the wealth that seemingly poured from the New World to Spain, they did not seem to be reaping the benefits of it to the degree I would imagine: at least not in terms of rebuilding their navy. All of their enemies knew they did not have the number of naval ships necessary to patrol the West Indies. Which was why the English, French, and Dutch now had colonies here. The Spanish could destroy any one of them, to be sure, but not all.

So we kept watchful eyes on the seas out of fear of the French. They had settlements on the west end of Hispaniola, and a colony on Tortuga, the small islet just off the northern shore. We were still purportedly at war with France, and they issued as many Marques as we did.

So we kept Hispaniola barely in sight for three days, and then the captain angled our course ever so slightly to the northwest and we headed for Jamaica. The next "Land Ho" from the crow's nest brought much jubilation. With equal parts relief and anticipation, I joined the others in watching the grey smudge become an increasingly taller green isle. I began to realize this was my new home. I recalled all the other times I had ridden into strange and unknown places and the delight I had found in mounting my personal discovery of them. I reassured myself that I had few regrets.

Despite descriptions of its topography and flora, I was surprised to view a place so hilly and lush. I supposed this to be the norm for a land that never experienced winter. It was early March, and yet the temperature was the hottest I could ever recall experiencing. The air was so moist that once one perspired, one did not seem to dry unless one stood still in a heavy breeze. It was only logical that any location so climed would grow greenery like a hothouse. No wonder everyone wanted to plant things of value here.

The climate cannot explain the white sand of the beaches, though, or the azure beauty of the sea. From the deck of the ship, it was one of the most beautiful places I had ever beheld.

Port Royal sits on a cay, at the end of a long peninsula of land that arcs south and west from the island proper, enclosing a large bay. The northern side of this bay is fed by two rivers. They deliver a great deal of silt, making it unsuitable for larger craft. So upon establishing Jamaica as a colony, the English built Port Royal on the cay in order to take advantage of the best anchorage the huge harbor offered. The Spanish, not being the greatest of sailing nations despite the vast number of ships they once commanded, had not favored the site and had built farther inland and at other places along the coast.

The cay, according to my studies, had recently been joined to the peninsula by filling in the shallow brine marsh that separated them. This afforded the town greater area and allowed a land passage to the mainland, though it was quite roundabout. Most sailed or rowed across the bay to the plantations and Spanish Town, a small town about five miles inland up the Copper River. The Governor had recently moved his house there. According to my father's associates, it had been decided that the Governor should reside someplace that the buccaneers did not.

From the sea, I could not truly tell where the Palisadoes, as the long peninsula was called, started. It initially looked like any other stretch of shore we had sailed past. Then I saw that it was more sparsely forested, with palms, cacti, and the like; and I remembered that the end of the Palisadoes, and the cay which Port Royal resided on, did not have a water source. All water had to be brought across the bay. It was also my understanding that Port Royal and its environs were often plagued by small earthquakes. I did not find all of this overly alarming. The plantation I was sent to build would be inland and have water.

We saw other ships before we saw any architectural evidence of Port Royal. Then finally we saw demonstration of human habitation. Belfry joined us at the rail and instructed us on various features. There were scattered small buildings on the Palisadoes, and then an armed wall marking the eastern edge of the town proper, and presumably the original cay. Following that, there were more buildings, mostly houses from the looks of them, and a church: St. Peters and Church of England, according to Belfry. He had taken service there on his prior voyages. He complained that the town was rife with Jews driven from Brazil, all manner of other Protestants, and even some Popish men. And that most of the buccaneers appeared to be Godless, as there was no report of them entering any church. I did not venture to explain that

that bit of news sat well with me.

We soon could see a great number of more densely-packed buildings along the northern side of the cay, where the harbor was – including several large structures, which Belfry said were the King's House and various warehouses. The southern shore we sailed along was inhabited, but not to the extent the northern edge was.

We came to Fort Charles, which had originally been Fort Cromwell, and renamed, of course, after the Restoration. This seemed to be small. All the structures bearing the name fort that I was familiar with were far larger edifices. Yet I assured myself it was a significant structure considering its locale. And it appeared to be undergoing additional construction.

"The passage up into the harbor is just past the fort," Belfry said. "On the right, we will pass the Chocolata Hole, which is a shallow bay where the buccaneer and freebooter vessels anchor. It is well-suited to their sloops and ketches. It doesn't have a proper wharf, but they moor and row longboats or canoes to the beach if their craft is too large to beach."

I frowned at this. "Why Chocolata?"

"My Lord?" Belfry asked.

Davey was chuckling and I was sure I already had my answer, yet I felt compelled to press the man. "Why is it named thusly?"

"What, the Hole, sir? I do not know. It's where the buccaneers and freebooters dock; they named it thus. It is an odd name, now that I think of it, though I haven't considered it before. They do grow cocoa here, but..."

He noticed my amusement.

"Do you feel it has some other meaning, my Lord?"

"I feel it may have a certain connotation," I said.

"What is it called again?" Dickey asked.

"The Chocolata Hole," Belfry supplied with careful enunciation.

Dickey suppressed a small smile and flushed, "Ah, I find myself in agreement with Lord Marsdale." He started laughing. "Though I dare not say how a young man of my upbringing would have heard of such a thing."

Tom was chuckling now, but Harry looked as confused as Belfry and Fletcher.

"Would someone please explain?" Belfry asked.

"I believe it may be in reference to sodomy," I said, which evinced a great guffaw of laughter from Davey and several of the other men standing nearby.

"Oh," Belfry said, while staring at the place in question as we began to round the point. "Oh my. That's...." The surprise evident on his face transmuted to indignation. "How crude."

I ignored him and turned my attention to the craft clustered in and about the crudely but amusingly named location. I judged the Hole to be maybe a hundred yards across, and there were two sleek craft anchored in the center, the *Charles* and the *North Wind*. A smaller craft was all the way on the beach, which was bustling with activity.

Another vessel was anchored almost in the passage, and awaiting a change in the wind or tide I would assume. Named the *Griffon*, she was a frigate and about the same size as our vessel, though she was far sleeker. Her deck held many more men than ours. I studied these men, who I assumed were buccaneers, as we passed at the distance of a hundred feet or so. For the most part they wore canvas breeches and tunics or vests, with brightly colored kerchiefs on their heads; and, oddly, gold sparkling at their ears. They were all armed, pistol and musket as well as swords, and looked like an army of mercenaries.

With the sleek lines of the vessel and their dark eyes watching us with predatory intent, I was minded of the sharks. I was sure this one could leap forth from the water and bite whatever hairy arse it chose. I wondered if Fletcher would claim God responsible for that, too.

It was obvious to them we held a cargo of bondsmen, and they shouted many words of encouragement in several languages as we passed: most suggesting that our cargo would do well to jump ship, and if they ever did run, they would have a home amongst the Brethren, as these men apparently called themselves.

"Look at her; she's not even flying the Union Jack. She's already under the damn buccaneer Jolly Roger," Belfry muttered. "No respect."

I looked at the *Griffon's* flags; she was flying red colors, no markings, just brilliant crimson against the blue sky.

"Jolly Roger?" I asked.

"You don't think that has another connotation, do you, sir? I was under the impression it was a French term. Perhaps...."

I shuffled it about a bit in my mind until I understood.

"Jolie Rouge," I pronounced correctly in its native language. "Pretty Red. I would think the connotations would involve blood or power."

"But nothing more... salacious?" he asked.

"Possibly," I teased with a grave face. I left him to contemplating the possible salacious meanings behind every term he must have heard in these parts and looked over my companions. Fletcher was viewing the *Griffon* with alarm, as were Harry and Dickey, but there was a spark of curiosity in Tom's eyes, and Davey's gaze positively ached with yearning. He caught my eyes.

"You can join them," I mouthed.

"How?" He shook his head at my foolishness.

Belfry was called by the captain, and I stepped closer to Davey to speak quietly. "I do not know yet. Let me see more of the lay of the land so that I can formulate a strategy. Will we dock?"

He sighed. "Captain's not stupid. He won't even dock until after you have your men off. And this wharf is damn expensive. We'll come in to offload your cargo real quick."

"That does complicate things. Still... Do you maintain the same watch schedule in port?"

He frowned. "Aye."

"Good, then I shall know when you should be on deck. Be ready to leave at a moment's notice. If the opportunity presents itself, I cannot have you chasing about after your possessions."

He shook his head with a derisive snort. "I only have a small bag."

I snorted in turn. "I usually travel as light."

He did not seem to believe me, and I sighed.

A hand rested on my shoulder; and I forced myself not to start, and instead, glanced casually back to see Fletcher.

"The bo'sun's watching you two," he said just as casually.

I smiled as if he had just delivered a joke. Old Fletcher had a dishonest bone in his body after all, and the wherewithal to exercise it.

I ignored Davey for now, and returned to watching the shore of my new home. The rest of the Port Royal side of the passage into the harbor was lined with buildings and pens on the beach; someone said they were for sea turtles. Then we rounded the second point and came into the harbor itself. As Davey said, the captain did not steer for any of the wharfs, but instead sailed into the bay and anchored nearly a quarter mile from shore.

Captain Starling asked to meet with me in his cabin, and I quickly obliged. He sat at his desk with a tired sigh and the wave of a fan. The cabin was sweltering, and he had dressed to go ashore in periwig, large hat, full coat, and boots.

"We will go ashore and meet with your father's agent," he said slowly. "Steins gave me a letter for him to introduce you, as we have arrived well before any other news of your coming could. The bondsmen will stay here until you have a place to take them. You are contracted for a week in that regard; additional days will cost additional money. I am sure your agent will have made arrangements, though, and you will probably have them all cleared in a day or two. After your men are secure, we will dock and unload your cargo. Before that, we have one final bit of business. You were contracted for twoscore men and there are forty-one. Since you have befriended the lot of them," he seemed disapproving of this, "I leave it to you to choose which one I get to sell."

I was appalled but I suppose it was to be expected. "I want all of them. How much would one of their contracts normally fetch? Name an amount and I will pay you."

He nodded slowly. "I thought you might say as much. Forty pounds."

I knew this was high, yet I saw no point in bargaining. Between this and the amount I had promised Belfry, I had nearly halved what little my father had given me for my own use.

I retrieved my purse, and he handed me a sheaf of contracts.

"Whichever one you choose is yours; the rest will be handed to your father's man," he said.

It seemed an odd thing for him to say, until I realized the implications. I had purchased this contract, not my father. I rifled through the sheets until I found Fletcher's.

A half hour later, my cabin mates and I were gathered on the deck with our belongings and prepared to depart. The captain would be rowed ashore with us, to meet with my father's barrister, a Mister Theodore. Most of my baggage would be landed with the rest of the cargo. I, of course, retained my weapons and personal bag.

I left Old Grisholm in charge of the men and took Fletcher with me. I told him it was to aid in the arrangements, and he did not question it. The others were anxious to get off the damn ship, and I assured them I would get them ashore as soon as I could.

As I was not sure under what circumstances I would see him again, I pulled Belfry aside and pressed a bag of coin into his hand.

"Thank you for a fine voyage and all your assistance. I wish you well in your coming nuptials."

"Thank you, my Lord, your fine acquaintance has honored me greatly. Perhaps we will meet again the next time we sail here."

"But of course, feel free to pay me a call. You will be most welcome."

He bowed deeply, and I responded as if he were a gentleman of station equal to my own. He seemed to take great pleasure in this, and we parted company.

I did not see Davey. It was still his watch, and he should have been above deck; but he was not to be seen, though I did notice the bo'sun eyeing me with a smirk. I vowed to settle accounts with that man when I came to pick up Davey. It seemed he harbored a mistaken perception of his own worth.

Shortly thereafter, we disembarked onto the longboat and were rowed to the common wharf across from the King's House. It was the original Governor's mansion until he moved to Spanish Town. There were no ships before the landing, and so the large house was afforded an uninterrupted view of the bay and mountains to the north.

The rest of the half mile or so of the northern side of the cay was quite crowded with ships and wharfs and buildings of several stories in height. There were three docked ships: all English merchant vessels of large tonnage, and all in the process of unloading and loading cargo. Four other vessels rode at anchor in the harbor. They presented quite an engaging sight against the lush green mountains, which I guessed to be the Blue Mountains from the crude maps I had seen.

The landing places bustled with activity, as people, dressed both well and common, embarked or disembarked from the small craft that were used to cross the bay. All in all, it looked like any small English port I had seen. Oddly, I did not see any buccaneers.

Captain Starling met with a man on the wharf and sent for someone to fetch my father's barrister. I was not looking forward to meeting this Theodore, as I was sure he would be much as Steins had been. Starling also sent someone to fetch Tom's uncle's man. Then the captain sat in the shade and waved his fan.

I took the opportunity to pull Fletcher aside and explain what had occurred. I handed him the contract and bade him tear it up.

He shook his head with wonder. "But Lord Marsdale, you have paid my passage here."

"Then I expect to hire you cheaply to run my mills," I chided. "And you owe me forty pounds."

His eyes went wide at the sum. "My Lord, I may as well be your bondsman," he shrugged.

"Let us draw up our own contract for a term based on the number of years it would actually take you to earn the money, as if it were a loan."

He finally smiled; and then true elation gripped him, and he swept me up in a great embrace. As I had not been chest to chest with another man in months, I was torn between wanting him to stop breaking my back and wanting him to squeeze tighter. Thankfully he released me before my hungry body tried to wrap itself around him.

We rejoined the boys, who were regarding us curiously. I explained about Fletcher now being a free man. They seemed surprised and pleased at this news, but quickly returned to appearing ill-at-ease.

"Is something amiss?" I asked.

"This is not as I expected," Dickey said.

"How so?" I asked.

"I expected more," Dickey replied. This was apparently a sentiment shared by Tom and Harry.

I chuckled. "Well, Jamaica, and this cay, has only been in English possession for eleven years now. I quite frankly expected less. But never underestimate the perniciousness of British industry. I imagine in ten years the whole cay will be packed with buildings like this, all the way to the southern shore. Land will be at a premium, and these lots on the harbor here will be worth hundreds of pounds."

"And it will still be small," Dickey said with disdain.

"Aye, but all commerce for Jamaica will flow through it," I said.

"How many people are there here?" Harry asked.

"Oh, from what I heard, there are over ten thousand men, women, and children on Jamaica, and maybe a thousand here in Port Royal. Beyond that, possibly a few thousand Negro slaves."

"And well over two thousand buccaneers," a wherry man who had been listening to us added. "But they come and go. Don't know what we'll do if'en they all land at the same time. Probably run outta drink."

I gawked at the figure. "Over two thousand? Residents or no, that is twice as many people as I was led to believe the town possesses."

"Oh, aye, sir," the wherry man said. "There's a mess of 'em. Can't control 'em. They run amuck in the streets at night, and the good folk stay indoors. The Governor had to be moved to Spanish Town after one of the bastard captains took to shooting the place up. Some crazed Portugese arse."

I was amused. "But it is my understanding the Governor has reason to want them here?"

"Oh, aye, aye, Governor Modyford loves 'em dear, due to most of our money coming from 'em too. Not like he don't line his pockets, if you understand me meanin', sir." Then he looked as if he realized he had spoken more than he should.

I gave him a reassuring shrug. "I know few here, and would not pass along the opinion of an honest man."

He smiled at that. "Thank ye, sir, I was forgettin' meself."

An officious-looking man wearing a nice coat, stockings, and real gold buckles on his shoes charged onto the wharf and approached Captain Starling. They exchanged pleasantries and paperwork, and then Captain Starling ambled down the street. The man, who I assumed to be Theodore, stood and read through the letter from my father. His face betrayed nothing, though he occasionally glanced in our direction. Once he finished, he approached us and bowed to Dickey.

"Lord Marsdale, pleased to make your acquaintance, I am your father's agent, Jonathon Theodore."

Dickey was taken aback, and I found myself laughing as I looked us over. Dickey was indeed the only one of us still dressed as a man of quality, in full coat, hat, and stockings. I was wearing a shirt, breeches, boots, and little else other than a pistol and sword. My coat and hat were thrown over Tom's luggage. I had not even bothered to pull my hair back.

"Um, sir, I believe you are mistaken," Dickey said quickly. "That is Lord Marsdale." He pointed at me; and Theodore turned to regard me, with initial embarrassment that quickly became bewilderment.

I stepped forward and bowed before offering my hand. "Pleased to make your acquaintance. I have only heard the best about you, and my father has been quite happy to have hired a man of such fine recommendation."

He recovered quickly, and bowed before shaking my hand. "My apologies, my Lord, I did not expect you to look like you had been roving," he said with diffident good humor. "And thank you very sincerely for your too kind words."

I decided I might actually try to like him. He seemed forthright. "Roving?"

He nodded. "Aye, my Lord, I assist some of the buccaneer captains in land grants and other legal matters with the prize courts. They clean up when necessary, but for the most part they come to me looking as you do. That is always when they have the money to spend."

"Ah, well, it is good to know I will blend in with the local populace," I said.

He glanced at my weapons. "Are you proficient, my Lord?" I noted that he wore a sword at his waist, but from the look of the scabbard and hilt, it was either unused or exceptionally clean and new.

"I am very proficient," I assured him.

"Then, my Lord, you will fit right in," he assured me. He turned his attention to my companions and gave me a curious look.

I introduced him all around.

He recognized the name of Tom's uncle and his agent. "Mister

Eaton, if your uncle's man does not soon appear, you are welcome to accompany us to my home for refreshments," he assured Tom. "I will send a boy round to inform him of the change in your location."

With that, he turned back to me and gave another glance to Fletcher. "Um…"

I had introduced Fletcher by his name and given no account of his status or relation to me other than to refer to him as a traveling companion. I did not want this man treating him as a servant. "He will be staying with me as my guest, for the time being. And where might we be staying?"

"My home, my Lord."

"Oh, will an extra guest be a burden? I would not want to bring an unsuspected imposition upon you. Not that you had any warning of my arrival, either."

"Not at all, my Lord, I have a spare room with a hammock for guests. We can string another hammock or not as you prefer, though the one is kind of small for two men to actually sleep in."

I was momentarily rendered speechless. In all my travels, I had never had a man, and a gentleman at that, assume I would share my bed with another: especially if they guessed my relative societal rank. On occasion, I might be expected to share a bed with a traveling companion in an inn, or while as a guest. Yet there had been something in Theodore's delivery that seemed to indicate he thought we might do more than sleep.

"Well, then, a second will be required. I cannot imagine fitting two people in one except to…"

He did not blanch or flush at my words. He nodded agreeably. "My Lord, you would have to be fond of one another indeed to sleep in it after."

He was implying what I thought he was. I hooked his arm and led him away from the others. "Fletcher is not my lover."

"Oh, my apologies,… my Lord… I did not mean to presume." He frowned, and we stood there awkwardly. "I am truly sorry," he finally sputtered. "I was just assuming you were a buccaneer again."

That remark, coupled with the name of the Chocolota Hole, visited upon me the realization that I may have landed in a town full of armed sodomites. I laughed.

"Are you implying that the buccaneers often take men as lovers?" I asked quietly.

"Aye, my Lord," he hissed back with a pleasant nod. "More partners than lovers, really."

"I may fit in quite nicely indeed, then." I grinned.

He flushed and sighed, "Oh, my."

"But that is not the nature of my relationship with that man, or any of these young gentlemen. And buccaneers aside, I would have your counsel on the perception of such activities by the other planters. When the time presents itself, of course."

He appeared greatly relieved. "My Lord, there are a great many matters I would be delighted to offer counsel on, as to Port Royal and Jamaica. For the moment, suffice it to say that it is known and tolerated, but frowned upon outside of the port and amongst men of quality. As in, it is considered acceptable here, as it is in England, in situations of common boys and men under the duress of an insufficient number of women, but frowned upon in situations where a man has the wherewithal to marry and behave as God intended. So they all expect their bondsmen to do it, and sailors, but only as a matter of last recourse for men in desperate need of companionship. However, the buccaneers are different."

"How so?"

"Perhaps..." He looked around. The boys were watching us expectantly.

"We should continue this elsewhere and later," I agreed. "And thank you for speaking so frankly with me. I do not stand well on ceremony."

Theodore smiled. "Thank God for that then, sir. I have been here so long I have forgotten how to behave appropriately around a man of your birth."

"Please continue not to remember."

"If it pleases you, my Lord. I will treat you as I do any other client I have."

"It will please me greatly. Stop calling me 'my Lord'. Call me Marsdale."

"Marsdale it is, then." He smiled.

I felt the Gods had led me home.

Six

Wherein I Face A Decision

Fletcher and the boys followed Theodore's Negro away from the wharf and down the main thoroughfare. I maneuvered to stay a little behind with Theodore, so that we might talk along the way. As we began to depart, Theodore was hailed from a ferry pulling up to the landing. I waved the others on as he stopped and greeted the disembarking men.

"Captain Bradley, Siegfried," Theodore said with sincere cheer.

I regarded them curiously. Captain Bradley was of similar height to myself, though a bit thicker through the chest and wider of shoulder. He also had me in the advantage of years: perhaps five, but maybe ten, if he carried them well. His hair was unruly and dark and he wore prominent sideburns, yet his beard was short and well-kempt. He was smoking a pipe. His eyes were warm, yet cunning, under heavy brows. The man with him, Siegfried, was small, thin, and wily-looking with a sharp nose and black hair. He had a swarthiness that suggested him to be of Romany descent. Both were armed with multiple pistols and swords, and dressed in good hats, light coats, fine linen shirts, and woolen breeches; but they wore boots instead of hose and shoes. And they sported small gold hoops in their ears.

Theodore exchanged pleasantries with them for a moment; they had apparently been out to Bradley's plantation, which I guessed Theodore had been involved in the legalities of. Then they turned to me.

"This is the Viscount of Marsdale," Theodore announced proudly. "And this is Captain Bradley and his matelot Siegfried."

I was not familiar with the term matelot, and was not sure if I should ask for explanation.

The men looked me over. Bradley smiled widely as he offered his hand, but there was challenge in his eyes. "You look like you'll do well here."

"Thank you, Captain, I assume that is meant as a compliment." I shook his hand heartily. He was the first man since England who had heard my title and yet not made any remark of it. However, as much as that pleased me, I did not feel he had done so because he did not care, but because he did not wish to acknowledge it.

Bradley laughed. "Just Bradley will do."

Siegfried shook my hand without a word, but his eyes flicked over me, and I was sure they missed nothing. They held mine for a moment, with a hint of respect and sincere welcome.

"What brings you here?" Bradley asked.

"My father wants a plantation, and I found England to be as boring as it had been before I left it the first time." I shrugged.

"So you've traveled then?"

"Yes, most of Christendom. I have lived in Italy, France, and Austria."

"Austria? Do you perhaps speak German?" Siegfried asked in German.

"Ja, not as fluently as I would like," I replied in the same language. Theodore and Bradley blinked in surprise.

"Truly?" Bradley said in English. "You wouldn't happen to speak Castilian, would ye?"

"Oh, aye," I said in English, and then switched to Spanish. "I am probably more proficient in Spanish than German." They all looked at me with incomprehension and I switched back to English. "I also speak French and Latin. None of you speak Castilian, I presume."

"Nay, we do not." Bradley grinned. "A man of languages, eh? Who has traveled and might know his way around a pistol and blade."

Theodore threw himself bodily between us. "Nay. God no. We have business to attend to. Once that is completed, to my satisfaction, then you can haul him off somewhere and get him killed."

"How long will that take?" Bradley asked with a teasing grin. "We're sailing to catch the Galleons and the Flota in the week."

"Excuse me?" I asked.

"The Captain here is one of the buccaneers who cleans up well," Theodore said wryly.

This seemed to amuse Bradley and Siegfried a great deal. I was more intrigued than amused.

"Are you seriously offering that I sail with you?" I asked.

Bradley nodded. "You would be welcome. If you cannot sail when we do, then there are other ships that could use a man who can speak Castilian and defend himself. It's not an easy life and we don't have officers like they do," he indicated the merchant ships around us, and then studied me intently. "We're all equals here."

"I do not think being one of the men would trouble me at all, amongst a crew of equals."

He nodded approvingly. "Our ship's the *North Wind* and she's anchored in the Hole. Any of the men on board would be able to find me, or I'll be about town."

"I will be staying with Theodore here. If all goes well I will consider looking you up before you sail. It has been a pleasure, sir."

"Likewise."

With that, we parted company. As we walked up the street, Theodore eyed me with consternation.

"Cease and desist," I chided as I took in what there was to see. The street was wide and packed with a jumble of buildings, most containing shops in front and living quarters in the rear. There was a fish market and a multitude of taverns, near which I saw men dressed as the buccaneers on the *Griffon* had been.

Theodore led me down a narrow lane between a smithy and another block of houses.

"Your father implied you were a hearty man in his dispatch."

I smirked. "I wonder exactly what he meant by that."

"I took it to mean that you would survive and do well in a colony such as this."

"Have you reformed that opinion?" I asked.

"Nay, it has been quite handily reinforced."

"Were you ordered to be responsible for my behavior or me?" I inquired.

He shook his head and sighed. "Nay, I was not. I knew your father would send someone, but you are not what I expected. But by all rights I did not know what to expect."

"You expected Dickey."

This elicited another heavy sigh. "In truth I did. You most certainly will do well here, but... I would advise against roving, at least until you have seasoned."

"Seasoned?"

"Become acclimated to the tropics for a time. Many men who come here die in the first six months."

"I have heard that. But that could happen with or without roving, could it not?"

"Aye, but when I write your father, it would be better if I could tell him you were buried in the cemetery on the Palisadoes, and not that you were fed to sharks, enslaved on a Spanish plantation, hanging from a Spanish gibbet, or simply missing at sea."

I gave serious weight to his words. I had been enthused beyond my expectations at the mere prospect of sailing with the buccaneers, and I wondered at myself. I had only just arrived, and I did wish to make good on my plan to do my father's bidding and to care for my flock. Yet my heart betrayed me, jumping as it had at the first chance offered for adventure.

"In truth, I do not know if the life of a planter will appeal to me," I said solemnly.

He nodded. "I can see that even now, and I have only just met you. You are not a boy."

I took this as a rebuke. In it, I heard the echo of Alonso's words.

"Aye, I should have grown beyond such trivial pursuits. I should settle down and become a man and do my duty."

He stopped and frowned. "Nay, sir, I only meant that you are old enough to keep your own counsel on such matters, and you have presumably seen enough of the world not to be led astray by foolish flights of fancy."

"Thank you, I apologize. I was attributing someone else's thoughts on the matter to you."

"Your father's, perhaps?"

"Nay, an old and dear friend who presumably abandoned adventure to take up the harness of family duty."

"And you have tried to do the same and found it chafes?" he asked kindly.

I shrugged. "I feel I have not been harnessed yet. It is more as if I skitter around the paddock waiting for destiny to come to me, and now the fences seem ever closer and I hear the call of distant meadows."

"Feral creature, are you then?" He smiled.

"I suppose I am." At that, we saw Fletcher and the boys standing outside a small house, and we were obliged to rejoin them.

I say small house, but in reality it was an average dwelling as compared to its neighbors, being of two stories with a high roof. We took the brief tour of the place. There was a narrow path running between it and its neighbor, leading back to a yard with a cistern, where water was delivered as needed. There was a small brick cookhouse, well separate from the main building. There was also a latrine. The interior of the dwelling was composed of a front room that served as his office and general place of public business, a back room for dining and private entertaining, and two rooms upstairs: one his own sleeping quarters and the other for guests.

The Negro slave who led the boys here slept in the cookhouse. He was named Samuel, and apparently understood a good deal of English. I had never met a Negro slave, and I was curious concerning him, but he stayed out of sight as much as he could manage.

Theodore also had a bondswoman of middle age called Ella, who did his cooking and such and slept in a small room attached to the back of the house proper. She was round and fleshy in the extreme, with very unpleasant teeth and the overall demeanor of an angry cow.

Ella had not been set to expect anyone to return with Theodore, and she made quite a fuss bringing in sweetmeats and lemonade – or rather haranguing Samuel to do it, while she walked in circles, clucking about how lazy he was and however could she be expected to serve so many in such a small house. Theodore finally bade her leave and wait in the yard, and things were quieter.

We supped and chatted aimlessly for a bit, until I remembered an earlier question.

"What does mate lo mean?" I asked. "I am assuming it is French, but I do not recognize it."

Theodore gave a small snort of amusement and spelled the word for me, adding the silent Gallic T at the end. "It means partner, at least amongst the Brethren of the Coast. Some have taken to using it to mean sailor, but that is not what it means here, except in a general sense. The English buccaneers have taken to referring to all the men they sail with as a shortening of the word, mates. They still use the full French, or perhaps it is Dutch, word for their partner. From my understanding, the original buccaneers on Hispaniola and Tortuga used the term."

"Partner?" Dickey queried.

"In all things," Theodore said with a glance my direction and a degree of discomfort.

"Oh," I said as understanding dawned upon me. I recalled the details of my conversation with Bradley and his matelot, Siegfried, and I realized a number of subtle things. "Oh," I said with more emphasis for my own benefit.

"The buccaneers take their matelots very seriously," Theodore continued. "To them, all property held by one is held jointly, and all funds are shared. If one is to marry, they make arrangements as to whether the wife, too, will be shared, or sometimes they end up killing each other. If one dies, the other inherits. If the booty is great enough and a buccaneer loses his matelot while roving, the crew will often agree to give the survivor the dead man's share as well. All of the buccaneers recognize the status of matelot as common law. Of course, without proper paperwork, none of that is recognized within English law."

"It sounds like they are business partners, and perhaps married," Dickey said with amusement.

"Precisely," Theodore said.

"Ah," I said. "Is that what you meant when you said they were different?"

He nodded. The others were regarding us with curiosity. I ignored them and continued the conversation.

"So this is not below-decks buggery or schoolboy loves amongst men with little alternative, or even the romances of pretty boys and old men who favor one another? This is men marrying other men, with or without other alternatives."

Theodore nodded again. "Precisely, though with some of them, it is much the same as elsewhere for that sort of thing. If women are available, they will avail themselves of them; and on the other side of the coin, I am sure men become quite attached to other men elsewhere without sexual congress. But here, the one and the other are condoned within the Brethren, and by necessity by those who have dealings with them, because the last thing you want to face is an angry pack of buccaneers."

I found myself chuckling yet again. Every place I had been, I had found sodomites, and every one of them had lived a life of discretion unless they were safely amongst the company of likeminded individuals.

"So you are saying the buccaneers are sodomites?" Dickey asked. "Including those men we saw on that ship?"

I nodded.

He smiled and sighed deeply. "So I may have come to a place where I will not be accused of being a sodomite because I do not possess a manly nature."

I had to laugh, and Theodore could not hold his amusement in any better than I. The other three looked aghast, but Dickey readily joined our mirth.

"So I take it that you do not favor men?" I asked, to confirm what I already guessed.

Dickey shook his head and stifled his laughter behind his fingertips. "Nay, sir, I do not. Did you think otherwise?"

"Nay, in sincere truth, I did not leap to that conclusion. I have known a number of... less than manly men who did not favor men. Whereas, some of the manliest men I have ever met did. Whether they were in harmony with their interests or not was another matter."

"Do you favor men?" Tom asked me with equal parts challenge and curiosity, as if he were daring me to answer yet scared I would.

I threw caution to the wind and answered him sincerely. "Aye, and women. I fancy both, though I have a tendency to... love the men more, I would say. The women have been diversions over the years, and rarely engage my heart. On the other hand, I rarely meet men I wish to... That I am willing to trust in that fashion." I did not care what their response would be, I felt as if a giant weight had been removed from my chest.

It did throw them all into a state of surprise and silent consternation, though – which was most evident in Fletcher, who looked as if he wanted crawl under the table or over his chair to get farther from me.

I addressed him directly, "And take no offense, Fletcher, but I have no interest in you." This seemed to relieve him greatly, and so I added, "Or the rest of you, for that matter."

Theodore was regarding me as if he thought my admission ill-advised; and perhaps it was, but it was done now, and I felt the better for it. I rewarded him with an amiable shrug, and he returned one in kind.

"I favor women," Tom said to no one in particular.

"You have proven that," I said without rancor.

"Davey?" Fletcher blurted.

I was surprised, but recovered quickly as I grasped Fletcher's reason for his mention. "Him, either. Though that does remind me..." I realized I might have come upon the means of Davey's salvation, in the form of Bradley. I would have to find the man.

I was prevented from sounding out Theodore on the matter by the arrival of Tom's uncle's agent: one David Skinner. He was a portly, snobbish little man to whom I took instant dislike. He looked the boys over with annoyance, and then regarded me with even more distaste until Theodore made introductions. At which point, Skinner seemed ready to kiss more than my hand. I did not deign to let him touch me, and barely returned his formal bow. I wished the boys luck and reminded them they could always count on me if the need arose. I watched them walk away down the sandy street with an unexpected sense of loss.

It reinforced my need to rescue Davey as soon as feasible.

"I need to find Bradley tonight," I told Theodore. The sun was already beginning to set. He was genuinely baffled by my request, as was Fletcher, who had not met Bradley. "I need to rescue a sailor from the vessel I sailed on."

"Oh, God help us," Theodore sighed. He led us inside and bade me give him the particulars.

"Not tonight," he said after I finished. "Wait until they land the cargo. That will take several days, as we have to land the bondsmen. I have made arrangements with another plantation to house your men until the land grant is completed. Then Starling will have to arrange for return cargo and load it. So, you see, you have time, and later will be better than sooner."

I took him at his word and surrendered to his logic.

"I will send for Donoughy, the man I hired to manage the plantation for you, if he meets your approval of course. Then we shall visit the land near Spanish Town, if you feel up to it after your voyage."

I nodded. "I should. So has the land already been granted?"

"Nay, but Donoughy and I have chosen a likely parcel. The grant will be a formality. Governor Modyford has some of the neighboring acreage, and he will be delighted to have an Earl's land near his."

"So they will just grant me twelve hundred acres of land?"

"Well, aye, or more or less. It is true they offer thirty acres per servant, but in practice it is a bit different. The parcel we have chosen is a hundred and eighty acres. It will be difficult to get forty of that in cane this year. How many bondsmen did you arrive with? Forty as expected? Or did more survive?"

"We sailed with forty-eight. It was my theory that if we fed the ones we had well enough, then they would be less likely to die. I cut a good deal of Starling's bonus profit in the process, though, as I refused to allow pressed men."

"That explains some of his grumbling," Theodore smirked.

"We arrived with forty-one." I decided it was safe to tell him of Fletcher. "Fletcher here was the forty-first. I bought his contract from Starling, and then released him from it."

"We wish to draw up another contract so that I can repay Lord Marsdale," Fletcher added quickly.

Theodore appeared bemused. "We can do that. Do you have skills for employment?"

"I am a miller," Fletcher said.

"Ah, wonderful. So you plan to hire him and have him repay you from his earnings."

I nodded. "So, Fletcher aside, I have arrived with forty bondsmen contracted to my father."

"With forty men you may be able to plant thirty acres the first year. A quarter of your men will die. You will need to acquire Negroes as soon as you can. With a hundred men, you should be able to keep eighty to a hundred acres in cane. You will use the bondsmen to build your mills, houses, and roads and the like, and then Negroes in the field when you get to that number. Eventually your bondsmen will either matriculate in their contracts or die, and you will have replaced them with Negro slaves."

I was alarmed at his prognosis for the men I had come to know during the voyage. Reading that one out of four men died once coming here was one thing; knowing them would be another thing entirely.

"Most planters here have several plantations," he continued. "As the land does not always cooperate with our attempts to subdivide it as we will. And much of the prime land of Jamaica will probably not be put to use for decades, because we cannot get into it except on foot. So you will receive this first parcel that you will plant, and then a number of other parcels that you will develop if the first does well, or hold in reserve, or pass on to your descendants."

That had not been explained to me prior to now. I wondered how much of it my father understood. "So my father will have a hundred and eighty prime acres, and then a number of like sized parcels we may or may not see in the near future."

"Aye, and," he eyed me speculatively, "as you are not your father, you can apply for your own grants, and increase the total amount of land your family holds. As a free man, Fletcher can do likewise."

I was well pleased with this, as was Fletcher. "It will not be a matter of combined family holdings, though," I said. "So how many acres could I receive? Thirty, at least?"

He smirked. "Marsdale, you can have a thousand if you wish and you are willing to befriend Modyford."

"Ah, so matters are handled here much as they are everywhere."

"Precisely."

"I will befriend who I must. Having land separate from my father is an unexpected gift." I realized I could possibly gain enough to grant the surviving men their acres if no one else would.

Theodore eyed me speculatively. "Am I to understand you are not wedded to your father's wants and ambitions?"

I smiled. "You are to understand that this is something of a test. I had been away from my father's estate for ten years and returned a mere month before I sailed. He had no one else to send that he did not wish to lose to disease, the Spanish, or worse."

He appeared sympathetic. "I understand. We will maintain your interests separate from his."

"Thank you." I thought it likely I had made another friend.

The next day, we took a ferry across the bay to the Passage Fort to meet our manager. Theodore told me Kevin Donoughy had been a bondsman on Barbados, and once a free man he had stayed in the planting life, moving to Montserrat in 1660 to buy his own land. He had purchased forty acres, married a woman sight unseen from England, and brought her there. Illness and a run of misfortune had befallen him, and the wife had died along with most of his laborers. He had been unable to plant for a season, and thus he had ended up working for other planters. Now he was here to do the same.

He was waiting for us on the wharf. He proved to be a big, broad-shouldered man who looked as if he had done hard work for many a year.

He surveyed me as we approached, and I knew he thought I had never worked a day in my life. Since I have not, I do not bridle at that perception of my person when I encounter it from common men, unless the one beholding me in that manner thinks men who do not work are weak. Bradley had much the same look about him when we were introduced, until he learned I had traveled and had skills he could use. I had not seen a like perception in Siegfried's eyes, though. He had looked me over and found me of interest without such prejudice. Yet neither of them, or Theodore, or this Donoughy, showed any respect or awe such as Belfry, Steins, Starling, or Fletcher had revealed at the mention of my title.

I found some amusement in this. Men were not judged here as they were in England, or the rest of Christendom. On Jamaica, titles and fine clothes seemed to mean little; whether or not a man could heft a blade seemed to mean much. Though it was true I had not met the local gentry yet. Still, no matter how the wealthy perceived the social order, the other men I was encountering did not seem to lay much store in social hierarchy. They appeared to want to know what a man could do before they granted him worth. I thought it likely I would be proving myself quite a bit. This was in contradiction to how I learned to present myself in my prior travels. In most places I went, I had not wanted any to know of my true skills. I had been happy if they perceived me as some useless court-reared bastard. That would not do here.

So I stood firm when Donoughy tried to grind the bones of my hand to powder and I returned his greeting in like measure with a hand strong from wielding a sword. This seemed to gain me some modicum of respect. I noticed he did not press so very hard with Fletcher, as he seemed to have more respect for my miller from the moment he saw him. They were two of a kind and recognized one another as such.

Donoughy ignored me and addressed Theodore. "So the ship arrived, sir. Did they send all that was asked for? And how many men?" He spoke clearly, with only a trace of a brogue he must have worked hard to overcome.

"All seems to be here," Theodore replied. "There are forty men, in relative good health. And Mister Fletcher here is a miller that we will hire."

This last delighted Donoughy. The smile he awarded Fletcher was warm indeed. "I'm pleased to meet you, then." He returned to business. "The bondsmen, were they pressed? Are any of them convicts?"

"Nay," I answered. "They signed willingly. They are good men. Some of them are skilled."

His look implied he did not think I was the best judge of that. "Men will say a great deal to stay out of the fields."

"True," I replied with a thin smile. "But it has been my experience that men will speak the truth if they do not fear censure and feel their words will be honored. I spent most of the voyage amongst them and I feel most if not all are what they say."

Donoughy grimaced and quickly covered it with his own thin smile. "Begging your pardon, sir, it has been my experience, that when men who are desperate or foolish enough to travel around the world to work find someone to curry favor with, they will say whatever they think will aid them."

He watched for my reaction and I glanced to Fletcher and Theodore. Fletcher was frowning and Theodore was studying the sky as if he might soon comment on the weather.

"Fletcher," I said, "Do you feel the men dissembled with me as to their abilities?"

He looked relieved to be included. "Nay, sir."

I turned back to Donoughy. "Perhaps you will adjust your opinion once you get to know them."

"I don't need to get to know them, sir. I need to make them work. I can't be their friend. Men don't work for friends. Men need to respect their leaders. They need discipline." Seeing my brewing protest, he continued quickly, "No man wants to work here, sir. And here less than other places, as it is miserable and hot and there are all manner of insects and other forms of pestilence to plague a man. God did not mean for white men to live on these islands, and he makes it hard for us. We must be ever vigilant in order to wrest a living from this soil. And the men who come here are fools and not prone to work hard."

I wondered what this said of him. I had heard such sentiments before, not in application to the tropics, but in many a gentleman's study, and of course from Steins. According to most wolves, all sheep are lazy. This is merely because they are sheep. If they were wolves they would not work for another at all. And the wolves always sense this, even if they cannot name it as such. The sheep are weak because they do not fight back, therefore they lack ambition, therefore they are lazy in the eyes of their masters.

I did not think Donoughy truly a wolf, no more than I had thought

Steins one: ironically, for the same reason other wolves think sheep are lazy. If Donoughy and Steins were truly wolves, they would not be working for my father. This was especially true of Donoughy, as land was free here. They had been well-taught by wolves, though. In a way, they had been raised by them just as I had. It tempered my anger.

"Mister Donoughy, I am the kind of fool who chooses to befriend men in my employ. I consider the bondsmen on that ship to be in my employ, just as you are. Though we are not off to a fine beginning. Please understand, I will have no one mistreated. And that will be by my definition of ill-use and not yours."

As I expected, he immediately looked to Theodore. I was acutely aware that my father's barrister could render me impotent with but a word. This was my father's business, not mine. Theodore said nothing. He still seemed preoccupied with the sky.

Donoughy studied the smaller man's profile for a time, and turned back to me with a sigh.

"I was hired to manage this plantation, sir. And I was told," he glanced pointedly at Theodore again, "that my continued employ and my pay would be based upon her profit. When a plantation does well, it can make a man wealthy; but it is not easy, and there is much that can ruin it. Not all cane fields produce to their owner's expectations. And I don't know when more Negroes will arrive for sale, and a good number of the men you brought will die no matter how we use them. I need to work the ones that do survive hard."

"Mister Donoughy, I have never been forced to make men work, but I surmise they will wish to do far more if rewarded and treated kindly. A well-loved horse will run itself to death to please its rider. A well-loved hound will face a boar for its master. I have seen many a well-rewarded and thus loyal servant turn the tides of fortune in matters of intrigue. Just as kind words and coin will quickly turn a misused man into his master's worst enemy. I do know a little of men."

He frowned thoughtfully, and I sensed that he agreed with me. His continued employ was of far greater concern to him, though. He was indeed a sheep.

"And now that I understand your concern," I continued in a kinder tone, "perhaps I can allay that somewhat. The success and profitability of this plantation is my responsibility. Your job is to insure that it is managed to the best of your ability within the parameters that I set. I cannot guarantee that we will all be here two years hence, but I can assure you I will be discharged from this endeavor if it goes poorly long before you will. I will take all blame if that is to pass, and shelter any other who is involved from my father's displeasure. Believe me, he already dislikes me and thinks you both fine fellows. If we do it according to my desires and it fails, he is not likely to blame you. And understand this as well: if this venture should fail, my father will not be turned out of his house over the matter. He does not risk what he cannot lose."

I heard a quiet chortle beside me and looked over to find Theodore smirking, his eyes still fixed upon the sky.

Donoughy considered me. He finally reached some decision and nodded. "I will trust you on that, sir, as you surely know your father better than we do. I do not wish to mistreat a man, but I will make them work."

"I do not think any man on that ship is a stranger to hard work or lives in fear of it. What they are afraid of is starvation, the plague, forced military service, and all manner of things they left England to avoid. And some of the younger men did come here seeking their fortunes, because they knew well there was none to be had in England. Why did you journey here?"

He studied me with a frown that finally melted into a smirk and a self-deprecating chuckle. "Debt. I was indentured and sold to a ship's captain for transport to Barbados for a debt. I was a shiftless bastard in my youth."

"Good Lord, man," I smiled. "If I ascribed my own history to every man I met, I would walk about with a sword in hand at all times and trust no one."

This seemed to surprise him until he realized I jested. It brought forth another chortle from Theodore. Fletcher frowned at me. I smiled good-naturedly; I had only been partly in jest.

Our initial battle laid to rest, we rented horses at the livery and rode inland. I thanked the Gods that it appeared I only need be vigilant with one of the men I was to work with. Theodore seemed to truly be my ally.

Fletcher and Donoughy began to talk and established some degree of rapport. Thus Theodore and I were regaled with an exchange of information betwixt them concerning grain mills and sugar cane plants for all five or so miles to Spanish Town. I had decided the mechanical aspects of this whole endeavor were in seemingly knowledgeable hands by the time we reached the little hamlet the Spanish had called Villa de la Vega. It did indeed sit on a wide plain next to the Copper River, or Rio Cobre as people still seemed wont to call it.

Spanish Town had been the Spanish capital, and was technically the English one as well, as the court and Governor were here. However, it was a dusty and somewhat vacant little place as compared to Port Royal. This was due to all the industry of Spanish Town, or anywhere else in the Jamaica hinterlands, taking place on plantations, not among closely packed wharfs and warehouses.

We ate at a small inn and proceeded across the plain to the acreage. We passed several plantations, and Donoughy stopped to show us cane and explain how it was planted and harvested over a two year cycle, how many men it took per acre, and so on.

When he described planting and weeding the fields with gangs of men, I asked, "Do we not use plows here?"

He shook his head and sighed. "Can't right off. As you see, the trees are thick here. When we clear a field it leaves a number of stumps. Cane can be planted around them. We wouldn't be able to plow through them, and we don't need to spend the time removing them."

"Aye, I can see that if speed is of the essence," I said, "but surely after the initial crop is planted, there is time to clear the next fields properly so that they can be plowed."

"Not enough men, sir. It will take the entire field gang to keep the fields weeded and fertilized and kill rats. And you want to keep them busy, sir, especially after we get Negroes. Can't let the buggers sit about and do nothing; they revolt."

"I see," I said and rode ahead. I did understand, and I wanted little to do with it all: which is, of course, why I knew I must be involved.

I was sweltering in the heat, and felt sympathy for my livery horse, since I had doffed my coat and laid it across the poor animal's broiling haunches. If not for the hat, I was sure my brain would boil in my skull. Theodore assured me one acclimated to the heat and humidity soon enough; but I had every reason to doubt him at the moment, as I was miserable.

I thought of men toiling all day in these conditions and then trying to sleep at night in the same, and I wanted even less to do with the business. And even beyond my concern for others, I was damned if I was going to live out here on the land. Sleeping at Theodore's had been uncomfortable enough last night. I had grown accustomed in the final weeks of the voyage to sleeping on deck. The cabin had been too hot and enclosed, with no breeze to whisk the sweat away: much like Theodore's guest room. I felt no wind on this plain, either. I wondered what I was to do.

We rode along the river, and finally reached the plot a good three leagues north of Spanish Town. It was wide and flat and snaked along between the river and a hill that could not easily be farmed upon. The hill was part of the acreage, though, which is why this plot had not been snapped up by an earlier planter. We climbed it, and Donoughy pointed out where he would put the mills and works and where the first field should be cleared. I nodded appreciatively at his planning, and then let him wander off to show Fletcher a thing or two in detail, such as the lay of the land where they might put a water mill.

I had brought my muskets; and I proceeded to load and fire them, as it had been many months since I had done so and I was in the mood to punch holes in something. Theodore watched me with interest but declined to join in, saying that he had almost broken his shoulder the one time he had been foolhardy enough to fire a musket. So I set about familiarizing myself with the unique aim, trigger movement, and other peculiarities of both pieces.

The wheellock was, of course, precise in all the ways I had remembered: from the smoothness of her firing mechanism to the trueness of her aim. However, I had forgotten how tedious and prone to irritation the winding of the wheel was. The flintlock was a fine weapon, and her less delicate firing mechanism seemed as hearty as it was simple in comparison. The sights were not as precise, but I soon found the aim necessary to compensate, and could put ball after ball into the same square foot of tree trunk at a hundred paces.

"You shoot well, but you reload too slowly," Theodore observed.

I was in the process of doing same. "I have been aiming for precision as opposed to speed. As you are well aware, a poorly loaded musket will end my life far faster than the tropical vapors."

"Aye, of course," he shrugged. "You'll just have to get faster if you're going roving."

I finished ramming the ball and patch home and paused to regard him. "Will I, now? Well, from your counsel, I should take a good half year and let myself season before even considering it. This would afford me a great deal of time to practice."

He grinned. "You won't last that long. You want nothing to do with this endeavor."

"Am I so obvious?" I finished loading the pan and fired off another round. "And are you so ready to be rid of me?"

He regarded me thoughtfully. "Aye, I think you will be a detriment to this endeavor."

"Theodore, I have decided to harness myself, not to my father's wishes, but to those men."

He seemed to give great thought to his next words. "You possess a large heart and a beneficent spirit. You should be commended for it."

"Yet?" I prompted.

"You cannot be so naïve as to think your sentiments are the way of the world."

"Nay, I do not. That is why I feel someone must champion those that cannot do it for themselves. The sheep need shepherds," I muttered.

Theodore frowned. "Marsdale, it sounds as if you missed your calling."

I laughed. "Theodore, let me tell you how I have spent these past ten years." And so I did. I told him how I had earned a living as a hired sword and duelist, and begged and borrowed my way across Christendom, leaving dead men in my wake.

At first he was bemused; and then true amusement took hold of him, and he laughed so that he was forced to lean upon his horse.

"Sir," he finally said, and made show of wiping his tears away, "I feel you may have come to the correct island for the wrong endeavor. And yet you are so charitable. Do you seek atonement?" he asked seriously.

This gave me pause. I had not considered my actions in that possible light. "I do not think so. I merely do as I do. I follow the dictates of my conscience and act as I will."

He chuckled and then waved off my frown. "I mean no offense." He nodded thoughtfully. "Does your father realize you are so liberal in your love of your fellow man?"

"How do you mean that, sir?" I grinned. "I do not know if he realizes the depth of my philanthropic bent, but he is aware I favor men."

"Ah, I meant the former and not the latter. Though now that the subject is broached, does that have much to do with why you traveled so?"

"In part, aye, in a large part."

He smiled and thought for a moment. "Have you taken so many under your wing before, for such an extended venture as this will be?"

"Nay, and truly I fear I lack the resolve."

He sighed. "Far be it from me to steer you from the path of righteousness, but Marsdale, you need not do this. Donoughy is not an evil man and I do not feel he will mistreat your men. Furthermore, I will not let him, or allow further concerns of your father's displeasure to drive him. It is customary to give a manager a base salary and then reward him with a small percentage of the profits. We can simply pay him more to begin with. Your father has allowed me, or rather us, a great deal of discretion in that regard."

"Thank you," I said solemnly and quickly waved off his response. "Thank you for standing by my wishes. I know well that you do not have to."

"Nay, you are correct, I need not take your orders. I am not in your employ," he sighed. "Yet, I feel you are correct. It has also been my experience that men who are used well and fed well work harder. I believe in showing all men respect, regardless of their station in life."

I believed him, as I had seen no evidence to contradict his words. He even spoke well to his slaves. I wondered where he came from: England, obviously, but what stratum of society? He was surely not raised by wolves, and there was much about him that reminded me of Rucker.

"I trust you," I said. "Yet I will not abandon this endeavor. I will try not to block its progress either..."

He waved me off. "You need not be miserable. What will you do here? Work alongside them in the fields? Go, have your own adventures as you are accustomed to doing. You are well-suited to another way of life here in the West Indies. Embrace it."

I could scarce believe he meant it. "But what if I die on some Spanish gibbet, or drown at sea?"

"You could just as easily perish here of some fever. Or fall from a horse. Or choke on a husk of bread."

"You truly wish for me to go roving?"

"I feel you will excel at it; but nay, I am not trying to drive you away. Do as you wish, but I feel you will become bored with this endeavor and resent it. You need not go roving immediately. Perhaps you should stay in town and familiarize yourself with life here. Then if you feel the need to travel about a bit, do so; just attempt to return on a timely basis, as I will need certain things from you on occasion."

"Such as?"

"I will need your signature on documents from time to time. And it would be prudent for you to write your father. Also, you should stay in good standing with the local gentry, Modyford included."

"You truly make it sound easy and the choice of merit. If I were to do this, I would have some things done in my absence. I would have them well fed. I will not have their contracts extended for petty infractions. I wish them to have a tutor. I was teaching them on the voyage."

He sighed. "I do not see where there will be time for that last."

I considered telling him time would have to be made for it, but I could see where there was much to be done initially. I sighed and we regarded each other.

I nodded and shrugged. "After all is in order and Negroes have been purchased, then."

He seemed relieved at my willingness to compromise, and I wondered how much he thought I might complicate matters. Did he truly wish for my contentment or his?

"What will you name her?" he asked while looking over the plantation. Fletcher and Donoughy could be seen returning to us.

What would I name a promised land I might not live on, that I was being prompted to be an absent but beneficent ruler of? It came to me and I chuckled. "Ithaca."

"I am not familiar with that name."

"It is a Greek island. It is the land Odysseus, also known as Ulysses, sailed from to fight the Trojan War and did not return to for twenty years."

"Oh, Lord," Theodore sighed and rolled his eyes.

"Though, thankfully, I will not need to leave a wife or child behind if I do this thing," I added.

Donoughy and Fletcher rejoined us. Theodore mounted his horse, and seemed disinclined to continue our discussion. I was thankful. I packed up the muskets and we rode back to Spanish Town.

"We have been talking," Donoughy said. "If all of your men are truly willing..."

"They are," I said.

"As in, if we need not fear them trying to escape, I would suggest bringing them here directly. We can unload the ship the same day and bring over what we need, and perhaps warehouse the rest of it for a week or so." He looked to Theodore for support.

"If we house the men elsewhere, we will have to pay for their food." Theodore shrugged. "If we keep the cargo in a warehouse, we will have to pay for that."

"What will be better for the men?" I asked.

"We'll pay the warehouse fees." Theodore smiled.

"Can this be arranged on the morrow?" I asked.

"I do not see why not," Theodore said.

"But we do not have the land yet."

"Nay, but it is a given as long as you make a good impression upon the Governor."

"I will do my best. So when should I meet him?"

Theodore grinned. "At the party in your honor at the King's House tomorrow night."

"Oh, bloody Hell!" I yelled. "I suppose I will have to dress."

They found great amusement in this.

Donoughy accompanied us to Port Royal and strung a hammock in Theodore's yard. As it seemed cooler outside than in, I envied him. I was feeling the heat even as the sun set. Still, I slept well. I had long ago learned to ignore things I could not resolve. Whenever I was faced with such choices, something always occurred to tip the scales one way or another and relieve me of the decision.

I watched the skies for portents from the Gods.

Seven

Wherein I Meet Many Important People

The next morning, I gingerly ate the bacon Ella prepared for us and washed it down with stale wine. My stomach roiled almost immediately. I decided to fast for a time, to see if it would settle.

The four of us took a ferry out to the *King's Hope*. The men were delighted to see us.

I still did not see Davey, and this concerned me once again. Belfry was not aboard for me to ask; neither was the captain. I considered asking about, but Theodore saw me looking around and slipped to my elbow to ask what was amiss.

"I do not see the sailor I wish to rescue."

He sighed. "They likely have him locked below, due to fear of him jumping ship. Many captains do that so that all of their men do not run off and become buccaneers."

"Oh, for the love of..."

His glare silenced me. "Follow your original plan, Marsdale. But do not, whatever you do, let anyone know you are involved. Not if you wish to befriend anyone."

"Aye, sir," I sighed.

He snorted. "Now speak to your flock."

I stood on the quarterdeck and looked down upon the forty upturned faces. I was not used to addressing so many and I felt my cheeks warm. I smiled as best I could. "Well, men, we have land."

They cheered.

"How soon can we stand on it?" Humboldt asked.

"Today."

They cheered even louder.

"However, it is virgin land. Your first order of business will be building a shelter. We will get all of you ashore, and then the cargo. The well-dressed man there is Mister Theodore, my barrister and my father's agent in this endeavor. He is a good man, and you may trust him with your concerns if there is need to speak of anything away from the plantation and... I am not available."

Theodore nodded thoughtfully. I was relieved. I had not discussed that bit with him in advance and had merely hoped he was conducive to it. All of the men eyed him curiously.

"The man next to him is Kevin Donoughy. He will manage the plantation for us. I have also found him to be a good man. He has managed sugar plantations on Barbados."

This last was greeted by many a nod and Donoughy actually smiled at them. In fact, I had seen him talking to several of the men, and despite his words about not befriending any, he did not seem to be holding them at bay.

"Fletcher, as he is a miller and we have need of his skills, has been promoted to overseer." That I had discussed with Donoughy and Fletcher. Thankfully this was greeted by nods and several hearty congratulations and no complaints.

"Now, let us all go ashore. I will not be accompanying you up to the plantation as of yet. There is still business I must attend to in town."

None seemed inclined to argument with this, or even to have concerns. Fletcher coordinated getting them into boats and across the bay to the Passage Fort. From there, they would walk up to the plantation. Donoughy would see to the cargo. I rode back to the wharf with Theodore. Thankfully, he did not pester me about leaving or staying.

He left me at the house and went to see to the business of other clients, after admonishing me to remember the party this eve. Once he was gone, I slipped out to wander about the town alone, with only a pistol and sword for company and nothing on my person other than a hat, a shirt, and breeches. No one noticed me. Only the quality of my attire separated me from the few buccaneers conducting their business about town: that, and my hat and lack of earrings. To become even more in keeping with the local fashion, I retired my heavy headgear, and replaced it with a kerchief to protect my broiling scalp.

I still felt a little ill and often found myself squatting in the bushes. Even with the ocean breeze, the heat was oppressive in the extreme, and I was sweated dry. In the market I found a fruited drink of rum and pineapple juice, and purchased an onion bottle of it. I had discovered I liked pineapple, a strange sweet fruit native to Jamaica. I had not experienced rum before, and to my amusement, the concoction made me far lighter-headed than a similar amount of wine or beer. It was pleasant and made the heat disappear.

So I wandered about the market and surrounding store fronts, looking for nothing in particular and feeling beckoned by all, until I spied a little place selling a variety of interesting articles: including, to my delight, books. The offerings were small, and primarily consisted of recently printed romances, poetry, and religious and political treatises from London. However, they had a box of odd books in many languages, and I perused these with anticipation. I almost toppled with laughter when I found a copy of Plato's *Republic* in German. I immediately purchased it and located a nearby shady place at the mouth of an alley, to collapse with my bottle and book. I proceeded to read in peace.

Some indeterminable amount of time later, I felt eyes upon me, and looked up with a small amount of annoyance to discover I was not merely being gazed at in a casual fashion. Nay, I was being stared at with an intensity I supposed, once it seeped through my rum-addled brain, a sober man might find alarming. I studied my watcher with blurry concentration that became sharper as I sensed danger about the fellow.

He was dressed as a buccaneer, but darkly. Whereas most wore ecru or linen-colored canvas and gaily-colored cotton on their heads, his loose breeches, tunic, and kerchief had been dyed a deep maroon that appeared black unless directly in the sun. Black lacquer and gold adorned the grips of his pistols, of which there were two, and the hilts of his swords and knives: of which there was one rapier, of fine quality, two cutlasses, as I had learned the buccaneers called their heavy long knives, and three dirks. All of them looked well-used. There was a musket slung across his back. The baldric and belt this wealth of armament suspended from was likewise black leather. He wore no footgear, but if he had, I was sure they would have been boots and ebony.

He stood maybe a dozen feet away, with his arms crossed and his feet firmly braced. I doubted any could move him from the spot; and indeed, the people passing by parted around him like water round a rock. From the hang of his clothes, his stance, and the cords of muscle in his calves and forearms, I judged his build to be muscular yet lean. His bone structure was fine, as his hands seemed almost delicate. He was clean-shaven and his face was attractive: not handsome, not pretty, but somewhere in between. He appeared to be of an age with me. I could not tell his hair color, but his skin was browned the nutmeg of a fair-skinned man. He wore gold hoops in his ears.

I noted all of this, but what really held my attention were his eyes. They were wide-set and the whole of the socket around them was painted black as coal, like a mask that ran from one temple to the other, even across the bridge of his nose. From within those pits of shadow, two blazing emerald orbs regarded me. And I was at a loss as to their motivation or emotion.

"Who are you?" he asked in a husky voice that barely crossed the distance between us.

I blinked. The question had been in German, but his accent was French. Maybe I was more inebriated than I thought. Why was a strange man addressing me in German?

I chose not to bridle at his tone, as there seemed more curiosity to his query than rancor. And then I was at a loss as to how best to answer his query. I was loathe to use my title, for I did not wish to be known by it amongst the buccaneers. For a moment I toyed with using my old alias of Ulysses, but that was the moniker of someone I was no longer. And then too much time had passed to be considered polite.

I quickly used my true surname. "Williams. And you are?" I replied in German.

"I am called Gaston the Ghoul."

I pushed myself up the wall and stood.

"Pleased to make your acquaintance," I said politely. I made sure of my legs and approached him, transferring the bottle to my left hand to reside with the book, leaving my right free. He was just shy of my height. He had not uncrossed his arms but I sensed the change of his balance as he brought his weight to the balls of his feet. I fervently hoped he meant me no mischief, as I was too drunk to fight him. His eyes were still unreadable.

"Why are you here?" he asked in the same tone as before.

At the moment it seemed as esoteric a question as my name, and my mind flailed about in the grasping of it. An abundance of answers presented themselves, leaving me at a loss as to what he truly wanted to know. I switched to French. "Begging your pardon, but you will have to be more specific. And I would prefer speaking French or English if it pleases you, as my German is somewhat underused and not suitable for a discussion of merit in my current state of intoxication."

He nodded and frowned in thought for a moment before speaking French.

"You read it." His eyes darted to the book in my hand. I remembered it was in German.

"Oh, oui, I am literate in German, but this work is taxing my skill with the language. Thankfully I am familiar enough with it in Latin."

Green eyes studied me. "Why are you in Jamaica?"

I supposed the correct response involved saying something of the plantation, but it seemed hollow, somehow, and disingenuous in its specificity. Perhaps this was the result of reading Plato while intoxicated. "I came here to try and make amends with my father and shoulder the yoke of family duty, or something of that ilk I suppose. I think I shall fail."

He was taken aback, and his face froze for a moment with incredulity. Then he apparently judged me sincere, and his features settled into a mild grimace of confusion. "Why?"

"I have never had the man's respect and goodwill; and in truth, I am not sure what value I place on it in comparison to my own desires."

"Which are?"

"Adventure and romance as opposed to duty and diligence. I enjoy traveling and learning new things. However, I find myself harnessed to duty here by my own choice."

"Are you a philosopher?"

"On occasion. I take great delight in the perils of sophism. Plato here is not one of my favorites, though I took great delight in finding this book. I would not wish to live in his republic."

"Why?"

"I was raised without a great deal of nurturing and found it not to my liking. And I feel the education of a youth should contain far more than music and athletics. And though I agree with his conceit that any man should be able to love as he sees fit, I find his overall presentation of utopia to be somewhat loveless and far too regimented for my taste. And I cannot see loving a nation over one's fellow man. Truly, if I have to read ancient Greeks, I far prefer Homer."

"Do you prefer mythology over philosophy?"

"Only in the reading of it. I prefer the exercise of reason over superstition."

He smiled, and then sobered and looked me over again. "Do you wish to become a flibustier?"

At my confusion, he smirked and rolled his eyes.

"You English, you call every man who sails under the Jolie Rouge a boucanier. I know of few men in this port who ever hunted on the Haiti and made boucan. On Île de la Tortue, we call the ones who rove flibustiers and the ones who hunt boucaniers. Most men do both, at least they used to. Not so many boucaniers anymore."

I turned it over in my mind a couple of times, until I realized that flibustiers was the French pronunciation of freebooters. "I can see where a distinction could be made about such a thing." Some vague thought stirred and slowly made itself known. "Are we not at war?"

His body tightened and his eyes narrowed with suspicion. "You have done nothing to anger me... yet."

I smiled affably. "I should hope not. I meant our nations."

"I have no nation," he said with a trace of amusement.

"Forget I said anything."

He smirked again. "You will learn wars only cross the Line when there is gold involved. The same is true of peace. I have been sailing on a French ship under a marque from your governor. Yet if he could muster the men and ships, he would retake Île de la Tortue from the French."

"But all he has of a military force are the buccaneers, excuse me, freebooters, and I take it they are not in agreement with that."

"It serves the interests of all to play one against the other as necessary. A year ago your Governor Modyford was seizing prizes. So everyone went to Île de la Tortue and Port Royal lost all of the booty. Now he is issuing marques to any who want one, especially the French."

I grinned. "I truly adore public servants. They are always so... predictable."

"So you think you will become a flibustier?"

"Possibly. I met a Captain Bradley two days ago, and he said he could possibly use a man who spoke Castilian and had a fondness for steel. He is planning on sailing, soon, though; and I am not sure if the affairs I came here to handle can be left alone as of yet, though my father's agent would have me sail."

"Why?"

"He feels I will be a detriment to the endeavor." I smiled.

"And why is that?"

"I do not have it in me to callously enslave men, and I care little for farming."

His eyes narrowed with suspicion. "Do you have it in you to kill men?"

"Oui, with great celerity and regularity as the need presents itself." I shrugged.

He smiled. "So you would rather kill them than own them?"

"Quite possibly, oui."

"And you have a fondness for steel?" His eyes flicked to my blade.

I smiled. "We have more than a passing acquaintance, as it has both saved my life and attempted to relieve me of it on many an occasion."

"We should spar. When you are sober."

I grinned. "I am sure I would enjoy that immensely."

His eyes flicked over me critically. "If you are going roving, you will need a musket."

"I have two at my disposal."

"Lighter attire."

"I plan to remedy that."

"And earrings."

"Why? I am truly curious," I chuckled.

He shrugged. "I do not know where the tradition started, but they make it easy to spy another fliebustier in the smoke of battle."

"That is useful to know. I will consider it. May I ask a question? Why do you paint your eyes so?"

"The Carribe. One of the Indian nations that lived here used to paint their faces thus. The Carribe ate people. The Spaniards were terrified of them. Several of my party did this when we attacked Saint Jago on Hispaniola. It bothers the Spaniards." He shrugged and smiled thinly. "It bothers the English. And the French. Everyone really."

I chuckled again. "How long have you been in the West Indies?"

"Ten years."

If he was truly of an age with me as I surmised, that meant he came here at about the same time I left England the first time. But whereas I had spent the years wandering the known world, he had made his home in this wilderness. "Why did you come here, to seek adventure or fortune?"

He frowned briefly, and I felt him withdraw from me even though he moved not an inch. "My father bade me to," he said quietly, and abruptly turned to leave.

I felt an immediate sense of loss and fought the urge to follow him. Instead I called out, "Where shall I see you again?"

He paused and turned to regard me. "We will meet again."

Then he left, and I stood alone on a dusty street, with a book and bottle in my hand. There was hope in my heart, though. I had met an educated man who I thought I had much in common with. I returned to Theodore's with a smile on my face.

"You look pleased with yourself," Theodore commented as I entered. I decided against mentioning my meeting and told him of the book and the rum concoction and reading in the shade. Theodore shook his head as if he had already consigned me to a life of piracy and drunken debauch. He sent me upstairs to dress for the party.

As I donned clothing I did not wish to wear ever again, I thought of Gaston the Ghoul. In a few brief minutes he had become my savior. I stuffed my head into a wig and my feet into hose and shoes, and realized I was quite smitten with him; and here I thought I had long outgrown schoolboy infatuations. I vowed to approach him with all the sophistication and nonchalance I possessed. And not to play the eager puppy begging for a bone of kindness, as I was always so wont to do on the rare occasions I found a person I wished to know.

My pleasant thoughts of my meeting dissipated as I finished dressing. By the time I joined Theodore in his office I was steeped in the misery known by the common name of sweat. Theodore pronounced me pleasing to the eye, and my innards knotted and clutched at my lower spine. I assumed that, since the gentry here sought to imitate all things English, there would be some unfortunate servant stationed near the latrine to hold my coat while I shat. Needless to say, my mood was as foul as my imagination.

"Hmmm, it looks as if it may rain," Theodore commented as we walked to the King's House.

"Will it bring cooler temperatures?"

"Sometimes. Primarily it will turn the streets to sandy mud filled with filth," he said. "Be thankful you will not experience the full glory of the rainy season until late summer."

Upon witnessing the expression on my face, he laughed uproariously; and I silently vowed that when it rained, I would trip him on the walk home.

And then we arrived. But for the heat and foliage, it would have been difficult to tell this party from a similar function at my father's manor. The ladies were quite lovely in the finest gowns, and the men were well-dressed in the latest styles. The servants were in sharp livery and circulated with silver trays proffering refreshments. The decoration was tasteful, if perhaps a little musty. All in all, it looked like many a fête I had attended over the years.

I drank wine and Theodore introduced me about, and I smiled and nodded and said witty things, or at least they laughed politely. My snide remarks about the climate were always well-received, though they said that one grew accustomed to it in time. I realized this might be true, as I seemed to be perspiring far more than the people I was speaking with.

I met Governor Thomas Modyford, who seemed a witty man himself. He looked me over with a delighted smile but a shrewd eye. I smiled in return, and decided he was a man one did not give ground to, lest one lose his respect.

After the introductions were made, Theodore said, "Lord Marsdale is delighted with that acreage near yours, and we have taken the liberty of sending his bondsmen there."

"The one with the hill? Oh, wonderful," Modyford said. "I will have my man draw up the papers tomorrow. My Lord, have you given any thought to where else you may want land?"

"Not as of yet." I shrugged. "I feel I will need to take some time to make that determination, as I am not familiar with the island. I hope the delay will not prove to be troublesome."

"Not at all, my Lord. I can make suggestions, as I am sure Theodore can. But it would be best for you to take your time and perhaps even venture about."

"I will do that."

Theodore surprised me. "Lord Marsdale wishes to go roving. So I imagine he will not see to it until he returns."

To my amazement this did not seem to surprise Modyford at all. "Truly, my Lord? On what ship?"

"I have been invited to sail on the *North Wind*." I wondered what ship Gaston sailed on.

"Good, good, my Lord. Bradley is a fine captain, I am told. Of course, I have never sailed with him." He guffawed at his own joke. Then he stepped closer to whisper, "Roving with the buccaneers may not be to your liking, though."

"How so?"

"Well, sir, they are a rough lot, and may trouble a man of your breeding," he said with sincere concern.

I shrugged. "I have traveled before."

"As a man of wealth or poverty, my Lord?"

I understood the point he wished to make, and I did not wish to give it to him, though he was correct to assume I had always journeyed as a moneyed man in some fashion. "Both. Sometimes it behooves a Lord's son not to be known as one."

"Ah, very good then, my Lord. You may do well. I wish you the best of fortune. The rest of the land can be settled when you return."

Another man approached and Modyford beamed a smile at him. "Ah, Morgan. This is the Viscount of Marsdale. Lord Marsdale, this is Henry Morgan, the admiral of our buccaneers."

I fought frowning at that. The only credence I could give to this statement was the man's earrings and his overall mien, which was predatory and wary despite the fine clothes and proper young bride at his side. He looked me over, and I knew he thought me weak, much as Bradley had initially done. I chose to ignore it for the time being.

I wondered how one became the admiral of the buccaneers, and whether or not the buccaneers were aware of this. He was not much older than I, and I wondered a good many things about him, but he did not seem inclined to talk in my presence; and so Theodore and I graciously excused ourselves to mingle with other guests.

My official duty for the plantation done, Theodore abandoned me to speak to his other clients. I thought this wise, as I wished to berate him somewhat over his announcement to Modyford. Left alone, I stood and looked about.

Upon arriving, I had been surprised at the number of women present. Though the men still outnumbered them two to one, I had not even expected that many. Apparently the proof of money and power on Jamaica was the possession of a wife. The few single daughters of marriageable age were in demand, and I did not even attempt to force my way through the knots of men surrounding them to get a glimpse. So it was with real amazement that I spied Bradley and Siegfried exiting one of these clusters of courtship.

In truth, I almost did not recognize them, as they were as formally dressed as I. The earrings gave them away, though; and I had to chuckle, as I had discovered another battlefield where gold at the ears could allow buccaneers to recognize one another. Of course I did not have a set yet, so they almost failed to recognize me.

Bradley grinned when he did realize my identity. "I expected you here."

Siegfried shook his head and smiled. "It is in his honor, you fool."

Bradley shrugged and grinned. "All the more reason to expect him."

"That makes one of us," I said. "I was dismayed when I learned of it yesterday."

"You don't like parties?" Siegfried teased.

I thought about that for a moment. "Nay, sir, I do not. I have had my fill of them. In truth they have come to represent work and not play for me."

They regarded me curiously.

"How so?" Bradley asked.

I sighed and shrugged. "There have been periods of my life when I could be considered a duelist by vocation."

"Ahhh," Siegfried said. "So you are quite good with a blade."

"Aye," I grinned. "Good enough to live this long."

"Have you given any more thought to joining us?" Bradley asked.

"A great deal," I said. "You said you would be sailing soon?"

"In two days."

"That soon," I sighed, thankful I would have a good excuse as a result. I could not see where everything could be settled to my satisfaction, even if I wished to rove by then. And there was also the issue of Gaston. I shook my head at my own stupidity. One chance encounter and I was going to make decisions based upon him. I was pathetically lonely.

"I will have to see where my affairs are by then," I said with a regretful tone. "And my health. I seem to have a touch of the flux."

"It'll either pass or you'll die," Bradley said with a shrug.

I laughed. "Easy for you to say, I see."

"I'm just saying it should not be an impediment to your decision. When we first leave port, we need to provision; and then we'll need to careen. By the time we actually start looking for the Spanish, you'll either be well or over the side." He clapped my shoulder with amusement.

"Ahh, I see your argument clearly. Now if you will just explain it to yon Theodore."

To my delight, Tom joined us. I made introductions and looked him over critically. Dressed as a gentleman of quality, he was exceedingly handsome in a boyish way. Yet there seemed to be something lacking in his presence, actually two somethings. "Where are Dickey and Harry?"

"Harry has fallen quite ill and Dickey is tending him," Tom said sadly.

"Truly? With what, pray tell?" I asked.

"The flux."

I looked at Bradley who started laughing.

"I was just complaining of having a touch of that myself," I quickly told Tom, in order to smooth the frown he was giving Bradley. "How ill is he?"

"Grievously, I am sorry to say. The physician has bled him twice already. He says there is hope, though, and he has recommended a treatment of brandied oats and no drink of any kind, in order to reduce the level of... well you know, liquidity of the stool."

This remedy made a good deal of sense to me, and I eyed my wine suspiciously. It had been doing little to slake my thirst or ease my suffering. I either required a far stronger drink or none at all.

"I would be with them, too," Tom said. "But my uncle insisted I accompany him and meet the local gentry. He also wished to gain your introduction, as he feels I was fabulously fortunate to have the honor of traveling with you," he said with a sarcastic flourish.

"Will there be fawning?" I asked with a grimace.

"As if you were in the forest at springtime," Tom said.

We all laughed, but I sobered quickly. "Well, perhaps we should get this over with, then, so that you may return to Harry."

"My uncle is yonder, speaking with Morgan," Tom said.

At the sight of the so-called admiral of the buccaneers, I turned to Bradley with a smile. "Did you know you have an admiral?"

Bradley sighed. "Aye, of sorts. He was a favored student of Mansfield and his uncle was the Lieutenant Governor – and well, Modyford adores him. So he has the job of organizing and leading the buccaneers as a whole; not that anyone wants to listen to him as yet. Don't be fooled by all of that. He's a good man, and a smart one. He has a talent for leading and for battle. He's also a friend."

I nodded respectfully. So Morgan did possess a degree of credibility amongst his peers. We joined Morgan and Tom's uncle, a florid man of great girth and thick lips. He did indeed fawn in quite an embarrassing fashion, and I had to pull free of his grasp several times. Morgan was initially annoyed with this, until he spied Bradley and Siegfried in my wake.

"Don't tell me you two have taken to worshiping the nobility too," Morgan said, as the uncle babbled on contentedly about something I was not listening to.

I glanced back in time to see Bradley smirking. "Marsdale may be sailing with us."

"What?" Morgan scoffed. "Do you think that wise?"

Thankfully, Morgan's poor bride had met the eyes of the uncle and was now caught in his trap. This left me free to take a half step back and engage in the other conversation.

"Why would it not be wise?" I asked innocently.

"It's a hard life," Morgan said.

"Ah yes, so I have been apprised. I was told I may have to curtail my usual entourage, and the accommodations are quite poor, and there will be none of the little crullers I so enjoy."

He glared at me briefly before hiding it behind a pleasant chortle. "You have quite the sense of humor, Lord Marsdale."

"Aye, I should hope it will serve me well as I lie dying of the flux while the ship is being careened."

Bradley and Siegfried were laughing now, and Morgan realized he did not know how to consider me; though he obviously liked me even less.

"I hope it will serve you well, that and courage, the first time you face the Spaniards."

"Are they so horrible?" I asked. "I have never harbored a particular dislike for them."

"They will kill you if you let them," Morgan said.

"As long as they die when I shoot them, we shall get along famously. I have never feared the dead, or had quarrel with them for that matter."

"So you feel you possess the proper mien to become a buccaneer?" Morgan asked.

"From all that I have heard, aye."

"There are no women on the ships, and we do not offer commissions."

"Excellent and excellent."

His gaze narrowed and I felt all eyes upon me. "It will be interesting to hear your opinion this time next year," he finally said.

"It is always interesting to see who Dame Fortune favors over time."

He took his leave. As he walked away with his little bride I labeled him a wolf, albeit a self-made one. There was a roughness about his manner and speech that told of an upbringing without nannies and tutors. He assumed I was not someone who could ever affect him greatly. He was not the first of his kind I had encountered. Coming up from the realm of sheep as they do, they often make that mistake about the wolves they seek to emulate.

As I looked about, I was pleased to note the uncle had been distracted as well. I was left with Tom, Bradley, and Siegfried again. I bid Tom farewell for the evening, and bade him carry my best wishes to the ailing Harry. Once he was gone, I turned to Bradley and Siegfried.

"All duties now done, I wish to retire from this place. What plans do you gentlemen have for the remainder of the evening? There is actually a matter I wish to seek your advice and aid on."

Bradley was regarding me with amusement. "We were going to a tavern; you would be welcome to join us."

"I would be delighted." As I turned, I discovered Belfry hovering at a socially polite distance. "As soon as I talk to this man."

Siegfried indicated something across the room and I glanced in that direction along with Bradley, in time to discover one of the eligible young women beginning to escape from her knot of admirers.

"We'll meet you outside," Bradley said, and they were off in pursuit. I wondered at this, but there was obviously no time to question it.

I joined Belfry. "And how are you this fine evening? I am glad you were able to attend the party."

"As am I, my Lord. It is a blessed relief to step on dry land sometimes. Tonight I will even sleep in a real bed."

"You are staying in town, then?"

"Aye, my Lord, I have to prepare the cargo for loading tomorrow afternoon. We have a limited time at the wharf."

So Davey's rescue definitely had to be affected this very night. My stomach clenched and roiled, and I felt sweat bead on my forehead anew. I hoped fervently that Bradley would agree to aid me, as my body was going to be an unwilling participant in any endeavor I mounted.

"So did all of the officers come ashore?"

"Just the captain and I for the party, then he will return to the ship."

I exchanged further pleasantries with him and bid him farewell once more, even though I harbored the suspicion I would see him again. I was actually grateful it would not be this night, though, as I wished poor Belfry no ill.

I located Theodore, and he followed me outside. His man Samuel was waiting, with an urgent note from another client. I began to shed clothing and accoutrements at a speedy rate and hand them to the unfortunate Negro, until my attire was reduced to shirt and breeches. At which point I strapped my sword back on and stuffed my pistol in my belt. I handed Samuel a small coin. "Please return those to the house, or toss them in a midden heap. I care not. I am not feeling particularly charitable towards them at the moment."

Bradley and Siegfried had joined us and witnessed this exchange.

Samuel regarded me with wide eyes, and Theodore had to give him approval and shoo him away.

"You don't understand the basic principles behind slavery, do you?" Bradley asked. "You don't have to pay them."

"True, true; but what I do not understand about slavery is why he does not kill us in our sleep. I would."

Theodore was sighing heavily, with his head thrown back in supplication to the heavens. We left him there. Several blocks down Thames, as the main thoroughfare running parallel to the bay was named, we turned left through an archway and entered a short alley between two buildings. I spotted a likely shadowed spot that reeked of urine, and asked which tavern they would be in. They said they would be in the Three Tunns, the building on our left. Once I finally made my way inside, I found them at a table in the back with two other men. I resigned myself to waiting, and shook hands with a Captain Searles and a Frenchman named Pierrot, who I assumed was another captain, though he was not introduced as such.

Pierrot was a big man of middle age with dark Gallic coloring, expressive eyes, and a Roman nose. He possessed one of those visages that could change from the melancholy of an old dog to the jocularity of a court jester in the blink of an eye. I supposed that was why he was called "clown."

Searles was even brawnier, with a square face, small eyes, and a forbidding attitude. At the moment he was ranting in a booming voice. He barely slowed down to receive my introduction; Bradley quickly handed me a tankard and waved me into a seat as the man continued.

"And they're off at the King's House celebrating the arrival of some damn Lord's whelp," Searles was saying. "And I've got men to feed. Not that I even know I want to risk bringing another prize in. That bastard Modyford. Oh, the King said this and oh, the King said that. And that fucker Willoughby. Oh, we're here to claim this victory for the King. And Morgan's a good man, better than his uncle at being a buccaneer, but for Christ's sake he's a whelp. The French won't sail with him. Will ya?" He turned on Pierrot, who gave him an amused shrug. Bradley and Siegfried were laughing.

"What's so damn funny?" Searles demanded.

Bradley pointed at me. "The English Lord's whelp."

Searles looked me over and took a swig of beer. He snorted and shrugged. "Doesn't look like I expected."

"He's going to sail with us," Bradley said. I was interested in noting that we had progressed quite handily from the potential of my sailing with them being merely discussed to it being a known fact.

"Listen, Searles," Bradley said. "I know you've been ill-used by the local government, what with them seizing the prize last year and all. But I have faith that business has all changed to our benefit, especially with the war." He shrugged apologetically at Pierrot. "And Modyford not wanting us to take our prizes to Tortuga. So I'm going hunting the Flota this summer. You will do whatever you wish. When the war clears up, we will sail again for bigger plunder, under Morgan, whelp or no."

Searles sighed heavily and looked distantly across the tavern, as if seeing rolling waves and not a wooden wall. "Aye, aye... All is as you say, but damn it man, the life is hard enough without... " He nodded to himself and looked Bradley in the eye. "Damn it all, I want to trust my government, or have none at all."

Bradley nodded sympathetically. "That's why we buccaneers have to stick together. As one, there's not a force on this sea that can stand against us. Separate, we're just pirates running from port to port trying to stay off the gallows."

They all looked thoughtful for a moment. Then Pierrot toasted, "To the Brethren of the Coast!"

We all drained our tankards.

I was, as always, plagued by questions and further bothered by the lack of opportunity to ask them. Thankfully, Searles took his leave shortly thereafter, and I was able to give the other men a questioning look.

Bradley said, "The King has not always been sure how to address the issue of war in the West Indies with the Spaniards. Or more specifically, he's not sure what his ambassadors should be telling the Spanish court as opposed to what he wants from his own colonies. So the governors here have received contrary orders, sometimes only months apart. All in all, they want us here to defend them, but they don't want us to draw Spanish wrath; and then they want the prizes, but they don't want to condone piracy, and so on. So when Modyford arrived in sixty-four, he thought his duty involved putting an end to privateering, and he seized several Spanish prizes brought to port, including two of Searles'. Then England was at war with the Dutch, and everyone was issued marques against them, and Searles and Stedman sailed for Tobago and took it. Three days later, the governor of Barbados shows up and claims *that*. They had to argue to keep the booty. The man has good reason to be angry."

I grasped the situation quickly, as I had seen others like it. "So there is a chance you will sail, and while you are away, the rules will change and you may not have a safe port to return to."

"Aye, we often take that risk when we're roving for months at a time."

"And how fare the French?" I asked Peirrot.

He shrugged. "Our leaders are somewhat more consistent. But Île de la Tortue has changed hands many times. I think it will remain French now, and our King will support privateering without second thought or doubt. But who can truly tell? If a treaty is needed...." He held his hands up to indicate it was in the hands of the fates or at least the powers that be. "Of course, we take a risk whenever we sail here. I was amazed when Modyford offered us a marque, but we've been sailing out of Port Royal for a year now, prior to the war."

"There are French buccaneers on many of the ships. Dutch, too," Bradley added.

I nodded. "So in some ways the Brethren of the Coast truly transcends nationality, and perhaps national loyalty?"

"Oh, by all means." Bradley grinned. "Most men here have no love of the nation of their birth, or often it of them. That's why they're here."

"Are you loyal to your King?" Pierrot asked.

I shrugged. "I grew up during the Reformation. I have traveled Christendom for the last ten years and seen no consistency of government, other than it is always controlled by the powerful for their own ends and they use the weak to do their fighting."

Pierrot nodded approvingly. "You will do well here."

"Aye, I feel so, but I am somewhat dismayed to hear that some things are very like where I have already been."

Bradley frowned, but Peirrot shrugged and grinned. "Here the weak have weapons."

I smiled back, but I was thinking that armed sheep can still be herded: it is in their nature. The talk turned to other things, and another ewer of beer was ordered. Eventually Pierrot bid us adieu. I quickly seized the opportunity.

"I have a matter that requires urgent attention this very night."

Bradley and Siegfried regarded me with surprise.

"We are at your service," Bradley said curiously.

I explained about Davey. They exchanged a long look and Bradley spoke. "We have no qualms about helping a sailor jump ship, but it would present a real hornet's nest if the ones doing it were apprehended."

"Aye, I was thinking a tactic of distraction might be in order if that were to occur," I said.

"How important is this man to you?" Siegfried asked.

"He is merely an acquaintance; one I feel some responsibility for, wholly of my own making. I know it may seem quite the endeavor for an acquaintance but..."

Bradley waved me off. "That is your own concern. However, in the name of our concerns, we cannot be directly involved. What my men do is another matter, however."

"As long as you do not know of it?" I asked. I was somewhat dismayed at his attitude and caution.

"Aye, if asked now, I can say you approached me about helping a sailor jump ship."

"I see, and if I am ever questioned about such things, I should perhaps say that you told me you could and would not be involved in such endeavors."

He winced, though I had not tried to sound harsh. "We will... Aye, you should say that, if the need should come to pass to explain such a thing. It would be best for all if it did not. Marsdale, you have to understand, in depredations against the Spaniards I have no scruples;

in what amounts to a depredation against the English I am a property owner now, and a member of..." He glanced at Siegfried, who looked uncomfortable. "We can't be pirates forever, and we have to think about the future. We have concerns. I am somewhat surprised that you do not share them, especially considering your birth."

Bradley was a tame wolf indeed. The only thing that would stop a wolf from engaging in this endeavor was the possible loss of money or life or the angering of bigger wolves. In his defense, I suppose those reasons could be considered here, but they were not his reason alone. I could see it in his eyes and hear it in his words. He was not a rule maker, but a rule follower.

I was disappointed, and it sat heavy in my heart. I endeavored to keep it from my countenance.

"My relationship to the station of my birth is my own affair," I said with an affable smile. "What aid can you give me, if any? And I blame you not. I fully understand."

He sighed. "Go to my ship and ask for Striker and Pete. Explain yourself; tell them I suggested you speak with them. It will be their decision as to whether or not they wish to take the risk. Knowing them, they'll do it for a bit of fun and damn the consequences."

With that, I drained another tankard and departed. I felt tired and light-headed, and it seemed damnably hot again. With some alarm, I was beginning to suppose I was feverish. By my reckoning, I was halfway to the Chocolata Hole when my bowels directed me to the shadows of an alley. I was beginning to feel both furious and determined. If these men of Bradley's would not help me, I vowed to steal a small boat and row out there myself. Concerns, whatever they may be, English law, and the flux be damned.

I staggered out of the shadows.

"Drink this," Gaston said with his husky whisper in French, and handed me a wineskin.

I started so badly my heart pounded in my chest and my vision wavered for a moment. I was delighted to see him, but I wondered how long he had been following me; and then I wondered why.

"What is it?"

"Water. Boiled."

I attempted to ponder his meaning. "I was told just tonight that the local physicians prescribe a lack of liquid for this ailment."

He blinked at me once and frowned slightly before sighing, "No wonder there are so many deaths." He shrugged. "I heard my remedy from a physician of the Arabian schools. Think of it thusly, what would you do if you had a vile lump of something lodged in a pipe?"

"Flush it out." I took the water and began to drink. In between gulps I asked, "What does boiling have to do with anything?"

"Nothing lives in boiled water."

I stopped drinking and frowned at him. "What?"

"Have you ever looked at water through a lens that magnifies?"

"Non." I grinned and drank more water to hide my excitement. He was either well educated, possibly better than I, or he possessed a more curious mind than mine, as I had not thought to look at water through a lens or been in the company of anyone who had.

"There are all manner of little things swimming in it," he said.

"Like very small fish?"

"Non, like very small shrimp or slugs."

"That is disgusting. So they are not there after it has been boiled?"

"Correct."

"Did you make this discovery or were you taught it?"

"Monks, and I performed the observation myself."

"I never got to learn from monks."

"You are not a Papist, and I only received the blessing of their wisdom after I was expelled from every other proper school in France and Austria." He smirked.

"Are you a devout Papist?"

"Only by birth. And you; are you a devout heathen?" He crossed his arms, but there was an amused cock to his head.

"Non, nor any other faith."

We grinned, as we had established another degree of commonality. And his mention of school had confirmed my guess about his education, and also a suspicion I had been harboring as to the station of his birth. I believed us to be peers.

"I am off to cause mischief," I said. "Are you otherwise engaged?"

If I had still believed in God, I would have prayed Gaston was a wolf so that I did not suffer a truly crushing disappointment this night. If Gaston were not a wolf, considering what I surmised of his birth, then my entire theory of wolves and sheep was at risk. Not only would I lose this most excellent possibility of a true friendship of equals, but I would also be in danger of losing my perception of order in the universe.

He shook his head.

"Of what nature?" he asked as we resumed my course.

"At the very least, it will involve the breaking of what surely is a maritime law of some sort; and at the worst, it may involve the taking of property and life."

"If we are seen," he said.

I grinned. "Non, prior to that. If that were to happen, the incidence of the first two would grow exponentially." I quickly explained about Davey and relayed my plan.

He was silent even when we were standing on the beach of the Chocolata Hole and regarding the *North Wind* anchored beyond. Her deck was well-lit and appeared to be hosting a party. I was alarmed that it might not bode well for the night's mission. I was also concerned that Gaston had not made comment, considering what I had proposed.

"Are you with me?" I asked carefully.

"Excuse me?" he said, and looked at me curiously. "I am sorry, I was trying to decide if any of them appear sober enough to be of any use to us."

The tension drained from my shoulders, and I smiled. He was a wolf. I was truly smitten.

We borrowed a small boat from the beach and rowed to the sloop. I was sure we could have slipped on board and caused mischief for all the attention their watch appeared to spare us. That was, until we reached the side, and the head and shoulders of a man were immediately silhouetted above us.

"WhoAreYa?" the voice boomed, with a heavy brogue which had no respect for the separations usually awarded between words and syllables of the King's English. The question had been an eerie blur of sound that only became understandable words after I concentrated and used my wits.

"WaitIKnowYa," soon followed.

Gaston smiled.

"Greetings, Pete," he said in English, without raising his voice above his usual husky whisper. I was surprised he could be heard with all the ruckus occurring on deck behind the listener.

"AyeYaBeThatMadFrenchie. YaBeTheGhoul. Gaston." There was a note of triumph in this, as if Pete were proud of himself for remembering. "YaBeGood."

I was somewhat surprised that Gaston did not take offense at being referred to as a mad Frenchie. Of course, perhaps I had mistranslated. I was also curious as to why he was known as The Ghoul.

"Correct," Gaston said to Pete. "This is my friend... Will. He needs to talk to Striker and you. Bradley sent him."

I blinked at the shortening of my surname.

"Will?" I whispered.

Gaston shrugged apologetically. "The Brethren prefer names that can easily be shouted in battle, and no man uses his real name across the Line."

"Ah." I nodded. I spared it a moment's more thought, and decided it would do nicely. I had not used a variation of my surname as an alias before.

Then I thought on what else he had said. So the man greeting us was one of the men I sought. And here I had thought I would have to do all of the talking.

"So you know them?"

"Oui." Gaston nodded. "Our ships sailed with Mansfield. During the raids, I fought beside these men."

We threw up a line to secure our craft. Gaston whispered to me before we climbed on board, "Striker thinks for both of them most of the time, but Pete is not as stupid as he appears. He is a genius at combat, as long as it does not involve fencing, and that is only because no one has taught him."

We climbed aboard with that, and I got to see Pete as more than a silhouette. I managed to keep my jaw from falling agape by a sheer

act of will. To say that Adonis had blessed the man would have been
an unjust understatement. Adonis was personified in this man. Pete
was a tanned, golden-haired god, with a long, lean muscular body
and a powerfully handsome face graced by azure eyes. And it was all
too evident: he was only wearing a loose pair of breeches held up by a
rope belt tied low on his hips, so that golden curls could be seen at the
base of his rippled stomach. The only things marring his flesh were a
number of scars here and there: the type any man engaged in combat
will obtain over his life. They were not detracting features. His beard,
which I usually detest, was not even a detracting feature, in that it was
well trimmed and curling and served to outline his jaw. At the moment,
he was rewarding us with a boyish grin so intense in its radiance that I
expected to hear the holy host singing on high.

"WeGotRum. GotCakeToo. WantSome?" Pete asked.

"Cake, truly?" I asked.

"Naw. NoFlour. Cheesecake."

"That will do," I said. Pete ran into the midst of the partying men.

"He is gorgeous," I whispered.

"Oui, I have never even seen statuary that could equal him."

"Oui, the great masters would have given anything to have him
model."

Another man was approaching, and he momentarily drove Pete
from my mind. This is to say he had an equally strong impact on my
consciousness, as driving images of Pete from my mind I would have
thought nigh impossible at the moment. It was only because this man
looked a great deal as I supposed Shane would look as a man and not a
boy, only better. He was as tall as Pete, with an equally muscular build;
however, he lacked the perfection of conformation Pete possessed. The
same was true of his face, which while handsome, was a little too strong
in some areas and not others. His hair was ebony and hung over dark
eyes; but he had light golden skin. He did not wear any more clothing
than Pete.

He studied us as he approached, the trace of a frown upon his brow.

"Gaston," he acknowledged politely and they shook hands.

"Striker. This is Will."

I shook hands with the man. "Bradley suggested I talk with you."

He raised an eyebrow. "Concerning?"

Pete returned with a bottle and a plate of goop, which he proffered.
"Cheesecake."

The goop did indeed smell like cheesecake, and I ate it readily. It
proved to taste like cheesecake, too; and it had been months since I had
eaten anything so good.

"That is truly delicious," I said. Pete appeared pleased and offered
me more. We retired farther astern, to the *North Wind's* low quarterdeck,
and sat to finish the cake and pass the bottle.

"I need assistance rescuing a sailor," I said. "I have a friend on a
merchant ship in the harbor. He would like to become a buccaneer. I

have offered to help him. The captain has judged him at risk of fleeing and had him locked below deck."

"Could we assume this was a close friend?" Striker asked with a knowing grin.

"Nay, we could not. I have developed a pastime of availing myself as a philanthropist or benefactor of sorts. He is spirited and ambitious, and I admired him for that and decided to help."

Striker appeared to be somewhat incredulous, and he glanced at Gaston for his reaction. Gaston shrugged.

"When?" Striker asked.

"Tonight."

"You are in this?" Striker asked Gaston, who nodded. "If we are seen?"

"That will not be acceptable," I said.

"Will the bodies be missed?"

"Aye, most probably. As I will most likely kill the bo'sun even if we are not seen, my thinking is thus. She is empty of cargo. The only other person of her crew I have grown fond of is ashore tonight. I cannot see where the rest of her crew would be harmed by her loss. I harbor no true ill-will toward the captain, yet he does not own her. And the owners benefit from the selling of pressed men, which I find abhorrent. So I am considering burning her as a diversion." I was keen to see their reactions. As I had already relayed this to Gaston, I was not concerned about his.

Pete and Striker smiled like wolves, and I was relieved.

"LikeBurnin'Ships," Pete grinned.

"You realize if we become lost on this path we'll end at the gallows," Striker said. He did not seem to think this was likely. "Is there any money? If we're going to burn her, we might as well rob her."

I smiled. "If it is still aboard, the captain has a good forty pounds of my money and possibly more."

"What did you pay him for?" Striker asked.

"A man's contract, which I then destroyed."

"Who the devil are you?" he asked with more suspicion.

I sighed, but met his gaze levelly. "I am the Viscount of Marsdale. My father is the Earl of Dorshire, and he sent me here to oversee the establishment of a sugar plantation."

The wolves studied me with unease, and glanced as one to Gaston and back again to me. Striker frowned at whatever he found on Gaston's face, but by the time I looked to see my new companion's reaction, his face was schooled, and he appeared to be idly watching the men at the bow. I cursed under my breath. I felt quite comfortable with him, as if we were old and true friends; but in truth I knew less of him than he probably did of me.

"WeNotBeAidin'Planters," Pete said and slid the cheesecake beyond my reach.

"Bradley sent you to us?" Striker asked, as if he could not fathom why.

My ire flared: not necessarily at them, but at the situation I found myself in. I would not have these men think ill of me because of my damn father.

"Aye, Bradley sent me. He invited me to sail with him and I am considering it wholeheartedly. I asked for his aid, and he said he wished to have no part in this endeavor as... I believe he is concerned for his respectability. As for my being a planter," I snorted derisively. "I have little interest in it. My father wished for me to come here as his agent because he thought I might die and save him a bit of trouble, and there was no one else he wished to risk. There is no love lost between us, and I have not lived under his roof but for two months these last ten years. I came because... I will inherit. When I do, I can do much good with the title, or so I tell myself. In the meantime, acting as his agent, I can at least see that those he has contracted are treated well."

They seemed somewhat taken aback by my vehemence. I glanced at Gaston and found his eyes large upon me. He quickly regarded the deck.

"WeBeBondsmenOnce," Pete said, so that I shifted my attention to him. He scratched his head and pushed the cheesecake back toward me with a guilty smile.

"I am sorry," I said quietly.

A slow smile spread across Striker's face. "Let's get your man."

I shook my head and smiled sadly. "The entire point of the endeavor is that he be no one's man."

"Aye," he grinned. "Let us get our weapons." They slipped off the quarterdeck to the deck below.

I hazarded another look at Gaston and found him studying me intensely. Once again, he looked away quickly when our eyes met. I wished to speak but did not know what to say, and the wolves were still within hearing.

He stood abruptly and took his musket to Pete, who stowed it in the area from which they were retrieving their weapons.

"So, that forty pounds, you willing to share it out?" Striker asked.

"Aye," I shrugged. "I already considered it well spent. Recouping a fraction of it will be an unexpected pleasure."

"Were Bradley and Siegfried at that party tonight?" Striker asked as they returned to the quarterdeck. They now wore no more clothing, but they were wrapped in belts and baldrics laden with as many weapons as Gaston carried, but no muskets. Striker chuckled before I could respond. "Damn, you're the Lord it was to welcome, aren't you?"

I sighed and took another pull on the bottle. "Aye. And I met all of the important people I was supposed to meet and promptly escaped."

"So Bradley doesn't have the balls for it anymore, does he?" Striker said with a lopsided grin. "Getting all respectable. Were they chasing women at this party, proper ladies?"

"Aye," I said with a raised eyebrow.

Pete and Striker exchanged a look.

"I feel sorry for Siegfried," Striker shrugged.

"YaEverDoThatI'llFuckin'KillYa," Pete said with a look that made him appear anything but the affable idiot he seemed previously.

Striker blew him a kiss, and they smiled with sarcastic sweetness at one another.

I suppressed a laugh. As I looked about at my three new companions, I realized the Gods had tipped their hand; and I was momentarily in awe of their magnanimity.

Eight

Wherein I Throw Myself To Destiny

The wolves informed the men drinking in the bow that they were going into town. The four of us slipped over the side to the boat Gaston and I had borrowed from the beach.

"You know her anchorage in the dark?" Striker asked, as if he expected me not to know the answer.

"There are four ships at anchor. I checked their positions from the King's House this evening. She is on the end, farthest west, closest to the Passage Fort."

They took a set of oars, and Gaston and I took the other. I looked to him before we were swallowed in the darkness beyond the *North Wind's* lanterns. He was studying me again; and once again, his eyes darted away when they met mine. I still could not read his expression.

We spent the passage quietly discussing various tactics, each based upon what we might find. We found the *King's Hope* easily in the moonlight, and glided silently to her side. Pete drove two axes into the hull and we all held our breath to see if the noise was heard. Then he climbed up to stand on them and peer over the gunwale. He waved us up a moment later.

There were lights and men on the quarterdeck and forecastle. The three men astern stood near a lantern, and I recognized one of them as the first officer. The rest of the crew seemed to be clustered about the bow, as they had always been during our voyage. They were playing cards. I could hear snoring as well. Coming over the gunwale into the waist, we were in shadow and alone. We crowded together and crouched very low between two cannon.

It had been decided that Gaston and Striker should take the captain's quarters and Pete and I should search for Davey – and once finding him, set the ship afire below the waterline. I had wanted to stay with Gaston; but Pete had been adamant about firing the ship, and I was the only one who knew Davey.

To my amusement, Pete kissed Striker on the cheek. Then he waved for me to follow, and we slipped across the deck to the hatch and dropped into the hold below.

It seemed quite large, now that it was devoid of cargo. I assumed Davey was somewhere in the darkness around us. I listened. I heard rats and the faint clank of metal from the stern. Pete had heard it as well. I started to move in that direction, but Pete stayed me with a hand upon my arm. In the dim light from above, I saw him take a lantern from its hook just below the hatch. Then we padded aft, even our bare feet sounding loud, despite the muted voices from both castles and the omnipresent water on the hull about us.

I stopped when my outstretched hand encountered wood, a pole that swayed at my touch. I guessed it to be part of the whip staff apparatus which steered the ship. Somewhere in this area, the whip staff above us was connected to the rudder in the water at the very rear of the vessel.

Pete handed me the lantern, and I lit it. The sudden illumination was blinding in the enclosed space; and it was a moment before I could perceive much of anything. Then the light showed a man chained to the hull beside the steering apparatus. It was Davey, though I almost did not recognize him for the bruises. He was sleeping or unconscious.

Seeing his battered face, any remaining remorse I might have felt about destroying the ship vanished. If doing this to a man was considered a routine part of one's livelihood, then perhaps it was a livelihood that deserved a considerable setback. Burning one ship was not going to make any other merchant vessel treat its crew more humanely; but there was the principle of the thing, and in this instance it mattered to me.

I assessed the chains on Davey. He was manacled, and the chain between his wrists was connected to another that ran to a bolt in a beam of the hull.

"We will need keys," I muttered to Pete.

"Naw ya won't," a voice growled from behind me. It was not Pete. It was Cox, the bo'sun.

I spun low and drew a dirk.

"Thought you'd come." He grinned at me and brandished an axe.

I was somewhat alarmed, as I did not see Pete and wondered where he had gotten off to. Then arms closed around the very surprised bo'sun: one around his throat and the other about his chest, pinioning his axe arm above the elbow. Pete's head loomed over the man's shoulder and grinned at me. I stepped in quickly and relieved Cox of his weapon with a twist to his wrist.

"Did you think I would come alone?" I asked in pleasant whisper. "Not that I would truly need help with the likes of you. Now, where are the keys?"

He glared at me and I rested my blade across his chest, leaving an ever deepening line of blood as I pressed. He gasped and struggled and finally snarled, "My pocket."

I let him fumble in his own pocket with his free hand. He gave me a key ring.

"YaWantTaKill'Em?" Pete asked.

"I want him dead." I shrugged and prepared to thrust with my blade.

"I'llDoIt," Pete said and adjusted his grip to the man's jaw. Then he jerked up and back and there was a popping sound. The bo'sun slumped to the floor.

"LessBloodTaSlipOnWhenWeBeRunnin'." He pushed the body out of the way.

I had to admit he had a point.

"I have never seen a man killed like that before," I said. I did not think I possessed the strength, but I vowed to remember it in case the need ever arose.

Davey had woken. He blinked at the light and recoiled.

"It is Marsdale," I hissed.

He shook his head. "You came?"

"Aye, and now we must go."

"I didna' think you'd come."

"I said I would aid you."

"Aye, but..."

"We do not have the luxury of discussing this now." I got him out of the chains and pulled him up to his knees.

Davey regarded Pete curiously and then moved slowly past him, not out of recalcitrance, but out of stiffness and injury. I sorely wished we had possessed the time to kill the bo'sun slowly.

Once Davey was at the hatch, Pete took the lantern from me and admonished, "WatchNow." His eyes gleamed with enthusiasm. "YaGotTa WatchWhileItCatches. ItBeBlueAn'ThereBeLines."

I watched. He threw the lantern against the beam Davey had been chained to, so that it broke and sprayed oil all about. Pitch and tar burn faster than wood, and a ship is nothing but the three together. The pitch caught first; and as he said, flame shot along the planks in blue lines. It was beautiful, mesmerizing even, as the wood caught hold and the flames billowed up to flow across the ceiling.

Pete roughly grabbed me and pushed me ahead of him and up the hatch. He was laughing. I realized I had been too busy watching to realize the danger.

We found Davey leaning on the gunwale, regarding us with horror as the smoke began to billow up from below. I looked about for Gaston and Striker and did not see them. Pete helped Davey over the side to the boat. I stayed in the shadows and waited until our missing companions came bounding out of the cabins. We all slipped over the side, Striker passing a chest down to Pete before he disembarked. The hull was hot beneath my hands, and the stars and moon were obscured by smoke. The crew was yelling and beginning to run about.

Then we were off. We rowed north like madmen, away from Port Royal, so as not to run afoul of the doomed ship's own longboats or be seen by anyone looking across the harbor at the commotion. The burning ship's bell sounded frantically, and then there was a loud explosion as the powder magazine caught. I truly hoped all of her men were clear. I supposed I would hear tell of the outcome in the morning.

In the darkness, we worked our way around toward the Passage Fort and then headed south again, so it would appear that we had come from there. Our pace relaxed and we were able to make introductions. Davey seemed a little dazed by the turn of events, and asked several times if my companions were actually buccaneers. This caused the others a great deal of amusement.

"You're one of us now, mate," Striker informed him. He kicked the box, "And you'll receive your first share of booty once we get back to the *North Wind*." We had agreed that Davey would receive a share, since without him the whole enterprise would not have been conceived; and he would need money to equip himself for his new life.

I could not see the expression on Davey's countenance after Striker's words, but his shoulders spoke unreadable volumes. He sat perfectly still. There was no tension in his wide back, and he did not stoop or straighten; he just did not move. I could see the wolves watching him in the moonlight, judging his reaction with a mix of amusement and wariness. I had imagined Davey would be happy with this turn of events; but I surely did not know him well enough to know. He slowly turned to look at me over his shoulder.

"You robbed the ship?" he asked quietly. "And burned it?"

"Aye," I said with a shrug. "Had to cover for your rescue."

"It is the way of the coast," Gaston said in French.

Davey frowned at him. I translated, though it helped little as Davey did not understand what the coast in question was. Nor did I, other than knowing we were amongst the brethren of one.

Pete stopped rowing and clapped Davey heartily on the shoulder. "NotOneO'ArShips. You'llGetPastIt."

Davey nodded. "We're not goin' ta hang?"

"If we're found out we might," Striker said. "Ship's gone. No witnesses, no bodies if we're lucky between the fire, the explosion, and the sharks. Just the five of us. Course the Captain and his matelot know of it. But despite their trying to be proper gentlemen, they won't say anything." Striker looked at me and frowned. "Anybody else who might know you wanted to get him free?"

"Two, both beholden to me in some fashion." I knew Theodore and Fletcher would be dismayed, but I was sure in my heart they would be admirably silent about it all unless they knew the details. "As long as they know not of the money and I say the burning resulted from the heat of the moment, as it were."

Striker grinned and nodded. "Same goes for Bradley. And I'll trust your judgment on yours. I have a feeling that you've been involved in enough endeavors of this nature to be a good judge of a man in that regard."

"Aye," I smiled.

Davey turned to find me in the moonlight. He was grinning this time. "You robbed and burnt the ship."

"Christ's balls, I think he's beginning to see which end's up," Striker laughed.

I chuckled and glanced at Gaston. I found him watching me again. This time he did not look away when our eyes met.

"Thank you," I whispered.

He snorted and looked away with a thoughtful frown. "Non, thank you."

Though we witnessed a great deal of commotion along the harbor wharfs, none came toward us. We rowed through the dark. In the aftermath of the excitement, my bowels chose to remind me of their existence. I found myself unable to row as I hunched over the oar in pain.

"Will?" Gaston hissed. I felt more than heard or saw the others stop rowing.

"It is nothing. Merely cramps. More of the same involving my bowels," I whispered back, though it did little to prevent the others from hearing as all was quiet about us.

Gaston's fingers were on my forehead and then the side of my neck. "You are not fevered."

"Thank the Gods. I am rarely ill, truly."

I heard Striker swear quietly.

I tried to sit up. Gaston pulled the oar out of my hands and bade me sit still with a gentle touch. The wolves commenced rowing again.

"Do you need…?" Gaston began to ask.

"Non," I said quickly. I did not even wish to imagine them balancing the boat while I hung my arse off the side.

"Drink," he whispered and handed me his water skin.

I drained it.

Gaston was still concerned.

"When did it begin?" he asked in French.

"Today."

"Have you been feverish?"

I wished to say no. "I have found it intolerably hot all day, and yesterday, and blamed it upon the tropical climate."

He nodded soberly. "You are worse than I assumed. I am sorry. It need not kill you, though. I will care for you."

I returned his nod in kind. "Thank you."

Not only did I believe he would, I believed he could. As chilling as the idea was that I was truly ill, I was greatly warmed by the knowledge that he wished to care for me.

The few men aboard the *North Wind* greeted us as we rowed up. They had all been distracted from their drinking by the explosion, but none had stirred themselves to leave the ship and go in search of information. This was probably in the best interests of all concerned, because the men were drunk. Striker informed them Pete and he had gone ashore in search of cheesecake, but the bakery was closed. Very few of them remembered that Gaston and I had even been on board before, fewer still would probably realize Davey had not been there with us. As possibly none of them would remember much of the night at all, it mattered little. However, Pete and Striker went amongst them to tell what they had supposedly heard in the streets about the explosion. Thus the way was safe for Gaston and me to get Davey, and the one thing that would surely sober a bunch of drunken pirates, the cash box, into the aft cabin.

I closed the door behind us, and leaned on it with a sigh of relief – which immediately turned to a quiet growl of annoyance. The room was dark, the leaded windows along the stern doing little to illuminate anything at night. I could only guess at the location of a lantern. Gaston was far more knowledgeable about the logical places to keep lanterns in a ship's cabin, or he had spied one before the door closed, because he lit one a moment later. I sighed with relief again.

The room was very small and the ceiling low. It was furnished with a bunk along one wall and a table with two chairs on the other. Davey gingerly lowered himself into a chair. I crossed slowly to the other and sat, as my legs felt quite weak. Gaston considered the cash box he had placed on the table.

"Did you have to kill anyone?" I asked.

"We did not have to," he said distractedly, as he pried the hinges loose on the back of the box, effectively opening it without touching the lock.

I chuckled. "Did you anyway?"

His lip quirked. "We encountered two men who were observant and therefore not destined for a long life under the circumstances. And you?"

"The bo'sun."

Davey had been frowning at both of us. "You killed the bo'sun?"

"Nay, Pete did." I said.

"Good," Davey said with a slow nod.

I considered him in the lamp light. He looked far worse than he had in the dark, which was of course to be expected. He was filthy and haggard and he had been soundly beaten. Both eyes were bruised and swollen, his lip was split, and there was a gash on his cheek and another along his jaw. I imagined his clothing hid worse.

"If I had seen the extent of your injuries before he died, I would have saved him for a slower death."

He smiled weakly. "That woulda been good."

"I daresay you will need a surgeon."

Gaston shrugged. "Non. He will live. None of his wounds look so bad as to require stitching. I am sure he can rest below." He began to stack coins in countable piles.

I supposed he was correct. I had oft been far better off when wounded to not have some physician attempting to readjust my humors through bleeding or some strange concoction. I had just assumed the wounds were of a sufficient nature to require a surgeon's attention; but now that I looked at Davey anew, I saw Gaston to be correct. Davey was not bleeding. The more I thought on it, the more I realized that the bo'sun had inflicted his damage for pain and show. He would not have wanted to injure Davey so that he could not work on the return voyage.

Davey's eyes got big as he considered the money. "I'm fine, sir."

Gaston paused to frown at him.

"What are the rules amongst the buccaneers for addressing a superior?" I asked.

"I am not his superior," Gaston said. "And there are no rules. Men are usually respectful of a captain, once we are at sea and he has been elected, or if it is his ship."

The mention of an election was intriguing, but in thinking of that question I remembered an earlier one. "What coast are the Brethren the brethren of?"

Gaston frowned at me and then smiled. "The Haiti of Hispaniola. The high country and northwest coast along the passage."

The wolves crammed themselves into the cabin with us. They stood in awe for a moment at the amount of coin on the table. I regarded it. There had been far more in the box than I had guessed. There was gold amongst the silver.

"Damn..." Striker said appreciatively. "This is a fine end to a night's amusement."

Pete fingered a coin. In the harsh lamplight I noticed a T branded in his palm. He was a convicted thief. He grinned with predatory splendor, the lamp-lit gold reflecting in his eyes. He tossed the coin onto the table and turned to haul me off the chair and to my feet in a great embrace.

"ILikeYa. ILikeYaLots." He dropped me and descended on Davey, who had the good sense to look panicked as he saw me trying to catch my breath. Pete stopped short of him and squatted to eye the wounds. "LikeYaMoreThanHim. Won'tTouchYaThough. YaNeedRum." He handed Davey a bottle. Davey winced at the first taste but quickly took a second swig.

Striker was making rapid calculations based on Gaston's piles. "There's more than a hundred."

"PiecesOfEight?" Pete asked. "Good."

"Half the coin is pieces, but I meant pounds," Striker said.

"Damn," Pete said thoughtfully.

"That would be around four hundred pieces of eight," I said. "With five shares, that is eighty pieces each, or twenty pounds."

Davey had very big eyes, and he took another drink.

"I have never seen that much money," he muttered.

I supposed he had not. I wondered why the captain had carried so much; and then I realized it was probably a good part of the amount he would have used to procure cargo here in Port Royal, though I assumed some of those transactions would be conducted with letters of credit.

Striker helped Gaston divide the different currencies into five equal piles: first pieces of eight, then shillings, then odd currencies. Since not all of the coinage was evenly divisible by five, they decided on their own exchange rates and evened out the piles in terms of value. I was impressed; I did not believe I could have done a swifter or more competent job of it.

As there was actually a little over a hundred, we each chose a pile that roughly equaled twenty-three pounds. I was pleased. I had little left of what my father had given me, and any additional money was welcome indeed.

Striker dug around in a chest on the wall and produced bags for us to scoop our booty into. I noticed with some amusement that Striker scooped almost all of Pete's share in with his own. He handed Pete ten or so small coins, and Pete seemed content with this.

Striker eyed Davey. "You will have to stay on board, and below deck, until we sail. We'll see to buying your weapons and the like on the morrow. You can reimburse us."

"Whatever ya think best." Davey nodded soberly. "So I will truly sail with you?"

"Aye."

"When?"

"Day after tomorrow." Striker grinned. "We're after the Flota, and if we don't catch one of them, then the Galleons a month or so later. We should be at sea three or four months."

"No matter to me. I haven't been on land in two years," Davey said.

"YaWannaWalkOnShore?" Pete asked.

Davey chuckled. "Aye, I would at that. Just for a time." He stood slowly. His eyes met mine. "Thank you. I haven't said that yet. I'm sorry, but thank you. Not that you didn't get something out of it all, but..."

I sighed and shrugged cordially. I had been prepared to say something properly polite and emotional, but after his last bit of cynicism, I decided I did not want to tell him he was always welcome. First he had not believed I would show, and now he thought I had the ulterior motive of the money. It was disheartening, and protestation would gain me nothing. I hoped the others did not feel as he did.

Gaston glared at Davey, who avoided his gaze. My spirits were raised. At least one man in the cabin understood I had not done it for the money. And he had not, either. He had joined me merely because I asked. He had sought me out this night. He had chosen to make my acquaintance the day before. He was as much a wolf as I. He had said he would care for me in my ailment. And now he had the greenest eyes gazing at me from that black mask. The idiotic schoolboy thoughts I had harbored began to frolic once again in my head.

He looked away with embarrassment. My heart cramped near as hard as my bowels. There was an ugly sound somewhere deep in my mind, and I was sure it was the ghost of Shane's scornful laughter.

Pete led Davey out, and Striker rummaged in the same chest in which he had found the bags and produced a bottle of good Madeira. I wondered whose cabin we were in. Striker seemed very free with its contents. He lounged on the bunk and took a pull. Gaston took the chair Davey had vacated.

"You sail the day after tomorrow?" Gaston asked.

Striker nodded. "We'll crew up... today really. Sail tomorrow. Articles the morning after, once we're out of the Hole."

I sighed, though Bradley had told me much the same about the nearness of their sailing. It was very soon.

Striker drew my attention sharply to him, especially after I realized he wasn't speaking to me. "Are you thinking of joining us? I thought you sailed with Peirrot on the *Josephine*."

I realized the French captain I had met in the Three Tunns was Gaston's captain.

"I do," Gaston said. "But he is not sure when he will sail, and I grow weary of doing nothing. Would I be welcome?"

My heart soared and pounded and I found it hard to keep a grin from my face. Perhaps it was as he dissembled; but I found that hard to believe in light of his other actions concerning my person. He did not want to lose contact with me.

Striker studied him. "You're mad. Bradley saw the incident at Granada."

At first this statement confused me. Then Gaston looked away sharply to glare at the windows. I realized Striker was actually saying Gaston was insane, not that Gaston was mad for wishing to sail with them. Once again my heart was gripped by cramps similar to my bowels. My new friend was not denying it.

"I suffer from bouts of... anger," Gaston said.

"Aye, you become a dangerous raving lunatic," Striker said. "But as I see it, no crew you've sailed with so far has marooned you or thrown you overboard, so you must be worth the trouble. And from what I saw of how you fight, I judge you to be worth the trouble. Besides, someone should come with us to look after Lord Will here."

For the briefest of moments, I seriously considered shooting him. I could tell Gaston was thinking the same thing. Then he glanced in my direction, only to look away quickly with embarrassment. Striker noticed this, and he smirked at me.

"You are a brave man," I told him.

Striker chuckled. "I prefer to think of myself as foolhardy rather than courageous."

"You should be careful; you do not have Pete here to back you," Gaston rumbled.

"Ouch," Striker hissed with only partially feigned injury. Then he sobered and shrugged. "'Tis true though. I should keep a firmer hold on my tongue. You're damn fast and Will there would no doubt back you. But if Pete were here I would kick your arses." He grinned.

I had to chuckle. "At least you know where your strengths lie."

"Aye, I lie with him."

To see a man such as Striker say such a thing so openly was a wonder to me. There were things I wished to ask, but years of habit held my tongue.

Gaston stood and left the room. Striker appeared alarmed. I gave him a helpless shrug and followed Gaston.

Dawn had been creeping up on us, and I emerged into a world of muted light. Except for the call of gulls, all was muffled by the predawn grey. There were more men aboard than there were before; and they were spread out all over the deck, both singly and in pairs. Their sounds too were muted, as if they took a cue from the light in their lack of definition.

I found Gaston gathering his musket from the place where Pete had stowed it for him. He did not meet my gaze. I wished to know what the matter was, but I dared not ask with so many strangers eyeing us curiously. Instead I followed him about like a loyal dog, as he went to the rail and looked over the side for something, presumably a boat. Pete and Davey had not returned with the one we used earlier, but I was sure all of the men arriving recently must have come out on something.

Striker caught up with us.

"Will we see you then?" he asked me, as Gaston would not look at him.

"I do not know. We," and I put a touch of emphasis on the word, "must discuss it. Will you see to Davey's equipping?"

"Aye. You would be welcome. Both of you. I did not mean to rile you."

Gaston nodded, still without regarding him. Striker clapped my shoulder. "I hope to see you both. Knowing you has already proven entertaining and lucrative."

"Thank you for your assistance, and I have been honored to make your acquaintance."

He nodded with a sincere smile and left us alone. I found Gaston regarding me. The soft light was not the only reason I could not read him. The mask about his eyes hid much. I supposed that was the real reason he painted them so. We discover a great many things about another man's intentions by watching his eyes, or rather the play of skin and muscle around them. Gaston's were shrouded in secrecy.

He turned away and led me to a canoe tied below. We slipped over the side and released it. He handed me an oar. I quickly discovered this type of craft was far less steady than a normal boat. I followed Gaston's example and knelt. He showed me how to row with the single oar, and we quickly made our way to shore, or rather he did with me aiding him by accident on occasion. Once at the beach, we shoved the light craft up above the water line.

The night's events had taken their toll, and I stood on wobbly legs. He regarded me critically for a moment before his hand snaked out to touch my brow. He frowned at the result.

"You are now fevered," he whispered in French.

"Oui."

"You should rest and drink more water."

I did not want to lose sight of him. "There's a spare hammock at Theodore's, and I daresay food."

He considered me for a long moment and started walking. I followed until we reached the first cross street and he paused to look to me for direction. I led us to Theodore's.

We slipped into the back yard, and removed our weapons and accoutrements next to the brick cistern. I filled a basin and washed my face and hair. I realized I smelled of smoke. I was not pleased at this, as unless I had been standing next to a cook fire there was no place on Jamaica I could have been encased in smoke long enough to pick up the scent except for, say, a burning ship. I was sure an experienced seaman could even tell I had been subjected to burning tar and pitch. It marked us guilty. I stripped my shirt, and scrubbed my chest and arms as if this would somehow clean it all away.

Samuel emerged and went wide-eyed at the sight of Gaston. Then he saw me standing next to the Frenchman, at which point he broke into a wide smile.

"Master Marsdale," he whispered. "I'm glad it's you."

Gaston handed me a bucket and spoke in French. "You need water, boiled water."

"Sam, can you do me a favor?"

"Anything for you, Master Marsdale."

I wondered why he was so happy to see me, and then I remembered the money I had given him last night. I smiled. A well-greased palm was always the way to a man's heart.

"I need some water boiled." I explained what I needed in detail; and he looked confused at first, and then became resigned to my mad English orders. He filled the bucket and headed for the cookhouse, pausing to ask if we would both require victuals on the way. I assured him we would.

Apparently our conversation had alerted Theodore to my return, and he appeared in the yard. I thought him awake quite early, but then I realized the calls of birds about us were now cocks and not gulls. He looked me over with a critical eye, and then regarded Gaston with a mix of emotions that finally aligned themselves into something I would label resigned curiosity.

"Theodore, Gaston," I said in the briefest of informal introductions.

Neither man seemed to take umbrage at my lack of manners.

"Pleased, I'm sure," Theodore said with the barest of bows. Gaston regarded him without expression or movement. Neither man seemed to take umbrage at that exchange either, at least not that I could tell.

"We will be eating and sleeping here today, if that will be acceptable with you," I said.

"You are of course quite welcome. What happened to...?"

"We found that friend I mentioned and he is quite well. You may be interested to know that a ship burned in the harbor last night. Well, burned until her powder caught; at which point she exploded."

He looked pained as he studied the scattered clouds far overhead. "Is that so? And in all your carousing, did you happen to hear which ship?"

"The *King's Hope,* I believe." I looked to Gaston for confirmation, and he nodded agreeably.

Theodore sighed, and his face looked as if it ached in his efforts to stop from smiling.

"Well, I hope someone had the good sense to rob her first." He returned inside, leaving Gaston and me gaping after him.

Amused, I sank down beside the cistern with a strangled laugh and spoke in quiet French: "I did not realize he would be so conducive. I have been here so short a time I have not had the luxury of knowing my compatriots as well as is my norm for engaging in activities of that nature. I truly know no one at all. Thankfully, I have had the incredible good fortune to meet men of excellent character, maybe not of the highest moral standing, but seemingly excellent in their loyalty and willingness to put faith in me. I was not sure what I would encounter here when I sailed, and I have been quite pleasantly surprised." I looked up at him. "Not the least by you. On the voyage, I truly despaired of meeting anyone such as you, a man of intelligence, education, courage, and breeding."

He rewarded me with a disparaging snort and doffed his kerchief to wash the smoke from his face and hair. "You are gracious, and I will accept some of your praise, but not all: only because, though there are many intelligent and courageous men on this island, there are few with the ability to reason for themselves – and even fewer still have received a proper education in anything but the most rudimentary elements of letters and sums. As for breeding, however, judging from the poor mix of the bitch and dog that bred me, if I had been a puppy, I should have been drowned to preserve the line."

I chuckled. "Surely you jest."

"Non, both of my parents were touched by madness, and I am their true descendent in every way." He squatted next to me. "But I think your intent was as to the station of my birth. And you are correct in your assumption. My father is a Marquis."

I nodded. The morning sun was now upon us, and I was awed by the color of his hair, which was a dark red, nearly the color of blood.

Even if he had not removed his kerchief, I would have known from the stubble of his beard in this light. There was a scar on the left side of his forehead, near the hairline, where some blow had split the skin. He saw my eyes upon it, and ran his fingers through his hair above to mask my view.

"I need to cut it. So do you. There is less trouble with heat and lice when it is short." His hair stood more than hung, and was at most an inch long.

I scratched my head at the mere thought of lice. My straw-colored hair fell to my shoulders. I did not feel I would miss it. "If I sail."

"Do you wish to?"

"Aye, I feel it is my nature and I wish it, yet... I have assigned myself a duty. Not to the plantation, or my father's wishes, but to the men, the bondsmen. I would see they are well cared for and well used. I have been assured by Theodore that this will be the case. However..." I trailed off and watched him inspect the mortar between two bricks.

"That is admirable." There was regret in his voice.

"Do you wish to sail?"

"I must." He closed his eyes as if it pained him. When they opened again, they were beseeching. "I possess a violent soul, and it is best I visit it upon enemies and not allies. I am restless with little to do here; and though there is little to do most times upon a ship, it is at least going somewhere."

The haze burned away in my heart, and I was gripped by clarity of purpose. The Gods had spoken. They had delivered the thing that would tip the scales of my dilemma, and it was Gaston. I do not possess a violent soul, but a romantic one. I would not abandon forty-one men to an uncertain fate in order to satisfy my whims and alleviate potential boredom; but I would do it for him. It became very easy to justify when I regarded the man squatting next to me. I could hear his breathing, and smell smoke, leather, and gun powder masking his muskiness, and feel him block the sun and breeze a little, and almost touch him. He was so very close. And though I had no promise of that which I desired, there was still the tenuous thread of hope. And that slender siren call wakened the beast of loneliness that had lived within my heart since I first learned that some people are loved and I was not. It howled that my sheep could not and would not ever love me as Gaston might. And thus the choice was no longer within the purview of my rational mind, and therefore not mine to make.

"Gaston, I would have you as a friend if you are so inclined. And to that end I am loathe to see you sail off for months when fate, and the vagaries of the sea and piracy, are prone to be fickle. I am willing to do as you choose. If you wish to sail on either the *North Wind* or the vessel you came here on, or for that matter another ship altogether, I am willing to accompany you."

He appeared stricken for a moment, and then he looked away. "You humble me."

"Non, I am truly being quite self-serving."

This disturbed him; and he stood, to my dismay. He did not retreat farther from me, though. "I would rather not sail on the ship I arrived on," he said without regarding me.

"May I ask why?" I pulled myself up to stand.

"I have ruined my welcome there with all but one." He looked concerned and studied the ground.

I wondered at the nature of this madness he claimed, but I chose not to broach it. There would be time for that later. "So we sail on the *North Wind* then?"

He met my gaze again. "Oui. We should sleep, and then there are things which must be done."

I nodded. I was thankful he had not suggested doing anything before sleeping. He went to check on my water and our food, and I donned my shirt and made my slow way inside.

Theodore was at the table, sipping a cup of something. I eased my sore body into a seat, poured a cup for myself from the pot on the table, and found the substance to be chocolate. Most places I have been, it is a rare treat indeed. Here, where they grew cocoa and sugar, I supposed it might be ordinary.

"You move through life with astounding speed," he said.

I regarded him quizzically. I had not told him of my decision, and wondered if he had spied upon us. "Whatever do you mean?"

"What is the nature of your relationship with this Gaston? Who I assume is French by his name."

I smiled and sighed. "He is a friend. I may move through life quickly as you say, but I have noticed a deep-seated tendency of people on this island to leap flailing into the abyss of conjecture at a moment's notice."

He smirked. "So I am not the first to leap to this conclusion?"

"Or several others. The mere mention of wanting to rescue Davey caused a great deal of likeminded thinking. Elsewhere in the world, it is common for men to be friends without having carnal knowledge of one another."

Theodore laughed. "Not when they admittedly favor men."

I supposed I would become accustomed to it, and wondered why Striker's and Theodore's assumption bothered me so. Then I remembered the embarrassment Gaston had suffered at Striker's suggestions. I rubbed my temples and decided to change the subject.

"I am sailing tomorrow with Bradley. We meet on the ship this eve."

He smiled. "I hoped as much."

"I know. I will not be about to trouble the endeavor for months."

My tone had not been harsh, yet he winced. "They will be cared for, Marsdale."

"Aye, with labor so scarce, no one involved has reason to lead them to ruin." I met his gaze and held it. "And I trust you."

"Thank you," he said solemnly. "I will not dishonor your trust. You are the type of man who burns a ship because of a perceived injustice. I am not a fool." He smiled to take the edge from his words.

I grinned. "Nay, you seem wise to the ways of the world. I mean no threat to you, though."

He shook his head. "Nay, I understand. I suppose you have not the time to see Fletcher and Donoughy before you go."

"Nay, and it vexes me. I feel I am running off in the morning light. I will write Fletcher a note." With pungent guilt, I realized that was more than I had done for Alonso. I winced at my thought.

Gaston joined us. He set a bottle of warm water on the table before me. I noticed that he and his clothing were a good deal wetter, and I surmised he had cleaned himself more thoroughly. Samuel had followed him in with a tray of food and a pair of wide eyes, which Gaston glared to the floor upon noticing.

Ella wandered in and made remark of Sam's handiwork, before Theodore shooed her off to the market.

My new companion had eyed her with horror and seemed greatly relieved when she departed. He sat in the chair opposite me. He regarded the utensils and plate with a kind of befuddlement, and then he straightened them, adjusting their distance from one another.

"Has it been a while?" I teased.

He rolled his eyes, a gesture even his mask could not hide. "Drink your water."

I did as he bade while Samuel served.

I noticed Theodore watching me with curiosity.

"Water?" he asked.

"It is a remedy for the flux," I gasped when halfway through the bottle. I set it down. "The rest will wait until I have food," I told Gaston.

He blinked at me in a non-committal fashion and fastidiously cut his sausage into small bites. I took in his posture, which was excellent, his grip on the utensils, which was proper, and his overall demeanor, which would have done my old nurse proud, and I endeavored to also sit and eat at the table as I had been drilled to do endlessly in childhood.

Thus I waited until I swallowed before saying, "The first time I was away from home, or rather the first time I was not at a proper table amongst gentlemen and ladies, I was in a tavern and I took great delight in slouching, belching, and using my fingers. It was an act of utter rebellion. I was once forced to endure an entire day at the table because I could not sit still while breaking the fast."

Gaston smiled. "I never had trouble at the table, but I lived in mortal terror of the upstairs maid and my governess."

I laughed and asked sympathetically, "Were there issues with the bed linen?"

He glared at me, and for a moment I thought he might blush.

"When I was five," he said coldly.

"I did not think it was when you were fifteen. Though that reminds me of the times I had the most difficulties with maids and the subject of bed linen."

"I was in school by the time that became a problem, and the staff seemed to expect it with a dormitory full of boys. When I was older, the monks even viewed it as a matter of course."

We had conducted this conversation in English, and Theodore was wide-eyed over it, as it had surely notified him somewhat as to the nature of Gaston's birth.

"Theodore, were you forced to endure hostile and unsympathetic servants as a child?" I asked.

Theodore nodded. "Not so many as I feel you two were forced to endure, but I too had difficulties with the maids, as everything we did was reported to our mother by them."

"I suppose my mother was informed, but she was so rarely involved in my instruction or punishment that I came to view her as this curious person who had no real interest in the matter." I could count on two hands the number of times my mother had spoken more than a formality to me prior to the birth of my sisters.

Gaston had grown very quiet and withdrawn at this turn of the conversation, and I felt it best to steer it elsewhere.

"What will we need to do later? I wish to judge if we should have Sam wake us at a specified hour in order to have time before the markets close."

"I need to stop by my old ship and retrieve my things, and we will need to finish equipping you. The visit to the *Josephine* can wait until after the markets close." He thought for another moment. "I would suppose we should be up and about by midday."

"I will instruct Ella and Samuel," Theodore said. "There is one bit of paperwork I will need from you prior to your final leave-taking. It can wait until late afternoon or evening."

I nodded and pushed my plate aside to finish the water. I thought of all I wished I had time to accomplish before sailing. Beyond the obvious visit to Ithaca, I dearly would have liked to bring this remedy to Harry and the boys. However, I felt that they would have given it no heed, even if I had. The same was likely true of my sheep. I gazed upon my history with them through the lens of Donoughy's words and my own experience with men about their betters, and thought it likely they had wished to befriend me to curry favor. I remembered several strange looks I had received and the whispers that occasionally followed me about deck. I had been lonely and wished to believe they valued my acquaintance for more than their own ends.

So what then had I talked myself into regarding Gaston?

I marveled at my thoughts. I was such the fickle fool. I vowed to stop thinking on it for a time, lest I tie myself in knots.

With a belly full of eggs, sausage, and water, I retired upstairs with Gaston in my wake. He regarded the narrow little room and its small window with dismay. "We will have to be about by midday; it will be too hot to do otherwise," he remarked.

I nodded my agreement. I had not attempted to remain in the room through the heat of the day since arriving. I did not relish the thought. We opened the window and propped the door wide; and then I slipped to Theodore's room across the landing and opened his door and window. If we were lucky, there would be a breeze; and it would actually flow in the needed direction.

I doffed my shirt and was about to do the same with my breeches, when I saw that Gaston was not removing his clothing. I had known several men who, when confronted with no other means of privacy, used their clothes as their only shield. I kept my pants on out of respect for his choice.

We both arranged our weapons in the netting of our hammocks so that they would be in easy reach if the need arose. I was amused as I thought of our earlier conversation. This was not something we learned from governesses or nannies, or even monks. In fact, it could said to be proof against such.

At last able to relax somewhat, I crawled into my hammock and found myself quickly asleep. I was once again unconfused as to my course in life for the near future. I was not alone anymore. I was at peace with what the Gods had offered and I had accepted.

Nine

Wherein I Become A Buccaneer

When I woke, the room was hot but there was a somewhat chilling breeze on my sweat-soaked skin. I was hungry and needed to relieve myself, but thankfully in the usual manner that did not require a desperate run to the latrine. Despite the needs of my body, I was reluctant to open my eyes and truly leave slumber behind. It was bright. I wondered at the time.

I was rewarded when at last I did raise my lids. Gaston was sitting by the window, reading the German Plato book. I drank the sight in. He was beautiful and brought to mind a fine rapier or even my grandfather's wheellock musket: a finely crafted thing of grace and tempered strength inlaid with jewels and designed for killing. He would require skill to wield to any success. I was amused at my hubris, as I was assuming as much as the others. My rational mind told me that though he was as lonely as I, he was not interested in being handled. My heart and loins whispered a great many other things.

I am not attracted to all men. I have a connoisseur's appreciation of a fine body, and I worship talent and knowledge when I find it, but these things do not often bind together in any man in such a way as to elicit more than a passing interest from my soul. Gaston was a rare find and he had the full, and I was sure lasting, attention of every part of me, most especially my manhood.

Feeling my gaze, Gaston looked up to meet it. I yawned and stretched, pretending I had not been looking as long as I had.

"What is the time?"

"No human thing is of serious importance," he read.

I chuckled, considering my most recent thoughts. "I disagree."

"Why?" he asked with a small smile.

I considered this as I rose and donned my shirt and weapons. "Art."

"I will concede that," he said with a solemn nod. "It is just past midday. I was going to wake you soon. I believe that abominable woman has food for us."

I thought of Ella and smiled. "Ah, she is not a work of art."

"I am not sure if she is a work of man."

"So would that lend her serious import?"

"Only in a fool's mind."

He followed me downstairs, but not out to the latrine. I returned to find him eating meat and cheese at the table, and I joined him. I drained another bottle of water.

"So what will I need?" I asked.

"What do you possess for weapons?"

I described what I had, and he nodded agreeably.

"I would leave the wheellock here. You should have a cutlass in addition to your rapier. I have never had to duel with a Spaniard, but I have had to hack through many things. You should carry several knives and more pistols. Each man is responsible for his own shot and powder, though it will be replenished from captured goods, if there are any. I suggest carrying a water skin of your own and some boucan if you can get it. You will need new clothes, and I would suggest earrings."

"What is boucan?" I asked.

He frowned and then smiled. "Dried meat."

I frowned. "What does dried meat...?"

"Boucaniers make boucan," he grinned. "We learned how from the Indians. The Spanish abandoned much of the Haiti, the highlands of Hispaniola. They only chose to remain in the southern parts of the island. This was many years ago. They left their cattle and pigs behind. The cattle ran wild, and the land teemed with them. Men from many nations found they could disappear on the Haiti and live without kings or rules except of their own making. They killed cattle and dried the meat and sold it to passing ships for shot, powder, or whatever they might need that they could not make. They became the Brethren of the Coast. When the Spanish would try and drive them out, they would retreat across the channel to Île de la Tortue. The story goes that Pierre Le Grand was the one who discovered how to strike back at the Spanish by taking their ships in 1635. So the Brethren became flibustiers for part of the year and remained boucaniers for the rest."

"Thus your insistence that we are not all buccaneers," I grinned.

"Oui, yet that was more than thirty years ago. Now it does not mean quite the same, but I choose to be stubborn about it." He shrugged. "Today you will become a buccaneer, even if you never make boucan."

"Thank you." I thought over what he had said. "You mentioned that they lived with no laws except of their own making."

"The Way of the Coast." He sighed. "But that is changing, too. The more civilized people cross the Line, the harder it is for men to remain free. Now there is no peace beyond the Line, but all other things of the Old World are here." He snorted.

I thought of Morgan and Bradley. They did not fit the image of lawless wild men Gaston painted. Brethren of the Coast or not, I was sure they saw themselves as English citizens.

"You talk of the Haiti and the original buccaneers with nostalgia." I noted to Gaston. "Do you feel that time is past and we are on the crest of something new?"

He nodded sadly. "The Brethren were in trouble the minute they were perceived as useful."

I was amazed he had put it so succinctly. But of course he knew as much of noble wolves as I did.

He told me to bring my musket, and we headed out to the market. I was thankful we had robbed the *King's Hope,* as I purchased whatever he told me to as we worked our way through the shops and stalls. He was disdainful of the prices charged, and I could understand why. The merchants saw a buccaneer coming and assumed he had a great deal of booty to spend. They priced their wares to maximize their profits. We haggled and argued with vendors at nearly every shop, and in a few instances took our business elsewhere.

When we reached the gunsmith's, I expected more of the same; but Gaston appeared to relax, and he even smiled in greeting as we entered the well-ordered shop. The smith, a man named Massey, knew my friend by name and greeted him happily. After introductions were made, the man examined my flintlock carefully and pronounced it a fine weapon, though apparently not so fine as Gaston's musket from Dieppe. I asked him of this, and he showed me both weapons from his craft's perspective. Gaston's had a thicker and more carefully-constructed barrel. This meant it could handle more powder. More powder meant more range and damage.

"Do you have another like his?" I asked, and both Gaston and Massey smiled. The sum was exhorbitant, and I considered what little coin I had left.

"It will have to wait," I sighed.

"Non, I will buy it for you," Gaston said, and nodded to Massey.

"I will repay you," I said seriously.

This seemed to cause Gaston consternation, and he did not look at me for a time.

We sorted through the cask of shot, finding balls that best suited the bores of our guns. Gaston explained that the musket was the key to the buccaneers' prowess. Four well-placed one-ounce balls shot from fine muskets could easily equal the damage of one six-pound cannon ball at twice the range, against anything other than hardwood or metal. Fifty men firing muskets from the deck of a ship were devastating, if all the enemy had were light cannon. The musketeers did not have to be in range of the cannons in order to do damage. And even if shot would not do a cannon's damage to a man, it could put him down and make him bleed enough to keep him from fighting.

As he described some of the fighting he had seen, and how effective the muskets could be, I realized I had not thought we would be engaging in pitched battles of that nature. He made it sound as if I had joined the military.

Then Gaston introduced me to the concept of a cartouche, which was a package of shot and powder wrapped in paper. The paper was used for wadding after the contents were dumped down the barrel. I began to understand how the buccaneers could reload quickly. If all of the necessary items, including a measured amount of powder, could be handled in one package, it made the process much faster.

The necessary paper for the wrapping and several more pistols were added to the pile of things on the counter Gaston said he would purchase. In the end, I hoped our hunting would be good this summer, as I owed him half as much as we had taken from the *King's Hope*.

Soon after, we had everything on his list, and had deposited it all at Theodore's. We went to the Hole. Since it was daylight and we could not simply abscond with one, we paid to borrow a canoe and paddled out to the ship Gaston had been sailing on, the *Josephine*. She was anchored beyond the passage, near the little sand bar of Gun Cay. I was more concerned than I wished to admit about paddling a craft as small as a canoe out of the bay into what was ostensibly open ocean. The canoe was nothing more than a hollow log and we were kneeling in her. A shark would not have to jump far to bite our arses.

The *Josephine* was a long and low two-masted craft. She appeared larger than the *North Wind*, or at least what I had noticed of the *North Wind* the night before. I counted eight cannon along the side we approached: which, unless she had additional fore or aft mounted guns, made her a sixteen-gun ship. This was a goodly size in these waters, from what I had been told.

We secured the canoe alongside and climbed aboard. The men who watched us arrive did not appear pleased at our presence, and Gaston offered them no greeting save a glare. Peirrot emerged from the main cabin to meet us. He looked me over quizzically as if trying to remember where he had seen me before; and then recognition lit his eyes. Then he looked at Gaston quizzically and back to me again. He mouthed a silent "ah" and smiled widely.

"I am astounded how quickly people leap to conclusions in the West Indies," I said in French.

Gaston rolled his eyes. "They are bored and have little better to do."

Peirrot shrugged. "You cannot blame a man for hoping, non?"

"I am going to sail on the *North Wind*," Gaston said quietly.

The older man thought it over for a while and nodded slowly. "It's probably best, but I will miss you horribly and worry a great deal."

"I know," Gaston said solemnly and went below.

Peirrot studied me for a moment before stepping closer to speak quietly. "You must take good care of him."

I frowned. "I will endeavor to do so, though I feel I will need more care than he."

He shook his head. "Not always."

"There was mention of bouts of... madness...?"

Peirrot nodded and lowered his voice even further to speak very seriously. "When they strike, he knows not friend from foe, as he is busy fighting his own demons. At times he is quiet and docile and merely wishes to do things that..." He sighed. "He poses the bodies of the men he has slain. Thus many have taken to calling him The Ghoul. Yet that is harmless and quite preferable to what he does when the rage grips him. He becomes very dangerous, though more to himself than others, as he will do everything he can conceive to anger those around him. It is as if he seeks death at their hands. If you are his friend, when these things occur, you must protect yourself from him and him from everyone else. I strongly advise knocking him senseless and trussing him someplace dark and quiet until he recovers."

I was truly amazed. I could not envision Gaston behaving as he said. My friend appeared to be the epitome of control and discipline; but I supposed that was how he chose to hide the other, or perhaps the two states were in reaction to one another. I was curious as to this posing of the dead. But I was far more concerned with Peirrot's remedy to the situation. I did not condone that at all. It did not seem a compassionate solution or one I would be willing to utilize, but I did not argue.

We turned to find Gaston watching us from the hatchway. He joined us without speaking. He did not give us any look of recrimination, yet I was sure he knew what Peirrot had been saying. It chilled me to the bone. As before, when Striker had made mention of this madness, Gaston made no attempt to deny or relieve the accusation of its seriousness in any way. I remembered his words from that morning, about his parents being mad and how he had worn his welcome thin on this vessel with all save one, who I now knew to be Peirrot.

Gaston handed me a heavy rucksack and looked up at Peirrot. "I owe you more than I can ever repay."

Peirrot shook his head and hugged him, a thing Gaston reluctantly allowed. Peirrot released Gaston from his embrace only to grab his face and kiss his forehead.

"Repay me by finding happiness somewhere, my friend."

"I do not know if that is possible, but I will endeavor to try." Gaston led me over the side, and a minute later we were rowing back to Port Royal.

He waited until we were well away, and then he said, "I did not overhear all he said, but I would not doubt the validity or veracity of it. He has always held my best interests at heart."

"Then I will not. He explained the manifestation of your malady; however, he did not mention what brings about these bouts, and that is a thing of which I am obviously curious."

Gaston paused in rowing and regarded me over his shoulder. "I cannot say, precisely. There is a tension that develops in my spirit and I have been told I become... brittle in mien. And then I explode. It is often after battles. I am sorry; I should have been more forthright."

"Non, you have been adequately forthcoming as to the condition, just not to the particulars. I have dealt with one who suffered from an ailment of the mind before. I do not fear it."

He gave me a weak smile and returned to rowing. "You are either a fine man or a fine idiot."

I laughed. "I have been awarded both titles many times over."

"Would you tell me of this other madman?"

"His name was Joseph, and he was one of the finest painters I have ever had the joy to behold the work of. His portraiture could capture the subject's soul, and seemed on the verge of movement or speech. His landscapes could evoke a melancholy for missing the locale, even if you had never ventured there. He was truly gifted with an extraordinary talent. Yet when I met him, he disparaged his own work in the name of others. After seeing more of his creations, I began to inquire of our mutual acquaintances as to the nature and relation of these critics who used him so poorly. None could give me answer, as these individuals were not known in the social circles we traveled in.

"In time I came to his studio and he showed me several paintings he had done of these mysterious friends, and freely spoke of their names and histories. These portraits were rendered as beautifully as his others, and I was aghast at how the subjects could ever criticize him. He assured me they did, and that shortly he would destroy these canvases in order to placate them. I implored him not to and even offered to purchase them; but he refused. I passed the whole matter off to an unfortunate eccentricity on the part of a genius, and vowed to give these individuals my opinion if our paths should ever cross. I commissioned him to do several works for me.

"Some time later, I was at his studio, and we were drinking and having a pleasant meal when he began speaking to another person. There was no one else in the room. He referred to this person by name, and it would have been one of the mysterious individuals he had committed to canvas. At first I wondered if the girl were hiding behind the tapestries and this was all some game Joseph was playing. Shortly I came to realize that the person in question did not exist, as he placed her in the room where she should have been visible. He even poured a goblet for her and set it upon the table as if she would actually take it.

"Needless to say, I was quite astounded, and I questioned him on the matter. In his state of inebriation, he became irate and accused me of lying that I did not see her; and he threw me out, claiming I was just like all the others. I passed this affront off to drunkenness on his part and spent more time with him. I chose not to comment when he spoke to the imaginary people of his fancy, and in time he became perplexed that I did not interact with them as he did. I came to realize he harbored a suspicion that they were not real, and he simply did not know what to make of it or do about it.

"Then, one day, after what must have been a furious argument with several of them, he destroyed every canvas in his studio and fell into a despair in which he did not eat or drink for many days. The few of us who now knew of his condition considered our options and wondered if he should be allowed his own care. I even went so far as to visit an asylum to see if they could offer him aid. What I saw in that house of horrors convinced me to never surrender anyone but my most hated enemies unto such a place.

"So we did what we could for him, and in time he recovered and painted again. Some days he was better than others, and some days I found even myself involved in his arguments with his ghosts. And so time passed and he completed the portraits I had asked of him and we remained friends. I make it sound as if it was a happy time, but it was not. My heart ached every time I left him."

We reached the Hole and the beach and returned the canoe. We began to walk to Theodore's.

"What happened to him?" Gaston asked. "You speak of him in the past tense."

"He had a young lover he was quite enamored with, and the boy was as stupid as he was beautiful and rich. He could not understand that my interest in helping Joseph was platonic, any more than he could understand the nature of Joseph's affliction. In the end, he left Joseph during a particularly bad time and Joseph hung himself. I found my friend a week later, after his landlord contacted me to complain of the stench and that the door was barricaded. I was so enraged I went and killed his lover. Not in a duel or anything so civilized. I found the boy, got him alone, bound him hand and foot, put a noose around his neck, and kicked a chair from beneath him. I have never felt remorse for it."

Melancholy had taken hold of me as I related my tale. I sought out my memory of the end of Joseph's lover's life, because it always filled me with anger that allowed me to bury the rest again. I had stood watching the boy writhe and die of slow strangulation. Alonso had been calling me from the door, urging me to flee. I had told him no, I wanted to watch the breath drain from the bastard's lungs and the soul flee his flesh.

This time the memory did not fill me with my remembered rage, but with a sense of dread. And I realized this was due to my finding another madman to fall in love with. And though I claimed not to fear madness, I did fear the price it could exact upon me.

I found Gaston watching me intently when my thoughts returned to the present. I shrugged it all away and scratched my head. "And that is what I know of madness."

"You are truly a unique individual. Nothing you have said has made me like you less." He continued up the street to Theodore's.

Perplexed, I followed. "I would say the same of you."

I vowed I would do better by this madman than I had done by the last.

When we reached Theodore's, I collected my possessions from the spare room, and we retired to the yard to sort and pack and make ready. After we shaved, I followed his lead and cut my hair to within a finger's width of my scalp. I had never been that shorn in my life; and I fingered my handiwork with dismay, until a breeze ruffled through it, and I immediately perceived the benefits of not having any hair to block its cooling touch.

I changed into my new clothing: a loose pair of canvas breeches and a sleeveless tunic of the same cloth. I had followed Gaston's lead in this, too, and eschewed the common and unremarkable cream or tan of sailcloth, opting for fabric dyed in deep wine colors instead. The new clothes were as cooling as the new hair length, and I felt lighter and more at ease in the heat and humidity.

Dressed and shorn, I handed him the gold hoops he had bade me purchase. "I do not think I can get these on myself."

He nodded with a degree of resignation and pulled a fine-pointed dagger. I winced. He rolled his eyes.

"Sit down."

"How many of these have you done?" I asked as I doffed my shirt.

"None."

"Truly? So in your estimation am I honored or a fool?"

He grinned. "You are a fool, but it has nothing to do with allowing me to poke holes in your ears."

He braced a fold of a belt behind my earlobe, and I sat and endeavored not to move while he bored the hole and inserted the hoop. It was not as painful as I had imagined, yet it was of the type of annoying discomfort that is very hard to hold still for. This was made all the more difficult by his proximity and the rest of my body's reaction to it. His very presence tightened my groin. I could feel his breath tickling my cheek. He did not touch me except to hold my ear and steady the knife, yet I could feel every point of contact as if it burned. I clenched my hands on my thighs, more in an effort not to reach for him than in response to the pain. And then we repeated all of this for the other side.

He moved in front of me and regarded his handiwork with a critical frown.

I raised an eyebrow. "Well?"

He met my gaze and nodded approvingly. "You are bleeding, and we should put rum on them."

"Why? I think we should put rum in me, as they are beginning to ache in the aftermath."

"Nothing lives in liquor."

"Oh."

"And unlike water, alcohol kills things it touches."

I raised an eyebrow again.

"The little things swimming in water," he added. "And larger things, like leeches, slugs, fish, frogs. None can survive in alcohol."

"So how can we drink it?"

He shrugged. "People die if that is all they consume, do they not?"

I realized the irony of thinking that a sobering thought.

"I still want a swig or two."

We called for Samuel, and he provided us with a bottle. Gaston liberally doused my ears, and we both took several good pulls.

Theodore showed up right after this, and sniffed the air while viewing my new attire. "I can see you're well on your way to becoming a buccaneer," he said wryly. "Bald, half-naked, bloody and rum-soaked."

I laughed and even Gaston smiled. I mopped myself dry with my old clothes and bade Samuel burn them. I donned my new shirt and kerchief. As I strapped on belt and baldric, I told Theodore, "I wish to leave my trunks with you, now that they are landed; and I believe you had something you wished me to sign."

He smiled and led me inside, to his desk in the front room of the main floor. There was a sheaf of blank parchment and an inkwell. I perused this curiously, and then realized what he wished.
"You are not serious?"

"You agreed you would."

"Aye, aye..." I shooed him out and retrieved my seal from my bag, and sat at the desk.

Gaston regarded me curiously.

I switched to French. "He wants me to write my father."

My friend nodded and went to peruse the book shelves. I put pen to paper and wrote two things: the date and "My Lord". Beyond that, I knew not what to say; and I tickled my nose with the quill, watched a cart pass by outside, and touched my aching ears to see if they continued to bleed. I found Gaston regarding me.

"I know not what to say," I sighed. "What do you say when you write your father?"

There was immediate tension in his shoulders, and I realized his parents were a subject to be avoided.

"I am sorry, I will not...."

He waved me to silence and sprawled across one of the armchairs in front of the desk. "I am exiled here."

"So you are spared this," I said lightly. To my relief, he smiled. "In a way I am exiled here, too, but..."

He spoke into my silence. "The day we met, you said you were not sure if you cared if you remained in his good graces, as you had done without them for too long to assign them much value."

I grinned. "I talk a lot while drunk."

"You talk a lot."

"And yet you have not disliked anything I have said," I teased.

He smiled. "You say interesting things."

I sighed. "He was a distant and disapproving figure before I left home when I was sixteen. Then I spent ten years abroad; and when I returned, we did not know each other and I harbored more ill will than I realized. I had also not been sure of his reception. I discovered why he dislikes me. He discovered that I had changed. We have a new respect for one another. He sent me here."

"You are twenty-six?" he asked.

"Oui, and you?"

"Twenty-seven."

I nodded. "As I thought. We are of an age."

"So what would you tell him if you did wish to gain his friendship?" he asked.

"The interesting points and my observations of my adventure so far. The people I have met and the things I have done."

He grinned. "That may not be wise to commit to paper, even if it would be well received."

"You see my problem. And I have little interest in writing a dry report of the acquisition of the plantation and such things, because if that is all I am allowed to speak with him of I might as well not know him at all."

"So write the truth, but couch it in such a manner as to be open to interpretation."

I was amused at the prospect; and I wrote a brief but thorough report of my adventures thus far in the West Indies, saying what I could and implying the rest. Gaston read the pages as I finished; and he was quite amused, and deemed it a work my father would surely take great interest in. Though he disliked the glowing terms I used to describe my acquaintance with him.

"And how do you feel your father will interpret this?" He read, "*I have been extremely fortunate to make the acquaintance of a fine man of my own age, who hails from a family similar to my own and possesses an abundance of education, intelligence, and skill, and who I feel shall make a fine companion in my future adventures.*"

"He will think we are lovers." I smirked. "And he will be in good company, as this is what everyone in Port Royal seems to think."

He blushed, and I regretted my flippancy.

"I am sorry. I do not mean to cause you..."

He shook his head. "It does not need to be discussed."

I bit my lip and held in the sigh, as on the one hand I most certainly did wish to discuss it and on the other I feared the outcome of such a discussion. "Of course not. The opinion of others is of little import."

He studied me for a long moment. "I am used to others entertaining conjecture about my person. I give them little real knowledge, and men are drawn to anything that smells of enigma. Our newly-acquired friendship waves a whole bouquet under their noses, and I must learn to accept that."

"Would you prefer we adopt the stance of actively dispelling any rumor or insinuation upon hearing it?"

"Non, that will just make things worse. Let them think as they will.

In some ways it may serve to our advantage. So are we finished here?"

I decided not to inquire further, and hoped the other advantages would make themselves clear to me, as he was surely not inclined to explain them. "Non, I have two other letters to England; both will be much as the first. And I would leave a note for Fletcher and the boys."

"Who is Fletcher?"

I explained my relationship with Fletcher while I wrote the man.

"You are a philanthropist." Gaston smiled as if it were not a bad thing.

He waited patiently while I wrote to Sarah and Rucker. I wished I had time to compose a true compendium of my observations for my old tutor, but it would have to wait. I wondered if I should take paper and ink with me on my travels, but I knew I would not take the time to write unless forced. The missive to Sarah was to the point, and merely said that I was feeling much better about the world now that I was here and I hoped all was well with her. I also mentioned that I had enjoyed getting to know her as a young woman and I looked forward to seeing her again someday.

Gaston was still dusting the pages for me and then folding and sealing them. He had taken interest in examining my signature and seal, and I hoped he would not begin to call me by my title.

"Who is this Mister Rucker?" he asked.

"My tutor. He is far more responsible for who I am than my father."

He smiled. "So we now know who to thank."

I elbowed him and wrote a quick note to Tom.

"And this?" he asked as he read it.

"One of the boys I sailed with." I grinned.

"Ah," he said and read Sarah's letter. "And this is your sister?"

"Aye. She is seventeen and... I know her little, but wish I had known her more as she matured," I said without looking at him.

When I finished the notes, he was still staring at Sarah's letter. His expression was odd, and I could not discern the emotion behind it.

"Is something amiss?" I asked.

He shook himself as if waking from reverie, and sighed. "Non." He quickly folded her letter and sealed it.

"Do you have family that you miss?" I asked.

He took a deep breath as he regarded me. "Oui."

"Do you...?"

"No more, Will." He stood and left the room.

I stifled my curiosity and reasoned it into submission. I would either learn his secrets in the fullness of time or I would not. I arranged the letters in bundles, one for England and the other for Jamaica, and followed him out the back door. We found Theodore in the yard sitting on the cistern. I wondered at this until I felt the relative coolness of the breeze.

"You should put chairs out here," I noted.

"Aye, I consider it and then forget it until the next time."

"You should task Ella with it."

"I doubt her ability to choose a comfortable chair. Are you finished?"

"Six pages, signed and sealed."

"I'll put it on the first ship out. Which would have been the *King's Hope*, but alas."

I remembered someone else I should write, and hurried back inside to compose a note to Belfry. When I returned to the yard I said, "I have also left a note and some coin for Mister Belfry. He was second officer of the *King's Hope*. I wish I could provide him with more, as he is now without a job. I hope we will take a good deal of Spanish gold, as I have much I need to do with it."

Theodore frowned. "Damn, Marsdale, a man is truly blessed to make your acquaintance."

I grinned. "Not always. Have you heard any news concerning the ship?"

He shrugged. "Five died, and the captain is bankrupt and stranded."

"As I said, not always."

He nodded soberly. "You are akin to some curious angel who metes out justice as you see fit, are you not?"

"I would suppose that describes me." I grinned.

He nodded solemnly, and embraced me as if we had known one another years and not days. "May God protect you."

"And you. Fear not, or fear, I will return."

He chuckled. I availed myself of the latrine and received more boiled water from Samuel, and then we gathered our things.

When we reached the street, Gaston said in French, "I may be embarrassed that others consider me to have a lover, but I am honored that it is you." I forced myself not to embrace him.

The sun was setting as we approached the Chocolata Hole. I shaded my eyes and peered across the small bay, at what would be my new home for the next several months. The *North Wind* was a silhouette against the sunset. The distant, glowing clouds and the gold water reminded me of the Arno on that night which now seemed an eternity ago. How long had it been since I left Florence? Seven months?

The *North Wind* was a sloop maybe threescore feet in length. She carried eight cannon. The single cabin we had visited last night was set low, so that her quarterdeck was only a yard or so above the main deck. Her draft was shallow and her canvas large for her size. Gaston told me he had heard she was very fast. She was a sleek vessel built to carry men and not cargo about the seas.

And tonight her deck was filled with men. We had heard the music before reaching the bay. There was a pipe and lute and drums and a deep rhythmic thumping that indicated dancing. All the men closest to the low gunwale had their backs to us as we came alongside, and I imagined the center deck had become a dance floor. We climbed aboard and shouldered our way into the crowd, to discover the spectacle of Pete and Striker dancing a jig. Their timing and precision were excellent, and it was obvious they had done this many times before. When the tune finished, Pete dove on Striker, bowling him over so they rolled down the deck laughing. More men took their place as the musicians began the next song.

Gaston and I made our way toward the panting and still laughing pair. They were kissing deeply when we reached them, and there was a stirring in my groin at the sight of it. Striker broke it off to look up at us with a grin. "You visiting or sailing?"

"Sailing."

Pete bounded up and his blue eyes flashed over my new attire and earrings. He guffawed. "LookAtYa. IDare'EmTaCallYa'ALord."

"Dare or no, I would rather they did not," I said. "In truth, I would rather keep that bit of my identity hidden."

Striker was still lounging on the deck. "But I like calling you Lord Will."

Pete kicked at him playfully. "BeNice!"

Striker attempted to sweep his partner's legs out from under him, but Pete leapt up and spun in the air to land a good three feet away.

"Gettin'Slow!"

I was in awe. The only time I had seen an athletic feat like it was at a carnival performance.

"How do you do that?" I asked.

The Golden One shrugged and gave me a teasing grin. "YaCan't?"

"I do not know. It seems baffling to me. The only time I turned in the air in that fashion I was falling out a window."

"YaLandOnYarFeet?"

"Nay, I landed in rose bushes. Somewhat on my back, I think."

"Why'dYaJumpOutAWindow?"

"I had just been shot in the arse. And the fellow was not alone, and his manservant had a musket and not a pistol. I feared he might have been able to aim at least as well as his master."

There were several others standing around us now, including Bradley and Siegfried.

"Why did the man shoot you?" Bradley asked with great amusement.

I gave them a sheepish shrug, as I had not intended to get that far into the tale. "I had just bedded his wife, a delightful young lady who was truly wasted on a man of his years."

Loud guffaws rang through the night.

"You got shot in the arse and dove out a window into rose bushes? How far?" Bradley asked, as if he doubted the veracity of my tale, no matter how amusing it may be.

"I have the scar, if you wish to see it. I fell possibly ten or twelve feet, as I was on the second story. However, the roses were on a sort of mound, I think, so the distance was lessened somewhat. I do not recommend it. Thankfully I was clutching my clothing in front of my most treasured areas, and the body tends to roll into a ball upon falling.

I was also lucky the bushes were mature – and had sufficient depth to
hide my location from the window above, once I sank completely into
them. My howls of pain and cursing alerted my companions, and they
pulled me clear of the tangle and away. Mercifully I do not remember
much of that part of the evening. Yet I do have the very distinct memory
of spinning through the air as I fell. That seemed to occur very slowly."

My audience was laughing uproariously, except for Gaston, Bradley,
and Pete. My companion was indeed amused, and I think the reason he
was not laughing with the same gusto as the others lay in the fact that
he was not drunk and he never did anything loudly or with abandon.
I think Bradley was not as amused because he still doubted me. Pete
was a mystery, though, until he pulled me aside and asked quietly,
"YaBedWomen?" He truly seemed aghast over this.

I shrugged. "Aye, when the opportunity arises and they are
sufficiently comely to arouse my interest."

"YaBedMenThough?"

"Aye, when the opportunity arises and they are sufficiently comely
to arouse my interest," I repeated with amusement.

"WhichYaPrefer?"

"Men," I assured him.

He seemed relieved, and I wondered why he cared; but Bradley had
joined us.

"May I have a moment with Marsdale?" he asked Pete.

The Golden One frowned before shrugging and leaving us.

"I am going by the name of Will amongst the Brethren," I told
Bradley.

"Ah, I will not name you otherwise then. I am sorry."

"You did not know. And Pete has heard my title before." I regarded
Bradley curiously and waited for him to speak.

"You're a man of surprises," he finally said.

"In what way?" I asked.

"Why is he here?" His glance indicated Gaston.

"He is with me."

"But your tale would seem to indicate..."

I cut his words with a shake of my head and a jaunty grin. "I swear
I have been subjected to more conjecture in this place than in the courts
of several kingdoms."

He rolled his eyes. "I apologize. Do you trust him?"

"Obviously."

"What do you know of him?"

"A great many things. What do you wish to know that I know?
About his madness?"

Bradley sighed. "So you are aware."

"Aye, will this prove an impediment to our sailing with you?"

"When we spoke last I was not aware..."

"Neither was I. And you have not answered my question, sir."

He smiled. "Nay, he is more of a known evil than you."

I cocked my head and smiled. "I am not sure how to interpret that."

He shrugged. "You may be more than I bargained on."

"I am often that. Why do you think my father sent me here?"

Bradley laughed. "I'm beginning to understand."

He returned to the crowd; and for a moment I stood relatively alone, where I had ended up on the quarterdeck. I was beginning to wonder what I had walked into.

Gaston joined me with his arms crossed and strangely timid look about him.

"Am I welcome?" he asked.

"Aye, with some reluctance."

He sighed heavily and looked away. "What must you think?"

"That you must be a holy terror when it grips you."

He seemed to draw in on himself. I threw caution to the wind and draped my arm across his shoulders.

"We will endure and.... Conquer," I said. He regarded me as if I were mad, and I grinned like a fool.

Pete and Striker joined us.

"Sorry," Striker said, and jerked his chin toward where Bradley was standing. "He's angry about last night."

"What did you tell him?" I asked.

"That we slipped aboard, and Davey was below, and we were forced to kill anyone who saw us, and we burned her to prevent more deaths. He thought that imprudent. I told him nothing of the money."

"Now, that was prudent."

Striker chuckled. "I did not mention Gaston's involvement, either."

"Even more prudent, I fear," I said. Gaston was not looking at any of us, and I realized I still had an arm across his shoulders. He was not pulling away, but he was tense beside me. "Where can we stow our things? And I would see Davey."

I was able to nonchalantly take my arm away as we began to walk, and Gaston seemed relieved. The wolves led us to the steps down to the deck. There was a five-foot-wide alcove between the last gun carriage, the gunwale, and the wall of the aft cabin, which rose to the quarterdeck three feet above.

"WeSleepHere," Pete said.

"You're welcome to join us," Striker added. "There'll be at least sixty men aboard. The hold will fill with victuals, so we all sleep on deck, except for the Captain and Siegfried."

I looked up the length of the ship at the number of men standing about. At its widest, the deck was maybe sixteen feet. I remembered the decks of the *King's Hope* crowded with sleeping men, and I carefully kept my dismay from my face. I had known I would be sleeping on deck, but until now I had not been truly cognizant of what that would mean. Striker and Pete had laid claim to what could be considered premium deck space, and they were willing to share it.

"Thank you, that will be wonderful," I said quickly.

We stowed our sacks, muskets, and most of our weapons and gear in the space. Pete and Striker led us below to see Davey. The ship's surgeon had arrived midday, and apparently plied our sailor with something to help him sleep while he recuperated.

He was in the hold. It proved to be a wide but very low space, with walls defined by the sharply-sloped hull. It was mostly sand and ballast, with a gangway of planks laid the length of it, and casks stacked along the sides. There was an area near the bow that was mostly floored, though, and that was where Davey was sleeping on a pile of bedding.

Davey did indeed appear to be drugged when we reached him, but he seemed happy to see us. He looked a bit better, as he was clean and his wounds bandaged. He regarded me quizzically and raised a tentative hand to briefly touch my left earring.

I grinned. "You think that is something, you should see this." I doffed my kerchief and showed him my hair.

He chuckled. "So we be buccaneers now?"

"Aye, or some may say freebooters."

He frowned, but Gaston snorted with amusement.

"You French are strange," Striker said.

"Have you ever made boucan?" Gaston asked.

"Nay."

"Then how can you be a boucanier?"

"Because I want to be," Striker said with a comical tone of righteous indignation.

I laughed and then had to explain the meaning of the term to Davey, who sighed with annoyance that such a thing should be discussed or worried over at all.

"We'rePirates," Pete said.

"Nay, we're privateers," Striker said. "I daresay I'm the only man here who's actually been a pirate. Though I don't know about him." He pointed at Gaston.

My companion rolled his eyes. "I've been a boucanier and a fliebustier, which means I've been a pirate since we were roving without a marque."

"So two of us have been pirates," Striker said.

"I'mAPirate," Pete huffed.

"You've been a thief but never a pirate," Striker told him, and Pete pouted. "We've always sailed under a commission here, so we've been privateers."

"Where were you a pirate?" I asked.

"England. I roved the Isles, the North Sea, and the French coast for five years."

"How did you come here?" I asked.

"He is answering," Gaston said quietly in French. "But it is usually considered rude to inquire of a man's life before he crossed the Line."

"I do not mean to pry," I added quickly to Striker in English.

"What'dHeSay?" Pete demanded.

"He said it is considered rude to ask of a man's history before he came here," I said.

Striker nodded agreement. "Aye, it is; but I have nothing to hide, at least not from men I steal gold with."

"Speaking of which, I believe we are all pirates," I said.

"Right you are," Striker sighed with a grin. "Last night was piracy. As for me, our ship was captured, and I was sent to Newgate and offered ten years of slavery in exchange for the noose. I took it, and that's where I met Pete."

I remembered what Belfry had said about transporting prisoners as bondsmen. "How long ago?"

"Nine years."

I blinked with surprise and regarded the two men critically. "How old are you?"

"Twenty-seven. We're not sure about Pete but I think he's of my age."

I added and subtracted years. Striker would have been sailing as a pirate between the ages of thirteen and eighteen before he was sent here. Pete not knowing his own age was baffling to me, but I supposed it could occur if he was left to his own devices at early enough an age. They had obviously not served their terms of indenture.

"I think we are all of an age or close to it," I said.

"I be twenty-five," Davey said.

"Close enough," I said. Yet though we were all close in age, I marveled at how much of their lives Gaston, Striker, and Pete had spent in this part of the world. As adult men they had known nothing else.

We left Davey to sleep and returned to the party above. I was able to obtain a bottle of Madeira, and Pete and Striker led us around, introducing us to a great number of people who I would not remember on the morrow and who would not remember us. Yet the endeavor left me feeling more comfortable with the assembled crew and my surroundings. Gaston and I ended the night sharing the bottle, while sitting upon the cannon closest to our new sleeping quarters, if the cubby could be called that, while Pete and Striker fucked in it.

In my travels, I had witnessed many acts of buggery that I was not personally involved in. Yet I had never witnessed two men engaged in what the poetic called the art of love. Much less two men who looked as Pete and Striker did. They were kissing and licking and fondling and all manner of things not necessary for the mere act of sodomy. I knew not whether I should avert my vision or stare with open abandon. We were not the only ones with a view, and others were watching, so it seemed somewhat permissible to stare. However, I did not want to watch, as it made me extremely conscious of my own needs – which were not going to be met anytime soon by anything other than my own hand. And of course there was Gaston, who I would have considered myself in the bowers of Heaven to do the same with. He was very pointedly averting his gaze and attempting to ignore the entire affair, the way one avoids watching another man relieve himself. It was the most damn disconcerting situation I could remember finding myself in, and I knew without doubt that this would be just the first of very many nights featuring the same.

I sought to distract myself, and concentrated not on what the two men were doing but on where. The space was the width of a bed and there would be four men in it. I could not imagine Gaston in such a situation, much less myself.

"Where did you sleep on the *Josephine*?" I whispered in French.

He smiled obliquely and continued to study the moon. "I found several small spaces where only one would fit, and sometimes I slept in the main cabin during the day."

"Why did you agree to this?"

He shrugged. "There is nothing for it. Why did you?"

"In truth I did not understand. I knew we would sleep out in the open on a deck but... Gaston, I have never slept in close proximity to anyone."

"You have had lovers." He regarded me with curiosity.

"I have not slept with them, except for one, and that was a large bed and on rare occasion." Alonso and I had shared a bed for something other than sating our carnal appetites only a handful of times in two years. I did not wish to explain why I was not comfortable in close proximity to a man unless I was able to pay attention to him.

He was now regarding me with amusement. "I do not like to be touched."

I had realized that, yet it was obviously something I had not wanted to hear. "Then how will we make the best of this?"

"I get the wall."

"That is not very helpful."

He grinned. "We will endure and conquer."

Another pair of men began to have sex on the cannon across the way. I watched them for a moment with dismay.

"This will continue for hours," he said, even more amused at my discomfort. "One pair starts it and then another watches and they decide to start, and then another, until all of the pairs who intend to, have."

"You are serious?" I asked without much hope that he was not.

"Quite."

I finished off the bottle and wondered if there was another. I worked my way to the relatively unlit stern and relieved myself, first of urine and then of semen. Pete and Striker were curled together in approximately half the space when I returned, and Gaston was preparing for bed against the wall. With a heavy sigh I crawled in between Pete and him. Despite the belly full of wine and the empty cock, sleep was slow in coming as I felt every twitch of the men about me.

I heard the Gods laughing at the jest they had so deftly played upon me.

Ten

Wherein I Gain A Matelot

I woke to the feeling of bodies pressed against me. For a moment I was quite content with this. I felt cozy and warm and pleased with the world. Then I woke further and experienced panic, as my head was pounding with wine, and I was not sure where I was, and I felt pinned by unknown assailants, and this reminded me of things I strove not to remember. I squirmed and struggled until I was sitting with my back to the gunwale. Only then did I possess the presence of mind to remember where I was and identify my bedmates. Pete was responsible for most of my panic, as he had been sprawled partially atop me. Gaston had been curled into a ball against my side. I was thankful for the lantern on the aft deck. Otherwise, it would have been too dark to see, and I do not know what I would have done.

Gaston was awake and regarding me with heavy-lidded annoyance, which quickly changed to concern. He already had a pistol in his hand.

"What is wrong?" He frowned and sat up, taking in our surroundings for signs of a possible threat. I realized I was breathing hard, and probably appeared as panicked as I felt.

"I cannot abide someone being on top of me," I whispered.

He regarded Pete, who was still sprawled across the space, oblivious to us and my pushing him around to get out from under him.

Striker was awake now too. "Sorry, he does that," he muttered, but his eyes were narrowed with interest at my state.

"Will is not used to sleeping with others," Gaston said.

I was embarrassed. I held up a hand to stop their wayward

thoughts. "It is no matter. I will become accustomed to it." I stood and took a good amount of time pissing over the gunwale until I could compose myself. I imagined looks passed between them, but thankfully they said nothing. I felt a fool and had no intention of explaining myself. They did not know that weight on my back was a thing of great fear that not even Alonso had been able to cure me of. I had resigned myself long ago that Shane was always going to be over my shoulder.

Gaston wordlessly handed me one of our water bottles when I sank down to sit with my back in the corner. I sipped it slowly and massaged my temples, though that never made a headache go away.

"I'll sleep in between," Striker said. He poked Pete gently in the ribs a few times until the Golden One's limbs retracted and he rolled over with a sleepy grumble.

"Don't trouble yourself on my account," I said. I wished the subject could be passed.

Striker grinned. "Nay, on our account. Believe me, if he starts thinking you, or anyone else, is me in his sleep, I'm afraid someone might be forced to stab him in self defense. I would rather avoid that."

I nodded with an appreciative smile at his reasoning. What he suggested would be very bad indeed. But, oddly, I never thought of pulling a weapon when that fear hit, and I have never truly understood that about myself. I knew that I did not do it all those years ago. But that did not explain why I did not react in that fashion now; or perhaps it did, as the fear had so deeply entrenched itself in my brain as to impede my natural instincts for survival.

I watched as Striker crawled over Pete, and with a little nudging got him against the gun carriage. I felt absurd and lonely as he curled against his partner's back and returned to sleep.

Gaston moved closer until we were almost touching.

"You can have the wall," he whispered in French.

"I feel ridiculous," I whispered back. "Two men having to protect me from the sleeping habits of probably the most beautiful man I have ever seen."

He smirked and then sobered. "I did not understand what you were trying to convey, and I am sorry."

"I am not sure I realized what I was trying to convey, as I did not anticipate the severity of my reaction, or... that he rolled around so." More was being said than I intended at the moment; but I reasoned that there were things he must be expected to know about me, if we were truly to be friends.

Gaston frowned and sighed. "There are things I react to with no rational thought. You asked yesterday if I knew what brought on my episodes. I do not, in their entirety, other than what I said; but I do know that there are things that I have issue with that abet the process."

"What are these things, or may I ask?"

"The most serious would be whips. I think neither of us cares to discuss the reasons why such things exist in our minds. Let us say it is enough that we know what to avoid with one another."

I stifled my curiosity as I realized what he was saying and offering. Both of our pasts were haunted with demons we did not wish to share.

"I agree. Though there are a wealth of terrors associated with the reason in question, I do not wish to discuss them; but as I think of identifiable pieces, I will relay them to you."

"And I shall do the same," he said solemnly. "I can add two now. Being restrained in any way, and being trapped in a dark place."

I was alarmed. "Do you know what Peirrot suggested to me as the best recourse when you should suffer a bout?"

He nodded grimly. "Bind me, and put me someplace until I recover, which was usually the hold." He sighed. "He and the others before him were truly trying to protect themselves and help me. But their methods made it all the harder to recover from one, as I would always find myself plunged into a night terror there was no waking from. Yet I would rather that than die or recover to find I have done something regrettable to someone of importance to me."

"There must be a better way."

"Wait until I have tried to kill you before saying that," he said with a grim smile. "Now let us see if we can sleep some more."

"After you say something of that nature?"

He chuckled and lay down next to Striker. I slipped in between him and the wall, and was surprised to find myself drifting back to sleep.

I woke to sound all around me; and this time I knew where I was, even though my head was pounding. Gaston was awake already and sitting with his back to the gunwale, and I almost had my head on his thigh. I sat up slowly, and he handed me the water bottle again. The events of the night worked their way through my mind, and I sighed. He looked at me curiously.

"I do not wish to remember last night," I said.

He smirked.

Pete and Striker were not in sight. A great many other men were, and many of them seemed to be talking.

"What now?" I asked.

"We are no longer in the Hole. We sailed out with the morning breeze. Now we will probably do articles, elections, and provisioning decisions, as there is no food on board ship yet, except for what any man brought for himself." He handed me a strip of boucan.

I tested it with curiosity, and found it quite good and full of taste: not what I had expected from a piece of smoked and dried meat that resembled a strip of leather.

I spied Davey and called to him. He squinted around with his bruised eyes until he saw me and smiled. He came to sit next to us with his back to the cabin wall.

"Cleghorn said to get up here for articles," he said. "Don't know what that is. You?"

I looked to Gaston, who took his time swallowing and taking a sip of water before responding. "The articles are the rules of the ship for the voyage. It is a contract. Every man has a say in them, though the majority rules, and every man must sign on them showing he agrees."

"Don't read," Davey said. I suppressed a sigh as I remembered that Davey had possessed little talent for learning the few times he attended the lessons I gave Fletcher and the others.

"You do not have to; they will read them aloud," Gaston said. "Most of these men cannot read."

"Maybe I should start a school," I said.

Davey frowned at this, but Gaston shrugged. "There will be plenty of time." Then he frowned. "Do you crusade for literacy?"

"Aye," I grinned. "You think me a fool?"

"Not for teaching people to read."

There was a call for attention from the quarterdeck, and we sat on the gunwale to have a better view. Everyone quieted down and took seats on the cannons, gunwales, and about the deck, until all were looking up at Bradley, who stood at the center of the quarterdeck rail. I noticed with interest that Bradley, and Siegfried beside him, were now dressed no differently from any other man on board. Striker and Pete appeared, and lounged on the rail near Bradley. They were immediately above us. I could have grabbed Striker by the leg if I wanted to.

Bradley said, "Most of you are known to me, but some are not. This is the *North Wind* and she is my ship. Therefore, unless I fail in my duties as Captain and the majority decides I am unfit to command, there will be no election for Captain. Is this understood by all?"

I counted sixty-six men while he talked.

A ripple of "ayes" ran the length of the ship, which I joined. I glanced at Gaston. He shrugged.

"We will sail, no prey, no pay," Bradley continued. "Does everyone understand this?"

We all assented, though Davey looked at me with confusion and I had to quickly explain: "If we do not capture a prize or any booty, none of us receives any money."

"Now then, as to course," Bradley said. "Our intent, that is mine and that of the remaining men from the last crew, is to sail in search of the Flota this season; and if we have no luck there, then the Galleons. Is that agreeable to all?"

There was a chorus of guffaws and "ayes", but one man said, "What about raiding?"

"This ship does not have a commission for raiding, and we are but one. I believe Morgan will be organizing a fleet for raiding this winter," Bradley responded.

This brought a round of cheers, and he waited until they quieted. I was not sure if this was in response to the possibility of raiding or the mention of Morgan's name. I hoped it was the former and not the latter.

Bradley went on, "And I believe I heard a majority on the Spanish treasure fleet. Does anyone else have an objection?" There was no response and he continued. "It has been suggested that we do a little raiding to provision, though." This brought laughter and cheering, and people suggested locations. "Good. I do not like to provision on credit from the cutthroats of this port, as a ship could be in debt for an entire prize and the men drinking nothing but watered rum and eating mealy beef." More laughter and cheering. "Though we are out for two hundred pieces of eight for a new sail and rigging and some shot for the cannon, and that will be recompensed from any prize monies." No one seemed bothered by this. "Now, on to elections and articles. Which first?"

There was a great deal of yelling, but even I could tell the elections were the clear winner.

"All right, then." Bradley smiled. "I know of no other surgeon on board, so I say Cleghorn. Is this acceptable?" There was a great deal of assent and no dissent. Gaston said nothing, and neither did I; though Davey cheered loudly. I would have liked to hear the man's remedy for the flux, but with only one surgeon on board, there would be no choosing.

Cleghorn was a thin little man with large eyes and a small chin. He shrugged agreeably and obviously didn't cherish the attention, which earned him some goodwill on my part.

Bradley moved on. "I know of only one man who can bring this ship in to kiss galleon arse in a reaching wind, so I say the Bard for master of sail. Is this suitable to all?" A unanimous "aye" and even Gaston joined in quietly.

I glanced at Gaston.

"He is famous," Gaston whispered. "One of the best pilots."

The Bard was a tall, lean man with an almost gaunt face and a sardonic mien. As Cleghorn had before him, he looked somewhat embarrassed with the attention.

"Why is he called the Bard?" I asked.

"I do not know." Gaston shrugged.

"Those were the easy ones," Bradley said, and there was laughter. "Now it gets hard. Our last carpenter died; who here thinks they are capable?" Several men called out and stated their qualifications, and then were questioned in detail by Bradley and the Bard. This took a while; and though I listened, it did not seem something I could really have an opinion about, as I knew nothing of the subject.

Davey was looking around and studying the rigging overhead. I asked him, "How many men does it take to sail a vessel of this type?"

"She's a sloop. Six with watches, I would say. I was wonderin' what the rest of us do. Only need eight or so for the guns 'less you were goin' to have big crews or fire both sides at once."

"Board ships, hunt, careen, raid," Gaston answered.

"So we're marines then," Davey said, as if this suddenly made everything make sense. Then his face fell. "I don't know anything about fighting."

Gaston and I exchanged a look.

"You will learn that before you learn how to read," Gaston said. I nodded agreement.

"Pete bought me a musket and lots of shot so I could practice," Davey said. "Said he'd teach me."

"Good," I said. "I think there are a few things I would have him teach me." Oddly, this earned me a frown from Gaston.

The captain was calling for a vote again, and we paid attention long enough to give our half-hearted support for the man everyone else seemed to like the most. I felt guilty, as that was not the way one should participate in a democratic process. I vowed to do better with the next, until the captain announced it would be for ship's cook. Then I despaired, as this was also not a thing I cared greatly about.

"We need one who will be amenable to boiling drinking water," Gaston said.

"How the Hell are we to determine that?" I asked.

The whole crew was involved in questioning the three men who stepped forward. Many of them seemed not to like the fellow who had held the position before, and he proved to be quite surly about it. I supposed it was this flaw and not his cooking that caused their dislike. It was obvious he would not be elected. The second seemed as surly as the first and answered several questions about how he cooked with "you'll bloody well learn to like it," which seemed a damn strange way of trying to get elected for something. Perhaps he did not want the job. The third man was an agreeable, portly chap who had been a tavern keep.

"I think this last fellow looks good," I commented.

Gaston deigned to move himself from the gunwale long enough to look at the three. I pointed to the tavern keep and he shook his head. "No one trusts a fat cook when the provisions are low. Either he has not been roving long enough to know what to do, or he has been filching."

I supposed he had a point, and watched with amazement as the surly second man got the job. Then he immediately made the tavern keep his assistant, and everyone seemed happy.

"All right, on to the last position we need to fill, quartermaster," Bradley called. Everyone settled down.

I whispered to Gaston, "What does the quartermaster do?"

"Leads boarding parties, sails prizes to port, settles disputes, metes out punishment."

"So this would be the first officer in some ways?"

"Oui." There was a spark of amusement in his green eyes, and I wondered at it.

"I nominate Cudro," a man said from near the bow. I looked forward to see several hands pointing at a large man with a stern mien, square jaw, and a barrel for a chest. He looked older than Bradley.

Gaston stepped forward to glance around the men on the cannon again, swore in French, and finally said intelligibly, "I hate that bastard. I wish I had known he was aboard."

"We nominate Hastings," another group near the mast cried out.

This man was also a bit older, but he was slim and wiry, with a knowing smile and a patch over his left eye.

"Do we know him?" I asked.

Gaston shook his head. "It matters not, as we know one other."

I regarded him quizzically and he pointed to the quarterdeck.

"I nominate Striker," the Bard said. Now I was very interested, as what had seemed merely an egalitarian exercise took on political overtones and personal meaning. Gaston smirked as the new understanding lit my face.

There was a great deal of discussion. It was hushed as the candidates were asked to state their qualifications. Cudro had been a Dutch merchant captain and sailed as quartermaster on a number of French privateers. Hastings had been an English Navy officer and served as quartermaster on an English privateer. I was beginning to despair for Striker, and then he spoke: revealing, to me at least since it was a known fact to most of the men on the ship, that he had been an officer on the pirate vessel in the North Sea when he was seventeen and he had sailed prizes for Myngs, as a captain, and been quartermaster on the *North Wind* the last five times she sailed.

"I am curious," Hastings called up to Striker. "Perhaps you would indulge me. With your record, why haven't you had your own ship?"

"I haven't found one worth the bloody effort," Striker said with a grin. This brought a round of laughter from all but the men supporting the other candidates. "Except for this fine ship," Striker added, "but I haven't been able to talk Bradley into selling her yet." That brought more cheers. "Why haven't you?" Striker asked Hastings when it died down.

Hastings smirked. "I haven't been sailing as a free man long enough to have the money." Many of the men nodded in agreement with this, as it apparently seemed a reasonable answer to them.

"And you, Cudro? Why are you not a captain again?" Striker asked.

"Like you, the opportunity has not presented itself," Cudro boomed in a voice easily heard the length of the ship – and, I guessed, across the cay. He had not been shouting. With that degree of projection, if he possessed good pitch it was a waste that he was not singing opera.

"Because no one will sail with him twice," Gaston hissed with disgust.

I stepped out and asked. "Why so many ships, Mister Cudro? Are you easily bored, or were you not welcomed back?" This initiated a round of hushed whispers, as the man had named six ships he had sailed on.

"As I said," Cudro boomed, "I've been seeking opportunities."

"So your only aim is booty and you care not for service to your fellow buccaneers?" I asked.

"I did not say that," he roared.

"Nay, that is why I asked," I said, wishing I had a deeper voice. "I know what Striker is willing to do for a fellow man without offer of recompense."

The seed had been planted and taken root, and I could see the heads nodding in agreement and hear the occasional snippet of an anecdote mentioning Striker. Cudro was furious, and he sat down. Hastings was watching me with interest. I raised an eyebrow and he waved me off with a grin that said he would not take me on.

I glanced up at Striker as I returned to my seat, and found him trying not to laugh. He quickly stopped Pete from talking to me. Davey was frowning at me in that annoying disapproving way he had.

"What?" I asked.

"Nothing... my Lord," he said quietly.

"What the Hell is that for?" I hissed.

"You're dead set on being a lord wherever you go, aren't ya?"

"Aye, it's in my nature," I snapped.

Gaston was glaring at him. "Ungrateful whelp," he said in French.

"He is an angry young sheep," I replied in the same language.

"Sheep?"

"I will explain later."

Gaston shrugged and regarded me seriously. "Thank you for that. I cannot make myself heard in these situations."

I realized I had never heard him speak louder than the low husky voice he was using now, and that he was being literal and not figurative.

"You really can speak no louder than that?" I asked.

He nodded. "The reason is something I do not wish to discuss. But oui, my voice was destroyed years ago."

"I am sorry, whatever the cause." I gave him a small bow. "I stand at your service if you need any yelling or singing performed, though I do not possess the one you hate's excellent projection."

Gaston smiled. "I will explain my dislike of him when we have time."

"Am I to understand the tale is lengthy?"

He shrugged.

Bradley called for the vote by a show of hands, and Striker received over two-thirds of the assembly's support. Striker let Pete jump down to us, and I was hugged until I thought my ribs would break.

"He would have won anyway," I protested when I could breathe.

"AyeButYaHelped." He climbed back onto the quarterdeck, with one last pat on my head.

"We will now read the last articles, and any man can make suggestions. We'll put changes to a vote," Bradley said. "Article one: In matters of prey or battle, the captain shall have absolute authority. In all other matters, every man shall have his say and his vote. If in battle the captain should be unable to serve, then command passes to the quartermaster until the strife has passed, at which time an election will be held. If not in battle, and the captain is struck ill, then the command of the ship passes to the master of sail until an election can be held."

My fiendish mind grasped that no provision had been made as to how many of the men need be present to make an election. I could also see where the absolute command of the captain could be abused, if the definitions of *battle* and *in pursuit of prey* were loosely measured. But I saw no point in mentioning these things, as this set of laws had obviously been functioning nicely prior to my hearing of it; and if the men on this ship ever felt there was a serious breach of their trust, I was sure no man could stand against them.

No one had any comment on the first article, and it was ratified unanimously.

"Article two," Bradley continued. "Any man deserting his post or acting with cowardice during battle will be marooned."

"What's marooned?" Davey asked.

"Left on a deserted island with a skin of water and a pistol and one shot," Gaston said.

Davey nodded soberly as we all ratified that article.

"Article three: All booty belongs to the whole of the ship until it is shared out amongst us; and any man withholding any item from his mates shall be considered a thief, and he shall have his nose and ears removed and be cast out. Any man stealing from his mates shall suffer the same punishment."

There was no complaint or question about this article, either. I raised my hand along with the rest; though I was curious if things that the others would not value, such as books, would count as withholding something.

"Article four: No man shall strike another while on ship. All disputes will be settled on shore by duel of pistol and sword. The quartermaster shall direct any duels."

"Excuse me," a man said. "Can the duels just be sword or fist, for the times when the mates don't want to kill each other and just want to fight?"

There were nods of assent at this, and it was generally agreed to change it. "Article four: No man shall strike another while on ship. All disputes will be settled on shore by whatever means the combatants desire. The quartermaster shall direct any duels," Bradley read.

We all ratified it. I wondered what happened when there was a dispute on shore; did it immediately become a duel? Once again I kept my mouth firmly shut.

"Article five: There shall be no dicing or cards for money."

There was some grumbling amongst the men. I thought it a fine rule, as I could see where it could lead to a great many duels amongst ones such as these, so that half the crew might be dead before they reached anything to plunder, and weeks spent getting there on account of having to stop every hour for another duel. It was ratified.

"Article six: No women or boys to be brought on board, or even women dressed as boys. The punishment shall be marooning."

"With the woman or boy?" some jester asked. There was a round of guffaws and resounding "nays". I imagined this rule existed for the same reason the prohibition against gambling existed: too many duels. It was ratified.

"Article seven: Every man is responsible for keeping his pieces in working order and ready for service. Every man is responsible for the deck he sleeps on and anything he can reach from where he sleeps. Additionally, men are responsible for the cannon they sleep closest to. Punishment for shirking these duties is left to the quartermaster."

But not defined, I noted. I looked at the cannon with new concern. I know nothing of cannons.

This article was ratified without comment, and once again I was forced to assume that this rule had performed an adequate job of maintaining the equipment and the ship prior to my arrival; and my advice or thoughts were not required.

"Article eight: All men are to have one equal share, with the following exceptions. The captain will be granted five shares for use of his ship. The quartermaster and master of sail shall each receive two shares. The surgeon and carpenter shall receive two hundred pieces of eight or two slaves for their services, above their full share. The cook shall receive a hundred pieces of eight or one slave for his services, above his full share. Any man losing the use of an arm or a leg, even if it just be a hand or foot, but not a finger or toe, shall receive six hundred pieces of eight, or six slaves per limb, prior to the sharing of the booty. Any man losing an eye will receive two hundred pieces of eight or two slaves prior to the sharing of the booty."

"Begging your pardon," someone said. "But what if the captain is killed and we go on to other booty? Does the new captain get the five shares of all the booty, or just from when he became captain? And the same with the quartermaster?"

Striker spoke up. "I say my matelot gets any shares I was entitled to, and the new quartermaster gets shares of any booty taken after he becomes quartermaster."

Bradley sighed and sagged on the railing. "We have had this debate. The matter is too hard to govern if you include matelots. We do not possess a record of who is matelot with whom."

"We hold a vote," Striker said. He turned to the ship. "How many of you say Pete is my matelot?" Every hand on the ship shot into the air. "There you have it, and some of them have never sailed with us before," he told Bradley triumphantly.

The captain was laughing. "We'll put it to a vote then. All in favor of the matelot of a ship's officer receiving their shares of any booty taken prior to their demise."

Many people raised their hand, but someone called out, "Hold. That's only if they die in battle, right? What happens if we vote them out?"

Another man spoke. "And I would like ta say that me matelot is more valuable to me than me right arm, so maybe we should include matelots for getting' somethin' if a man loses one." I saw who said this, and I was sure he was a man I had been introduced to the night before. His nose was crooked in many places; and he had the palest hair I had ever seen, under a strange floppy leather hat. His accent was Scottish. His matelot was a big man with dark hair, who I vaguely remembered had a Dutch accent. Their names came to me slowly: Liam and Otter.

"Nay," another yelled. "That is not fair to those of us who have no matelot. That money comes out of the booty prior to shares."

I could hold my tongue no longer and stepped forward.

"How about this?" I called loudly and people stopped to listen. "The original change called for matelots inheriting a deceased officer's shares. And many seemed in favor of it. Why not add that any man who loses a matelot, as decided by public vote, receives any shares his deceased matelot was entitled to? And also set in the article that a man, whether he be officer or not, is only entitled to shares while he is alive or holding office."

There was immediate discussion amongst the men and much nodding of heads, until Hastings, the one-eyed former Navy officer asked, "Do you have a matelot?"

I was about to say "nay" when a chorus of voices erupted from the quarterdeck saying "aye." I winced and looked to Gaston helplessly; and he sighed and shrugged with resignation.

"Apparently," I said with no real conviction.

"You're new to us. Who are you and who is your matelot?" Cudro boomed from the bow.

"You can call me Will and..." I looked to Gaston, who stepped to my side and, to my amazement, threw an arm across my shoulder as he gave Cudro a defiant glare. I was extremely curious as to what had once passed between these two men: upon the sight of him, Cudro growled loud enough to be heard on shore, and looked ready to charge us like an angry bull.

"Well that bein' the case, I do na' think it matters, as neither of those two will likely die in any venture we may find arselves in," said Liam, the Scotsman with the crooked nose. This brought a round of laughter and asides. I looked over my shoulder at Bradley and Striker, beseeching them for rescue.

"All right, then," Bradley called. "Who here is in favor of Will's suggestion?"

Almost all of them voted their assent.

Gaston pulled me back into the alcove and out of sight of most and released me.

"Um..." I began.

He cut me off with a tired, "Do not speak of it."

Davey was watching us with a good deal of confusion. "What's a matelot?"

Gaston rolled his eyes and stared out at the sea, and I was left alone with the question.

"A partner," I said and hoped he would not ask for more.

This appeased him for a moment and then he asked, "With

buggery?"

"Aye, that is apparently an option," I sighed.

He looked from me to Gaston and back again, and made a small "hmmm" sound.

I tried to ignore him and returned my attention to the proceedings. Cleghorn had been tasked with writing up the new articles, and he was now adding the revision I had suggested. Once the document was complete, every man was expected to sign it or make their mark.

Unfortunately, while I could ignore Davey, I could not ignore my own thoughts – which were profoundly affected by my having a matelot and all that that implied within the Brethren of the Coast. I was married. In fact, I was more than married. A wife would have no say on my holdings or be involved in my business dealings.

I have never wished to be married. Almost all of my adult liaisons with members of either sex have been excruciatingly short in duration, rarely lasting beyond a night or two, and usually over within the hour. A few had lasted months, and none had been exclusive. I had been with Alonso the longest, and though I had considered us partners, I had not considered us married. I might have been induced to give my life for him under certain circumstances, and I had momentarily been tempted to travel to Spain with him. We had cared for each other when wounded. However, we fornicated where and with whom we chose. We only shared items that had been bestowed upon us jointly, such as Teresina's spare house. Our purses had been our own, and we had seldom known the amount the other possessed. We had respected and trusted one another, and in time loved, but we had never held ourselves out to anyone as a couple – even though many in our acquaintance had known we were close companions and possibly partners. In truth, few beyond Teresina's household had known we buggered one another.

This was different. It was assumed by all that we buggered one another; and I harbored the great suspicion that any attempts at dalliance with another would be greatly frowned upon by our crewmates and not tolerated by my matelot. In all honesty, I did not think I would tolerate it from him, either. In my understanding, we would share all things, even money. We would care for one another. We would inherit from one another in case of death. We made decisions about our life and livelihood in concert. We were denoted a pair in the eyes of our peers. We were married in all ways in which I understood it, and then much beyond it. No wife could have exercised the hold upon me Gaston did now.

I was trying to determine exactly how this had occurred in such a brief period of time.

"Get up here and sign," Striker said.

We signed the articles as "Will" and "Gaston", and moved aside to join Striker and Pete at the rail.

"You're good," Striker said with a devil's grin.

"You would have won anyway," I said.

"Then why?" Striker asked.

"He is not very fond of Cudro." I gestured to Gaston. "He promises to explain later, to me anyway."

"I don't like Hastings," Striker said quietly, with a serious frown.

"Have you sailed with either before?"

"Nay, but I have heard things. I was quite surprised they thought they could come here and challenge me." Striker gave us a warning look, and I glanced over my shoulder to see Hastings smiling at us before signing the articles.

Gaston was glaring past me at Cudro, who was standing in line to sign.

I shrugged. "I am surprised he is staying aboard."

"I don't have a reason to turn him out," Bradley said, from between Striker and Gaston.

I was surprised, as he had not been there when I turned my head. I decided to change the subject, and addressed Bradley and Striker. "Thank you both for confirming that I had a matelot," I said sarcastically. They laughed. "Perhaps we would have preferred the banns published a while longer and a more formal ceremony."

"It's not as if you are married," Bradley said.

I frowned. "And how is it not? Other than I would not be expected to share property with a wife."

He grimaced with consternation. "Having a matelot is not marriage."

"If my understanding of such things is correct, and perhaps it is not, then matelots are partners, considered couples apart from all others, share all things – and they, even by the article we just ratified, inherit from one another. I see it as differing from marriage in that it indicates a condition of greater legal entanglement, not less."

The Scotsman, Liam, Otter, his Dutch matelot, the Bard, and Siegfried had joined us in the back corner of the deck. Everyone watched Bradley for his answer, and the captain looked uncomfortable under their scrutiny. He gave Siegfried a beseeching look.

Siegfried sighed. "Marriage is a union sanctified in a church." Bradley looked relieved, and the rest of us frowned. Siegfried looked no more pleased with what he had just said than we were.

"Pardon me," I said. "I was born to nobility, and I have spent years in the courts of Austria, France and two Roman cities. Amongst people of such birth, marriage has little to do with the church unless there are political considerations between members of two differing faiths. Marriage is a legal contract between families and individuals intended to provide for demonstrable parentage and the care and support of children, and to cement alliances. And on truly rare occasion, it has something to do with love. The institution also serves to keep people from fighting in the streets about who had carnal knowledge of whom." I shrugged. "But I am not a religious man. Still, from what little I have seen and been told since arriving here, matelotage serves many of those functions for preserving an orderly society, and thus in my opinion matelots occupy the same level of legal distinction amongst the Brethren as a married couple would in England."

"What'dHeSay?" Pete asked.

I made note that I would have to greatly simplify my oration if I required Pete's immediate support in any matter. I also noted that Siegfried was studying the planks with a small smile and not looking at his matelot. Bradley regarded me with consternation. I was sure I had not fallen within the parameters of what he bargained for, once again. Liam grinned; his matelot thoughtfully chewed an apple. The Bard scratched his head and wore a sardonic smirk. Striker was deep in thought. And most importantly, my matelot regarded me with amusement. I was greatly relieved that he was not looking upon me with murder in his eyes.

"I agree," Striker said suddenly. "I'm more married to Pete than I was my wife."

"You had a wife?" I asked.

"Aye," he said soberly. "And a babe, but they caught a fever and died while I was at sea. It was before I came here."

"I am sorry," I said.

He shook his head. "I think perhaps it was for the best. If they had lived another year, they would have been abandoned when I was shipped here; and who knows what would have become of them. It wasn't as if I was a good husband anyhow."

"You'reGoodTaMe," Pete said with concern, and rubbed Striker's shoulder.

Striker smiled again. "As I said, I'm more married to him than I was to her."

"It does not fit within my definition of marriage," Bradley said. All gazes shifted to his matelot.

Siegfried looked thoughtful. "Nor mine." He turned away from us, and worked his way through the signing men down to the deck below. An awkward silence followed. Bradley left us, too.

"I cause nothing but trouble," I said quietly.

"Tell me of it, I married you," Gaston said disparagingly in French.

I grinned. In truth, I was secretly pleased with the Gods.

Roving

March~May
1667

IV

Eleven

Wherein I Discover I Am Not A Wolf

My bowels and the heat asserted their hold over my body and spirit during the debate about where to provision, and I crawled into the hold and napped in the bed Davey had used. If he came and found me there, I was not aware of it. The ship was under way when Gaston woke me. He informed me we were on our way to Hispaniola to raid a swine farm. I drank water, ate boucan, and went back to sleep, as there was a familiar unsettled sensation in my stomach and I realized I was seasick again.

Sometime later, I was awakened by our surgeon, Cleghorn. Bradley had informed him that I had the flux. I propped myself against the sloping wall, and told him I was also prone to seasickness and seemingly suffering from that too. He asked the usual questions concerning the consistency of my stool and what I had been eating and drinking, and then he felt my pulse and listened to my breathing as I answered. I did not embellish my responses with the whys and wherefores, I merely stated that I was drinking a great deal of water and eating as I could.

"I want you to stop consuming anything until they pass," he said. "It is my guess that this will not be overly irksome for you, as you probably do not feel the need to partake of anything with the seasickness and all. I will give you something to help you sleep. You should rest for several days, and then if it has not passed, I will bleed you to clear the bad blood."

I let my perplexity show clearly. "How will we know if it has passed if

I have not partaken of anything to pass?"

He smiled. "The urge to do so suddenly will pass, and you will feel calmness in your bowels."

"How will I feel calmness in my bowels if I am famished?"

"Bradley warned me you might be a troublesome patient."

I let that pass. "What say you to the theory that it may be possible to clear a vileness of the bowels with large quantities of water? To flush it out?"

"That's absurd. Where did you hear such a thing, some court physician in England?"

"I have never been to court in England." So Bradley had told him a number of other things about me as well. "Where did you learn your trade?"

The air was growing distinctly cooler between us. He set down the vial that he had been examining and regarded me with a calm face and firm eyes. "I was trained as a surgeon in His Majesty's Navy. Where did you receive medical training?"

"I have not. Yet in my travels I have met and required the services of a number of surgeons and physicians in several nations: enough to know that medical opinion varies greatly from place to place and person to person. I mean no offense, but none of you know for certain what will work or not, unless it is a simple matter such as removing shot or stitching a wound. All other matters of the body seem to be a mystery and spark as many schools of thought as religion and philosophy combined. As a result, unless I am unconscious and incapable of making a decision on my own behalf, I choose to keep my own counsel and decide which remedy to partake of. A week ago, I would have followed your advice to the letter, but since arriving here, I heard of another course of treatment, and it made a great deal of sense to me, and I wish to continue it."

He looked annoyed, but was attempting to continue to be pleasant as he packed his bag. "I can see your reasoning. I truly can. So where did you hear this remedy from?"

"You will scoff, but Gaston."

Cleghorn narrowed his eyes and shrugged. "I don't know him."

"My... matelot."

This induced him to roll his eyes as I had expected. "Good luck to you, then." He stood as much as one could in the low hold, and braced his hand on the ceiling beams. "You may find it prudent to have someone inform me when you pass into unconsciousness. That way, I may possibly be able to save your life."

I smiled congenially until he left with the lantern, and then I drank the rest of the water in the dark. I realized it was late, as there was very little light coming through the hatch. There was another lantern at the other end of the hold, but it did little to iluminate the shadows around me. I heard voices nearby and knew I was not alone. I thought I should try to doze again. And then Gaston was at my side.

"Were you here?" I asked sluggishly.

"Non, I saw him leave. If I had seen him come down, I would have been here. I am sorry. Did he give you something?"

"Non, I defended myself well and would not let him," I said in a teasing tone, as he seemed very serious. "I am afraid he is unhappy with me as a result. He said I should partake of nothing until the flux passed."

Gaston heaved an exasperated sigh and turned to sit with his back to me, as if guarding me from the rest of the hold and all the world's idiotic surgeons. His concern was touching, and I was gripped by an urge to caress him since he was in easy reach. This need did not seem to spring from my loins but from my heart. I simply wanted to touch. I forced the thought away, as whatever my intent, I knew the act would not be welcome. I foresaw a great deal of frustration in my future over that.

"Where did you learn medicine?" I asked to distract myself.

"A surgeon on Île de la Tortue, a physician really, trained in a Moorish college of medicine. He taught me a great deal and I read his books."

"So why are you not posing as a medical practitioner?"

"I do not like people and I do not wish to be obligated to help them." He said this with no humor whatsoever and I laughed loudly in response. He glared at me, and finally smiled.

"I am so very glad you like me," I said.

He snorted derisively, and then smiled again. "You are my matelot; I will do right by you."

I frowned at that; but he could not see it, as he was not facing me. I was free to study his profile, though. Sitting as he was, and facing the only dim source of light, he was an interesting study in shadows. There was much we needed to discuss.

"Have you had other matelots?" I asked.

He shook his head, "Non, none."

"Lovers?" I winced even as the word came out. I knew not how he would respond to it.

Gaston was quiet for a moment but he did not glare at me. "Non, none."

I was, of course, surprised. He was a virgin?

"In all this time here, you have not had a lover of any persuasion?"

He sighed and regarded me with mild exasperation, but no anger. "Non. I understand how you would find it hard to imagine."

I winced. "I am not that promiscuous."

"Truly?" he asked with a small smirk.

"Well, oui, I guess, as compared to some, possibly."

"How many?"

I grimaced. "I do not know. I am not being coy. I just stopped counting years ago. It seemed a boyish thing."

"Matelots?"

"Well seeing as how I never heard the term until I arrived in Port Royal," I teased. He looked away again, but I did not sense he was annoyed; more that he would wait me out. "Almost one."

He gaze returned to me. "Almost?"

"I had a man I was... He was my partner, but not as this is, or how I imagine this is, or... Never mind."

He was deep in thought. "Was he your lover?"

"Oui."

"Was he your partner in business as well?"

"Oui. And he was my friend, which I view as being a separate issue. I have had business partners and lovers who were not friends. I have often had one or two of those components, but he was the first in which all three were encompassed. Yet, even if we had been here and knew the term, I do not think I would have called him matelot."

Gaston frowned. "Why?" he asked when I did not speak.

I was trying to determine why I felt that. I had said it and known it to be true, but what exactly was different? Then it occurred to me.

"He would not have been comfortable with the public display of the title and what it might imply."

Melancholy welled in me over this new knowledge. Alonso had not been furtive about all aspects of our relationship, but he had insisted on discretion as to the sexual nature of it. I had thought this in perfect keeping with how such things were done at the time; but in regarding it from amongst the buccaneers, I found it confining and insulting in retrospect. Though in truth, I had been nowhere else that men could so openly profess or display their carnal relationships with one another.

"It would not have been acceptable to him," I added. "Just like Bradley becoming distraught at my calling it marriage."

"It is marriage," Gaston whispered. He moved to his knees. "We should go up and eat. It is night and cool now; you can sleep on deck."

"Oui, I should let Davey have his bed back."

He stopped and regarded me. "Have you been with him?"

"Who, Davey? Non, non. Though I will admit I considered it on the voyage. I was powerfully bored and lustful, but he..." I sighed heavily. "I have some pride. I do not fuck sheep."

"What?"

"It is this theory I have concerning people and..."

His hand brushed my chest and came to rest lightly on my lips. I was stunned and then I heard people descending the stairs, and I understood. His hand moved away, and he dropped beside me again, with his back in contact with my hip this time. The new arrivals were speaking Dutch. I recognized one voice, Cudro, as his magnificent baritone was hard to mistake for any other. I found the pistol I had tucked into the blankets. I did not know why Gaston hated the man, but I would trust that he had good reason.

Another lantern was lit, and we saw Cudro, and Liam and Otter. A moment later, they saw us. The Scotsman waved.

"We be checkin' barrels," he told Gaston in English, or rather his approximation of it. He indicated the stacks of them which took up half the hold. "Bradley wants ta know if we 'ave enough to salt and barrel a whole farm o' hogs. I told 'im we should make boucan, it'll last longer an' taste better. 'E's worried 'bout the time it'll take."

"We could do it while we are careening," Gaston said. "With enough men, we could do the pits quickly and have time for it to smoke."

"We'll have to, not enough barrels anyway," Otter said.

Cudro sneered and addressed Gaston in French. He kept his tone jocular, as if he were discussing the weather. "Will your new friend be helping? I see you finally became lonely enough. Now we can finally see what it is you want in a man, though I can't imagine one such as that wanting the likes of you. Or has he seen you yet?"

Gaston was very still, and I could feel the tension through his spine. I kept all expression off my face save mild curiosity, as if I did not speak French. This is what Cudro was obviously assuming. The Scotsman and his matelot apparently did not speak the language: after some mild curiosity of their own, they turned to examining barrels. It could also be assumed that no one else in the hold spoke the language, either.

"Probably a good idea to move fast," Cudro continued. "I hear he's sickly and new here. Cleghorn thinks he won't survive seasoning. But to jump a man who doesn't know a thing about you seems unfair."

As usual, I reached a point where I could no longer hold my tongue. "I feel I know him well enough," I said in French. I pushed myself up and moved so that I was kneeling on the other side of Gaston, where I would not hinder his blade if he should need to draw it. I let my arm drape across his shoulders, with the pistol dangling negligently beside him. "And I am not on my deathbed. I truly feel I should take issue with Cleghorn concerning that."

Cudro sucked wind like a wounded boar, and his face froze in surprise. Gaston grinned. It was not a nice grin.

"I am sure there will be enough time for other matters once we careen," Gaston said.

"I don't wish to fight you," Cudro said in English. This and the overall change in mood had the Scotsman's and his matelot's attention, along with that of the other men in the hold. Their quiet conversation ceased.

I sat still and wondered if Gaston would force the issue. As of yet, this was his quarrel and not mine.

"Then you can apologize," Gaston said in English.

"What'd he say?" Liam asked.

That, I felt I could and should address. "He said he thought it was unfair that Gaston should take advantage of me when I am sickly and possibly dying by entering into a relationship with me when, according to this gentleman, my matelot has much to hide. He also wondered why someone like myself, whatever that may imply, would possibly want Gaston, and ..." I looked at Gaston innocently, "did I miss anything?"

"Nay, not of what he should apologize for this day. The past is another matter, though; and we will settle that someday, but not on account of this. Unless you find that unacceptable?" Gaston asked me.

"I will be satisfied in this matter if you are satisfied." I grinned.

Cudro looked to Liam and Otter for support, and found cold eyes and frowns. The big man underwent an apparent reconsideration of his current place in the world and in the eyes of his peers.

He addressed us with a mien that approached humility but did not quite attain it. "I apologize for any insult you may have perceived from my comments." His words, too, approached an apology but did not quite attain it, either. Just as his original slurs had been very close to insults, but not enough to make most men pull a piece on him. The big Dutchman was very clever, and I was impressed in spite of my dislike for him.

Gaston continued to stare at him. For my part, I sighed with less-than-subtle impatience.

"What more would you have me say?" Cudro asked.

Gaston did not blink.

"May I?" I asked.

Gaston nodded.

"I would have you apologize for the intent behind your words, as that is what I perceived as insulting."

Gaston nodded again.

Cudro's lip quirked for a moment. "I meant you no..."

We cut him off with shakes of our heads.

His lip twitched again. "I am sorry I insulted you."

I grimaced and held up my left hand with the thumb and forefinger held close together but not touching. This time I heard his quiet curse.

"I apologize for attempting to insult you."

"Aye, I am sure you regret it now," I said, and Gaston smirked. "I believe I can speak for both of us in saying that we accept your apology, but we have no intention of forgiving you." Gaston nodded agreeably.

The big Dutchman snorted and left the hold. Liam and his matelot turned to us after watching him depart.

"You should probably kill him," Otter said quietly.

"I intend to," Gaston said.

"So, then, I should tell the captain you two'll be in on the boucan making?" Liam asked as if the whole other conversation had not occurred.

"Aye," Gaston said. They began to leave.

"Should we be taking this?" Liam indicated the lantern.

"Aye," Gaston said.

They departed, and we were plunged into semi-darkness. There was only the flicker of the lone lantern at the stern of the hold. The other conversation resumed, somewhere in the shadows. I could not make out the words.

I realized I still had an arm across Gaston's shoulders and we were very close. I was almost pressed against his side. I removed my arm.

"Non," he whispered.

I replaced my arm. He sighed. We sat that way in silence for a time. I did nothing to dispel it, as it was nice to touch him and, as I had come to find earlier, I needed to touch someone.

"Cudro was enamored with me when first we met," he whispered. "I rejected him repeatedly, until his affection turned to something else. Since then, he has always been cleverly insulting and..." He took a long breath, and was slow to start talking again. "He knows some of my weaknesses, and he, with intent and malice, once endeavored to set me upon one of my bouts. He succeeded. I tried to kill him, and was stopped by other crewmembers. At which point they allowed him to beat me soundly. I left that ship at the next port. I would have had no recourse there, except to take them all on. I began sailing with Peirrot after that."

I was furious. "Now I want to kill him."

He snorted with wry amusement. "He is mine."

"You have far more discipline and restraint than I."

"Do I?"

"Truly." I was being honest, except for one notable exception in my history. I squeezed his shoulder, and he moved into me a little. We sat like that for a while longer; and I was torn between contentment and smoldering anger over what had been done to him.

"Gaston? Will? YaDown'Ere?" a familiar voice asked from the hatch.

"Aye," we said in unison.

There was a pause. "ShouldIGo?"

I wanted to say "aye" but Gaston had already slipped away from me to stand.

"Nay, we are coming," he said. I felt a tap on my forehead and I reached up to find his hand. He pulled me to my feet, and we joined Pete at the hatch.

"CaptainWantsTalkBoucan."

I followed and listened to an hour of discussion about when hogs could be slaughtered in relation to creating boucan and salting. I would not have thought the matter of victuals to be so damned complex, but then I remembered every officer I ever met speaking of an army moving on its stomach.

Knowing someone would tell me what to do when it was necessary for me to do something, I curled up in the corner of our alcove and tried to doze again. Instead I found myself watching the stars and the sail against them. There were millions of them, and I found my eye drawn to constellations I had learned over the years; and then I was naming the stars I knew. Sometime later the conversation stopped, and Gaston eclipsed the stars until he came to lie beside me. I pointed to the last three stars I could name, and he named them. And so we lay there looking at the heavens and recounting the myths behind the constellations as we had heard them, until I was finally tired enough to sleep again.

I rolled onto my side with my back against the wall, my head at the gunwale and a pistol and my rapier in reach. He followed my lead and even scooted closer to me, so that we were almost touching. And so I lay there feeling very cozy and safe from harm. I slept deeply.

The next morning, we continued to beat upwind toward Hispaniola. As the prevailing winds in the West Indies are the trades running east to west, any ship attempting to sail east must fight them. The *North Wind* was a fore-and-aft-rigged sloop, so she could make far better work of beating upwind than the *King's Hope* or another square-rigged vessel would have been able to. Still, it was estimated it would take a good sevenday to reach the place the swine farm supposedly resided. I hoped the hog farm would actually be where it was said to be, lest the crew eat the poor bastard who suggested it.

As we did not wish to share it, Gaston and I ate sparingly and secretively of the boucan he had cleverly insisted we bring. Our alcove-mates were not sitting about with growling bellies either, so I assumed they had their own cache of victuals. I had depleted our bottles of clean water, though. There was an adequate supply aboard, as the captain had seen fit to lay on several casks in Port Royal. However, it was not boiled, and we doubted we would be able to talk the cook into performing this service. I was forced to drink it as it was.

That morning, everyone aboard began a routine that was familiar to them. Gaston explained what we were about, and I joined in. We all saw to our weapons. The damn humid air was hell on powder, and there was no good way to keep it fully dry. Additionally, the salt spray was hard on the wood and metal parts; and they had be kept clean and oiled. So firearms were checked for fouling and cleaned every day. Shots rang out as men discharged and reloaded their pistols. We did not keep the muskets loaded, so we did not to have to waste the shot and powder the constant discharging and cleaning would require to maintain their readiness. Our pistols were another matter, though. I was amused to note that most kept one loaded and with them at all times. Since I doubted the sharks would jump on deck and molest us, I knew there was a small lack of trust among us all. Or perhaps it was habit, and we were truly showing a great deal of trust to our fellow Brethren by only carrying one loaded weapon apiece.

Cutlasses and knives were cleaned and sharpened next. Then those of us near cannon gave them a cursory inspection, to insure their carriages had not become blocked and they were in overall readiness. Meanwhile, the men who knew rigging and all manner of seaworthy things inspected the craft. Then buckets of seawater were brought up, and we swabbed our areas to keep the wood moist and clean before the heat of the noonday sun took hold.

In the midst of this, I learned another thing of note. The buccaneers did not keep the hideous four-hour watches other ships maintained. Gaston explained that with so many men, those who wished to work

beyond their daily chores could, and those that wished to do nothing
could do that as well, as there was not enough work to go around
to keep all of us busy. As for command of the ship, it rotated among
Bradley, the Bard, and Striker, based upon whichever of them was the
least tired. I was amused to hear that the master of sail was generally
in command of a buccaneer vessel, unless he was asleep or there was
battle.

Even after most of the cleaning and the like had been accomplished,
I continued to hear steady firing. I stood to look across the quarterdeck,
and spied Davey and Pete at the stern rail firing their muskets.

"Are you any good?" Gaston asked, and I regarded him sharply. He
was grinning as he handed me my musket.

I chuckled. "I believe I am proficient."

"Merely proficient," he teased.

"Would you prefer I give myself airs?" I asked as I followed him to
join Pete and Davey.

"Non, if the need arises I will brag for you. It would be best if I had
reason to brag, though."

I laughed. "Afraid I will embarrass you?"

His smile was challenging. We began to load our muskets. I had not
fired this new piece, and I deferred to Gaston as to the correct amount
of powder.

"I have little doubt as to my ability to hit a target," I said. "But I have
been told my speed at reloading is somewhat deficient. Of course this
remark was made by a barrister, and therefore I know not how much
weight to award it. I also have not tried reloading with a cartouche."

He was patient in his instruction, and I managed to roll my own
package of shot, powder and paper, and then get it properly into the
musket. I would need a great deal of practice. This bothered me little, as
I had always found improving my prowess with weapons to be both an
enjoyable and very necessary pastime.

Davey was firing at a small wine cask tied to the stern. It had been
let out to a distance of a score of feet or so. I did not think it would
pose much of a challenge, even as it bounced about in our wake. It was
proving a difficult target for Davey, though; and I wondered at this until,
feeling the fool, I remembered he had never fired a weapon before.

I did not envy Pete the job of teaching Davey, until I saw that
instructing the sailor about something as simple as firearms was far
easier than trying to impart to him knowledge of anything conceptual.
And Pete was the perfect teacher, as he did not offer instruction on any
irrelevant matter that was not required to the task at hand. Under his
tutelage, Davey managed to hit the target three times out of twelve. But
after those successes, it was obvious there would be no more in this
practice session: he was not accustomed to the recoil and had become
sore. Also, a small crowd had gathered, which was making him quite
nervous.

I was not pleased with the onlookers, either, as they included

Bradley, Siegfried, Liam, Ottter, the Bard, Cleghorn, Striker, and of course Pete, Davey, and my matelot. I decided to ignore all but Gaston.

"You can let the cask out a little," I said.

"Let's see if you can hit it first," Bradley said.

"Are you doubting me, sir?"

"Aye." He grinned.

I snapped my piece to my shoulder, aimed, prayed there were no unknown deficiencies in my musket, and fired. The Fates smiled upon me; and by sheer luck, my shot snapped the twine at the knot and the little cask began to fall behind. I could not have duplicated the hit if I had fired a hundred times.

There was a chorus of "oohs" and much laughter, as I gave them a jaunty grin and began to reload.

"But can you reload fast enough to shoot it now?" Bradley asked.

"Nay," I said, concentrating on creating a new cartouche instead of simply reloading as I normally would, by pouring powder directly into the barrel from my horn.

"Ifn' ya don't mind, then," Liam said. "Two up, first, knot at top, second, sides." He pointed at someone as he spoke. Then he brought his musket up. He was in front of me, but I heard a shot from behind me simultaneous with his. I glanced back and saw that Pete had fired, too. I looked at the target and saw they had both hit the knot Liam had called, and the little cask was split asunder. Then Striker and Otter fired, each taking out the corners. Then Liam and Pete fired again, and my jaw dropped with astonishment. How had they possibly reloaded that quickly? I watched in amazement as Otter finished reloading. He and Striker did not fire though, as there was nothing left of the cask above water to shoot at, even though it would have still been in range.

"Damn!" I exclaimed.

There was a good round of chuckles and I caught Davey looking as impressed as I.

"It appears we'll need more targets," Bradley said.

Gaston handed me a new cartouche. I noticed that the others had them tucked in pockets or slots on their baldrics, within easy reach. But that was not the only explanation for their speed. Even with the necessary ingredients readily available, there were still a number of physical steps needed to seat the ball and powder the pan. I watched Liam reload with swift and economical movements; and I understood. Liam did not move a finger unless it was involved in the process. His whole body was focused on the actions it needed to perform. I was sure he had done it so many times it came as naturally to him as walking. I needed a great deal of practice indeed.

Gaston saw my attempts to imitate what I had seen; and he stopped me and made me slow my movements to check their position. Liam and Pete joined him at this; and they had me fire at nothing and reload several times, so they could watch my hands and arms. They gave pointers and I repeated the sequence, improving my speed each time in my estimation.

Until Pete stepped in close and looked me in the eye. "DoItWrongAn BlowYarHeadOff."

"I am well aware of that," I said with a wry grin, wondering at his point.

"That'sYourProblem." He grinned.

"'E's right," Liam said. "You've got ta trust yarself. The thing is, in battle, they're shooting at ya, an' the real threat is not ya misloadin' an' blowin' yar 'ead off, or blowin' out the barrel, or maimin' yarself, or even flashin' the pan, it's them shootin' ya on account a ya didna' reload fast enough to shoot 'em first."

"Well, when you put it that way," I sighed. I could see what he meant. I looked at Gaston.

"You are thinking too much," he said.

"I am prone to that."

"I have noticed."

"MadDrunkOrScared," Pete said.

Gaston and Liam smiled.

"Aye," Liam said. "Maybe we should 'ave a drinkin' contest."

"Bulls," Pete said.

Liam laughed. "Otter me boy, ya remember Isaiah? Poor bastard. Got a bull mad at 'im and got charged right after 'e shot. His men weren't near 'im, an' we were a way up 'cross the field. So 'e ran, an' reloaded, an' kept firin' o'er 'is shoulder, an' missin' 'cause 'e didna' dare slow down. That were some o' the fastest reloadin' we e'er did see, what with it bein' on the run an' all. But the bull got 'im anyway, on account 'e weren't aimin', an' the stupid bastard weren't carryin' a pistol. In the end, 'e stabbed it ta death with a short knife, but it 'ad broken up both 'is legs. We 'anded 'im a pistol an' left 'im to make peace with the Almighty." Liam shrugged. "I guess lookin' back on it, maybe it weren't a laughin' matter. Seein' 'im runnin' around afore the bull caught 'im was right amusin' though."

"Will'll get inspired in battle," Striker said.

"Aye," Bradley agreed. "In a line for volley fire, him being off a little won't matter, and in an open battle he'll find the speed, especially if someone's life hangs in the balance."

That was a sobering thought. I had no military experience; and Gaston's stories made it clear that, in battle, the buccaneers often acted as an ordered unit. I was quite conditioned to fight by myself and for myself. That would no longer be the case.

Thinking on how Pete, Striker, John and Liam had fired in volleys, I realized that beneath the orthodox military organization of a volley line, buccaneers fought in pairs, or rather they fought in pairs of matelots. Gaston would be depending on me in battle, not to cover him on occasion, but for us to fight in concert as a team. I looked at him.

He shrugged. "I know you will hit when you do fire," he said quietly in French. "I will plan accordingly."

"Thank you, but I will practice daily, without bulls... I have not seen you shoot yet," I added with a teasing grin. He snorted derisively, and his eyes caught on something. He brought his musket up and fired. I turned my head in time to see the gull fall from the sky into the waves. Then he reloaded with speed and precision. I smiled stupidly at him, as I could think of nothing clever to say. My estimation of him was further polished. I could not have chosen a better man as matelot, had I months or even years to make the decision.

Weapons inspection and practice completed, we returned to our alcove in time for swabbing. It was soon apparent that this duty for our small part of the ship would be left to Gaston and me. Striker was busy with his duties, which involved insuring everyone else performed theirs, and Pete was now busy instructing Davey on some other piece of buccaneer lore. We would also be responsible, in cooperation with the men on the other side of it, for the cannon. Gaston gave me a cursory explanation of the firing of it.

"Maybe I should practice on this as well," I said when he finished.

"If all goes as it should, you will rarely ever see the cannon fired on this or any other buccaneer vessel. They are too small to do any real damage, and they have little range. In a naval engagement, we will all be firing muskets and not these cumbersome things. It is the Bard's duty to make sure we are never in range of the bulk of the prey's guns. We could not withstand even a single well-placed volley from a galleon."

"Then why do we carry them? They take up space, and then there is the weight to consider – and the powder magazine."

He shrugged, "As an occasional threat and deterrent to smaller craft and land targets. If we need to run, they will be pitched overboard. Sometimes they are needed as ballast."

"We could do without them, and you are merely making excuses."

He shrugged. "It is the way of the coast."

"Which, the excuses or the cannon?"

"The cannon. The brethren like their pieces, even if they have little use for them," he said slyly. I laughed.

After the morning's exertions, such as they were, I found myself disposed to nap again. I considered going below to escape the sun; but Striker had a blanket. We rigged it over the alcove between the cannon and quarterdeck, so that it blocked the sun nicely while allowing the breeze free passage. And so I slept for a time on deck.

I woke to find Gaston sitting nearby with arms crossed, staring at nothing. The act of sitting up to join him caused a roiling in my stomach and a throbbing in my head. So when he inquired, "How are you feeling?" all I could do was nod curtly and stand to heave bile over the side.

"Close to despondency over the sorry state of my constitution," I said as I sank down beside him. He handed me a bottle of water and I drank until the hideous taste was diluted, though it still haunted my mouth like a shade of meals remembered. He gave me a small chunk of boucan and I chewed slowly, hoping I would not waste it by heaving it over the side as well.

"Is there anything I can do?" he asked.

"Distract me from my misery. What do you do to pass the time?"

"I am a solitary person by nature, and the events of my life have reinforced that." He was staring into space again, and I was not sure how to interpret his words.

"So you would rather I did not trouble you?" I ventured.

He started. "Non, non, that is not what I meant. You asked how I pass the time. I sit and think. I do not make friends. There is little I want to say or hear from most men. So I am both content and resigned to having no one to speak with. That does not mean it is something I do not desire. I think. It is simply not a thing I am familiar with."

"But I could wear on you, seeing as you are not used to the constant chatter which I am so very prone to produce."

Gaston smiled. "I do not know yet."

"Please tell me to be quiet if I begin to wear on you."

"I will do that. In the meantime, I believe you were asking me to distract you."

"Aye, since I am so fond of conversing it provides a balm for many things."

"What would you have us converse on?"

"What were you thinking on before I woke?"

He shrugged. "The grain of wood. See how the grain differs between the wood of the gun carriage and that in the deck planking? I was wondering what causes the difference. Obviously they are two different types of wood, and they are from different types of trees. But why are the trees different? And furthermore, why are they always different? What makes a cedar grow to be a cedar no matter where it is planted?"

"I take it the standard answer of 'because God made it a cedar' will not be considered a pertinent or learned response," I teased. "Why can sharks not leap from the water, or rather, why do they not, or even can they, when they look so like porpoises? What makes one a shark and the other a porpoise?" I related my argument about sharks and sailor arses that I had engaged in with Fletcher, what seemed like ages ago.

"Precisely," he said. "Though I have considered that as well. I believe in the case of sharks and porpoises that there are physiological differences, such that one is designed to jump and the other is not. There is profound divergence in the musculature of their tails. A shark waves his tail from side to side, whereas a porpoise waves his up and down."

I thought on it, and saw he was correct.

"Leave it to a physician," I teased.

He shrugged. "Was there but one creator with a plan for all things as we are taught? Can that be the only explanation, when we are presented with so much order in the nature of things? Or is there another explanation and we are just too blind to see it?"

I contemplated this. "I believe there is an order to all that is, and that we will discover it someday. Because not all men are sheep, and sometimes the wolves get distracted and do something worthwhile."

He regarded me curiously. "There you are, mentioning sheep again."

I chuckled as I remembered that my explanation had been cut short the day before. I quickly laid out my theory of sheep and wolves as I had presented it to Alonso. "I now think there needs to be a third category, as I keep discovering people who exist in between. I was thinking foxes, but that is merely a small wolf; and these people are not truly wolves, even small ones. Or maybe they are. For example, Davey, who is a sheep in so many ways, and yet he has strength about him and resolve in the face of whatever he encounters."

"He is a goat," Gaston said.

I grinned. "Oui, a goat would be a belligerent sheep. I see Pete and Striker as self-made wolves."

He nodded. "Certainly."

"How would you name Bradley? He is his own master and proud of it, yet he seems so quick to accept society's mores and ways. At least from what I have witnessed. He is a wolf, but I feel reluctant to award it to him."

Gaston shrugged. "He seems like many wolves I have seen."

"This is true," I mused. I had seen many wolves like him, myself. Men who would prey off the weak or herd them as needed, yet were easily herded by stronger wolves. "Though maybe he is a fox."

"Non, he is a wolf; it is you and I who are not like the wolves that raised us. I think you err if you measure all wolves against yourself, as you are an exception and not a rule."

I looked at him sharply. I had never considered that. "Then what are we?"

He was silent for a while. "We are predator and not prey, yet are we within the natural order of things if we are not wolves as we were born and raised to be?" He rubbed the planks between us thoughtfully with his fingers. "Are we perhaps the nut that bears a different fruit than its parent should have created? Are we some mythological creature as a result?"

I had never been so in love with any man or woman as I was with him. I sought to cover it. I was afraid he would look into my eyes and see the truth of my feelings and it would scare him.

"Perhaps we are Gods," I said lightly.

He snorted and smirked. "Gods create, do they not? Or hold dominion over something."

"Oui, do we not?" I teased.

Gaston shook his head. "Non, we are not Gods. Perhaps we are centaurs. Half-human warriors with great knowledge, who teach. It accommodates your crusade to educate the sheep and accounts for our martial skills. And in my way I am a healer who lives as a hermit."

I laughed; as I was suffused with happiness. He had just lifted a

tiresome weight from my spirit. "I concur. We can be centaurs. I like
that. I like that a great deal. And here I have spent years trying to
determine why I was such a poor wolf."

"You never were a wolf, you were merely raised by them," he
reiterated. "And I have spent years wondering if my separateness from
others was another symptom of my madness, and now I find another of
my own kind. It brings me great relief."

The silence was heavy between us. I knew not what to say. I wanted
to crawl into his lap; or, better yet, inside him to a place where I might
never be lonely again. Even if he would have allowed me in his lap, the
other would not have been an option. I told myself quite firmly that
therefore I did not need the one, either, as what I really wanted was not
a thing of mere physical contact, but a combining of souls that could
not be attained within the mortal coil. So I did not need to touch him.
Reasoning is a wonderful thing, but poorly-used it leads to lies, as mine
was doing at the moment.

"So, where did you live in your travels? Tell me what you have seen,"
he said.

I was both delighted and dismayed by the change in topic. It was not
as if we did not have tomorrow and the next, and for that matter, several
months of time to sort out and address all of the other things that lay
between us. I cheerfully began to list the places I had visited.

The next five days of our voyage were similar to the first. In the
mornings there was practice with firearms and ship maintenance. In the
afternoons Gaston and I talked about whatever struck our fancy, though
we avoided anything of a deeply personal nature by mutual accord. In
the evenings we sat about and talked with the other men. I slept a great
deal and felt very little change in my health, for good or bad.

And so we reached the island of Hispaniola and made our way along
the coast to the desired location. It was marked by a small port. The
swine farm was approximately three leagues to the east and a league
inland, according to the men aboard who had raided it before. As there
were more than an adequate number of buccaneers available to take a
swine farm, or an entire village if the need arose, and my health was still
less than acceptable, it was decided that I should stay behind. I whined
piteously over this, until Gaston and Striker both felt my forehead and
judged me an idiot. I was ordered to be still or they would have Pete sit
on me. And so an hour later, I found myself deserted by almost everyone
I knew on the *North Wind*. Except for Davey, who was left behind
because he also was not fully recovered, he knew nothing of hogs, and
he lacked a mastery of the necessary fighting skills.

We dropped our men and sailed a good half-mile out to sea: in order
to give us room to maneuver and to avoid betraying the exact location of
our landing party should we be seen. Then those of us left aboard had
nothing to do but wait for the signal that would bring us back to shore. I
was bored; and after days of stimulating companionship, I suddenly felt
very alone and acutely aware that I was on the other side of the world,

on a ship in hostile waters, surrounded by men I did not know well.

Davey was talking to the sailors, the men who were the actual crew of our vessel. These men were counted more as able seaman than musketeers or soldiers – or as Davey had aptly named us, marines. The sailors worked for the Bard, and from what I heard, usually stayed behind when the others were raiding or boarding. There were ten in all, not counting the cook, carpenter, or the master of sail.

Those three men were also still on board, along with two other buccaneers who were in worse shape than I with some illness, and Cleghorn, making us eighteen. As Davey and I had not had much use for one another of late, if we ever truly had, I did not seek him out; and I was left to my own company, which I did not feel in the mood to keep. I had caught Cleghorn smirking at me every time I spewed something at the sharks, and therefore I wanted nothing to do with him. The sick men were in no state to be conversed with, and one was considered close to death. The Bard and the carpenter were playing cards with Cleghorn, and so they were unavailable. That left the surly cook.

At first I was dismayed as I made this assessment; then I realized this might be the only opportunity I would have to talk to the man alone about the matter of clean water. I did not have any great hope on it being a successful venture. Handled badly, the rumors would spread about what a fool I was, if it was not being said already. So I approached the man with a smile and great deal of trepidation.

He greeted me with an annoyed glare. "What da ya want?"

He was a gaunt man with an angular face and a gravelly voice. His eyes were dark and hard and a curious reddish-brown color; so they resembled rusted shot. I realized I lacked the energy to be clever and even the ambition at the moment to attempt to rally him. I decided to hurry my crushing defeat and crawl back to my alcove.

"I need boiled water."

"For what?"

"I have a theory."

"A what?"

"A concept, an idea."

"And ya want ta boil it?"

Davey and some of the sailors were looking our way. I squatted next to the cook at the fire pit and sighed.

"I think boiling makes the water healthier. And I am ill, so I wish to drink healthier water."

I thought he would surely scoff and laugh; instead he frowned and asked, "Why?"

So I explained about little things living in the water and how they could be seen with a lens that magnified them. I said that it was my understanding that boiling killed those things. Instead of telling me to piss off, he seemed to put serious thought into my words.

When I finished, he nodded soberly. "I don't know 'bout glasses an' little shrimps; but I do know the longer water sits, the more it smells.

I trust me nose." He stood and led me to the one water cask on deck. "This is the oldest water we have." He opened the cask and sniffed deeply, and then invited me to do the same. "Ya smell that?"

I could smell something. "Aye, but I cannot place it."

"Like bein' near a pond," he said. "It's still water. Still water is stale water."

"Aye." I could imagine that now, and the smell it brought to mind was the same as I smelled in the barrel.

He retrieved a large pan for soups, and filled it with water from the cask. "So let's boil us some with nothin' else in it and see if it smells."

I smiled broadly, and we sat and talked while waiting for the water to boil and then cool enough for us to trust our noses over it. His name was Michaels, and he was from Dorchester. He had been enlisted in the army at fourteen and somehow ended up as the cook's apprentice. He did not especially like preparing food, but he had resigned himself to it being his lot in life, even here in the West Indies. He took pride in his work and said he could cook damn near anything and make it edible.

He asked of me, and with some reticence I told him the truth of my birth and the current circumstances of my life. He was quite amazed, as he had seen a few nobleman and they were all right arses in his opinion. I thanked him for not considering me one.

When the water cooled enough, we smelled it; or rather we did not. We smiled at one another.

"I be damned," he said with a chuckle. He filled my bottles, and we decided that while boiling the water that smelled was probably prudent, boiling the water that did not smell was possibly unnecessary. And since the boiling was time-consuming, he would use the freshest cask for drinking water and the rest would be boiled when he cooked with it. But he said he would boil water for me as he was able, and I thanked him heartily.

"What ails you?" he asked as he watched me sip water.

"The flux and a touch of seasickness."

"What be yar remedy? You didn't take something from the surgeon, did ya?"

I chuckled. "Nay, I did not. I am drinking water." I explained about flushing out my pipes.

He nodded thoughtfully again. "This'll help, then." With that, he dug through his bag and produced several packets of herbs. He selected a pinch here and there from amongst them and steeped them in a mug and sweetened it with cane sugar.

"What will this do?" I asked after I drained the mug. It had not been a tasty concoction, so I had made fast work of getting it down.

"Purge your bowels." No sooner had he said it than I felt a great roiling in my belly. Seeing the look on my face, he grimaced. "It can work mighty fast. You should drink all a' that water though. If ya run out I'll boil more."

I was too busy running to the side to be angry with the man. As the bouts subsided, Michaels plied me with sweetened mashed apple and a broth made from boucan, and a great deal of water. I ate and even trusted him when he gave me another concoction that he said would not do anything at all. It induced sleep, and that evening found me napping again.

I woke to the sound of hogs. Then my senses were overcome by the smell of them, and presently by the sight of them, as one snuffled up the deck and tried to investigate my foot. A moment later, I was perching atop the cannon. And while the weapon was no taller than the swine, it did afford me a vantage point and lend me some feeling of safety. There were twelve of the damned animals running about on deck, and the Bard was prodding one on the snout with his foot to keep it off the quarterdeck. Two men were trying to get another down into the hold. The other hatch had men spilling out of it with barrels and anything else that had been below.

Pete saw me on my perch and laughed heartily. I made my way across the ship and climbed atop another cannon to view the goings-on. The heavy air was filled with a symphony of squealing and cursing. Apparently it had been decided that first night, when I was watching stars, that we would keep as many pigs alive as we could fill the hold with, until we could find a place to careen and then slaughter them fresh for boucan. We were also to slaughter as many as we had salt and barrels for today. Then a determination would be made as to what to do with any left over. We were able to come fairly close to shore, but not close enough to swim pigs to the ship. So while one group of men slaughtered and salted like fiends, another kept the swine herded together, two groups rowed swine-laden boats back and forth, and another group hoisted them aboard. Pete was hoisting, Striker was not to be seen, and I finally spied Gaston amongst the men doing the butchering.

I could not see any area of this undertaking that seemed to need an extra set of hands, and so I retreated to the quarterdeck and helped the Bard keep it swine-free.

"Is there anything I can do that may or may not be more useful?" I asked, after we had pushed away another confused beast. The usually-sardonic man was looking somewhat wild-eyed.

"I hate fucking pigs," he stated emphatically.

I could think of two ways his statement could be interpreted, and I chose the less salacious. "You knew they would be on board, did you not?"

"It was mentioned." He took a deep calming breath. "You want something to do?"

"Aye. I am not feeling particularly useful at the moment, as there is so much industry going on about me; and I feel you can defend yourself from hogs quite adequately without my assistance, such as it is."

"All of my men are chasing hogs and we're dead in the water. I want as many eyes on the sea as we can get, so that we have some warning.

Go to the bow. I'd send you aloft, but we all saw your performance today, and you're the last person I want hanging over my head."

With a rueful chuckle I did as he bade, and spent the rest of the endeavor standing in the bow, sweeping the sea for approaching craft.

By the time all was done, we had an astonishing number of the creatures in the hold, a line of barrels down the middle of the deck, and roast pork for all. It was deep into the night. Thankfully clouds and cool breezes had come in as the evening progressed, and the work had not been done in sweltering heat. We weighed anchor and set sail as the last of the men came aboard. My bloody and exhausted matelot was amongst them, and I watched as he crawled over the gunwale and made his way to our alcove. I imagined he would be confused when he discovered me missing. Or perhaps I was giving myself airs.

I wondered when I would be relieved and considered going to ask, but since we were under way I stayed at my post. We came around and sailed west. The men who slept in the bow had filed in and surrounded me. They were all too tired to speak, and sank to the deck to eat and sleep. There was a heavy sigh, and someone collapsed next to my feet. Almost annoyed, I looked down and was happy to find Gaston. So he had sought me out. It was a trivial thing, but it made me happy.

"The Bard would like you stay here until we anchor," he said, and handed me a bottle of water and a hunk of the pork he was eating.

I ate happily and hoped it would cause me no trouble. The smell of the meat roasting for hours had left me alternately hungry and nauseated. I drank water and remembered I had to tell him of my meeting Michaels; but after regarding him, I decided it could wait until morning.

"You are quite the sight," I said. He had managed to soak off some of the blood while wading to the boat; but he was still smeared with black in the lantern light, and I was sure his clothes were caked with it. He glared up at me and stuffed the last bit of food in his mouth. Then he rubbed his eyes with greasy fingers. This only succeeded in smudging the mask all over his face.

I chuckled. "You are making it worse."

"Watch the sea," he admonished. He doffed his kerchief, and used it to wipe his face.

I returned to scanning the horizon, not that I felt my eyes were going to save us from doom. Between the clouds that had rolled in and the lack of a moon, it was too dark to truly see anything; and I wondered how the Bard was navigating at all.

"Wait, we are going to anchor? Where?"

"At sea off the coast. Probably soon. We will find a suitable place to careen in the morning." He had his eyes closed and his head pressed back into the sloping wall at an awkward angle. I let him nap.

I felt several drops of rain. There was a great deal of activity toward the stern. From the bow, I saw men hurriedly passing muskets and powder bags down the ship. After studying the movement at the far end,

I came to understand they were filling the cabin with our weapons and powder to keep them dry. I assumed Pete and Striker would see to ours, which were wrapped in oilcloth with theirs in the alcove.

Soon after, we furled the sail and dropped anchor. I could see nothing around us, not even stars, and it had started to rain in earnest. Thankfully it did not seem to herald a storm with thunder, lightning, and high winds. Still, there was sustained cursing and grumbling heard the length of the ship, as men realized they would shortly be soaked. As the initial wave of complaints ebbed, the Bard shouted orders from the quarterdeck and I was relieved of my watch.

Like two wet dogs, Gaston and I worked our way back down the ship to our alcove, only to find Pete and Striker fucking in it.

Gaston rolled his eyes heavenward. "I would beseech God," he whispered, "but if He exists He is responsible for all of this...."

"And why would he bother, on our account, to change the course of events he liked well enough to set in motion?" I finished his thought.

"Precisely," he said.

The lanterns were being extinguished and soon there was nothing but darkness and rain. I was cold.

"To Hell with it," he sighed. He crawled into the alcove, and with a chuckle I followed.

"You'reWet," Pete noted between strokes.

"It's raining," Striker gasped.

"Truly?" Pete asked and stopped to listen. "SoItIs."

This set Striker to laughing. "Pay attention to what you're doing, you numbskull."

"LikeThis?"

Striker grunted and stopped laughing, and the panting continued for another minute, until they achieved their end in a harmony of groans and quiet swearing.

During this, Gaston and I sat with our backs to the wall and waited. I shivered, and to my dismay found myself horrified rather than aroused. The whole situation was evoking the memory of my first time with Shane once again.

My remembrance was vivid. Cold English rain had pelted us as we rode like madmen to reach an old hay shed, the only shelter in sight. We entered with our mounts, and the place quickly smelled of wet horses and old hay. We were soaked through, and we had not been dressed for the sudden change in weather. It was almost cold enough to see our breath. Laughing around chattering teeth, we doffed our wet garments and dove into the hay to try and warm ourselves. One of us suggested getting closer to share our heat. Cold flesh had found cold flesh, and carnal feelings had emerged as the warmth returned. Hands rubbing to produce heat slowed and explored as goose-bumped skin turned to satin. Like blind baby birds in a nest, we groped each other in that hay. Touching on the other what we wanted the other to touch. Mouth finally found mouth and we squirmed together until the pleasure came and we had to wipe our hands and bellies clean.

In the present, the cold and the rain gripped me anew, and I was almost overwhelmed with the urge to run. I waged war against it, as it would have done me no good. On a ship there was nowhere to run, and these were the people I could trust most in this place. So I sat and listened to men making love while pressed shoulder and hip against a man I wanted, and I remembered how these things could go so very wrong. I vowed to be still and hope that everyone would sleep soon and forget my existence. My body chose to betray me, though: not in its usual fashion or by way of the usual culprit, but by shivering, violently.

To my dismay, I found myself relieved of my weapons and pulled down amongst them, so that Gaston was pressed against my back and Striker my front. I did not have the strength to fight or even find the voice to protest. My mind was frozen in terror, just as surely as my body was stiff with cold, with muscles held rigid to keep myself from shaking apart. To my relief, no one rubbed or explored, there was only the pressing and holding, and the warmth. In time I stopped shivering, and the fear receded.

I trusted the Gods.

Twelve

Wherein I Come to Understand a Number of Things

I woke feeling warm and cozy. There were a blanket and arms wrapped about me and the beat of a heart at my ear. It was oddly disconcerting: I could not remember waking this way before, yet I felt completely comfortable with my surroundings and not the least alarmed. I hazarded to open my eyes, and there was darkness which slowly resolved into deep shades of grey. In the position I lay, pressed to someone's breast, I could only see a shoulder, a wall, and a bit of ceiling. I could smell blood. It took a bit of time, but I slowly recalled who and where I was and the events of the night before. At length I surmised I was with Gaston in the cabin. It was the only explanation that made any sense; all others involved the last week of my life being a dream. That being said, I did not remember moving into the cabin. Nor did I remember removing my clothing.

Anxiety began to clutch at me, and I squirmed in his grip enough to look about. He was clothed. We were indeed in the cabin. It was filled with stacks of oilcloth-wrapped muskets. I could hear snores and wheezing, and I guessed the other ill men were with us, somewhere beyond the weapons.

Gaston's hand was on my forehead. I tilted my head back to regard him.

"What transpired?" I asked in French.

"You became feverish and delirious. We decided to bring you in here and warm you."

I swore and sighed heavily and hid my face in his chest again. "I sincerely apologize for being such a bother."

He snorted with what I hoped was amusement. "You do not know the half of it," he whispered. I looked up at him and found his eyes kind, though his face was grim. "Can you sit? I need to relieve myself."

I nodded and reluctantly pulled away to sit slowly. I felt sore all over, as if I had ridden hard for days. I wrapped the blanket tighter around me and pulled my knees to my chest to sit against the wall. He stood slowly and carefully picked his way to the window. It was daylight again, but I was not sure if the light was muted due to it being dawn or to the clouds and rain. As he opened a window and the quality of sound changed, I realized the incessant noise residing at the edge of my thoughts was the steady patter of rain. So it could be any time of the day.

"When?" I asked.

"I do not know the time. You became ill in the middle of the night. We are under way." He finished and returned to sit next to me.

"I was delirious?" I hoped I had not said anything of an embarrassing nature. It was a stupid thing to be concerned with, when my life had been in danger.

"Not raving," he supplied quickly. "Though incoherent." He appeared exhausted.

I spied my clothes drying over the back of a chair. For someone as unfamiliar with intimacy as I supposed him to be, dealing with me, naked and delirious, must have been quite the chore. "Thank you. For caring for me. I know it was…"

"We were almost…" He stopped and sighed and rubbed his temples. "If not for Striker, and oddly, the cook, and to some degree Siegfried, the Bard, Liam, Otter, and most especially Pete, we would both be in irons amongst the pigs awaiting marooning. This would all be due to my… temper. The damn surgeon wished to bleed you, and I would have none of it. He said you were under his jurisdiction if you were unconscious, and I disagreed. As your matelot, I have the right to make those decisions when you cannot, and bleeding can be added to the list of things which lead to… my loss of control. I did not have a bout last night, thankfully, but it was close, and Bradley now views me as a loose cannon he does not wish to sail with."

I tried to imagine the roaring altercation that must have occurred in front of the whole crew in the rain and dark.

"And I missed all of this, pity," I said as lightly as I could.

He smirked briefly, and then truly smiled as he turned to regard me. "Oui. You do not know how lucky you are." His mask had been rubbed away by last's night's exertion and the rain, leaving dark smudges all about his eyes. Despite this, he looked younger.

"So, will we be allowed to stay, or will we be left wherever we careen?"

"I think it will depend upon Bradley's mood this day."

"Which is bound to be pleasant in light of the weather."

"If we are left on Hispaniola, it is not a great difficulty." He shrugged. "Perhaps it is a great difficulty, but it does not mean death. Depending on where, we can make our way to Petit Goave or across the Haiti to reach Île de la Tortue."

I decided not to say anything of how my current physical condition would factor into the odds of our success. "I owe you a great deal."

He shook his head. "Non, you do not. That was the first time I have become embroiled in a conflict on someone else's behalf. I think that is a good thing, somehow. It made me feel useful."

"Would that mean you are emerging from your cave, oh great Chiron?" I teased.

He chuckled. "It would not be because you are Hercules."

"Non, it would not. I am quite far from being a demi-god of strength, though I have angered a number of goddesses."

"And recently a surgeon," he added.

"Though I have befriended Apollo, Adonis, and the cook."

We were laughing now, and one of the ailing men complained. We apologized and tried to stifle our snickers, but it was to little avail. And thus was how Michaels found us when he entered the cabin. I sobered as he handed me a mug of some brew.

"Good to see you more yourself," he said.

"Thank you, for this, whatever it is, and the help you offered last night." I glanced at Gaston curiously.

"It were nothing," Michaels said. "Damn surgeon. That is broth ta help ya get yar strength back and warm yar belly."

"No purgative properties?" I asked with a grin.

He chuckled. "Nay. Other than bein' yourself and in good humor, how ya be feelin'?"

"He is no longer feverish," Gaston said. "The solution you prepared last night seemed to relieve some of his duress."

"Aye, that's an old one I learned from a fellow of Romany descent. I can give you the ingredients if you wish."

"I would appreciate that very much," Gaston said.

I felt as if weeks of my life had vanished rather than hours, as Gaston and Michaels conversed about herbs I would never remember the names of. Apparently this area of Gaston's knowledge was once again due to the monks. I took an inventory of my skills and abilities, and found few of them related to bringing about anything good or useful in the world. I was a collection of useless facts, and my skills were all related to harming people in some fashion.

Michaels inquired of the other ailing men, and left to fetch more broth since they were awake. He informed us it was midday and we were cruising the coast looking for a likely spot to careen, though we would be able to do nothing until the rain stopped. All the while the ship was filled to overflowing with hogs and hungry, cold, and wet men. I was sure our days on this vessel were numbered, as there was no way I could foresee this all putting Bradley in a more reasonable state of mind.

I had donned my still-damp clothing, and we were discussing whether one or both of us should return to the deck, when Striker entered. He appeared exhausted and in a foul temper, but he smiled at the sight of me. He squeezed into the small floor space Michaels had occupied and kept his voice low.

"You look better."

"Aye, I feel better than I suppose I felt last night, though I remember none of it. We were just discussing if it would be in our best interests to return…"

"Nay, it's miserable, and you'll only ail again, and we've had enough of that." He regarded Gaston. "And you should stay out of sight."

Gaston did not appear pleased with what that implied. "I apologize for…"

"For what?" Striker said and grinned. "Though threatening to hack Cleghorn to bits and feed him to the pigs was perhaps not in the best interests of diplomacy."

"And I missed all of this," I sighed theatrically.

Striker chuckled. "Aye, you lucky bastard. Your matelot was going to take on the whole damn ship to keep you from being bled."

"As I would have wished, had I been lucid." I was almost moved to say that it would not have killed me, though, and I would rather have been bled than both of us thrown over the side. But I understood Gaston's reasons, to the extent I was able, and I did not feel it was within my rights to discuss them with Striker. "Why would Bradley not respect my matelot's decisions on the matter? And likewise, why would Cleghorn not?"

Striker considered it quite soberly before smiling and chuckling to himself.

"Maybe he's right," he said and shrugged. "Pete thinks it's because they fuck women or want to."

I had a glimmer of what Pete meant in mind, but I could not yet focus it. "What would he mean by that?"

"Pete feels women are the root of all evil," Striker said. "They create nothing but trouble, and they rain all manner of destruction upon men foolish enough to fall prey to them."

I found myself chuckling. "I have known other men who felt thus. I do not agree with them; however, I can occasionally sympathize. Why would Pete feel thus?"

"I think his mother died early in his life. And his father, if that was who the man truly was, had a succession of wives or mistresses after that; and they all disliked Pete and his siblings, or at least cared none for them. Then Pete was cast out on the street at a young age, and he lived with a gang of boys. The older boys sometimes had girls, and they caused all manner of trouble for the younger ones; and so he never learned to trust or even like women, and he always had other boys. He's never been with a woman, and he intends to die without ever having been despoiled by one."

"In some ways that is tragic," I said.

Striker shrugged and smiled.

"How does this relate to Bradley and Cleghorn?" I asked.

"Cleghorn has a wife in Port Royal, and Bradley is looking to get married and settle down as a planter."

"Ah, so in the name of the choices they have made or intend to make, they choose not to give credence to the state of matelotage, because if it were marriage then..."

"Bradley is already married, to Siegfried," Striker whispered. "And any man who has known them for a while can see the strain this is causing betwixt them."

"I have seen signs of it, and I do not know them well. And how does all this sit? Not the matter between Siegfried and Bradley, but the matter of the dispute last night – with the rest of the crew?"

"Most, even ones such as Cudro, who truly dislikes the two of you," he regarded us in a fashion that said he wished to know why, "have come forward once they heard the details of what transpired, and said that Bradley and Cleghorn were in the wrong."

"Truly, that is good to hear. So why must Gaston stay out of sight?"

"Because if he is not in here caring for you, the crew may feel he was told to leave you, and they will become angry with Bradley, and I wish to avoid that."

"Why did you not say that in the first place?" I said with exasperation. "You made it sound as if we needed to hide lest we be thrown off the ship."

Striker frowned. "I'm sorry. I did not mean for you to take it in that fashion."

Gaston appeared relieved. "I am not familiar with public opinion running in my favor."

"Well." Striker smiled. "If Pete hadn't stopped you and you had tried to make good on some of your threats, then I would be bearing different tidings; but as it is, you were not in the wrong."

"I was not mad last night. Angry, but not mad," Gaston said quietly.

"Aye, I know it," Striker said soberly. "You could be reasoned with. I saw you on Granada when you lost your senses. You could not be reasoned with, then."

Gaston was frowning. "What did you instruct Pete?"

Striker shrugged. "Pete and I discussed it and decided that if Will is unavailable, or in truth, even if he is available, that if things come to that end, it would be best if Pete dealt with you to keep you from harming anyone."

My matelot appeared sullen, yet he nodded slowly and said, "Thank you."

"Hold," I said. "The decision as to what is to be done with him is mine, is it not?"

"Aye," Striker replied. "Pete will help you as you need him, and follow your direction in such matters."

I was relieved. I did not need to be fighting both of them at such a time. Still, some of what he said troubled me.

Gaston spoke before I could. "Will, do not let your regard for me blind you when I am blind with madness."

"Aye," Striker added. "I believe in that event, Pete will have a clearer mind about the matter."

I nodded resignedly. The whole possibility seemed remote and impossible, as if we were discussing battling dragons or some other mythical monster. I could not imagine Gaston behaving as they said. I could not picture in my mind what form this insanity took. Did he rave and foam at the mouth? Did he speak in tongues? Did he gain unnatural strength? They implied that he did not know his fellows; but he did not have many friends, so I could see where perhaps he would not want to acknowledge them if he were overwrought with emotion. I doubted it applied to me. I could not see how Gaston would ever hurt me.

The rain stopped in the afternoon. A likely little cove had been found and a boat dispatched to scout the area. They returned bearing the news that though the beach was good for careening, it was a bit shallow; and the entire ship could not be pulled ashore without clearing brush. The maintenance to the boat could still be accomplished, but the whole of it would take several days longer than usual. This would put us in greater danger, as we were in French territory and unsure as to whether or not there was a war. The extra days would, however, give us the necessary time to make the boucan. There was talk of whether or not to wait and find a better location, but the question of the hogs remained. They stank, and they would not survive sailing about the sea, as we had no food or water for them. We would have a ship full of dead swine once the heat took hold. The whole matter was put to a vote, and the common opinion was to get the Hell off the stinking boat – or rather get the hogs off so we could clean her. Even if this took a week and we were in enemy territory.

Once this issue was decided, the discussion began of how best to accomplish this. After great debate, the following strategy was devised: We would be organized into three groups. The first would be relatively small, and was tasked with offloading the cannon and establishing a defensive perimeter, then mounting watches and providing protection to the rest. Striker would lead these men. The second group, which would include most of the crew, would clear space for us to careen, build a small hog pen and assist in the offloading of the hogs, and careen the ship. This bunch would be led by Bradley. The third small group would be composed of actual boucaniers, the men who had actually made boucan. They would build the pits necessary, cut the firewood for the pits, slaughter the hogs, and prepare the boucan.

Gaston and I would be amongst this group, along with Liam and Otter, and unfortunately Cudro. There were three other men I had not

met, but Liam and Otter seemed familiar with them. Since he knew
all and was not in dispute with any, Liam was placed in charge of the
endeavor. I was relieved at this, as I had been afraid Cudro would be
awarded command, and I knew he would cause nothing but trouble for
us.

As if hearing my thoughts, the big Dutchman immediately grumbled
that we would need another man, as I was next to useless in my current
state. Liam hushed him and said he didn't plan on my doing much of
anything, anyway, and I would do what I could. I was not pleased. On
the one hand, I was obviously well-regarded, but on the other, I felt as
useless as Cudro deemed me. I silently vowed to do my share of the
work despite my condition.

Weapons and tools in hand, we were one of the first parties ashore.
In the name of the common good, Gaston and Cudro did not argue over
the details, but they did not converse either. After much thinking and
consideration of the lay of the space available, the number of hogs, and
the need to hold the entire operation to as short a duration as possible,
three large pits were decided upon. One man was assigned to clearing
and digging each, while the others began to collect the necessary
materials for building the smoking platforms. Gaston and I ended up
digging, in the same pit, as I was not deemed an entire person for the
purposes of the endeavor.

We worked quickly, as we wanted to accomplish as much as
possible before nightfall. After a mere hour, I was forced to admit that
even under the best of health I was no match for any of the men about
me. I had never performed hard labor in my life. The musculature
I possessed, such as it was, resulted from hours of daily practice
with weapons, not digging. I did not have calluses to protect me from
the rough wood of the shovel, and I quickly blistered. The heat was
oppressive, my back and shoulders ached, and my bowels still did not
like me in the least. Yet I refused to stop, until Gaston threatened me
with the shovel if I did not go and sit in the shade.

Feeling woefully inadequate, I sat in the gathering twilight, drank
water, and watched him work. He was intent upon his task, and moved
with fierce determination, as if he disliked every shovel of sand and
wanted it gone as quickly as possible. He did not falter or slow; this
after slaughtering hogs for hours the night before and then not sleeping
while dealing with me in my delirium.

It occurred to me that even if I was superior to him in skill, a thing I
doubted, he would still win in any duel we might have, due to his being
far more powerful than I and possessing a great deal more endurance.
I felt a boy again, watching a man and realizing what I was not. I sadly
recalled how I used to feel while watching Shane practice. There had
been the constant feeling that I would never equal him. What I had
been thinking of Gaston was a disturbing echo of those memories. In
not being able to be them, I wanted to possess them, or be possessed by
them. The thought made me shiver, and not with pleasure. I had never

experienced that with the other men I had known: not even Alonso.

Night fell upon us, and the men gathering supplies were forced to stop when they could no longer see. The pits were finished by lantern light, because they did not require a great deal of precision. They merely needed to be roughly square. After some discussion, we decided to stop for the night and get a start at first light. One of the men brought us roast pork from the cookfire. We sat about and ate, and Liam entertained us with stories of the Haiti and crocodiles.

Gaston noticed my damaged hands when I winced while taking the water bottle from him. "What is wrong?"

"Nothing of concern, I blistered my hands."

He took my right hand and explored it with his fingertips. I winced and cursed as he probed.

"You fool," he snapped. "Come with me."

I was not pleased with his tone, as he had not been teasing at all. Yet I let him pull me to my feet and lead me to the sea.

"Wash them," he commanded.

I knew it would hurt, but my preparation for the pain was wholly inadequate. It brought tears to my eyes and I knelt in the sand and cursed vividly, slinging several insults his way. He bore it without comment until I was through.

"What were you thinking?" he asked. He was angry, truly angry, with me.

I was still in a fine pique. "I feel inadequate. I am damn near useless. I know nothing. I can do little. And I have the constitution of a girl."

He sucked wind at this and walked a little from me. "You have a fine constitution. If you did not, you would already be dead. And do not assume girls are weak in that regard."

I wondered what had prompted that last remark.

"For your first year here," he continued and abruptly dropped beside me to stare into my eyes in the moonlight. "You are as a child again, and you will need to allow people to care for you. There is no shame in it, Will."

His eyes were ferocious, and it took an act of courage not to look away.

"I understand." Though I did not.

He backed away a little: no longer angry, but now distraught. He clutched at the sand.

"I do not want to lose you," he whispered without looking at me. Then I understood, and I was awash with shame.

"I am sorry. Truly. I am stupid when it comes to... It has been said that I will probably be the last to recognize my own death, as I will not realize it is upon me and argue with the reaper out of confusion and indignation." Alonso had yelled that at me once after what he considered a harrowing encounter with a band of robbers. I had been amused. I had also been drunk. We had not been harmed, and as a result I had literally seen no harm in the matter. Regarding the event from the light of sobriety, I had come to understand how dangerous it had been, and why he had been afraid. At the time I had viewed it as a lark, and if sober would have viewed the outset of it the same.

"And even you have noted I am not always a cautious man," I added.

Gaston took a deep breath and calmed himself somewhat. "You do not see the dangers here at all, do you?"

"Non… Not as you do, obviously. Gaston, I have courted death all my life, at least since I left home."

"Why?" he asked fiercely. "Do you wish to die?"

"Truth? I have not feared it. And there have been times when I wished it."

"And now?" He was intense again and his eyes were brutal and glittering in the moonlight.

"I do not," I whispered.

He pounced, knocking me back into the sand and sitting astride my chest. Panic began to overtake me; and I fought it even as I tried to resist him pinning my wrists beside my head. He was as strong as I had guessed. I could not move.

"Swear it!" he hissed, his nose an inch from my own.

"I swear I do not want to die," I whispered. "Now get off me," I said with more conviction. "Now!"

Something snapped in his demeanor, and he was no longer fierce. He released me to sit back. His fingers hovered and then stroked my face.

"Do not…" he whispered, almost too low for me to hear. "I cannot… Not again…"

I was torn between comforting him and getting out from under him. I was not sure what the next moment would bring in terms of his demeanor. I stroked his arms up to his shoulders and guessed as to the correct words. "Hush now. I will not leave you. I will not die."

He threw himself onto my chest and buried his face in my neck. I held him, as there was naught else to do. In time, he had calmed enough for us to return to camp. He did not speak, but followed meekly as I led him there. I curled around him protectively, and he slept. I was awake for hours, and not just because of the insects swarming about.

A small fear was growing, now that I had witnessed his madness, or at least a taste of it. I could begin to understand the monster I faced. I wondered what the others had seen the night before. Had he been so unbalanced and ephemeral of temperament then? If so, it was no wonder Bradley feared him.

I fought the fear. I alone could not succumb to that. I would be betraying him to do so. He was my matelot. He had warned me to the best of his ability. Others had warned me. I was the one who had not been able to comprehend.

Now that I understood, I set about thinking of ways to handle him in addition to what Peirrot had suggested. I realized Pete's help would probably be required under certain circumstances, as I could not control Gaston physically.

I woke alone, and looked around to find Gaston already working on the platform for the pit he had dug. He appeared calm and deep in concentration, as he used palm fronds to bind sections of wood to the notched posts he had driven into the bottom of the pit. I relieved myself, found water, and went to join him.

"So was that a small example?" I teased lightly.

He stopped to regard me with searching eyes. I smiled at him and let my regard for him show in my gaze. He closed his eyes as if in pain and looked away; but a small smile traced his lips.

"Very small," he whispered.

"If it is any consolation, I am glad this occurred here, just betwixt us, and in small measure. I now have a greater understanding of Peirrot's advice and your own dire warnings. I am glad I was not introduced to you in that state amongst a whole herd of antagonists. I shall be better prepared now. Can you tell me what brought that on, or do you know?"

His hands stopped working, and he thought.

"I was reminded of my sister's death." He looked at me, his eyes holding mine. "Will, I cannot discuss that."

Questions whirled about, but I nodded my acquiescence to his unspoken demand. I would not ask. I allowed myself to note that his sister had probably passed away due to a sickness of some sort, but where and when this occurred would have to remain a mystery until he chose to reveal more.

"What can I do to assist?" I asked.

He smiled thinly. "Show me your hands."

I presented them. I was surprised to see the amount of damage. The blisters across the base of my fingers had all broken open, and the skin beneath was raw.

"I should wash them again?"

He nodded.

"And bandage them to keep them from receiving more injury?"

He nodded. "Bring the bandages here, and I will help."

I went to do as instructed. As he bandaged my hands, I noticed him stopping and clenching and unclenching his own in a distracted manner. I studied his hands carefully and noticed nothing amiss with them, until I spied a disturbing ring of scars around his right wrist where it joined the hand. Then I saw a similar ring on the other. My bowels cringed, as I could only think of one thing that would cause such damage: his hands being bound tightly and for a long enough duration for the rope or strap to cut into his flesh. It did not explain the clenching behavior, though.

"Why do you do that?" I asked casually, when he had stopped and shook his right hand again.

He seemed confused by the question; and then he looked at what he was doing, as if he had been unaware of his actions before.

"My hands go numb."

"Excuse me?"

"When I am engaged in a task that flexes my wrists repeatedly, such as binding this frame together, my hands go numb and tingle. Sometimes it occurs if I sleep on them in a certain way." He shrugged and looked mildly uncomfortable discussing it.

"Have they always been thus?" I asked carefully.

He was looking at his hands carefully now, and he sighed. "Non. They were damaged. I do not wish to discuss it."

"As you wish. May I assist you with the task that is causing them difficulty?"

He nodded, and once he finished bandaging my hands, he taught me how to bind the fronds to secure a joint in the slats. I proceeded to assist him in wrapping and making knots as he directed, at least as much as my damaged hands would allow.

The other two platforms were coming along as well as ours, and the men not involved with that had been amassing firewood. Once our platform was ready, it was judged time to begin the slaughter. I was sent to herd one pig at a time from the pen to whichever of the butchers was ready for it. This is not as easy as it may sound to those as uninitiated in swine as I was at the start of the endeavor. I learned a great deal about the animals over the course of the day, and after getting rammed and almost bitten numerous times, I was pleased to send many of the animals to their reapers.

Once a hog was killed, it was butchered into large slabs of meat, which were in turn cut into thin strips. These were laid across the platform of sticks in layers. Fires were kindled below and fed with wood, as well as bone and bits of hide from the animals themselves. Gaston, Cudro, and Otter were our butchers; and they worked tirelessly to render the animals down to slabs, so another could cut it into strips. As the hogs weighed many times what a man would, and we had no means of raising them, the process required a great deal of manhandling of the carcasses in the broiling midday sun. The men stripped down to their breeches, and were soon covered in blood and sweat. All except for Gaston, who was just as hot and covered in offal, but chose not to remove his tunic.

I wondered at this. I could not recall him removing his clothing in my presence. Then Cudro spoke while taking a break between animals and some light was shed on the matter, though not in a way I would have preferred.

"You look miserable," Cudro taunted Gaston in French. My matelot did not deign to regard him. "Why don't you strip down? Oh that's right, you wouldn't want to do that, would you? Somebody might see."

"Do you truly blame him for not wanting the likes of you ogling him?" I countered.

This elicited several snickers from the other French-speaking men, who had grown quiet and tense at Cudro's taunting. Gaston was ignoring all of us.

Cudro regarded me with a smug smile and I hoped I had not stepped into some trap. "I think he's hiding from you."

"And why would he hide from his matelot?" I asked, as I was determined to play it out.

"Because his matelot is a gentleman, used to pretty things," Cudro said.

I frowned and raised an eyebrow. I glanced at Gaston. He appeared embarrassed. If he was already in that state, I reasoned, I could do little to make it worse. "I think he is a pretty thing."

"Then you've a stronger stomach than most," Cudro said. "Or hasn't he let you see?" There was challenge in his eyes.

I have bluffed men with little in my hand and taken their money many times. I let nothing show upon my face except contempt for my opponent. "I do not make purchase sight unseen."

He shrugged. "Then I was wrong. I am not the only one who can overlook it." He turned to the pig I had brought for him, and the matter was closed for the moment.

I looked around and found Gaston watching me. His eyes flicked from my gaze. Now I apparently had another secret to uncover. Cudro's implications troubled me. Was Gaston scarred or marked in some way? Or did he have a condition of the skin or something else of a hideous nature? I told myself it mattered not, but I was lying. On occasion I have found myself deeply bothered by physical imperfections or anomalies.

By evening, we had reduced all of the swine to strips of pork, and the platforms sagged under the weight. We fed the fires again, and Cudro and the other men went to clean up in the sea. Liam, Otter, Gaston and I remained to watch the pits until they returned, at which point it would be our turn to get away. My matelot had been silent since my exchange with Cudro, not that he had spoken a great deal prior to that. When the other men returned to camp, he stood and took up his musket.

"Come."

I followed, my own musket in hand.

He led me a ways up the beach, outside Striker's perimeter. We were very much alone when he stopped. He studied the sea in silence.

"You do not have to show me anything," I said quietly.

He shook his head sadly and propped his musket against a tree, and removed his belt and other weapons. "Will, I am severely scarred, enough to evince shock and pity in those who witness it, if not revulsion."

I held myself steady. I was sure I could learn to accept scars. I have scars. He was indicating these were far more serious, though. Even as I looked at him fully clothed, I could see a few. There was the one on his forehead, and the slash across his right forearm near the elbow, and several more just below his knees, and the ones at his wrists. With a growing sense of horror, I wondered if they were all related and of a kind somehow. I forced the fear away and said lightly, "Well, as of yet, you have managed to engender curiosity and not revulsion."

He met my eyes. "Will, I do not choose to discuss what happened, with anyone. This did not occur here. No one in the West Indies knows the details of my life before the Line. Do not ask. Do not comment. I beg you."

"I will do my utmost to honor your request," I said solemnly.

He closed his eyes and doffed his tunic and breeches. I was thankful he relieved me of the necessity of keeping my reaction from my face, as I do not know if I could have.

He was covered, with practically not an inch spared betwixt shoulder and knee, with the white stripes of whip scars. These were not the thin lines and pocks I had seen on the backs of sailors or the occasional man exposed to the gaoler's lash, but wide, white-ridged tracks that I guessed could only be made by a horse-whip. And they were not restricted to his back, but wrapped all around him. As I struggled to comprehend it, I was able to reconstruct how the damage could have occurred: not the how and why of it, but the physical aspects of the scenario. He had been bound and suspended with his hands above his head, so that the whip had access to his entire body. He must have shielded his face as best he could in his arms, and that was why there was little evidence of the carnage in his visage and about his neck, and the top of his shoulders or the top of his arms. The tender flesh of the underside of his arms had been quite torn, though. Likewise, he must have made some attempt to protect his privates. It was quite evident from scarring in that region that he had been naked. There was no patch of unmarred skin to even indicate a loincloth, and yet his manhood was only marred by a scar near its base, which connected across the top of his thighs. All of the rest of his flesh had seemingly borne the damage somewhat evenly, and I could not even think to count the number of times he must have been struck. The scars crossed one another and combined and split apart, in a pattern it would take hours to trace.

And yet, underneath it all, he had the most exquisite body I had ever beheld. Much like Pete's, Gaston's form reminded me of the classic Greek sculptures, with every muscle defined and an overall conformation approaching perfection. Only Gaston was compact, whereas Pete was long and lean.

Gazing upon him, my manhood stirred in response; and I bit my lip in frustration. I was sure it would never possess this object of my desire.

I now understood a great number of things. I knew why his voice was broken. He had screamed until it cracked, and it had never recovered. I knew why his wrists were damaged. His weight had surely been suspended upon them for a great deal of time. I was sure that even if this event were not the full reason, it was at least partially responsible for his madness. And I understood why whips and being restrained could drive him to the edge of his sanity. I was not sure about bleeding or his sister's death, but I had the strange thought that it might all be related somehow. I knew I would know in time. I knew he was an enigma I would spend my life unraveling if he would give me the chance.

I wanted to hold him or bellow in rage for him. His eyes were now open and he was watching me with a guarded expression. I swallowed the anger and sympathy and composed my thoughts and words. If I was indeed his friend, he was counting on me now.

"May I say one thing?" I asked. To my relief, his face relaxed into resigned amusement. He nodded. "I wish I had some talent at the arts, so I could sketch or sculpt you. Or in some way show you what I see when I look upon you. Then you would know that I do not find you revolting. The scars are horrible, but underneath, you are exquisite. And I would have you know that, if I could."

"You are kind and delusional," he sighed. "And a fool." He smiled sadly on the last.

I handed him my musket and doffed my gear and clothing. My manhood proudly saluted him with an obvious disregard for his words. His eyes widened with surprise.

I shrugged. "He does not dissemble well at all, and usually does his own thinking, much to my dismay."

I could see the effort he put into pulling his eyes back to my face. He looked young. If he had been another, I would have swept in like a hawk and pressed the advantage of surprise; but this was my matelot, and not a conquest. And even more, this was Gaston; and after last night I was not sure how he would react. I walked into the surf and rinsed the day from my skin.

A minute later he joined me, and scrubbed the blood and sweat caking his own skin away.

"Will, I am sorry."

"For what?'

"That I do not favor men."

I cursed silently under the weight of those words. "You do not know how many times I am sorry that I do. It has been the bane of my damn existence."

"And now the irony of your existence," he said. "Here you are amongst the Brethren where it is acceptable, and yet you are with me."

I did not find his comment amusing, and I looked at him sharply. He was studying the surf quite somberly.

"It is not fair," he added. His eyes met mine. "I will do what I can." Then his gaze darted away and he appeared distraught. He quickly returned to the beach and set about cleaning his clothing.

I stood there for several minutes with one thought: When? I was unable to convince my manhood it was not now, and chose to ease myself there in the surf. Then I came in and washed my clothing.

He was not looking at me or speaking.

"Is there anything else I should know prior to engaging in another verbal sparring match with Cudro?" I teased.

Gaston frowned, but with thought and not anger. "I can think of nothing at the moment."

I watched the play of muscle under his scarred skin as he wrung ouy his tunic. In a way, it looked as if he had armor imbedded in him instead of scars. There were thin strips of skin between the tracks.

"May I ask a question?"

He nodded.

"Do you still have sensation...?"

He froze, and I bit my tongue. There was a trace of betrayal in his eyes. He was barely within arm's reach. Without moving any closer, I held up my hand where he could see it and slowly moved it to his shoulder to stroke lightly from the undamaged skin and onto the scars with my fingertips. It was textured but soft. He held his breath, but he did not pull away. I moved closer and ran my fingers up to the soft unmarred skin of the side of his neck and then down across his shoulder and back. He closed his eyes. I continued, moving my body closer and spreading the area I touched in increments until I was caressing his entire back in light strokes.

"May I ask you a question?" he whispered.

"Oui."

"Is it not disgusting to touch?"

"Non, it is a different texture. In truth, normally I avoid scars, but in this case... Well, there are so many, it is simply your skin and not an anomaly; and so I do not find myself reacting to it as I would with another."

"It feels good," he whispered. "The scars are dull in sensation, but the skin in between is very sensitive, and the mix of the two is pleasant."

I clawed my hands and scratched a little, and he arched like a cat. I grinned.

"Since you say you have not had a lover, then I would guess no one has touched you thus..."

"Oui."

"Thank you for allowing me to."

"You are welcome," he said.

I do not know if he opened his eyes to watch the beginning of the sunset as I massaged and scratched his back. I know I did gaze at it and felt content.

He must have opened them at some point. "It is getting dark: we need to return." He sounded sleepy.

I stopped my ministrations, and there was an immediate tension in his shoulders.

"I can do that again anytime you wish."

He relaxed and twisted to face me. "Oui."

I grinned. Our faces were very close and I was overcome with an urge. I kissed the scar on his forehead. His eyes widened with surprise and then he smiled. Then his eyes flicked to my crotch, where my manhood was thankfully quiescent at the moment.

"I saw to that earlier," I assured him. "It may return, though. If it troubles you I am sorry, as I have no control over it."

"I understand. I will not be offended. I do not suffer from that problem, though."

I was incredulous. "You do not? You have never looked at a woman and felt the blood rush hither of its own accord whether you wished it or not?"

"Non."

"A naked woman?"

"Non." He stood and dressed quickly.

I stood and did the same, but at a slower pace. "Then in all due seriousness, how do you know you favor women and not men?" I asked.

He smiled grimly. "Because my blood does not rush when I gaze upon you either, or Pete or Striker, and they seem to engender blood rushing in many a man."

"Oui, Pete could get rise out of a dead man, or woman. Do you pleasure yourself?"

He rolled his eyes. "On rare occasion."

"What do you think of when...?"

"How good my hand feels," he said flatly.

"So you are not awash with carnal desires in any form?"

He sighed heavily. "Non."

"That would perhaps explain why you have not felt the urge to take a lover. As we have discussed before, I have been at the mercy of my desires since my privates learned to crow."

"It is my understanding that most men are, and I am the exception rather than the rule," he said.

"Oui. May I continue to pry?" I asked as we gathered our weapons and started up the beach.

"Could I stop you?" he asked with wry amusement.

"Probably not. How old were you when...?"

He stopped and turned to me. "Will, that is not to be discussed."

Even in the twilight I could see the warning in his eyes. I held my hands up in supplication. He let it pass, and we continued walking.

We were challenged by the man at the perimeter, and I was pleased with this. It meant we had some security. We passed him and continued on, until we could see the dull glow of the boucan pits at a distance through the trees.

"May I have your leave to annoy Cudro?" I asked quietly as we approached.

"In what manner?" I could hear the amusement in his voice.

"Oh, I would make a thing clear to him, but it will require touching you."

"I do not mind you touching me." He stopped and turned to me. I could barely read his expression in the dark. "Unless..."

I guessed his exception. "I will not touch your privates, or attempt to induce you to arousal."

"You mock me."

"I assure you I do not. I take such things quite seriously." I was sure he could hear the amusement in voice, even if he could not see me grinning like a fool.

"I should hit you." He started walking again.

"Please do not."

As I hoped, everyone was still awake, and we were the last ones in. What was not in my plan was the presence of Bradley. He was conversing with Liam and Cudro, and all three watched our entrance into camp by the low light of the boucan pits.

"Captain," I offered politely as we neared them. In all of yesterday's debates upon the ship, he had avoided looking at and addressing the two of us. I was interested to see what he would do this night.

"Will... Gaston," he said and nodded in greeting. Then he returned to speaking with Liam and did not offer a polite inclusion into the conversation. This could be interpreted several ways, the simplest being that whereas he was calmer now and past his anger, he still wanted nothing to do with us.

We sat in the sleeping space we had utilized the night before and prepared to retire. I complained at the heat and smoke, as we were close to the fire pits. Gaston patiently explained that the smoke would keep the insects away. As I had woken that morning with only a dozen bites and I could see the damn insects swarming all about, I acquiesced quickly to this logic.

Once our weapons were checked and situated, I slid behind Gaston and pulled him almost into my lap. He did not resist, and leaned against me in a natural enough fashion that it would not have been observed that we had not embraced in this way before. He felt good in my arms, and for a moment I closed my eyes and rested my head on his shoulder. I reveled in the feel of his back pressed to my chest. We had slept the last two nights in each other's arms, but not consciously on the first or with great comfort on the second, as after his minor bout I had been too tense to enjoy it. Perhaps tonight would be different.

He turned his head to whisper in my ear. "Your plan is meeting with success."

"Is it now?" I murmured and opened my eyes. Bradley had slipped away and Liam had crawled into Otter's lap. Cudro was staring at us: not with anger as I had suspected, but with unabashed longing. I almost felt guilt, until I remembered everything the man had done. I slipped my hand beneath Gaston's tunic and across the wall of his stomach. This elicited a small contented sound from deep in my matelot's throat. Cudro turned away. My manhood, which had been partially alert, sprang to full attention.

Unfortunately its growing tumescence was at an inopportune angle and pressed between us. I slipped a hand down to adjust the situation and murmured, "Sorry, do not be alarmed or offended."

He tensed and then relaxed.

"You are aroused at holding me thus?" he whispered.

"Oui." I did not mention the sound he had made, lest I make him overly conscious of such things and less prone to do them in the future.

"Does it not trouble you?" he asked.

I considered the question, not in terms of how to answer it to my best advantage, but in all sincerity. "Not especially. It would prefer I pay it more attention, and it aches some with need, as it always does in that state. But as it does this on a regular basis, I am quite used to ignoring its demands when they are inconvenient."

He was quiet for a while, and I thought the matter closed; and then he spoke. "So we can sit thusly and you will not be angry with me for.... doing nothing?"

"Oui." I did not attempt to explain that we tread a fine line between the comfortable ache in my loins of the moment and a degree of arousal which would make action or avoidance necessary. Even as I left the words unsaid I regretted it. Every second I slipped farther from that "oui" it became harder to recover from, as if I had walked into a room and the door was closing behind me. I knew the room was going to become more like a cell with every passing encounter between us, because every time we touched, I would want more, and my manhood would be more eager. Yet I did not want to disturb him this night, with there being a promise of greater intimacies between us in the future. If he allowed me this now, he might allow me more tomorrow, and the problem would see to itself in time.

Oddly, I felt as if I were seducing a maiden and not a boy. A man should have understood the demands and whims of his manhood enough to understand mine. Gaston spoke as if he did not have one, and I wondered how seldom he was aroused. My concern over this was tempered by my knowledge that he had not engaged in any contact with others or had many objects of desire. Thus his manhood may have descended into a form of torpor from which my presence might awaken it. Unfortunately, I took the risk that once arisen from slumber, it might want nothing to do with me.

The next morning, I arose in a leisurely fashion: lying there in the sand for a good amount of time, watching the fronds and leaves and the small clouds wave about in the blue sky. I only resigned myself to sitting upright because Gaston kept nudging me with his foot and calling me lazy. I noted that he did not seem predisposed to move any farther than a seat on the log we had slept beside. We were both possessed of a fine humor.

As there was nothing for us to do immediately concerning the boucan, we took our time maintaining our weapons, shaving – which neither of us had bothered to do in several days – and eating more roast pork. Gaston even reapplied his mask, and I wasted a little time wondering if I liked him better with or without it. I could not decide.

We went to watch the ship being hauled ashore for careening. I had never seen a ship careened before; and Gaston explained the process as we watched most of the crew tow the *North Wind* onto the beach. She was allowed to list to one side so that half her hull was exposed. I was surprised, in seeing her thus, at how deep and thin her keel was. I could now see why the walls of the hold sloped so quickly down. I asked Gaston of this, and he said he knew too little of ships to explain why she had been constructed thus, but it might have something to do with why she was so fast under sail. Many ships he had seen were rounded upon the bottom, like large troughs, especially the Spanish ones; and they were not known for their speed or maneuverability.

After the ship was lying on her side, a team of men set about scraping away the barnacles and seaweed adhering to her. Then another team reapplied pitch and tar to the planks and seams of her hull, until she gleamed black in the sun. In the tropics, this had to be done every three months or so, to prevent her from leaking and to keep her from being fouled by all the things that would attach themselves to her. Once this side was completed, she would be pulled over to lie on her other side and the process repeated. It was hard and hot work, and I did not envy the men doing it; though the sheer number of them seemed to make what we watched go quickly.

We returned to the pits, and Liam sent us to gather more firewood. And so we spent the day in the slow but steady acquisition of such, so that I was not taxed and Gaston was not driven from his good humor. As my hands were still healing, he did not allow me to wield the axe; and I was left with hauling cut wood back to the pile. Between trips, I found myself with little to do but sit in the shade and watch him work.

"I am trying not to feel guilt," I said.

He finished hacking through a branch and came to join me. "For?"

"Doing so little. I suppose there was some truth to what you said while mad."

Gaston frowned. "Will, I do not always remember what I say during those times."

"You said I was as a child for this first year in the tropics, and I should allow myself to be cared for, and there is no shame in it."

"Oui." He smiled.

"I feel I will need to adjust to more than the tropics, but to a different way of life. I have always considered myself to be a hearty soul, and capable of enduring hardship without complaint; but in truth, I have slept most of my life in a feather bed and never had to perform any sort of labor. I feel weak and pampered in comparison when I look upon all of you. The only exercise I ever engaged in involved the sword, and I have been exceedingly lax in that of late."

"As have I, as I have had little call for the skill," he said. "In the few duels I have been involved in, the other man has not known how to face a real blade, and has only been familiar with using a cutlass, which you saw yesterday in its true use as a meat cleaver. It is not a weapon of speed or finesse. In facing a man with one, a swordsman need only have the most rudimentary skills and be fairly quick. In the raids and taking of ships, the Spaniards have not been duelists either. As for your other comments, you will change as time passes, and I do not doubt that, in a year, others will think you have lived here as long as I."

"Truly? Will I look like Pete?" I teased.

"Non." He was quite serious in his delivery.

I laughed.

He remained serious. "I only meant that no one looks like Pete, you will..."

"You do not need to explain."

"Oui, I do. I wish for you to understand that I do not find you.... revolting."

I bit my lip to keep from laughing again, as it was obvious he was in earnest and this admission had taken effort on his part. "Thank you."

Embarrassed, he turned back to chopping wood, and I left him alone for a bit by hauling more back to the pits. His admission had pleased me on a number of fronts, but I thought it best not to tell him so or allow the matter to be dwelled upon.

And so when I returned, I asked, "Where did you learn to fight?"

"In school."

"I never attended school. I had a gifted tutor for my education in letters and a number of instructors for combat, and an excellent sparring partner."

He gave me an amused frown before moving on to another branch. "I was not speaking of the sword. You asked where I learned to fight."

"So you are a master of pugilism as well?"

He snorted. "I once took a boy's eye with a compass during geometry instruction."

I sprayed the water I had been drinking and laughed. "Truly? I do recall you mentioning something of being expelled from a number of schools."

"Oui. For that I was in the cellar for a month on bread and water, until my father agreed with the headmaster to send me elsewhere."

"Gaston, I am beginning to envision your childhood as a living Hell."

He shrugged. "Perhaps. It was not pleasant. I remember little good of it. I have heard worse, though. In that instance, the boy was the son of a Duke, and the matter was not taken lightly."

"Why did you take his eye?"

"He did not like me, no one ever liked me, and I had called him stupid. He and his friends had offered to trounce me on the yard, and I suggested we attend to the matter where we were. Desks went flying and he tried to hit me. I had learned that since I never had the advantage of size, I should always avail myself of whatever weapon was at hand. I was holding a compass. I did not mean to take his eye, but I did mean to hurt him and his eye was available."

"It all sounds reasonable to me. I wonder how I would have fared if my father had sent me to school."

He paused. "If he had, and he had sent you outside England, we might have met, since we are of an age."

I wondered at that, as I thought of who I was at that age, before Shane, before so many of the events which shaped my current demeanor. Would our meeting have carried the same weight then? Would we have recognized one another at all, and would we have mattered to one another as much as we did now without the years of experience? I thought not, though I was sure I would have been infatuated with him even then.

"Oui," I said. "But I feel he would have kept me in England if I had not been tutored. Until I was expelled from all of the English schools of course."

"Do you feel you would have...?" He stopped and laughed. "What am I saying? I have seen how you interact with others now; you would have been in more trouble than I, as you would have argued with every instructor."

We laughed. "Other than my birth into a noble house, which afforded me an education and the parentage of wolves, I view being blessed with Mister Rucker as my tutor as the most fortuitous occurrence in my life. And then there is you." I immediately regretted adding that last, even though it was true.

He stopped and regarded me sharply. "You view making my acquaintance as a fortuitous thing?"

"I am pleased to meet another of my kind."

He was quiet and went back to chopping. I took this as my cue to move more wood. He was waiting for me when I returned.

"Tell me about this Rucker."

So I sat in the shade and told him of my tutor and my happy childhood prior to Shane.

"How old were you when you went to school?" I asked after another wood trip.

"Seven. I had a tutor of sorts before then."

"Why then? Was it a tradition in your family?"

"My mother died." He did not look as sure of that reason as the flatness of his tone had indicated.

Having learned more of him every hour, I passed on the obvious questions and asked, "How many schools?"

With a relieved sigh, he listed the schools he had attended and why he left each one, which almost always involved his fighting and marking or maiming some other nobleman's son. There was one exception, and that was the academy in Geneva that he set fire to. This amused me no end, and we discovered that we had indeed met some of the same individuals over the course of our lives. In one instance, I was able to relate how a certain Marquis' son had told me he received a long scar upon his left arm in a duel. He had not told me it had occurred at the age of ten and that he had been fighting a redheaded demon half his size with a table knife. This amused Gaston greatly, even more so when

I told him I had maimed the man's other arm in a duel after bedding the boy he was enamored with, a promising young musician.

At length he completed his list of institutions. "And so I ended up with the monks when I was fifteen, and it was considered a punitive measure; but I rather enjoyed it."

"What order?"

"Franciscan."

"I was afraid you would say Jesuit."

"Non, these were a quiet lot, not prone to scheming or traveling. They had a vineyard. If events had not transpired as they did, I would have returned and joined them."

"Truly?" At first I could not see him as a monk; and then I knew I could, and it might have been a happy existence for him, but for one detail. "I thought you are not a man of faith."

"I had faith enough then."

"That was before the event... So it robbed you of your faith. I am sorry." I apologized not out of sympathy for his loss of faith, but for disobeying his request and mentioning the matter.

He understood, as he did not appear to take umbrage or give me a warning look. "Oui. God failed me, and in time I realized it was because He did not exist... or does not care."

"I know all of my teary prayers in the dark were never answered," I said. "But I feel some of that is because I never possessed true faith."

"What were you praying for?"

"Deliverance from evil...I..." I realized I did not want to discuss that, and took another load of wood to the pits. I was concerned that he would not take my cue and leave the matter be; but I need not have worried.

"How big is the pile?" he asked when I returned.

"In my estimation, it looks as big as it was last night, and we made it through the night with wood to spare."

"How are you feeling?"

"Tired; I have not napped today. But my bowels seem content for the time being."

"Then let us return and you can sleep."

"That sounds agreeable."

We gathered our things. He paused before we started on the little path I had made through the trees.

"All of your scars are on the inside, are they not?" he asked.

I nodded. "Not so severe as yours, I feel."

"Why? Because they may not have involved as much bodily pain?"

I hesitated, but decided the words were correct. "I do not feel my tribulations drove me mad."

He displayed the hint of a smile. "I was mad before, Will; I just did not succumb to it with the ease I do now."

I thought of what he had related concerning his school history and realized he was most probably correct. My problems remained seemingly miniscule in comparison with what he had suffered, though.

"I still feel I make something out of nothing sometimes," I said.

"Perhaps we will compare notes some day, when we both feel capable of the endeavor."

I could not help myself: I embraced him. He returned it, and we stood for a while holding one another; until he released me abruptly and led us to camp without another word or look. I did not feel slighted by this.

We found they had floated the *North Wind,* and on the morrow they would reload the cannon and ready her to sail. Bradley was curious as to when the boucan would be completed, and Liam assured him we could pack it in sacks by the next evening. This seemed to please our captain, and we knew we would sail the day after next. After the pleasant day I had just spent, I was not enamored with returning to the confines of the ship; so I vowed to relax and make the most of the time we had left on land. I slept happily on solid ground.

I woke in the dark with weight on my back and an arm around me. The fear closed in, and I was almost in the closest boucan pit before I realized my assailant was Gaston. I crawled back to him sheepishly. He was awake now, and I could see his concern in the dim light of the pit coals.

"I am sorry," he whispered. "I forgot."

I nodded and lay next to him again, in the same position but not touching. I felt his hand on my back.

"It is all right. It has passed," I whispered, not wanting to discuss it once again.

His hand moved, and he began to rub along my spine and then out to my shoulders with a feathery caress. I was surprised he was touching me, or for that matter had lain with me of his own accord. It held great promise. I smiled to myself and rolled onto my belly and turned my head to regard him.

"Feel welcome to continue that," I whispered.

He smiled and increased his efforts, and I sighed contentedly.

"I am truly sorry," he said.

"I know. It will not be a problem if I know it is you. If I am surprised, as in waking, then I am gripped by panic and…"

He was nodding. "I will lie in front of you unless you are awake."

In time I calmed and was lulled back to contented sleep by his caress.

We woke as we had the day before, with lazy contentment. The pile of firewood was adequate to finish out the day, and we would begin to cool and bag the boucan in the afternoon. This left us with little to do, and we strolled to the beach to walk in the surf with our muskets across our shoulders.

I took in the blue sky, bluer sea, and stretch of white sand. "I could grow accustomed to this."

He chuckled. "It is endurable."

"Some would liken it to paradise."

"As long as they are on the beaches and there is a breeze. I personally prefer the Alps."

"Truly? They have a charm and beauty, majesty really, but there is that snow and cold to contend with."

"I am fond of snow and cold. Not being about in it, but being within when it is without. One cannot appreciate warmth until there is cold to give it meaning."

"That is true of many things. Do you think you will ever see the Alps again?"

He shook his head. "Non. I think I will die here."

I regarded him sharply, as there was a tone to his statement that sat uneasy with me.

He shrugged. "There are no old buccaneers. They either become planters or they die."

"There are places to go in the world other than France, if you did not wish to remain here."

"And live like this?"

I thought about it and grinned. Here we were, two armed men, walking down a beach with nary a care. We could do whatever suited our fancy, as long as it did not impinge upon the livelihood of our fellow buccaneers. If we decided not to board the ship on the morrow, they would not attempt to stop us. We were free to do as we pleased, bound only by the dictates of our bodies. The only laws of man we need obey, we had a say in the making of and could take or leave as we chose. For all other concerns, might made right; and if we were not strong enough to do as we pleased alone, we could choose to band with others or we could change our objectives. I could think of no place else in the world where this would be the case.

"So we endure all of this for freedom," I said.

"I have heard it always has its cost; but those who speak of it thus are usually the leaders of nations and sending others off to war."

I smirked. "The wolves always know what is best for the sheep. I should know; I feel the need to herd them and as you have pointed out, I am not even a wolf."

"I think it is more that you feel the urge to shepherd them. And they like to be herded."

"Spoken like a wolf," I teased.

"If they did not wish to be sheep, they would become wolves."

As I had thought the same many times myself, I agreed with him. My mind was still working over an earlier turn to our conversation. "So what do centaurs do with their lives?"

"Hide in caves."

"Oui, but when that grows dull."

"Become shepherds and physicians and train great heroes."

"Are we hiding in a cave?"

"Oui, and in truth, Will, now that you are here I feel no need to leave it."

My heart swelled and ached much as my manhood always did, but unlike a cock there is no easy way to relieve the pressure in the heart. One is either filled to overflowing with an intensity of feeling or one is not, and it does not matter whether the emotion is pleasurable or not: it feels the same either way, and it was not comfortable. I wondered if perhaps there was some pleasured release of the heart that no one ever spoke of, because few had experienced it and they kept the secret for only the most enlightened. Or perhaps the wise avoided the pressure by practicing temperance in all emotions, including love. I found that a melancholy thought and discarded it. I wanted to feel what I felt for him now, uncomfortable or not.

I was madly in love with him. I loved his demeanor and humor, which were so well matched with my own. I loved his mind and the excellence of the thoughts that occurred within. I loved his scarred body, as it bespoke a strength I could not equal and could only admire. I loved his husky voice, as it made every conversation a thing of intimacy. I even loved his reticence concerning all things carnal, as it made me his first and would allow me to discover him. And in a less than becoming manner, I even loved his madness, as it made me useful to him.

"I am honored," I said quietly.

He was frowning in thought at the undertow burying his feet. He looked up to me and smiled.

"What do you feel centaurs should do?"

"Be with other centaurs."

"And when that grows dull?" He grinned.

"I do not foresee that."

He shook his head and sighed with a smile.

"You think me foolish?" I asked.

He shook his head again. "Mad, perhaps. Definitely tending toward delusion. I am wondering what I did to deserve you, and thinking that I am the one who is honored."

"I wish my heart could come," I blurted. He frowned with consternation and so I explained about how I was uncomfortably swollen with emotion.

"I know that feeling," he said soberly. "I feel it."

"Then what do you do?"

"Kill something," he said with a nod.

I blinked.

He shrugged. "It is usually not a pleasant emotion I find myself filled with."

"And now? Do you feel it now?"

"Oui. It is pleasant. I have no name for it. Can you name yours?"

"Oui." I bit my lip. I was hesitant to speak it, as I had always been soundly rebuked for it before. "Love."

He took a long breath and studied the horizon. I cringed inwardly.

"You are sure?" he asked.

"Oui."

"You have felt this before?"

"Oui, and it has gone unanswered... every time."

His eyes were filled with trepidation when they found mine. "Not this time."

I took a long ragged breath. I moved my musket to my left hand and embraced him with my right. He did likewise, and once again we stood holding one another for awhile.

"Do not leave me," he whispered.

"I will not."

"I will try to make you."

I frowned and held him tighter. "You will not succeed."

"You are sure?"

"I cannot foresee any act that you could commit or thing that you would say that could drive me from you." I was lying, but he did not challenge me on it.

That night we took turns rubbing one another's backs, and we slept curled together in the smoke. It was as close to paradise as I have ever achieved.

I prayed the Gods would not be cruel.

Thirteen

Wherein We Explore Jealousy

The next day, a large frigate sailed past around midday. She was at a good distance, and our men were not been sure if she sighted us. We moved as if she had anyway. Since the cannon had been loaded that morn, and all else was in readiness, we packed the boucan with haste, and we set sail a day early. This proved to be a prudent measure. When the other ship came round again, she was bearing for our location. With winds thankfully in our favor, we were easily able to sail out and away from her. We were not sure of her intent, as she flew French colors. It was best we outran her, which the *North Wind* seemed capable of doing,

Gaston and I knelt at the gunwale and watched our pursuer. "Do you recognize her? Could she be the *Josephine*?" I asked.

"Non. She is not the *Josephine*," he said. "She is larger."

"I was hoping we might have been lucky," I shrugged.

He frowned at me. "Why would that have been lucky? Peirrot sails under commissions from both countries; he could take us as a prize."

I was surprised at this. "Oui, but would he?"

"If he thought we were worth something; but he knows how long we have been out of port and that we could not have taken a prize yet ourselves."

"If it were Peirrot, and he had thought we had worth, what would occur if we were to fight?"

"Are you asking where my loyalties lie?"

"Non." And I was not, as that had not occurred to me. "I am asking if he would... What is the result when buccaneer ships are at odds and fight on the sea? Do we surrender gracefully and they take the money, as in a highway robbery, and we all go our separate ways? Or is every man put to the sword? Or are we ransomed, though I know not to whom?"

"Oh," he said as if he had not considered that a question. "It depends on a number of matters, such as whether the crews know one another. If they are unknown, we fight and any left alive are sometimes given a choice to join the winning crew and sometimes killed. But first we would fight as if our lives depended on it. If they are known, it may occur as you described, with a surrender of the booty in exchange for the lives of those remaining after the fight."

This brought a whole host of questions to the fore in my mind. Yet again I was confronted with a good many things concerning the business of piracy that I had not given sufficient thought. I chuckled sheepishly.

"This has all been fairly, I guess you could say, academic. What happens if we are captured?"

He regarded me as if I were a fool.

I winced and sighed. "Before you consign my intellect to the midden heap of contempt, please hear me out. I plan well, in the short term, and I have been deemed to be quite excellent at tactics and even strategies in order to meet specific goals, but I do not exercise the same forethought in regards to the major events of my life or..." I sighed again. "I choose to overlook them. I knew this life would have its share of dangers, and I could even name them if asked. Yet... I just do not think they will ever befall me, and so I worry little about them, until confronted in some fashion."

"I do not have a midden heap of contempt," he said distractedly, as if he were giving great thought to the matter. "It is more of a mountain."

"Oui, and I am perched atop it, I understand."

"You are nowhere near it. You are still a fool, but not for this, though you are foolish. Coming to the West Indies at all was your first mistake."

"And pairing with you probably my second."

He grinned. "That was incredibly stupid."

"Oui, I see," I laughed. "So in answer to my foolish question."

"The only ones who might capture us are the Spanish, and we are pirates, dogs, and heretics to them and not due the respect of even the lowest soldier. They will either enslave us and send us to their plantations or mines, or they will torture us, or they will kill us, and they may do all three."

"Though they probably would not kill us first if that were to occur," I noted.

He snorted. "What did you think would happen?"

"I did not, really. I suppose I thought perhaps we would be ransomed or kept as prisoners of war or some such thing. I guess I am thinking like a wolf. The few times I have been in truly dire straits in my travels, there has always the notion that any man could be bought and I could always write my father. And yes, I realize how incredibly childish that sounds."

He shrugged. "You thought like a wolf. Your life had meaning and value, as opposed to the common sheep."

"Oui."

"You are a sheep here, Will."

"Non, non, I am a centaur; the Spaniards will just think I look like a sheep."

He smirked. "They will see you and hear nothing but *baa*."

"Non, though I be a barbarian, my Castilian is quite proficient."

"Truly, why? Where did you study it?"

"I have known a number of Spaniards, in Florence and elsewhere."

He grimaced. "I have heard the bastards are crawling all over that peninsula. I have a talent for languages, and as theirs bears a great similarity to French, I have an understanding of it. But I do not like conversing with them." There was vehemence in his words, and I was surprised.

"I have found them much like any other people."

He frowned. "I suppose that may be true. But Will, the Spaniards are civilization in the New World, and I hate them for it. I have been thankfully insulated from civilization during my life here. In thinking on it, I am sure they are as any other nation in many regards. But here, across the Line, they are somewhat different. They plunder and murder in the name of God and profit, and send all of it home to Spain. Their people here are indolent bastards, who abuse who they can. Did you know that almost all of the Indians are dead? I feel that if any of the Carribe survive, they are in hiding; and I have only heard of a few Arawak left alive on Hispaniola."

"Oui, Rucker and some of his associates are well informed on that subject. It is supposedly a matter of outrage in England. Though I feel they would like the Indians no better, and it is merely another reason to berate Spain."

He nodded. "As always, civilization serves its own ends. As do wolves. However, I feel your English brethren would not treat them as the Spanish do." He shook his head. "The Spaniards enslave the Indians, and then sleep with their women and create more slaves. They do the same with the Negroes. How can a man bear fruit with one woman and call it an heir, and with another and call it a slave? If the offspring is less than human, what pride did the man possess to spill his seed in the dam in the first place? They may as well lie with their livestock."

"You do not feel we are much the same?" I asked.

He glared at me briefly and shrugged. "You have not seen it as I have. Each nation is different in regards to such matters. The English only sleep with English women, or at least white women. A Frenchman will marry an Indian woman and claim the children as his. I am sure the English bemoan the lack of Indians, because there were none left to enslave and they were forced to resort to bondsmen. Therefore they claim the moral high ground, as they did not murder the Indians. Instead, they enslave their own. A French contract of indenture is usually three years. With the English it is seven, or more. The Spanish do not have bondsmen; all are slaves, so there is no hope to escape their yoke. However, they usually do not enslave their own countrymen."

I was beginning to feel amusement at his respect for his former countrymen without ever using the word "we" or claiming them as his own. "I did not realize you were so patriotic."

He snorted derisively. "I am not."

I smiled. "I happen to agree with you, though. The French make piss- poor wolves. No talent for empire building since Charlemagne," I teased.

He finally chuckled. "William the Conqueror."

"Ow!" I laughed. "True, true, and the Normans stayed to mingle and marry. You know all the nobility is of the same pack these days, anyhow; you should know that more than anyone, considering your educational experiences."

"As should you, after working your way through every court in Christendom."

"Not every court. Oui, there are differences, though; you are correct. I did favor France. If I had not encountered a bit of trouble there, I might have stayed longer."

He raised an eyebrow.

I sighed. "There was a death due to a duel I was involved in and... Actually, that is the primary cause for my leaving many places I have lived. I once fancied that I am always only one step ahead of the reaper."

"Is that due to your lack of forethought?"

"More to my upbringing, really. Being raised a wolf, I have always thought I had the right to take whatever I wanted, as long as I had the power to do so. But I was a wolf alone, and thus it was easy for them to ally against me after I had taken down one of their number."

He studied the sea. "You have never been religious? Have you ever believed in sin?"

I looked where he did: our pursuer was far behind us now, and it was obvious that unless there was divine intervention on her behalf, she would not catch us.

"Non, I have not."

"Feared damnation?"

"Always, as I was constantly threatened with it. Then I grew older and realized that if there was a God, the people making the threats had no right speaking for Him."

"Perhaps I am not speaking of God."

I regarded him with curiosity, and found I would have to speak: he was not looking at me, but still out to sea. "How so?"

"Do you think it is possible to sin against nature, or man, or perhaps even yourself?"

I gave the matter thought. "Sinning against nature, man, or self would denote a morality to be transgressed against as a thing inherent in those concepts. I see morality as an inviolable basis for right and wrong, and I do not feel that such a thing is inherent in nature, man, or self, or invested in any thing for that matter. So, non. I think it is possible to do wrong. I do not think it is possible to sin. I truly do not believe in sin in that context."

"How do you know you have done wrong?"

"I feel guilt."

"How do you prevent yourself from doing wrong?"

"I am not always successful, though many of my wrongs have been inadvertent. I do have a good knowledge of what will cause me guilt."

"So your basis for morality lies within you?" He did not seem incredulous or judgmental, merely curious.

"Oui. And you?"

"I think that if you do something you know is wrong you are sinning against yourself; and if it would be wrong in the eyes of your fellow men, then against man; and if it be wrong in the name of all that is natural, then against nature."

He was somber to the degree of profundity. I felt shallow sitting next to him. This was something that touched me lightly, and I often thought little of it; and here it seemed to touch him to the core of his being.

"What would you place at the apex of the hierarchy of sin in that regard?" I asked carefully.

Gaston studied the sea for a long moment; and there was change in him, a thing deep inside that I could only bear witness to in the small changes wrought upon his physical mien. His posture straightened and his eyes sparkled, and there was now the hint of a smile on his lips. It was as if he had gone so deep he had come out the other side. Or perhaps he had rebounded off some impenetrable wall in his psyche and I was witnessing his return.

"Willful fornication with swine," he said with jesting earnestness.

I laughed at the unexpectedness of it; and then I understood his game and joined it happily, as I did not want to dwell upon the subject either.

"Hold, pray hold, I am endeavoring to envision unwillfull fornication with swine. They are large, ungainly creatures and quite willful in their own right. Sheep are fairly tractable, and one might mount a half-hearted attempt at copulation on a sheep and be relatively assured of success. A swine, however; that would require a particular brand of willfulness. As I have recently learned, forcing a stubborn swine to do a thing it wishes to do may tax a man, and forcing upon it a thing it will surely take umbrage with could endanger life, and in the example of copulation, the most favored of limbs."

He laughed with me, and the darkness that had taken hold of him was dispelled.

We sailed on, and it was soon the middle of April. Bradley had it on good authority that the Spanish Terra Firma fleet known as the Flota had wintered in Veracruz. It was also known that if the Flota stayed through the year, then she made ready to return in April or so, reaching Havana to acquire more cargo in May and then sailing for Spain in June. From Havana, the Spanish treasure fleets always followed the same route home; and this involved sailing up through the Straits of Florida, until they could catch the westerly winds and cross the ocean.

Since we were early for their arrival at Cuba, Bradley wished to sail south around that island and into the Gulf of Mexico to catch the fleet on its way to Havana. If this failed, we would hover near the port herself, wait until they departed, and chase them north.

Thus we cruised ever westward, until we had passed north of Jamaica. We hugged the southern shore of Cuba, keeping her a thin smudge of grey upon the horizon. Thankfully it was not as boring as crossing the ocean had been, though men in prison are afforded more space – and, I even fancied, more variety in their daily life – than the threescore men crowded together on the *North Wind*. With every meal, my certainty increased that I would soon grow exceedingly tired of salted pork and fruit washed down with lemon water.

We followed the daily routine. Every morning we woke and saw to our weapons. Then we swabbed the decks and any available woodwork. Then we practiced, trained, or in Gaston's case, engaged in calisthenic exercise. I joined him in this as soon as my strength returned. Then we would while away the rest of the day, sitting about and talking or playing cards. In the evenings, when the sun no longer burned down on us so brightly, the musicians played and there was dancing and general revelry, though with a distinct absence of alcohol. Even if all of us being intoxicated had been advisable, the *North Wind* did not have a hold large enough to carry the amount of alcohol necessary to keep us drunk.

There was a pleasing monotony to this life, and I found it reassuring and not confining in its simplicity only because of Gaston. Without him, it would have bored me to stupefaction, and I do not know what I would have done. I was at a loss as to what he had done prior to my arrival, as he seemed driven to converse for hours at a time. Perhaps I was seeing the end result of not having anyone to speak with for many years. I was pleased to be the recipient of so many pent-up words, and I enjoyed having such an avid listener.

He shared my vast fascination with art, and took to questioning me in great detail about what I had been fortunate enough to see in my travels. Thus I talked myself hoarse many an afternoon describing the contents of the collections I had seen. We once spent half a day discussing a painting we both had the opportunity to view, in order to clarify nomenclature and form a common frame of reference. He was not satisfied with mere words in these discussions. If it was a painting, he wanted to know the colors: not by their names, but as hues we could see around us, so that he could vividly picture the piece in his mind.

If it a sculpture, he wanted me to sketch it with my hands. I taxed not only my voice but my mental faculties attempting to adequately relate the sublime. Thus the time passed quickly and amusingly.

Occasionally the monotony was relieved in other ways. North of a small set of islands known as the Caymans, we encountered another vessel flying the Jolie Rouge, the *Griffon*. I knew I had seen the name before; and then I recalled she was the ship we had seen preparing to sail from the Hole on the day of my arrival on the *King's Hope*. Both ships anchored off the long western beach of the biggest of the islands, and most of the crews went ashore. The *Griffon* had several kegs of beer, and we traded them boucan for two. A party was held, to the delight of all.

Before disembarking, Striker went about and solicited volunteers to serve as sober watchmen aboard the ship in the event of any sort of trouble or emergency. Gaston agreed to this duty, as did I; though my matelot assured me I did not need to on his account. I had little interest in going ashore without him, as I had been hearing tales for several weeks of the astounding levels of debauchery sometimes occurring at buccaneer revels. I was in favor of being an observer at this juncture and not a participant, especially if my matelot would not be joining me.

Eight of us stayed aboard, all pairs of matelots. Liam and Otter were with us, and the Scotsman approached us after the last boat went ashore.

"We be calling the cabin first," he said with a hopeful smile.

"The hold," one of the other men said, and he and his matelot disappeared down the hatch. Shrugging, the other pair retreated to the bow.

Liam regarded Gaston and me, where we sat side by side on the quarterdeck steps.

"First watch will be right with ya?" Liam inquired solicitously.

"Aye." I nodded and Gaston shrugged. And then we were alone. We had not been alone since careening. In the intervening time, we had touched on occasion and overall possessed a greater comfort with one another; but there had been an increase in tension as well. Now, as I sat staring at the bonfires on shore, and listened to the music gusting toward us and the creak of the ship in the shallow waves, an awkward silence descended between us. All warmth and life seemed very far away. I knew I must make light of it or it would lie heavy upon us all night.

"I did not realize the implications of taking the watch," I said.

"Nor I," he murmured. "Not having had a matelot before."

"So this is not some ploy on your part to get me alone and ravish me?"

He started a little, and even in the moonlight I could tell he blushed.

"I jest, I jest," I said quickly, and poked his arm.

He captured my hand and held it in both of his. I let him and leaned close to kiss the corner of his jaw. He held his breath, and his grip on my hand tightened. I sat back and waited. I did not watch him.

The tide, such as it was in these regions, was going out, and our anchored bow was pointed toward the revelry on shore. I could hear a lively jig and see dancers in the firelight. Below us, a new set of sounds was emanating from the cabin. In the bow, the couple that had retreated there could be seen engaging in their own dance of courtship. They were silhouetted against the fires on shore; and the effect was rather interesting: much like watching a play with the actors behind a screen. I glanced to Gaston to see if he was watching them too, and found his eyes on me.

"What would you have of me?" I asked gently.

He looked away, towards the bow, frowned and looked at the stars above. I had decided he would not speak and began to plan my next utterance when he said, "I know you do not wish to have anyone behind you...." He did not finish.

I frowned curiously. "Yet?"

"Could you sit here?" He pointed at the step between his knees.

"As I believe I said. I will be fine with such things if I know it is you and I have warning." I sat where he indicated. As it was what I wanted, I leaned back into him. I was relieved when his arms wrapped around my shoulders, and even more pleased when his head pressed next to mine. I embraced his legs on either side of me as if they were the arms of a chair, and we sat thus for a time.

I watched the men in the bow. They had gone beyond courtship and were beginning to engage in the culminating act itself. Bathed in moonlight and silhouetted as they were, their performance was quite beautiful.

"I wish I possessed some talent at painting," I whispered.

Gaston stiffened. "You would paint that?" There was a touch of reproach in his voice.

I frowned and pulled away from him enough so that I could turn and regard his face. "You do not find them beautiful, as they are, with the play of light and the red of the fires on shore beyond them?"

He was frowning, first at me and then at the couple in the bow. He sighed. "I see... There is... Primarily because it does not look as it normally does, at this distance and..."

I was curious and alarmed. "What do you see when you see two men thus engaged? Say it is Striker and Pete, who we have ample occasion to watch." I knew he did not watch them: he always averted his gaze. I had assumed it was out of politeness.

"They are like beasts," he said with a tired sigh.

"Oui, two beasts. I think they are quite beautiful. In my eye, men appear at their most powerful when they strain to reach that momentary perfection. Every muscle and sinew is taut, and for them there is nothing else except their bodies and the sensations. Fighting in concert, side by side, it is as if they storm the gates of Heaven demanding entry."

He was quiet. I watched him. He watched the men in the bow.

"Do you think it grotesque?" I asked. Then I remembered our conversation regarding sin. "Or do you think it unnatural? A sin against nature?"

"Non," he breathed. "It is not a thing I wished to do, so I did not seek to view it in a positive nature. I do not think it unnatural, as some might say. I have seen a man and a woman, and I find it just as discomfiting. I do not wish to behave in that fashion. Yet..." He held me tighter. "Will, what would you have of me, if I were a willing subject for your desires?"

At first his question took me by surprise. I had obviously given the matter great thought, even in my dreams; but I had not sought to compose it into words to convey to him. I had also thought in terms of acts. This was not the time to speak of that. I did not feel he was ready to discuss things with names. So beyond that, what did I want? What had I ever wanted from a lover, and never truly received?

"I would want that we were like Pete and Striker. To be equals, both partaking in the joys of giving and receiving as we wish. And I would want quiet times of great intimacy to enjoy each other's caress, whether it gives rise to passion or not. But primarily, I would want the freedom to enjoy you in all ways, whether they lead to your pleasure or mine or both or none. And truly, I do not lay all of that out as a river you must cross alone to reach me. I have never had a relationship such as I wish for now. And I am not ready to meet my half of the arrangement. I feel it will take effort on both our parts."

He held me and I waited, concerned I had said more than I should.

"I will fight it with you as best I am able," he whispered. "But Will, I foresee a very long war."

So did I, and I was not pleased with this grim vision of the future. At least I was not alone. This heartened me greatly, enough to allow me to push the other thoughts aside. I settled into him and watched the stars and the horizon. He seemed content to hold me, and I was content to be held.

It was truly new ground for me and I strode on it gratefully, despite the small frustrations of my manhood. In all of my prior relations with men or women, someone's manhood, usually mine, had taken precedence over all other aspects of intimacy. I had never been with a lover with whom I could engage in intimacy, without it culminating very quickly in the act of copulation of one form or another. And then it would be gone. Alonso and I had never sat about and simply held one another. I wondered at that. I had known I wanted to. Since Shane, I had known I wanted to be held and have the freedom to touch without censure. Yet I had never attained it. Nor had I strived for it. Now I felt the need to hold it like a painted egg.

Sometime while we sat thus, a fight broke out on shore. We did not hear of it until morning, when several men, the Bard included, returned to the ship to recover from their excess of drink. Relieved of duty, we went ashore to watch the pending duel. Otter and Liam went with us, with the Scotsman thanking us profusely for letting them use the cabin all night. I assured them that we were not put out, and then immediately regretted it as they regarded us curiously.

I realized I did not want anyone to know we did not engage in buggery. Thinking further on it, I came to see that this was related to my thoughts and wishes of the night before. If I was involved with a man, I wanted to crow the fact to the world, without threat of his displeasure or anyone else's. And at the same time, if I was involved with a man and it was plain for all to see, I wanted others to think that we at least enjoyed one another, lest they think there was something amiss with one or both of us. Of course, as this was truly the case, I wanted them to know even less.

We found our friends and waited while the duel was started. The men had decided on swords, or rather cutlasses and knives. The first round would not be with pistols, as the pair evinced no interest in killing one another in the sober light of morning. The proceedings would continue until first blood was drawn. I asked what it was about. Pete did not know. Striker was involved in organizing and coordinating with the *Griffon's* quartermaster, due to the duelists being from different ships. Our cook, Michaels, turned out to be a font of information, as he slept near one of the men involved.

Apparently the fight was somewhat over a third man. Michaels related that it was a bit more complex than both of them being in love with the third. There had been a prior relationship between two of the men. And the men dueling had actually been interested in one another as well. I lost track of Michael's explanation as the duel began. I was not even sure which of them had come from the *North Wind*.

The duel commenced, and all watched them swing wildly at one another with cutlasses. The crowd cheered and caught their breath when the tide appeared to turn one way or another. I, on the other hand, was appalled at how slow and clumsy they were. I could have run either man through before he ever swung. If the buccaneers thought this was swordplay, they were sorely mistaken.

In addition to the charging around and hacking about in the sand, both men were hurling a great number of snarled insults. Additionally, many things were said when they clenched that the rest of us did not hear. Their tempers rose. When all was truly said and done, one of the men struck first blood by hacking the other's chest so thoroughly that he damn near cleaved the man in two. Striker and the other quartermaster allowed it, and no one complained overly much. I made note that *first blood* had a very broad interpretation amongst the Brethren.

Shortly after, a shot rang out from the *Griffon;* and several minutes later, we learned that the third man had taken his own life in response to the outcome. All eyes turned to the winner of the duel, who was apparently our man from the *North Wind*. His name was Harris. He made a great show of bravado, and acted as if it all meant little to him. This was not well received by the men of his acquaintance. He went to sit on a dune by himself.

I had once been in attendance at a large ball at which a wife had grown tired of her husband's open philandering and thrown a glass of Madeira in his face, before slapping his mistress and retreating with a degree of dignity many monarchs would have envied. That night I had been very amused to watch the other onlookers. In the duel's aftermath, this rabble upon the beach was much the same as those elegant lords and ladies. Some faces carried a smug assurance that such social indignity would never befall them. Other countenances showed a fear that it would. Others yet suggested it already had at some time. And there were still others that seemed bewildered that such a thing had occurred at all.

Davey was one of that number. He seemed at a loss that anyone would kill another or themselves over such a thing as love. He said as much. I pitied him anew. Michaels, meanwhile, appeared older than he usually looked and saddened by both the events and Davey's words. Striker gave Pete a look that made me wonder why he worried so. Otter stood munching an apple, with his arm over Liam's shoulder. Liam said he hoped Harris would choose to leave on the *Griffon* and not return to the *North Wind*, as we had no need for troublemakers of his ilk.

Gaston's hand slipped into mine. Unfamiliar with such a thing occurring in public, my eyes swept about to see who might have witnessed it. I immediately experienced guilt at this, as I remembered Alonso doing it, much to my chagrin. Cudro was watching us, as were Bradley and Siegfried. I kept the frown from my face and turned my gaze to my matelot. His eyes were lit with mischief.

"Are you sober?" he asked.

I nodded with amusement, as he most certainly knew I was.

"Are you well?"

I nodded again.

"Would you like to spar?"

I laughed.

"I was beginning to despair that you would ever ask," I said as he led me down the beach. "I am sadly out of practice and I hope I will not embarrass you, as unless we go far away we will surely attract an audience." I had not seen him practice with a blade since we met, either. I did not think he would embarrass me. He also did not seek to remove us completely from the others, though he surely could have simply by walking over a few more dunes.

He snorted derisively. "Do not be making excuses for my defeating you." His eyes held a mixture of amusement and challenge. He released my hand, and we shed all weapons save rapiers and dirks.

Then we were in motion. He was indeed as good as I had hoped; but to my surprise, I was better. As expected, he had me in strength and endurance, and we were evenly matched in speed. However, spending the last ten years without a worthy opponent had made him rusty, and my spending the last ten years living off my blade had taught me things he never had a chance to learn. His style had been tainted by the cutlass, yet he was incredibly opportunistic in using the ground we fought upon to his advantage. I remembered what he had said of his days fighting in school. In a true battle between us, the victor would owe his win to luck and surrounding conditions. In sparring, I had the advantage as long as I kept control of the match and did not allow him to corner or run me excessively. There was a very sweet moment when he realized I was his better, not because it fed any preening pride on my part, but because there was admiration in his eyes and I knew he was pleased that I was good.

We had indeed gathered an audience, almost as large as the duel had. The howling and cheering ebbed in my ears beyond the pounding of my blood. Gaston and I stood, our sword tips in line, watching for the next move. His eyes left mine to look me over, and when they returned I saw the battle light dim. He stood straight and dropped his sword to his side.

"Enough," he whispered between breaths.

I knew he was not as winded as I, and that he did this to spare me having to lose if we continued. We embraced. I kissed his cheek.

He whispered, "No one will bother us now."

I felt the fool as strongly as I felt my admiration for him grow. I was indeed out of practice, and not merely with the sword. In the ballroom with the lady flinging Madeira long ago, I had played several of the reactions I witnessed to my advantage. Here, I had only taken the first step of observing, when he had already formulated his battle plan and begun to implement it. I did not let my unfamiliarity with the terrain excuse me. I had grown lax, and there were truly as many intrigues here as there were in any great house in Christendom. Men aboard a ship were just as trapped with little to do but meddle with one another as any pack of wolves known as a royal court.

Pete loomed over us. Not that he is truly that much taller than I, or even Gaston. It is just that the Golden One seems to take up so very much space, as he radiates some aura about him like the sun. "TeachMe!"

Gaston and I laughed in agreement.

"All right then," I said as I caught my breath. Using my matelot as an example, I proceeded to give a basic lecture in fencing, involving the differences between a rapier and cutlass, how they are used, and what tactics we had utilized during our match and why.

At one point Cudro called out, "We don't need to learn that. Spaniards don't fence."

"I beg to differ," I replied. "My last sparring partner was a Spaniard, and he fenced very well. And as for what one needs, you do not need to do anything. It has been my experience that if man only did what he needed to do, Adam would have stayed in the Garden of Eden, alone." This brought a round of guffaws and laughter, and Cudro thankfully abandoned us.

I agreed to start teaching actual stances and the like on the morrow, and sprawled on a dune to rest. The other men drifted off. Gaston sat behind me, legs on either side of me again, with his arms wrapped around my shoulder and chest. I leaned into him with contentment

"Did you fear I could not fend off any challengers?" I teased.

He shook his head with amusement. "I was tired of seeing eyes upon you."

"Surely you jest."

"Non. Many think I have done well, far above what I should deserve."

"Because of my father?"

Gaston snorted. "Because others do not find you revolting."

"If what you say is true, then I have truly been leading a blind and blissful existence." As I thought on it, though, I realized I had not looked beyond him to see what others may have thought of me.

"I have not noticed," I added with a bit more sobriety. "Your regard has been all I have sought or been aware of."

"I am honored." He was quiet for a time. "Your last sparring partner was a Spaniard?"

"Oui."

"And he was good?"

"Oui. You would defeat him handily, though."

"Was he the one who was almost your matelot?"

I moved so that I could look up at him and gauge his reaction. He did not appear as if he wished to hear my answer. "Oui."

He grimaced and sighed. "A damn Spaniard... Do not let anyone else know."

"Rest assured, I will not. I am dubious about my wisdom in letting you know, considering your feelings for that nationality. Promise you will not view me as tainted."

"It will be difficult. I cannot imagine it." He grimaced again.

I was amused. He was truly perturbed and not just playing the part. "He was quite handsome."

"They are all fat."

"He was not fat."

"And stupid."

"Nor was he stupid. Please grant me some degree of taste and pride. I did not bugger Davey because he was stupid, and look at him."

"They are arrogant."

"Well, he was that. You might like him, if you did not know him as a Spaniard when you met."

"He is still alive?"

"Oui, I would hope so. He was going to live in Panama on his family's plantation."

"So he is in the New World?"

"If everything went according to the plans he relayed to me, oui."

"Do you wish to see him again?"

"Non, but perhaps out of curiosity. Are you jealous?" I teased, wondering if he would deny it.

"Non." He would not look at me.

I chuckled. "Well, you are doing a fine job convincing me otherwise."

"I am envious. I believe there is a difference, non?"

There was indeed. I turned in his embrace until I was kneeling before him, so that our eyes were level. I pinioned his gaze with my own.

"Truly, there is no need for that. There is a definite inequality between what existed with him and what exists with you. If anyone were to observe the entirety of the two situations from an impartial position, they would see that if either of you had reason for envy, it would surely be him. And, having experienced the emotions you engender within me, I would rather be alone than return to what I had with him. For any overtures of love he may have relented to make... pale in comparison to the regard I hold for you."

He shook his head as if he did not believe me.

"Why will you not accept my word?" I asked.

"I have done nothing to deserve you."

I smiled. "Considering the effect I have on many lives, that may speak well of you."

He relented and smiled. I turned and settled into his embrace again. I dearly wanted to know what haunted him so; but I knew, as with other aspects of our relationship, the knowledge would be long in coming.

We sailed the next morning, cruising further north and west, toward the strait between Cuba and Campeche. Our daily routine resumed, and two days after leaving the islands, Striker, Siegfried, Gaston and I were lounging about in the morning after weapons practice. There was too little deck to truly spar, but I had endeavored to give Pete an exhausting lesson – for me – on the rapier; and now the Golden One was training with Davey.

The match was uneven to the extreme, though Davey had taken well to wielding steel in general. However, Pete was amazingly fast and, as Gaston had noted to me that first night, possessed a genius for all combative pursuits. Thus Davey was covered with little cuts, which he gleefully ignored in the name of trying to deliver the same to Pete, who was noticeably unmarred. I was greatly entertained, as one might imagine, by the sight of two men looking as Pete and Davey did cavorting about, with muscles straining under taut golden skin while wearing only breeches.

Still, after Davey took another good cut, I was moved to wince and say, "Mayhap someone else should spar with Pete."

Striker snorted and frowned. "Let him bleed."

I raised an eyebrow in response. I remembered my observation after the duel, which was that I was, quite frankly, not observing enough. I regarded Pete and Davey from a different perspective, that being Striker's. Pete had called a halt to the match, and now they stood talking and joking about Davey's wounds. Pete was being Pete: happy, effusive, and the center of all attention. Davey's eyes were filled with adoration for the Golden One. This was, of course, what rankled Striker.

"It is hero worship. It will pass," I murmured.

"Aye," Striker said, "and I cared not what the others whispered, especially after the duel, but observe Davey."

He stood and took my water bottle and walked up-ship. As he passed Pete and Davey he stopped long enough to throw his arm around his matelot and whisper something in his ear. Pete snaked an arm around his waist and listened with interest, and then the two parted and Striker went below to fill the bottle. I had kept a partial eye on them, but as instructed, I had watched Davey. Striker was correct; there was an issue at hand. Davey's entire demeanor changed in Striker's presence, and his eyes flashed anger and defiance.

I wondered how Davey could be so foolish; and then I attempted to see events through his eyes. Pete and I had rescued him; Striker had been robbing the ship with Gaston. Pete had taken Davey to shore and purchased weapons for him. Pete often spent time with him when Striker was busy as quartermaster. Pete was training him; Striker was not. Davey did not sleep with them and see their nightly antics. Davey came from a world where liaisons were of a more casual and less permanent nature. It was entirely possible he did not understand the true depth of their relationship or its duration.

I had little time to think more on it, as Pete joined us with a grin.

"YouSparWithMe?" he asked Gaston and Siegfried.

My matelot smiled. "Aye, tomorrow. You will not fare as well, though."

"Good." Pete grinned.

We all looked to Siegfried. He shrugged. "God knows I need the practice."

Striker returned. He dropped beside us on the steps again.

"We have not discussed this, and obviously we should. You two are in the boarding party, correct?" Striker said.

"Aye," Gaston answered.

I had assumed everyone was in the boarding party when we took a prize. Not wanting to appear the fool, I kept my mouth shut. Striker seemed satisfied with Gaston answering for both of us. I decided I was also.

"I would be in the boarding party," Davey said.

Striker looked from Davey to Pete and shrugged.

"He'sReady. NotAloneThough," Pete said.

"I'll go with you," Davey said.

Pete shook his head. "Nay. I'mWithHim. BoardInPairs. WatchTheOther'sBack." He clapped Davey's shoulder. "Doesn'tHaveTaB eAMatelot. JustAMateTaWatchOutFerYa. AMateThatDoneItBefore."

Striker was amused, though he tried to hide it from the crestfallen Davey.

"Who would ya suggest?" Davey asked.

"LetMeThinkOnIt. Sit."

Like an obedient puppy, Davey practically sat where he had been standing. Pete sat on the bottom step between my legs, and began to look over the crew. Liam and Otter were in their alcove, next to Davey, and they began to look around too. Siegfried sat on the top step next to Gaston. The Bard joined us and leaned on the rail by Siegfried.

"What are we doing?" the Bard asked.

I stifled a laugh. It was appearing as if it would be matelot by committee, and I wondered if Davey realized what he was in for.

"Davey here needs a mate to go boarding with, or possibly a matelot," Siegfried told the Bard.

There were now eight men staring at the rest of the crew, and some of the crew were staring back.

"We should probably discuss something," the Bard said quietly, "Otherwise they'll all think we're up to something."

Davey helped by turning his back on the rest of the ship. "I'm just looking for a mate to board with," Davey said.

Pete shrugged. "That'sHowTheyStart."

"And even if it's a matelot, you don't have to bugger one another," Siegfried said.

"Then why bother?" the Bard scoffed with a teasing grin.

Siegfried chuckled. "Because some men don't wish to bugger anyone, but that doesn't mean they can't be fine business partners and loyal companions."

"If I have to put up with another bastard in my life, somebody is fucking somebody," the Bard said.

"I seem to remember you being quite fond of the last bastard in your life," Siegfried chided.

"Aye, I was. He was still a bastard, and I like being alone."

"You're on a ship."

"You know what I mean."

I did not dare tip my hand and look behind me to see my matelot's reaction to their discussion. All I could tell was that he was very tense. I found the conversation interesting, and it made me wonder more than a few things about the true nature of Siegfried and Bradley's partnership.

"How did you meet Bradley?" I asked Siegfried. "If you do not mind my asking."

He sighed. "How did I meet him, or how did we become matelots?"

"Both."

"I was shipwrecked, and the ship he was sailing on rescued us from the cay we were stranded on. We became friends, and I liked that ship and so I stayed with them and became a buccaneer. Sometime later we became matelots."

His story did not answer the question I wished answered, but thankfully Davey was far more tactless than I.

"When did ya start fucking?" he asked.

Siegfried snorted with amusement. "When we became matelots."

That answered several questions, and I silently applauded Davey on his artless audacity.

"Can you bugger someone and not be matelots?" Davey asked.

A strange silence settled over the group; not that they had all been speaking before, but as if they had to give his question some thought, or it disturbed them.

"Why would ya?" Liam asked.

This gave Davey pause. It gave me pause.

"Being new here, I have to ask, are you implying that buccaneers only have carnal relations with a matelot?" I inquired.

"Well," Liam said. "If they 'ave a matelot they're not lyin' with anyone else, and if they don't have a matelot and they want ta bugger a man, one would think they would like 'im enough to be matelots."

I could see his reasoning, and I found it amusing. I had not spent any time watching the carnal habits of my crewmates, other than the wolves in our alcove, so I was not sure if this was accurate. Then it occurred to me that Davey had asked the question first. I had seen him engage in casual buggery with at least two other sailors and one of the bondsmen on the voyage to Jamaica. If he was asking, this seemed to indicate that he had not been as promiscuous here, as he had not seen others doing it or partners had not readily presented themselves.

"What if a man just favors men and wishes to sample all of the men who do not have matelots?" I asked.

They all looked at me, including Pete who had to turn around. "EndsUpDead. YouSawTheDuel."

"Aye, but it is my understanding that the man who initiated that duel won, and he is not dead."

"He will be, if he courts anyone who may possibly be attached," Striker said. "He has a reputation now, and no one trusts him."

"And I suppose the threat of dueling keeps men from straying from their matelots." I smiled. "That has never worked amongst men and women, as I can attest to many times over."

"Do they live on ships?" Striker asked.

I could see that reasoning also. "Nay, but they do live in small social circles, or towns on occasion. Yet, unlike upon a ship, they have the possibility of clandestine trysts. Here, there is no place to hide. And there are other major differences, I suppose. Women do not carry firearms or duel; and once betrayed, their greatest weapon is to sleep with another. And since all the men are engaged in the activity of cuckolding one another in some fashion, they all share the guilt; and when dueling does occur, it does not always lead to death. Infidelity is expected and accepted. Here, it is not. I assume a betrayed matelot kills his partner."

There was a round of chuckles.

"You assume correctly," Striker said. "Though it's not always the way of it. Sometimes they simply dissolve the partnership, but usually blood boils and someone dies. And any man caught trying to seduce a matelot is usually dealt with by one of the pair or shunned by his shipmates."

I knew many a priest and vicar who would have been quite pleased with the buccaneers, at least in theory. If you wished to have carnal relations you must marry.

I was very glad Davey was hearing all of this. I spared him a glance; he appeared thoughtful, studying the planks beneath him.

"Ach. StrikerEverDid." Pete growled. "I'dKillTheBastard. KillStriker. ThenKillMeself. CauseICouldNotLiveWithoutHim." He became somber. "HeEverDies, I'mADeadMan." He glanced at his matelot.

Striker smiled and leaned down to whisper in Pete's ear. They chuckled.

That definitely drove the final nails in the coffin of Davey's infatuation, or so I hoped.

"Sexton," Liam said and we all looked at him curiously. He regarded us with confusion as to why we did not know what he was speaking of. "Sexton, ta be Davey's mate. He be good. His matelot be dead."

"Aye," Striker said, "But he's a musketeer, not a boarder."

"Ahh, forgot, sorry," Liam said. "The Ram? I've heard 'e's good, an' I've na' seen 'em about with another."

"He's with Cudro," Striker said. This evinced several stares and a bit of tension from my matelot, who had just relaxed. "Not as matelot. He's one of Cudro's men." Striker sighed and dropped his voice. "Bradley wants to go for two prizes if the pickings are easy. If this be the case, then we'll hold a vote for a second quartermaster, and it will probably go to Cudro. He'll need his own boarders, because even if I take half as many as I will board with to sail the prize, he'll still need at least twenty. So, Cudro's men are out. The Bard's men are out. The musketeers are out. Who does that leave?"

"HastingsHarrisGreenMaroon."

"Harris is out," Striker sighed.

"NotGreen. BeenWhoring. CriesWhenHePisses."

"So that leaves Julio the Maroon or Hastings," Striker said. "I would advise against Hastings. I do not think he likes men at all, and he may be one of Cudro's friends by now."

"Don't like him anyway," Davey said coldly.

"Julio the maroon then," Striker said.

"What is a maroon?" I whispered to my matelot.

"Half Indian," Gaston whispered back.

"The one talking to the cook," Striker said quietly.

"Aye, I like 'im," Liam said. Otter nodded.

"He's an able seaman too," the Bard added, "but not one of my regular boys."

Davey was looking to Pete, who was nodding. "Like'ImALot. HandsomeDevilToo."

Davey turned to regard what I had already been eyeing: Julio the Maroon was a fine specimen of manhood, and I had caught myself staring a few times when I noticed him about the ship. I had wondered before about the exotic quality of his face, the reddish-brown of his skin, and the lack of hair on his strong jaw and massive chest. Now I understood.

"He's free?" Davey looked back at us with wonder.

The wolves nodded.

"As far as we know," Striker said.

Davey smiled and abruptly sobered. "Would he take me?"

"In truth, many men won't take him because he's Indian," Striker said.

"If they are that damn blind, what right do they have being buccaneers?" I asked.

This brought a round of laughs and a quiet "Hey," in my ear. I craned my head back to regard my matelot, who was glaring at me.

I teased in French, "What are you concerned about? He probably does not read Plato and I doubt he fences, though perhaps he can be taught."

I thought he was going to bite me. I grinned.

Striker walked up-ship and spoke to the man, and Davey stood and looked nervous and awkward. Julio the Maroon seemed to be doing a fair amount of nodding; and he walked back with Striker, who seemed positively gleeful about introducing them.

I pulled Gaston's arm tighter about me, relieved I did not have to worry about such matters.

"Are you overcome at his presence?" Gaston whispered in French.

I chuckled. "Non, I was merely thinking how pleased I am that we decided things on a street, and my future was not dictated by a council, though the chorus did decide some of our fate."

He rumbled with quiet amusement.

Now that Davey was a member of a pair, though they did not initially call themselves matelots, he and his partner were included in our little cabal for cards, discussion, and general companionship. Previously, this group had only been composed of six: Liam and Otter and the residents of our alcove. Julio also joined us in fencing practice, and had quite a knack for it. Additionally he proved to be sensible, soft spoken, and to my amazement, not only fluent in Castilian, but literate as well.

Shortly thereafter, rearrangements of sleeping space were made; and Davey and Julio moved into Liam and Otter's alcove across from ours, and began to refer to themselves as matelots. They were committing sodomy within the week, with a degree of amorousness that I think surprised Davey, as he was used to a far less intimate form of buggery. Julio liked to kiss.

Now, if only my own love life were so simple. I knew the Gods were taunting me.

Fourteen

Wherein We Learn to Interpret Signs

The following week passed quickly, as we sailed through the strait of Campeche and into the gulf of Terra Firma. We went ashore into the thick forest, and replenished our water and managed to procure some fresh meat and fruit. I was happy to eat anything that did not taste of salt. We had worked our way through the salted meat first, since it would not last as long as the boucan. I was now very tired of pork.

The only other ship we saw was a sloop of woodcutters bound for on Campeche. Since it was one of ours, we did not give chase; though some wanted to, simply because it would be an amusement. We began to criss-cross the sea leading to Havana. I was assured we would be at this for weeks.

I recalled my earlier idea of teaching, and out of politeness asked Bradley if he felt this would present a problem. He was actually very enthusiastic about the matter, and offered whatever support he could give. So I set about determining if anyone would wish to partake of lessons. Of those I knew, Bradley, Siegfried, Cleghorn, the Bard, and Striker were literate. Possibly not well-educated on any matter that was less than useful in relation to their occupation, but they could read and write charts, bills of lading, and the like. All of the Dutch, including Cudro and Otter, were literate in Dutch, but not English. Cudro wanted nothing to do with me, but Otter and some of the others wished to learn English. Hastings, who had been an English Navy officer, was a man of letters and apparently possessed of an excellent education. He thought I was on a fool's errand, as most of the men on board were surely too stupid to teach. I noticed that he gave this opinion very quietly. I awarded him a withering smile and told him we would see. The rest of our number, who were primarily English, could not read. I found with interest that this included Pete. I did not understand why he could not when his matelot could.

I approached Striker cautiously on the matter when Pete was away.

"I assume you have tried to teach him to read."

Striker sighed. "Many times. It always ends with us yelling at one another. I do not understand it. He... I do not know if I can explain it, either." He chewed on his lip, and came to a decision.

When Pete returned to the alcove, Striker whispered in his ear. Pete looked glum, but he nodded.

Striker looked to me. "All right, then. Observe."

Gaston and I watched as Striker wrote "Striker and Pete" on the deck with charcoal. He handed the charcoal to Pete and said, "Now copy it."

Pete wrote, "Stirkre and Pete." Additionally, three of the letters were reversed. He tapped on his own name and said, "SeeIKnowThatOne. P E T E." He had rendered the "P" backwards. He frowned and shook his head with a groan. "DamnIt! TheyBeMovinAgain." He attempted to copy the names yet again, and different letters were displayed out of order; and some of the letters which had been backwards were now in the proper direction. He finally gave an exasperated sigh.

"StrikerSaysTheyDon'tChange. IDon'tKnowHowAnyManDoesIt."

Striker looked to me and shrugged with a heavy sigh. "I could not teach him."

Gaston seemed very agitated by it all, as if the sun had risen in the west and he wished to know why. He wiped the deck down and drew an "E" and asked Pete to reproduce it ten times. A third of Pete's renditions were backwards. The astounding thing was that Pete understood something was going wrong.

"I'mStupid!" Pete snapped and threw the charcoal overboard.

"Nay, you're not!" Striker snarled back.

"I do not think you are stupid," I added.

"It is a disorder of the mind," Gaston said calmly. "There is nothing wrong with your vision, and I have seen nothing to indicate your intelligence is in any way retarded. There is simply some disorder that prevents you from seeing things as others do, much like some men not being able to perceive color."

Pete was initially displeased with this verdict; and then he appeared to think it over, and decide he could accept it. He looked from one to the other of us.

"CanYaTeachMe?"

I was not about to tell him no. "It will be a challenge. For all involved. And you must be patient with yourself, and not fling the charcoal overboard, as there is little enough of that."

Pete winced and ran to get more from the cookfire. Striker was giving us a warning look.

"I will endeavor to try," I assured him.

"You truly understand that he is not an idiot?" Striker asked.

"He is far too perceptive to be an idiot. And he learns other things very quickly."

Striker sighed, and some of the tension left him. "I just can't have others thinking..."

"Nay, of course not," I said. "This will be our secret. I will endeavor to teach him separate from the others."

This relieved Striker even more. Pete returned and handed me another chunk of charcoal and each of us a banana. My mind was churning quite furiously.

I asked, "Do you know your letters?" and wrote the alphabet.

"Aye. StrikerTaughtMe." Pete named them one by one.

This was a relief, and made what I planned next far easier. I wrote, "I like bananas," and asked, "What does that say?"

Pete regarded me as if I was stupid. "ICan'tRead."

I pointed at the "I".

"I."

I kept pointing, one letter at a time.

"L, I, K, E," he said.

"What sounds do they make?"

He glared at me, and then he glowered at the letters. Then the tension left his face, and the calm of awe and understanding replaced it.

"Like," he whispered.

I grinned, "Aye."

"Bananas" was a bit more difficult, but he had the idea now. Within an hour or so, I had proved to all of us that Pete could indeed be taught to read. Striker had laid excellent groundwork. Pete could recognize the letters, whether his mind saw them as forward or backward. As long as he read them one at a time and then strung the sounds together in his head like the notes of a melody, he could puzzle out simple sentences. That in itself proved his intelligence, in that he had to expend far more intellectual effort than an average man in order to achieve the same result. He was pleased when I explained it to him in that way. I did not think he would ever read quickly, as he could not recognize whole words. But he could look at something written and make sense of it after a time in this fashion.

And so I went about offering daily lessons to a good twenty men in the afternoons and worked with Pete alone in the evenings. Another week passed.

I was at ease with my life. I was in the best health I could remember, amongst the best friends I could recall having. And there was always Gaston. With the exception of one aspect of our relationship, he was a constant font of contentment and satisfaction. I endeavored to not allow my needs to sully my state of mind. I assured myself that things were progressing, handsomely, when one considered the many factors involved.

Now that he was more receptive to my touch, and willing to initiate contact with my person, my only frustration with my matelot came at night, as I had feared. In truth I should not say my only frustration, as I was occasionally at full sail with nowhere to go in the middle of the day. But it was at night, when the darkness provided the illusion of privacy among so many men, and we lay side by side, that I felt it most acutely. It was more difficult when we could hear Pete and Striker in their amorous glory, and worse yet when we had to fend off their rolling about in the throes of passion.

Since the Cayman island, Gaston had not seemed prone to discuss the subject of our intimacy. When I was sure he was asleep, I would ease myself and feel guilty for it afterwards: a thing I put much thought in after our discussion of sin. I had initially wondered why I felt guilt, if I was so sure masturbation was not a sin. Then I realized I felt guilt because I was sinning against myself: I was not ashamed of what I was doing, but I was allowing myself to think I should be. It troubled me. I was doing something wrong to no other person than myself. This would not be the first time.

I heard the devious laughter seeping from my memories, taunting me that I had walked this path before. My waking mind did not truly think so, as there were a great many differences between what had transpired between Shane and me and what was transpiring now. Gaston did not engage in the hypocrisy of desiring me and then despising us both for it, as Shane had done. Gaston did not want me.

He did not seem to want anyone, not even himself. Despite the physical intimacy that life upon the sloop demanded, I had not once caught him easing himself in any fashion. I clearly recalled his admission that he was seldom moved, but it truly seemed impossible that any man would not be moved at all. I did not dare broach the subject with him.

I knew our wolves were aware we did not engage in carnal acts. How could they not know? Pete's face often contorted with unspoken words when Gaston left my side after politely rebuffing this or that advance I had made, or when I escaped my matelot to spill my seed over the side yet again. Pete apparently always talked himself out of offering whatever counsel he wished to give, because he never said anything. I did not make inquiry and force the matter, because I did not want to admit to him, or anyone else, that I might have been in need of advice upon the matter. It was between Gaston and me; and despite, or perhaps especially because, we were forced to sleep side by side with other men, I wanted it to remain a private matter.

One night as we sailed north yet again, the entire ship was in fine spirits. The musicians were particularly inspired, and rounds of dancing rattled the planks. Pete and Striker had been trying with limited success to teach me to dance a jig. I was sure that with the addition of a little liquor, I could manage it handily. Sober as I was,

I felt stiff and awkward, but I pressed on gamely. Gaston would have none of the endeavor, except to watch with great amusement. As I could not envision someone of his mien and reserve dancing, I did not even attempt to cajole him into participating.

When I was tired of it, I left the wolves to dancing with one another and joined Gaston where he sat on the cannon by our alcove. He welcomed me into his embrace. Flushed and happy, I was overcome with the urge to kiss him, so I did. It was a light and chaste press of my lips to his. From his reaction, an observer might have thought I bit him. He became very still and his hands were on my chest, holding me off. His eyes held a warning look I knew all too well.

The apology immediately sprang to my lips. I always did things I had to apologize for. Anger surged from somewhere deep in my soul. I did not know the reproving look in Gaston's eyes from him; I knew it a thousand times over from Alonso and Shane. I was so damn tired of apologizing.

I began to pull away, only to have Gaston grip my tunic. "Do not."

"Obviously," I hissed. The anger must have reached my eyes, because he recoiled ever so slightly.

"Will, calm yourself. People are watching."

"You care far too much about what others think, when you should be worried about my thoughts at the moment."

I expected anger, but his eyes only held betrayal. It doused my rage. I embraced him as hard as I could manage, as if somehow, in one physical gesture, I could crack him out of his shell. He did not fight me. He returned it. And so we held one another with bruising intensity for a time, while I silently swore at myself.

I experienced the feel of his lips on my neck with more wonder than titillation. Then his fingers slid under my tunic and caressed the soft skin of my sides and belly. It tickled. I bore it because I did not dare stop him. His face was pressed into my shoulder, so I kissed his temple. I longed to pull his head back and cover his mouth, but instinct told me I had pushed my luck as far as it would go tonight, and he needed to lead us wherever we would wander now. So I mirrored his touch back upon him, and let him explore as he would.

I was jostled from behind by some of the dancers, and we started. His eyes flashed anger over my shoulder at the others. With a chuckle, I steered us into the corner of our alcove. We stood together, and the flirtatious petting continued. I was on fire, and several times I watched the dancing and held him at bay. This, of course, only spurred him on. He was teasing and coy and grinning as he drove me to distraction. I was amazed at his change of spirit on the matter, and resolved to enjoy it while it lasted.

As the music ended and the lamps were extinguished, couples broke away or groups of men sat about and talked. Our wolves did not join us immediately, and we sank to the floor in the shadows and some degree of privacy. Gaston's fingers played along the tender flesh between my navel and the top of my breeches. He slid his leg farther up mine, so that it almost brushed my turgid member. He worried my shoulder with small nibbles. He batted my hand away when I tried to touch him. It reminded me of many an experienced lady I had dallied with, and I felt taunted to the point of reprisal. I had passed beyond mere arousal and aching need and into the realm of desperate craving.

With an amused growl of hunger and frustration, I decided I had had enough and swiftly rolled atop him, so my leg was between his thighs and my chest upon his shoulder. I intended to kiss him. I stopped short at a small pain in my ribs. I looked down and saw the glint of steel in the moonlight. He was still and his eyes hard. With a long, slow breath I pushed myself up and off him and moved to sit at the end of the alcove. He quickly sat and pressed himself in the corner. He embedded the knife in the gunwale.

I was gripped with a red-hot fury like I had experienced few times in my life. I could not see him for the blood haze in my eyes. I sat very still, thinking that if I moved, I would spring upon him and strangle him. When I could trust myself to look at him, I found him glaring at me. His eyes glittered dangerously in the lamplight. Snarling, I stood and walked away. I did not know where I would go, as there was nowhere to go on the ship; but the quarterdeck stairs were before me, and I mounted them and made my way to the stern rail, where I stood and gulped air until the blood stopped pounding in my ears. My eyes focused on the moonlit waves in our wake, until they took on a mesmerizing quality and my breathing became normal again. Then I did not wish to think of what had occurred.

"I take it the honeymoon is over," a voice beside me said quietly in English. I looked round with surprise, and found the Bard standing nearby, with his back to the rail and a pipe in his hands, which he was cleaning intently. I glanced further around. Men were spread all about, but were sleeping or talking quietly. We were relatively alone, though I could have touched three men if I bothered to stretch out my leg.

When I did not speak he continued, his voice pitched for my ears alone. "Everybody ends up back here some night. I've been figuring one of you would, sooner or later. You two have been too damn happy, chattering away in French for hours and making doe eyes at each other."

I had not thought how others saw us; and I sighed, "Go to the devil," with far less rancor than I usually would have delivered the words. I did not want it to be about what the others saw. And in the end, it had not been.

He chuckled. "I'm just poking fun at you, which is of course why you'll get riled. Funny how that works." He looked up from his pipe to grin.

"I am already riled, you are just adding fuel to a blaze," I said with some humor, as I was not angry at him. His presence was actually a relief.

"Your first fight is good."

I gave him an incredulous look and wanted to scream that this was not a fight: the man I thought I loved had just pulled a knife on me. That was not an argument. That was an act of betrayal.

Instead I said, "And why is that?"

"If you can't fight, it won't last."

"Is this why they call you the Bard, because you stand about on your stage and dispense wisdom on love and life?"

He frowned at me. "I never thought of that." He cocked his head. "Nay, I don't think so. Our old surgeon started calling me that after we met, never explained why. We were introduced and he said, "Oh, so you're the bard", and that was that and it stuck."

"What is your name?"

"Francis Bacon."

I chuckled in spite of my dark spirit. "I think I have your explanation. Some believe that William Shakespeare was not intelligent or deft enough to write all that he is credited with; and they say that an associate of his was the actual author, a man named Francis Bacon."

The Bard chuckled. "That explains it, then. Our last surgeon was a man of letters."

As Cleghorn was nearby, I did not ask if this man was well-schooled in his profession as well. "What became of him?"

"He had a condition of the heart that he knew would kill him one day, and sure enough it did."

"That is a sad thing."

"I do not know that. He was a jolly fellow, as he was not sure if the next day would be his last; and therefore he lived as if it was, and enjoyed himself." He lit his pipe and took a pull. "It changed the way I regarded my own days."

"In a way, are we all not unsure if tomorrow will be our last?"

He nodded. "Aye." He grinned at me as if that were the entire point.

I sighed. "What makes you the master of romance?"

"I know nothing of romance; I know a great deal of matelots."

"So why do you not have one?"

This earned me an even wider grin. "Because I know a great deal about matelots."

He shrugged. "I had a partner once. He's dead now. Haven't found anyone since. I just watch everyone out on that stage, from up here, and I have plenty of time to think and to see who lasts and who doesn't over the years."

"And being angry enough to want to kill him is a good thing?" I asked with no small amount of exasperation.

"Aye. If you didn't love him as much, it wouldn't make you as angry, now would it?"

He was correct. As I was calmer now, I could see that. Alonso was the only relationship of any duration I had experienced . We had not fought. If angry, we simply avoided one another until it passed. We had not experienced the bloom of romantic love, either. We had been partners in business and living arrangements for months prior to his decision to seduce me and my decision to let him. I had thought we had love. As I now knew all too well, it paled in comparison to what I felt for my red-headed demon.

"Hmmm," the Bard muttered and moved farther away from me at the rail. I regarded him curiously, and he flicked his gaze up and behind me. I turned and spied Gaston watching us from the alcove. I could not read his expression at distance in the moonlight, but his stance was stiff.

There was nowhere to go on a ship. We would have to talk. I beckoned for him to join me. He turned and sat. This rekindled my anger.

"May I sleep up here tonight?"

The Bard was chuckling quietly. "Sure."

He shrugged and returned to his bed in the fore starboard of the quarterdeck, which happened to be right above my own sleeping place in the alcove. I was thankful he did not appear to speak French.

I sat where I had stood and watched the waves. I vowed that I would not apologize. I had done nothing wrong. I would not appease him. I had some pride.

I had been dozing, finally, when I felt another's presence. I looked up to see Gaston. He squatted in front of me. The dim lamp light was on me and not him. I could not read his face. I felt he was searching mine, though. He reached toward me, his movement tentative. It was curious. My sleep-addled mind was not alarmed, yet I was bothered. If I had not known it was he, I would not have thought it was; and I could not discern exactly why. It had something to do with the gentle and exploratory touch of his fingertips on my lips. I frowned at the shadowed face that was now inches from my own.

Someone moved nearby, and he started and crouched: more like an animal than a man. His face had turned into the light. He appeared to be afraid; but it was a child's fear, not a man's. I was baffled.

"Gaston?"

He looked to me again, and then closed the gap between us, diving into my arms to wrap his own around my chest. His breathing was fast and ragged. I embraced him, and he calmed slowly. It seemed as if I were sheltering a child.

Then, finally, it came to me. He was mad. He was having one of his bouts. This was just another face of it.

I cast a net through my recollections and strained the night's events, trying to ascertain when he had stopped being himself. It must have been when I held him so tightly after I snapped at him. He had been the Gaston I knew up until that moment. And then, during the embrace, there had been that first little kiss upon my neck, and then the questing fingers had begun.

I was such a damn fool.

The predawn light found us still locked in one another's embrace. I woke before him, which was rare. I wondered if he would be himself when his eyes did open. I looked about; men were beginning to stir. If we wished to avoid days of questioning looks, it was time to move back to our alcove. I clasped his shoulder and shook him gently.

He was disoriented, but it was Gaston who looked about with confusion, and not some other part of himself. He frowned, and I knew he was trying to remember. Then he regarded me with suspicion quickly followed by guilt.

"Now, now," I soothed and rubbed his back. "Let us return to our little hole, and then we will talk. I will tell you everything I remember, and what I fool I am, in that I did not know until the end that you were not yourself. And I apologize for that, most sincerely."

"You need tell me nothing. I remember." He frowned and his hand went to the knife at his belt, the one he had pulled on me. "Are you well?"

He looked me over quickly, stopping at the small hole in my tunic and the even smaller prick-point on my skin.

"I could have killed you," he breathed.

"Yet you did not." I thought of the danger in his eyes after he had pulled the knife. I had been too rage-blind to understand. He could have easily killed me, but even in that state he had chosen not to.

"I have not behaved in that manner before," he whispered. "Never." His eyes were imploring.

I guessed his meaning, but I asked anyway. "Flirtatiously?"

He nodded. He was studying me intently. His hand darted out and caressed my cheek. It was as quickly gone, and his gaze was tinged with guilt as it dropped from mine.

"Come now," I whispered. "Let us go and talk. I do not want to be here when the others wake."

He nodded again and we found the lee of the ship and relieved ourselves. Without us in their way, Pete and Striker had sprawled across the entirety of the alcove. I prodded both of them gently until they rolled on top of each other with sleepy curses. Then I pulled Gaston down to lie with me. We cuddled together, our noses touching.

"My memory is broken," he sighed, "like that of a dream. Please tell me what you saw."

I whispered the entire chain of events as best I could recall them. He closed his eyes and occasionally swore to himself. I rubbed his back and kissed his nose.

He was silent for a long time after I finished. We lay there and listened to the ship waking about us. Over Gaston's shoulder, I saw Pete smile when he saw us together. I was sure that they had all thought, as the Bard had, that we had quarreled. None would know the truth, as I had almost been blind to it myself. None could know the truth. In the future, I would have to do so much better by him.

"It is like a horse," Gaston whispered. He smiled weakly when I looked to him again. "I know you are an excellent horseman, yet..."

"You know no such thing," I grinned. "You have never seen me ride."

"I have heard you speak of the animals, and I see how you apply yourself to things you enjoy. You are an excellent horseman, whereas I am not."

"Thank you, but..."

His fingers found my lips. "I am not fond of them and have little experience with them. I am making an allegory. Be quiet."

I chuckled and nodded.

"My thoughts... emotions, my mind, is like a big unruly horse which I ride. Most of the time," he stressed this and I nodded. "I have the reins well in hand and go where I wish. But there are times when it is a skittish creature; and it takes the bit in its teeth and runs where it will – and all I can do is hold on. And there are times when I am so tired... of always having to tell it where to go... that I wish to simply drop the reins and let it wander about. But that can be dangerous, for without me there to guide it, the animal becomes more and more prone to starting at nothing and running wild. I am not sure, Will, but I believe I tried to hand the reins to you last night for a time. You were so very angry at me. I wanted to make you happy, and I could not do it as I was."

I was stunned, and then deeply touched. I pulled him tighter. "Gaston, I do not want you to be other than what you are, despite how selfishly I may behave. I will do better next time, I swear it. I am sorry I was such a fool in so many ways. You said a thing which... was something I have heard before. The irony was that you meant the opposite of how it had been wielded against me in the past. But it mattered little to my heart. All my heart saw was that it was being wielded against me at all. And I do not wish to live in fear of that particular blade any longer. At every step of my life, I have been told that my desires are wrong. It cuts worse when it comes from those I desire and... who I have reason to believe desire me. Though throwing you in with the others is not truly fair, as I do not think you desire me, nor do I think you wish to censure me for desiring you."

"Non," he assured me. "I am flattered. And as for I not desiring you... Will, I do not know. As I have said, I am not motivated by desire, though apparently I did desire you last night in some fashion. Or rather my horse did." He frowned. "I sometimes wonder if our beings are like Plato's cave. Am I the true thing in the sun, and the face I show the world while mad merely the shadow on the wall?"

The idea was intriguing and I puzzled on it. "Perhaps we all are. If it is the case, I would very much like to slip my bonds and turn about in my chair, so that I could see you in the light."

"I do not think I am a pretty thing in the light."

"I do not feel that I am either. If I envision my soul, it is a misshapen thing."

"I want to see it. I do not believe that an ugly thing could cast so fine a shadow."

My eyes were moist and my heart somewhere in my throat. "You are making me ache again."

"Do you wish to kill something?" he grinned.

"Non, the other one."

Later, after a pleasant morning thinking on his words, I told him, "You know, you cannot fall from that horse of yours."

"And why is that?"

"You are a centaur. It is part of you."

He smiled. "I will attempt to remember that the next time it bolts."

"And perhaps," I added. "We can endeavor to convince your horse body to stay with mine, and instead of there being reins to be passed about or dropped, we could simply hold hands and thus relieve your skittishness."

He took my hand, and his face softened as he watched the waves with a hopeful smile. In his demeanor, I recognized a little of the child that had crawled into my arms this morning. I decided the shadows he cast when he was mad were just different facets of him, shown in a very harsh light.

Two days later, we sighted prey. She was a flute, a three-masted Dutch cargo vessel. This one was flying a Spanish flag, sitting heavy in the water, and sailing for Cuba as fast as she could manage in a reaching wind, which is to say she was beating a course that crossed our own. When she spotted us, she turned and ran downwind. The Bard seemed to think this was amusing. As I saw how quickly we gained on her, I understood his reasoning.

After a month of boredom, the excitement was intoxicating. The buccaneers ringed the deck, whooping and shouting imprecations, knowing their howling was carried with the wind to the fleeing vessel. They were a pack of wolves, or rather a single entity, a shark, closing in for the kill.

I stood well out of the way in our alcove, and watched it all with wonder. I had girded myself for battle in both spirit and the flesh dozens of times, but never with so many others. I found Gaston regarding me with amusement.

"We will be some of the first on board." With his broken voice, he had to strain to be heard over the mob.

I nodded. After years of working with Alonso, I fully expected my matelot to proceed to reiterate everything he had ever told me about boarding. Gaston said nothing. He was an island of silent repose in the sea of battle-lust about us, readying weapons. I embraced him. He returned it without comment.

Striker and Pete joined us, and we made room for them to prepare themselves.

As boarders, we would not carry muskets, so we left them wrapped along the wall. We would, however, need every other weapon we had. I loaded all four of my pistols and festooned them about my baldric and belt, along with a cutlass, rapier and four dirks. I offered Pete my extra rapier, but he said he would have to think too much about it, and it was best to go with what he knew. In addition to pistols and cutlasses, he carried axes. I pitied the Spaniard who faced him.

Once I was prepared, I checked the position of our quarry. She was much closer than before, but there was still a little time. Some of the howling had died down as Bradley moved about organizing everyone. Striker paused before going to join him, and addressed me.

"Do not kill anyone with earrings," he said as if it were some profundity.

"UnlessTheyBeASpaniard," Pete added. "OrAManYaHate."

"As always in battle, it is good to be loved, if not by the Gods, then by your fellow man," I said. They laughed and left us alone for a moment.

Gaston was reapplying his mask. He studied my face, and then offered a gob of paint. I grinned and let him apply it. The substance felt odd around my eyes, but he seemed pleased with the result.

We joined the other boarders crouching amidship behind the mast. Pete and Striker were cats ready to pounce. They exuded fire and danger, and the looks between them were full of challenge, as if this were some game that could be won. Then they kissed as if it were their last.

I glanced at Gaston and saw that he had been watching them too. He took my hand and squeezed. I kissed his cheek. To my amazement, he grabbed my head and kissed my lips. The moment was shattered by gunfire.

As we had closed in from behind, the flute had tried to turn and bring her few cannon to bear. Liam and the musketeers were now shooting the Spanish gunners, while the Bard masterfully got us behind her again. All the while we were dropping sail so we did not ram her.

In the final yards, the musketeers volleyed back while we boarders, twenty of us in all, worked our way up the middle of the sloop to the bow. Men well-used to the task grappled us to the flute's stern, while the muskets kept the Spaniards at bay. Our carpenter and another man drove a wedge behind the flute's rudder. She was now helpless in the water, with the *North Wind* a giant leech on her arse.

To my left, Cudro led his men up a rope to the stern castle. Gaston and I followed Striker and Pete up an axe ladder they had laid into the flute's flank. I was initially concerned about this method of boarding, but the battle lust was upon me; and when it was time, I cared not that I was clambering up the back of axe heads with a knife in my teeth and a pistol in each hand.

As we were the first aboard, the field was still clear, and the enemy was obligingly *over there* as opposed to being *over here*. I heard a shot whiz by my head, as I fired both pistols and saw the shots strike true. I dropped the guns and pulled my second set.

Cudro's men were attacking the quarterdeck from above, while we attacked below. Some of the Spaniards ran for the bow. Gaston gave chase, staying well wide of the oil and broken glass the flute's crew had spread about. I began to follow; but then Pete crashed into me, sending us both sprawling over one of the cannon. I saw what he had been diving away from: an officer with a rapier. Pete now knew very well not to fence with a cutlass.

There were too many earrings around to get a clean shot. I tossed Pete my pistols, even as I glanced about for Gaston. My matelot was way up the ship. I yelled at Pete to help him, but Pete had rolled away and was gone. Julio and Davey heard me, and I was relieved to see them sprinting to follow Gaston as I drew my sword and stood.

The officer regarded me with a desperate arrogance that is unique to wolves. He would die: he knew it. His only goal was to take as many of us with him as he could. I did not expect the exchange to last long. I was correct. He rushed me with a lack of caution. As I had much to lose, I retreated before him, only too late feeling the pain in my feet and understanding what it meant. He grinned as I slid on glass and oil. Unfortunately for him, pain does not deter my ability to fight. It merely makes me angry.

I pressed the attack and dove past his defenses, which were competent but not gifted. I ran him through and pulled my blade free. I was looking about for another target before he slumped. There were none; the damn ship had not been military, and had not carried much beyond her sailors.

I spied Bradley, and he crossed to me to snap, "Get your loose cannon!"

I regarded him with incomprehension, until he pointed toward the forecastle. I turned. Gaston was hacking away at something. Despite the pain in my feet, I ran.

When I reached him, his eyes were filled with the glittering danger they had held when he pulled the knife on me. He was breathing heavily. There were dead bodies at his feet. I did not know what to say.

"He's mad!" Davey howled. He was hanging from the rigging, presumably in order to stay as far from Gaston as possible. Julio stood nearby, a look of horror on his handsome face.

"He just hacked them up," Davey continued. "There were three of them. One of the heads went overboard."

"You are not helping," I told him. Gaston was not looking at us. "Gaston!"

He regarded me with annoyance.

"What happened?" I asked.

"He had a whip," he snarled.

I looked at the pile of bodies. There was indeed a severed arm with a cat in its hand. I thought of the force necessary to sever limbs even with a cutlass, not to mention heads.

"You are bleeding," Gaston said.

I looked back to him. He was no longer angry. He appeared

concerned. I looked down at my feet. The world spun. I truly have no stomach for the sight of my own blood. There was a good amount of it.

A minute later, I found myself sitting with Gaston's back pressed to my chest, and my right leg curled up and around him so that my foot was in his lap.

"This will hurt," he said. "Bite something."

I decided he would not appreciate my teeth in his neck, so I bit his baldric where it passed over his shoulder. He pulled a sliver of glass free. It hurt so that my bowels clenched and I left teeth marks in the leather. It did not stop there. Shortly I was not sure which was worse: his probing about to find more glass, or the pain that occurred when he located a piece.

Pete arrived in the midst of this and returned all of my pistols to me, and the ones Gaston had dropped to him. He watched for a time.

"ToldYaBoutTheGlass, Didn'tHe?"

"Aye," I hissed.

Gaston glared at him. He had indeed lectured me about the trick of spreading glass on a deck, and a number of other things the Spanish did to try and keep us at bay.

Pete looked about and spied Gaston's earlier handiwork. "Argh. IWill NotDigInThatMessForGold. AMan'sInnards. TheyBurn."

"We will see to it," I hissed.

"Nay. WhenYaCanMove, CaptinNeedsYa." He jerked his thumb down the ship. Things were calm. There were several prisoners tied to the main mast. Cleghorn was treating other injured buccaneers.

"For what?" I asked.

"Interogatin. YaSpeakSpaniard."

"So do I," Julio said from nearby.

I sighed and nodded happily. I do not mind torturing men on occasion, when it is warranted; but, perversely, not while I am in pain.

Julio and Davey followed Pete to the prisoners.

Gaston had continued probing. He stopped. "I think I have it all. Some of the wounds will need stitching."

I swore vehemently. All was quiet for a moment, and I listened to a man protesting in Castilian that there was nothing of value on the ship to us other than what was in the hold. I wondered what she was carrying. I was staring at the pile of dead bodies.

"What occurred?" I asked.

Gaston sighed. "I cornered those three. They were without pistols. I looked back for you and saw you engaging with a sword." He smiled ruefully.

"Imagine my surprise," I chuckled. "I was trying to follow you when Pete ran into me."

His fingers found my lips again. "You do not need to explain. It is battle. Situations occur that we cannot foresee."

"Still, I will endeavor to stay closer to you next time." I gestured to the pile of bodies.

"I had thought I was doing well," he said somberly.

"You seemed calm before," I said.

"Non, non, not with my madness, with… you. I have rarely cared these past years if the men about me lived or died. And now I have you to worry about. I told myself that I would not be a fool and hang on you, worried that you might be harmed. Yet you engage in battle and I watch like a daft cow, all the while telling myself that you are competent. That if I have chosen to feel this way for another, at least I have chosen a man who is competent."

I tightened my embrace around his chest and kissed his cheek. "Thank you, though I feel I do not deserve such praise. After all, I was pushed into glass like a boy with a toy sword." I chuckled. "Because I did not feel as brave, or foolhardy, as I usually do. I feared injury and death, as I feel I have much to lose. I wanted to get to you as quickly as possible, because I feared losing you."

He smiled. "Then we are both fools and we should quit this profession."

"Perhaps we should." I found myself gazing at the bodies again. "So you were watching me and…"

"Then the fool hits me with a whip and I killed him… and his companions."

"We would have killed them anyway." As if to punctuate my words, one of the prisoners wailed with pain.

"Oui," he sighed.

"Do you think they have any valuables on them?"

"I sincerely doubt it. I will check." He pulled his cutlass and first pushed the arm with the whip overboard. Then he probed through pockets and pronounced them poor. He tossed the rest overboard for the sharks. He helped me work my way down-ship, and we joined the others.

The one man was still wailing, "We have nothing of value to you."

I sat on a cannon next to Pete. "What is the ship carrying?"

"DyewoodAn'Hides."

Bradley and Striker seemed intent on questioning the prisoners. Matches had been lit between the protesting man's toes. As my feet ached, I could not watch.

"Is that odd?" I asked. "The cargo?"

Gaston shook his head. "For a ship in the Flota. This one was crossing to Cuba early, alone. True, it could have come up from Campeche with this cargo, but she is very far north."

I regarded the crying prisoner curiously.

"There is nothing of value to you," he whined yet again.

"To us," I said loudly in Castilian. "What is there of value on this ship to others?"

The man's eyes shot wide with surprise, and he became very still. Julio translated what I said very quietly for Striker, who turned to give me a triumphant smile.

"What?" Pete asked. I explained. Pete grinned. "ThoughtTheyWas WastinʼTime. ThoughtThereWasNothinʼHere." Pete crossed to the prisoner, and braced his arms on either side of the man. I could not see Peteʼs eyes or hear what he whispered, but whatever the man saw or heard caused him to lose control of his bladder. Amusingly, this put out the matches that had been burning his toes.

"Books," the man stuttered. "In the barrels."

Gaston and I exchanged a look. He understood enough Castilian to understand, and he hurried below to look. I wished to follow, but decided against it. He and two other men returned a few minutes later with armfuls of books. I snatched one from him and paged through it. It was some sort of religious treatise. Gaston was paging through another. He grinned and we exchanged books. This one was a romantic adventure and quite racy. Another in the pile was like it, only with etchings of a clearly salacious nature. I took up the religious one again, and read a paragraph; it seemed to be speaking out against something.

Everyone was watching us. I smiled.

"I believe they are smuggling books of a salacious nature and possible some heretical material as well." I was greeted with confused stares. "They are dirty books in Castilian," I said and passed about a particularly naughty drawing.

Our men were amused, but not pleased at all. The prisoner confirmed my theory, though. They were indeed carrying books printed in Terra Firma to Cuba, where they would be smuggled back to Spain. Other than amusement value for those of us who could read Castilian, they were worthless. To someone with access to Spanish markets, they were probably worth a fortune.

Mystery solved, I took up samples of each book, and with Gastonʼs help, made it back to the *North Wind*. I gave a naughty book to the Bard. He was amused. He also had an appreciation of the ironic value of the cargo.

Gaston handed me a bottle of wine from the Spanish ship and went to rummage through his bag. I took several pulls and found it quite admirable. He snatched it back from me. "Do not drink it all. I need it for your feet."

I sighed. And again when I saw him unwrap a small surgeonʼs kit.

"Lie on your belly," he said.

I did not wish to do that. The thought of lying on my belly with my back exposed while someone caused me pain made my heart race. He must have read it in my eyes, as his face softened and he said gently, "It is the best position for me to get access to the bottom of your feet. Where would you feel safe in that position?"

"Nowhere." I held up a hand to ward off discussion. I looked about and crawled onto the quarterdeck, and situated myself above our alcove facing the rails so I could see what was going on. He let me have another pull on the bottle. Then he gave me a leather wrapped stick to bite. I needed it.

While he worked, I tried to concentrate on what little I could hear of the roaring argument above us regarding the prize. There seemed to be some disagreement over what to do with the vessel. I finally turned to Gaston when he finished with my right foot, and spit the stick out.

"What is that about?"

He shrugged. "With a normal prize, the quartermaster sails her, along with part of the crew; and she will be used in concert with the first ship to take any additional prizes, and then sailed into port to be handed over to the English admiralty court. Then she will be auctioned off and the proceeds split with the Crown. But this one is not worth sailing in pursuit of anything; she will just slow us down. And she is not much of a prize. Her cargo, the dyewood and hides, are worth money...."

"But at a relatively low yield per ton," I said.

He nodded. "So I would guess that Striker does not want to sail her back to port. He would rather stay aboard to take bigger prizes. I would also guess Cudro is thinking the same."

"Ah, do the men who sail a prize into port forfeit anything captured after?"

"I do not know. That would be up to all to decide. I would say oui. They will not risk their hides with the rest of us. I also think it fair they split either the value of the cargo or the ship amongst themselves if they are to take her in alone. It is a gamble for someone, any way it is done."

"Who else is capable of sailing her to port?"

"I would imagine Hastings."

"So anyone who volunteered to be quartermaster."

He nodded. "I need to finish your other foot."

"Will this affect us?"

"I feel we should stay with Striker."

I nodded and bit the stick again. I was not sure how much use I would be in crewing a ship, if I was actually expected to do something involving sailing. I realized I should probably continue the education I began on the *King's Hope*.

I waited until he finished a stitch and removed the stick again to ask, "Can you navigate?"

"A little."

"Would that be comparable to the little you know of medicine?"

"Possibly," he grinned.

"And you call me competent," I teased and bit the stick again. I had indeed married well.

He finished with my other foot, and bandaged both of them. They ached. Gaston cleaned his tools with the remainder of the wine. He mentioned he would need to have Michaels boil the needles before he used them again.

For a moment I considered licking the last drops from the bottle.

"I would like some wine," I said. Gaston frowned and went to find some on the Spanish ship.

Most of the men were returning from the flute, some only to retrieve their belongings. There was a great deal of ill will in the air. In the strange post-battle anxiety I often experienced, I was concerned that the ship would cast off and Gaston and I would be stuck on different vessels. I knew it was absurd, but I found myself eyeing my musket where it was wrapped in the alcove. If I had it in hand, I could shoot anyone attempting to cut the ropes. Thankfully Gaston returned before I could crawl down to get it. He had rum and news.

"There will be a vote," he said. "Hastings will sail her to port. The vote is over the division of the prize."

I was relieved. I did not like Hastings, and sending him off with a load of wood seemed fitting. In the end, that is what we did. The vote was close; but it was even decided that he, and any who went with him, could retain the money for the cargo. The ship herself would be sold at auction; and that money would be shared amongst everyone who returned to Port Royal on the *North Wind* or any other prize she took. Ten men went with him, leaving us with fifty-five and considerably more deck space.

Bradley was concerned about the number of men remaining. He wished we had started with more. I could scarcely imagine how we could have crowded more on the sloop to begin with. And as it was my understanding that the *North Wind* could be sailed with six or so, that left a good fifty of us to take other vessels. After what I had witnessed today, it did not seem very hard.

That night there was a great party with the alcohol the Spanish had been carrying. I could not stand, let alone dance. So I sat with Gaston in our alcove and drank, while I looked at the dirty pictures in the one book and he watched the stars. When all finally quieted, I had been hard for hours, despite the pain in my feet.

Our wolves joined us, and we all bedded down. I waited patiently until they slept, lying as I often did, with my forehead against the wall, Gaston against my back, and my member firmly in hand. I felt him stir, and immediately stopped and waited to see if he was just rolling in his sleep. A perverse part of my soul wanted him to know what I was about, to see if it garnered any reaction. The rest of me was terrified that he should see or hear my dissipation.

I felt his hand in the center of my back. I held still, knowing him to know that I was awake. I withheld a sigh. His hand stroked tentatively.

"Will," he whispered, "am I helping or hindering?"

My relief was so great I would have found release then and there if my hand had been in motion. "I do not know yet."

"Is it a matter of touching?"

"At the moment, it is a matter of condemnation."

"Oh." He was silent a moment. "What can I do to show you I approve?" He moved closer, his body pressing along mine, his weight on my back. This position would normally have engendered fear, but at the moment, in the grips of arousal, it engendered quite the opposite.

"That will do," I gasped; and stroked a dozen times and came harder than I had in months.

    I slept better than I had in months, as well. I dreamed of the River Arno, running blood-red. But this time, it was because it ran red with blood, not because it reflected the setting sun. I wondered what the Gods were trying to tell me now.

Fifteen

Wherein We Descend Into Hell

Hastings sailed away with the prize, and the *North Wind* returned to working her way up and down the path the Flota would take to Havana. We were at it for the next two weeks, and it was very much like looking for a needle in a haystack. The prisoners we interrogated on the prize had not even known when the Flota would sail from Vera Cruz. The Spanish were very secretive about such matters. However, as it was the second week of May, and the Flota usually spent a month in Havana before sailing for Spain in June, we knew they should be en route now if they had not already slipped by us.

If we missed them going to Havana, we would be forced to wait a month until they departed, as we obviously could not attempt to take a ship in Havana's harbor. Tales were told of many a rover taking one just outside the forts' cannons, though. This seemed madness to me. Tales were also told of rovers missing a fleet they had waited weeks for, due to misjudging the time and careening or provisioning when the great ships passed. So we did not stop looking. Thankfully we had refreshed our water a few weeks before, and the boucan was holding up admirably. We had been reduced to rationing fruit, though.

It was decided that, if we did not spy the Flota in the next week, we would sail to Havana and take a look at their port to see if the fleet had slipped by us. If they had, we would find a place to provision along Cuba's northern shore or in the cays of the Bahamas, and then catch the Flota in the Straits of Florida. If that failed, we would be forced to make a decision between returning to Jamaica empty-handed or sailing back around Cuba to await the Galleons coming up from the Main. They usually arrived in Havana in July.

I had begun to understand why no one could tell how long a roving voyage would be. We were at the mercy of so many variables that it was impossible to extrapolate a duration, unless one set limits on it in some fashion. I personally, probably owing to coming from cooler climes, hoped that with or without further prey we would return home by winter. I was actually beginning to become a little obsessed with this idea. The dreams I had on the *King's Hope*, of sailing forever with sharks in our wake, had returned.

Of course, we did not need to return home by winter, as it would not become cold here. And the general mood of those about me was that we would not return poor. They had too many debts, and no money to keep them fed in Port Royal until the next cruise. This sloop was home for many of the buccaneers. They thought of no land as their own. They did not have houses they owned to return to. Here on the ship, they did not have to pay for any of the necessities of life with anything other than their share of the labor.

"How many months of the year do you spend on a ship?" I asked Gaston one afternoon.

He smiled and tousled my hair. "We should trim."

"That long?"

He chuckled. "Is this another thing that you have failed to think through?"

"Oui."

"Other than raiding ashore and careening, I have spent close to twenty-two of the last twenty-four months on a ship," he said.

"That long," I sighed.

I let him trim my hair back to stubble, for the second time since we had set sail a mere eight weeks before. I knew I had little to complain about. Yet the voyage to Jamaica, which was all I had to compare this with, had come to its end before eight weeks.

As he ran his fingers and a blade next to my scalp, I let myself think of how very much had changed in my life in a mere two months. I had a partner and lover. I was not alone. Despite my current restlessness, I was generally content. Other than the floor constantly moving, and being crammed together such that it was difficult to find a place to stand alone, and the monotony of our diet, and the lack of alcohol and horses, it was little different than any other place I had lived. I laughed to myself, though it was true. Even when I lived as I was accustomed – in large rooms with large beds, and ready wine, and horses to ride, and all of the other niceties of civilized life amongst the nobility – I had still spent most of any given day sitting about doing nothing or conversing with my associates. In that, life onboard the sloop truly did not differ from life in Florence, Paris, or Vienna.

And of course, such places had been devoid of Gaston. I lolled my head back onto his shoulder and kissed his jaw.

"Have I been complaining? If I have, I am sorry. There is no place that I would rather be than here with you."

"Liar," he whispered. "You would rather be someplace with more room and fewer people, with me."

"Oui, with a door that closed and a bed and tub and servants and..."

He laughed briefly and sobered. "I have forgotten how to live that way. Theodore's was very strange."

"Do you find it uncomfortable or merely odd?"

"I do not know. You will laugh, but I am no longer accustomed to living amongst men, if I ever have been."

Pete was napping almost atop my foot. I could see twelve men from where we sat. I laughed. "I do think I understand your meaning, though. You mean civilized men."

He smirked, "These are civil."

"Oui, they are all armed."

He shrugged. "I understand the order of things here."

"Will you spend time ashore with me as I have to?"

"Of course. There is no place I would rather be than with you." He kissed my forehead.

I closed my eyes, and reveled in lying across his lap and feeling the breeze on my scalp.

The night after we took the flute had definitely begun a new phase of our relationship. He was far more receptive to my touch, and he actively participated, though at a distance of sorts, in my obtaining pleasure. Sometimes he would press against me from behind as he had that first night; and other times I would lie upon my back, and he would lie beside me with his head on my shoulder and a leg across my thigh, as I took myself in hand. He never came in contact with my manhood, or allowed me to caress him in a carnal fashion. I was content in this for the time being, as simply having his tacit consent brought me happiness.

Two days after my second sheering, we raised sail on the Flota, as ships popped one by one above the horizon. There were twenty-seven in all: five galleons and twenty-two well-armed merchantmen. They formed a ragged line along our southern horizon, as they beat their way upwind with as much canvas crowded on their yards as they could carry. We were running before a reaching wind, toward them. The Bard and Bradley conferred, and we shot toward the middle of the line and through it; and the Bard did truly begin to sail circles around them, as we hung on the rails and had a good look at each in turn.

I was sure one of the men of war would turn and pursue us, but then I noted two things: the galleons were too fat and big to ever chase our sloop, and thus they posed no danger to us as long as we did not come in range of their guns; and, we were not the only rovers pursuing the fleet. There were three other buccaneer ships following along like sharks.

So we were unmolested as we observed which of the Flota's vessels sat low in the water, were well-armed, were lagging behind, seemed slow in making a tack, and anything else that might prove noteworthy and help us choose a target. To say they knew of our presence during this activity would have been an understatement. We could see the Spanish officers watching us while we watched them. They were hapless fat sheep trying to swim as fast as they could, while the sharks circled ever closer.

And they were fat ungainly things in the water, too. I now truly appreciated how sleek our sloop was in comparison. Not merely in terms of aesthetics, but also in relation to the function underlying her overall design. The Spanish ships were large and bloated from bow to stern, with towering fore- and aft-castles rising high above the water, as if small houses had been dropped at the front and back of her decks. The *North Wind* was designed to move swiftly on the water, and therefore she could not carry a large amount of cargo or guns; the galleons were designed for carrying weight, whether cargo or munitions. They were more floating buildings than craft designed to ride the winds. They could carry a great number of cannon, though; even the merchantmen had us outgunned several times over.

Despite the guns, their only hope lay in letting a few sacrificial lambs slow their pursuers while the rest beat their way to safety. In looking at the larger tapestry of the situation, it was a ridiculous notion. There is no true safety on the seas; they could be followed to Havana. But when one considered the speeds, where we sailed, and the exigencies of capturing a ship, it was obvious that if we rovers stopped to engage, it would be more difficult for us to catch the fleet again; and there was always the chance we would lose them until they were at harbor. Thus the ships at the front of the flotilla had the best chance of escaping: if we engaged there, we would become targets for the next ship in line. So it behooved us to pick prey from those in the rear.

However, the ships trailing the rest were the ones they viewed as the most likely to be lost. Since the Spanish would not choose to lose their most precious cargo, the ships lagging behind would not have it. So we did not want the easy pickings at the rear.

Of course, most of the gold was on the galleons, as those were floating fortresses of seven hundred or more tons, over fifty cannon, and at least five hundred men. They would be the real prizes; and yet they were out of reach, not by distance but by magnitude.

So we were tasked with picking the likeliest ship to have cargo we wanted, and waiting for it to become separated enough that we could pick it off without one of its fellows coming to its rescue. This was easier said than done, as all worthwhile things always are.

There were seven merchantmen loosely grouped in the lead, followed by a pair of galleons, including the general's; then seven more merchantmen, once again loosely bunched, one galleon, five more ships, two more galleons, and the remaining two ships – one of which was trailing badly. The whole fleet took up several miles from front to back and was spread out quite widely, as they were all beating upwind and even disciplined navies do not have ships that tack together. From the middle, we swept swiftly around the back with the wind and then worked our way forward, tacking across their paths, always out of range.

Our deck was a bedlam of men arguing about this or that possibility, all of them staying off the cannon and staying evenly distributed, as there were enough of us to unbalance the ship and the Bard had threatened to start shooting if men did not stay out of the way of the sailors and the yard. Bradley and Striker had been studying every ship as we passed, and Siegfried had been making notes for them. Gaston and I joined the group on the quarterdeck in crossing back and forth to regard our potential prey as we sailed among them.

As we gave the lone galleon a wide berth, I watched her with longing.

"Ah, to dream," I sighed in French.

Gaston rolled his eyes and snorted. When he spoke, he kept his already-quiet voice pitched for my ears alone. "It could be done. I doubt Bradley has the balls, but it is possible."

"You think so?"

"They are arrogant, and rightly so with one of those. They think we would never dare. But look how low she sits, and all of her lower gun ports are closed. She is carrying cargo below, a great deal of it, and no cannon. So she only has the upper deck to defend herself with. Look at the men on deck: most of them are not in uniform; they are passengers. There are so many people on her deck, the guns she does have are probably impeded. In a boarding, the passengers will impede everything."

Pete was standing with us. "What?"

"How would you take her?" Gaston asked him in English.

"ComeInNormal. SweepHerPoop. BlockHer. HangOnHerFlank."

It was what we had done with the flute, and was the standard buccaneer method of boarding a ship. I could have said the same.

Then Pete added, "Grenadoes. UseSlings."

This departed from the usual tactics, but I could see his plan. One could kill or drive below a good number of men by lobbing grenadoes onto her decks.

"ThenGoSlow."

Striker joined us, and I realized we had been overheard. "Get as many men on board as possible: not just boarders, but our musketeers as well. And then take her deck by deck until they surrender," he said. "Release the rudder once you have the staff, and steer her away from the others. The lead galleon won't come after if you've got this one's cannon. Even if you haven't taken the gun decks yet, they wouldn't dare."

Bradley was leaning on the rail, chuckling and shaking his head. "I'm getting old."

Striker sidled up to him and said seductively, "Look at her. Look how low she sits. She's just waiting to be liberated from those Spanish bastards. They'll be telling their grandchildren about us."

Our captain laughed harder. He looked over his shoulder at Siegfried and then the Bard. His matelot's eyes gleamed; but his master of sail appeared distraught. Not as much as he had concerning the swine, but not enthusiastic in the least.

"What does she have?" the Bard asked.

I wondered at this until my companions turned as one and studied the galleon's stern. Despite our somewhat oblique angle, it was evident she had four guns pointed behind her, or at least four gun ports.

"And he's got enough wind to turn her to get the angle."

"You'reGettin'OldToo," Pete said.

"Nay," the Bard said sarcastically. "Makes no difference to me. Same as any other ship from where I stand. I can get us on her and under her guns. Then I get to sit here. I don't have to fight soldiers on her decks. All I have to do is sail home with the survivors."

"We also have the two last galleons to deal with," Siegfried said, somewhat reluctantly: as if he were loathe to mention a sensible thing at the moment.

"Nay," Striker said and pointed. We could all see that a pair of rovers had taken the straggling ship. One of the galleons had already turned to drop back and give chase. "We will not have much time, but dusk is falling. There will be confusion. If we are lucky, they might not even notice until she leaves the Flota."

"They won't notice because of the storm," the Bard sighed. We all turned to see the great dark clouds cutting across the horizon. I had been so busy studying ships I had not noticed. The wind was becoming wilder.

"All right, then," Bradley sighed. "Let's put it to a vote."

He walked to the front of the quarterdeck and yelled for silence. Once he had it, he pointed at the galleon we had just passed. There was a simultaneous explosion of laughter and swearing. Once that died down, he outlined the plan of attack. There was less swearing, and many of the men started to grin. When he called for a vote, the ayes far outnumbered the nays. Gaston and I were among the majority.

Once it was decided, we moved quickly. The Bard began our turn, and we dashed to ready weapons and get into place. The four of us stood in the alcove, strapping on belts and baldrics and loading them with pistols and swords.

"I would like the two of you to stay with Pete and me," Striker said, quite somberly.

"Try and pry me off your arse," I said.

Pete laughed and slapped my back so hard I was sure he had marked me. Striker was amused. There was a predatory gleam in my matelot's eye. I compressed my lips into a smile that I had once been told was quite feral. With the experience of the flute behind me, I now knew what to expect, and I was ready.

Striker collected the rest of our usual cabal of eight; and Liam and Otter seemed somewhat surprised by this, as they normally never boarded. Striker explained that we needed them to provide covering fire for the six of us, as we would be boarding first on the stern. I was relieved we would have two of the best marksmen protecting us.

Gaston clasped my shoulder. His eyes were hard. "Stay with me."

"I will be right behind you," I said solemnly.

"How are your feet?"

They were still tender at times, but had healed admirably well; and Gaston had pulled the stitches a week before. I did not relish climbing a rope with them, but battle was not about comfort.

"I will not disappoint you."

"You could not."

"No matter what stupid thing I do? If I tripped and fell and shot you in the back?" I teased.

"Not even then."

It was awkward. We were so very close, yet so very far apart.

"Then you will not be disappointed when I do this," I said and kissed him firmly on the lips.

He smiled. "Non."

I wanted very much to do it again, as like sunsets, it was a thing to be savored before one giving one's life into the hands of the Fates. He led me to the rail before I could.

Striker had joined Bradley in going amongst the men, and ordering them into squads of between six and eight with one man as leader. All of these groups were composed of several boarders and a couple of musketeers to cover them. After an initial area had been secured, we would start bringing the musketeers aboard. The only ones who would hold back and not board were the few men the Bard needed. Even Michaels and Cleghorn were assigned to squads. Bradley, Cudro and Siegfried all led boarding parties.

By this time, we were running close to the wind at the galleon's stern. It was almost amusing. We were near enough for me to read her name, the *Santa Lucia*, before even one of her gun ports opened. A second followed shortly; but in all, it appeared that either they were lying in wait or they truly were not expecting us. The galleon tried to turn to give her guns better angle, but the Bard and the *North Wind* were too swift for her. Our master of sail kept us on a line with the starboard point of her stern, so that no matter which way she turned, we were still at a bad angle for her guns. Not that it seemed to matter in the end: as by the time she finally fired, we were already furling our sheets to slow down. She did not get a second set of shots off, as we were under her by then.

Our musketeers were in range by this time; and after the first volley, every Spaniard who had run to the poop rail to see us was dead or dying. We did not see any man exposed on the rear of the vessel after that. A moment later, we were under the huge, ornate tower of her stern; and I was eyeing angels carved above us, complete with wings and pipes.

We came in so fast that the men in the port bow had to use grapples on the galleon to bring us to a lurching stop. Ropes snapped taut as metal tore through carven cupids. Then another set of men threw more grapples ahead. The musketeers protected these, even as the *North Wind* shuddered and skewed to larboard under the *Santa Lucia's* stern. This was planned, as it allowed the men who would wedge her rudder to work. We grappled her stern again from amidship and allowed our sloop to be dragged along at an angle by the galleon, which had to be ten times our weight. Thankfully this was only a temporary measure, as the *North Wind* was complaining loudly with creaks and moans.

While the rudder was wedged, we six threw another set of grapples aloft: three ropes, two men apiece. My hands were sweaty as I grasped the knotted rope and followed Gaston up the escarpment of the heavenly host. My blood pounded in my ears; and calm descended over me, as it always did when my life was in danger.

Below us, they released the poor sloop from her unnatural bonds, and she straightened at the galleon's starboard flank. She was no longer below us. We clung for our lives over the sea. Soon, I hoped, I would hear grenadoes erupting somewhere ahead.

The Spanish gunners had dropped the gun ports when they knew we would board and there was nothing left that their cannon could do. The first men of our squad to reach them wedged them closed. Steady volleys from Liam, Otter, and Bradley's squad on the *North Wind's* quarterdeck kept the defenders from dislodging our grapples or throwing things on us from above. However, the gallery and captain's cabin windows were our own concern.

Gaston threw himself sideways and pressed into the woodwork, as a shot narrowly missed his head. Being immediately below him, I could see his attacker. Holding on with one hand, I fired and caught the man in the shoulder. Gaston fired left-handed a second later, and wounded another man I could not see but could only hear as he howled in pain. As the window was open, Gaston motioned me up. I flung the empty pistol into the opening above and climbed until I was next to him. I could now peer into the room, and I narrowly missed getting shot myself.

"Can you hold there and fire?" Gaston asked.

I took his meaning and nodded resolutely. I grasped the window frame with one hand and a pistol with the other and shifted my weight to my feet, which were braced precariously on angel heads. Once in position, I popped up and fired at the first thing I saw: a man who was preparing to fire toward the port side, where Pete was hanging in a position similar to Gaston. I hit. I threw that piece into the room and pulled my third pistol from my belt.

Gaston and Pete waited no longer, and scrambled through their respective windows. I popped up again as they rolled across the floor.

I shot another man in the doorway. Striker was right behind Pete, and I clambered in after Gaston. A whole herd of Spaniards tried to enter the room while I was getting off the floor, and Gaston and Pete emptied every pistol they had. I threw Gaston my last loaded one, and started frantically reloading the ones strewn about the floor. Davey and Julio joined us a minute later, and the room was cleared. We did not have time to be amazed that we had a foothold on the galleon. To my relief, I heard the explosions of grenadoes and a great deal of screaming.

Reloaded, and each with a cutlass in one hand and pistol in the other, we began to work our way forward. We shot anyone with a firearm, hacked anyone with a blade, and bludgeoned anyone unarmed, until we reached the door to the main deck. We had passed under the quarterdeck and the captain's cabin, and those would have to be dealt with next; but so far we had cleaned out the officers' and wealthy passengers' cabins and anyone pouring into the companionway from the gun deck below. As of yet, we were not sure if any other buccaneers were aboard. Needless to say, we viewed the door to the deck with a good deal of trepidation; but the steady explosions and the screaming were reassuring.

Pete threw the door open; and to our relief, we were not facing a mortar with grapeshot. Instead, we looked into one of Dante's rings of Hell. Parts of the deck were missing; and howling people, soldiers and civilians alike, ran to and fro, tripping one another and stumbling upon those on the ground. As we watched, another grenadoe landed and exploded, blowing more wood and bodies about. There was a pile of dead and wounded by the starboard rail, due presumably to our musketeers below. An officer stood amidst it all, shouting at whoever would listen.

"Watch above," Striker ordered and dove out onto the deck, rolling as he did to cover the quarterdeck above us. He had a target and fired almost immediately, as two rounds of shot narrowly missed him. The rest of us poured out and turned to fire, catching several of the ship's officers as they reached for their next weapons. A short fight ensued with the commanders; and when it was done, we had the quarterdeck and captain's cabin, and Striker was signaling the *North Wind* to send more men up.

Within the next five minutes, the Spaniards realized the grenadoes had stopped, and they became a bit more organized. Within ten minutes, we had lost three men and had six more wounded. Shortly after, the decks were awash with blood, and we had at least two hundred prisoners herded together on their knees in the waist of the ship. Down below, they unwedged the rudder; and Striker and the Bard steered the two ships in tandem out of the line and away from any pursuers.

We had captured a galleon.

At some point, I had beheaded a man with a cutlass; and in the immediate aftermath, I kept hearing his head hit the planks. I knew it would pass. Many years ago, I caught my sword on a brass jacket button as I ran a man through. The grating steel had sounded as if his very flesh had screamed. That sound had stayed with me for a while, but now I could not remember it exactly. The wet thumping sound would pass, too.

The main deck was a ruin; and as I watched, two men fell through a hole. Cleghorn and Michaels had commandeered the poop deck above us to care for our wounded. A pair of our men were checking the Spanish dead for valuables and then heaving them overboard. One of the Bard's men was at the whip staff. All seemed to be falling into some sort of order; and as we had done much, I did not feel the need to do more at the moment.

Gaston was sitting next to me on the quarterdeck, clenching and unclenching his right hand. I frowned at this, until I remembered about the numbness that sometimes afflicted it. I pulled the hand into my lap and massaged it.

The wounded captain lay a few feet away, watching us. He was at the center of a spreading pool of blood, and I could see his vital organs through a long rent in his side. I vaguely remembered being responsible for it when we rushed the quarterdeck.

His mouth worked in silence a few times; and then he gasped, "You English dogs are all insane," in Castilian.

"I am not English," Gaston replied in Castilian.

The dying man turned his eyes skyward and prayed, "I am sorry, God. I have only endeavored to serve you. Why have you turned from me? Please forgive me for my sins." It was very personal, and did not have the sound or pattern of traditional Catholic prayers.

As he whispered his life away, another of the Spanish wounded, a junior officer, rolled over and crawled toward him. This man was also in his last breaths, but he reached his captain and attempted to cradle him in his arms. The captain died. The young man looked at us with haunted eyes. All seemed quiet and still in our little corner of chaos.

"You never attack the galleons," the junior officer said, as if it would somehow refute the obvious. "He was a great man."

"For what?" I was compelled to ask. "For letting his ship get taken and his men slaughtered by a pack of English dogs?"

The young man recoiled in horror. "He was a man of honor. He was very religious, he had a wife and family, he had been a captain for many years."

"And this makes him a great man?" I asked.

A shot rang out, and the boy crumpled across the body of what I supposed was his mentor. I looked at the pistol in Gaston's hand.

"Let him die with his illusions," Gaston said softly.

I shrugged. "It has been said I would argue with the devil."

"Will, you would argue with God," he whispered.

There was no trace of humor about him, and I studied his profile in silence. He was very distant from me. Rigging popped overhead in the ever-stiffening wind, and he flinched. He gently drew his hand away, and pulled his knees up to wrap his arms around them. He was still staring at the two dead men in front of us. I was not sure whether I should leave him in peace, as I was not sure he was feeling peace. I was also not sure what I could do or say.

Davey joined us. He appeared exhausted and shaken. I looked around, and did not immediately see Julio.

"What is wrong?" I asked. "Where is Julio?"

He pointed aimlessly toward the ship's waist. "He's helping with the prisoners."

"Ah, and you? How are you feeling? You did very well."

"I suppose. I've been in battles before, in the Navy. And then the other ship. But it was nothing like this. I realized Julio needed me, and I could not deny him, or Pete, or all of you."

It reminded me of something Plato said. I did not remember the exact words, so I delivered my own thoughts on the matter as best I could. "If we fight alongside men we love, we do not fight for our lives or gold or glory or kings, but for each other. Death is less painful than watching a loved one die; and no fear is as great as being alone after the battle. And no man would appear as a coward in his lover's eyes."

"Is that why you fight so well?" Davey asked.

It was a compliment, and it surprised me. "In general or today?"

He shrugged.

"For most of my life, when I have entered into battle, it has been for lesser reasons, the most prevalent of which would be preserving my own life. Today," I glanced at Gaston, who was still very removed from us, and I thought of my actions and motivations and my pretty words of a minute ago. "I truly did fight for the men around me."

"So not for the gold?"

"Davey, if this ship is carrying barrels of rat dung I would still have fought as I did, for the challenge and because the men I care about wanted to come here. I truly do not do much for money."

"So you won't be needing a hundred extra then?" Bradley asked. He and Striker joined us on the quarterdeck.

"I would not say that. What would I be entitled to an extra share for?"

"Courage in boarding the ship. I intend to present it to vote when we share the booty. All six of you deserve a reward. Without you, we wouldn't be standing here now. You did fine. Both of you." He frowned at Gaston, who was still looking at the dead.

"He is a little withdrawn at the moment," I said quickly with a shrug. I did not wish Bradley angered at us, as his countenance in regards to me at the moment was once again as open and inviting as the day I met him. And, apparently, all I had to do to return to his good graces was prove I was a fool. "We thank you for your praise. So gentlemen, what will be sharing out?"

"Well, she's laden with cargo from the Orient. A great deal of silk, spices, and ivory," Striker said with an amicable shrug. "The whole lower deck is filled, along with the hold. She only has half her cannon, and we found barrels of spice in the magazine."

"Ah, so she is not full of gold then," I sighed.

Bradley and Striker looked at each other and shrugged.

"She's not full of gold, Will," Bradley said with a grin, "because if she was she'd sink." They started laughing.

"Gold's heavy," Striker added and tossed me a coin.

I caught the doubloon and smiled at their jest. "How much?"

"Two whole chests of it," Striker said. "The only organized buggers on the whole ship were guarding it. Cudro lost a man taking the hold."

Cudro and a couple others were standing behind them, looking pleased with themselves.

"All doubloons or pieces of eight?" I asked.

"Doubloons," Bradley and Striker said in unison.

"I think maybe a hundred or more coin per share, doubloons," Striker said.

"My God," I said as I made the calculations. "That would be what, four hundred pounds?"

"There are gems, too," Bradley added.

"We're rich," Davey said.

The men who had overheard were dancing around in circles and cheering. The Bard forced his way through them and joined us.

"What's everyone so damn happy about?" he snapped.

We all rewarded him with a questioning look, and Bradley tossed him a doubloon and said, "Over four hundred pounds apiece, you cantankerous bastard."

The Bard's anger fell away, and he whistled appreciatively as he examined the coin. Then he sighed, and the frown returned. "Well, we're going to be wealthy dead men, if we're not careful."

"The rest of the Flota has sailed on, and the other rovers will be lining up to cheer us, I imagine," Bradley said. "What are you worried about?"

"Where should I start?" he drawled. "That storm blowing in from the West, which is odd. The wind is restless and changing. The *North Wind* is seeping due to the strain she took. And this galleon is a piece of shit. The Spanish have no damn business sailing anything, let alone this vessel. She's badly designed, old, at least fifty years if she's a day, heavily laden, and I do not know what they were doing over the winter but maintaining this ship they were not. She's seeping." He looked at Striker. "I don't envy you having to sail her anywhere."

These revelations had sobered Striker and Bradley immensely. "Can we make Jamaica, or should we careen along Campeche?"

The Bard shrugged. "We can't careen a ship this large. So that is out. I don't think we'll see a blow like a hurricane: it's too early in the year. But even a small storm will not be pleasant. I'm sure the sloop can make it to port. This one, too, if she's lucky. We will not want to tackle the Strait until after the storm passes, though. I say we head south and get into the Bay of Campeche."

"Then let us do so," Bradley said.

"I would suggest one other thing," the Bard said. "Split the gold between the ships... in case..."

"Let's move it all," Striker said. "The sloop has a better chance."

"Nay, let's split it," Bradley said. "My real concern is where we can stop to share out the gold before sailing into port. I don't fancy the crown taking their share. They can have their ten of the cargo in the hold and the prize herself."

"Caymans," Striker suggested.

Bradley agreed to that with a nod.

"What will we do with the prisoners?" Cudro asked.

"I have questions for them," Bradley said. "Morgan asked that any prisoners be questioned as to what they know of the Spanish intent toward Jamaica. We will put any that are left alive ashore, as the opportunity presents itself. Any that cause trouble can be thrown overboard."

With that, he and the others left the vicinity. Striker paused before following.

"Is he...?" he asked, and gestured toward Gaston with a nod of this head. I looked: my matelot had not moved. I was not sure if he had blinked. I shrugged helplessly.

"Let me know if you need anything," Striker said and left us.

I understood his meaning. Gaston flinched when I touched his shoulder, but he did not turn to look at me. As I knew not what to do concerning him, I stood and prowled around the quarterdeck, checking bodies to insure that they were indeed dead and not wounded. Once satisfied in that regard, I leaned on the rail to observe the activity on the main deck.

The corpse detail were still stripping bodies and throwing them overboard. Behind me on the poop deck, one of our men wailed in pain as Cleghorn and Michaels worked on him. I considered asking if the surgeon needed any assistance, but thought better of it. He already had Michaels with him.

Four buccaneers were dead, and I recognized two of the names. We were now at fifty-one, with at least six wounded. We must have killed over a hundred Spaniards and wounded more, and it was unknown whether the rest would survive to return to their homes. Part of me was appalled. It was a small part; and in actuality I felt guilt at this, that it was so small.

I have harbored no regret over many of the men I have killed. I have been involved in numerous conflicts wherein I have colluded with other men to rob or murder for a variety of reasons. I have brought battle to an enemy and I have defended from the same. I cannot say I have always been the one making the decisions or choosing the tactics, yet I have only engaged in these activities with sufficiently small numbers of comrades so that I always exercised some control over my destiny. And

I have always maintained the option of walking away if I disagreed with the choices being made. Yet now here I was, involved in an army of sorts under the guise of adventuring. The only thing making the situation palatable was that I did feel I had a say in the matters at hand, and I still felt I could walk away if it suited me.

The corpse detail dropped a body on the way to the rail, and I was reminded of the sound the man's head had made again. It was always the little things that haunted one. I could see his face clearly, and I did not want to. I felt guilt and sighed. I could not speak for others, but I had sinned here today. I had not transgressed against God, or myself, or nature, but against my fellow man. What right did I have to kill a man who was trying to defend himself from my attack? What justification did I have for that attack? My mind wandered farther: was my largesse toward my fellow man truly an attempt to atone for all my sins? I remembered having these discussions with myself on occasion over the years. It had never resulted in my changing my ways.

I looked about, to shake off the feeling of malaise settling over me; and discovered I had larger and more immediate problems. Gaston had dragged the bodies of the captain and the young officer back to the stairs leading up to the poop deck, and was proceeding to arrange them in some fashion. I joined him as he was finishing his composition. He had draped the captain across the lap of the officer. There was something familiar in the pose. It took me a minute to recognize it.

"The *Pieta*?" I asked.

He stopped in the process of getting the officer's head to loll just so, and turned to look up at me with the wide eyes of a child who has been caught doing something wrong.

"You see?" he whispered desperately.

I recognized this aspect of my matelot now, and I wondered if the horse had bolted or if he had just dropped the reins. My bowels constricted with fear nonetheless.

"Oui. I do not understand, why the officer as the Virgin Mary and the captain as Jesus?"

"He," Gaston indicated the officer, "offered him up to God; and the other one was the martyr to prophecy."

I was wondering how I should deal with him, and too occupied to puzzle together what he was seeing metaphorically. I knew I had to keep him calm and talking, and I was afraid that any indication that I did not understand might anger him. However, I could not think of anything intelligent to say. Instead I knelt with him in front of the bodies. It was so very macabre, yet he was filled with wonder. He seemed happy to have me beside him gazing upon them. He took my hand.

"What in the name of God are you doing?" Cleghorn howled from the deck above us. For a moment, I wondered why it was acceptable to strip the bodies of gold and throw them overboard, but it was not acceptable to arrange them like a famous sculpture and stare at them reverently. Then I saw Gaston pulling a pistol. There was terror in his eyes. I leapt upon him.

"Gaston, look at me. Look at me." I had him on his back and I sat astride his thighs with our faces close together.

His eyes met mine, and hardened from childlike innocence to danger.

"I am not going away," he snarled. As of yet he was not fighting me, but I was not sure how long I had.

"Non. You are not going anywhere. You are staying with me. I will not leave you."

He softened and asked. "You promise?"

"I promise. Now put the pistol away."

He looked between us at the pistol pointed at my belly and fear suffused his face again.

"I did not mean to."

"I know. I know. I am not angry with you. Are you angry with me?" He shook his head and set the pistol beside us. Distantly I heard Cleghorn swearing. I did not need his interference, and I did not want to divert my attention from Gaston. I glanced about and saw the door to the captain's cabin mere feet away.

"Let us go in the cabin there? It will be quiet, and we can talk."

"Will, should I get a priest?" Michaels asked. "I think there's one left alive. Your matelot looks possessed."

I was stunned for a moment. Here I had thought he was a reasonable fellow. Gaston had seen the look on my face, and his eyes slowly narrowed. I felt as a mouse must while waiting for the cat to finally pounce.

"Nay, nay," Cleghorn said. "Go get Striker and Pete. Hurry now!"

"Non!" Gaston hissed and I felt every muscle beneath me go taut.

I threw myself flat atop him to whisper in his ear. "Gaston, listen to me. Everything will be fine. I will not leave you. I will not let anyone hurt you. You are just not yourself at the moment. You know that. I know you know that. Please."

I felt him move, and Cleghorn yelled, "Will, he's got a knife." I knew which side; and I shifted to pin his left arm. This was all Gaston needed to throw me off of him and roll to his feet. His eyes were dark with hate and a dangerous thing to behold. He still had the knife in his left and he was focused on me. He did not see Pete, who grabbed him from behind, pinning his arms to his sides. I dove in and wrested the blade from his hand.

Gaston was snarling at me in French, "You bastard. I know what you want. I know what you all want. You are only friends with me because you want to fuck me."

I recoiled in shock. If he had suddenly reached into my chest with a great clawed hand and torn my heart out, he could not have hurt me more. He saw it in my eyes and knew himself to have the advantage.

"It's true, isn't it? You're just like the rest, a damn sodomite who just wants to fuck. You cannot go a single night without begging for it."

I had heard it all before in another language.

I hit him. I hit him so hard his head turned sideways, and Pete was pushed back by the force of it. Gaston slumped in Pete's arms.

"GetHisFeet!"

I did as Pete instructed. Cleghorn had the captain's cabin door opened. We hauled Gaston inside and dumped him on the bunk. Pete handed me a coil of rope. "YouNeedHelp?"

"I can do it."

"GetHisWeaponsToo."

I nodded. Pete was still standing there. I did not want to look at him. I did not want to see anyone, because that meant that they knew, somehow. It was very important to me that no one had heard what he said. I did not want anyone to know, because they would never forgive him. I remembered that Pete did not speak French. He was safe.

I looked at Pete and nodded again. "I know what to do."

There was compassion in Pete's eyes. "It'sHard. He'sMad. NotYourFault."

I was close to weeping. I concentrated. "I know. Thank you. Could you leave us alone?"

"Aye. I'llSeeToYourThingsOnTheSloop. We'reStayingHere."

I nodded my understanding. "Thank you again for your help."

He clapped my shoulder in a reassuring fashion, and left. I was alone in a room full of demons. Most were in my head. As much as I wished to stand there and will myself into oblivion, the one on the bed and the world around me took precedence.

I stripped his weapons off, and bound him hand and foot. I was careful to coil the rope so that it didn't cut into his scarred wrists if he should wake and struggle. I checked his jaw: a bruise was already evident, but my blow had not split his lip or damaged his teeth. At least I had aimed well. My knuckles hurt.

While I was at this, Pete brought in all of our equipment and bags from the sloop, as well as the weapons we had left on the quarterdeck. He set them by the door. He suggested I search the room if I needed something to do. I thought this a fine idea.

In my mind I stood in an imaginary small room, and in the center was a vast cesspit and Gaston had kicked the lid off. If I concentrated on doing something, I could walk about the edges and not fall in. Unfortunately, the edges were crumbling; and the less I moved and the more I thought, the closer to swimming in the refuse of my past I became.

In the sea chest at the foot of the bunk, I found four bottles of wine. I consumed half of one before I finished searching. I found the man's journal and a small box of coin. I found several books and a Bible. His clothing was unremarkable. I had already seen his weaponry.

There was nothing left to do. I sat at the table and stared out the window. I finished the bottle. I went to the window. We were under way. I was high above the water. The gallery through which we had entered the ship was below me. I watched the waves and the shark fins. I did not want to see what they fed upon, any more than I wished to hear the screaming that occasionally came from the main deck or know of the man on the captain's bunk or feel the memories starting to emerge from the pit in my head. I watched the waves and opened the second bottle.

When Striker entered, I was quite drunk. I handed him the coin and the journal, and then hugged the remaining bottles of wine.

"I realize these are part of the booty and I should relinquish them to be shared but... I intend to drink them, so maim me if you must."

Striker pulled the one I was drinking away from me, and finished it in a long swallow. "You can have the rest. I don't need anyone else addled. We're sailing into a storm on a leaky ship."

"I am sorry we are so much trouble," I said because it seemed the proper thing to say.

He smiled sadly. "Two years ago, we sailed with Mansfield's fleet. Peirrot and another French ship joined us. We raided the Main along the coast near Campeche. We met Gaston then. In Granada, he went mad, and it took three men to put him on the ground, and he cut one of his own crewmates. Peirrot was the only thing that kept the rest of the crew from killing him. They trussed him up and dumped him in a shed. He alternately cursed or pleaded with someone to let him out for two days. Peirrot cared for him as best he could, but it as obvious he didn't trust him either. When it was over, Gaston was sullen and did not speak to anyone for weeks."

The tears welled anew. I had avoided them so far. I felt guilt. Somewhere deep inside, a rage began to grow.

"Will, you've assumed a commendable burden. You may be the only thing that separates that man from death, and you may even save him somehow. If you had not been with him, we never would have taken him on. He fights like ten men and he's smart, but many feel he's not worth the trouble if he can't be controlled. Bradley does not know what transpired as of yet, but Cleghorn will probably talk."

"So what are you saying? We should go elsewhere once we reach Port Royal?"

"I'm saying Bradley may request it. I want you to know that I will not. Hell, it's a bit premature, but with the money from this prize, we may buy our own ship. You would both be welcome there."

"Thank you," I whispered.

He clapped my shoulder as Pete had done, and stood. He paused and stared at Gaston.

"He's still out. You must have hit him pretty hard. I've never had to hit Pete. There have been times I've wanted to kill him, but I've never had to hit him."

I looked up at his blurry form, and managed not to laugh hysterically. I did not speak of the pistol in my belly or Shane's words coming out of his mouth or the hate in his eyes or the knife.

"I hope I will never have to do so again. For now, I will care for him as best I can," I said. I was not sure who I was telling this to.

Striker left. The remaining floor had crumbled and I was wading about in the offal. The wine had deadened the pain. It all seemed very far away.

I was not alone anymore. Alonso sat where Striker had. He watched with a sad shake of his head as I opened another bottle.

"What will you do? Drink yourself to oblivion?" he asked.

"Si, that is my intent. It calls and I must answer, because it is the only safe place."

"You have fallen in love with a madman. What are you trying to do? Make reparation for Joseph? Atone for your sins? Do you intend to bear him as a cross? Or is he a mirror you cannot turn away from?"

"He is my matelot. He was wounded and he still ails from it. I will care for him. I think he loves me more than you did."

Alonso was gone, and Shane was sneering at me. "Is that why he said those things? You like lies, Will. You like believing that people love you. No one does. No one ever has. You can't make them by being born their child or by fucking them or giving them money or teaching them to read or by marrying them." He snorted derisively. "Why lie, Will? You don't want love, not unless it comes hard and long and sprays you with jism. He said it; you're a damn sodomite who just wants to fuck. That's all you live for, and you'll do anything for that. You'll let anyone do anything to you for it. You did with me. You begged me for it. No matter what I did, you kept hoping I would change. You kept hoping I would love you. You even prayed. Not that God would ever answer you; you sold your soul to the devil of lust."

The wine bottle shattered on the wall behind him, and he vanished. I was in over my head and drowning. I staggered to the bunk and threw myself down next to Gaston. I wept.

I dreamed. The world was rolling and shaking. The furies howled and pounded at the door. Gaston was very angry at me. He kept yelling my name over and over again, yet I could barely hear him. He was standing over me with a knife. I told him I was sorry. I had stayed with him. I would stay with him even if he never loved me, because maybe I could save him and maybe that would make me a better person. He was not listening. I found myself chained to all of my weapons. I was in Hell and I was burdened with them forever, as they were the instruments of my sin. And I was chained to Gaston, as he was the other source of my sin. We staggered through a maelstrom filled with fear. Souls were sucked away into it. Pete and Striker struggled to raise a giant phallus off of a boat. The maelstrom helped them. Many people crawled into the boat. I did not, because I was chained to Gaston and Pete and Striker. We held onto the giant phallus. The ship disappeared, and there was only the phallus and we four lost souls and the instruments of our sin.

Then all was quiet, and I was on the river Styx. A shroud covered me, and my fingers dangled in the gently lapping water. I could hear rowing.

I woke to more of the same. I had to relieve myself. I thought that odd if I was dead. My head hurt. I also did not imagine there should be so much pain in death; and then I remembered I was going to Hell, so there probably was. Every day in Hell, you most certainly felt as if you had been drinking for days.

I carefully opened my eyes. I was on my side, wrapped around something hard, as if I hugged it. I was close to the water; my fingers and knees trailed in it. It was hot. I was covered by something that, when I slowly focused on it, appeared to be sailcloth. I sat up and held very still until the light stopped stabbing my eyes. When I was able, I looked about. I had to pull the piece of sail off to do so.

I was sitting on what must have been a mast. So were Gaston, Striker and Pete. They were similarly covered with sailcloth, presumably to keep off the sun. We were in open ocean, yet ahead there was land. They were all rowing with the butts of their muskets. The mast beneath me was festooned with bags holding our belongings and weapons.

I finally understood.

"Bloody Hell, it wasn't a dream!" I howled.

"Thanks for joining us, Will," Striker said wryly.

"Now Fuckin' Row!"

Gaston did not turn to regard me. He kept rowing toward shore.

I was in Hell and the Gods had led me here.

Sixteen

Wherein We Are Shipwrecked

Since my matelot was not speaking and Striker was uncharacteristically quiet, Pete informed me of the events that had transpired. We had set sail southward toward Campeche, shortly after Pete and I deposited Gaston in the Captain's cabin. Half the gold had been transferred to the *North Wind* along with Cleghorn and the wounded. Bradley had stayed on board to question the prisoners. That night, as the weather was getting worse and we neared the Campeche peninsula, we anchored; and Bradley returned to the *North Wind*. Thirty men had been left to guard the prisoners and sail the galleon, in addition to Pete, Striker, Gaston and myself.

Sometime in the early hours of the morning, the true storm hit and we lost sight of the sloop. We had to weigh anchor and attempt to ride it out. The thought of the giant galleon as a windblown piece of flotsam in the pitch black of a night storm clenched my gut. I was happy I had been drunk. One glance over my shoulder at Striker's strained face told me he wished he had been drunk too.

Due to the storm, we were blown out of the Gulf and toward Cuba, until the galleon began to break up and take on water. Then we were on the mast and at the mercy of the waves. Thankfully, the current was somewhat with us, and taking us up and north and closer to shore. However, the shore in question was Cuba, and we were getting ever closer to Havana. We needed to make land before we were sighted, hopefully well to the west of the city. As the island was heavily occupied, we would be in grave danger from the inhabitants; but we could find victuals and steal a boat to return home. Thus we rowed toward the land spreading across the horizon.

"What about the others?" I asked.

"Don'tKnow. TheyGotTheLongboats. OneWasBustFromTheMast."

I remembered lightning-lit glimpses from what I had thought was a dream, involving Pete and Striker and other men struggling to lift the mast from the longboat. I also remembered people being swept overboard. I did not ask about the prisoners. It could now be assumed that everyone who had left Vera Cruz aboard the *Saint Lucia* was dead.

The entirety of our situation slowly revealed itself to me as I paddled. We could not be sure if the *North Wind* had survived the storm. We might be the only men who sailed from Port Royal to make it home; that was, if we did not get captured by the Spanish or have some other evil befall us.

I was only alive because of Gaston. He had saved my life. I did not know how he had gotten free. I remembered another image: this one of him standing over me with a knife. I knew he had been very angry. I did not know what his humor was now. I was torn between knowing we had much to say to one another and not knowing if I wished to speak to him at all. I decided not to speak of anything while we were on the mast: in part because I wanted to see his face when we discussed it, as I was afraid his gaze would hold the same hatred, and I knew I would picture that expression when he spoke unless my eyes could behold otherwise. I also did not wish to discuss the matter in front of our companions, even in French.

We were very close to Cuba now; and I regarded the rugged coastline with hope, as I did not see any signs of habitation, which meant it was possible no one saw us coming ashore. There would be little we could do to defend ourselves if they did. Gaston had collected all of our weapons and bags and attached them to me. Pete and Striker had done likewise with their gear, though thankfully they had not attached it to me. So we had our muskets and pistols and swords, but we didn't have an ounce of dry powder among us.

With much relief, we rode the mast through the surf and onto shore. When we disembarked, I discovered there was still a rope about my waist tied to Gaston. It was symbolic for me; and I was loathe to untie it, as I felt the connection very tenuous between us, and I did not wish to do anything to further sever it – any more than I wished to draw him closer. He would not meet my eyes or even gaze upon me, and he regarded the rope around him with some annoyance once he was minded of it. Yet he did not immediately untie it, either.

"Thank you for saving my life," I said in French as we stood in the surf and watched Pete and Striker haul their gear ashore and into the shade.

"It may not have been a favor. You could have died in your sleep without a whimper." He pulled the knot free and left me there.

I struggled to shore with the rest of the gear, my head pounding and my heart aching. I dropped the bags next to Gaston and Striker, who were already assessing damage to the muskets. Then I rid myself of the rest of the rope, both from around my waist and what had been used to attach me to the bags. Striker was still sullen and not speaking. Pete stood a little ways away, and studied the hill above us and the shoreline. I joined him. We looked at each other, and of one accord walked farther down the beach.

"MineIsPissedTheShipSank," Pete said when we were out of earshot.

I sighed. "Mine is pissed I was drunk, or possibly because I hit him. In all truth I do not know. He is simply angry."

Pete snorted derisively. "NoTimeForIt. WeNeedWaterAn'Food." He stomped back to our matelots and drew on his baldric. "We'llScout."

I slung my baldric and checked my blades quickly.

"I will go," Gaston said.

"Nay!" Pete said. "YouTwoStayHereAnPout."

Though I had said nothing, Pete's words earned both of us livid glares.

Striker came to his feet. "You arse! I'm not pouting! I'm despondent! You would be, too, if you had any God-damned sense. We've lost everything! No ship. No gold. Everyone we know is dead. We're on Spanish soil. What am I supposed to do, leap about for joy?"

Pete's glare was level and steady, and a thing to be reckoned with only by the strong of heart. "WeBeAlive. You," he pointed one imperious finger at Striker, "NeverKnowWhat'sImportant." He turned and headed uphill, and I followed.

"AnHeSaysIHaveNoSense," he muttered.

We were halfway up the hill when Gaston caught us.

"Don'tYaBeLeavin'HimAlone," Pete growled.

Gaston stood his ground with arms crossed. "Do you know where to look for water?"

Pete thought about that for a moment, and sighed while studying the distant trees. "Nay."

"Then he can stay with Striker," Gaston said. He did not regard me as he said this, so I decided to stop watching him.

I looked to Pete, who shrugged. "Aye. CanYaKeepAnEyeOnStriker?"

"If he does not leap around too much, I am sure I can manage."

Pete chuckled, and I went back down the hill. Striker was standing in the surf, staring out to sea. I have never truly commanded anything, which is to say, I have never been responsible for the lives of others in the fashion of an officer or a captain; and therefore I could only understand a little of what he must be experiencing. However, I have witnessed the effects of loss on men who commanded, and the guilt and grief can take a shocking toll upon the weak. I did not think Striker weak.

I joined him. "For what it is worth, I would sail with you again."

He was still for a long moment, and then he shook; and I was not sure of the emotion giving rise to the tremor, until it burst forth from him in a hearty chuckle. When it passed, he sank to the ground where he had stood, so that the waves washed across his stomach. I dropped beside him.

"Christ, Will," he sighed. "I know there was nothing I could do. But now, all of those people are dead, and for what? There's no gold."

I frowned at him. "Are you saying the gold would have given their deaths meaning?"

"Aye, for me. If a man dies because of a goal, then his death had meaning."

"Many would think that; but most would think a worthy goal to be something other than gold, like defending God, king, or country, or maybe even family."

Striker shrugged. "Bradley keeps saying any damage we do against the Spaniards is justified because we're at war with them; but it's all about the gold, Will. That's why we're at war."

I smiled as I saw his meaning. "I would say it is all about power, but one grants the other, does it not? Those with power have gold, and those with gold have power. The Spaniards had the gold, so they possessed the power to say all the gold in the New World was theirs. But every time we take a ship, we prove them wrong and deny them their power and their gold." I thought on it for a moment. "You could view it thusly, that their deaths had meaning because they denied the Spaniards gold."

Striker chuckled. "I could view it thus, but it would only be a temporary bandage of a deep wound requiring stitching."

"Most justifications are." I shrugged.

"Soldiers care not for all of that," he said. "A soldier only wants the gold so he has enough power over his own life to avoid fighting for others. The nobles can fight for God and king. They rarely have to die for it." He paused and recited from memory, "All men want gold, men with gold want power, and the powerful want everything."

"Who said that?"

"My uncle, the pirate I learned everything from," he said ruefully.

I smiled. "He sounds like a wise man."

"He's dead and gone, before I left England. He died of the ague. If we had still had him as captain, we would not have been captured; but his first officer who replaced him was a foolhardy numbskull, and I was young and stupid and cheering him on. We were rash and we paid for it. Didn't get any gold out of that, either, and very few of us lived to tell the tale."

"So you view those as wasted lives as well?"

"Aye."

"Tell me, do you only think about our men, or do you count the dead Spanish as well?"

He frowned and regarded me with puzzlement. "Do you count the Spaniards?"

"Sometimes I think I do. The men aboard that ship did not set Spanish policy or benefit all that much from Spanish gold. They were just sheep torn asunder in a war between wolves. As all sheep are, I guess. Sometimes I can ignore such things, and at others it does not sit well with me. I realize I am engaging in foolish notions for a pirate." I also realized I had not explained my sheep metaphor to him and probably appeared quite the fool. To my surprise, he grasped my meaning immediately.

"Aye. You cannot feel sorrow over sheep, Will. They're sheep. We wolves have to eat."

"Do you see the world in terms of predators and their natural prey?" I asked.

"Aye, the strong and the weak."

"Was your uncle a wolf?"

Striker chuckled. "Will, I come from a long line of wolves. We've always roved the seas."

The thought of dynasties of self-made wolves intrigued me. I needed to discuss this with Gaston; and then I remembered we were not talking. I lost all interest in the topic, as it seemed so incredibly foolish and trivial in relation to the issues of my life.

"What really makes me angry," Striker was saying, "is that I don't even know where we went down. If I did, we could try and salvage her. And you're correct about gold granting power. Every time I sail a prize into port I think..." He trailed off.

"That you wish to have the command all the time?" I hazarded.

He nodded. "Aye, and then something like this happens. It is as if God is smiting me for my delusions of grandeur."

I laughed. "Ah, Striker, if we are at war with the Gods, we may never get home."

Melancholy gripped me. I only knew one man who would readily understand my jest. I felt a sense of loss that far outweighed my fear that he would snarl vicious obscenities at me again. It was quite obvious, even to someone as blinded as I often am by my own desires, that we could not be together in the way I had hoped. Yet I still wanted him as a friend.

My change of mood must have been quite evident, as Striker was regarding me with curiosity. And then he confused me with his question.

"Where is home, Will?" It did not seem to be rhetorical. I realized it was quite profound.

"I do not know," I said. "When I traveled before, I always thought home was England: specifically my father's estate and the house I was raised in. But that place never engendered any of the feelings philosophers and poets assign with the name. Neither has any other place I have slept."

Striker was chuckling ruefully. "My home is with Pete. He's correct, I'm such an arse."

"Home is where the matelot is, eh?" I smiled. I thought of the last two months with Gaston, and my smile widened. "Well, if we are at war with our matelots, we shall never get home."

He laughed. "'Tis true, 'tis true."

"Do you think there might be shellfish or such in this water? Or do we have a means of catching fish?"

"Aye," he said and stood. "I have hooks and line. We can try." He regarded the distant waves for a moment. "My stomach tells me it cares not for gold or power or ships, or even matelots unless they bring food."

"Mine speaks thusly all the time."

An hour later, we had caught one fish and had high hopes of catching more; we had powder drying upon a stone; and we still had not seen our matelots. We were concerned, but not overly so. We were even more concerned when we saw a number of men coming down the beach toward us. We doused the fire and hid as best we could with our muskets: even though we had not the means to fire them, we could at least use them to bluff if the opportunity presented itself. As they continued to approach, we counted nine in all. Then we began to notice other details, and our anxiety transmuted to curiosity; and then hope and finally joy, as we ran out to greet our own men.

"What's this with muskets?" Cudro roared with amusement as he clasped hands with Striker. "You're all wet."

"You have dry powder?" Striker challenged back.

"Nay, I was going to club someone with it." He brandished one of the few muskets they had.

Davey swept me off my feet in a great embrace and seemed overjoyed to see me.

"Where's Pete?" he asked.

I met Julio's gaze over Davey's shoulder and rolled my eyes. Julio seemed more amused than upset, and shrugged it off with good nature.

"He went with Gaston for water. Do you have any? And what of Liam and Otter?"

He frowned at me. "Nay, no victuals either. Otter and Liam were on the *North Wind*."

I was somewhat relieved, though they could still be dead.

"We landed not long before you, and saw you coming in – and decided to come here," Julio said.

Striker clasped hands with each man, and then he grew somber. "How many were on your boat?"

"Thirteen," Cudro sighed. "We lost two to sharks and two just slipped away. Never saw the other boat."

"Was that the damaged one?" I asked.

Cudro shook his head. "Nay, we had the damaged one. Leaked so bad we started to go down, so we flipped her over and hung from the sides. That's how we lost the men."

Striker shook his head sadly, and then gave a shrug. "Well, as you saw, we were thankful the mast floated."

This engendered some chuckles; and then we rekindled the fire and set more men to fishing, and we all got about the business of determining what we had. They had a few weapons among them and little else. We had six muskets and twelve pistols. Due to the way we all carried our blades, every man had those. As for other gear, none of the men from the longboat had a thing, unless he had kept it in a belt pouch.

We were all dining on fish by the time Gaston and Pete returned. They were both relieved at the sight of our mates and dismayed that they had not brought enough water. I was curious as to where they had obtained the bottles they did bring water in. I was not the only one.

"Where the Hell did you get that?" Striker asked as Pete produced a pie from a bag.

"WeFoundAHouse."

I offered Gaston half of my fish, and he sat next to me with a sigh. He handed me a bottle of water, and I took a long drink before passing it on.

"And here I thought you would be exercising some woodsman skill learned upon the Haiti to locate a spring. I could have spotted a house," I teased.

He smiled grimly, but he still would not look upon me as he spoke. "It was both a blessing and a detriment. We need to move on before the occupants are noticed missing."

"Ah, anything else of value?"

"We have some idea of where we are. Perhaps you can make more of it." He handed me a sheaf of papers. They were old, and included a grant for land that mentioned a township and a crude map.

"Does the name Cabanas mean anything to anyone?" I perused the map and cursed. "We are damn close to Havana."

"That may be to our favor," Striker said, after he, too, cursed. "More people, but that means more ports."

"We should move tonight," Gaston said.

"No one has slept since before we took the galleon," Striker said. "But I agree. Let's set watches, and everyone should sleep a little now."

I did not argue that Gaston had spent last night unconscious and I had been in a drunken stupor and in some ways we were more rested than the others. Of course I did not need to explain this to my matelot.

"We will take first watch," Gaston volunteered.

There were no objections, and we slipped up the hill and found a fine vantage point. There are two options for covering all possible angles of observation: one involves sitting back to back and the second facing one another while looking over the other's shoulder. He chose to turn his back to me. We sat in silence for a while.

I had not wanted to speak to him thus. I wrestled with my options, and after much deliberation decided on a course of action.

"I am sorry," I said.

The silence stretched for a while longer, and I felt anger begin to kindle deep inside me. What else did he expect me to say or do?

He finally spoke. "I woke in the dark in an oddly moving ship. I did not know where I was, my jaw hurt, someone was next to me, sleeping, reeking of wine. I hoped it was you. It was apparent from the motion and sound that the ship was sinking. I was bound and it took me a good while to get a knife off your belt and cut the rope. Then I lit a lantern. There you were, without a care in the world. I seriously considered slipping the knife in your ribs."

Guilt blossomed and fought with anger for my attention, each claiming to provide me with greater emotional satisfaction.

"Why did you not? It would not have been the first time you considered it that day."

He was quiet a while before answering. "I do not have many friends, much less... You were the only one who would have stayed with me, drunk or sober. I realized I was only angry because you could have gotten us both killed. Why were you drinking during a storm?"

"It was not storming when I started drinking," I said sadly. "I am sorry. I will not do it again."

"It was because of the knife, was it not?"

"Non. I drank because you tore away an old scab I thought a scar, and opened a wound. I drank to staunch it, because I knew not what else to do."

"How?" There was no anger left in his voice, and from the change of the sound I knew he had turned to regard me.

I trusted in my resolve. This would be best for both of us. "Your words. I had heard them before. It was what you said, and the hate in your eyes when you said it. I know not whether you speak the truths of your heart or your fears when you are mad. It does not matter, either way. I heard, and I will trouble you no more in that regard. In all honesty I cannot covet you now, with that image and those words in my mind. It will pass, and that wound will heal over again. But I feel that.... Well, I feel I received the wound the first time because I desired something I could not have. And here I am again, doing the same thing and getting wounded the same way. I should learn by now. So I will trouble you no more. I would that we remain friends."

He took a long ragged breath that echoed my own. "What did I say, Will?"

I cursed silently. How could he have said something to hurt me so badly and not even remember it? How was that fair? It made me feel childish for being upset at all.

"I do not wish to repeat it."

"I cannot know what you are speaking of, if you do not." He sounded angry again, or possibly more frustrated than angry.

I watched the horizon. The sun was setting, and it was quite lovely. If I just watched the colors and let the words come out, I did not have to think about their meaning. "You said that the only reason I wanted you as a friend is so I could fuck you. And that I was just a damn sodomite who only wanted to fuck and that I could not go a single night without begging for it." I sighed. "There, now, I have said it. I do not ever wish to speak of it again."

I stood and moved farther away.

He said something and I could not hear it.

"What?" I asked, and looked back at him. It was a mistake. He was crying. I may as well have turned to a pillar of salt, as I felt my resolve crumble and begin to blow away on the wind. I fought it with all my might. It would just be worse the next time.

"Fears," he said. "You asked if I spoke my truths or my fears."

"Gaston, you see how it cannot matter, do you not? And I forgive you, I truly do, but I cannot forget."

"I am sorry. So I have managed to drive even you away."

"Non! I am not leaving. I still desire your company and conversation. But I cannot... want you anymore. And we cannot... touch or... We just cannot. I cannot. It hurts too much, and in that I am weak."

"When next I am mad and scared I will say something else."

"I would say that there is nothing else you could have said to wound me more deeply, but I am sure that you could find something."

He stood. "Do you think I did that with malice?"

"When you said it, oui. I do not think you planned such a thing in advance, non. I did not mean to imply..."

We were looking at each other, and I wanted to hold him. I was such a fool.

"No more, I beg of you," I sighed. "Let this go. I care for you very deeply, and I wish to remain friends, and I will not abandon you. But I am a damned fool if I let you hurt me again, because then I hurt both of us. I am not asking for much to change, and it is not something you wanted to begin with. You do not favor men."

"I liked the touching. I was growing accustomed to it." He was in earnest, and I wanted to howl with frustration.

I kept my voice level. "Non. I cannot do that anymore. I am sinning if I do."

He frowned.

"Against myself," I said. "I once swore I would never subject myself to being... loved within the confines of another's rules and terms. If I am going to love you in that way, I cannot constantly exist in the fear of condemnation on your part. And I do not believe you can guarantee that will not happen. I know you are as lonely as I. And I have great difficulty separating the desires of my heart from the desires of my loins. I fall in love with any man I am attracted to, and I am attracted to any man I love. If you desired me, then it would be different. But you do not desire me. I am merely here. I am your friend and I am available in that regard. But Gaston, you will end up hating me such that you do not have to be mad to say it, if we continue down this path. So let us redefine our friendship and partnership. We are not going to become Pete and Striker or any other pair of matelots who lie together. We do not have to."

"You can go without?" he asked. He was not mocking.

"I may take myself in hand a great deal, but other than that, oui. I am resigned to it."

He studied me for a moment, and abruptly turned back to his side of the watch. With a start I remembered we were up there for a reason that had nothing to do with my personal concerns. I swept my hemisphere and hoped the Spanish Armada had not sailed up to the beach. They had not; and I was left with my own thoughts. I vowed to be content with this solution. Wanting to stick my cock where it did not belong had damn near been my undoing more times than I could count.

"Have you been shipwrecked before?" I asked, to distract myself and to determine whether he was speaking to me or not.

"Non."

"Have you heard of people surviving such things?"

"We will steal a boat and be home inside of a month, you will see," he sighed.

I thought of Striker's definition of home, and smiled ruefully.

"I am home," I whispered. Such as it was, it was no more comfortable than any other home I had lived in, but no worse, really, either.

When it was fully dark, we slipped down the hill and found the others ready to move. Gaston presented me with a whole new cause for concern.

"Has Cudro asked for an election?" he whispered as we joined them.

"Non," I sighed as the implications became clear to me. "Do you think he will try to supplant Striker in the middle of this endeavor?"

"If things do not go well, oui."

We were thirteen in number: a fact that several men had bemoaned for its lack of luck. If Cudro and Striker did not vote, that made eleven. I knew where five of the votes would go, or at least I felt I did. I could not be sure of the other six; but a few of them seemed to like Striker a great deal.

"He may not feel he has the numbers," I whispered.

"Ah," Gaston agreed. "I had not counted. He will when he feels he has a chance."

"I suppose now would be an inopportune time to kill him."

"Oui, we may need him. For example, if we are pursued by Spaniards, we can always slice him so that he runs slower than the rest of us and thereby delay them."

I glanced at him and smiled, which he returned. It appeared that not all things would suffer between us. I was greatly relieved.

We made our way along the beach by moonlight: heading west toward a port, if the map for the land grant had been correct. We had a small amount of dry powder, but there was no guarantee it would work until we fired it, and we did not want to risk the noise. We walked in the surf so it would cover our tracks. I was thankful for this, the walking on the beach, as my feet were still tender from the wounds; and despite not wearing shoes for close to four months, the soles of my feet were still not as tough as the other men's. I would not be able to walk overland amongst brush and brambles and the like.

We covered a considerable distance at a good pace that night, and stopped in the early hours of the morning when we lost the moon. We slept in shifts between matelots, so that around half of us were awake at any given time. Those of us awake on the first watch cast lines into the surf at dawn and caught a number of fine fish, which we cooked quickly before the smoke of a fire could betray our presence in the daylight.

I was to sleep through the next watch while Gaston went scouting with Julio and Pete. Due to our lack of faith in some of our companions, namely Cudro, Gaston and I were not fond of the three of them leaving together while the three of us, Striker, Davey and myself stayed in camp. But there was little to be done for it, as we needed to sleep and they were well suited to forming a scouting party. So I slept near Striker with one eye open, as the saying goes, and did not rest well for it.

They returned to report that we were within a league of a small harbor and there were two flyboats docked there. I had to ask what a flyboat was, and Gaston simply explained it was the size we wished, a single-masted small sailing craft that could hold thirteen men, though it would be crowded. After asking a dozen questions, and the scouts rendering a rough approximation of the harbor in the sand, Striker said he wished to sneak in after dark and take whichever one of the flyboats was more readily available or better suited to our needs in respect to cargo and general seaworthiness.

Cudro did not appear to be fond of this plan. "Let's raid the place. There's not that many buildings, but it's likely they have something. Then we can take both boats."

I leaned close to Gaston and whispered. "Now may be an opportune time to kill him. How shall we go about it?"

"Leave it to me," Gaston whispered and quietly doffed his baldric and belt. "I am sure he will provide an opening."

"We did not look for militia," Julio protested.

Cudro waved him off and stood to take center stage. "What are we to do, return to Port Royal with our tails between out legs, no gold, and all of us crowded in a little flyboat? We don't even have enough muskets to go around; and once we return, those of us without won't have the money to buy one. I say we equip ourselves here and return home with something in our pockets."

Striker sighed. "You want Spanish muskets? I think we should try to get home alive. This will be easy, as long as we're cautious. We can address the weapons issue later. Currently we don't have good powder for the weapons we have."

"All the more reason," Cudro said doggedly. "Unless you're... well I can understand you being shaken after the ship went down. We all can. That was a big loss. But you cannot let that affect your judgment."

Gaston smirked and stood. "You have no business calling Striker a coward. You are the coward."

I thought he had countered a bit prematurely, but there was no issue here of disguising what was about to happen, so it did not matter.

"I did not call him a coward," Cudro rumbled.

I looked around at the others. They were transfixed and listening intently to hear Gaston's hoarse voice over the surf, except for Striker who eyed me curiously. I mouthed, "We are helping." He smirked.

"You spoke as to imply it," Gaston said. "I will not mince words. You are a coward. You refuse to fight me unless I am bound."

This got a confused reaction from the crowd and Cudro blanched. "You liar."

"While sailing with Nantes, we boarded a ship and you conspired to bring on my madness; and then when I attacked you and was brought down, you waited until I was bound hand and foot before requesting your right to revenge. And you have avoided dueling with me since, out of fear. You are a coward."

All eyes shifted to Cudro. He was pale despite his tanned skin and beard. "That's a lie."

"Prove it," Gaston whispered. "No weapons. Here. Now."

This brought raised eyebrows and even made me catch my breath, though more with amusement than concern, as the disparity in size between the two men lent an absurdity to the potential of a match between them. Cudro had to be twice Gaston's weight, and stood head and shoulders above him. What was telling was that Cudro was scared. I wondered if Gaston was carrying a compass concealed upon his person, or perhaps a quill. Yet even without an improvised weapon of opportunity, I had faith in my matelot. If he thought he could beat Cudro, I was sure he could.

Cudro was fighting a desperate battle to maintain his composure. "No weapons. I accept that. First blood? Or do you intend to kill me with your fists?"

"Until you beg for quarter," Gaston said coldly.

Anger began to replace fear in the big Dutchman, and he rumbled, "I won't beg you for anything, boy."

The other men had already pulled back to create a rough ring, and Gaston was circling Cudro with a malicious smirk. The big man dropped into a traditional pugilist's stance. Gaston charged him, went low under Cudro's fists and rammed his knee into the other man's groin, then rolled away from him. The rest of us erupted into laughter and sympathetic groans as Cudro toppled while swearing in falsetto. Truly enraged now, the big man did not stay down, but heaved himself to his knees to snarl insults in Dutch.

Gaston waited.

"Do you wish to continue?" he asked during a lull in the laughter.

Still wincing, Cudro lumbered to his feet. This time he turned a hip toward his opponent and kept a hand below his waist protectively. Gaston rushed him again, and Cudro dropped low and remained defensive. Gaston feinted to his midsection and then punched him in the nose. We all heard the crack. Cudro did not topple, and he came hard and fast at Gaston, who leapt up and somehow climbed around so that he had an arm around Cudro's throat and the fingers of his free hand at Cudro's eye. The Dutchman roared and fought the hand away while throwing himself to the ground to dislodge Gaston, who rolled clear only to dive back upon the big man and land several rapid jabs to his face. Then Gaston was away again, leaving Cudro rolling about and cursing in the sand.

The audience now had wide eyes and Pete muttered, "Fuck." I guessed his underlying thought. We were lucky Gaston had not had a chance to have a go at either one of us when he was mad. He was going to be very difficult to survive, if he ever did.

"Again?" Gaston asked as Cudro pulled himself up. The big man was spitting blood, and his eyes would shortly be swollen closed.

"Go to the Devil," the big man said.

"The next time you go down, I will not withdraw," Gaston said calmly. "We will see how much you enjoy pissing blood."

I winced at this, and remembered the real reason behind this exchange. I wondered how much damage Cudro had been allowed to do to Gaston. It made my stomach clench even as the anger gripped me. I wanted Gaston to beat him to death.

Cudro was now pride and anger and little sense. He waved Gaston in. My matelot charged and rolled, slamming his weight into the side of Cudro's leg so that it buckled and the big man roared. Gaston was up and kicking him when he went down. Cudro tried to defend himself by rolling into a ball, but it was to little avail. I twice heard the crack of ribs. When Gaston had done as much damage as he wanted, he withdrew and regarded his downed opponent.

"You still have not asked for quarter."

"Quarter," Cudro gasped.

Gaston walked away, and two men rushed to help Cudro.

"Do you feel you have obtained satisfaction?" I asked Gaston curiously in French as he despondently donned his weapons.

He shrugged. "I never do. Hurting him doesn't make my memory of the pain go away."

I was intrigued by this. "Is that why you did not seek him out before?"

He nodded. "It served purpose here. He might have won the vote and led us all to our doom." He regarded me seriously. "There are bodies on the gallows in town. We could see little detail from where we lay, but there were nine." At my look of consternation he continued. "The other longboat had nine or so men."

Understanding dawned. "They would have had fewer weapons and no powder. Have you told Striker?"

He shook his head. "Pete did not think he would take it well. And I wished to see what attitudes prevailed before..." He sighed. "Revenge is pointless if it gets you killed."

Striker was approaching, and we regarded him expectantly.

"Thank you," he said. "Though you should have killed him, as he cannot walk now."

"It will keep the ones who want trouble busy carrying him." I shrugged.

"Should he see a surgeon?" Striker asked. "Not that I care, but..."

"Nay," Gaston shrugged. "He will recover if he does not move about much. Once we get him on the boat, he can sit like a barrel of lard until we reach Port Royal."

Striker was looking out to sea. "Perhaps he was correct."

Gaston stiffened slightly; and Pete, standing behind Striker, slumped.

"In what regard?" I asked.

"Perhaps we should not go home empty-handed. Perhaps I am being a bit cautious."

I scowled. "What did you tell me yesterday about getting captured and how if your uncle had been alive...?"

"Aye. Aye." Striker smiled. "Be my conscience, will you?"

"If necessary. I want to return to port, alive."

"We will not haul your carcass back." Striker grinned. "So if you wish to see Port Royal again, you will be alive when doing it. There is no need to stipulate such a thing."

We stayed quiet and rested as we could until dusk, at which time we made our way along the shore to the port. It was a small horseshoe of beach with a single wharf. The flyboats were the largest craft in residence. The gallows were across the small bay from where we lay in the sand. They were clearly visible from sea or land, as the Spanish, like the English and every other nation, adore trying to scare pirates and smugglers with gruesome examples of the local justice.

Striker, of course, studied the entirety of the area. Those of us who knew of their contents could clearly see when he came across the gallows, as his body grew taut.

Pete sighed, "ItBeThem."

Gaston was studying the gallows as well. "They died fighting. Judging by the wounds, some of those bodies were hung after they were dead."

"Were they there this morning?" Striker asked from what seemed a great distance.

"Aye," Pete sighed.

"We were up there." Gaston pointed along the hill to the South. "And from the angle and distance, it was difficult to discern."

"But you suspected," Striker said.

"Aye," Pete sighed. "IWantedYaTaSleep. NothinWeCanDo. Let'sGetABoat."

"I will not slink out of here," Striker said with conviction.

I thought it ill-advised to mention that we had killed or been responsible for the deaths of a good five hundred Spaniards within the last two days;, yet I felt compelled to say something, and quoted Gaston.

"Revenge is of little value if you are dead. We do not know how they were taken. It is entirely possible that this small town is overrun with competent Spaniards."

"That will be the day," Striker snapped. "I have never understood how they conquered the Indians."

"That was over a hundred and fifty years ago," I sighed. "They were better then."

"I want to hurt them, Will."

I looked across the bay.

"I agree," I said quietly. "People should be hurt. It solves nothing, but it will at least let them know that hanging our brethren in such a fashion will not protect them or scare us away."

"Not you, too," Gaston whispered in French.

"What is a centaur to do?"

He rolled his eyes.

As one, the four of us turned to regard the small town at the back of the bay.

"Fire," Pete cackled. "BurnItAll."

"Damn it Pete," Striker teased. "You're supposed to pillage before you burn." Then he regarded Gaston seriously. "Does anyone else know? Julio?" At Gaston's nod, he continued, "I want the men to steal the boat. The four of us will cause mayhem."

I laughed. "Someday I will go somewhere and not cause mayhem."

"WhenYarOld."

Striker ordered the men to wait a good while and then proceed to take whichever boat they found best, while the four of us went to check for provisions and powder. He put Julio in charge, and spoke quietly to him so that he understood the entirety of what we were about and why. Julio was solemn and agreeable, as always. Davey was not, and asked to join the raiding party. Striker refused, and said that if he took issue with it, they could settle things later, but for now Davey had best do as ordered. Davey grudgingly acquiesced.

We left our muskets and pistols with the other men, and snuck down the rocky moonlit beach with knives in hand. When we found the first militiaman, secreted behind a dune watching the closest boat, we scared him as badly as he scared us. Pete recovered quickly and slit the man's throat before he could give a cry. We realized we had chosen wisely, even if at the outset our plan had appeared rash. They were lying in wait for us.

We proceeded to stealthily circle the bay, silently killing sentries as we went and appropriating their weapons. They may have had an excellent plan; but, as Striker noted, they were incompetent in its execution. Two of the sentries were quite drunk, and all of them were stationed alone. None of them saw us in time to raise the alarm.

Twelve muskets later, we were heavily laden with pistols, shot, and dry powder. We returned to find our men waiting on the beach while Davey and Julio inspected the first boat. Thankfully Cudro was sleeping, and we were not forced to endure any gloating on his part. I was sure there would be time enough for that as we sailed home.

We equipped everyone; and those of us who still had them took back our own pistols and muskets, as they were far superior to the aging Spanish weapons the sentries had possessed. Unfortunately, they were all loaded with the questionable powder, and our first shots might flash in the pan; but we had no way to discharge them silently, so we resolved to do what we could.

Thus armed, we joined Davey and Julio at the first craft. They were greatly surprised to see us, and even more relieved that we had discovered the trap before it was sprung. We set sentries while they checked upon the second vessel. The first was empty, but the second was a good yard longer and loaded with tobacco. There was some quiet discussion, as we could always sell the tobacco, but it left little room for us on a boat that small. Cudro, awake now that he had been moved, insisted we take both craft; and Striker finally relented. The Dutchman, being unable to move about, was deposited on one boat with another man and three muskets. We sent two men to the other boat, with orders not to move it as of yet and to stay low.

Then the remaining nine of us slipped into the town proper. There were maybe fifty buildings in orderly rows. We quickly located the garrison, and discovered the rest of the town's militia engaged in a party, complete with wine, women, and truly awful singing. With righteous anger, we assumed they were celebrating the death of our comrades. I did note that they must have been about it for two days if that was the case, as our men had been on the gallows that morning.

There were a good forty of them, and we were not sure if they comprised all of the armed men to be had in the vicinity; so instead of appropriating the wine and killing them directly, we blocked the doors from the outside and tossed two huge grenadoes onto the roof. These consisted of an onion bottle packed with powder inside a small cask packed with sand. The twin explosions brought the ceiling down atop the drunken Spaniards, and the overturned lamps and candles set the timbers ablaze. By then, we had found another source of wine and rum and even fresh bread, cheese, and sausage. We set fire to a few other buildings as we departed, but primarily we ran like heavily laden rats.

We had both boats quickly asail, but we paused at the mouth of the bay to cut our dead from the gallows and stack them one upon the other. We discovered they had indeed been tortured and disfigured before they were hung. I felt no guilt about the burning town behind us. We burned the bodies. The pyre was visible a long way down the coast as we sailed south.

It was a beacon to insanity. As I watched it, I ate bread and wondered where the Spanish were growing wheat and why revenge never lived up to one's expectations. There was a light touch on my arm, and I looked to Gaston expectantly. He merely opened his hand in request for the hunk of cheese I was carving. I handed it to him and looked away.

We sailed south around a peninsula that thrust toward the strait and then down and east toward the Cayman Islands: our rendezvous point with the *North Wind*. Striker had a set of navigational instruments, and proved as competent in their use as I had suspected. The winds were cooperative, and we were not subjected to any storms. We once encountered whales, and I experienced several nights of horrific dreams, as I had not imagined the creatures to be so huge when so very close – especially not in comparison to our little craft, which were only a score of feet long apiece.

And so we crossed a hundred leagues of sea, without incident except for Cudro's occasional carping. I was forced to admire the man's persistence. Oddly, he did not seem so hateful to Gaston or myself any longer, or really hateful to anyone. It seemed to simply be his natural mien.

We did not find the *North Wind* on the large Cayman island. We sailed all about the area looking for any sign of them, and found none. We provisioned and took a vote. It was decided that we return to Port Royal. We could not know how long we should wait, if at all. They could arrive the hour after we left or never.

In all that time, I wished for some sign from Gaston that he was not in agreement with my resolution. I could not look at him without thinking of his madness on the ship; yet I knew if he but reached for me, my resolve would crumble. I desperately wanted my resolve to crumble. But like a truly fine companion and matelot, he respected my wishes; and though the confines of the small craft sometimes pressed us together while sleeping, it was as if we were brothers and not lovers. He talked as if nothing untoward had ever passed between us, and to all appearances everything was as it had been before.

I felt my victory pyrrhic, yet I was afraid the Gods were not yet done with the matter.

Jamaica

June 1667

V

Seventeen

Wherein The Die Is Cast

We arrived in Port Royal on my twenty-seventh birthday. I made mention of this, and all were amused that I had been given so fine a gift as to return home safely. Gaston regarded me thoughtfully. I supposed I should not complain; I was still amongst better companions than I ever had been on a birthday, and I had much to be thankful for. Yet I was miserable.

On a whim, I asked Gaston, "What day were you born?"

"March fifth, Gregorian."

I chuckled despite my mood. "I suppose that is more accurate. I have always counted it by the day, no matter which calendar I was living under the aegis of."

"This year it was right before you arrived," he said quietly. Then he would not look at me.

We asked about, and no one had seen or heard from the *North Wind*. This sat heavy in our hearts, but we knew we could not give up hope as of yet. Thankfully, Hastings had brought the flute, our first prize of the voyage, into port; and it had been sold at auction. Striker decided to look for him later. Word of our adventure spread throughout the buccaneers in the Hole, and we were soon besieged with well-wishers and the curious. Striker promised to give a full accounting at the Three Tunns that night, and that relieved us of many of them. Gaston's glare relieved us of the rest.

We sold the tobacco and parceled out the shares of it. Our cabal kept one of the flyboats, while others of our men kept the second. We parted company with the men for the time being, and our little band staggered down the street to Theodore's. We could not think of another place to go; and with news of our story spreading through town, I thought it best to see him in person as soon as possible.

Peering through the window showed Theodore with clients we did not recognize, so we slipped into the yard and availed ourselves of the cistern and wash tub. Samuel appeared pleased with our arrival, and provided us with lemonade and a lemony cheesecake, which made him Pete's friend. This seemed to alarm the poor man greatly.

Belfry, Dickey, and Tom blundered into the midst of us shortly thereafter, and Dickey squealed quite absurdly. Belfry and Davey stared at each other in surprise, and I stupidly wondered what that was about for a moment. Then, of course, I remembered – and immediately wondered how we would ever manage this mess.

"Boys, how good to see you," I blurted. "How is that you are here?"

"We live here," Tom supplied. "How are you? How was roving?"

"All three of you?" I asked, and they nodded. This elicited quiet groans from Striker and Pete, as we had hoped to sleep there for the night.

"Roving was... quite adventurous. You will have to accompany us to the Three Tunns tonight to hear the whole tale. We took a galleon from the Flota, and then we were beset by a serious storm, and we sank and had to steal a boat on the Cuban coast and sail back here." They appeared suitably impressed with this brief account, and I wondered now what they must imagine at my tame and banal words compared to the reality of the event.

"So how is it you are living here?" I asked.

"I had a falling out with my uncle; and well, you are aware of Mister Belfry's circumstances," Tom said.

"Aye, indeed. How is it that you are still in Port Royal, my good man?" I asked Belfry. "I thought you were to be married, and assumed you would return home after the unfortunate business with the *King's Hope*."

I gave my companions a look fraught with meaning; and for a moment, Gaston and Striker regarded me with little comprehension. Then realization dawned, and my matelot's eyes grew wide. Striker was on his heels and quickly informed Pete. Meanwhile, Davey had explained to Julio.

"Oh, I am; I have sent for her!" Belfry exclaimed. "With much gratitude to your generous bonus on the voyage, and the addition of a partner, I have found the way clear to become a business owner here in Port Royal."

I was surprised. "That is splendid. What line of business?"

"Dickey and I are opening a haberdashery."

"My God, that is... quite surprising. To think that I have in some small way been involved in bringing a haberdashery to Port Royal, of all places."

Striker was laughing. "Good God, Will, you will have to be upon your death bed before you stop spreading mayhem in your wake."

Gaston was smiling next to me; and Belfry and Dickey were eyeing Striker and him curiously.

"It is a jest," I said quickly, "it would be difficult to explain, as it concerns something which occurred in our travels. So that is wonderful for you. And how are you faring, Tom? And is Harry here as well?"

This sobered them, and I immediately felt ill-at-ease.

"He has passed away," Tom said.

"Truly, I am sorry. How, may I ask?"

"The flux."

Gaston turned his back and appeared to somberly contemplate the cistern, but I new he was fighting laughter. I considered elbowing him in the ribs, for if he let loose even one chortle, I would be quick to follow. And if the other jest would be difficult to explain, this one would be truly impossible. The tragic facet of the matter was that I sincerely felt sorry for Harry.

"I am sorry," I managed to repeat in a sober fashion. This was aided by the realization that I could have shared his fate. "So, how goes it with you?"

"I have been considering roving," Tom said. "In truth, I have few other options."

"You are a fool," I said. "Come to the Three Tunns tonight, and we will explain why."

"I do not feel I will be dissuaded," he said with a defiant jut to his chin.

This sobered me even more than Harry's death. "Nay, you will probably not be."

Belfry was eyeing Davey again. "How is it that you managed to escape the *King's Hope*?"

I started to think of several possible excuses and outright lies; and then Davey said, "The bo'sun released me when he found the ship on fire, and I was able to get above decks and throw myself overboard. I swam a ways and some buccaneers that had come out to see the ruckus picked me up, and I joined them."

Belfry seemed contented with this, and I was greatly relieved. The tale was well constructed in its plausibility; and I wondered who thought of it, as I could not credit Davey with it. I looked past him to Julio, and found my author of deceit. I flashed him a small smile, and he shrugged.

Theodore joined us on the tail end of that conversation, and he quickly crossed the yard to embrace me. I wondered at this, as in truth I had spent but a week with the man, and that was two months prior.

"Marsdale," he gasped. "A man arrived from the Hole a few minutes ago, and told us that the *North Wind* had sank in a storm and all hands save a few had been lost."

"It is interesting how these things spread," I said, and shared a shrug with Striker. "We have no knowledge that she sank. The prize we were on sank. As you can see, we survived."

"Tell me," Theodore commanded.

I sighed and made introductions all around, and launched into an unembellished account lacking in all personal detail. Theodore seemed satisfied with this, and I invited him to the Three Tunns for the better telling. In the meantime, I told him we had been hoping for a place to sleep. He said he knew of a house being let nearby and we could address that on the morrow. For today and tonight, we were welcome to any space he had, though he would not have any beds or hammocks for us. Tom and the boys offered up their hammocks in the guest room if we wished to catch some sleep prior to the night. We accepted their gracious offer quite heartily, and went upstairs to sleep somewhere comfortable.

There were, of course, six of us – and only three hammocks. Thankfully they were well attached to the posts, as Striker and Pete immediately jumped into one, and Davey and Julio followed suit with another. Reluctantly, but with fake good cheer, I crawled into the third with Gaston; and we positioned ourselves back to back, as we had often slept on the flyboat this last week. He seemed completely unconcerned by this.

We woke after dusk, and made our way to the Three Tunns. Everyone at Theodore's went, with the exception of Samuel. The tavern was filled to overflowing, and we were allowed inside only because we were the ones with the tale to tell. Cudro and the other men were already there; and I was surprised the Dutchman had not attempted to steal the glory, as that would fit very well with his way of doing things. Then I took a good look at his still-bruised face, and realized he did not want to call attention to himself at this juncture. Someone might have asked what bull ran him down.

Henry Morgan was there, and he made a show of inviting us to his table in the center of the room. We joined him, but it was obvious there would not be room for the ten of us. This did not prove to be a problem, however, as every eye in the place was upon us; and many of our party were not sure what to make of it all, and did not wish to remain so visible. However, Striker and Pete were immensely pleased with the attention, and took center stage in a space cleared next to the table. Gaston and I sat with Morgan and the other captains, which is not what I would have planned, but it seemed safe at the moment. The rest of our party shoved themselves into the crowd in a less conspicuous fashion.

Somewhere in Striker's lineage of sea-roving wolves, there must have been a bard or two: he had quite a gift for storytelling, and was delighted to have so large a crowd. With Pete's occasional commentary, he made a great show of relating the taking of the flute, the finding of the naughty books, the taking of the galleon, the storm, the wreck, and the raid of the town where we stole the boats. He left out things I would rather no one knew, such as Gaston's madness and the fight with

Cudro. I saw the Dutchman look as relieved as I, when Striker passed over his involvement and simply said that some of the men had been of a different opinion on certain matters.

Morgan kept the beer flowing at our table, and seemed quite jolly; but I noted he watched the crowd's reaction to salient points as much as I did. When Striker finished, the questions began.

"So you took a man o' war with fifty men?" Morgan asked.

"Fourth-rate with a piss-poor crew," Striker said. "And we took her with six men on board, musketeers on the sloop, and a great many grenadoes."

"Impressive," Morgan said sincerely. "Which six men?"

Striker named us and pointed to each in turn. Morgan seemed surprised when it came to me. I did not think it was because he knew me by my title alone, but because he assumed much about me due to the title. I smiled at him with great amusement. He called for a toast to our bravery, and I was forced to elbow Gaston before he rolled his eyes.

"Can you name the dead?" a man asked.

Striker named every man that had died; and there was a moment of silence to honor them, and then another toast to all we had known who had passed on.

"And you know not of the *North Wind*?" a captain at our table asked.

"Nay, we were surprised she did not meet us here."

There was a toast to her well-being and speedy return.

"And how much gold did you lose?"

"Still aboard the galleon? At least three thousand doubloons, probably more."

Beer was spit, and there was a collective groan.

"YaDrinkToThatAndI'llPuke," Pete said.

This brought a great round of laughter.

There were a few more questions; and then the general party began, and Striker and Pete sat with us.

"So now what will you do?" Morgan asked as he poured Striker a mug.

"I do not know," Striker said. "I think we will wait a while to see if the *North Wind* shows."

"And if she does not?"

Striker frowned and shrugged. "I have considered purchasing a ship."

Morgan nodded thoughtfully. "I was hoping that would be your intent. We could use men like you and your fine companions here. As you may know, Bradley has been a friend of mine for many a year, and I value him greatly. I hope with all my heart that he will return to us safely, as I would miss him dearly if he does not. On a more practical note, I will miss his ship and expertise for our coming plans."

"Bradley said you plan to take a fleet against the Main," Striker said.

"Aye, I believe it is the best way to insure the safety of this colony; and the Governor agrees with me. It will also bring added prosperity here, just as Mansfield's and Myng's raiding did. And it's a better use of ships and men than chasing solitary vessels or fleets around the sea."

"We sailed with both," Striker said. "And I concur."

"I thought as much," Morgan replied. "It is my intent to call together a fleet in the cays of Cuba this winter, and once provisioned decide upon a target. Now that the war with the French has passed, I will be inviting those of them who are willing to sail with us as well."

A truce with the French was news to us, and Gaston and I exchanged a look.

"So, my good Striker," Morgan continued, "would you be willing to join us if you had a vessel? We could use you."

"Aye, I think I would, but first I could use a suitable vessel. Would you happen to know of any?"

"Unfortunately, no." Morgan smiled. "But if one were to become available, would you be able to purchase and equip it?"

Striker hesitated for a brief moment and then nodded resolutely. "I could."

"I see. So you are not a buccaneer who spends all of his money on wine and women," Morgan said.

"Nay," Pete said with annoyance. Striker smirked.

Morgan gave a small, apologetic shrug. "Of course."

I remembered that Morgan was married, and I had to stifle a smile. I wondered what Morgan had thought of matelotage prior to marriage.

As if Pete's solid rebuttal had diverted the course of his mind, Morgan turned his attention to Gaston and me. He regarded us with a small frown over the rim of his mug. I wondered what he saw; and then realized I had been drinking more than I assumed, as there was something to see. I was sitting, as was my custom in taverns filled with armed men, with my right leg crossed over my left, ankle to knee, my beer in my left hand and my right hand lying across my lap near the pommels of my pistol and sword. Gaston was to my left and sitting forward with his left elbow on the table, beer in hand, and his right arm draped across my shoulders. I had scarce noticed this, as it had felt as natural as my own limbs being where they should be. Morgan had noted it, though, and he was studying Gaston with interest. My matelot did not flinch from his gaze; and, as he was wearing his mask again, I knew Morgan saw little he could read in the smoky lantern light.

Morgan smiled and regarded his empty mug. "Lord Marsdale..."

"Will," I corrected sweetly.

"Will." He shrugged. " I would not have thought you to be one to become mired in the local customs so soon."

"Mired, hmmm?" I grinned and glanced at Gaston. "Oh, I am good and stuck, all right. I rather enjoy it."

This brought appreciative chuckles from the other men at the table. Gaston had grown very still, and I wondered if he had realized what he was doing. Neither of us could move now, not and keep up appearances.

"So I see you will not be pursuing our eligible young women,"

Morgan said slyly.

"Nay, I fear not. From what I witnessed at the last party I attended, they are not in need of an additional suitor any more than I am in need of a wife."

"Truly? One cannot rove forever. It is a young man's sport. What then?"

"I suppose one of us will learn how to order servants about, or cook."

This brought even more laughter, and to my surprise, Gaston even relaxed a little.

"What of progeny?"

"In all seriousness, Morgan, if I am to marry as a matter of my title, then it will be in England and to someone chosen by my family, expressly for the purpose of producing suitable offspring."

"Ah, aye, I had forgotten your father holds title as well," he said.

His forgetting was absurd, but I let it pass.

"And you are the oldest son, are you not?"

"I am indeed."

"And yet you are here."

"I possess an adventurous spirit."

"So we have noted. I would imagine it would behoove your father to have another heir in place, would it not, considering your current avocation?"

"Aye, it would." And I was quite sure my father did, as he had not been sure he had an heir for many a year.

"And what of you?" Morgan asked Striker. I found it of interest that he did not ask this of Pete and Gaston.

"I've got Pete. As for children, anything that issues from one of us should probably be drowned at birth, no matter who the dam is."

Even Gaston chuckled with the rest of us at that. I laughed, though I did not concur in the least. I felt the world needed more Petes and Strikers and fewer Morgans. This was never the way of things, though. No matter where I went in the world, the people most likely to produce offspring were the ones I felt should do it the least.

"Have you been blessed with progeny?" I asked Morgan.

His eyes flicked away for a moment before he smiled. "Nay, we have not been so blessed."

I decided not to pursue this, out of respect for his wife.

Striker stood. "If you will excuse us, I should buy my men a round. Thank you for the beer, and I'm sure you will hear when I find a ship."

Morgan nodded. "I will tell you if I hear of one first. Where might I find you?"

Striker sighed and looked to me, and we both shrugged.

"You should be able to locate us through Jonathan Theodore," I said.

I lolled my head back upon Gaston's arm, and looked to him with a grin. "We should escape with them," I whispered in French. My position had put our heads very close together, mere inches apart. I saw him start at our proximity.

He kissed me, the lightest press upon my lips.

Then he was standing, and I had the choice of sitting there like a stunned ewe or standing with him. I stood and finished my beer. I managed to thank Morgan for it and its fellows; and then I found my feet weaving through the crowd, following Gaston to the side of the room with our companions. Then we were in the midst of them, and there was much talking, and he would not look at me. He appeared distraught. I was sure I appeared the same. I knew this to be true when Theodore asked me what was amiss.

"Nothing that need concern you," I said quietly and kindly. "I would not choose to explain, even if I could."

"So be it," he shrugged. "When will you be visiting your Ithaca?"

For a small moment I did not know what he spoke of. "My father's Ithaca. Soon. How are they?"

"They are well..." He chuckled. "I will allow Fletcher and Donoughy the pleasure of regaling you with their triumphs and failures."

"Thank you. I will go there as soon as we resolve the issue of living quarters."

"We will see to that first thing in the morning," Theodore said.

Tom was standing behind him, and appeared ready to speak. Theodore graciously stepped aside.

"I will have you know I am not dissuaded," Tom said.

"You are a fool," I said lightly. "Striker managed to omit a number of pertinent details."

"Such as?"

"Eating nothing but salted or smoked pork and fruit for weeks on end. Sleeping on deck in the rain." He was smiling at me, and I remembered my amusement several months ago at Morgan's suggestion I was not hardy enough to be a buccaneer. I sighed. "You have to kill people."

A furrow creased his brow for a moment, and then his eyes flashed with defiance once again. "I feel I am capable of that."

I knew he understood there was a difference between feeling and knowing; and on that note, there was little else I could say.

"We will not sail until Striker locates a ship."

Before he could reply, one of the men dancing in the center of the room wheeled into Pete and knocked his beer from his hand. Pete roared his disapproval, and the man yelled, "Sorry mate, it's a party!"

Pete picked the man up by collar and belt and threw him onto a table. "NowIt'sAParty!"

The men at the table roared and came after Pete and proved him correct, as the amusement truly began. I turned to face the majority of the room and made ready to duck anything thrown my way.

Theodore and Tom were still standing beside me, with Dickey and Belfry behind them looking rather alarmed.

"I would leave now, but..." Theodore said.

I could see his cause for concern. All of the action was between us and the door. "I am sure if you inquired politely, Pete would be happy to throw you out the window," I shouted to be heard over the noise.

"I will pass, thank you," Theodore shouted and ducked a hurled mug.

"Perhaps the back," Tom said.

I glared at him. "I thought you wished to be a buccaneer." Before he could protest, I grinned and punched him in the jaw. He fell back in a heap, taking Dickey with him.

There was a tug on my tunic and I whirled to find Gaston on the table. He pointed at the window and I joined him quickly. Theodore scrambled up behind me as Gaston opened the sash. We crawled out into the alley. To my surprise, we were followed by Cudro, who had been at the table we stood upon.

He glared at us. "I am not up for another fight." He leaned heavily on the wall, and I remembered he had been using a crutch, which he did not have at the moment.

"Where are you sleeping?"

He shrugged. "We intended to go to the beach."

I swore. We could not leave him standing there, or rather not standing there. His cronies could be hours and not remember to look for him at all, depending on how many blows they took or beers they drank. I looked to my matelot and remembered I still needed to strangle him. I sighed. Gaston shrugged.

"Come on then," I told Cudro.

He regarded me curiously, until I offered him my shoulder to lean on. He seemed as reluctant to take my help as I was to give it; but he was as quickly bound by my offer of assistance as I was bound by some shred of human decency. We made our slow way back to Theodore's in silence. Once there, I deposited him in the office, where we would be sleeping for the night.

"Thank you," he said sincerely.

I shrugged. "You are welcome after a fashion. I still do not like you."

"It is mutual." He smiled.

"It is good that we have this understanding, then."

Theodore had roused Samuel and they brought Cudro some water. I looked about; Gaston was not to be seen. I knew he had accompanied us to the house. I exited through the front door and found him leaning on the wall, with his arms crossed and one leg bent. It was a moonless night illuminated only by the lantern at Theodore's door. Half of Gaston was in shadow, the other half harshly lit in yellow.

"I am sorry. I was possessed," he whispered ruefully.

"Truly?" I approached him until he was within reach. I crossed my arms to prevent my hands from bridging the distance between us. "And what, pray tell, possessed you?"

"I have been trying to determine that."

He finally deigned to look upon me, and we studied each other in silence for a time.

"I wanted to," he whispered. "You had been so far away, and then you were so close, and it felt...correct."

I was greatly heartened by this, and I moved toward him again until we almost touched.

"I have missed touching you, also."

He was so close I could feel his breath. He did not flinch from me. My mind grasped the memory of the softness I had felt for just a moment in the tavern and the two times we had kissed before boarding. I imagined how his lips would feel under mine again. I could start with the gentlest of kisses, a mere twitch of my lips on his, and then I would rub across them lightly. My manhood sprang to life, not a slow unfolding, but a near- painful rush of need and desire.

I would kiss him. And then he would stop me.

I smiled sadly. "I would kiss you if you would but let me. I wish to count your teeth with my tongue."

His eyes widened, and he drew in on himself in an effort to pull farther away from me. I allowed myself amusement at my foreknowledge. I had phrased it somewhat crudely on purpose. If desire had been upon him, as it was upon me, he would not have reacted so.

"I do not know when," I continued softly. "Whether it be when you first feel my lips or after our tongues are entwined, but you will stop me. And no matter what your reason for it, it will be as a knife in my gut, and it will cause far more pain than any blade you carry. I do not blame you for this. It is the way it is. In truth I fear it is my problem, a thing resulting from my scars."

Another realization visited me, and I winced from it. "I know now that I am not as scared of the possibility of you hating me for what we might do – as I am of me hating you for what we will not do. I am a horrid bastard, I truly am."

He frowned with concern and shook his head ever so slightly. "You are not the only one afflicted here."

I could still only see half his face in the lantern's light. I reached into the shadow and traced his brow and cheek, as if I could truly find the part of him lost in the dark somehow.

His eyes flicked down and I followed his gaze. My manhood was evident in my britches. I chuckled softly and let my fingers fall from his face. "I am quite predictable."

As I started to turn away, his hand closed over my crotch; and my manhood leaped, as it was captured in strong fingers through the cloth. I gasped and found myself leaning with my hands on either side of him. I regarded him curiously, our faces mere inches apart.

"You have my complete attention," I whispered.

"Hush." With his free hand, he laid his fingers across my lips. His other hand moved, gently stroking, and I closed my eyes and moaned. He turned his hand so that it covered my mouth with his thumb below my chin and then his other hand moved a great deal more. I groaned quietly into his palm until I came, and slumped against him. He wrapped his arms around me and held me for a long while.

I heard approaching voices and footsteps and I began to straighten. He grasped my head and held me close to whisper fiercely in my ear, "Will, I will never hate you for that, sane or mad. I will never hate you." I hugged him to me and kissed his cheek.

Then the rabble was upon us. It took a good hour to clean the lot of them up and bandage those who needed it. Gaston was actually called upon to stitch a gash on Pete's head and a cut on Davey's lip. He boiled the suture needle and thread before using it on each man, and liberally doused their wounds in rum. As they were drunk, they did not complain overly much about being steeped in more liquor. Belfry had wrenched his wrist in some fashion and required a sling. One of Cudro's friends had received a nasty hit on his head, and Gaston ordered that he be sobered up and kept awake until the darks of his eyes became the same size.

"You are a surgeon, aren't you?" Striker asked. He was drunk and sitting on the ground near the cistern, with Pete's snoring head in his lap.

Gaston rewarded him a disparaging snort. "Of sorts."

"We will need a surgeon," Striker said.

"I do not wish to be a surgeon," Gaston said.

"But if you have the skills, and so few do, how can you deny your fellow buccaneers?"

Gaston squatted in front of Striker and stared into his bleary eyes. "It is very easy. You just say no."

Striker waved him off. "When the four of us get a ship. You get to be surgeon. Pete will be quartermaster." He looked at me. "I don't know what we'll do with Will. He doesn't know much about sailing. We need the Bard, God damn it."

"Hold, hold," I said. "What do you mean, when the four of us get a ship?"

He shrugged. "I have enough money to buy a ship and outfit her, but not by much. It would be better to spread the cost and risk between more people. That way everyone doesn't end up in debt when she sinks or there are no prizes."

"I see your point. How much do ships cost?"

"Four to five hundred pounds."

I was surprised, as I had thought they cost more. In all, the idea appealed to me, but it was not my decision alone. I regarded Gaston.

He shrugged. "I have nothing against purchasing a ship." He appeared thoughtful as he packed his surgeon's kit away. "I have the funds; it is not something a man like me does. Yet with Striker as captain, we could attract enough men to sail."

"Aye," Striker said. "Men like me."

"Why is that?" I teased.

He frowned, not out of umbrage, but due to being so intoxicated he considered the question bona fide.

I patted his head. "Nay, I jest."

"I would ask why you seem to favor me," Striker said.

I gave this due consideration, and decided a shorter response would be better, and it encompassed all that need be said, anyway. "You are a good man, in my book anyway."

He nodded somberly. "I am honored."

"As well you should be."

This time he knew I jested; and he smiled and leaned his head back on the cistern.

"Will you be joining us inside?" I asked. "Or will you sleep out here?"

Striker poked Pete's shoulder a few times. The man did not move.

"Out here." Striker shrugged and pulled a pistol. He flopped sideways, so he lay partially on Pete with the pistol in hand. It did not appear comfortable, but he was snoring before we finished cleaning ourselves and extinguished the lamps to retire inside.

In the front room, Cudro and his cronies occupied a large part of the floor behind the desk. They were playing cards and trying dutifully to keep their comrade awake. Davey and Julio had another corner and were sprawled in their sleep. There was little room left, with the exception of the middle or the doorways. This appealed to neither of us. We eyed the back room speculatively, and Gaston moved the chairs from about the table and hefted one end of it. I regarded him curiously, and he indicated I should take the other end. I did so, and followed his lead to move the table to the wall. Then he climbed under it. I followed suit.

"Are you attempting to insure that they wake us for breakfast, or should I find a cloth and we can make a small house?" I asked. "Did you do that as a child?"

"You were allowed to make houses with the dining furniture?" he asked incredulously.

"In my room, but nowhere else."

"I can scarce imagine that," he sighed. "You can put out the lamp."

I regarded the lamp and then turned to face him again. "There are things we should discuss."

He shook his head. He appeared exhausted as he arranged weapons and our bags. "We should sleep. We will both be here in the morning. Now put the lantern out and lie with me."

I realized there was little I could refuse him on. I did as he bade, and he pulled me to him, to rest with my head on his shoulder. As I have never been comfortable sleeping in that manner, with my arm under my person, I squirmed about until my back was to him but my head was nestled on his upper arm.

I lay there a while and considered the events of the past few hours, specifically between him and me, as the rest were not things I would lose sleep over. Where were we now, and what would I discuss with him on the morrow? Did I trust him not to wound me again? My resolution to protect myself was so much dust in the wind. As I gave it all great thought with an exhausted and beer-addled mind, I came to realize that I would rather risk injury than deny myself this. I was home; and I was, for the moment, content.

Sometime in the morning, at least I guessed it was morning as it was not dark but not fully light either, I woke to a gentle rapping on the table leg. Beside me, I could feel Gaston's body tense. Clutching a pistol, I looked toward our feet and saw one of Cudro's men regarding us with anxious exhaustion, or perhaps exhausted anxiety.

"Benjo's eyes, they be all right now. He sleep?" the man asked.

With an incoherent groan of annoyance, Gaston rolled from under the table and followed the man into the other room. I crawled out and made my way into the yard to the latrine. Once finished, I emerged to find my matelot waiting.

"He will live," he grumped and slammed the latrine door. As he relieved himself, I stood in the grey light and looked about. The fires had been started in most of the cookhouses near us, and servants could be seen working in the other yards.

Pete and Striker were still sprawled on the ground where we had left them, but Pete had apparently been startled by the door slamming; and his tousled and bloody head peered over the cistern. I waved. He belched and fingered his bandages curiously. I entered our cookhouse and woke Samuel, and retrieved a couple bottles of water. I handed one to Pete before meeting Gaston at the house's back door.

Pete was exploring the wrapping and what might lie under it in earnest now.

"Do not touch it," Gaston snapped. "I put five stitches in your head last night."

Pete's hand obediently left his head; and he sat still, looking all the world like a little boy who had been scolded.

"You may want to drink some water," I suggested quietly, before following Gaston inside. Once there I teased, "With that demeanor, you will never be able to maintain wealthy patients."

He glared at me over his shoulder before crawling beneath the table. I joined him.

He shook his head, and a small smile finally graced his lips. "Can you envision it, me calling upon the rich to cure gout?"

"As you are dressed and armed now, and even with the Carribe face paint," I chuckled. "I can see it all as clearly as if I stood in some great drawing room and listened to the matron of the house squeal and the servants rush about for the salts."

We laughed quietly, until he sobered and sighed. "I think I shall never return to the Old World. I do not know what I would do there. As we have discussed before, I cannot conceive of living within the confines of civilization."

"Which is that in name only. I understand." This brought to mind Morgan's words, and I frowned. "I cannot conceive of returning, either, at the moment; but there is that matter of the title and all hanging over my head, and my life rarely follows the course I think to set for it.”

We regarded one another. In his eyes I beheld my own consternation at the realization that there was the potential for our futures to be quite incompatible.

“Alonso asked me to join him in Panama,” I said. Gaston frowned, and I held up my hand to bid him to hear me out. “I refused, obviously, since I am here and not there. I knew that if I were to accompany him, we would not have lived as we had in Florence, and he would marry and have children, and I would be this curiosity in his life. I want you to know that I would never expect that of you. Even if you were willing to do such a thing, I cannot see being married to some woman for the sole purpose of producing heirs, while you have a room down the hall. And that,” I paused as the ramifications of what I was about to say became clear to me. “If it is a choice between my inheritance and you, I choose you.”

He hugged his knees and smiled sadly. “I am truly honored, but you are a fool. I will not hold you to it. Think of all the sheep you could herd, Will? And we cannot know what the future will bring.”

His words reminded me of the epiphany I had experienced with Rucker. I did indeed have sheep to herd; yet I could not now bear to think of doing it alone. “Do you judge me insincere?”

“Non, not at all. But who will we be in ten years? We could be dead. Your father could disinherit you. All manner of things could occur. You may experience a change of heart for very excellent reasons.”

I was forced to admit to that possibility. I nodded with heaviness in my spirit.

“I would do the same for you if it were an option,” he said quietly.

I smiled. I wished to embrace him but I was unsure as to where we stood on such things. “May I hold you?”

He considered this, but did not readily agree. I forced myself not to make much of it.

“I understand. It is not necessary,” I said softly, and began to crawl from under the table. He pounced upon me, bowling me over so that we both struck the far table leg.

By his design, he ended up astride my waist, grinning down at me with his hands on either side of my head. I had not fought him at all.

“It is,” he said.

Never one to shy away from a fight, my manhood found this all terribly interesting and began to think about waking.

I slid my hands tentatively up his arms. “May I?”

He frowned with consternation. “Are you truly so terrified of me?”

“Oui,” I said, perhaps too quickly. This seemed to trouble him even more. “I am not afraid of you so much as I am afraid of... causing...”

He cut me off with a nod, and I was thankful, as I did not know how best to phrase it. I did not want this to end. I did not want him to withdraw. And I did not want to receive another knife prick in my side.

“I have decided that it would be best if I were more aggressive,” he said seriously.

"All right, then," I said with equal sobriety, even though I was deeply amused. "Do with me as you will." I could not help a teasing grin on the last.

He sighed and smiled. "I realize that is rather like a blind man leading a horse."

I laughed, and he joined me in it, until he sank to my chest and let me embrace him. His hands found the straw stubble of my scalp, and he explored the texture with gentle fingers. I felt very peaceful, and we dozed until we heard footsteps.

I roused myself enough to turn my head and spy Theodore at the base of the stairs, regarding us and the room with confused and bleary eyes.

His voice was hoarse. "I have come to the conclusion that there are things I do not need to know, as the questioning of them would tire an already-weary mind."

"A little too much to drink last night, Theodore?" I teased.

He groaned. "You buccaneers may be familiar with hard drinking, but I am not."

"Nay, I feel we, or rather they, are not either, unless in port. There was no alcohol on the *North Wind* and verily we went weeks without, with the exception of the time we were able to purchase a keg from another vessel. As you can well imagine, that did not stay amongst us long. As for myself, this last five months, since before I left England even, I have consumed less alcohol than during any similar period in the last ten years. I have spent most days appallingly sober."

"All of Port Royal's residents think we buccaneers do nothing but drink and fuck because that is all they see," Gaston said, from where he still rested upon my chest.

"I did not mean all the time, because I have dealt with enough sober buccaneers to know better," Theodore said, and roused himself to go and sit in one of the chairs in the middle of the room. "But when you do drink, you drink to excess."

"True," Gaston said.

"Why is my table in the corner?" Theodore asked.

"I thought you were not going to ask that," I remarked.

He sighed. "I am compelled."

Gaston slowly raised himself off me and to his knees. "I do not wish to be stepped upon while sleeping."

Theodore looked around the empty room in a slow but somewhat comical manner. "Did you think that imminent?"

"One never can tell with drunken buccaneers about," my matelot said with a smile.

"Ah, I see your point," Theodore said. "Speaking of drunken buccaneers being about, after we break the fast, we should go and have a look at the house the Jews are letting."

"Ah," I said. "Aye, I have heard mention that there are Jews in Port

Royal." I tried to remember who had told me. Belfry, perhaps.

"Aye, they came here from Brazil, and then there was another group from London, and another from somewhere else, I forget where. There are at most a mere fifty of them, but they seem content to stay. One of them died recently, and he possessed a large house on the next street over. From my understanding of it, his family is wisely loathe to sell it before all the land on the cay is granted. They wish to make some money on it while it is empty, though. I feel you could let it for a time, until you decide where you wish to live, or if you wish to stay here at all. They do not have a true house built on the plantation yet."

"I could not imagine residing there, even if they did," I said. "A lot and house in town would have its uses, but of course if we are soon able to purchase a ship, I suppose it will not matter, as we will have a place to sleep there."

"You're going to buy a ship?" Theodore asked.

"Not alone, as I lack the money to do so, but the enterprise has presented itself; a likely candidate has of yet not." I pulled myself upright and assisted Gaston in returning the table to its rightful position, as Samuel was standing in the doorway with a kettle and looking rather vexed. "What became of Ella?" I asked.

"I moved her on to another who felt he had more use for her than I," Theodore said with a tired sigh. "I do not regret it." He regarded Gaston and me with renewed speculation, as we sat in chairs at the table and helped ourselves to the hot chocolate. "Marsdale, may I ask a question of a personal nature as your barrister and agent?"

"It is simply Will now, amongst the Brethren. And you may ask anything."

"Will, then. Are you two matelots?"

"Oh!" I chuckled. I remembered that we had not been, or at least not named it such, when last we saw Theodore. "Aye."

"And so if something were to befall you?"

"He is my heir, aye."

Gaston appeared thoughtful as he rubbed his temple and sipped chocolate. I raised a questioning brow. He shook his head and sighed. "I realize I must make similar arrangements, though the majority of my assets are on Île de la Tortue. Still, I have some money here."

Theodore seemed to be in deep reverie as he studied his cup. As I still harbored fear of condemnation from amongst those not of the Brethren regarding such matters, I began to feel he had concerns regarding our relationship. Then he surprised me; and I learned once again that I should not judge another based on my own anticipations.

"I need a wife," Theodore said sadly. "Not so much for copulation, though assuredly that would be of interest, but for solace and companionship; and God knows I need someone to keep the house and myself."

"Can you not send for one?" I asked. "Surely you know families in England who could suggest a suitable woman."

He shook his head. "Aye, I do. But I must confess a certain romantic inclination in such regards, and I have little interest in wedding a woman I have not laid eyes upon or conversed with."

"Theodore, I find that perfectly understandable," I assured him; and then I smiled as I thought of the last matchmaking venture I had witnessed. He eyed me as if I might have found humor in him. "Nay, um…" I stood and peered over him into the front room, where I could see Davey and Julio still deeply in the thralls of slumber. "Let me tell you how Davey got his matelot." I indicated the couple, and Theodore nodded with interest. Gaston was smiling now, and we quickly related the tale. Theodore was greatly amused. "If you wish, we could charge Pete with the task."

"Nay, thank you, nay," Theodore said quickly, with a laugh.

"Probably for the best, as I doubt he has acquaintance with any women in town, much less anywhere else."

Samuel entered with two heaping platters of pork chops, bacon, and eggs, and was immediately followed by Pete and Striker. He set the food upon the table and regarded us, or rather the spaces in front of us, quizzically. With a heavy sigh, he went to fetch plates and flatware from the sideboard. I wondered how long they had been without Ella.

Then a graver matter occurred to me. "Can any of us cook in a reasonable fashion, beyond the obvious fish upon a stick or making boucan? We're talking of letting a house; and I fear that without the constant supervision of an individual versed in the arts of cooking and cleaning, we will shortly be living in a den with bones heaped upon the walls, because we forgot there are no sharks about to clean up after us when we fling things."

The others were amused, with the exception of Pete, who seemed to possess both an aching head and a serious regard for the topic.

"Dahgs," he said.

Striker patted him gently on the shoulder. "They cannot cook or be sent to the market or refill lanterns with oil."

"I will place inquiries," Theodore said, and then frowned. "How many of you will be dwelling there?"

"At least six, I would imagine," I said. "Possibly more, as the need arises; but they would be billeted as they are now." I smiled.

"That is lovely," he sighed. "I would suggest purchasing at least two hearty slaves of a congenial nature, if they can be found."

"WhoCanCook," Pete added around a mouthful of pork chop.

"You may be forced to take what you can get, and I would place priority on the congenial nature," Theodore replied grimly.

Pete frowned and looked to his matelot for explanation.

"He thinks we may be difficult to live with," Striker said with a chuckle.

"MeHardToLiveWith?"

"Nay, non," we all assured him.

The house we were to let sat in the triangular corner at the

intersection of Lime and New streets. The lot was larger than
Theodore's, possessing a goodly yard with a chicken coop and small goat
pen in addition to cookhouse, cistern and latrine. The house was also of
greater size, and had four rooms upon the upper floors and three upon
the lower, with an additional small room protruding into the yard for
servants. We were pleased with the place, as it would afford the space
we required.

The original owner's brother, a Mister Abraham Arpenasus, who I
learned had come here from Brazil, was not pleased about the prospect
of letting the place to buccaneers. Then Theodore made much of my title
and that I was a plantation owner and the like; and the man became
assured that not only would we pay, in advance, but we would also not
burn the building to the ground as the result of some Bacchanalian
festivity. I was sorely tempted to let him know that such a thing was
perhaps more likely to occur because I was an Earl's son.

As the necessary papers were signed and money exchanged, I
inquired if he knew of any slaves or bondsmen for sale, or perhaps
a housekeeper for hire. He regarded me coldly from behind his well-
groomed but flowing beard and brows.

"You be sodomites?" he asked abruptly.

As Pete and Striker were engaged at the chicken coop, which the
Golden One had developed a fascination with, Theodore, Gaston, and I
blinked with surprise.

"Aye," I answered brusquely, before Theodore could attempt to
dissemble or in other way deflect the situation, as I was sure he would.

"All who would live here be sodomites?" Arpenasus asked. "No man
amongst you with a fondness for women?"

"Aye and none," I said.

"Then wait here, if you please." He hurried two houses down the
street, and went inside.

We all regarded one another, and Theodore sighed, "At least he
signed the contract first."

"I have an inkling as to why he asked," I said.

"And what would that be?" Theodore snapped.

"Let us see if my suspicion proves out," I replied firmly. When
Arpenasus emerged from the house with a woman, I knew myself to be
correct. I rewarded Theodore with a triumphant grin, and he regarded
me quizzically before turning his attention to the pair approaching us.

The woman was possibly of an age with Gaston and me. She was
no longer a girl, but still young. She possessed a confident gait, and
she looked each of us over in turn as she approached. She was quite
fetching, as she was slim of form and had a pleasing countenance. She
was swathed in black from the scarf upon her head to the boots on her
feet; and I wondered how, in Port Royal's heat, she did not melt away
like butter in the sun.

Pete and Striker joined us; Pete had a chicken tucked under his arm
and a wide grin.

"It'sGreen," he proclaimed proudly. The fowl did indeed have a green sheen to its black feathers. Pete held it out by the feet, and turned it this way and that, so that we might better observe this interesting color.

"He is not always like that," Theodore said quickly.

The rest of us regarded Theodore incredulously.

"Well actually he is," I said.

The woman suppressed a smile. Pete noticed her for the first time, and stepped back and pointed with approximately the same degree of consternation the Bard had evinced upon finding hogs upon his ship.

"Bah."

Arpenasus chuckled. "I see I have nothing to fear. This is my niece, Rachel. She is a widow with no children."

I noted that Rachel winced ever so slightly at this.

"She would be available at two shillings a month to keep house, under the condition that nothing untoward occurs concerning her person. She is not to be subjected to any lewdness or advances."

"Sir, I feel I can reasonably assure you that that will not be an issue," I said.

Arpenasus returned to his house, and I made introductions. Rachel nodded respectfully to each of us, and I could see that she was attempting to decide who we all were in relation to one another.

Pete was still playing with the squawking fowl.

"That is a laying hen," Rachel told him in an authoritative voice that showed she was not at all cowed by the large, half-naked barbarian. "Put her back in the coop."

The Golden One did not pout, as he usually did when scolded. His features settled into a scowl, and his body shifted ever so subtly to a fighter's footing. I quickly surmised that Striker had not been exaggerating when he told us Pete did not like women.

Beside him, Striker appeared alarmed, and I could see him casting about in his mind for some way to remedy the matter.

"Can you bake pies?" he asked Rachel quickly. "Cheesecakes?"

Rachel shrugged. "Aye, sir."

"Such a thing would go a long way to making Pete here a happy man," Striker said.

"Pete being a happy man would be in the best interests of all," I added.

Her gaze returned to Pete, and understanding suffused her fine features. She nodded. Her voice was gentler, but not patronizing.

"I am sorry to snap like that, sir, but I am used to scolding my brothers and cousins. You can look at the chickens all ye want, but if they are scared they will not lay, and there will be no eggs for breakfast."

"IfSheBeMeanToMeSheGoes," Pete said to all of us, and stomped back to the coop.

A truly awkward silence settled over us for a moment.

"I am sorry, sirs," Rachel said. "I will endeavor not to anger him again. I wish for this be acceptable to all of us, as I do not wish to return to my uncle's house."

"I am sure everything will be fine," Theodore said with forced cheer.

Striker was kind. "It would be best if you did not order him about or scold him. I would say do not hit him but that, uh..."

"I would not dream of it, sir," she said quickly.

"If you should ever feel he is about to strike you," I said and looked to Striker. His small nod let me know that was indeed a possibility. "If that were to occur, you should run and seek one of us immediately."

She gave us a sad smile. "Sir, if that is to start I may as well move back to my uncle's. I know what to do in such a situation. I cover my head and wait for it to pass."

"Nay," Striker said firmly. "You should run. I doubt the men you have lived with before have killed men for a living."

"Oh," she said. "Then I shall run."

"To us, as we are the only ones who may be able to mollify him." Striker frowned. "Please understand; no man here will condone him striking you. We will not tolerate it. However, it is a possibility. I love that man with all my heart, but he is possessed of demons sometimes, as we all are. I would not see you harmed by things you are not responsible for."

She nodded soberly. "Is it possible that I befriend him then, sir?"

"I do not know. I have never seen him around a woman for any duration. I do know that he has ever had a woman be kind to him." Striker went to talk to Pete.

"You do not actually think he would harm her?" Theodore said, with a good deal of indignation.

I shrugged, and Rachel cut off his next protest. "In truth sir, I would rather it be this way. I would rather a man hate me and hit me than say he loves me and hit me."

"I concur," I said with a smile.

She entered the house and Theodore followed her, apparently in a furor to discuss furnishing it; or perhaps he just wanted to bask in her womanly presence.

"If he does strike her, he will only do it once," Gaston said quietly in French.

"I know," I said, "because she will be dead from the first blow. I would say we should terminate her services and send her home for her own safety; however, that does not seem to be safe or acceptable either, and she seems willing to embrace the risk."

As I was, I thought. I, too, had accepted the Gods' challenge.

Eighteen

Wherein We Share

We left furnishing, provisioning, and all other things associated with preparing a house for residence in more capable hands, and retrieved our gear and proceeded to the gunsmith's. We left our muskets to be disassembled, checked for damage from immersion in salt water and the general mishandling they had suffered, and then cleaned, oiled, and the wood sealed anew. Additionally, we left half of our pistols there for the same service.

Gaston went to the back room to discuss something with Massey, and I guessed it to be the cost of these services.

When we left the smith's, I asked, "So how much do I owe you now?"

He regarded me sharply. "You owe me nothing. We are matelots, Will. All I have is yours."

"I know that in theory, but we have not discussed money." We had not been matelots prior to roving; and now that we were, the only matters of money had been the selling of the tobacco, which we had both taken a separate share of, and my using that to pay for half the advance rent on the house. Striker had paid the other half.

Gaston paused in the street and regarded me with concern. "I am sorry, Will. I am not used to speaking of it. Do you have any money?"

"Possibly thirty pounds at Theodore's."

He regarded me with surprise. "No wonder you are concerned. I have close to a thousand pounds with Massey, and a great deal more with another on Île de la Tortue. If anything befalls me, it is yours. I have already informed Massey; the amount on Île de la Tortue will be more difficult for you to obtain, as the one who holds it for me does not approve of matelotage."

I was near slack-jawed at the amount. "I have married well, indeed."

He smirked.

"Who is this other on Île de la Tortue?"

He frowned. "My... mentor, Dominic Doucette. I will tell you of him sometime, but not here and now."

I nodded, and we continued up the street. I still did not feel I was due his money; but it was as if a great weight had been lifted from me, knowing that I need not worry about how we would come up with our share of a ship or how I would pay to have my weapons cleaned.

By midmorning, we were on a ferry to the Passage Fort, and shortly thereafter at the livery. I chose the best two animals available, and was anticipating some fine riding, as the day was breezy and clouded and not overly hot. Gaston eyed the animals suspiciously, with his arms firmly crossed; and I knew my plans were not to be realized.

"Ah, I remember you saying something of not being a horseman."

He sighed. "Non. I am not a horseman. I have never possessed any talent for horsemanship or fondness for the beasts, and I have not ridden since coming here."

I regarded the two spirited geldings I had chosen and, with a sigh, inquired of the stable boy as to their most placid and tractable mount. He pointed to a swaybacked mare in the paddock.

Gaston sighed yet again. "Even I can see that is an ugly horse; and I would not wish to trouble it, as it appears ill. I will endure, and possibly not conquer, but at least endeavor to make peace with this animal." He approached the sorrel, which eyed him askance.

"Non, take the bay; he seems good-spirited. I do not feel that red-headed demon has any interest in making peace with you." I tied our bags behind the saddles.

"You feel the other one is angelic in its browness?"

"Non, I feel he is somewhat more angelic in that he is not champing at his bit and did not take a nip at the stable boy."

Gaston kept his distance as he circled the sorrel and cautiously approached the bay, from the wrong side. It was difficult not to laugh.

"Am I to understand that you have truly experienced less than positive moments on horseback?"

He snorted and slipped under the bay's neck, to get between the two animals on the supposedly angelic horse's correct side, where he proceeded to mount it with some degree of competence.

"Staying on the animal's back has always been a positive experience," he said, once up.

I mounted the demonic sorrel. Just out of the paddock, our mounts were a little skittish, as they were in need of exercise. They pranced and sidestepped a bit, and tossed their heads, as high-spirited and healthy animals are wont to do on occasion. During this, Gaston hung on and maintained little control of the animal, so that I was forced to grab his reins. I realized how apt his metaphor for his madness was. Or rather, I was able to view it in a different light.

I got both animals walking up the road at a brisk pace, and they soon settled down. Gaston relaxed, and I was able to hand his reins back. He awarded me a grateful and slightly sheepish look.

"Thank you; I do not know how to control them."

"They are merely restless. They become content when they realize they are actually going somewhere."

He nodded and regarded his horse's pricked ears. "They are a bit like very large dogs. I am fond of dogs."

I chuckled. "I like dogs, though I never developed an affinity for them. I have always been fond of horses, though," I said lightly. "I used to ride to the hunt, and have often found a good ride of any speed to be a balm for my soul. I have always kept a fine horse if I resided anywhere for sufficient duration. Have you kept dogs?"

"Oui, on the Haiti, but they are more feral creatures. I have never owned a horse, and I did not learn to ride until I was twelve."

"See, therein lies the problem. I had a pony named Blackie when I was two, an age where I had no sense and no fear. With him began my affinity with horses, especially black ones, though the color obviously does not have a damn thing to do with their performance or behavior. I have always been fond of ebony animals, though."

My mind was running through the various black beasts I had owned, and I recalled Goliath. The old heart-rending emotions filled me; and I watched a wagon pass us on its way to the Passage Fort with great interest, in an attempt to distract myself.

"Is something wrong?" Gaston asked.

"Old memories," I sighed. "The best horse I ever owned was a spirited black stallion that was damn near too large to be considered a proper hunter. He was more destrier than riding animal. He could jump and run, though, and I imagined he could have done so with equal alacrity even if I had been astride him fully equipped in plate mail. I was the only one who could ride him. My cousin found this unacceptable, and while I was away, he sought to break him for his own use. I returned to find a tortured and ruined horse that I had to put down. I almost shot his hunting dogs in retaliation; but I could not bring myself to harm them, as they were as innocent of the war being waged as my horse had been. So I created a funeral pyre for Goliath using every ounce of alcohol in the house, because that was my cousin's favorite thing. Of course he could always procure more, and the horse and been a unique creature. I left home after that, as the damage to those around us had grown too high."

I was overwrought, and I wished to give the sorrel his head and just run. I had not intended to say as much as I had. Gaston rode silently beside me, and I could feel him waiting. I knew I should continue and explain. I knew I could say I did not wish to discuss it, and he would leave me with it; but I no longer wished to carry it. It would be best if he knew.

Yet, even though I had spoken of it all before, it was still damnably difficult to force the words from my throat. "I had... have... a cousin, a second cousin on my father's side, named Jacob Shane. He came to live with us when I was eight. I had always desired a brother, as I was a lonely boy in a big house, with only servants and tutor to annoy and no one to play with. Shane was a serious boy, and deeply troubled by the death of his family. We shortly became the closest of friends, as boys are wont to do. He was better than me at everything, except our studies and riding. My parents found his demeanor far more suitable than mine. He excelled at the sword and all other physical pursuits. It was considered by many a shame that I was my father's son and not he. I later learned he felt the same, and was resentful that a mere difference in birth had put me in the path of so much and him so little. Yet when we were young, all of this was not known or understood, and we lived in a kind of Eden with few cares.

"Then our lives were ravaged by adolescence. As I discovered my manhood, I came to understand that I was fond of boys and not girls. I became infatuated with Shane in something other than a platonic sense. One day, a situation occurred in which we discovered his manhood was as interested in being pleased as mine, and cared not who did the pleasing. For a time after that, our lives achieved an even greater degree of perfection, as we had this new territory to explore together. Then he discovered that it was not a place a proper Christian young man should go. He began to avoid me during the day and continue to seek me out at night. And then he began to publicly revile me amongst our associates and still seek me out at night. And finally I began to resist and... the war began, of which my horse was the greatest casualty, and I was forced to retreat wounded."

We entered Spanish Town and I was thankful for the interruption. Once we were through and on the road to the plantation, I hazarded a glance at him. He was quiet and thoughtful.

"I did not kill him," I said quietly. "I had not killed before and I felt.... I felt I had led him astray and it was my fault. And I harbored hope with a fool's fervor that he would change."

"Will," Gaston said gently. "I understand. I do. This thing that happened to me, the scars, I brought it on myself and I do not blame the one who did it, as I would probably have done the same."

That bothered me, but the calm in his eyes forced all the other thoughts away.

"I love you," I said.

He smiled. "I know. Because I now understand that what I said to you on the galleon was tantamount to hitting me with a whip, and yet you stayed."

The dark pressure weighing on my soul had been released for a while, and I felt more content than I could remember. I moved my horse closer and caressed Gaston's cheek. He captured my hand and kissed the backs of my fingers. He did not release me.

"Do you think it is possible to... perhaps not erase memories and pains, but to paint over them?" he asked.

I nodded. "I have been able to, on occasion. Alonso's patience and persistence allowed me to... receive a man's love again. I had been bestowing myself upon those who would have me for many years and..."

He flushed and looked away, but he did not release my hand.

"I am sorry," I said. "I know..."

"Be patient," he whispered. "Not that you are not already."

I squeezed his hand.

"May I ask you something awful that you may not wish to speak of?" he asked.

"Do I get to ask a question in return?"

He thought on this, and nodded. "Oui."

"And your question is?"

He clenched my hand almost painfully. "Did this cousin of yours, this Shane, did he..."

I knew what he would say; and I looked away, as I did not want to see him when he asked it or when I responded.

"Did he force himself upon you?"

I took a deep breath and watched a bird wheel over the distant trees. "Oui."

"I had guessed as much," he whispered.

I still could not look at him. "Several times."

"Will, you need not..."

"Oui, I do. The first few, I told myself that I wanted it, even if he was so damn cruel and... and then the last time he bludgeoned me and I... bled for days, and I could not lie anymore."

I let myself remember. I never let myself truly remember. I filled with the old pain and fear and rage and shame and his weight upon me and the vile things he said – and... I was sobbing and clawing at the horse, as I had once done my bedding. Unlike the sheets of old, it was tossing its head and sidestepping in terror. I dismounted and let it skitter away, and I stumbled into the cane and vomited bile.

Gaston joined me, and I shied from his touch on my shoulder. He resolutely handed me the water skin, and backed away to wait with arms crossed. I hugged the water, not sure that my shaking hands could bring it to my lips without spilling it.

When I achieved sufficient mastery over my racing thoughts once again, I regarded him.

"I am..."

"Do not apologize to me." His tone was strong but his eyes were soft.

I nodded and managed to drink some water, though my hands were still unsteady. "I do not let myself remember it."

"I know. You give me hope."

"How so?"

"If you can... do anything with a man then there is a chance I can learn how not to... slip into madness at any reminder of it."

"I will do whatever is in my power to assist you."

He nodded. "Now it is your turn."

"For?"

"Asking a question."

I thought of my reaction. And then I thought that being reminded of the incident triggered his bouts. I was near loathe to ask anything at all. I settled upon a single thing.

"Who... did that to you?"

"My father," he said simply.

I nodded, and thought of all the times he had frozen at mention of this sire.

"Well, then, I can see why you do not feel any need to correspond with him."

He blinked and then smiled. He closed the distance between us and embraced me with a ferocity that would have done Pete proud.

I held him gratefully. I felt as exhausted as if I had sparred for hours. Thankfully, he said nothing; and after a peaceful eternity, we gathered our horses and rode on. In the aftermath, I did not wish to think. The cork crammed into my soul had been released, and I breathed far easier.

Sugarcane spread in patches on either side of us now, as we made our way north. Occasionally we glimpsed groups of men – some black, some white – toiling in the fields underneath the gaze of overseers sitting atop horses. These clusters appeared to me like men herding livestock, as the men working were stooped at the waist, performing whatever task they were at, and thus appeared as slowly bobbing backs of sheep or cattle in the growing cane. After noting this, I was disturbed by it, as I did not see them as men.

I was pleased I recognized Ithaca when we rode onto it. I had more trouble identifying the work done. The first cleared acreage we saw looked nothing like a farm field in England. There was no brush, to be sure, but there were stumps all about. I finally remembered that a plow would not be used here for just that reason.

We spied men working at the forest line, presumably enlarging the cleared area. We turned our horses toward them and worked our way across the clumpy dirt, threading through the stumps. I recognized Donoughy as I drew close: he was the only one not stooped and hacking at something. At least he was not on a horse. After a moment, I picked out the Jenkins brothers and Humboldt. They were all much browner now, and dressed similarly to myself in loose vests and breeches ,with kerchiefs on their heads. They were busy working with axes and cutlasses. They looked much like buccaneers clearing a deck. At least I did not see them as sheep.

As we approached, Donoughy wiped his forehead with a rag and stepped out to greet us. I realized he did not recognize me, and I thought I should not be surprised, as I had changed since last we met two months before.

Still I teased him, "Good day Mister Donoughy, have I changed that much?"

His jaw dropped; and then he laughed. I dismounted and we clasped hands.

"My Lord," he said. "Look at you. Theodore said you had gone roving, but my... Lord."

The other men were looking on with interest; and then one of them surmised my identity, and the whispers spread through the score or so of them. I was suddenly besieged by happy men who wanted to shake my hand.

After all made their greeting, Donoughy gave me an expectant look and flicked his eyes behind me.

I smiled. "That would be my matelot, Gaston."

Donoughy's eyes widened slightly, and I knew he understood the term. I looked back; Gaston waved, with a reserved grimace some might mistake for a smile.

"Are ya truly a buccaneer then, my Lord?" Humboldt asked. "Fletcher said you 'ad gone rovin'." Thankfully, I heard no recrimination in his voice for abandoning them.

"Aye, and I will tell you all of my adventures tonight. Where is Fletcher?"

"He's off with the others cutting lumber, my Lord," Donoughy supplied. "We get some here while clearing, but good beams come from larger trees. We have sheds to sleep in and we'll soon have the beginnings of the mills and boiling house. Theodore said a great house could wait."

"Oh, aye, by all means see to the necessities of the plantation before worrying about something as extraneous as a manor house."

He nodded with relief, only to tense again. "My Lord, there are some things we should discuss." He sighed. "And we've lost some."

"Ten men 'ave died of fever, my Lord," Humboldt said from the front of the ring of men. "Five are ailin'. Two others wounded so they canna' work."

"And one ran off, my Lord," Donoughy added. He looked as if he took it as a personal affront.

I shrugged.

"Theodore hasn't had a chance to buy any Negroes yet," he added.

So, not counting Fletcher or Donoughy, we were at thirty men alive and twenty-two men available to work. I had thought I viewed half our men in this field, not most. I was appalled.

"Good God," I muttered.

"We've cleared a good eight acres, though, my Lord," Humboldt added, with enthusiasm I could not fathom.

I looked back across the small field we had crossed, and thought of the acreage under plow around Rolland Hall. Then I looked at the weary men around me and the damn forest beyond them.

"That is spectacular," I said with a smile. "I am proud of you, to do so much against so much adversity."

This seemed to cheer them.

"We need to finish the day, my Lord," Donoughy said.

"Aye, we will leave you to it, then."

The men grumbled and turned back to the waiting forest. Gaston and I rode away.

"I did not expect so many to die," I said quietly when we were well clear of the others. "I know what I was told, but..."

"Men do not grow old here, Will," he said solemnly.

We soon reached the barracks, in another cleared area at the base of the hill. It was a long, open building with posts for hammocks and little else. We discovered a fellow named Pleasant had been made cook. He had one hand now. His left arm ended in a crude stump. I remembered he had been a farmer once, in Lancashire. Apparently he had an accident with an axe a mere month ago, and Donoughy and Fletcher had been forced to amputate what was left of his hand when it became putrid. They had made him the cook after that.

We saw to the horses, putting them in the paddock they had for a pair of mules. Gaston eyed the ailing men, and finally pulled his surgeon's kit from his bag with a heavy sigh. It took both of us to convince the men he was actually trained as a physician. Three of them had the flux, far more severely than I had experienced it, and Gaston explained to Pleasant about providing them with a great deal of boiled water and broth. The other two ailing men had a fever of some sort. Gaston said he would need to get supplies in town to even attempt to treat them. Then he quietly told me in French that they would most likely die. As for the other wounded man, he had a nasty gash from a shovel and was missing two toes, including his big one. The boys had cauterized the wound, and though it was an ugly mass of scar, it did not appear to be putrefying. He would be able to walk, but not well.

We walked a little distance away and I turned to Gaston with despair.

"Is it always thus? Can something not be done?"

He shook his head sadly and rubbed my shoulder. "They are truly doing well for not having seasoned. None are thin. Your men have done what they can for those ailing and wounded. The men in the field did not appear beaten or whip-scarred."

Fletcher and Grisholm arrived with two mules pulling a large log. Fletcher recognized me far more readily than Donoughy.

"My Lord, I thank God you're alive," he said as he embraced me heartily.

"Some intervention was involved in my returning." I grinned. "How are things here, Mister Fletcher? So many have died, but I am told this is the way of it."

He nodded and sighed. "We do what we can, my Lord. Donoughy is concerned..." He trailed off to regard Gaston, who was examining whatever was beneath a bandage on Grisholm's arm. Our carpenter seemed willing to let him look at it.

"This is my matelot, Gaston," I told them. "He is a physician." I was not sure if that was completely accurate, but I noted that Gaston did not correct me on it.

"Somethin' bit me, an' I was laid up for a good week, sir," Grisholm was saying.

I winced at the sight of a large circle of red and swollen flesh on his upper arm with a black spot in the middle of it.

"Spider," Gaston said. "The flesh here is dead." He pointed at the black spot. "It needs to be removed, and the hole stitched closed, and a poultice applied."

Grisholm nodded with resignation and a little relief. "Pennington got bit by something too, sir, but his is not so bad."

"I should look at all of them tonight," Gaston said.

"Some of us have worms, sir," Fletcher said diffidently.

"Including you?" Gaston asked.

Fletcher nodded glumly.

"What are you all eating?" I asked.

"The provisions we brought, my Lord, and what we can buy. That's what Donoughy is concerned about. We're feeding the men well, but it's costing a pretty penny."

Gaston paused in leading Grisholm to the cook fire. "Do they not have a provision plot?"

I looked to Fletcher and he shrugged. "My Lord, we can't grow wheat here, or turnips or...apples."

"Fletcher, all manner of things grow here."

"Aye, but they're strange, my Lord. We're sick enough."

Gaston snorted. "Fresh food grown here will provide for better health than rotting food brought all the way from England. And there are pigs and cattle running wild on this island, as there are on every island the Spanish lived."

Fletcher sighed at this rebuke. "Donoughy says that's not the way it's done on Barbados and the other islands. Not when you grow cane, sir."

I crossed my arms and regarded him sternly.

He held up a hand in supplication. "My Lord, I cannot debate as you can, and it is not my plantation."

"I will see to it," I sighed and relented to clap his shoulder. It was not his fault.

The men returned as the sun began to set. Gaston was finishing Grisholm's arm. I announced that any who had ailments should see Gaston, as he was a physician. They queued up immediately, and not just because my matelot was near the cook fire and Pleasant was ladling bowls of stew. Gaston began to treat them, with more patience than I thought he possessed. I was very proud of him.

Meanwhile, I went aside with Fletcher and Donoughy.

"So you have a matelot, my Lord," Donoughy said.

Fletcher frowned and then recalled the word.

"Oh," he said thoughtfully, and frowned toward where Gaston worked. He looked to me, and then away uncomfortably.

I remembered his desire to escape my presence when I had first told him I favored men. His behavior now bothered me more than I cared to admit. Morgan had been condescending to a degree, but he had not dared question if he was to remain amongst the Brethren. Fletcher, on the other hand, obviously did not approve but did not wish to say it. I wanted to know what damn business he had disapproving. Then I remembered that this was the way of the world. I had stood in a number of drawing rooms and balls, and heard the snide comments or seen the condemning snorts. They would do nothing, and they might not even ridicule, but they would feel they had the right to decide that what I did was unacceptable, as if I were unfortunate in some way. I used to accept that. Not only accept, but not question. It was the reason Alonso and I had not been open about our relationship. It was the reason I had always been discreet about the men and flagrant about the women.

Here and now, the irony was that Gaston and I were not even engaging in the activity that Fletcher most probably found inappropriate. However, I did realize that I might be making unwarranted assumptions, despite his religious convictions.

"Fletcher, what bothers you about the matter?" I asked pleasantly.

"Nothing, my Lord."

I continued to stare at him.

Donoughy sighed. "Fletcher believes it is a sin, my Lord."

"I don't believe it is," Fletcher said quickly. "It is. It's an abomination in the eyes of God. I'm sorry my Lord, I mean you no offense, but it is clearly wrong."

I sighed; my assumptions were correct. "Which? My having a matelot or sodomy? The two things can be quite mutually exclusive."

"Sodomy, my Lord," Fletcher said with exasperation. "I understand that some men are weak, and when denied women, they resort to sin to satisfy themselves the same as they resort to whoring, thievery, gambling, or drink. They will answer for those sins on Judgment Day if they do not embrace the Lord. But my Lord, you do not appear to be a weak man; and by your own admission you do not see it as a means of last resort but as a favored choice. You sin... arrogantly in such matters, and I do not understand why you wish to consign yourself to eternal damnation."

"Fletcher, I break a number of the Commandments on a regular basis. Committing sodomy should be the least of my problems on Judgment Day."

He had to think on that for a moment, and then his shoulders slumped dejectedly. "This is probably all too true, my Lord. You at least admit it is a sin, do you not?"

"Aye, sodomy is a sin, everyone knows that, so is murder, adultery, robbery, blasphemy, and," I sighed, "the Seven Deadly Sins which I am sure I embrace with equal conviction."

Fletcher rolled his eyes.

"Surely you jest, My Lord," Donoughy said. "You do not appear to be a man who bows before avarice or gluttony."

I chuckled, as I had not expected such a jest from him. "True, true, thank you, Mister Donoughy. I do not embrace all seven, but I do possess a fondness for lust, pride, and anger, and I have been known to occasionally indulge in envy and I often partake of sloth. And even more strangely, I have been known to commit other sins in the name of such virtues as zeal, generosity, love, and kindness. Though I must admit I have never managed humility, faith, or discipline."

"You revel in it, my Lord," Fletcher said with even more exasperation. "How can you revel in it?"

"Fletcher, I do not believe in God."

"I do not believe you, my Lord," he said with a dismissive gesture. "And how can you describe anything as a sin, if you do not believe God made it so?"

"I believe man made it so and," I thought back to my conversations with Gaston on the subject. "Some things are truly wrong, no matter why we decide they are."

"And is sodomy one of those things, my Lord?"

This brought me pause, as I realized I did view it as a sin. The question was, why? Was it merely because I had been told for so many years that it was?

I began to think aloud. "In truth, Fletcher, I have never given it much thought. I will not be so childish as to say that since it is something I wish to do, then it is obviously a proper thing. However, I cannot see where it harms one's fellow man or oneself. I can see where a case could be made that is not in keeping with nature, as it does not produce offspring, which is the purpose we assume for our privates. Yet, our bodies are as they are, and my cock is a thing of pleasure for my person, and it experiences and passes along to me an equal amount of pleasure whether it be burrowed in a man or a woman. I cannot see why it would do thus if it was not in its nature to do so. Likewise, if my arse enjoys something inside it, which it does, I fail to see how it could enjoy such a thing if it was not meant to. I feel the perversity would lie in my creation or design, if such things are wrong and yet make me so happy."

With that, I had successfully brushed aside all question in my mind as to the rightness of the act; but Fletcher looked as if he still required convincing. Actually, he looked as if he were on the verge of apoplexy, but I pressed on anyway. "And furthermore, were you not the one who posited that a shark could not leap because God did not make it so? Therefore why may my body experience pleasure in some fashion if it is not meant to?"

Fletcher sighed, and all the fight seemed to leave him. "My Lord, you are correct. You are most probably damned beyond redemption, and sodomy is the least of your sins."

I regarded Donoughy with expectance and curiosity.

Donoughy shook his head and chided Fletcher, "I would not know about damned beyond all redemption." Then he regarded me and shrugged. "My Lord, you will do as you will. It is no concern of mine."

"What of the men here? Is everyone as celibate as monks?" I asked.

Fletcher sighed, and Donoughy said, "Nay."

I eyed Fletcher. "I would hope there is no condemnation or censure of such activities."

"Nay, nay, my Lord," he sighed. "Though I do conduct Bible readings on Sunday mornings."

I shrugged, as I supposed there was no helping it; and many a man found peace and solace in religion. That was no matter of mine.

Fletcher was regarding me with a guilty countenance. "With all thanks to you, my Lord, I can read the Bible. And Mister Theodore says that once things are in a way in which there will be time for it, a tutor will be provided for the other men, as you have wished."

I smiled and clapped his shoulder reassuringly. "That is wonderful. How is the plantation progressing?" As I already knew some of Fletcher's concerns, I watched Donoughy.

They looked to one another, and shrugged amicably.

"Well enough, my Lord," Donoughy said. "We're clearing as best we can and truly making good progress. We'll plant what we have in August, and once that is done, we can start on the other buildings we need and the mill. There was the one man who ran off. We've had others that do not wish to work." His tone had changed, so that I heard the rumble of anger in the last of his words.

"Truly?" I asked. "And how was that remedied?"

"My Lord, unless they are injured or ail so that they can't work, if they don't work, they don't eat. They all agree on that, at least."

"That seems reasonable."

Donoughy gave an exasperated sigh. "If they don't work, my Lord, and we don't feed them, they'll just run off to find something to eat. And since nothing's been done about bringing the other one back, they don't have a reason to believe they can't."

"Nay," Fletcher said. "Most of the men did not like the fellow who ran off. It was Creek, my Lord," he added. I seemed to remember Creek as a big taciturn fellow who bemoaned the lack of copious alcohol on the voyage, and was always trying to trade other men food for their daily ration of beer.

"The others did not approve of him running off, my Lord," Fletcher continued. "And they don't approve of the Jenkins boy and Jackson complaining about working, either. It was the men who decided that they shouldn't eat when they refused to work one day."

"The Jenkins boy needs a good thrashing," Donoughy said.

"Oh, that will keep him from running," I said sarcastically. "And his brother, too."

"It would if we had a stockade, my Lord," Donoughy replied heatedly.

"Why not just chain them together in the field?" I snapped.

He shook his head. "We need to bring Creek back and make an example of him, my Lord, but Mister Theodore says you won't stand for it. He won't hire the men to do it."

"I do not know," I said, as I truly did not. I had given little thought to what would occur if one of them ran away. I had not conceived of the example it set for the other men when Donoughy first told me of it. I would rather not force the man to work, but it was true that we could not have them all running off. At the least, I supposed Creek owed my father forty pounds or so for his passage.

Then another aspect of the matter occurred to me.

"However would you find him? This is a large island, with an abundance of unexplored wilderness."

"Where he might have run to if he had an ounce of sense, my Lord. He's in Port Royal," Donoughy scoffed.

"You've seen him?" I was incredulous.

"Aye, my Lord. I chased him down the beach, but he slipped into the Palisadoes with some men; and I thought they might be armed, and I was alone. I've seen him since, and he just laughed at me."

I grimaced. This explained a great deal of Donoughy's frustration. Creek running about Port Royal doing who knew what was a different matter from a man deciding not to work and retreating to the wilderness to make his own way.

"I will retrieve him."

"He says he's a buccaneer now, my Lord," Fletcher said sadly. "I've seen him, too. I tried to talk him into returning."

"Was he armed?" I asked.

Fletcher frowned, shook his head, then shrugged. "Well, with a cane knife, my Lord."

I sighed. I could not perceive Creek being a threat with a cane knife. Pete with a cane knife would be death incarnate, but not Creek. But Donoughy and Fletcher were not me.

Still, he was no buccaneer with only a cane knife, though they were essentially cutlasses. "He has not the money to equip himself to rove," I said. "So unless he has a patron, I do not see how he could be a buccaneer. Yet I am new to this land and their ways, and perhaps there is a thing about it I do not understand. I suppose if he paired with someone with money." I frowned to myself as I thought of my own circumstances. "I will ask Gaston."

"And if you can get him back, my Lord, then what?" Donoughy asked.

"What would you suggest, flogging him? Stocks? A pillory? Chains? I would rather he pay us the money for his passage. And if he can earn that roving, so be it. But then I suppose we will have no one to work the fields."

Donoughy's gaze clearly said that this is what he had been trying to say all along.

I felt as if there were phantom chains around my own ankles, and the fight left me.

"Truly, what is done with a runaway bondsman?" I sighed.

"For a first offense, my Lord, his contract can be extended and he can be kept under watch and chained at night. If he runs again, he can be branded on the face." I winced. He shrugged his wide shoulders. "You bringing him back will show the others this is a serious matter."

I nodded. "I will do what I can. I make no promises, though."

I no longer wished to discuss the provisioning. I supposed that argument could wait for another day. It was with heavy heart I returned to the barracks. Gaston eyed me curiously as I sat beside him, on the edge of the clearing the building occupied. He was apparently done with the men, and they were sitting about eating.

"What?" Gaston asked quietly in French, and glared at Donoughy and Fletcher, who had followed me back to the fire. Fletcher seemed alarmed at this, but Donoughy seemed angry. I thought that if he were going to give himself the airs of so bully a sheep, he should at least arm himself.

"The escaped man," I whispered back in French. "He sets a poor example for the others." I quickly explained the circumstances.

Gaston frowned. "Unless he is skilled in some way useful to a ship, he will have to provide his own weapons to rove. But he need not have a musket and several pistols. Some ships will take him with a cutlass and a willingness to fight."

"And if this has occurred?"

He shook his head. "It has not if he is hiding on the Palisadoes. Buccaneers don't hide from planters, escaped bondsmen do."

I saw his reasoning. It was a fine line betwixt the two, though. All Creek need have done was make the proper friends. Had Belfry made sore remark of Davey's being amongst the Brethren the other morning, I was sure, every man there would have told a tale of how Belfry was mistaken as to Davey's identity. And a sensible man would not have gainsaid us. Creek had not been accepted by buccaneers when Fletcher and Donoughy last saw him – well at least not when Donoughy last saw him, but perhaps after. We could not know until we found the man ourselves.

"Will you aid me in finding him?"

"Oui," Gaston said, as if he were curious why I even posed the question.

"You will help me return him to slavery?"

Gaston nodded with understanding. "If he is not flogged. These men are not abused, Will, and he owes you money."

"My father."

He shrugged. "It is the principle of the matter. He agreed to a thing, and if what they say is true, he did not feel compelled to escape to protect himself."

He had placed the matter into the proper perspective for it to sit well in my heart. He did not protest when I embraced him. His body felt good, and I sighed with contentment. Then I glanced over his shoulder, and saw Fletcher watching us with a frown. I must have tensed, because Gaston released me enough to look at me questioningly. I did not wish to speak of the rest of my conversation with the men, though I was curious as to Gaston's opinion on such things. I was also afraid of it. His gaze was growing in intensity.

"Fletcher does not approve of matelotage," I said.

"On what grounds?"

There was apparently no avoiding it now. "He is religious. Sodomy is a sin."

Gaston became tense at once; and I swore silently and released him. I was surprised he did not move away from me.

"Do you think it a sin?" he whispered.

"Non. And if it is, I have committed far graver. I do not believe it is even a transgression against nature." I quickly explained my reasoning, as I had to Fletcher.

Gaston grinned, and I was heartened by the sight of it.

"What are your thoughts on the matter?"

He frowned. "I do not feel it is a sin." He still appeared uneasy, though.

"Other than it being a sin, then, what issue do you have with it?"

"It is not a thing I have wished to do."

I cringed inwardly and wished to walk away. I remembered his description of it as a thing done by beasts. He was merely stating the truth.

"I know. You do not favor men. I am sorry. I am not thinking as I should."

He gave me a bemused smile and was about to speak when someone a short distance away made a sound.

"Um, my Lord, sir, we all would like to hear the story, if ya don't mind," the younger Jenkins boy said.

"Aye." I smiled.

"We will talk later," Gaston whispered. I sighed, and we followed the boy closer to the others.

I was not necessarily in the state of mind to tell tales, and I knew even at my best I could not do the story as much theatric justice as Striker had done; but as I looked over the faces, I felt compelled, and I knew I wanted to tell them. So I leapt into it with all the enthusiasm I could muster. And like most tale-telling, it got easier as I went. At least an hour passed before I finished, and they seemed heartily amused and asked many a question. I must admit I made mention of the death and gore and danger a great deal more than Striker had; and as a result, not a man in my audience professed an interest in going roving, which I was thankful for. Fletcher and Donoughy were regarding me with wide eyes as we finished, and the men stumbled off to their hammocks.

"And you intend to do this again, my Lord?" Fletcher asked.

This set Gaston to chuckling.

"Oh, aye," I assured Fletcher with a lopsided grin. "I rather enjoyed it."

"You are a madman, my Lord," he said.

"And someone once asked me why I didn't go roving..." Donoughy said.

"It is good to know Davey took well to it," Fletcher said. "However did you get him off the ship, my Lord?"

I bit my lip. "That is a tale for another time."

Donoughy supplied us with a pair of hammocks. With so many dead, the shed was longer than needed to house all the men, and there was an empty set of poles next to the place where Donoughy and Fletcher slept. When I returned from relieving myself, I was amused to find that Gaston had strung our hammocks together between four poles so that they formed one wide berth. Fletcher was appalled.

When Gaston went to relieve himself, Donoughy whispered to me, "My Lord, the men that um...." He sighed. "Well, they slip away into the woods for a bit."

"We are merely going to sleep in it, I assure you." I considered going to find Gaston so that we could talk, since the opportunity was obviously not going to present itself once everyone was bedded down, even in French. My manhood suggested maybe I could request a repeat of the night before, as well. I told it to be still. Its interest kept me from seeking my matelot, as I did not wish him to think that was all I wanted. I arranged my weapons, and lay on the hammock, and waited for his return.

Shortly he did, and immediately rummaged in his bag. He found his jar of hog's fat, which he swore by to keep the insects at bay. I could barely stand the feel of it on my skin. As I had already been bitten a number of times, I reached for the jar with resignation. To my surprise, he swatted my hand away. He looked along the shed. I followed his gaze.

As the lamps had not been put out yet, we could see the men preparing for bed. I noticed several men furtively slipping in together from the forest. If I had not seen them arrive together, I never would have guessed they shared any interest in one another. I also noticed some of the men glancing our way quite curiously. I did not feel condemnation, but I did feel as if I were in another place and time.

I remembered one evening at a château in Geneva in specific. The ladies had all retired, and the fire had burned down, and the men had been drinking cognac and smoking. Several of us favored men, and glances were exchanged; and on one pretense or another, a man would slip away and another would follow shortly thereafter, with the rest of us making silent bets as to who was next. There had been an air of romance and intrigue about it all; but in looking back upon it, I quickly decided I never wished to live that way again. I had ended that particular evening buggering a beautiful young man in a stairwell. Once finished, he had scampered off to bed with a whispered good night, and I had stumbled to my room alone and weary of spirit.

Donoughy put out the lanterns, all save one on a central pole, which he turned very low. I heard, but could barely see, Donoughy crawl into his hammock in the dim illumination. Along the shed there were embers here and there, as men smoked pipes. I heard Gaston leave the hammock. I turned to face where he would have been, and could barely see him in the darkness. I felt his hand upon my wrist, and allowed him to pull me off the hammock and out of the shed.

All was shadow except for the sky. The sliver of moon and the brilliant panoply of stars did little to illuminate the treeline or the bulk of the shed nearby. A steady cacophony of insects drowned all other sound. I could feel Gaston in my arms. My manhood was delighted, and began to rise for play.

"We did not have to...."

His lips pressed to mine and stopped my words. I pressed back gently in a soft kiss. He withdrew somewhat, but his breath was still upon my lips as he whispered, "I want to explain something to you, but it has been a long and trying day. If you do not wish..."

I kissed him lightly to still his words, as he had done to me. Then I caressed his cheek with the tip of my nose, delighting in even the feel of his day-old stubble. He was very still, but he did not move away. I covered his mouth with mine again and brushed my lips across his. He did nothing until I licked the corner of his mouth, and then he turned his head.

"I am not ready for that," he sighed.

I did not protest, choosing instead to return to caressing his cheek. I shifted my hands and rubbed the small of his back in incrementally lengthening strokes. He pressed against me, and I was sure he could feel my arousal.

"You may touch me anywhere," he whispered.

I gasped ever so quietly, yet he heard it and gave an answering snort of amusement. Then he rubbed his body against me, in a way that confirmed my suspicion about his knowledge of my arousal. My hands found his buttocks and ground him closer. He slipped his arms around my neck, allowing me to run my fingers where I would. I proceeded to, with great delight, as I had dreamed of caressing the entirety of him.

When I reached his chest he gasped, "Not there," as I brushed his scarred right nipple. "It feels... odd."

I slid my hand to his left nipple and he held still, and let me fondle it. His breathing caught a little, and he made the happy humming sound.

As I continued to explore and touch, though, I began to realize that he was not breathing shallowly or writhing or moaning as I would if similarly handled. There was a response, but it was dim. Instead of redoubling my efforts, I slid a hand between his waistband and the rippled wall of his stomach and dipped into sacred realms. I found him flaccid. My fingers teased and cajoled and explored for a little while. He twitched against me as if I tickled him on occasion, but his manhood gave no reaction. I withdrew my hand and held him close.

He truly held no interest in me. I endeavored to hold the disappointment at bay.

His voice was tight. "You must understand that it is not you."

"Non," I said gently. "It is men in general. Oui. I understand."

"Non, non." He swore quietly. "Will, I do not think it would matter if you were a woman. I do not feel..."

Now I understood. I shoved aside my rising guilt at my prior thought, and tried to comprehend what this meant to him.

"When was the last time...?" I feared I knew the answer already.

"That night."

He did not need to explain what night. Apparently it had scarred more than his voice and skin. My manhood was shriveling in sympathy and fear. Still I asked, hoping for something, "And nothing since?"

"An occasional twitch. I sometimes wake from dreams and there is evidence it performed on its own; and I am relieved as it is not wholly dead, only to my waking mind." He sighed. "Will, you must understand that your touch feels very good. I just do not react as I know others do. As I see you do. As I know I would have before. I do not want you angry with me."

"How could I be angry with you?" I murmured. "In all honesty, I now feel guilt at the incidences where I have been angry or frustrated with you before. I now understand. I am sorry. I wish you had told me weeks ago," I said with wry amusement. "It would have made our lives easier."

He murmured into my neck. "I know. I was afraid. I feel less a man for it, and when asked I have lied. You are the only person I have told."

"Not all of your scars are on the outside, either," I said. "I knew this, but not to the degree."

He held me closer. "As I said before, you give me hope. Now that I have you, I find myself hoping this wound can be healed."

"I love you," I whispered and crushed him to me, as his words had made my heart ache again, and not in sympathy to his pain and loss. I loved him with an intensity I had never felt before and could not express. "We will find a way."

I struggled to even think of a way to confront the problem. Bestowing or receiving touch had not brought him alive. It was a thing of the mind and not the body. That was where he needed to heal.

"We will suture it with patience," I said, and hoped he could hear my smile. "I will use my blood for balm if necessary."

"Non, not yours," he said sadly. "I have given the matter great thought and I fear it is more a matter of lancing and draining and possibly even bleeding. There is one other time when it functions, though thankfully I have never acted upon it; and that is when the madness grips me."

I could not help myself, I groaned and looked to the stars, not for guidance but as a reminder that unreachable and unfathomable things can be quite pretty to look upon.

I kissed his temple. "It is all tied together in some Gordian knot in your mind, is it not?"

He nodded against my cheek.

"I am sure it would help greatly if you would but tell me what occurred," I said. "If it is difficult to speak of or remember, we could fill you with rum. I promise no matter what occurred I will never judge you harshly."

"I cannot." He choked on the words. "Truly, Will. It is part of the knot. It is a dream, and to even think of the few images I have is to court madness. I know I sinned, and I know my father's rage was justified, but the how and why of it I do not allow myself to know."

"Hush, then. We will not attack it directly, or even tonight. Let us sleep and see what the morrow brings." I rubbed his back, and slowly he calmed, and stopped clinging to me with desperation.

I watched the stars and wondered at the strange turns in our lives, and whether or not we could be considered blessed or cursed to have discovered one another. I decided blessed, as I could not imagine living without him now.

Gaston sniffed away his duress and shifted in my embrace. He pulled his arms from around my neck, and I felt something pressed against my chest.

"Hold this," he whispered.

"What?" I took it and recognized the jar of hog fat. "Oh, I need that. I have been bitten a dozen times."

"We will remedy that," he whispered.

I felt his sticky fingers on my brow, and I closed my eyes and let him coat my face in a thin sheen of the noxious stuff. I ran into his fingers as I started to scoop some out to work on him.

"Non. Allow me," he whispered.

With amusement I let him do my neck and arms and even my legs. I had not thought the spreading of it could feel so pleasurable as when someone else did it. I sensed his game when his fingers slid up under the legs of my breeches; so did my manhood. I captured his hand as he reached for the jar again.

"Non."

"I want to."

"You do not owe me anything."

He sighed and pulled his hand away and slid it under my tunic. "I want to because one of us can. I learned that last night."

"If it is for your benefit, then I of course I will not deny you." My chuckle stopped abruptly when his fingers found a nipple. With a sigh I rested an arm on his shoulder and leaned into him. Then it was his turn to chuckle quietly as his hand slid into my breeches and I gasped. I locked my knees and threw my head back to watch the stars. A pleasurable time later, they all seemed to move of their own accord, and

I slumped against him.

I could foresee myself becoming quite pampered. Yet I despaired of ever knowing whether the Gods were on my side or not.

Nineteen

Wherein We Have Dreams

The next morning, I told everyone we would return shortly, and we rode to the Passage Fort. We made a leisurely go of it, and I endeavored to instruct Gaston in riding, or of greater import, becoming comfortable upon the beast. He did well, but I knew it would take him several days to truly become accustomed to it. So I told the livery boy we were not yet finished with the animals, and we paid him for the entirety of the day on the promise he would let the sorrel and the bay to no one else.

In contrast to his demeanor during the pleasant morning ride, Gaston became uneasy as we approached the ferry wharf.

"Is something amiss?" I asked.

He shook his head and sighed. "There is so much noise here. I react poorly to crowds and…"

There was a crash nearby, and I whirled to find a man cursing at another over a broken wagon wheel. The contents of the dray, a series of large copper kettles, had clattered to the ground. When I turned back to Gaston, his arms were crossed and his eyes closed. I tentatively slipped my arm over his shoulders.

He took a deep breath, and released it slowly. His eyes opened and found mine.

"I do not like towns. They are unpredictable. It takes time for me to adjust to them. I must be vigilant or the horse shies."

"I will endeavor not to let you be thrown," I said seriously. I kissed his temple.

"Take it elsewhere," someone grumbled.

I had a pistol aimed at the speaker's head before I saw him. He threw his hands wide, backed off, and quickly skirted us. I realized we were standing in the road as I returned the piece to my belt. Other people were regarding us, but I thought it unlikely they would say anything now.

Gaston was smirking at me. "You are as skittish as I."

"Oui, we make a fine pair, do we not?"

"Oui." He smiled and kissed my cheek. "Let us go before someone dies."

I kept my arm around him as we walked companionably to the ferry.

"You can recognize this man?" Gaston asked as the boat was pushed off.

"Oui." I described what I remembered of Creek.

"It is midday. Sensible men, who are not English," he gave me a teasing look, "avoid the sun and rest in the afternoon here, much as the Spanish do."

"I would think him prone to sensibility, or drunkenness, such that now is when he would be rising."

"Then let us go to the wall leading to the Palisadoes."

Thus when we arrived at the landing, he led me left and east on Thames, into a part of the town I had not ventured before. We took a lane to High Street and proceeded toward the wall. The cay narrowed considerably on this end, so that there was only one set of lots on each side of the road, though they were deep and filled with larger buildings than houses. I was amused as we passed a prison. It seemed incongruous in this place. When we reached the Landward Fort, I was pleased to see that it was indeed a wall of stonework with cannon. It separated Port Royal from the spit of land leading to Jamaica. There was an open gate, and no one was being challenged as they entered.

"What do you propose?" I asked when Gaston stopped inside the wall and looked about.

"That we purchase food, and sit and wait until he comes or goes through this gate."

We found a shaded spot beside a storehouse, and Gaston left me to watch while he went in search of food. As we had passed a vegetable market of sorts on the way, he thankfully did not have far to go. He returned with a bottle of watered wine and several wrapped bundles.

"These things grow here," he said as he presented the packages. I understood his intent and tasted everything. I was not fond of the cassava, finding it a bit plain, but I devoured the fried plantain. I was already familiar with and found great favor in pineapples and mangoes. Thus we whiled away the afternoon talking of foods we liked and why many of the English were stupid for refusing to eat the native foods.

I spied Creek entering through the gate as the evening came upon us. He was dressed in a way that was now familiar, in breeches and vest with a kerchief upon his head. He wore no weapon belt, but carried a cutlass in a crude scabbard over his shoulder, supported by a leather thong across his chest.

The four men he walked with were similarly attired and armed. Except for the lack of weaponry, they looked like any group of buccaneers as they strolled casually through the gate laughing at some jest.

I pointed him out to Gaston and stood. My matelot was a shadow several paces behind me as I walked into the road to intercept Creek's path.

"Mister Creek, I would have a word with you," I said amicably.

He frowned at hearing his name and studied me with curiosity. Then his eyes went wide with recognition.

"Lord Marsdale," he breathed. His eyes flicked back to assess his distance from the gate.

"What's this, then?" one of his mates asked.

"He's... he's...the lord o' the plantation," he stammered.

"Well, actually, it's my father's and..." I shrugged.

The other men quickly grasped the situation and fanned out defensively, or perhaps menacingly, though I did not feel threatened as Gaston was behind the two to my left. None of them had noticed him as yet. I was not sure how much of an asset they would be to any ship they sought to sail with.

"I.. I.. uh, well, my Lord..." Creek stammered with no end in sight.

I smiled pleasantly. "You either need to return with me or pay the money for your passage."

"He's a buccaneer now," one of the other men said. "He don't owe you nuthin'." He was to my right, large and looming.

"So am I, and I beg to differ." I kept my eyes on Creek. "So, what ship do you intend to sail on? Most are out hunting the treasure fleets now. But I hear Morgan is looking to organize a large raiding party this winter. Will you be living out there in the trees until then? And what are you doing for money? Beer and wine are horrifically expensive in this damn town, because they expect all who buy here to be buccaneers or planters."

"I can't go back, my Lord," Creek said with quiet fear.

"I guarantee you will not be branded or flogged."

"He don't need no guarantee from you," the man who had spoken earlier said. "He don't need to go nowhere." He was the only one with a weapon belt, and he pulled a cutlass from a beaten scabbard. I had hoped things would not decay so quickly.

I felt more than saw something dart through the air. Then there was a knife in the man's right shoulder. He dropped his blade with a muffled curse.

Creek and his mates finally noticed Gaston. I grinned at their consternation. My matelot now had both pistols drawn. I pulled one of mine and aimed it at Creek's head.

"Now," I said with the same pleasant tone I used before, "I care not for the rest of you. I only have business with Creek. I do swear he will not be abused over this misadventure, and if all goes well, you will likely see him again. However, if things go poorly here this moment, you will all likely see one another in Hell."

The man to Creek's right proved to be far wilier than his fellows. He stepped back, and I thought he was withdrawing. Then he pushed Creek toward me, and the fellow on the other side of him somewhat toward Gaston. Unlike men with a wavering commitment to violence, my matelot and I fired simultaneously. We only swore in the aftermath, when three men lay upon the ground, one of them Creek.

The man to Creek's left ran. The man with the knife in his shoulder began to do likewise.

I pulled my second pistol. "Hold! The knife! Return it. Do not be stupid in how you do."

The man stopped, gingerly pulled the blade out of his shoulder, and dropped it on the ground. Then he too was away.

I joined Gaston in reloading while considering the wounded men. The one that had been pushed toward my matelot was shot in the right buttock. The one doing the pushing had blood spreading from his shoulder. Creek was dead. I had put my ball in his eye. I blamed too many damn years of dueling.

"Well, that did not go well," I muttered.

Gaston smirked. "He is a fine example now. I doubt any will consider running."

I rolled my eyes and discovered ten curious yet cautious members of the militia advancing on us from the wall.

"Oh bloody Hell," I sighed.

It was near night by the time Theodore finished laying it all to rest. Thankfully, we were able to claim our own defense, and only one man was dead. Gaston even went so far in aiding the situation as to dig the shot out of the wounded men: one of whom proved to be a runaway and was promptly returned to his plantation. Still, despite our exoneration, or perhaps because of it, I felt great guilt.

Finally we sat with Theodore in his yard, on the bench he recently purchased, and shared a bottle. Creek's body was shrouded in burlap by the fence. I found I could not stop staring at it, just as I could not ignore the knowledge that he would have gone with us if his companion had not chosen to act.

"In the future," Theodore sighed, "if this event does not deter all others who might consider running, what would you like done with those who do?"

"I would know why," I said, as I now had given the matter a great deal more thought. "If a man has some reason beyond not wishing to work, I would know of it before passing judgment. If he is merely trying to avoid completing his contract, then I would have him apprehended and returned."

Theodore sighed again. "You do realize that the stipulation of knowing why hinders my ability to hire men to bring one back."

"I will see to it."

"Will, I feel it would be far less expensive to send someone else." He laughed.

On my other side, Gaston was chuckling quietly. I elbowed him and took the bottle from Theodore.

"I will plan better next time. Truly, I am well steeped in guilt over this event."

They quieted, and Gaston's arm stole around my back.

"You are a good man, Will," Theodore said. He stood and regarded us. "Stay here tonight. The boys moved to your new house." He left us.

"I do not wish to face the men at the plantation tomorrow," I said. "I have killed one of my sheep."

Gaston pulled himself closer so that his lips were at my ear. "I love you."

Initially I thought it alleviated nothing, and then I realized it meant everything. For once in my life, I was loved no matter what I did.

I stopped staring at the shrouded body and turned to face him. "May I touch you?"

He sighed and considered it before murmuring, "You need not ask... ever again. Though..."

"I will endeavor not to ask more than you wish to give," I murmured. "I will not take offense if you stop me."

"Offense, non, yet..."

"I did not say I would not become frustrated, just that I will understand." I grinned.

He chuckled and I led him inside and upstairs. It was the first time we had been alone in a room since before we sailed. We crawled into a hammock together. I did not attempt to bring him to life; I merely satisfied my need to explore him in the dark. He seemed to enjoy it, and even allowed me to remove his tunic. As my fingers ventured where they would, his did the same; and I soon forgot the events of the day for a time.

In the morning, Gaston went to the apothecary to purchase a few things to treat the men. I went with Theodore to review the plantation's books, at the home of a clerk he engaged for that purpose. Griswold, the clerk, was a tall and lean man with stooped shoulders. He seemed very fastidious, and his script in the ledgers was quite neat. He left us alone at a table in the corner, and returned to hunching over another book across the room.

After seeing the appalling mount of money spent on provisions, I asked, "Do none of the planters grow food here?"

Theodore shrugged. "If they have the men. Most absentee planters, such as your father, view the entire endeavor as a business venture. They are willing to invest money into their plantations until the first crop is produced. They always expect it to be an enormous success. The truth is that it sometimes is not. Growing anything is a fickle business subject to the whims of weather and blights – and even rats, here. Since the land is free, the greatest expenditure is labor. All other expenses are secondary. They wish to get a crop planted as soon as possible, and thus reap profit as soon as possible. With more and more of your bondsmen dying," he grimaced and sighed. "And I did not mean in that fashion. You have fewer men to clear and plant. Since cane takes a year and a half to grow before there's even a chance of profit, pulling the men off planting the first crop to plant provisions would slow the process. And quite frankly, your father does not care. He planned on importing all of the provisions. He has set aside lines of credit with merchants in England, to keep the plantation supplied until it begins to make a profit."

I knew some of that, but as usual I had not considered the implications. Though I have been privy to discussion of many business dealings, I have no head for it. Still, this sort of planning seemed shortsighted.

"Do you think that wise? It seems to me that, well, should not a farm – which is essentially what a plantation is – should it not be sufficient unto itself? It is growing food, after all."

Theodore smiled and shook his head. "Nay, it is growing money. Sugar cane is not food; it is muscovado, molasses, and rum. You can consume them, but truly it is alcohol and another form of spice, albeit a very sweet one. Think of it more as a mining endeavor, and you will begin to understand the thoughts of those that invest in it."

"Ah, that does shed a different light upon the matter. Yet, would it not be better if the miners grew their own food?"

"Aye." He grinned. "When the time presents itself."

"Is there not a time after the field is planted that...?"

He shook his head. "Will, do you remember anything Donoughy told you?"

"Nay," I scoffed. "That was months ago and I was quite feverish."

He chuckled. "Once the cane sprouts, it must be weeded and fertilized, though not so much with a new field. By next year, you will want a number of livestock penned somewhere to provide the manure. But this year, whatever acreage is cleared will be planted and then weeded until the cane is too large to walk through. When the men are not engaged in that, and after it is of sufficient size, they will be involved in building the mills, boiling house, curing shed, and distillery. And then they will clear more acreage, so that another crop can be planted next year. And then they will plant the second crop and ready themselves to harvest the first."

"Oh, good Lord," I sighed. "We need more men."

He clapped my shoulder and smiled. "Aye. I am authorized to purchase as many Negroes as I can when they become available, or bondsmen if they present themselves."

"How often is that?"

"There have been three ships this year; and I have been outbid, or there were previous contracts, on all of their cargos."

"Outbid?" I teased.

"In one instance, two planters conspired to buy the entire lot for an outrageous sum. It was truly foolish. In another, I did not bid a great amount because the lot of them appeared sickly."

The true nature of what we discussed occurred to me. "How are the Negroes treated?"

"Will," he sighed in a chiding fashion. Then he relented. "Truly, most do not view them as men. If they did, they would have to treat them as such."

"As you may well guess, I will view them as men. I have had dealings with men of color before, and found them to be much like any other men."

"I guessed as much." He smiled ruefully. "So when will you be returning to sea?"

I swore quietly, and he chuckled.

Gaston was waiting for us when we returned. I was surprised to see that he had not merely purchased a few herbs, but a medicine chest for the plantation. Theodore was surprised at this as well. Then Gaston listed the various ailments in existence there, and how he had bought the prescribed remedies. Theodore quickly reimbursed him, even though it was a goodly sum of four pounds and six shillings.

"Are you truly a physician?" Theodore asked.

"As much as any other who claims it." Gaston sighed reluctantly.

"Well, at least you will have a trade when you tire of roving." Theodore shrugged.

Gaston glared at him and took the medicine chest outside.

I shrugged apologetically to Theodore. "He is not fond enough of people to wish to aid them."

"And yet he's treating the men at Ithaca, and he saw to those men he wounded yesterday."

"Aye, I know," I sighed. "We will hire a cart to take Creek's body back, I suppose."

"I'll send Samuel to fetch one. Should you return his body?"

"Despite my guilt and reluctance to face the lot of them with this news, the endeavor was mounted in order to deter other escapes. In that regard, I feel their seeing his body will impart far more of a lesson than my merely telling of his death."

"You realize you are as fickle as your matelot?"

"How so?"

"He wishes not to be a physician and yet he cares for the ailing and wounded; and you avow you do not think things through, yet you do when it suits you."

"Have I mentioned that you are not what I expected from my father's barrister?"

His laughter followed me out the door. Thankfully, he did send Samuel for a cart; and soon we were off to the ferry wharf, with the incongruous cargo of a body and a medicine chest. To my annoyance,

W.A. Hoffman

we actually had to pay passage for the corpse. And, of course, the livery boy was happy to rent us a mule for the deceased. The only thing I was pleased about in the matter was that the boy had kept the bay and the the sorrel set aside for us, as instructed. Even this small happiness was impinged upon, as with the mule we were not able to travel faster than a peaceful walk, though I had wished to further improve upon Gaston's horsemanship. And then the thick clouds opened upon us, and we were drenched in mere minutes. Gaston was greatly amused by my swearing.

It was late evening when at last we reached Ithaca. The men were already at the barracks due to the rain, which had not yet relented. Though the chest was built for use at sea, Gaston had been ill-pleased with its exposure to rain for the last several leagues. He quickly dismounted; and I joined him and held the mule, while he removed that part of its burden and took it into the barracks shed.

Fletcher hurried out.

"What is this?" he called as he approached the mule.

"Not my intent," I said quickly. I was aware of all the eyes upon us; but thankfully Fletcher, and Donoughy behind him, were the only ones I had to face.

"I believe he would have returned, but one of his compatriots was... There was an altercation and..."

Fletcher uncovered the body's head, and saw both its identity and my handiwork.

"You shot him?" he cried.

Other men began to spill from the shelter.

"I did not intend to. Another man he was with was also escaped; and he and several others caused a bit of confusion, the end result of which is that I shot Creek."

"How could you?" Fletcher appeared sincerely horrified; and staring into his eyes, I was mortified.

"I had a pistol aimed at him because one of his fellows waved a cutlass at me; and then this other fellow pushed people about in an effort to distract us and... I fired, Fletcher. And since I have rarely been called upon to fire in a situation where I need only wound a man, I aimed so as to give him a mortal wound. It is... a skill I possess."

All was silent except for the rain. Fletcher regarded me with wounded eyes, and I could see little else. And then I could not stop speaking. I was compelled to explain, somehow.

"I kill men for my livelihood, Fletcher. It is what I do. Even before coming here. Truly, I did not wish poor Creek any ill; it was just that the circumstances were such that... this occurred."

"You have made mention of that... my Lord," he said sadly. "And light of it. I thought you jested."

"I do make light of it, Fletcher. Because... it is a heavy burden, and I do not believe even God can relieve me of it."

"You will burn in Hell," he said sadly and with great resignation. He took the lead rope and led the mule away.

I did not fear the fires of Hell; his condemnation was painful enough. I was afraid to meet the rest of the eyes I felt upon me. The rain had turned cold, and that stirred old memories as well. I considered mounting the sorrel and riding until there was no light.

"He were always a right idiot," someone said. I looked toward the speaker, and found Grisholm shrugging. "Had a thing for the drink, he did. Said there weren't enough of it here to suit him."

"I did not intend to shoot him," I said. "I merely went to bring him back."

He shrugged. "And rightly so, my Lord."

Beyond him, I saw others nodding. I hazarded a look at other eyes. I found fear in some, and sadness in others, but very little recrimination. Everyone began to return to the barracks. Someone had taken the horses to the shed. I thought it might have been Gaston, but then I saw him, a shadow to my left, just as he had been when we faced Creek and his friends. I found warmth in that.

Donoughy did not go with the others. I met his gaze.

"You have seen to the problem, my Lord," he said with no amusement.

"Aye."

"My Lord, how many men have you killed?" I saw no condemnation about him, only curiosity and a bit of wariness. It seemed I had earned his respect.

"Well, with the roving this last month, I would imagine close to thirty."

He nodded thoughtfully. "Yet you won't see a man flogged?"

"Aye," I said resolutely. I knew I could not explain it to him. I did not understand it myself.

He returned to the barracks, and I stood there until Gaston led me out of the rain. I took great comfort in his merely holding me throughout the night.

The next three days, we spent the mornings learning a great deal about clearing land. I was determined that they have some form of garden plot; and so I inquired of Donoughy where I might put one. He thought me quite the fool, but suggested a likely location; and Gaston and I set to work.

Gaston insisted we stop during the heat of the day; and so we would nap for a time, and then go riding in the evenings as the clouds rolled in. My matelot refused to allow me to go riding alone, as he said it was unsafe. I was not sure who it was unsafe for, others I might meet or myself; but I let him go with me, on the condition he ride bareback. By the third evening, he and the bay were getting along quite well, and he had not fallen once. He named the animal Francis, as in Saint Francis. I was amused. I named the demonic sorrel, who had in truth become quite tractable after getting to know me, Diablo.

My matelot also treated the ailing men with some tincture of tree bark he called quinine. One began to mend, but the other was too ill for any good to come of a remedy, and he died. Gaston was saddened by this, though he had predicted it would happen to both. Thankfully he was not prone to melancholy, and could take some pleasure in the other man's survival and not be blinded by the loss, as I surely would have been.

As it was, I was still smarting from Fletcher's condemnation. He would speak to me and I to him, but there was now a wall between us that I did not know how to breach. As for the other men, they initially scoffed at our clearing ability when they heard of it; but after seeing our excellent progress the second day, they urged us to join them on the main field. We declined. Gaston said they might be resentful when we stopped at midday to nap and ride. I agreed.

We only engaged in one other tryst after the lanterns were out, due to my being sore from the unaccustomed labor and him from the riding. So only on the fourth night, when we felt better, did we amuse ourselves again with much mutual groping.

On the afternoon of the fifth day, a horseman appeared as we prepared for our ride. Other than Pleasant and the ailing men, we were the only ones in camp; and we watched the man approach with interest, as he appeared to be a boy and he was riding hard. He pulled up and regarded us with a frown, his eyes casting about for others.

"Excuse me, good sirs, I'm seeking a Lord Marsdale."

"That would be I."

He seemed relieved. "Very good, sir, Mister Theodore sent me, sir. He wishes you to know that the crew of the *North Wind* has arrived in Port Royal."

"The crew? What about the ship?" Gaston asked.

We packed and departed, only pausing at the field long enough to tell them we were off and not sure when we would return. Fletcher was out cutting timber with Grisholm, and I was not able to say goodbye. I did not allow myself to dwell on it.

We rode hard, as Gaston was now able to ride at a gallop with ease. Our journey was accompanied by intermittent rain, so we were quite soaked. Despite this, we slowed a mile or so from the Passage Fort and walked the last bit to cool our mounts.

"I have never owned a horse," Gaston said. "Since we will often be returning here, or need to ride to Spanish Town on occasion when in port, would it be prudent to own horses?"

He was being oblique, yet I guessed his motivation as he patted Francis' steaming shoulder. "Perhaps. Though how often do you expect us to be in port?"

He sighed. "Does Theodore own a horse?"

"Nay, he rents one as needed. Though I suppose if one were available to him here, he might prefer to avail himself of it."

"I do not wish to think of Francis or Diablo being ridden by fat planters."

I stifled my amusement. I had long since noted that all men my matelot disliked in theory were labeled as fat.

"Neither do I. Should we purchase them and save them from that fate? I'm sure monthly arrangements can be made with the livery to board them. It is my impression many fat planters do the same."

"You think me foolish?"

"Not for this," I teased and then said seriously, "You know I have gone to great lengths and suffered much anguish for my love of the damn beasts."

"True," he smiled. "So we will own horses, and we will allow Theodore and those we like to use them if we are not about."

"I think that a fine idea."

So we haggled over horses and boarding fees for a time with the livery owner, until all were satisfied. Gaston was carrying enough coin to pay the man for both the horses and their boarding in advance for a year. After a bit of grumbling by the owner, on account of the extra effort, as he did not write, we obtained a receipt. The sun had well set when we caught a ferry to Port Royal.

We stopped at Theodore's and found only Samuel. He told us they were at the Three Tunns. We were able to make our way inside the tavern, despite it being packed to the ceiling beams with buccaneers. Striker and Pete were at a table with Bradley and Morgan. I was only able to spy a glimpse of them because I stood on a table to do so. Men were standing four deep all around to listen to them. I doubted we could easily shoulder our way in.

Then we spied the Bard, Liam, Otter, Cleghorn, and Michaels at another table. We were able to reach them. Davey and Julio were with them. Theodore, Tom, Dickey, Belfry and Cudro were at the next table over. All looked happy to see us, and though drunk, the men who had been on the *North Wind* jumped to their feet to embrace us.

"What happened to you?" I asked the Bard and Liam as we all sat again. Space was crowded, and the chairs short in number, so Gaston shared the seat with me – which suited both of us. Liam and Otter were similarly doubled up.

All of them appeared to be bandaged in one place or another. Liam had a rag around his head, and it looked as if his nose had been broken yet again. Otter's arm was wrapped, and so was his leg. Cleghorn was bandaged about the chest. The Bard's right arm was in a sling, and there was blood on the bandage on his shoulder.

The Bard was laughing quietly in response to my question. After giving him an expectant look, Liam shrugged and started telling the tale.

"The storm blew us north and east. We took on water an' sank, even with heavin' the cannon ov'r the side. We thought o' heavin' the gold as well, but it would na' 'ave done a bit a' good. Those that could got on the longboat, an' the rest on pieces o' the deck, an' we lashed 'em together. We did na' bring much with us in the way of muskets, victuals, or the like, as we were more concerned with drownin' and there were much confusion.

"After the storm, we drifted with the current for a spell o' days. We knew we passed north o' Havana, and we were right worried this would bring trouble. We finally found ourselves a cay by the sheer grace o' God. O' course God, in his infinite wisdom, 'ad a little more humor about Him than we would 'ave liked. It were a good cay ta maroon a man on, as it was but sand an' there be nothin' on it at all. We had few weapons, wet powder, an' hungry men, and we 'ad already lost three souls o' the twenty-three the ship sank with. We sat there for four days eatin' fish.

"Whilst we were discussin' the matter, we raised a sail; an' we were joyous for a time, though we could na' see 'er colors for the longest time, and 'ere we be sittin' like turtles on a beach. We laid low and readied the longboat. As luck and God would 'ave it, the ship spied us and came round ta take a look. As bad luck would have it, she were Spanish, and she saw we were right easy prey.

"They aimed cannon at us, an' commanded we come ta them in the longboat. In our favor, the Spaniard were a merchantman an' had no soldiers. But, they be smugglers goin' ta trade on Hispaniola, so they be well-manned an' armed for merchants. It was dusk though, an' most o' our men were lyin' behind a dune. So the captain thought they might na' know our real number.

"'E came up with a right smart plan, and we rowed out with the longboat under their cannon, with the ten men who could swim hangin' off her backside where the Spaniards could na' see 'em in the bad light an' waves. Those men swam below water a bit when they neared the ship, an' worked their way 'round 'er and came up on the other side. Those that came aboard from the longboat had no weapons, as the Spanish commanded they be left below in the boat. The ones climbin' up 'er far side 'ad only knives. We fought like madmen. When all was done, we knew God 'ad sent angels ta watch o'er us, 'cause eight of ours were dead, and most of us wounded, but we had a new ship."

"Eight men?" I asked. Based on what he had related, that would leave the survivors from the *North Wind* at twelve. We had only returned with thirteen. Hastings had, of course, returned with eleven including himself. The *North Wind* had sailed two months before with sixty-six, and only thirty-six had returned.

There were somber nods from everyone present. They named them off, and I recognized many; but only one made me wince. Siegfried was among the dead.

Cleghorn shook his head. "He couldn't swim. Bradley could, so he led the men who came up the back, and Siegfried did all the talking for us who surrendered to the Spanish. They started clapping us in irons, Siegfried first since he was leading us. When the Spanish captain realized something was amiss, he shot Siegfried where he stood. With a shot to the head from that range, there wasn't anything I could do for him, and I am sure he was dead before he fell."

"Aye, poor Siegfried 'ad the worst luck o' all," Liam said. "The rest o' us were blessed, in that the Spaniards could na' aim well at all. They fired once into the men standin' there, and then our men were able to take 'em afore they could reload. That first volley took three, though."

I could scarcely imagine it; and worse, I would have been one of those standing there hoping I could dodge when the shot came, as I could not swim at all. I looked to Gaston and whispered in French, "Can you swim?"

He nodded grimly.

I sighed. "I cannot." I could picture us in a similar situation, and the idea of it chilled me to the bone.

"Not that that scenario is likely," I said more for my benefit than his. Still I could think of a dozen others wherein we would be separated under dire circumstances, and one would die and the other would not.

"You will learn to swim," he said flatly. "If I had to learn to ride, you will learn to swim."

I looked back to the others. "So how many of the men who could not swim survived?"

"All o' us at this table, an' five others," Liam said.

I frowned with confusion.

He shrugged. "I said they could na' aim worth a damn. And they have these cheap muskets. Pistols did damage as they always do. But they were afraid o' us, as they weren't fightin' men, and so they were standin' away; and then they got distracted by the others. I got grazed in the head. Otter 'ad a ball hit 'is leg. It missed the bone. Then he got cut by one of them with a sword. The Spanish captain stabbed Cleghorn and Michaels, and they went down and he didn't look at 'em again. The Bard took a pistol ball in the shoulder. We lost more men to cutlasses in the fightin' that came after."

The Bard was regarding us with the drunken version of his usual sardonic smirk. "We heard you boys did not have quite as hard a time."

"Have you heard the entire tale or merely the gist of it?" I asked.

"The whole tale," Liam said.

"Than I shall not bore you," I said. "Aye, it was easy compared to what you all faced, though half the men who left the galleon that morning are not here today. Of course, those of us who did not get captured or eaten by sharks are not even wounded."

"Then what the devil happened to Cudro?" the Bard asked.

Cudro swore in Dutch, and I bit my lip.

"Fine, tell them," Cudro rumbled.

I was undecided as to where to begin.

"We fought," Gaston said and the others strained to hear him over the noise of the tavern.

"They fought," I said, loudly enough for them to hear.

Everyone, including our companions at the other table, looked incredulously from the big Dutchman to Gaston and back again.

The Bard started laughing. "Did you hit him?"

Cudro glared and then it slowly crumbled into a smile. "Not even once."

I glanced at Gaston; he was as surprised as I at this confession. Cudro looked to him and raised his mug in silent toast. My matelot snorted with amusement, and nodded respectfully in return. I was dismayed at this apparent peacemaking, as I still did not like the Dutchman.

Cleghorn and Michaels were studying Gaston with concern; and I wondered at it, until I remembered the last they had seen of him had been while he was mad. I was sure the surgeon in particular thought my matelot quite dangerous, as he had been threatened by him over bleeding me, seen him in his madness, and now heard that he beat Cudro bloody without explanation. I did not know if I should attempt to mitigate his opinion or not, as I was not fond of Cleghorn either.

"What were you all planning?" the Bard asked. "We are destitute and need money. All of our men need new weapons. The taverns alone will be selling them off as bondsmen, once they run out of credit and have spent all the money we got from the smuggler's cargo, which was not much. There's talk of taking this new ship out after the Galleons; but they should sail in a month, and Bradley has no heart for it."

"Well, we were not sure as to what had happened to all of you or the North Wind until today," I said. "Striker wanted to give you all time to return if you did, which thankfully you have. Whether you did or did not return, there was talk of buying a ship, depending on the disposition of all and whether one would become available."

The Bard sighed. "This new ship is English-made and not a Spanish tub, but she's still a damn barge compared to the sloop. She can sail. I am not in the best shape to sail her, though, and most of my able men are dead, as they were sailors and not fighters."

"Would Bradley let someone else take her out?"

"She's a prize," the Bard said. "We all bled for her, so she's ours, not his."

We looked toward the wall of backs surrounding the table with Morgan, Bradley and Striker.

"Do you think Striker would be willing?" the Bard asked. "The men will sail with him."

"It would actually be an election, then?" I asked.

Gaston nodded.

"If Striker is captain, I want to be quartermaster," Cudro leaned over to say.

"Quartermaster?" Liam scoffed and gave him an incredulous look. "Ya can't bloody well walk."

"I'll heal up by the time we provision. If it's not me, then who? Pete cannot, as no one will stand for the captain and quartermaster being matelots. No one will vote for him," he pointed at Gaston, "even if he is the best. I mean no offense," Cudro added quickly. Gaston shrugged. Cudro pointed at me. "You are not a possibility as you do not know a damn thing." I frowned at his assessment of my knowledge, but he was correct. We shrugged. "And so that leaves Hastings or maybe someone you don't know. And I know more men looking to sail," Cudro said.

I was amazed at the politicking, though I supposed it was to be expected. I did not favor Cudro being quartermaster or having a large voting block of the crew, but he made several good points. And if it came to a fight, I knew four men who could take him in a duel; five if I counted Julio, and seven if it started with muskets.

Thinking of Julio, I regarded him with raised eyebrow. He shook his head sadly and leaned closer to say, "You are too kind, my friend. I am a maroon; they will never accept me."

I rolled my eyes with exasperation, and he smiled.

"Then it may be assumed we have a plan, that is if Striker is willing." I grinned. There were nods all around. I fixed my gaze on the Bard. "Can you sail?"

He shrugged and winced, as he had forgotten his shoulder due to the beer. "I can, but I can't man the whip staff or the rigging. I'd have difficulty with a sextant at the moment. Damn it, and I always fancy I'm the one who is safest."

"May we assume you can orchestrate and teach?" I asked. He nodded.

I was thinking of myself, but I did not wish to be tied to the ship in battle. I needed to be with Gaston. I looked over our number and spied Tom. I smiled.

"I think I may have an apprentice for you."

"You?" he asked.

"Nay, I fight and stay with Gaston, though I have been learning what I can and am willing to learn more. Nay, I meant Tom over yonder." I pointed, and Tom looked surprised.

"Do not know him," the Bard sighed. "Is he quick?"

"He's literate."

The Bard snorted derisively. "You can teach a pig to read."

I disagreed, and I forced myself not to look at Davey. "Tom is smart enough."

"The blond one, not the others, correct?" the Bard asked quietly.

Dickey and Belfry were sitting next to Tom, and they were all looking expectantly our way. "Aye, aye, the other two are opening a haberdashery."

The Bard fell upon the table in the throes of laughter.

Tom had left his seat and come to stand between the Bard and myself.

"Truly?" he asked, and eyed the laughing master of sail with concern.

"Aye," the Bard recovered enough to say. They introduced themselves, and Tom squatted beside him to talk.

Cudro interrupted my listening to them. "Weapons."

I sighed and looked to Liam.

The Scotsman shrugged. "Otter and I have ours, an' there be three other good pieces, twenty pistols, an' most o' the men kept their steel."

"If he knows we're sailing for prey, and someone will offer surety for it, then the gunsmith will offer credit," Cudro said.

Gaston sighed. "I will speak to him in the morning."

"'E will na' 'ave enough good pieces on hand," Liam said.

"Then we will make do," I said.

There were nods all around, and then everyone began to talk in clumps. Striker and Pete joined us. Pete was unable to stand, and knelt on the floor. Striker stood swaying unsteadily. He patted my head several times, and appeared on the verge of speech. I smiled at him kindly. I did not think this a good time to tell him of his future.

I looked to the Bard and Liam. "Where are you sleeping?"

"The ship," all who had come with them answered in unison, with the exception of Cleghorn. He mentioned going home as he stood, and I distantly remembered Striker saying that the surgeon had a wife.

"Can you make it there?" I asked. They nodded. "Then we will meet you there on the morrow."

We collected our little band and staggered, some of us from the weight of those who could not walk, through the streets to our rented abode. When we arrived, Rachel's head appeared in the doorway to the servant's quarters, and she politely inquired, "Do you require anything?"

"Nay, we've been drunk before," I told her. Striker seemed to think this very funny, and he doubled over with laughter and damn near dropped both of us into the mud. With Julio and Davey's help, we were able to drag Pete and Striker up the stairs to their room. Then Davey told me which room they had set aside for us, and Gaston and I retrieved our bags from below and retired to it.

I was delighted to find a row of corked onion bottles filled with clean water. Apparently Rachel had followed our instructions as to preparing drinking water. Gaston lit a candle, closed the door, and opened the window. I passed him a bottle, and we looked about. The room was empty, save for the chests I had brought from England and a single wide and sturdy hammock tied to four hooks on the wall, so it was as we preferred: more a suspended bed than a bag of netting.

"I feel filthy and this room is very clean," Gaston said.

I nodded. I thought of what I wished to do if given the opportunity tonight. I did not want to do any of it while we both were stinking and covered in hog fat.

"There's a tub in the yard."

We were down the stairs a moment later. Rachel's head appeared in her window, beckoned no doubt by the lamp we had brought and the sound of water being bailed from the cistern into the tub in the middle of the night. Once she realized what we were about, she gave us a stern warning about not touching Pete's pies, which were cooling in front of the cookhouse. With great difficulty I suppressed the urge to say, "Yes, ma'am," before she disappeared from sight, leaving us standing like two scolded boys in the yard.

Gaston regarded the closed window with horror and then glared at me.

"Are you sure she was such a good idea?"

"Not at the moment, non. I am amazed Pete has not killed her yet."

I doffed my clothing. After checking to see if anyone was spying from the windows, Gaston joined me. We scraped off the muck and bathed, making part of the yard quite muddy in the process. I became interested, or rather I should say my manhood did, at the sight of Gaston's nakedness. When he noticed this, he doused me with a bucket of water; and we proceeded to chase each other around the yard in the dark with more of the same. Rachel, of course, appeared in the window again to tell us to quiet down. Gaston immediately hid behind me, and I hid behind a bucket; or at least, the part of me that had started the commotion in the first place did. She heaved a truly exasperated sigh and left us again.

"If she is mean to me, she goes," Gaston whispered in a well-enunciated imitation of Pete. I began to laugh, and he tickled me mercilessly; and we ended up rolling about in the mud and were forced to start the whole process over again.

Sometime later, we slipped into the house and back to our room. I could not interpret his expression as he turned up the lamp. I had been aroused by the sight of him in the shadows of the yard, but now I found myself fascinated in the flickering lamplight. I was possessed of a very great need to do more than look. I wished to explore with my eyes and fingers in tandem, as I had not been able to in our trysts in the dark. Only one small thing would make the possibility better. I realized that with my chests here, I had even that.

"Lie down," I whispered with a grin.

He had been surprisingly relaxed while cavorting about in the yard; but now he sobered and tensed. He flushed a little, and his eyes began to fill with refusal and guilt.

"Oh, come now," I whispered. "Why not tonight?"

He pointed to the lamp and then my fully aroused member.

"I wish for the light, and as for this, he is attached to me, and though he may occasionally think for himself, he is incapable of going anywhere without my aid."

Gaston sat on the hammock, and the new ropes creaked a bit. He tested the bounce a little, like a nervous young swain. I turned to rummage in the trunks to hide my smile. I found the small, carefully-packed bottle I sought and turned back to him. He was watching me with open regard.

"You are not revolting," he whispered, as if it was a curious thing to him, and I supposed it was.

"Thank you, I am grateful to hear it. And neither are you."

He sighed and lay back on the hammock with a grin. "The Fates must despise me, to saddle me with a matelot with such poor eyesight and judgment."

"And the angels must adore me, to bless me with a matelot who is so very humble." I joined him on the hammock and waved the bottle over his eyes.

"What is that?" he asked.

"Oil. Scented oil."

He gave me a guarded frown. "And what do you intend to do with that?" He glanced at my manhood again.

"I am going to anoint you with it. This is much better than hog's fat." I pulled the stopper and waved it under his nose. The scent of almonds wafted between us.

He nodded agreeably at the smell, and then his eyes narrowed. "And then what?"

"Nothing. I just wish to explore you in the light. You will lie there and enjoy it. Now roll on your belly."

After a little hesitation, he rolled onto his stomach. I started on his scalp, and massaged my way down his neck, shoulders and arms, even out to his fingers. Then I returned to his back and thus caressed my way over the entirety of his body, exploring and kneading until he glistened in the candlelight and lay limp and torpid. He tensed when I neared his buttocks, but relaxed after I smacked him for it. Some day I would slip between his cheeks and teach him to relax in other ways; but that would not happen if he did not learn to trust me now.

In addition to mounting desire, I experienced an echo of my own memories. Alonso had done this to me many times. He would bid me lie still while he caressed me with oil, until my mind finally surrendered to the sensation and my body relaxed. I had not wished to trust him, either; and he had been forced to get me quite drunk and have several goes at it, before I could allow him as much freedom as Gaston was allowing me now. Alonso had continued the exercise once or twice a week, until finally I had allowed him what he most wanted; yet never from behind where I could not see him, and never in the dark, and never sober.

"Roll over," I whispered. Gaston did and regarded me with sleepy eyes. I worked on his thighs, and he did not tense as I massaged around his manhood and up across his belly. I was careful to only rub lightly over his damaged nipple when I reached his chest. He smiled faintly when I finished with his face.

I sat back, and his eyes flicked to my crotch yet again. His hand raised but I pushed it away gently. I stroked myself. He realized my intent and appeared uncomfortable. Then he became as wondrous as he had that first night, when I had shown him my manhood fully aroused in response to him. I well knew how hard it is to lie there and accept that another could look upon me and want me. I forced him to do it now as my eyes drank him in. He was a glistening sculpture of male perfection, made all the more intriguing by the textures and ridges of the scars, which the lamp light and oil highlighted and masked at the same time. He flushed under my scrutiny, and I gave him a lazy smile and came on his chest.

His face contorted in a comical grimace as if I had deposited something far more vile upon his person. I laughed in the afterglow of my pleasure, "Consider it an offering."

His look told me what he considered it, and then he relented and smiled sheepishly. "I did not expect it to... land over here," he sighed and held up his arms to beckon me join him. I lay beside him with my head on his shoulder, and looked upon my offering. I scooped it up, and on impulse, quickly smoothed it over his manhood and massaged it in. He squirmed beneath me with a curse of surprise.

"What are you doing?" he gasped.

I pushed up on my elbow to regard him, and found myself close to laughter. "I do not know. I truly do not. Perhaps giving it an idea. It seemed a good one at the moment."

His indignant and incredulous look gave way to laughter. "Will, you are such a fool." He quickly sobered. "And I love you so very much."

I threw myself atop him and pressed my lips to his. He kissed me back, and we pecked at one another for a minute; and then his teeth gently captured my lower lip and released it. I let the tip of my tongue find his upper lip, and he did not pull away. I explored a little, until he opened for me, and our tongues met tentatively. In the following minutes, I taught him how to kiss properly. There was no passion in it, but there was a delightful sensuality that he seemed to enjoy as much as I did.

I finally pulled back and regarded him with my chin upon his chest. "You have twenty-seven teeth."

He laughed and pulled my mouth to his, and I was very aware of his counting. "And you have twenty-six," he said when he released me. He tousled my hair. "I do not wish to live without you."

"Nor I you. Tonight, hearing of Siegfried's demise, I grew concerned. I never truly consider death. My own I do not fear. Yours, I fear."

"We will not allow that to happen to us. If we die, we die together."

I nodded. The subject troubled me, and so I teased with a grin, "If you feel yourself mortally wounded, you will take me with you?"

He sensed my mood and smiled slowly. "Oui, with my dying breath I will kill you. Will you do the same?"

I let myself think of it, and immediately regretted it. "I do not know if I could."

He nodded thoughtfully. "Neither do I, and if I knew I would die I would want you to live."

I sighed and chuckled ruefully. "And I cannot imagine it without you. So we are back at the beginning."

"Let us not die."

"Even I, who do not like to trouble myself with the consequences of things, know that we should most probably change professions then." At that thought, I felt the brush of melancholy. "What did you intend to do with your life before I so rudely interrupted it?"

He was playing with my earlobes. "Did you realize your head is not symmetrical?"

I laughed. "Oui, I know. Neither is yours. An artist once told me that no one he ever saw was truly symmetrical, and he thought that if any man were that perfect, they would appear ugly to others."

"He was probably correct." Gaston smiled. "You look fine as you are."

"I am glad to hear it." I grinned. "What did you intend to do...?"

"Before I met a drunk Englishman on a street reading Plato?"

"Oui."

He looked away somberly and regarded the lamp. I watched the flame flicker in his eyes.

"I lived because I could not die," he breathed. "I gave no thought to the future. I was not careless with my life, but not careful either. Living here was no different than... before. I was happiest when I did not have to consider such things. When I was young, it was always a new school and a new battle, and here it has always been a new ship and new battles. I was mad before and I am mad now; it merely takes a different form. I was always alone." He frowned. "Except for when I was very young, and then I had my sister. Here I have occasionally found those who cared, but not enough to..." His gaze returned to mine. "I think I hoped that eventually I would be unlucky and it would end."

I held him and buried my face in his neck. I remembered the first bout of madness I had witnessed, wherein he was enraged with me over saying I had sometimes wished for death. I was once again overcome with emotion; but this time it was not guilt or shame. If forced to name it to another, I would have called it responsibility. I had never been this important to another being, ever. And no one had ever been this important to me.

He pulled my head up; and I kissed him deeply, which he allowed. Then he pulled my head back again, and looked into my eyes.

"What do you want to do?"

I thought on it, discarding all manner of orthodox goals as they never held meaning for me.

"I want to be with you. I want to exorcise both our demons. I want to be happy."

He smiled. "How?"

"Is not this moment enough?"

He increased the pressure on the sides of my head to hold me still, and his eyes bored into mine.

"You began this. I want the same things, but there are a number of decisions facing us, are there not? What will we do? We have money. We can catch a ship and go anywhere in the world. We are free to do as we please, if we choose to be. Do we wish to rove again? Do you care what happens on the plantation? Do you wish to inherit your father's title? Tell me what you wish, and I will do everything in my power to help you attain it."

I could see myself in his eyes, and it was disconcerting. I did not know if he realized this; though it fit well with his intent, which was to prevent me from evading the issue – which I was doing by thinking about his intent and not the questions facing me. Why did I not want to think on it? Why did I pose the questions if I did not want answers?

I smiled. "I want someone to tell me what to do."

He released me with a bemused sigh, but I stayed where I was and continued to gaze into his eyes and the little me watching me from within them. He started to speak, but I quickly placed fingers on his lips. He held still and waited. I was experiencing an epiphany of sorts. That one admission had brought it about. I did not only want someone to tell me what to do, I expected it. Someone always had, and I had always defied them. Events in my past were revealed in new ways; and I shuffled through them, seeing a connection for the first time in this new light.

"I... have never known what I wanted," I said. "I have always known I did not know what I wished for in life, but it... Damn, I do not know if I can explain adequately. My life has been defined by what I did not wish, or the avoidance of it. My whole life has been spent... running, with the wolves nipping at my heels in one form or another. I have been herded throughout by fortune and circumstance. Every which way I have turned, I have seen another obstacle I either did not wish to surmount or I found insurmountable. And instead of staying put or facing the things pursuing me, my wayward heart has always led me further afield looking for greener pastures. And so I run from one paddock to the next.

"Alonso angered me, when he said we needed to mature and accept our fates at the hands of our families and become responsible. I still do not wish to do that; but I do not know whether it is because I am so familiar with running that I can conceive of nothing else, or because I am afraid of being locked in some small paddock for the rest of my life, when I now have seen so many others. Though from what I have witnessed, in some ways all of the paddocks are very much the same.

"I feel I am truly thankful Shane drove me out. If it were not for him, I would be married now to some god-awful twit like my sister, with a number of children and a mistress in London. I would be drunk every night at one court party or another, because I would not be able to bear myself or my life. Instead, I have seen some of the world and I have ended up here, and I know much more of whom I am. Of course the fences and wolves here just drove me out to sea, but I found you, and now I am not alone.

"But are we truly free to do as we wish? We could catch a ship to anywhere, but where? As we discussed, we do not wish to return to the Old World. However, if we go many other places in the world, we will not fit in amongst the natives and we will be in greater danger than we are here; unless we remain with our own kind, at which point we may as well be in Christendom for how we will be expected to behave. So for now I wish to stay here with you.

"As for roving," I sighed. "It suits me. Though it is dangerous and I do not wish to lose either of us. Yet if we do not rove, what will we do with our time? Plant? I find myself seeking to justify it, so therefore it must be something I want to do yet feel will be denied me, or should be denied me.

"As for the plantation," I sighed again. "I truly do not know. That is some Gordian knot in my mind that I do not know how to untie as of yet. It is all wrapped about my father, and Shane, and the title, and who I am supposed to be and..." I trailed off with another sigh, as he was watching me patiently and I knew he understood. "So I believe, despite my new understanding of my life, that we are where we were before, as in tomorrow will be much as it was before."

He shook his head. "That new understanding makes all the difference in the world, Will. Are you still running?"

"As with all things, it is a matter of perception, is it not?" I smiled and returned to lying partially atop him. "I am not running at the moment. I am standing here with you looking about in a somewhat calm manner at the paths available."

"How do you perceive me?" he asked. "Am I an obstacle, or...?"

I stopped his words with my lips.

"Oui," I whispered with a grin when I pulled away. "You are an immovable object in my life now, yet I do not perceive you as being confining, but rather offering protection. I see us as two centaurs standing in a field with fences we can jump; and we are surrounded by wolves and sheep. Yet we tower above them, and we are well-armed."

He chuckled. "That may be a somewhat grandiose interpretation of the situation, but I will accept it for now." He sobered and frowned. "I can see it, but I see one of us as being lame."

I nodded. "I see both of us that way. We will overcome it."

"What color are we?" he asked. I regarded him quizzically. "The horse part."

I frowned. When I envisioned the metaphor I allowed myself to see, it but I had not regarded it in that degree of detail. I let my imagination flow freely about it and grasped upon the first thing I saw. "Like the hair on our heads. Your horse part is sorrel, and I am tan."

He thought on this and played with my hair. "I saw us as black and white. I wanted to be a black horse because you like them."

It was very sweet, and I kissed him for the image but I asked, "Why am I white? Do you like white horses?"

He shrugged. "I do not like horses, remember."

I rolled my eyes and he laughed at my discomfiture.

"Non, truly," he said, "I see us as the dark and the light. Two sides of the same thing. You are bright and shining and I am a thing of shadows."

"I will be your white horse and you can be my black," I murmured and held him closer. He smoothed my hair, and we lay together comfortably as the candle burned down.

I pictured him as a black centaur. I had never paid particular detail to what I thought the horse part of a centaur should look like. I had seen representations before, but they had not been my own. I thought of various black horses I had owned; Hercules, Goliath, Alexander, Gwidion and others pranced through my memory. In shape, Gaston would do best with Goliath's body, as I saw him as compact and strong; yet that body would have to be a great deal smaller to fit his torso upon it as it was now.

My mind strayed as I pondered these images, and I tried to remember Goliath more clearly, until I saw him as I last had, bloody and broken in his stall. Unbidden and unwelcome, the centaur image of Gaston replaced the first in the same scenario and I shuddered. He had already been whipped bloody in his life, and it had broken him. In my vision, he pleaded with me to kill him, and he was reaching for me through the bars of one of the asylum cells I had seen in Florence.

I woke with a cry. Gaston was eyeing me sleepily, but he was already reaching for a weapon, which was not there as we had not placed it at the head of the hammock.

"What?"

I took in the room and lay back upon him, and willed my heart to calm.

"A dream." I forced myself to look upon what I could remember of the images. "We must never return to Christendom."

He rubbed my shoulders reassuringly. "What did you dream? And move. We drifted off unprepared."

I did not wish to speak of any of it. I rolled onto my back, and he slipped from the hammock to retrieve weapons and place them in the netting. He returned to lay partially atop me.

"Will?" he queried my chest.

"I saw you in an asylum, and you were begging me to kill you. I could not bear to see you in pain. I will never allow anyone to hurt you. I would rather see you dead than tortured."

I gasped at my last words. "That is awful. I am sorry. How selfish of me."

He was very still. "I would rather be dead than suffer again; and if my madness ever does bring me to such a state, I would rather you kill me."

"It will not come to that."

He sighed. "I have night horrors, too. I dream of harming you while mad."

I had dreamed of that myself, many times. "It will not come to that."

He raised his head to regard me. "Do you speak from faith or defiance?"

"Delusion?" I proffered with a smile.

"Go to sleep."

I prayed the Gods truly granted dreams of hope and paid little heed to ones of fear.

Twenty

Wherein We Chart A New Course

I thankfully had no more memorable dreams that night. We woke
to voices and the smell of food wafting though the window, as our room
was at the back of the house. I found myself piss-hard as I often do,
especially with his naked body pressed against me. I knew he would
have none of it, and I quickly rolled out of the hammock and donned my
clothes to go to the latrine.

I discovered Cudro and a few other men sleeping in the front room.
I left them to their snoring. I wondered just who slept here. I knew the
wolves had a room and we had ours. I guessed Julio and Davey had the
third. Perhaps Belfry, Tom, and Dickey had the fourth. I wondered if any
of them were helping with the cost of food and water.

In the yard, Striker was sitting in the bathing tub with his breeches
on. He was staring at some distant point in the sky that I was sure only
he could see. I passed him without comment and used the latrine.

When I emerged he asked, "Did I say anything of interest last night?"

I walked over to him and discovered the tub did contain water.
Several possible retorts and jests occurred to me, but I opted for
kindness of a sort.

"I do not know. I heard nothing, but then I did not hear more than
three words from you all night, as you were quite inebriated when you
reached our table. You could have said all manner of foolishness to
Morgan and Bradley."

"That is what I'm afraid of. I was hoping someone of a more sober
nature was there. Pete was as drunk as I, and he never remembers

things."

I surmised that, to some degree, Striker was still intoxicated. "You should return to your bed."

"Nay, Pete's snoring."

"Well, you should at least cease sitting in a bucket of water."

He regarded me quizzically. "I rather enjoy it."

"Later today, when you are not inclined to sit in tubs of water while clothed, we need to speak of matters of import regarding things I do remember being said last night."

Striker nodded. "Where can I find you?"

"I do not know, as of yet. I know we shall go by the gunsmith's, and then there was talk of meeting at the new ship."

"The new ship?" he blinked comically for a moment, and then rose from the tub in a soggy rush. "That... that... aye." He frowned and nodded to himself. "I shall rouse Pete. After the smith's, please return here and gather us, and we will accompany you." He leaned on the cistern and continued to collect his wits.

"We can wait until later in the day."

"Nay, I would see her."

Gaston had emerged from the house, used the latrine, and joined us. "Who?"

"The ship they returned on."

"Have you...?" he began to ask in French. I shook my head. He looked toward the cookhouse. "Will we be fed?" he asked in English.

"When Pete rises," Striker said. "She's only nice to him."

"Oh bloody Hell," I chuckled. "And how does he regard this?"

"He is still wary of her, as if she were a wild dog that might turn on him at any moment."

"That seems wise," Gaston said.

I regarded my matelot. "I am of the suspicion that you are not very fond of women, either."

"I am not familiar with them. Except for the maids and governesses of my childhood, I have met few, and I did not like the maids and governesses. I do not dislike women in general."

"Nay, because then you would be forced to like horses."

He smirked.

I must admit I approached the cookhouse with a small amount of trepidation. I found Rachel cooking a large pan of eggs. There was a heaping platter of broiled fish. She started when she turned enough to spy me.

"Sorry, I came to inquire as to food. It smelled quite lovely upstairs. May we eat it?"

She nodded pleasantly enough. "Aye sir, will you be wanting to eat out here, or at the table?"

I considered it. "Here should be fine."

"Will you be sharing it?"

I nodded. She pulled a good pewter plate from a shelf, ladled eggs on it, and added fish. I accepted it happily.

"Can you get him out of that tub, sir?" she asked.

"He is standing now. Please forgive him; he is still intoxicated from last night."

She nodded. "I am not used to men indulging in strong drink."

"I assure you he is a sober and industrious fellow when at sea; we all are."

"Will he ever be sober when he is in port?"

"Has he been drunk every night?"

She nodded with a grimace.

I nodded thoughtfully, "I truly do not know if there is much I can do concerning that."

"And I should not complain, as it is not my place. I realize that, sir."

"True, but... Has there been issue?"

"Nay, nay." Then she shrugged. "They've retched in the house a few times and..." She flushed. "They do not seem overly concerned about where they are when they do a number of things, when they are intoxicated."

"Ahhh," I said as understanding dawned. "They are not overly concerned with where they do that when they are sober. I will speak to the others, and we will attempt to be more discreet about the house."

I returned to Striker and asked, "Did you bugger one another in front of the housekeeper?"

He thought and then his eyes went wide. He chuckled and looked over his shoulder to the cookhouse. "Not with malice. Is that what she's bothered about?"

"Aye, and I said we would attempt to be more discreet."

"I can attempt to do many things," Striker said. "My matelot on the other hand..."

I could see his point.

Gaston was chewing thoughtfully on a piece of fish. "This is not bad, but I would prefer bacon."

"She is Jewish," I said.

He swore flagrantly in French. When he calmed he said, "I had forgotten. However, she does not have to eat it."

"I think there are prohibitions about it cooking in the same pan. So I feel we will not eat pork at all while she is with us."

Gaston appeared ill-pleased with all things religious. In contrast, I thought it likely she thought us silly over the boiling of the water.

We ate, performed our morning toilette, such as it was, and left for the gunsmith's.

Massey was pleased to see us. Our muskets were ready. Minimal damage had been done by the rough handling, and he pronounced them as good as new. We explained that a number of the men sailing with us had lost theirs altogether, and inquired as to what he had on hand. He only had six of the fine pieces from Dieppe, and another nine of somewhat inferior quality from England and Holland. They were similar to the piece I had arrived with; and I realized I had another I could loan someone. Massey was not willing to part with all fifteen, as that would leave him nothing to offer any other buccaneer who might be in dire straits before his next shipment. I thought this kind but misguided; but as I was often the same. I did not argue. After some haggling, we reached a price on the high side of satisfactory for twelve of them, including five of the fine pieces and seven of the others.

Massey led us into the back room and opened a vault of sorts built into the floor. There he retrieved a box with Gaston's name on it, from amongst over thirty of its brethren. I realized Massey was truly a bank of sorts.

Gaston set the box on the corner of a work table and opened it. There was good deal of gold in the box, as well as silver and some gems. Gaston counted out enough to cover the debt to Massey, which was now several hundred pounds, more to replenish what he had spent on the horses, and then still more. He handed a good fifty pounds to me. "Keep this."

I did not view it as money I could spend, but as a thing I held for him.

He put a similar amount into the bag he wore inside his breeches and the rest in his belt pouch. There were still over five hundred pounds in the box.

"However does he not get robbed?" I asked.

"He only holds buccaneer money. If I were robbed, I would hunt the thief to the ends of the world. He holds money for over a score of men like me."

I chuckled. "And only those he holds money for know of it, I would wager."

He nodded.

Massey gave us a receipt and vouchers for us to give to the men we would allot the muskets to, as we were not going attempt to carry fourteen muskets and their shot and powder.

To my surprise, Gaston turned away from the direction of the house when we left the smith's.

"Where are we off to?" I asked.

"I was thinking..." He sighed.

"Oui," I prompted.

"I should have my own medicine chest."

"Ah. Will you wish to advertise you will have one, or..."

"I do not know yet." He led me to the apothecary. It was a crowded little shop, filled to the ceiling with shelves crammed with jars and vials of this or that potion or powder. I wrinkled my nose at the overall smell. Gaston began to converse with the proprietor, and I thought he might be a while.

Another scent caught my nose, a pleasant one; and I found the counter containing the toiletry and beauty items such as rouges, paints, creams, perfumes, powders and all manner of things for ladies and discerning gentlemen. To my delight, I also found a fine assortment of sweet oils and scented salves, far more than I would have suspected in a town of this size – until I remembered that I was not the only one who had use for such substances here, and though many of the buccaneers lacked refinement, the ones that did appreciate finer things had need of a steady supply and the money to demand variety. I set about sampling each fragrance and type in turn, to compare their smell and consistency. Gaston stopped beside me.

"We will need an adequate supply of that," he whispered quickly in French, and moved on.

I did not dare ask him what amount he felt would denote an adequate supply. Instead I bit my lip to keep from smirking and inquired, "Any preferences?"

While the proprietor was rummaging under a counter Gaston joined me and I had him sniff the ones I favored. He still smelled deliciously of almonds, and I was disappointed there was no fragrance that matched it. He glared at me when I opened my mouth to explain this; and I shrugged and caught up his wrist, and pushed it under his nose. He sniffed and sighed and looked over the bottles.

"None match," I said simply.

The proprietor was still looking for something Gaston had requested, and his search took him into the back room.

"Why do you not wish to speak of it?" I hissed quickly.

"It is a thing of intimacy," Gaston snapped. Chastised, I at first bridled at this, as it bothered me that he did not wish others to know what we did as if he were ashamed. I had been ashamed until now and not wanted any to know what we did, because we did nothing. Now there was a small part of me that wanted to announce that we were actually intimate from the highest mountain top. Of course, that would make it apparent that we had not been engaged in any carnal activity of merit before. As always, my life was steeped in irony.

I watched as he quickly and methodically sniffed every container with earnest concentration, and realized I was a fool. Gaston had no more qualm than I concerning any knowing we were matelots and therefore presuming what they would. He merely wished, as I did, to keep the details of such things a private matter as they should be. I experienced a dollop of guilt that I should abuse his intent so. He was not the ghosts of my past. I vowed to both respect my matelot's wishes on the matter of privacy and to exercise even more vigilance against habitual thoughts that had been learned at the hands of others.

He found two he seemed to favor: one was spicier and the other fruitier, with the latter particularly reminding me of berries.

"I do not know of this berry one," I whispered. "If one of us were coated in this, Pete might mistake us for a pie, and there would be no end to the bloodshed that would ensue."

Gaston found this very amusing, and had difficulty composing himself when the apothecary returned. He chose a spicy cinnamon-smelling salve and a musky oil that became sweet when warmed by the skin, and added several jars and vials of each to his growing pile on the counter.

Other than the oil and salves, which he said we would stockpile in my chests during voyages, he bought no more of each item than he could carry. I helped assemble the chest as Gaston directed. The box itself was much like the one he had bought for the plantation, only larger by half. The front and top opened to reveal shelves and rows of compartments, which we filled with vials and muslin bags of various herbs and powders.

I was appalled at some of the prices, especially when he paid ten pounds for a bag of buds of some flower. The bag would not fit inside the chest, either. Then Gaston explained it contained poppies, and they were the thing one made laudanum from. He said it was a thing not always available and well worth the price. Once I knew what they were, I was more appreciative of them.

It was late morning when we finally returned to the house, the chest carried between us. I was thankful it would be on a ship and we would not have to lug it about.

Once we reached the house, Rachel informed us that the rest of them had gone looking for us. With a sigh, we deposited the new chest in our room and went in search of our friends. We found them at Theodore's. Pete was outside, talking to several men I did not know. Striker was inside, talking with Bradley and Theodore. He saw me at the window and waved us off. We withdrew and waited, and Striker emerged a moment later.

"Bradley is distraught," Striker explained as we walked a little distance from the others.

Striker seemed sober, but appeared to be suffering from the after-effects. He kept glaring up at the sun as if its brightness were a personal affront.

"I would imagine," I said.

"Aye, he's had one blow after another, Siegfried being the worst of course. But in addition to losing his matelot, he lost his ship, half the men who sailed with us, all of that gold – and these last few months, some ailment has killed a goodly number of his slaves, so his plantation is a right mess."

"I feel great sympathy for him, especially on the loss of Siegfried."

"Aye," Striker sighed. "If I ever lost Pete..." He trailed off and regarded us, and we nodded. There was no real need for words.

"Will he wish to sail?" I asked. "It sounds as if he may need the money."

"I don't think so." Striker regarded me speculatively.

I smiled. "Here is the discussion you missed at our table." I quickly relayed all that had been said among the Bard, Cudro, and me. He listened without comment; and when I finished, he took a deep breath and scuffed sand about with his toe and a great deal of thought. I waited.

"Do you trust Cudro?" he asked.

"As far as I could throw him."

"Can you lift him?" Striker finally looked up to grin.

Gaston chuckled.

"I think not," I grinned. "However, the nine or so men I do trust could throw him a good distance, if you catch my meaning?"

"Aye. When you speak of it in those terms, I think any of us can throw him. Gaston proved that handily enough."

My matelot shrugged.

"True," I said. "I am not fond of his having a good number of the crew in his favor, though."

"Neither am I. We would need remedy that. For now, let us go and look at this ship. I will tell those inside that we are going. And where were you this morning? We sent the others on already."

"Purchasing a medicine chest."

"Truly?" He looked to Gaston.

"Aye," Gaston sighed without looking at us.

I gave Striker a warning look, and he shrugged amicably.

He slipped inside and informed them we were off. As he collected his matelot, he inquired of the men Pete had been speaking with as to which ship they were sailing on. When he found their answers somewhat nebulous, he let them know that we might be sailing soon and looking for men. This seemed to please them, and they said they would wait to hear more as to final decisions on such matters.

We made our way to the Chocolata Hole by way of the market, where we acquired fried fish for lunch. Once at the Hole, we retrieved our flyboat and sailed out just beyond the entrance of the bay, where the prize rode at anchor. She looked a great deal like the *King's Hope*, but somewhat smaller, being a three-masted English merchant ship with primarily square rigged sails. She carried far more cannon, though: ten, with eight along the rails and two under the forecastle in the bow. Her gunwale seemed full of holes as a result, and I knew her to have even less deck space than the *King's Hope*.

Overall I was not impressed with the look of her, and more importantly neither was Striker. Yet he was not appalled, either, as apparently she was similar to most of the ships he had sailed before crossing to the New World.

She was named the *Flor de Mayo*, which translated to *May Flower*. I informed the others of this and Striker shrugged, "*Mayflower*, damn common name for a ship. I saw two in English waters and heard of a couple more. It must have been her name when they took her."

Tom threw us a line as we pulled alongside; and when we climbed the ladder, we found Dickey and Belfry with him. I was sure the Bard was cursing my name.

"What a surprise to see you all here," I said.

"We just came to see the ship," Belfry said. "Apparently Tom will be staying."

Liam, Otter, Davey, and Julio were aboard, and a number of other
men I recognized, but not Cudro or his men, or thankfully Hastings.
The Bard was sitting on the quarterdeck steps looking quite tired
and out of sorts. I joined him as Striker went forward and, starting at
the forecastle, went from fore to aft, poking here and there, and then
went below to presumably do the same. Pete followed him, and after a
moment of confusion, so did Tom.

"She needs to be careened, Hell, she needs to be swabbed and
stoned," the Bard said, and patiently worked on loading and lighting his
pipe with one arm in a sling.

"And you?" I asked.

"I could use a good careening myself."

"The scraping or the packing with tar and coating with pitch?" I
teased.

"All," he chuckled. He fumbled with the flint for a moment, and then
handed it to me along with the pipe.

"Light this, would you?" He grinned. "It's been a while since I
was packed with anything. There we were." He pointed to an area of
the main deck near us, where I noticed there were still bloodstains.
"Spanish guns on us all around, and all I could think of was how long
it had been since I last engaged in any kind of carnal delight other than
my own good hand. I kept thinking I wanted to do it once more before I
died. I was not even concerned with who or what."

We laughed, though Gaston was a little more restrained and Dickey
and Belfry seemingly somewhat embarrassed. When I recovered, I lit the
Bard's pipe and took a pull before handing it back.

"I have heard there are whores in town. I have actually seen some of
them."

The Bard grimaced. "Have you truly seen them? I have more respect
for the little man. Nay, I need a matelot."

"I am sure Pete and Striker could make recommendations."

He shook his head and grinned. "Nay, I would rather see to the
matter myself."

Belfrey and Dickey were watching us with a degree of discomfort,
which annoyed me, but I did not comment on it. Gaston was leaning
on the quarterdeck rail and looking about. I moved to join him and
did likewise. There seemed to be a great deal of rigging above us. I
remembered the *King's Hope* had required relatively few men to actually
sail her, though. Then I regarded the deck and thought of the much
larger hold this vessel would have as compared to the sloop.

"Speaking of men, how many will we need?" I asked.

The Bard shrugged. "We could sail with twenty. She can carry a
hundred more."

I thought that insane. "Are there a hundred men available?"

"Probably, but do we want them? It is a somewhat similar situation
to the whores."

Striker was swearing. My eyes followed my ears. He was regarding the first cannon.

"Is there a problem?" I asked the Bard.

"Only if you consider rust a problem."

I snorted. "We have procured all the muskets Massey will let go in one batch, but I know nothing of cannon."

"Under normal circumstances, we would not have call for them," the Bard sighed. "But this old lady lacks the speed and maneuverability of the sloop. Half the cannon are good; the other half can be fired, but not for an extended engagement. We should have gun crews and a gunner as a result. Yet I cannot see us sailing with a hundred unless we're raiding. It's too many men to feed otherwise without a guarantee of prey." He seemed to be rambling to himself.

"So what are you saying, that we should sail with sixty men, eighty?" I asked.

"We'll sail with whatever we get. If God smiles upon us, a goodly number of them will be familiar with cannon."

I thought of how formidable a group the sixty-six who sailed on the *North Wind* had seemed and how crowded I had initially thought us.

"I suppose gathering buccaneers for such a venture is relatively easy, as opposed to hiring sailors for a merchant voyage," Belfry noted in odd juxtaposition to my thoughts.

"Aye, or pressing them into the Navy," the Bard agreed.

Regarding Belfry standing on the deck in his full breeches, hose, coat, and hat, I was struck by how out-of-place he looked amongst us; yet this man had done far more sailing than I, and was an accomplished seaman. I tried to imagine him dressed as a buccaneer and could not. I tried to imagine him sailing with us, and could not do that either. He was a product of the Old World and not this new one.

"I was thankfully able to avoid the Navy," Belfry said earnestly. "I was apprenticed as a cabin boy when I was twelve, and have been sailing since."

"Have you worked aloft?" The Bard asked.

"I have learned the ropes, sir, but only the truly magnanimous would call me an able-bodied seaman." Belfry shrugged. "In truth, I must admit a certain calling to the sea, as it is apparently quite in my blood. After the loss of the *King's Hope* I told myself I would happily live without ever setting foot upon another vessel; but I find, upon standing on these decks, that I am gripped with a certain fondness, perhaps nostalgia. And, to my amazement, I have even been giving thought as to the amount of time I have before the arrival of my betrothed and the stock for our haberdashery next spring, and reasoning to myself that I would indeed have time to sail on a voyage of short duration. Yet I see no way that I may be useful to this endeavor, as you do not appear to need my skills and I do not possess the skills you do require."

Needless to say, I was quite taken aback by his words. I was not the only one to feel this. Dickey was regarding his business partner with horror.

"Can you navigate, read a chart, man a whip staff?" the Bard asked.

Belfry shrugged and nodded. "Aye, but you have men to do that, and it is my understanding that young Tom will be in your tutelage for such matters."

The Bard sighed. "Aye, but it's damn good on a ship to have as many men as possible who can perform the same tasks, as you never know what may occur and people die. You would be an asset. Granted, it would take some adjustment on your part, as things are managed quite a bit differently here than on a merchant ship."

Belfry regarded me, and I proffered a shrug. "You have heard the results of our last voyage."

The Bard waved me off. "That was a strange and cursed voyage. It will be talked about for years. Normally no real hardship befalls us. There is risk, but for the men sailing the ship it is far less than for those who board or raid."

"I bow to the Bard's greater experience in such matters," I said.

"As well you should," the Bard said. "So what say you, Belfry?"

Belfry looked to his still-agitated business partner. "We will not receive stock, or I a wife, until February at the earliest, as they will not sail during the hurricanes. I have been considering seeing if Theodore could put me to good use and I could learn a new trade in the process, but there may be far more money involved in this venture." He looked to us. "Could there not?"

"Or there could be nothing," the Bard said. "But aye, if we take a fine prize, every man aboard gets an equal share and that is often at least twenty pounds. We're sailing for the Galleons along the Cuban coast. We should not be gone more than two months."

Belfry regarded Dickey hopefully.

"You really wish to do this?" Dickey asked.

"Aye," Belfry said with sheepish enthusiasm.

"I think you have taken leave of your senses, but you do not need my approval or blessing," Dickey said with a tired sigh. "You're all mad. Tom's entirely smitten with it."

"Do you possess any proficiency with that blade?" I asked of Dickey, as I noted that he still wore a rapier.

He rolled his eyes. "Some. My father was very keen on overcoming my deficiencies of character in his eyes by a great amount of drilling in manly arts."

I leaped to the deck and drew as I landed. Dickey swore and drew, and settled into *en garde* with practiced ease. I came at him, and we exchanged a flurry of stokes and blocks, until I had witnessed enough to judge him proficient with a blade, even if he was not particularly gifted with one. I stood down and we bowed formally. We had gathered an audience of all the men aboard, and there was clapping. Dickey appeared embarrassed but a little pleased.

"You can fence. Can you shoot?" I asked.

"About as well as I can fence," he said with resignation as if it were a horrid thing he were admitting to. "I know nothing of sailing other than what I saw upon the voyage here," he quickly added. "And I have never been involved in a true fight of any type. I have twice fainted at the sight of blood."

"I sincerely doubt you will do that in combat."

"Bloody Hell, is there any possible protestation I can mount?" he asked.

I pretended to consider the question seriously. "Nay."

"Am I to be conscripted then?" he wailed.

We were all laughing by this juncture, and Striker, Pete, and Tom rejoined us in time to hear Dickey's plaintive protestation.

Striker looked Dickey over and looked to me. "You are in jest."

"See, he is a sane man," Dickey said.

I shrugged. "Belfry will be joining us, and I thought it best Dickey do likewise, as almost everyone he knows will have sailed off without him. Though inexperienced, he is proficient with weapons." I did not add that he would be loyal to Striker and not Cudro, and I hoped I did not need to.

Striker looked to me with a small smirk that Dickey could not see, and then said with great seriousness. "I care not. He is welcome if he agrees to the articles and follows them. Any show of cowardice in battle and he is a dead man."

This apparently sparked something deep inside Dickey; and his ire flamed to life, until it was readily apparent he was consumed by it at the expense of common sense.

"I am not a coward."

"I did not say you were," Striker said, as he took the quarterdeck and joined Gaston in leaning on the forward rail to look over the rest of us.

"Fine," Dickey said quietly, so that only Belfry and I could hear him clearly as we were closest. "I will do this. Then I will write my father of the matter, and perhaps prove him wrong, too."

I regretted my goading.

"Dickey," I said quietly, "you do not have to...."

"Nay," he said with a defiant jut of his chin. "I do. And you are correct, what will I do whilst everyone is gone? And we do have many months to account for, and no money to idle them away with. It is best I do something." He looked about and gestured flamboyantly. "I suppose we shall be sleeping on deck beneath the stars."

This brought chuckling from those still standing about.

"Aye," the Bard said. "There are few aboard now, and a great deal of space to choose from."

"Gah," I said, realizing we needed to stake out a space, as Pete and Striker would be taking the Captain's cabin. Then I realized that, like the *King's Hope*, this *Mayflower* had two small cabins on either side of the steerage.

"I would assume the main cabins will be reserved for... officers... once elected," Belfry said hesitantly before I could say anything.

"Aye," Striker said. "The captain, quartermaster, master of sail, surgeon, gunner, since we'll need one, and anyone they favor to share with."

"I have that one," the Bard said and hooked a thumb over his shoulder at the starboard cabin. "Usually I share the quarterdeck with my helmsmen and the surgeon. Cleghorn has said he will not sail on this voyage, and two of my usual men are dead; so I have offered to share with Tom, and I'm sure we can fit two more in." He looked pointedly at Belfry and Dickey.

"We would be much obliged," Belfry said.

"As I am not a helmsmen or a surgeon or what have you," Dickey said, and looked oddly at Belfry; and I understood his consternation. They were business partners and not matelots, and I surmised he did not want anyone to become confused on the issue. "I should perhaps find other accommodations."

I was about to intercede when Pete told me, "YouTwoCanShareWithUs."

"That would be..." I looked to Gaston and found him frowning at the Bard. So was Striker.

"Hold," Striker said. "Cleghorn will not be sailing?"

"He says he has no heart for it for the time being," the Bard said.

Striker looked to Gaston without word or even expression. My matelot seemed to withdraw in on himself and he was studying his hands. He said something only Striker could hear, and Striker nodded. I quickly joined them on the quarterdeck.

"I will do it," Gaston whispered, when I was in range to hear him.

I was not sure if I should show my pleasure over this or not.

"I am pleased," I said with some restraint.

He regarded me, and the hard lines of resignation about his countenance melted to curiosity. "Why?"

"It takes far more to build than to destroy."

"Healing is repairing, not building."

I shrugged. "I think it is good for you."

"As do I." He looked back to his hands and frowned at them, as if he did not understand what fascination they held.

I patted his shoulder and addressed Striker, who was watching us with guarded concern. "Pete has offered to share your cabin."

Striker thought on it for a moment, and nodded. "I am in agreement with that, if we get a cabin."

"If you do not get a cabin, we will not sail."

He frowned and nodded. "Nay, we will not." He regarded the ship before us. "I want this, Will. If I do not win the election, I will buy my own ship. I find I no longer have an interest in sailing under another just to sail."

I smiled at him. "Good."

I noticed the Bard looking up at us from where he still sat on the steps. He was the only other who could have heard our exchange. He was smiling, and not sardonically or in any mocking fashion. Striker looked at him.

"I'll sail with you," the Bard said.

"I am honored," Striker replied.

"As well you should be." the Bard grinned. "Now, you have seen her. What think you? We heard the cursing."

They quickly listed repairs the ship should have, and her numerous apparent problems that could not be fixed but must be endured. As I understood one word in three, I threw my arm around Gaston, and watched Pete and Liam explain the finer points of buccaneer dress to an enthusiastic but confused Belfrey and an appalled Dickey. As Gaston was not chuckling at the particularly amusing statements, I squeezed his shoulders and inquired in French, "Are you well?"

He shook himself from his reverie. "Oui. I am sorry. I... Last night." I looked at him sharply. He gave a quick shake of his head. "Non. I enjoyed it. It is just that it resurrected some fragment of memory from... I dreamt. I cannot remember it clearly."

I thought of a number of relatively stupid things I could say, and settled for kissing his temple. He turned his head to regard me for a moment, and seemed on the verge of speech. He finally smiled, and taking my hand, led me on our own leisurely inspection of the *Mayflower*.

The ship was old and smelled a great deal of fish below deck. Thankfully this was not true of the master cabin, which had a set of leaded windows. Oft opened as they were now, I garnered they did much to air the room and keep it fresher than the hold. The cabin was as wide as the stern, a good fourteen feet and as deep as eight at some points. It appeared to have the same accoutrements all master cabins had. There was a desk along one wall, and along the other a bunk, and ample storage space and anchorage for hammocks.

Gaston closed the door and herded me toward the bunk, until my knees buckled and I sat upon it. Bemused, I chuckled as he pushed me all the way back and sat astride my hips. He appeared very serious, earnest really, and his mouth wiped the grin from my face as his hands slipped beneath my tunic to trace along my ribs and find my nipples. I clutched at his shoulders and groaned. I liked this aggressive stance he was taking, and he was not blind in leading me anywhere.

Then he stopped and sat back to doff his baldric and belt. Panting, I watched with anticipation. He dropped his weapons on the far end of the bed, and then flopped down so he was on his back beside me. He had not been grinning or even looking upon me at that moment. My cock, which had just begun to spring to life, was horribly confused at the sudden lack of heat and pressure. I was torn between concern and bemusement. I twisted onto my elbow to regard him. He was staring at the ceiling with deep concentration.

"Excuse me," I said teasingly, "but what the Devil was that?"

"An experiment," he whispered, eyes still on the ceiling and a frown across his brow. "I was trying to discover more of the memory. Being astride you in that fashion, doing as I did, was part of it somehow; and I have discovered I am uncomfortable with that."

"So you are not prone to continue that which you started?"

He shook his head, and his eyes met mine. He frowned, this time at me and not the mental will-o-wisp he had been pursuing.

"I aroused you, non?"

"Oui. You gave great promise of entertainment for a minute there. And while I appreciate..."

He grinned and snaked an arm behind my head to pull my mouth to his. I kissed him as deeply as he had me a moment before, and he responded graciously but without passion. I relieved myself of my pistol and rolled onto my elbows atop him, with one leg between his own. His hands found my chest, and I thought he would push me off; instead they slipped below my tunic again to play and tease. A moment later, I was earnestly humping the hollow of his hip. He urged me on in his fashion, and did not even offer complaint when I pushed my leg well up between and under his so that his left leg was curled over my hip. It was the closest to a true sexual position I had found myself in for close to a year, and I rode against him quite contentedly while plundering his mouth until I came.

Spent, I rolled off and scooped what I could of the effluence out of my breeches to wipe it on the blanket. I made note to wash all of my clothing before we sailed.

He lay still beside me, quiescent, unmoved and unmoving, and I felt as I had many times with very jaded or bored partners, men or women who did not experience passion with me and simply let me vent my lust upon their person. I felt almost as if I should pay him. It was a foul thought. It was not his fault he did not respond. I was very thankful he did allow me to vent my lust upon him. Still, I was uncomfortable and mired in guilt of some variety. It was as if my lust was a monster we were both victim to. In which case, I argued, he should not do so much to rouse the beast from slumber.

He sat without looking at me. I pushed myself upright beside him and whispered, "I am sorry."

He regarded me quizzically. "For what?"

"I feel like a beast that must be sated."

He grinned. "You are."

I recoiled a little, though I knew he was in jest.

"Will, if I took offense, you would be the first to know."

"I know. It is my matter, not yours. It is with... I assume... rejection."

His eyes widened slightly, and he jumped atop me and pushed me back onto the bed to kiss me. When he pulled away, he whispered, "I am sorry. I should reassure you, oui?"

"Now I feel like a child."

"Will, you always feel like something."

"I would prefer a man, but...." I smiled and sighed. "My mind just keeps running down paths it has long traveled. Every time I tell myself I am different, you are different, the world is different, I find myself addicted to my habits."

"Whereas I find myself trapped attempting to explore paths I have traveled before and cannot remember."

"I have not wanted to say anything foolish, such as it will come or give yourself time, but perhaps I should. Can you tell me of it at all?"

He shrugged. "It involved the last time I felt passion."

The door slammed open, and Gaston rolled off me and we reached for weapons. We had them in hand by the time we recognized Pete and Striker.

"Here you are," Striker said and came to jump upon the bunk and sprawl beside me on an elbow.

I looked to Gaston apologetically, and he smiled with resignation. We would talk later. Pete knelt with his elbows across my knees. Gaston set his pistol down, and pulled himself up to lean on the wall at my side. I was hemmed in yet, oddly, not concerned. I took Gaston's hand and he squeezed back.

"What do you want?" I asked Striker, though I was regarding Pete. The Golden One had laid his head upon his arms, so that when I looked down the length of my body I saw chest, stomach, groin and Pete's head. It was disconcerting and more threatening than erotic, as he was grinning with a great degree of feral zeal.

"All right," Striker said, "This is the lie of things. It is late June. The Galleons sail in August on no particular date. Sometimes they sail as late as September, but it was once reported that they sailed as early as late July. I need to check the taverns and see what talk I can hear of sightings or prizes taken along the Main. Right about now, they should be finishing up the fair in Porto Bello; and then the fleet will sail back to Cartagena, and then north to Havana to provision before following the usual route back to Spain."

"So we have approximately four to eight weeks in which to catch them, somewhere," I said. "And I assume it would be best if we were in those waters inside of four weeks."

"I would do better than that," Striker said. "There are occasionally lone ships that sail due north from the colonies along the south of the sea. And not book smugglers, either. They meet up with the Galleons at Havana. If we were able to sail very soon, we could follow their path and wait near the Cabo San Antonio, to the south of where we were wrecked. All ships coming from the south have to slip around it and into the Yucatan Channel. We could hunt lone ships, or if that fails, follow the fleet." He grew a little somber. "I will not risk us against a ship of the line again. I want lesser but surer prey."

I nodded. "As I asked before, what would you have of us?"

"This ship needs to be careened and have some repairs."

"Yes, the Bard was quite clear on that."

"That will take a week or so, even if we sail tomorrow, which puts us in July before we can hunt – which would be acceptable if we did not have the issue of provisions."

"Ah, you wish to provision before we sail in order to save time, and you do not wish to do it on credit."

Striker nodded. "I can provide the capital for repairs and the like, but it would take most of what I have to provision us as well. And, if we do not leave here owing anyone, then we can sell in Tortuga if we wish, and not give the crown a cent."

Gaston made a thoughtful sound and a nod. "They will not care overly much if we sail with their marque or not, as the island is now run by a company and not a government; though D'Ogeron does much to not make it appear so."

I remembered some of what he had told me concerning Tortuga's history, which had been strange and rocky to say the least. The island had changed hands amongst the Spanish, French, and English many times. It was now under the governance of the French West India Company, and due to the leadership of D'Oregon was considered to be the true buccaneer stronghold by many: it was a safe haven where their arrival with a prize would not put them in harm's way due to the whims of English foreign policy. Open warfare between the French and English did cause considerable problems for the English buccaneers in using that port, though. Thankfully that business was behind us for the time being.

"So if we embark upon this course, we will recoup our outlay from the booty prior to sharing it amongst the men," I said.

"Aye, we will provide receipts. So, mates, I must ask a delicate question: do you have the means to provision us?"

I looked to Gaston; it was his money. He nodded.

Striker sighed with relief.

"We have already procured as many muskets as were available," I said. I produced the receipt for that from my belt pouch.

His eyes went wide at the sum. "The men you award these to will owe you out of their shares."

"Should we not first assemble a crew and make sure it is agreeable to all, before we expend the money and discover problems?" I asked. "Not that I doubt your ability to win the vote."

"Nor do I, and I do not feel I am engaging in hubris to say so." Striker grinned. "What you describe is usually the way of it in situations of this nature. The crew is assembled first, and then we agree on the provisioning, as that has affect upon when and how we sail, and in this instance, what type of prey we need in order that all may profit. Raiding a pig farm costs nothing but time."

"Then our first order of business is assembling a crew," I said.

Striker nodded. "The news of our sailing is already being passed, and in the last hour twelve men have arrived. We're going to shore to spread word in the taverns." He sighed. "And speak to Bradley. And get a damn marque, though I would rather not."

"In case we must return here," I nodded, "it would be wise, especially if we intend to evade it and the crown's share. Could we even sail without one without arousing undue suspicion?"

"Aye and nay," he snorted. "And even if we could, I have this occasional fear of running afoul of an actual English Navy vessel and not being an honest privateer."

"Do you think it likely?"

"Nay, but it haunts me sometimes."

"Would that be why you have never left the tropics?"

"It would indeed. I will not be put in chains again, Will," he said soberly. "And I do not have it in my nature to abide the law." He was in earnest, and I was surprised by it. Pete even stood and regarded him with concern.

"Let us see that we do not run afoul of it, then," I said seriously.

He shook off the mood and grinned sheepishly. "Right. Let us get about it, then."

"We will meet you above in a moment," I said.

Striker frowned and looked from Gaston to me. "Did we interrupt?"

"Perhaps," I said flatly.

"YouHadTime," Pete said. "YouWereGoneAwhile."

"Perhaps we should not share a cabin," I said and kicked him in the leg. Pete laughed.

Striker made a derisive noise as he stood. "We will establish a signal."

"Knocking may also be appropriate. Fewer people may be shot that way." I brandished the pistol I still held with a smile.

He grinned. "I heard there was a shooting this week. Some matter about an escaped bondsman."

"Damn you for mentioning it," I sighed. "Aye, there was, though that was not my intent. We will tell you of it over a bottle."

"We will see you up top," Striker said with a chuckle.

They closed the door behind them, and I looked to Gaston. "This seems quite the risky investment."

He shrugged. "I have the money I have because I do not spend it. Perhaps this is another way I choose to venture forth from my cave."

"I bid you welcome to the world then."

"In the name of other centaurs?"

"Oui, though I have seen no other. But I believe you were telling me of something."

He shook his head. "It will wait until tonight, and perhaps a bottle. We should go." He paused in crawling off the bunk and regarded me. His lips twitched into a smile, and he kissed my forehead. "Will a kiss suffice for reassurance, or is there something you would have me say?"

I smiled and did not think long on it. "A kiss will do."

On deck, we found that there were indeed a number of new men aboard. Our musketeers had taken Belfry and the boys into town to equip them in all they would need to be buccaneers. I imagined the three of them with earrings and smiled. I imagined Liam regaling them with buccaneer lore the entire way and smiled wider.

Striker left the Bard to greet new arrivals. We took our boat back to the Hole and made our way to Theodore's. Bradley had long since left, but he had been headed to the Three Tunns and would be easy to find. His being sober was unlikely, though, and Striker was not pleased.

"I will make what I can of it," Striker said. He regarded Theodore thoughtfully. "We will have need of a marque. I have not captained before, and I know not the way of that."

"Ah, it will not be an issue," Theodore said. "I will send a note to the governor. He may wish for you to ride out to Spanish Town and pick it up."

Striker shrugged. "Whatever must be done. Thank you for your assistance. If I owe you anything...?"

Theodore waved him off. "I do not issue them, and in this case I need not represent you. You have many men to recommend you."

"Thank you," Striker said. He paused on his way to the door. "There may be other matters I will need your services on."

"You know where I am," Theodore said.

Striker grinned, and took Pete in search of Bradley.

"You will be sailing?" Theodore asked me.

"Within days. Do you have need of me before I go?"

"Perhaps you should write your father again."

I sighed. "Actually, I should take the time and write better letters to several others. But aye, I will sit and do it. Will you provide the paper?"

He opened a drawer on his desk and pointed theatrically.

I laughed. "Not tonight. In the morning, perhaps."

"Is there anything you wish for me to do in your absence?" he asked.

"Keep the house," I shrugged. Gaston nudged me, and I remembered. "Ah, and we have purchased two horses. They are at the livery, and you are welcome to use them if you have need. We left your name, but I am sure if you asked of them using our names, there will be no problem."

"Thank you, that is thoughtful. Whyever did you purchase a horse when you...?"

"Will be here so seldom? Aye. Well, we were concerned for their welfare."

His smile froze, and I saw much occurring behind his eyes.

"Are you not pleased I am leaving?" I grinned.

"Aye," he said slowly with a thoughtful nod. Then he smiled sincerely. "I will anticipate the excitement of your homecoming, though. You liven things quite nicely when you are about."

"Aye, aye," I grumbled. "Please look in on Rachel from time to time."

"I will be pleased to do so," he said enthusiastically.

"She is Jewish," I said.

"Some obstacles can be overcome."

I snorted with amusement. "It has been my experience that religion is rarely one of them. We will see you on the morrow, then."

"He is attracted to that woman?" Gaston asked incredulously as we walked down the street.

"She is comely enough, and he is lonely. You do not find me revolting, and I would think that a greater stretch of preference."

"There is much to your mind and spirit to recommend you," he said seriously.

"Thank you."

"And your body."

I stumbled and stopped to regard him. "Thank you."

He flushed and walked on ahead. I wondered at his thoughts, but felt it best to leave him to them.

We found Striker, Pete, and Bradley at the Three Tunns as expected. Bradley did not appear to have achieved drunkenness yet, but he was well on his way. He glared at us as we approached their table, and I was hesitant to join them. Either the man was possessed of the most Mercurial disposition or we brought out the worst in him. Striker looked confused at Bradley's ill temper, and glanced at me curiously.

I decided retreat might be a diplomatic necessity.

"Have you seen Cudro yet?" I asked.

Striker shook his head.

"Then we shall go and find him," I said, and we took our leave.

Gaston appeared glum, and I was angry at Bradley for making him feel unwelcome.

Pete caught us before we reached the door. "BradleyDoNa'LikeYa. Na"Im," he pointed at Gaston. "ButYou."

"I am not blind," I sighed. I know he does not like one of us. I am almost relieved to hear it is me. Would you know why?"

"You'reRichAn'ANoble."

"I can see how... Nay, I cannot. That did not seem to offend him, when first we met. He liked me, and then we burned the ship and he did not like me, and then he resented my defining matelotage as marriage, and then Gaston would not let Cleghorn bleed me. I can see where all of that somehow affected his opinion of me, but then he liked me again after we took the galleon. But perhaps that was only because we were all very rich then. Now he dislikes me again. I am left thinking it is us that he dislikes, not me and I do not see where any of it has to do with my birth."

Deep in thought, Pete doffed his kerchief and scratched the pale stubble on his head. He frowned at the shadowed table where Striker and Bradley sat.

"Envy," he finally pronounced.

"Truly, you feel he is envious of me?"

"Aye." He nodded more to himself than me. "That'sWhat'ESays. ThatNobleRascalCanDoAs'EPleases. Makes'ImAngry.

YouHaveTitleAn'Matelot. YaEven'AveFriendsAn'Skill.
An'APlantationAn'Money. You'AveAllManner O'Things'E'sWorkedHardFo
r. 'EDoesNa''AveItNowAn'YaDo."

"Oh good Lord," I sighed. "I barely have title. I have no money of my
own. And the plantation is not mine. How does one fight this? What can
I possibly say to convince him otherwise?" I regarded Pete. "Is he the
only man that thinks thusly concerning me?"

Pete shook his head sadly.

I shook mine. "Damn it, for years I traveled by many a name, none
of them my father's, and I made my own way in the world. I come here
where I should do likewise and... I should never have let anyone know
who I am. I do not know how that would have been possible, though,
considering my original business here." I looked back at the table. "I
worked hard for what I have, too, or at least I paid for it. Granted, I
have done some immoral and disreputable things to get what I have on
occasion." I listened to my words. "And I whine like a child."

Pete was watching me with a look about him that made him seem
another man, a smarter and wiser man than he usually appeared. He
favored me with a knowing smile, and mischief glinted in his gaze, as if I
had caught him at something. The look of him at that moment brought
something to mind that I could not name, and I stood staring at him like
a daft cow.

He laughed at me and clasped my shoulders to give me a
little shake. "ILikeYa. YaBeAGoodMan. IfTheOthersKnewYaAsIDo,
TheyWouldNa'Say SuchThings. BradleyBeAFool."

I had it. He made me think of all the tales of gods and angels
appearing as mortal men to judge the living.

"Would that get me into Heaven? Your approval?"

He regarded me quizzically. "YaWantTaGoTaHeaven? Why?
MustBeDull."

"Maybe it is more akin to the Elysian Fields or Valhalla?"

"What?"

"A place where warriors go and live a life of endless feasting,
hunting, and games."

He smiled. "SoundsLikeAPastor'sHell."

"I suppose it does. Thank you, Pete."

"For what?" he shrugged.

"For being my friend. It means a great deal to me."

He smiled slyly. "WhinyNobleDahgsNeedFriendsToo." He winked
at Gaston and returned to Striker and Bradley, accompanied by my
laughter.

"Did you see him just then?" I asked in French once we were
outside.

Gaston smiled. "I told you he as not as he appears."

"Oui, I think he is a God who walks amongst us in judgment."

"Thus your question?"

"Oui."

He grinned. "Pete is a God. We are fortunate to have befriended him."

If Pete was a God, Cudro was the man who would be king. We located him holding court in the Sugarloaf on Lime Street. He seemed pleased to see us, and we pulled him aside and conferred at length over the muskets in quiet French. He was amazed we had simply purchased them. I asked him to confer with Liam and compile a list of twelve men from the *North Wind* who needed them and to determine who the best shots were, so that they could have the better weapons. He readily agreed, and said he would go to the *Mayflower* that night.

Gaston and I exchanged a look, and with a subtle shrug, my matelot approved my handing Cudro the vouchers.

"There is a voucher here for each gun," I told Cudro. "Massey will hand them to whoever presents these. They are also good for an allotment of shot and powder."

Cudro understood their value and quickly tucked them away.

"Now, how goes the recruiting?" I asked. "We just left Striker conferring with Bradley. Striker wishes to sail this week, so that we will have time to careen and hunt for single ships heading to Havana before following the Galleons. This ship is not the sloop. We can carry more men but…"

"How will we provision if time is of the essence?" he asked.

"We were thinking of provisioning here."

"On credit?" he scoffed.

"Non, I would provide the money," Gaston said. "We may choose to sell a prize on Île de la Tortue."

Cudro nodded thoughtfully. "That would do well by me. I have business I should attend to on Île de la Tortue. You have that…?"

Gaston cut him off with a glare. "Obviously."

"Then buy the boys a round." Cudro grinned.

The cunning bastard had us, and I chuckled, though Gaston still glared.

"By the way, we need gunners," I added before the drinking began.

Cudro regarded me sharply. "She's that slow?"

"Oui, apparently. The Bard suggested it."

Cudro swore quietly. Then he introduced us all around to the twenty or so men present. A few of them we had met before, and others were new to me, many of them Dutch and French. Gaston seemed familiar with many, though, and they with him. They were quite surprised when he bought them rum.

Still smarting from Bradley's assessment of me, and not wanting to engender the same anywhere else in Port Royal, I cajoled Gaston to stay and drink with them. I even told salacious tales of my travels, which seemed to amuse them greatly.

Several hours later, we sat at a wobbly table and watched a line of men waiting for the one available whore. I became acutely aware of my surroundings and the state of my being, which was hungry and nauseated, as I had consumed nothing except beer and rum since noon. Gaston looked as I felt. Cudro was busy talking to a man who had been a gunner in the French Navy. We bid them adieu and took our leave. When we staggered out into the night, I was unsure of the way home for a moment. Gaston had thankfully not consumed as much as I, and he pulled my arm over his shoulder and took me home.

There was no one about on the main floor of the house, but there was a platter of cheese and boucan on the dining table. We shoved food in our mouths and drank a great deal of water. Then I was compelled to use the latrine for an extended period, as I am often wont to do after drinking. Gaston went upstairs without me.

Sometime later, I felt much relieved in a multitude of ways, including the possession of a clearer head; I slipped upstairs. The light seeping under the door was a beacon calling me home. I entered the room, and found Gaston naked and kneeling upon the hammock. I was initially delighted, until I saw that though he was physically there before me, his mind was somewhere very far away. His body was tense, and he looked down upon the netting with his head cocked and his hands held before him, fingers twitching ever so slightly, as if he were trying to feel a thing that could not be seen.

I guessed he was pursuing his elusive memory again, but fear clutched at me and I was unsure what to do. As he was not moving toward me and did not seem to be aware of my presence, I decided to slowly remove my weapons and set them upon the trunk. A scabbard thumped more than I intended, and I looked up to find him regarding me. His eyes once again reminded me of a child's, wide and innocent, as they had that night on the *North Wind* and later on the galleon when he had arranged the bodies into *La Pieta*. His gaze was filled with recognition and joy at seeing me. He held out his hand, and with a stomach full of leaden fear I went to join him.

"I made love to an angel," he whispered, once my hand was firmly in his.

I could not stop myself from frowning, but I nodded.

"She was beautiful," he continued. "There was white all around," he gestured to the hammock, "and her skin glowed in the candlelight."

I found great relief in his speaking of it in the past tense, and I crawled onto the hammock to sit beside him.

"I was as I am now," he said, "but she was dressed in...." He rubbed his fingers together and concentration suffused his face. "Soft. Cotton. A gown, a nightgown. She smelled of lilacs." His eyes met mine. "I cannot see her face. I knew that she was the closest to Heaven I would ever be, because in seeing her, I was.... It was wrong."

I wanted to hold him. Pieces of the puzzle were becoming apparent, and I surmised he had not angered God the Father that night by lying with an angel, but his father in flesh and blood. I slid my arm across his back; and he allowed me to pull him close, and rested his head on my shoulder.

He was sounding more himself. "I think I told you, I dreamed of it last night, after..."

"You told me," I murmured. "But you could not tell me what you had seen as yet."

"I have discovered most of that image, just that one image. The lamplight and my nakedness must have reminded me, and the scents today added to it. Then sitting atop you and..." He pulled away enough to regard me. "I had been planning to reciprocate your attentions of last night, but the thought of it all... I found I felt as I did this afternoon. I find I am uncomfortable with... being aggressive, or at least... above, for now, as something occurred that night and I do not know what. And in not understanding it I feel... I want to do nothing to mimic it, lest it engender some deeper memory I do not want to discover whilst... loving you."

I was of two minds on the matter, as I dearly wanted him to uncover the rest of his past. I understood his reticence, though, in that in doing so he might induce himself to madness and that would be unfortunate to say the least if it involved my lying naked beneath him.

"We need do nothing," I whispered.

He shook his head. "I..." he flushed. "You have done that before, non?"

"Oui and non. I have been the recipient of similar ministrations, but I had not bestowed them until last night."

"Would you think me selfish, if I asked you to do so again?"

"Non. It brings me great pleasure to touch you so."

"Then please do."

I kissed him and bade him lie down. Then I did as I had the night before, except I was a bit more playful, and took time exploring areas and means of touch that he enjoyed more than others. He in turn was more responsive and inquisitive, and thus the whole of it was more of a mutual act. This time his hand was upon my member when it deposited its offering on his chest, and he was the one who scooped it up and massaged it about his manhood.

I grinned and held him in the aftermath.

I felt loved by Gods both distant and present, and I vowed not to worry myself with demons, or angels, of the past.

Twenty-One

Wherein I Discover Roads Not Taken

We woke late and languidly. As the entire upper floor of the house reverberated with snores, some might say we woke comparatively early. I had slept well, with no night terrors or other memorable dreams. If Gaston's sleep had troubled him, he said nothing of it. As we were naked and I did not feel the need to dive away from him immediately to tend to my needs or avoid his discomfiture, I noticed that his manhood was fully functional in regards to waking full of piss. It gave me some indication of his size if he was truly aroused, and I was pleased with the overall shape and proportions of him. I said nothing of this, and cuddled with him as chastely as I could manage.

When at last we felt the need to go downstairs, I discovered a sheaf of paper, quill and ink, and dusting powder on the dining table. I used the latrine and asked Rachel of it. She said Samuel had brought it over. It seemed Theodore was busy with a client this morning; however, he did wish for us to stop by later. I was amused. I sat at the table with a plate of eggs and wrote. As before, Gaston waited until I finished a page, and then read it and dusted it.

I happily composed an informative, if abridged, telling of our voyage for Sarah and Rucker. Then, with some perverse need to expurgate myself, I told my father of shooting Creek, and assured him no one else would consider escaping. I told him how hundreds of Spaniards had died when the Galleon sank after we took it. I thought he might find delight in that. As I was in quite the furor at that point, I went on to say how I had survived that shipwreck and obviously returned, only to plan on sailing again, now that I had seen to my duty involving the plantation, that being apprehending an escaped bondsmen. I finished by telling him how very much life here agreed with me.

Gaston was amused but silent as he read through this missive.

"Do you feel it is more than I should say?" I asked. "Or perhaps I should say it differently?"

"Non. I think you have done well here. From this, I feel, he will think you are a very good wolf indeed."

I had not looked upon it in that light as I wrote it, and I chuckled. "Likely I will endear myself to him."

"Oui." He shrugged. "As he will not know how much you lie, and he would never understand why."

"It is not lying," I sighed. "I am merely editing the truth." I watched him fold the dry letters. "You truly have no one to write? I know... well, I know you will not write your father, and your sister and mother are dead. But is there no one else?"

He tensed as I spoke, but it fled him in a sigh as I finished. "There is one, perhaps, on Île de la Tortue, but we shall possibly see him soon. And if not, I feel no need to write him."

"You mentioned this person was your mentor."

"Oui, Dominic Doucette. He is a great physician." Gaston considered me for a moment. Then he took a deep breath, studied the table, and spoke. "That night occurred at Christmas eleven years ago. Within a week I was on a ship. I feel I am only alive because Doucette was traveling to the West Indies when my father's men arrived with me at Marseilles. He was an experienced physician, and I was near death. I knew none of this at the time. I was not in a sufficiently coherent state to make his acquaintance for six months.

"My father's man, Vittese, had booked passage to personally deliver me and the money my father had sent for me to Guadalupe, if I should survive. Upon finding a physician ready to sail, Vittese paid Doucette handsomely to care for me. I was mad with pain, and nearly drained of blood, and in constant danger of infection. Doucette later said he learned more from keeping me alive during that voyage than he had in all his prior years of practice. He kept me on laudanum for most of it, and all I remember of that period is much like a dream. I sometimes think that I would not have this gap in my memory if I had been able to think after the incident.

"We arrived on Guadalupe in March. Doucette heard there might be more use for him on Île de la Tortue, and so he moved us there that summer. Soon after, he began to wean me from the laudanum, and I truly went mad. It was very much like sobering in the harsh light of day, and I was angry... To this day, I regret that I exercised some of this anger on him; but I was very lost, to myself and in relation to the world around me. I did not remember coming to this New World. I could not remember why I had been forced to do so. I was hideously scarred, and my mind seemed to be in as much pain as my body had once been.

And there was this man telling me what I could and could not do, and denying me the thing that had kept the thinking at bay.

"He defended his position, which was that it was time for my mind to heal as my body had done. I wanted none of it. I bought the things I heard I would need, and took a boat across the channel to the Haiti. I lived like an animal for a year, but in time I gained some measure of peace with myself. When I was somewhat sane again, I returned and apologized to Doucette. That is when he taught me medicine."

Gaston shrugged. "To relieve my studies and boredom, and truthfully, my bouts of anger, I would go fliebusting with whatever ship was sailing. After a bad bout of my madness, I would return to the Haiti and calm myself again, which is how I came to know other men who lived there and make boucan. This went on for many years. Doucette always wished for me to stop roving, and stay and become a physician at his side. I was restless, and four years ago I started leaving for longer raids, and now I have not been back in over two years."

When he did not speak for a time, I rubbed his shoulder. "Thank you for telling me of it."

He took a deep breath. "I do not know why I have not before. It is not as if I harbor ill will toward him, or that I cannot remember those years."

"Was he ever interested in...?"

He shook his head quickly. "Non, he does not favor men and had no need, as he is the physician for all the whores and they render him services for free, or rather their masters charge him nothing. Not that the whores ever seemed to begrudge him. He is quite popular amongst them.

"Non," he continued thoughtfully. "In many ways, Doucette is my second father. He raised me again. Yet in others, I am a grand experiment of his, the greatest example of his work. He would always want to trot me out to show me off to other surgeons. He was greatly disappointed I would not stay, on many fronts. One of which was loneliness, as we were fond of each other in our own way."

I was curious, as there seemed to be an element I was missing. "How do your feelings for Doucette compare to your feelings for Peirrot?"

Gaston frowned, and his eyes met mine. "Will, I have never shared myself with anyone as I do with you."

"I did not..."

He shook his head. "Not physically, I know you know that. But my heart and soul. I speak to you as I do no other. Peirrot... protected me. We talked on occasion, but our friendship, such as it was, was... I feel he pitied me and wished to care for me because of my madness. Doucette... has seen me at my worst, yet... he does not see me as mad. It is an odd thing. I know I am mad. He feels it is a thing I can easily control and overcome. This is due to my never showing him my madness except for those first months, and then he blamed the pain and laudanum. After that, whenever I felt... brittle, whenever the horse would take no more, I would escape to the Haiti. So he never saw it. And as I said, I was a son to him, and he was much as my father was... without the temper. Non, that is not correct either. I felt for him much as I did toward my father. Doucette was not like my father, though. My father believed in the madness. He understood it well."

He had become increasingly distraught as he spoke, and now he stared at the table again.

"No more, Will," he whispered.

I knelt beside his chair and held him. He seemed happy with this, and returned my embrace, so that my ear was pressed against his chest. I listened as his heart ceased racing and slowly returned to its normal rhythm. My thoughts slowed too: though I knew we needed to discuss many things, I did not feel compelled to discuss them now. The answers would come, as he would continue to open to me of his own volition as time passed. As it was, I felt truly and deeply honored that I was the only one he had ever spoken to concerning any of this.

I wondered what we should do now, as my letters were written and my knees were beginning to ache on the hard floor. Though he was calmer, he still seemed to be in deep thought.

"I know I think too much sometimes, and it leads to melancholy," I said quietly. "Would you like to spar? Or do you wish to continue to think?"

He rubbed my back. "Are you sober?"

I chuckled. "I believe so."

"I have thought enough for a lifetime."

I pushed to my feet and leaned down to softly kiss his lips. He smiled. We left the house and walked to the beach, and then far down it, onto the Palisadoes beyond the wall. We did not return for hours, and by then we were exhausted and thoughtless.

I wished to nap, but Rachel told us Samuel had been around again. Theodore truly needed our presence. Striker's and Pete's as well; but they had already gone, a little before we arrived. Curious, we hurried to Theodore's, and were confronted by an incensed Striker before we cleared the threshold. He smacked me with a sealed envelope and gesticulated with an open one. He appeared to be in quite the snit, yet Pete was oddly calm and amused.

Theodore sat at his desk with his face in his hands and a long-suffering demeanor about him. He raised his head long enough to sigh at my entrance and mutter, "Wonderful, now I shall have two of you cursing me."

I regarded the envelope with which Striker had unceremoniously presented me. It bore my full name. I opened it and, with Gaston looking over my shoulder, perused the contents. I had been invited for dinner that evening at the Governor's house in Spanish Town.

"What is this about?" I looked to Striker; his envelope was very similar to mine.

"Modyford's man brought them," Striker spat. "I asked of it. You and

I are invited. Pete and Gaston are not."

"So to the Devil with them," I said.

"It's for the marque," Striker growled. "I knew well I would have to receive the damn thing from someone, but I did not think it would be over dinner."

"So you have to go," I said. "Why was I invited?"

Theodore rolled his eyes, and Striker awarded me with a look that said if he was forced to dine at the Governor's house, he was not going alone. I answered my own question by surmising that it was because I was my father's son, and people of a certain ilk still thought they might curry favor with me.

"I would hope you have not cast all your decent clothing onto a midden heap," Theodore said.

I shrugged. "Nay, and some might fit Striker with a little tailoring."

"Oh bloody Hell!" Striker howled. "You expect me to dress for this?"

An hour later, we had found that my shirts and breeches fit him, though a little snugly, and that the tailor had left a generous amount at the seams in one of my jackets. Rachel was busy at letting it out to fit his wider shoulders. Thankfully, we both owned boots and were not forced to make my shoes fit him; nor would I find it necessary to wear hose. We wore kerchiefs over our heads under the hats. An hour beyond that, we stood shaved and somewhat clean in our finery, and bore the amusement of our matelots with little humor. Rachel professed surprise that we could be made to look like gentlemen. Theodore appeared relieved.

Theodore had also been invited, and Pete and Gaston accompanied the three of us to the ferry landing. I kissed Gaston, and he admonished me to behave myself.

"I do not intend to drink beyond reason and dance upon the tables," I said.

He rolled his eyes. "Do not argue with anyone in such a manner as to endanger the granting of the marque."

"Oh," I said foolishly and grinned, and then teased. "Why would you think I would do such a thing?"

He blinked at me impassively and sighed.

I laughed. He knew me well.

"DoNa'BeDoin'AThingIWouldNa'," Pete told Striker, then apparently thought about it and decided that was not correct. "DoNa'BeDoin'AThingI WouldDo."

Striker laughed and then sighed with mock consternation and chided our matelots, "A little faith should be in order here."

"I have great faith in the consistency of Will's behavior," Gaston said, without any trace of humor. I was not sure how I should interpret that, so I decided to embark on the ferry and leave well enough alone.

"It's a deliberate affront," Striker said for our ears alone once we were under way. "They know we have matelots. It is rude and uncalled for."

"That may be," Theodore said gently, and then grinned. "But I believe your matelots are relieved they did not have to accompany you."

"He may be right," I told Striker. "But I believe you are correct, and I too take great offense. It is as if they seek to pass judgment on us or mete out their approbation if we behave as they do. What damn right do they have?"

Theodore regarded us with his arms crossed. "Has it occurred to either one of you that it is oftimes customary and perfectly acceptable to invite married men, without their wives, to dinners where business will be discussed?"

I could see his argument; yet, "Pete and Gaston are not wives."

"Aye, there is not the least wifely thing about either of them," Striker said thoughtfully, "If anything..." He trailed off abruptly and appeared a trifle embarrassed.

"There is no harm in it," I said. "If anything, we are the wives."

"I make no comment on that," Theodore said. "I believe I meant that you two are the more business-minded of your pairings."

"I would not say that," I said. "Gaston is far wealthier than I."

Theodore threw his hands wide in exasperation. "More socially acceptable perhaps? More likely to have the proper attire? Less likely to kill another guest?"

He continued to harangue us all across the bay until we disembarked at the Passage Fort. By then, I realized he might be correct. This was not necessarily a slight against us for having matelots, but for having the matelots we had.

I was happy to see Diablo and Francis, and I looked forward to at least a pleasant ride for the evening. Theodore rented an animal. Since Francis was ever the calmer of ours, I had him saddled for Striker.

He regarded the patient animal with dismay.

"I have never ridden a horse before," he said.

"How is that possible?" I asked.

He shrugged. "Any place I have ever needed visit was either in walking distance of the sea or there were no horses. I rode in a cart once...."

Thankfully he was not afraid of the animals, and he was a quick study. I gave him a rudimentary lesson in horsemanship, and he managed to plod along quite well with Theodore. I was then free to give Diablo his head, and we raced ahead of them. Thus I arrived at Spanish Town and the Governor's house first. With reluctance I handed my mount off to the boy in the yard and dusted myself to enter.

I cursed my luck as I discovered Morgan and Bradley smoking on the veranda. As there was no one else about, I was forced to either acknowledge them or appear rude. Neither looked pleased to see me. I gave them my most congenial smile and inquired as to whom else had arrived, hoping a name I recognized would be among them, so that I could excuse myself. Morgan rattled off the names of a number of Jamaica's prominent citizens; and I recognized several, but found none I would wish to seek out.

"Where is Striker?" Bradley asked.

"He will be along shortly. He is riding with Theodore, and they are making a slower go of it than I chose to."

"And why is that?" Morgan asked.

"I enjoy riding a great deal, and I chose to set a faster pace to exercise the animal and my spirits. Thus I arrived here before them. A ride can provide a great deal of satisfaction."

"I would not know. I have never ridden an animal in leisure," Bradley said.

I thought of the possible ways to counter him and chose two that might work in tandem. "I have been truly blessed, and I am thankful fate allowed me to become well acquainted with the art of horsemanship. You may wish to indulge in it. You have land to ride on, and I would guess you could afford the time. You may find that you enjoy it."

"Aye, I can well afford the time seeing as I have no ship to sail," he said.

I held my tongue as I knew there was naught I could say to appease the man. I was grateful Morgan also seemed taken aback by his friend's maudlin demeanor.

"So you will be sailing on this prize on the morrow?" Morgan asked briskly.

"Aye, the *Mayflower*."

"How many men?"

"We do not know of yet, as they are not all aboard."

Morgan shrugged. "That is always the way of it. Unless well commanded, the buccaneers tend to be a disorganized rabble. They revel in it."

"Are you not a buccaneer yourself?" I asked.

He smiled obliquely. "But of course. But I am also a man of vision. Many of the Brethren live their lives in thrall to the necessities of day-to-day existence. They do not think of the future, as they possess a Devil-may-care attitude and think they will die tomorrow."

I did not like the sound of that. "Aye, but most have lived hard lives and been condemned in one fashion or another, and they know not how to consider the future, as a strategic approach to life has been beyond their ken by both instruction and nature." I did not say, *because they are armed sheep* as I did not wish to ever have that discussion with these men.

"I am curious," Morgan said. "Why do you, of all people, champion criminals, escaped slaves, heretics, runaway sailors, and rebels?"

"Because I feel I am one of them on more counts than I care to relate to you."

He laughed. "I now recall you mentioning a certain amount of traveling in your life."

"Aye, and I have always been a heretic and a rebel in my thinking. It was oft noted in my childhood."

Bradley was frowning at me thoughtfully.

"I come from a long line of Welsh military men and farmers," Morgan said. "I do not harbor rebellious thoughts, only ambitious ones."

"So how did you come to this life? Did you come here seeking fortune and find an army waiting to be organized?"

"Aye, in a manner of speaking."

This troubled me greatly. I was convinced he planned to use the buccaneers to achieve his ends, which most likely included a very base lust for fame and fortune. Most of the Brethren would not or could not ever comprehend this, because they did not understand the ways of wolves.

We were thankfully interrupted by the arrival of another captain before I could engage in discourse that could have endangered the voyage, or my future on the island for that matter. I wandered into the garden to wait for Striker and Theodore. They rode up shortly, and I joined them. Striker dismounted and almost fell. He stood stiffly and tested his legs. I knew he would be complaining loudly in the morning, especially as we still had to ride back. I clapped his shoulder heartily.

"Think of it thusly. At least one cannot get seasick upon a horse."

"The Devil with you," he muttered. "However does one grow accustomed to this?"

I grinned at him as a number of salacious innuendos lined up to trip off my tongue. I thought better of it, and shrugged.

"It is like most things one learns to adapt to. May we speak a moment before we enter?" Theodore was ahead of us, talking to the other men on the veranda and we were virtually alone in the courtyard.

"As it will take my legs a while to carry me to the others; I think we have a moment," Striker said.

"What think you of Morgan?"

Striker sighed and grimaced. "I think him a necessary evil."

"How so?"

"The best booty is to be had raiding, not roving. Raiding any worthwhile city requires several ships full of men. Several ships require coordination and a common leader above the captains. Morgan was Mansfield's pupil on the matter, and Mansfield was a good leader. Myngs was better, and Mansfield studied him. Morgan is competent. He'll do his job and provide a rallying point. Most of the men like him, and he has befriended the captains, or at least his friends are captains." He shrugged. "What think you?"

"I find him arrogant, irksome, and dislikeable. He is not a buccaneer."

"Now you are starting to sound like your matelot."

I rolled my eyes. "Nay. According to my matelot, I was not a buccaneer until I participated in the making of boucan. I care not whether Morgan has made boucan, I care that he holds himself above the buccaneers, yet he claims he is one of them in order to lead them. It is hypocrisy and I do not tolerate it well."

"Liam and Otter say he was a bondsman on Barbados, and he joined up with Penn and Venables to take Jamaica here, just as Liam and Otter did. His uncles or cousins or whatnot were military men with Penn and Venables, and they gave him a helping hand."

"Truly? Then why in God's name will he not say that? I would think he would use that as a political tool."

"He has, on occasion. Many of the men believe he's just like them, only risen through the ranks. And he is clever enough for this to be the case."

"I am confused," I sighed. "If that is true, then I find most of my arguments against him quite hollowed. Though I still feel he intends to use the buccaneers to his own advantage. This does not make him any different from any other leader in history, yet it vexes me."

"Has Pete told you that you think entirely too much?" Striker asked.

"Nay, he has told me a number of things, but that one he has not said to my face."

"Will, do not take it poorly. According to Pete, every man spends too much time in thought. In your case, I feel he may be correct."

"In truth, I happen to agree with him. And I will admit it often causes me nothing but grief."

We made our way inside, and Bradley and Morgan were exceedingly complimentary on Striker's attire. He was gracious about accepting their praise, but obviously not pleased with the reason. I think this was evident even to them.

Morgan finally quipped, "So are we to understand that you will not wardrobe yourself with the booty from this voyage?"

"Aye, nor shall I take up planting or seek a wife," Striker said. Morgan shrugged with amusement, but Bradley withdrew from us; and Striker was quite obviously suffused with regret. He followed Bradley and talked to him in private.

I let them be, and wandered farther into the parlor. I spied Theodore talking to a portly older man. I quickly lost interest, as my gaze was captured by the fetching creature standing beside them.

She was a girl, and young by the looks of it, but no child. Venus had smiled on her in a fashion I have always adored. She was not tall *per se*, though she had good height for a woman, with a willowy body lacking in unnecessary, from my preference, roundness at bust and hip. Her face was comely, with a pert nose and chin gracing strong cheeks and jaw. Her eyes were large and blue, and peered from beneath wisps of golden hair escaping an elegantly coiled pile atop her head. And, more interesting, she was awarding me a come-hither look that would have brought a boy her own age to his knees.

Bemused, I crossed the room to join them. Theodore quickly introduced me to a Sir Christopher Vines, and his daughter, Miss Christine Vines. I was quite relieved she was his daughter and not his wife, though I had seen worse pairings. Vines seemed delighted to make the acquaintance of an Earl's son, and apologized for being unable to attend my welcoming party.

"And I have not had the opportunity to make your acquaintance since. We all must come in from our plantations on occasion," Vines teased. "Or do you have a thing there to keep you occupied, a wife perhaps?" He was in earnest.

"Nay."

"Ah," he looked to his daughter, and seemed at a loss on how to proceed. She appeared embarrassed and a little annoyed.

I was taken aback, as I had not met any young ladies while using my title since becoming old enough to be a threat to them. I was quite familiar with being chased off, not invited in.

"What do you do with your time, Lord Marsdale?" Miss Vines asked smoothly.

"I have been roving."

This seemed to amuse her.

"Truly," Sir Christopher asked, "you feel need to do that?"

Now I was amused. "I would not know about need, but I do enjoy adventure."

"Did you find it to your liking?" she asked.

"Aye, I did, despite the shipwreck and the like."

Sir Christopher was horrified.

"I would hear of that," she said quickly. "And I am sure you have much to discuss with Mister Theodore, Father."

He took the hint, or rather Theodore did, and they did not follow her as she retreated. I was close in her blue silk wake, though.

"I was told you are an educated man who has traveled extensively in Christendom," she said, once we were in relative privacy across the room.

"And this evoked your interest?"

"I have traveled, though not as extensively as you I am sure, and I do possess an education. I have found almost no one to converse with on any subject of interest on Jamaica."

I was intrigued. "Where were you educated?"

She gave me the name of an academy for young women in England, and then briefly mentioned her travels. It seemed her family was not of purely English descent, and she had a number of relatives in France and Austria. She was fluent in French and German, and had some grasp of Latin. I was stunned, and barely managed to sound intelligent while touching upon my travels. We spoke of Vienna, which she adored.

I wondered how it was that she was not married. I could see no easy way of asking, and finally managed to obliquely ask for her age. She was fifteen. She had returned here around the time I had arrived, due to her mother's ailing health. Her mother had since passed, and now she was seeing to her father's household for the time being. She obviously longed to take flight from this dreary provincial outpost: not because of the scarcity of parties or titled bachelors, but due to the lack of reading material and art.

It was one of the rare times I stood on the road of my life and looked back upon a crossroads I only now knew I had passed. I wondered what course my life would have taken if I had by chance met her before Gaston.

And as if there was a God and He was smiting me she had to ask, "So are you truly a buccaneer? Have you a matelot?" Her smile was impish.

I almost flushed. "Aye, and aye," I nodded with a bemused smile. "He detests gatherings of this nature, as do I."

"So why are you here?"

I thought on it and found no reason to lie. "Political expediency. The Governor suggested Striker come by to pick up the commission for our sailing on the morrow. We did not realize it was a fête of this magnitude. I was invited, our matelots were not, and Striker did not wish to come alone." I looked about and spied him with Morgan, Bradley, and the two other captains, happily talking and drinking. "As he purportedly detests gatherings of this nature as well, though he seems to not be despondent about the situation at the moment."

"Is he the tall, dark, and handsome one? He would be the only one amongst that bunch I do not recognize."

"Aye, he would."

"And so he has a matelot as well?"

"Aye, and a finer man you have probably not beheld. You should see him, simply to look upon a work of art, much as you should see Michelangelo's sculpture of David."

"Is that so?" she laughed. She sobered a little as she returned to studying the men near Striker from behind her fan. "The men here are in general far more hale and virile than the men elsewhere."

"True."

"They confuse me greatly, though. Many of that gaggle have courted me." She grinned. "They usually hunt in pairs. At these parties, once I fall within their gaze, they spring upon me, or rather they do not. It is as if I am a fox in a cage that they cannot touch, and yet they must all stare with rapt attention. Tonight they have not noticed me yet, as they have not looked. They do not arrive at a party and peruse the crowd for eligible ladies. Nay, they speak amongst themselves, and then one of them will decide it is time for the hunt to begin; and then they descend on the young women and attempt to be charming and witty."

She glanced at me and smiled. "I am not naïve. I have met many men who favor men over women, and from what I am told, this port is rife with them. Yet, when I am in the presence of a man who favors men, he does not look upon me the way a man who favors women does." She gave me a knowing look.

I smiled. "I favor both."

"I thought as much. So do many men here favor both? Because they all look at me as you do, yet, the reason for my confusion lies in that they do not..." She frowned prettily. "I am not a person they wish to seek out. Once they are in my presence, they are interested in me as a woman. But prior to that, they do not care. It is as if they are young boys and know they should seek the girls out, but know not why." She sighed. "I am afraid I am not expressing myself well."

"I feel almost all men here favor women, and only some truly favor men," I said. "But any man will take any port in a storm if given little other alternative. As for your observation, perhaps it is because they are having their carnal needs met elsewhere. They do not feel driven. From what I have heard, and bear in mind I am not on confidential terms with any of those men save Striker, I understand they feel a need to have a wife and children. It is a matter of status, and conforms to their sense of rightness in the world. So they court the eligible ladies, but they lack the impetus of a youth who feels he will only be sated if he manages to either marry or seduce."

She pursed her lips in thought and nodded. "Thank you, I believe that may explain it all." She studied me. "And you, dear sir?"

I sighed. "I do not feel a need to marry or produce an heir at this time. Perhaps that will change, as the title surely requires an heir. In your case, I am sorry I am not in the running. I feel you would be wasted on that gaggle, or truly most men I have met."

She flushed and hid behind her fan. "You flatter me, but I thank you for it." She looked toward the other men, and sighed herself. "I am not destined to marry here. I could make several acceptable, if not excellent, matches in England or Vienna, and I am to return there and do so in time. I am in no hurry to leave here for that, though, as I am not enamored with the idea of marriage. There is so much I would do in the world if only...I were a man."

"Ah," I smiled. "You are not the first of your gender that I have met to hold that sentiment."

"I would imagine not, at least I hope not. Though I have met many women in my short life who do not share that sentiment, or are even able to comprehend it. And how feel you on a woman's place in the world?"

"Unlike Aristotle, I have oft found women as intelligent and spirited as men."

"You believe we possess an entire soul then."

"Aye." I grinned.

We were called in to dine before she could say more. I offered my arm and escorted her into the dining room. There were no placecards, and so we took seats along the middle of the long table; and I snagged Striker on his way in, and placed him on the other side of her. He got the strangest look on his face upon seeing her and made a strangled little noise of surprise, as if I had suddenly sat him next to a shark. Miss Vines tried unsuccessfully not to laugh, and leaned to me to whisper, "Well, we know despite having Adonis as a matelot, he does favor women."

I remembered he had been married once, though after watching him with Pete for several months, I found it difficult to give credence to the idea. I attempted to introduce them, and realized I did not know his given name. Thankfully he supplied it quickly and we learned it was James. He kissed her hand. He was polite and charming, one might even say flirtatious, throughout dinner.

Her father sat across and down from us, and still appeared delighted she was in our company. The captains and planters who usually pursued her were quite crestfallen that she was with us, as it was obvious they were not going to be able to compete with Striker and me for her attention. I found this all very amusing.

As the dinner drew to a close, the governor made a pretty speech about how he hoped we would soon have another raid against the Spaniards that would teach them not to question our right to this colony or any other we chose to have across the Line. Then Morgan spoke of his plan to assemble men this winter. Once these necessities were completed, along with toasting the King, England, and all else that was deemed holy in the world, everyone left the table to mill about: as was usual for such occasions. Striker excused himself and made a grab for Morgan, and they approached Modyford and disappeared into the study for a time.

I was relatively alone with Miss Vines again. We withdrew to the veranda, though we remained decorously just outside the doors and within sight of any who would glance out. Miss Vines leaned on a colonnade and fanned herself. I sat with my back to the opposite column, where I could watch her.

"So tell me, Lord Marsdale,..."

"Here I go by 'Will'. We buccaneers eschew titles."

She smiled. "So tell me, Will, why did you choose to become a buccaneer so soon after arriving here? Did you learn so quickly that you were ill-suited for the rigors of being a planter?"

"Rigors of being a planter?" I laughed.

She had a pleasant throaty chuckle. "Oh, surely you know, the excruciating boredom, the deadly tedium of watching other men toil, the pain of observing the growth of greenery and the humbling knowledge that your entire livelihood rests upon those tiny shoots."

We laughed. "I am terribly ill-suited for all of that, I fear. My constitution would not abide it in the least. I am at best able to manage short doses of it, and then only if I am accompanied by hardy companions and take frequent time for respite in the form of riding."

She smiled for a moment, and then her countenance slumped into somberness. "Will you return to England?"

I guessed at her motivation. "I will not leave Gaston, my matelot."

Her lip quirked in a rueful grimace, but she quickly recovered. "How could you, if you love him?" This time she used her fan to proper effect and I barely saw the glance she gave me to gauge my reaction.

"I love him."

She sighed, and the fan dropped to her side. She regarded the night beyond the torches and not me.

"If... If you had not met him, and if there were no other constraints upon you, such as my family name or any other possible state of betrothal or the like, would you have fancied me?" There was no coquettishness about her question. She was very straightforward.

"Aye."

"And you do not find me forward, or inappropriately educated, or less than feminine in my demeanor?"

"Nay. I would find you a suitable match because of all those qualities. Miss Vines, do not be quick to wed."

"I do not want to wed!" she hissed and turned on me with teary eyes.

I gave her a sympathetic sigh, though I did not understand her. "I am sorry to disappoint you; or whatever it is that I have done as..."

My demeanor seemed to enrage her further, and she slammed her fist into the column. I winced. She pawed at her eyes and took several deep breaths.

"Someday I will teach myself not to cry," she snarled.

I do not understand the workings of the female mind, but I do know when it is best for a man to stay very quiet and keep all expression from his face, lest it be interpreted in some unintended fashion. I watched insects fly about in the torchlight. I listened to her breathing become calm and steady again.

"I apologize for... my lack of composure," she said. Her tone was pleasant and smooth.

I considered my words carefully, as any utterance I made would be fraught with danger. I decided that saying little was in order. I looked her over. She was stiffly composed, but her hesitant smile did not seem forced.

"You should stay a while out here. Your eyes are quite... puffed and red."

She nodded.

"Should I remain with you?" I asked.

She nodded. "Please." We both cast about uncomfortably. "So... tell me of your shipwreck."

So I did. And I did not spare her the more gruesome or salacious details, though I did hold private the personal ones. She seemed truly amused by my tales, and she asked a good many questions. All trace of the emotional outburst had vanished by the time Striker and Theodore found us. She bid us goodnight, and retired inside to her hovering and curious father. I wondered if and when I would see her again, and more importantly, if it was a thing I even wished.

"So, you do favor women," Theodore teased.

"She is far more pleasant to chat with than you," I said with a grin. "And aye, though please bear in mind I am not chasing her father about begging for her hand."

He smirked.

Striker had the marque of reprisal. He gave it to me to peruse. It granted the *Mayflower* the right to take by force any ship of any nation not judged to be on friendly terms with England, provided of course the Crown received a share of the booty and the prize was disposed of according to maritime law by the Admiralty Court. As we had what we came for, we bid Theodore good night. He wished us good fortune. He had chosen to remain at the party, and we would not see him again before we sailed on the morrow.

"That was the most beautiful girl I have ever seen," Striker said once we were on our horses and out of the courtyard. "It's the bosom I miss. I care not for the fleshy mounds on the whores. But on a young lady like that, you just know they are in there, soft and warm and nestled like two baby rabbits, resting on her corset and wiggling just slightly with every breath."

I laughed so hard I almost unseated myself, and Diablo was not pleased with me.

"Good God man, how long has it been?" I finally gasped.

"Not since Pete," he said with mock anger and a smile.

"You favor women," I stated.

"I adore them."

"Truly? I have not seen you gazing upon Rachel, and she is an attractive woman."

"No one has seen me gazing upon Rachel, because I am a careful man. Pete would have quite the tantrum."

"Striker, do you favor men?"

"Nay. I love Pete, do not misunderstand me, but I do not favor men."

"How did you become matelots with Pete? I know you said you met in Newgate."

He chuckled, and waited until we were on the moonlit road and no longer in town before speaking. "When our crew was brought there, I was sure I would hang; and my life had little value, so I took it upon myself to argue on behalf of the others. I was beaten for my trouble. Then they dumped me in a large cell away from my crewmates and friends. That is where I met Pete. He heard from others what I had done and decided he liked me. He cared for me. We became friends. When it was time for us to be shipped to Barbados, they chained us in pairs and Pete and I were manacled together at wrist and ankle for the voyage. I had no use for men. Since I was old enough to discover my cock I had kept a girl in every port, including the wife. I had never had call to resort to buggery. However, Pete had no use for women. And you may have noticed he is more stubborn than God."

"Aye, I have," I chuckled.

"Well, he gentled me down, as he called it. He would put his hand on my leg and I would tell him no and he would withdraw, and then a minute later it was back again. Eventually I was hoarse and found it not worth the effort to argue, and then he moved on to something else. Then I started enjoying his touch. By the end of the voyage, we had our cocks up each other's arses. Recalling it, I think it kept both of us sane and gave us something to live for."

"Have you ever regretted it?" I asked.

"Nay, not even tonight, truly." He shook his head. "I cannot imagine a woman adoring me as Pete does, or caring for me the way he can, or fighting at my side, or watching my back, or any of the things he does for me. I don't recall women being that strong. Pete is an extension of myself now. I think of us as two parts of a whole. I can rely on him as I do on myself. Women you leave in port, and they are generally frail, and they cannot fight or sail, though I am sure they can be taught. But they lack the strength. They are things one must care for, and here in the West Indies, I do not have time to care for another who is not my equal. A man needs a matelot and not a wife to survive. Women are luxuries, like fine clothes and sweetmeats."

He grinned at me. "At the moment, though, I would gladly bed that one, in the name of nostalgia if nothing else."

I laughed with him, though something stirred deep in my thoughts; and I was haunted by Miss Vines striking the column in anger at her own tears. For the most part, I agreed with his words, though I had met women who possessed a different kind of strength and power, subtle yet more resilient. But he was correct in that one did not go roving with them. One did not drink and party with them. One could not lie with them in wild abandon whenever one chose, without worry that they would become pregnant. In all, one could not live Striker's life the way he chose to, with a woman at one's side.

Neither could I. They were rather like strange possessions that exerted control over you, and not friends and companions, as you could not share your life with one. They were the trappings of maturity, if not wealth. I still did not wish to be saddled with the trappings or the actuality of maturity or wealth.

Striker was watching me, and I realized I had become lost in thought.

"Would you lie with her?" he asked once I met his eyes.

"I favor both men and women, and she is truly a bewitching creature. If I had not met Gaston when I did, I would have liked to know her better."

"Does Gaston favor women?" he asked quietly.

"Aye."

"Yet he is with you, and neither of you are chained together."

"Aye. We recognized a kinship when first we met. A poet would say we fell in love when we first laid eyes on one another. Others saw it, because we were confirmed as matelots a mere three days after we met," I chided.

He stopped his horse and stared at me. "You jest."

I reined in my mount. "Nay, we met the day before we robbed the *King's Hope*, the ship I arrived on."

He shook his head in consternation. "I know that. I do. But I cannot believe you two had only just met. You are correct, there is something betwixt you."

We started our horses again, and he studied the stars for a moment. "May I ask something?"

I chuckled. "Aye."

"Do the two of you...?"

"Not as you two do," I said quickly.

He nodded. "So you are still gentling him down, then?"

"Aye, in a manner of speaking." That was something I had no intention of ever mentioning to Gaston. In truth, I was leery of discussing most of the night's activities with him, and this vexed me.

"We will be careful not to intrude on this voyage," he said.

"We would appreciate it."

It was quite late when we finally arrived home, but we found our matelots playing chess in the dining room. With my chess set, I was interested to note. I thought this highly unfair on the part of my matelot, until I saw the number of pieces Pete had captured and the intense concentration the Golden One was paying to the board. As Gaston was equally intense, I kissed his head and went upstairs to relieve myself of my finery.

I returned to the dining room in a pair of breeches. Striker had done likewise, and we sat and ate cheesecake and drank wine, and watched our matelots finish their game. Thankfully they were playing rather quickly, and not spending an hour considering each move. Every time Striker started to say something, Pete waved him off. I knew better and kept my mouth firmly closed.

While the battle was being waged, I watched Gaston, studying the familiar lines of his face in the lamplight. He was quite handsome in his way, made all the more so because he was mine.

He regarded me curiously a few times while Pete was considering his moves. "You are being distracting," he whispered in French.

"I love you," I whispered back. Then I grinned and asked. "And what possessed you?"

We were bored and I thought you might have a deck of cards. I found them, but I also found this and wondered if Pete would possess a talent for it."

"Apparently," I chuckled.

Pete was glaring at us. Gaston checked to see where he had moved, and then made his own. "Check."

"Arg!" Pete said.

Gaston sat back and asked us in English how the party had gone. We told him of our various conversations with Morgan and Modyford and the like. We did not mention Miss Vines. Gaston was no more pleased than I at Morgan's attitude towards the buccaneers.

To my amazement, after considering the board for a good half hour, Pete conceded, and quickly explained how he could see Gaston's next moves. They discussed it, and Pete determined when he had made his mistake earlier in the game. I thought it unlikely I could defeat him.

"Will you tell me how it's played now?" Striker asked when they were through. I chuckled, as I had thought his earlier attempts at comment had been advisory.

"We can take it with us," I suggested.

This pleased Pete, and he restored it to its box and promised to teach Striker on the ship.

Gaston and I retired upstairs for one last night in our own room. Once alone, we lay facing one another on the hammock, and I told him of my conversations with Miss Vines and Striker. I did not mention the part about gentling down, but I did tell him all that Miss Vines had said and done.

He remained deep in thought after I finished and I waited patiently. "So she is intelligent, educated, and beautiful. Do you want her?"

"If you had never existed in my life, oui."

"What does my existence have to do with whether or not you want something?"

It was a prickly question, and his lips quirked as he waited for my reply. I thought on it.

"If I admit I want her now, even to myself, then not having her becomes a disappointment, and I cannot have her while I am with you. "

"So I am an impediment to your potential happiness?"

"Non. Non. It is more like having eaten a full meal of roast pork and then seeing a beef brisket and saying, ah, I could have had that, but now I am full with this wonderful pork and my needs are sated and I have no use for the beef. It is more an intellectual curiosity of roads not taken or meals not eaten. And besides," I added. "I could not love a woman as I do you."

He studied me for a long while and I saw no anger or animosity in his eyes. "If they are two different things, could you love both a man and a woman?"

"I have done so. At the time I loved them, I loved Teresina as much as Alonso."

"Could you share one you loved with another?"

"I shared Teresina with anyone she fancied, including Alonso, and likewise for him."

"Could your love for them be considered the deepest feelings of your heart?"

I saw his point. "Non. Until I loved you, they were the best example of my love I can offer. My love for you is of a magnitude a hundredfold of what I felt for them."

He nodded to himself. "I am pleased to hear it. I would rather not share you with a beef brisket. I do not think I could share you at all."

"Nor I you."

We kissed until I tugged at his clothes. He complied and we stripped. I fell upon him, and to my pleasure, he deigned to allow me to rub my manhood against his nakedness. When I reached for the oil, it was to ease my dissipation and not relax him.

Later as I lay there, drowsy and only mildly annoyed that one of us had to leave the comfort of the hammock to put out the lamp, he spoke.

"You became very tired of pork on the last voyage."

It took several long moments before I could divine his meaning. "And you do not favor horses," I jested.

He was silent. I rolled atop him again, now thankful that the lamp was still lit because it afforded me the light to read his eyes. He was serious and concerned.

"Gaston, my love, occasionally a metaphor is merely a play on words and it has no meaning other than what we ascribe to it. I will not grow tired of you."

"How can you know that?"

"Do you feel I would lie to you?"

He looked away, and his eyes suffused with guilt. "Oui and non."

He frowned. "I would say I trusted you implicitly, and I believe you would not lie to me on matters of import, but perhaps on small things. But in this matter, the lie that I think you might tell would be of grave import, to me. I am sorry. It is unworthy of me to think such a thing."

"Do you feel I would..."

"Non," his fingers covered my lips.

I pulled his hand away. "I wish you would not always do that."

I was not angry, merely annoyed.

He surged under me and flipped me on my back before I could brace myself. He rolled atop me and his mouth covered mine. I fought the momentary panic it engendered, but I did not fight him. His kiss was ferocious, bruising even, and I must say I enjoyed it, as it was the closest thing to passion I had felt from him.

When he released me, his eyes were intense. "I do not feel you would ever betray me, or be untrue to me, in any way, other than to lie to save my pride."

I studied him and thought of what possible response I could make to that, and realized there was none. "If you truly believe I would lie about such a matter, then there is nothing I can say to convince you otherwise. Thus your happiness or unhappiness with what you feel are my thoughts lies with you, as I can do nothing to sway you in any reasonable fashion. I can offer no proof other than words. And if they are not good enough, then I can offer no proof."

He slumped to my chest. "You are correct. I am sorry. It is just...."

He rolled off me to lie staring at the ceiling. He did not speak.

"It is just that what?" I asked. I was not being entirely successful in holding my anger at bay.

"I cannot truly believe that you would favor me over her. And I do not want you to remain with me because...."

I stopped his words with my hand. I had not realized what a vast chasm lay between us on that matter. I turned his head to face me. His eyes were hard. I removed my hand from his mouth and grasped his manhood gently.

"She does not have one of these and I happen to like these very much."

"Will, for all intents and purposes, I do not have one of those."

I swore and left the hammock to pace. It was as if we played chess and I was required to think two moves ahead of him, as he was surely a move ahead of me. I could not attack him and ask what proof of his love he could offer me. Since he did not favor men, his very presence naked in a bed we shared was proof enough. If I reminded him of Striker's assessment that one could not live the life we chose with a woman, Gaston could say I was merely with him because I chose this life. And I surely could not say that I preferred men because I could understand them better. I had to determine what it was specifically about men, and more importantly him, that I preferred. Why did I favor men?

I recalled every man I had been with. What did they have in common that had beckoned me so? They were all handsome, smooth, and lean of body with pleasing features, yet so were the women. In two cases, and it was my hope someday three, if I did not strangle him first, there was a pronounced difference. I told myself that Gaston had already refuted that argument, in that he could not perform the function that men could and women could not toward my person. Yet it was not merely the act itself. It was the ability to perform the act, not in the basest sense of insertion, but in the grander sense of having the strength to... make me. And there was an added facet....

I found myself sitting on the floor, thinking of things I had sworn I would not think of ever again. I was there with Shane on my back, pressing me down, pounding away at me. And under the pain, under the anger, there had been... triumph. He had lost the battle again. He had desired me so greatly that he had once again stooped to doing what he thought unconscionable. He wanted me despite his arguments against it. He wanted me. He proved it with every thrust.

I had thought that love. That someone would seek me out for the unthinkable, the unmentionable, when I was so wrong and repugnant to them. That had to be love for him to go against his nature so.

And Alonso, he had wanted me enough to be patient, to tolerate my protestations and fears and the conditions I placed upon our lovemaking. Had I loved him even more because he did not want me to touch him in front of others? Had I truly thought his hypocrisy proof of his love?

And what of Gaston? Was I not most pleased when he threw me on my back and plundered my mouth just minutes ago? He did not even favor men, and yet he was with me. Had I not just considered that the most valid proof of his love?

I was filled with self-loathing over the self-loathing my life was filled with. I could hear Shane's snarled words, *"You want this, you want this, you want this...."* one repetition for every thrust. Alonso's gentle chiding was a chilling counterpoint, *"Will, relax, you know you want this."* They were correct. I did want it.

And now I wanted it from Gaston. I wanted him to become so overcome with lust for me that his manhood would spring to life and he would be compelled to plunder my very soul. Because that was the thing a man could do that a woman never could.

The shame was bile I could not rid myself of fast enough. I was distantly aware of vomiting, and Gaston's hands upon me and his whisper in my ear. "Will, I love you, please. What is wrong?"

I could not tell him. I did not want to possess the knowledge myself. I crawled into his lap and clung to him. The Gods had shown me something tonight, and I wanted none of it.

Roving
June~July 1667

VI

Twenty-Two

Wherein We Careen In Peril

I woke in the hammock under Gaston's watchful eye. His hand was on my shoulder, and I realized he had shaken me awake. He did not look as if he had slept. I did not feel as if I had. The remembered ache in my heart had spread through my bones and head, until I felt as if I had been kicked for hours. His eyes were full of concern. I do not know what he saw in mine. I was afraid to give any emotion a foothold, lest it overtake me completely.

"Do not ask," I whispered.

He nodded and caressed my cheek tentatively. "It is dawn. I have packed. Pete and Striker have left already."

I captured his hand and kissed his palm. He appeared relived by this gesture. I sat. Our bags and weapons were by the door, and everything had been returned to the trunks, leaving the room neat and empty. There was a wet area on the floor where he had cleaned. I stood on legs that were firmer than I thought they would be. I dressed.

We were silent as we left the house. We nodded at Rachel. She did not seem disposed to speak with us, so it was just as well we were not talkative. Still I decided a more congenial housekeeper might be in order when we returned.

The streets were busy, and we were forced to weave around people and carts.

"May I speak on the condition I do not question you?" Gaston asked quietly in French as we walked. "With the exception of that question."

I guessed at his concern. "I am not angry with you."

He did not seem to believe me. "I was wrong to think such things. I was being foolish. I am sorry. Will you forgive me?"

"That is a question." I tried to smile, but the jest fell flat and took on an unintended meaning. "I forgive you," I said, quickly and firmly.

We had stopped walking. I felt on the verge of speaking, and I knew if I started that it would all come tumbling out and I would become deranged again, this time in the middle of the street and right before elections and articles and provisioning and all of the damn business we must attend to.

"I cannot talk," I said. "Not now. Later. Please."

I could see the understanding strike as his eyes widened. It was immediately followed by guilt.

"Stop," I said with exasperation that was only partially mocking.

He gave me a small smile and kissed my cheek, before taking my hand to lead me up the street. I forced myself not to think.

I counted eighty-four men on the *Mayflower*, including Gaston and me. All of the survivors of the *North Wind* were present, save Bradley and Cleghorn. Belfry and Tom stood ready and enthusiastic amongst the others, replete in their new clothing and earrings, along with a resigned Dickey. I was happy for the busyness of greeting everyone.

Striker stood amongst the men and called for elections first. Cudro nominated Striker as captain. To our relief, there were no other nominations, and Striker was resoundingly approved. This vote was followed by quartermaster, which Cudro won handily, although Hastings did make his bid again. The Bard was confirmed as Master of Sail, Michaels as cook, and a jolly man named Gusset as carpenter. The Frenchman Cudro had recruited became our gunner. He called himself De Morte. I thought it interesting he was "of death" as opposed to "the death." Gaston was voted in as surgeon, though this did cause some concern amongst the crew and was by no means unanimous. He took the dissension well.

I had been placed in charge of writing the articles, and Striker delegated the reading and negotiating of them to me as well. There were no arguments, and we approved all as they had been on the last voyage of the *North Wind*, with only a few variations in wording as I had not remembered the exact phrasing of the last set. Striker did, however, receive fewer shares as he did not own the ship and was merely captain. Mention was also made of reimbursement for any expenses prior to the sharing of the booty. All agreed to this.

Striker explained our intended prey and the matter of provisioning. Then there was much discussion and argument. Many did not wish to purchase provisions, as it could so thoroughly reduce the profitability of the voyage. They were of a mind to spend less time sailing and more time provisioning, and would rather increase the risk of having nothing in the end in order to owe nothing in the beginning. Others agreed with Striker that we should sail as much as we could, and increase our chances of prey even though the cost of the provisioning would decrease the shares. The Bard stepped in with the argument that won many of them, by pointing out that the money being ventured would come from men who were sailing on the vessel and not creditors on shore, and that we were not charging interest. The chance of something over nothing finally won; but many were disgruntled, and six men left before signing the articles.

So we sailed with seventy-eight men and a hold full of salted beef, sea turtles, fruit, fresh water, beer, and rum, which ran Gaston an outrageous hundred and seventy pounds. It made me wonder seriously why the buccaneers as a whole did not simply pillage the fat and rich merchants of Port Royal, as that is where all the money ended up. Striker had spent a similar amount on sails, powder, good lumber, pitch, tar, tools, and other repair items. I calculated that, in order to give each man a share of two hundred pieces of eight, or roughly fifty pounds, we would need to take booty valued at eighteen thousand pieces of eight or four thousand five hundred pounds. This amount would cover the expenses plus eighty-five shares for the men, including the additional shares for captain, quartermaster, and master of sail, and the monies paid above shares to the surgeon, carpenter and the like.

I shared this delightful information with Striker and asked him what cargoes, short of gold or silver, could provide that amount of money.

He said, "Will, they're not getting two hundred pieces of eight each. We'll do what we can."

I was saddened by this. In concert with this news, I was very happy we would not be sailing back to Port Royal to give the crown ten percent of our earnings.

With all the chaos of provisioning and getting under way, Gaston and I were not able to speak. And then we were not alone. That night, we lay curled in our large hammock in the master cabin and listened to Pete and Striker make love in the bunk. Striker was atop; there was a difference in sound, depending on which one of them was doing the riding. Pete tended to grunt a lot when he rode Striker, and to make contented little moans when their positions were reversed. Striker was not prone to noise other than panting, and that did not seem to vary much whether he was giving or receiving; though on occasion Pete elicited a groan or two from him.

I was aroused by it all, and slipped my hand in my breeches to let my manhood know I was not ignoring it, though I was not actively attempting to ease myself either. Pete made a particularly plaintive sound and I was suffused with as much amusement as arousal. I tried to stay silent as I laughed. Gaston joined me in this, and soon we found ourselves clinging to one another with the whole hammock shaking in an attempt to laugh in silence. He finally bit my shoulder with such ferocity that I gasped and all humor was driven from my mind. Then he kissed me thoroughly. My hand was still upon my member and I was sure he was aware of it. I stroked in earnest, as his kiss left my mouth and slowly trailed down my neck and across my bare chest accompanied by little nips and caresses. I came when he found my right nipple with his tongue and sucked it hungrily.

I lay there afterwards greatly relieved, as I had been afraid he would not wish to do anything upon the ship. I had also been concerned that the fragmentary memory that had driven him to discomfort would remain and keep him from touching me as he had just done. And all day I had been even more afraid that I would not wish to succumb to his touch until I sorted through my own thoughts. Apparently none of these fears were worthy.

Still, we could not talk. We could hear Striker and Pete whispering to one another between creaks of the ship. I was unsure as to whether the discussion necessary would end in my becoming overly distraught yet again, so I did not wish to risk it. I explained this very quickly to Gaston and he agreed to let it lie.

He woke me sometime later.

"It is before dawn," he whispered. "Striker and Pete have gone up."

I cuddled against him and wondered why that was important. I began to drift back to sleep.

He kissed me on the lips. "Will, talk to me, please."

I remembered what we were to speak of and came fully awake. His eyes were inches from my own. In the dim light seeping through the windows I could see concern and little reflections of myself in their depths. I could not watch him watch me while I spoke. I closed my eyes.

"I discovered a thing within myself that I am deeply ashamed of," I said.

He caressed my face, and his fingers settled lightly along my jaw.

I did not know how to proceed. I took a tentative step, not sure if it was the correct path to take.

"There is a thing that a man can bestow on me that a woman cannot." My heart cringed. I did not wish to make him feel inadequate, yet I reminded myself it was not truly a thing he wanted, so what did that matter?

I stumbled deeper into my thoughts, looking for the next words. I found the things I had not allowed myself to explore the night before.

"I do not know if that is what I initially wanted from a man. I know I was quite smitten with Shane, yet I do not recall ever harboring fantasies of his touching me in that manner. I never considered buggery at all when I was young. I had no knowledge of it. I had not seen it. Once I discovered my cock, I was interested in bestowing its affections upon others, not having them bestowed upon me. And when I first discovered the delights of touching another, with Shane, I was enamored with the shared pleasures, and not a specific act.

"I recall watching a dog go at a bitch one afternoon, and it brought forth memories of things I had half seen in the stable and pantry amongst the servants. I knew the fundamental relationship between my manhood and a woman's privates. And I wondered that day if such a thing occurred between men. And then I realized that this was the thing called sodomy and a number of other things became very clear to me. I became quite excited, yet I dared not mention it to Shane, as he would not discuss the very fact that we touched at all with me. And as I had heard this act of sodomy whispered about, I understood it was not a thing that many approved of. Shane was ahead of me, in years as well as in all things. Apparently he decided that it was a thing he was interested in trying.

"By then, he disapproved and reviled me publicly, far more than even my father did. And yet he sought me out. He told me it was my fault for leading him astray. He told me I wanted it as much as he did. He would tell me over and over again I wanted it while he...."

I shied off the memory before it sank its fangs in me. But it was too late in some regards. I tried to rally my anger to hold the tears at bay, but it was to no avail. I was simply tired and sad. Gaston smoothed the seeping moisture away with gentle strokes. I still could not look at him.

I soldiered on, knowing the worst was yet to come. "I do not know which of us he was trying to convince, but in the end he did indeed convince me. I did want him. I wanted him to... take me. I saw it as proof that he loved me, proof that he was so enamored with me that he must have me even though it shamed him to do so. And that.... And that is what I can not forgive myself for. That is why he is not dead. That is why I thought I loved Alonso. That..." I could not say that. I could not say, *And that is what I want from you.*

I pressed closer and he held me until the tears subsided. However was I going to separate what I wished to share with Gaston from those memories, now that I had this knowledge? Did I still wish for Gaston to sodomize me? Or was that a thing now forbidden to me, because I desired it for the wrong reasons? Did I desire it separate from the reasons?

"I love you," Gaston murmured. "And I wish I could prove it to you."

"Non! Non Non Non..." My eyes were open, and I found his gazing back at me, slightly amused and challenging. He had lured me out.

"But it was wrong," I sighed.

"Oui, what Shane did was very wrong. I am not sure about this Alonso. I think I shall hate him anyway, but..."

"Non, what I felt was wrong. That was not love."

He shrugged. "It was desire, non? Though they are not the same, it was proof of desire. They wanted you even if it went against their reason. So you thought that love? You know better now."

He was, of course, correct. "How are you so wise on the subject?"

"Every man who has ever written has wrestled with it. I have a read a lot," he grinned.

I sighed in capitulation. "I feel as if we are playing chess again, and you have me in check, and I do not know if I should continue to move, as it will not gain me anything but wasted time."

Gaston smiled. "If I had known we were to play chess over the matter, I would have enlisted Pete's aid. What do you think he would say?"

"That I think too much and do not know what is important." I chuckled and rolled onto my back with a sigh. "He would be correct."

"He is after all a God walking amongst us. You should heed him."

"I should? You would do well to heed his advice yourself."

He climbed atop me. "I will never be jealous of the Brisket again," he said seriously. "I swear it. And I will never question your love again."

I caressed his face and thought, *so say you now*, and realized that was exactly what he must have thought last night after my pronouncements. I smiled and pulled him tighter against me. My manhood was still awake and wondering what all the fuss was about.

"Prove it," I whispered and kissed Gaston again. His hand went to my groin and he kissed me.

I surrendered to his ministrations. My heart was not joyous; it was still a timid thing, sure there was something lurking in the shadows of my mind just waiting to pounce. Perhaps it was correct. At the moment, I chose not to submit to the doubt. There was time enough to poke about with sticks and scare the fears into the light. I need not do it now.

We spent a few days sailing northwest, across pleasant reaching winds to the Caymans. It was a shame they had no Spanish cattle or hogs, as they would have been an ideal place to provision. They lay close to the path of the Galleons and the single ships as they came up from the Terra Firma. We found a likely beach, on the leeward shore of the larger of the two small islands, and set about careening.

As we did not have boucan to make, my matelot and I were involved as much as the others in the hard labor of emptying the ship, hauling her onto the sand, and tipping her over. That was, until fingers were crushed, and men were cut by ropes, and joints were wrenched, and Gaston was called to mend them. As I was hale and healthy, I did not feel as useless as I had at the beginning of the first voyage. Still, it was with relief that I took a break and sprawled in the surf after we had her ashore. Belfry and Dickey joined me, and I could not help but chuckle at their appearance, as I had every time I had seen them for the past several days.

"I wish you would not do that," Dickey said.

"It suits you," I said.

"Nay, it suits you," he countered. "Your clothing has color. Liam said it was odd for a buccaneer to wear clothing of color and insisted we buy this ecru attire."

"I would have done the same if not for Gaston. I believe he wished for black clothing, and this deep wine is the best we can achieve."

At mention of Gaston, Dickey glanced to the place where my matelot was working on yet another injured man by the longboat. Then Dickey exchanged a look with Belfry, and I despaired that I would have the same argument with them that I had engaged in with Fletcher on the plantation.

"What is it?" I asked.

Belfry cleared his throat and studied the waves for a moment. "Well, it is just that we have heard some talk and... May we ask you a question, or rather inquire as to something?"

"I do not guarantee an answer, but you may ask."

"Well." He coughed again. "Several of the men maintain that your matelot is stark raving mad."

"Oh, that," I sighed, and looked up the beach to Gaston again. "He is, at times."

"Truly?" Belfry asked. "He seems reasonable enough, if a trifle reserved, when I have been around him."

"Michaels says he is possessed," Dickey blurted. "That he trifles with the dead and talks in tongues, and that he tried to kill you and you had to strike him to defend yourself."

"I used to like Michaels," I said flatly. They looked uncomfortable. "Do you two believe that gibberish?"

"Some of the other men have said that he used the bodies on the galleon to summon the storm that wrecked her with some kind of witchcraft," Belfry whispered.

I swore vehemently, and a chill gripped my spine. I sat and moved to face both of them. "Once again I ask; do you believe that utter nonsense?"

They regarded me in silence and shook their heads, but there was not much conviction in it.

"I do not believe it may be the case with your friend," Belfry said, "but I do believe that sometimes men are possessed, and I have heard of indisputable cases of witchcraft." He sighed.

"Gaston is mad," I said. "He is ill. He is not possessed. An awful thing occurred to him when he was young, and it scarred his mind so that occasionally he loses himself to reverie and is not able to control his emotions and reactions in the way a sane man would." That was not the whole of it, but it was the easiest. "He does not speak in tongues, though he does speak many languages. On the galleon, he was speaking French. Aye, he attempted to pull a knife on me. Aye, I struck him to get him quiet. Pete already had hold of him, and he was not going to hurt anyone. As for the bodies, I do not know why he did what he did, but we had spoken with both of those men prior to their deaths and I believe Gaston was..." I shook my head as this was truly the part I did not understand. "He arranged them into the *Pieta*, you know, Mary and Jesus. I feel he was trying to honor them in some fashion. There was no evil about it. I think he may have felt profound guilt over their deaths."

I wanted to explain that there had been blood and carnage everywhere, and that it was difficult for me to even comprehend the amount of it. And if anything was summoned on that day, it was God's wrath that so many should die for gold. I held my tongue, as I did not think it prudent to add any divinity to the argument at hand.

They both nodded thoughtfully, as if my explanation had satisfied them. They were educated men, though, and most of the crew were not.

I wondered if this was the type of thing that had driven Gaston from boat to boat. Not the madness in and of itself, but this superstitious misunderstanding of it. I knew with this traveling about the deck, he would now be blamed for the first sign of trouble.

I was relieved to find our wolves with the Bard and Cudro. That put all of them in one basket for me to deal with. I quickly related what I had heard. Striker swore a good deal, Pete looked confused, the Bard looked tired, and Cudro became angry.

"Damned pack of dogs," Cudro growled. "You only have to look at his hide to know he is mad and there is nothing more to it. This business is not coming from anyone that knew of him from Tortuga. They know better."

I glared at him. I could not believe he would do what he did and then take Gaston's side.

"What?" he bellowed. "What the Devil are you angry with me for?"

"I cannot forgive as easily as..."

"Hold, hold," Striker said and stepped between us.

Cudro regarded me around him and sighed. "All right, then, I admit it. What I did to him then was wrong. I was damn mad, though, and I was...hurt, in all truth. Still, it was wrong. But if he's settled with it, why are you still riled? You were not even there."

"He is my matelot, and the mere thought of someone harming him drives me to distraction."

He shrugged his massive shoulders. "He is lucky to have you, then, and that has been obvious all along. I mean him no ill will, and a matter such as this causes no end of trouble."

"I hate to alarm anyone, but I have seen men hanged and marooned over nonsense such as this," the Bard said. "We need to kill it now."

"I have heard many a complaint about him from the French, mainly that he cannot be trusted because he is mad; but I have never heard charges of witchcraft," Striker said.

"As I said, any man who has heard of him on Tortuga knows some of his story; they know he's mad," Cudro said. "We have seen him move bodies around; that's why he has been called the Ghoul."

"So what brought this on now?" I asked.

"We lost a great many men and a great deal of gold, and that serious a storm was out of season," the Bard said. "They are looking to blame someone."

I could understand it, from that perspective. I was not accepting of it in the least, but I could see confused and stupid men searching for someone to blame. "They do not know Gaston, and they have heard strange things about him, so he makes a likely target. Ironically, if they should call anyone witch, it should be Michaels, as he is the one with the ungents and potions he learned from gypsies."

Cudro nodded thoughtfully. "That may be useful."

"If it comes to a fight," the Bard sighed, "not all of us are able, no matter how willing." He indicated his wounded shoulder; and I realized he was correct. A third of our cabal, such as it was, had not recovered from their last voyage.

Striker was looking about. "Where the Devil did Pete get off to?" We all looked about, and spied him near Gaston. "Good, he's ahead of us as usual. You should guard your matelot, too. The last thing we need is for him to do anything odd."

"He should avoid Latin," the Bard added.

"Aye, as we all know that is a sure sign of witchcraft," I said derisively.

The Bard laughed. "He should avoid Shakespeare."

I had to chuckle. "And mythology, and the naming of angels or herbs, and of course speaking in tongues is not allowed."

"Whatever you do, do not allow him around a dead body," Cudro said, and then he sobered. "And if you do not know it already, do not allow him to see or hear anything resembling a whip."

"I already know about that. Tell me, Cudro, did he tell you of that or..?"

He shook his head. "I discovered it on my own."

"What is this matter with whips?" Striker asked.

"Have you ever seen him without his clothing?" I asked. The Bard and Striker shook their heads. I thought it best to tell them. "He was flogged near to death. He bears heavy scars."

Striker was surprised. "That is what people have spoken of, then. I understand now." He regarded me soberly. "Take care of your matelot. Do not start arguing with everyone. We will see what can be done."

I went to join Gaston. He had finished with the last injury and was boiling his tools. He regarded me curiously, and then flicked his gaze to Pete, who was hovering nearby. "What is the matter?"

"You have been accused of witchcraft."

He was stunned for a moment, and then he rolled his eyes; and then he sat down heavily. "That would explain why two men refused to allow me to treat them. This is new."

I waved Pete over to join us, and then I told Gaston of all that I had heard and my discussion with the others.

"Will, it would be best if they returned us to Jamaica," Gaston said. "It might be better if they left on the big island to the south and picked us up later."

"Bah," Pete said. "WeNeedYa. WeDon'tBeNeedin'ThemThatAreCausin ' Trouble."

"What if it is most of the crew?" Gaston asked.

He grinned. "LessMenWhenIt'sDone. WillBeHarderToTakeAPrize."

That night, as the ship was lying on her side, we all made ready to sleep on the beach. A cookfire was lit, down low between dunes so as not to signal our presence for miles in the black of night. Watches were set and a keg of beer was opened. The three of us gathered our possessions and Striker's, and a bottle of rum, and retired to the top of one of the dunes, so that we could look down upon the camp and also see out and about us.

I was taut with anxiety, as the tension had been gathering about the crew all evening. I had begun to think it might be best if we just slipped away into the night. When men were wont to be unreasonable over intangible concepts such as superstition or religion, they became more dangerous than if they were starving or filled with greed. You could feed a starving man or avert avarice for a time with gold; but you could do nothing to sate the needs of a man running to or from matters of the spirit, as it was all in his head and heart, and both oftimes bore poor witness to reality.

Pete appeared as tense as I. He sat with his musket across his lap, and his eyes constantly swept the camp. I knew he could tell where Striker was within a meter, and would have shot any man near his matelot who meant Striker harm. The first man to rush us from the camp would die. So would the next fifteen or so, if we were lucky. Thankfully, the camp was divided, and if we were rushed the bastards would be taken down from behind.

Still, I was afraid of someone sneaking up on us from beyond the dune; and I kept my eyes on the shadows, and rarely looked to the fire so as not to blind myself to the dark.

Gaston worried me. He had slid into a state of melancholy since I told him of the accusation, and now he presented the demeanor of a condemned man. He sat without weapon in hand and stared toward the surf. I rubbed his back or shoulder on occasion, and he did not shrug me off, but he did not respond either.

I started at a sound behind me and turned to find Liam and Otter joining us, albeit slowly due to Otter's injured leg. Liam looked us over before sitting in the sand with his musket ready across his lap and his eyes on the camp. Otter sat next to him, but his eyes were toward the night around us, as mine had been.

"There be trouble, but I reckon ya' know o' it," Liam said after he was situated.

"Aye, but please tell us what you have heard," I said, and reached behind me to pass him the bottle.

"There be a number o' stupid buggers thinkin' that Gaston is practicin' witchcraft. And then there be another group o' right bastards who be thinkin' Michaels is. There be men sayin' that Gaston poisoned Cleghorn. There be men sayin' Michaels named Gaston a witch ta hide his own evildoin'."

"What do you think?" I asked, with more amusement than I felt. As angry as I was at Michaels, I did not want him hung for things he did not do, either.

Liam made a derisive noise. "We be thinkin' the only prize this voyage may yield is gettin' home in one piece, as there may be deaths o'er this. We should keep ar' powder dry and ar' pistols in reach an' set ar' own watches."

"Thank you," Gaston said. He had not spoken since we came to sit on the dune, and his voice was almost lost to the wind.

The musketeers shrugged. Liam said, "I think that if you 'r anyone else was practicin' witchcraft, ya would 'ave used it to keep the damn boat afloat in that storm. I mean, iffn a man is to be consortin' with demons, he should at least get rich fer it."

Otter nudged his matelot and whispered something to him.

"Aye, aye," Liam said. "I be forgettin' to say the important things. Cudro is spreadin' the rumors 'bout Michaels. Hastings is the one sayin' things 'bout Gaston."

"Hastings, truly? So Michaels did not start it?" I asked.

"Nay, he started it. Na' the spreadin' o' it, but he were the match," Liam said. "Last night 'e be complainin' 'bout sailin' with Gaston, on account o' what 'appened on the galleon. Said he didna' like 'im bein' surgeon, neither. And then Hastings were curious 'bout it, an' got 'im talkin', an' Michaels said all manner o' strange things."

"So it is politics feeding the mindless fear and the need to blame," I mused aloud.

I wished someone had seen fit to inform us of all of this last night, but I supposed I should be grateful I discovered it when I did. I surmised it would have built for a few days yet, if I had not apprised Striker and Cudro of it, and they had not set out to quell it. Now it was not a distant bank of clouds harboring rumbles of malcontent, but a storm we had sailed into.

Davey and Julio joined us. I fully expected some manner of irritating remark to fall from Davey's mouth. Instead he surprised me by saying, "I told men I were there and saw what happened, and it were not witchcraft, just madness; but they would na' listen to me. They said I have been hexed." He sat dejectedly.

"Thank you," I muttered and looked down to the camp with mounting horror. The winds were howling indeed. I could see little clusters of men whispering amongst themselves. Some glanced our way, and some glanced over to where Michaels was crouched near the cookfire with a few other men. Striker and Cudro were talking to different groups. I could not see Hastings, but guessed he was beyond the light of the fire, as we were, watching.

The Bard, Belfry, Tom and Dickey stood and walked up the dune to join us. Thankfully they brought another bottle.

"The French and Dutch will not eat anything Michaels cooks," the Bard said. "If the ship were afloat, I would say we take her and let them on one by one at musket point, if they swear to never mention this whole sorry affair again, but we do not have that option."

"Thank you all," Gaston said. He roused himself enough to turn and face them. "As many of you know, I am quite mad. I have little control over it. I do strange things under its influence and I can be a menace to those around me. But I do not consort with demons, and I am not possessed."

"Ya need na' say such things," Liam chided gently. "If we thought

ya' did, we would na' be sittin' 'ere." This brought a chuckle all around.
"As for the rest, I figure that's y'ur matelot's problem." This brought
laughter. "And besides, you should na' be tellin' us anyways, as it's
those buggers ya need ta explain it to."

"You are correct," Gaston said, and I sensed a change in his
demeanor. He stood, and I was not happy at it, as I guessed his
purpose. We all followed him down the hill to the fire.

Men parted to make way for our group, and Gaston went to stand
next to the small blaze. I joined him, but the others held back and
waited. All eyes turned to us and silence fell amongst the crew.

"I am mad. I am not a witch," Gaston said as loudly as he could
manage. The men who had heard him responded to the requests of
those farther away, and his words were born out from the fire like
ripples in a pond.

"You need speak loud," a voice called from the far dune. I guessed it
to be Hastings, but I was not sure.

"He cannot," I said loudly. "Perhaps you should come down."

All eyes shifted to the location of the faceless voice, until a man
emerged from the distant shadows. It was Hastings. A man near him
repeated Gaston's words. Hastings did not comment.

"How do we know ya ain't possessed?" a voice called out from the
other side of the fire.

Gaston sighed heavily. He handed me his musket and then his
baldric and belt. He would not meet my gaze, and I accepted them
silently. Then he did as I feared he would and doffed his tunic. There
was a collective gasp all around us. I winced for him, but he was stoic
to the extreme. Then he dropped his breeches. He did not close his eyes
as he had with me that day on the beach; but he did gaze into the fire so
that he could not see them in the dark around it.

I turned my gaze to those I could see, and witnessed some gazing
with slack-jawed amazement, while others averted their eyes with guilt
or sympathy.

"I have not been wholly in my right mind since this occurred,"
Gaston said. Once again the words were passed and most men found
the sand beneath them quite interesting. Gaston pulled his breeches up,
and picked up his tunic but did not don it. "I do strange things I cannot
always explain, and I am prone to violence and anger that I cannot
control. I understand if many of you do not wish for me to be surgeon. I
will treat any who ask, yet I will resign the position and offer no claim to
the money due it." With that, he turned away from the fire and walked
back up the dune to our things. I followed him.

He pulled his tunic on and sat in the sand to hug his knees with his
back to the camp. I put his weapons down and doffed mine, and then I
sat to embrace him from the side.

"That was a lie," he said with quavering voice. "This did not drive me
mad. I was mad before. I am sure that is what led to it. I did something
unforgivable. I reminded him of my mother yet again."

"You once said both your parents were mad or deranged in some fashion," I whispered.

He nodded. "I have my father's temperament, his propensity for rage and violence and my mother's... He kept her locked in the North tower, because she was never in her right mind. When I was older, they told me they feared she would walk off the parapets on the whimsy that she could fly. She would become lost to herself, staring at the sparkles of light from the windows. She sometimes forgot her name or thought she was a person from a story. They whispered of witchcraft even after she died. I do not know if all of that is true. I never met her. We saw her at Christmas and Easter, because her ladies would dress her well and bring her to mass; but we were not allowed to talk to her, and she expressed no interest in us. She died when we were seven. She died in childbirth. One baby had been stillborn, and the other had died inside her. The strain and misery of it all killed her. In all the chaos that followed, we were able to sneak into the room. They had wrapped her head and dressed her in a blue gown, and the baby she had borne was swaddled all in white beside her. She reminded me of the painting of the Madonna and Child that hung in the house chapel. She was lying on her back, and it took a great deal of effort, but we pushed her up until she was sitting and placed the baby in her arms, so that she looked like the painting. Then they found us. Father was furious. I was sent away to school the day after the funeral."

I clutched him tighter and wiped the tears I shed for him on his kerchief. His tale explained much, but it also opened the door to vast mysteries.

"You said we?" I queried.

"Oui, Gabriella, my twin sister."

"And she is dead also," I breathed. I knew she was the one he had spoken of before.

"Oui, she was always sickly. Always sickly. I was always hale. The nurses used to say I had gotten all the good health that was to be split between us. I always thought I had robbed her somehow, that it was my fault she was ill."

"You know...?"

"Oui, I know," he sighed. "But Will, we know many things and still we cannot protect ourselves from the pain. You know that."

"Non, we cannot. Yet you know I would do anything to rob you of yours."

"Oui, and I love you for it. No one has cared for me as you do since my sister."

I heard people approaching, and looked around to see our friends. They were hesitant, and I waved them over.

"We have company. What do you wish to do?"

"I wish to drink until the world is a very distant place and I cannot remember their eyes upon me."

The Bard was closest, and I looked up at him. "We need a great deal more rum."

He nodded and looked behind him, and one of the others hurried back down the hill.

"Is all well?" I asked.

He sat between us and the fire, so that Gaston's back was to him still, and thus afforded my matelot what was left of his privacy. He nodded at my question. "There has been some discussion, and I believe Gaston is still surgeon, but we're not sure if Michaels will remain cook."

"I wish I could say I bear the man no ill will, yet I do," I said. "Even if Hastings was the real bastard."

The others sat and clustered near the Bard, so that Gaston did not have to look at them, either. All were there who had been with us earlier, with the exception of Pete, who had stayed below with Striker. I was sure those two would be slow in joining us, as they must insure that all had been resolved and calmed before giving the matter or the men their backs.

With everyone seated thus, I was confronted with a wall of shadowed faces, as the fire was distantly behind them and there was not enough moon to show a man's countenance clearly. I was not comfortable with this, but there was little I could do. Tom arrived with several bottles, and I handed one to Gaston. He had apparently composed himself well enough to deal with the others in a meager fashion, and he turned in my arms so that his back was to my chest. I kept my arms and legs protectively around him. He took a long pull on the bottle.

"That was a brave thing," the Bard said.

Gaston snorted. "Thank you, but I would rather not speak of it."

"Of course," the Bard said, and no one spoke of it again that night.

Gaston drank himself into a retching stupor, and I cared for him as best I could. Thankfully he was not a talkative or angry drunk, and therefore he was not as taxing as I had feared. When he vomited on Striker and me, he was sincerely apologetic. I followed him about, as he seemed to want to go swimming and had to be convinced otherwise; and I eventually got him to lie still on the beach with me and sleep. Once he finally allowed himself to succumb to it, he slept like the dead.

I could not find the peace of mind to slumber for a good while. I lay with him in my arms and regarded the stars, and wondered how he had survived. Once again, I thought my own hardships trivial in comparison. Then I thought of all he had said over the last few months, and knew I held many pieces of the puzzle of his past. I turned them this way and that, and felt myself on the edge of a great precipice from which I could leap to a number of conclusions. From the vantage point of ignorance, I did not like the look of any of them and chose not to jump, as I was sure any place I landed would bring no more serenity than I currently possessed.

Dawn was heralded by muskets and pistols being discharged. At first I thought nothing of it, as it was a usual thing to clear the weapons and reload them; and then I remembered the events of the night before, and I was quickly out from under my matelot and on my knees, pistol in hand. No one was approaching us, and Liam and Otter sat upon the nearby dune chuckling, at my rude awakening.

Gaston had not moved; and I doubted he would for several hours, as he was quite limp and dead to the world. I laid the pistol on his belly, and waded into the surf to wipe the sleep from my eyes and invigorate myself into productive thought. There was a ship to careen, and I supposed I should help with it, lest someone else think I was a pampered son of nobility. I would first need to find shade for Gaston in a place where I could keep an eye on him. I spied the longboat nearby. It was propped upside-down on barrels, to provide shade for some of the stores we removed from the ship. After a great deal of effort and sleepy French curses, I managed to get Gaston and our gear partially beneath it and out of the sun.

He was awake enough now to clutch at me.

"Let go and let me find some water," I urged.

"Michaels. Remedy," he mumbled.

I frowned, as I guessed he did not recall last night's events, which was probably for the best for the time being.

"I will find him." I patted his hand and pulled free, and went in search of Michaels and water. I found water, but did not see the man about the camp. I was finally forced to inquire; and, after I had received several strange looks for even asking, our gunner, De Morte, said he had seen Michaels walking down the beach last night.

I trudged in the indicated direction, until I saw someone in the dunes who looked to have Michael's legs. I approached cautiously, calling out his name, so as not to startle him and end up with lead in my teeth. Michaels did not rouse, and from the angle of his legs and feet I guessed him to be in as much of a torpor as my matelot. Then I smelled blood. I sprinted the last few steps until I was even with him. I knew he was dead without stepping closer, as the back of his throat was missing. He lay collapsed with the pistol loose in his right hand.

Guilt and sorrow closed over me, and for a time I did nothing but stand and stare. I had not wished this. I did wish I had not said what I did to Cudro and the others. The matter could have been resolved without this casualty. Here was a truly senseless death indeed.

Ever so slowly, reasoning returned and I knew there were things that must be done. I squatted and touched his foot. There was still warmth to it, and I surmised he had fired while the others were discharging their weapons so as to not attract attention. I stood and whistled loudly and looked up the beach. I caught the attention of Cudro, of all people, and I waved him over. He limped resolutely through the sand, with curiosity on his thick features. Then he saw the feet and frowned.

When he was even with me and saw the body, he cursed softly in Dutch and said, "Ate his own lead, who would have thought?"

I nodded. I had seen this before: twice actually. Once had been in a carriage. The man had removed the top of his own head, and blood had dripped from the ceiling. The other had been in a garden, and that man had used a small pistol, and the ball had not exited his head. It had taken those of us who found him a bit to realize how he had died, as we had not seen the hole in the roof of his mouth until he fell over. I had seen a man's throat blown out as Michaels' was only once, though, and that had been when I had killed a man by sticking a pistol in his mouth.

I shivered as cold fingers traced my spine and clutched my gut.

"Oh my God..." I whispered; and Cudro regarded me and shrugged.

I recalled all my memories of Michaels, and a startling thing occurred to me.

"Stay here, I'll get Striker," I whispered.

Cudro looked curious, but I shook my head and quickly walked back to camp. I found the wolves talking to the Bard beside the ship.

"You three should come with me quietly," I said. "Michaels has been murdered."

We all made our way in silence down the beach, until they could see the body. "You said murdered," the Bard said, "looks as if he took his own life."

"He was left-handed," I said with conviction. "And the angle of the shot is wrong." I took my own pistol and briefly stuck it in my mouth, as a man usually did when considering such things. "See? The angle is wrong. The only way the back of the throat is marred is if the bullet comes from above."

"All right, I believe you. But why? The matter was past," Striker said.

"They would not suffer a witch to live," Cudro said.

Michaels had been an easy target, coming down the beach by himself. Gaston had been with me. With terror in my heart, I realized I was a fool and ran back to the longboat. A little prodding and cursing proved that my matelot was still quite alive. I handed him the water.

As bleary as he was, he still recognized my distress. I told him of the matter quickly, and he sat up and massaged his temples. Then he drank the water in long gulps.

Striker and Pete joined us.

"I will slowly spread the word," Striker said. "I think we should let it lie as death by his own hand, and keep our suspicions to ourselves. You are still surgeon. Are you up to the task of examining the body?"

Gaston nodded slowly. "Help me stand."

I pulled him to his feet, and we made our slow way down the beach. The Bard and Cudro were still standing there, but so were several other men. Gaston composed himself with great effort, and made a good show of examining the body. Then he draped a kerchief over the face and collected Michaels' belongings. There was now quite a crowd, all muttering and whispering amongst themselves.

"It appears he took his own life," Gaston said for their benefit. The word was passed; and many a man crossed himself, and others bowed their heads in prayer.

We buried him that morning, and several men spoke over the body.

I could see guilt and regret on every face; and I made sure they saw the same on mine, and not the anger and fear I felt now that I knew there was a murderer amongst us. I kept hoping that I would see a different mien while scanning the crowd, and my vigilance was finally rewarded. Hastings stood well back with his cronies, and he smirked when Striker talked of what a shame it was that a man should feel so abandoned as to take his own life. It was not proof by any means. Yet, I wondered what Michaels could have told us about his conversations with Hastings, if he had lived.

Afterwards, no one had much heart for careening, as if any man would be enthused about standing about in the hot sun scraping and tarring, even without a death and the lasting malaise from the ill will of the night before. Striker went from group to group and got them organized. I asked the Bard what to do, and made a good show of scraping for a while, until I was sure my hands would blister and Gaston would yell at me. I handed the tool off to another man, and went to find my matelot. He was sitting in the shade of the longboat bandaging a man's hand. I sipped water and waited, until the man left with a very polite nod.

"Do we already have wounded?" I asked.

"Non, he is one who would not let me treat him yesterday."

"Oh."

We regarded each other. He sighed. "My head is in such pain. Did I do as I think I did?"

I smiled. "Oui, you vomited upon Striker."

He glared at me.

"You did the other too. That was before you drank a bottle. If it is any consolation, I feel it saved your life."

"I know, yet I still feel shame. I also feel guilt over poor Michaels."

"Why? You were not the one that told Cudro he made potions."

"What?"

I told him what I had told Cudro and the others the day before. "I did not think Cudro would use it so quickly. I did not think things would progress so quickly. I am loathe to admit it, especially to you, but I feel I must say something of it. I was relieved to realize he had been murdered. It eased a great deal of my guilt. It is very selfish of me."

"If there is a Heaven, a murdered man stands a chance of entering it; one who took his own life does not."

"I suppose that is another benefit to someone else pulling the trigger. I happen to believe it was Hastings; of course, there is no proof."

"What would he stand to gain?" Gaston asked. "From what I remember of events, many men knew he was the one stirring the pot. He cannot be hiding that with Michaels' death. And Michaels had aired his suspicions of me to others before Hastings."

"True, true, I cannot fathom his motivation, either."

"I will say one additional thing," Gaston said. "I am relieved that whoever did it made it appear as suicide, lest we would be blamed for that, too."

I cursed. I had not considered that, and there I had been the unlucky fool who had found him. "I hope the rest of this voyage is far more auspicious than its beginning."

But as I well knew, the Gods are fickle bastards and oft delight in mischief.

Twenty-Three

Wherein We Are Surprised

We were still alive a month later, and though the voyage had not become more auspicious, it had thankfully become less exciting. Other than Pete developing a rotten tooth, nothing of interest had occurred since the island. Of course that incident almost resulted in death, as Pete, damn near mad with pain from the festering in his mouth, took to the quarterdeck and held us off with pistols for two hours, before Striker finally told him that he would never kiss him again unless he had the disgusting thing removed. Then it took four of us to hold him down whilst Gaston extracted the tooth and flushed the socket with rum. Thankfully, Pete passed into unconsciousness during this.

After that, we all grew bored with making our way up and down the sea-lane leading to Cuba, looking for the Galleons. The tension from the witchcraft accusations had never completely abated, and now it was building again. Men began to mutter that we had missed them, and if we did not go north and check Havana, we would find we missed them altogether. In the name of maintaining harmony, Striker decided a peek at the Havana harbor would do us no harm, as it was the last week of July; and so we were sailing north at night, under a brilliant moon and clear skies, with a brisk broad-reaching wind.

The wolves had requested the cabin for the first part of the night. From their behavior on an open deck, I knew they did not desire privacy for carnal activities, but simply for its own sake. In order to maintain the peace, they spent their time circulating amongst the men every day. Striker did not wish to appear inaccessible, and so he rarely spent time exclusively with his friends or on the quarterdeck. It was trying for him, made even more so by the constant nagging knowledge that someone on board – who he was quite probably chatting with about the weather – was a murderer and could not be trusted. We watched one another's backs while taking great care not to appear that we were doing so. It wore on all of us.

Thus Gaston and I were on the quarterdeck, waiting to go below and sleep. Belfry, Dickey and the Bard were sitting with us. I stood watching the froth of our wake in the moonlight. Gaston sprawled on his back beside me and watched the stars. Unlike Striker and Pete, we had kept our distance from the crew, as there was still a question of Gaston's safety, and we had not been in a particularly diplomatic frame of mind after the careening. And, of course, Gaston had never been particularly social to begin with, and he still felt acute embarrassment over baring himself to all of them. None of them made it easier by their behavior, either; even our friends did not regard him in the same way after the incident. I caught several of them staring, and I knew he saw them at it all the time.

Thinking of his discomfiture, I sat and tousled his hair. He captured my hand and kissed my fingers lightly, before placing my hand back on his head in a silent bid to have me scratch his scalp. I complied, and he gave a happy little grunt, and rolled onto his belly for me to work my way down his back.

The mournful call of a whale hung in the darkness. It was soon joined by another. Their noises seemed to emanate from very nearby, which I was not pleased with, as the great creatures scared me. These sounds were soon echoed, quite comically, from the men; and there was a good deal of laughter.

I heard the pad of feet, and looked round to see Tom coming to join us. "You have the watch soon," the Bard chided. "I will be sleeping."

"I cannot sleep through the noise," Tom snapped.

"The whales keeping you awake?" I teased. "They only just started."

"Nay, the buggers in your cabin right next to ours. When I first heard the whales, I thought it was still them."

We chuckled at that. More whales had joined in the symphony, and the night was filled with them. I saw one blow to port. The huge back glistened in the moonlight. A little one broke the water and blew right beside the first, and I guessed it a baby.

"Do they mate?" Tom asked with annoyance. "Is that why they make all this noise?"

"Aye," Belfrey said. "I have had occasion to know a number of whalers. The creatures have great big members, and they do indeed mate as other animals do. These here are not mating, though. I rather imagine they are singing lullabies to their calves."

"Nay, nay, they are nagging at them as all mothers do," the Bard said. "Something has this pod all riled; usually they sleep at night. They can be quite dangerous while doing so. Not so much with a ship this size; but the sloop could have been stove in if she struck one."

"Perhaps they are discussing how best to ram us," I said, "as like all mothers they are very protective of their young and we sailed into their midst. I find them horrifying creatures."

"Men kill them easily enough," Belfry said cheerfully, as if that would ally all of my concerns.

"Men kill other men easily enough, and yet men are still the greatest threat to one another's lives," I countered.

"Whales do not engage in politics." the Bard chuckled.

"How do we know?" I asked. "Packs of dogs engage in politics of a sort. They are always yapping about one another as to who the leader is."

I turned to sit with my back to the gunwale and Gaston pushed up to his knees to give me a kiss at the corner of my jaw. I regarded him curiously. His eyes were filled with amusement.

"You should sign everything Socrates," he whispered in French.

"What is a centaur to do?" I whispered back.

He lay down on his side, with his head on my thigh, one arm about my rear, and the other hand on my knee. My hand went straightaway into his hair, in a never-ending attempt to smooth all the little red clumps that stood out this way and that.

I looked up. No one was speaking. I found all eyes on us. Our companions appeared as a pack of dogs eyeing a juicy chunk of meat, and several shifted uneasily when my gaze fell upon them. The Bard was honest enough to throw his head back and sigh.

I chuckled. "You really need to see to that careening."

"A careening would not be enough," he sighed. "I need to be sailed." He sounded as mournful as the whales.

I felt sympathy for him; yet he had done little to find a matelot on this voyage, and much to bring himself even greater misery, as he had become enamored with Tom.

He was not the only one. Many of the unattached men followed young Tom with their eyes: including, to my dismay, Cudro. In truth, after observing the man with a less cynical eye, I had come to realize Cudro favored men as much as I. And like myself, he possessed refined taste and aesthetic sensibilities. He had found Gaston as handsome as I did; and now he thought the same of Tom, who was probably the most beautiful man aboard, next to Pete.

Tom was blind to none of this attention, and he basked in it with the arrogance of youth. It amused him greatly, but he had no interest in any of these men. If Dickey's tales were to be believed, which I thought highly possible, young Tom had managed to engage in several liaisons with some of the planter's daughters on Jamaica in the short time since our arrival, and quite possibly seduced one. That was what had resulted in the falling out with the uncle. I had asked Dickey for names and descriptions and been relieved to find that Miss Vines was not amongst his conquests.

Tom could still not foresee ever having a use for men, even if he were trapped with one for the rest of his life on an island in the middle of the ocean. This did not bode well on a ship already fraught with tension, and it was becoming obvious Tom was going to lead to a duel or two and possibly some deaths. He had no intention of taking a matelot and removing himself from contention, and every intention of continuing to rove. I felt I might have possibly been in breach of the articles in bringing him aboard, as the whole injunction against bringing boys aboard was to avoid starting fights.

In stark contrast, no one eyed Dickey at all. He was handsome enough, but his effeminate airs, manners, and whining labeled him as weak, though I know he did most of it for show. No man was interested in a weak matelot, even if he was attractive. And of course Dickey had no use for men, and was determined not to be considered a sodomite – and therefore was scrupulous in maintaining his distance from Belfry and any other man, even Tom.

In thinking of them thus, I realized a thing that gave me much amusement. It would serve both their ends – well, not Dickey's so much – but more the ship's in general, if Tom and Dickey were viewed as matelots. I wondered if such a thing could be arranged. Dickey was sensible enough, and I was sure he could be made to see the danger Tom was causing. And he did care for his friend. Tom, on the other hand, was as annoying as Davey to me, in that he felt he knew all and damn anyone who strayed from the course of what he did know.

As added inducement, they had both been eyeing Gaston and me with longing, and I knew the need for companionship had come upon them this last month. Of course, they would probably choose not to allow themselves the comfort of having someone to touch and they might not have the wherewithal to overcome their objections. I knew all too well that what Gaston and I appeared to now have with such ease had been hard-won.

Tom was leaning on the railing and watching the wake, and the Bard and I were regarding one another under the bridge of Tom's body. This seemed to amuse the Bard, and he eyed the younger man's hard belly and narrow hips with subtle longing. I caught his eye and gave him a bemused shake of my head. The Bard shrugged and sighed and looked away. He knew what Tom was, just as I did; and we had discussed the matter on several occasions.

Beyond him, Dickey was slumped in the corner, watching either our wake or what could be seen of the receding whales. His expression was poignant and contemplative. Just as I regretted inviting Tom, I was even more rueful about pressing Dickey into this voyage. Most times he did not seem mired in despondency, and was generally cheerful; but I was coming to realize that it was often an excellent façade he had learned to show the world, and he was truly a melancholy individual.

Belfry sat a little farther over against the starboard rail, and smoked his pipe with his knees pulled to his chest. He had taken to the ship and the buccaneer way far better than I thought he would, though he still possessed a number of underlying notions concerning the separation of crew and officers and the like. These views were not disabused on this voyage, as due to a number of circumstances there were two distinct groups of men aboard: the men, who had little to do but wait and amuse themselves, and those involved in sailing the ship and their cronies, who happened to include all of us sitting upon the quarterdeck now.

Whenever the subject of sex reared itself by example or mention, Belfry still became either flustered or withdrawn and oft mentioned his bride. The Bard had quickly noted to me that Belfry could not know if she was to show in the winter. Belfry had sent her a letter to ask her to come, but he could not have received a reply as of yet, as she had probably only received his missive when we sailed on this voyage. I wondered what he would do if she did not agree to sail to Jamaica. He did not love her with passion or abandon. She was simply a fine thing he had acquired, and he spoke at length of her sensibilities and breeding, as if she were a hunter he had purchased.

It all reminded me of my conversation with Striker on the night before we sailed. If I had not myself witnessed many a man smitten to the depths of stupidity by love of a woman, I would wonder if such a thing existed between men and women at all. The whole prospect of marriage seemed so mired in tradition, family, children, and propriety that it was difficult to remember that it occasionally occurred for love; though in my experience it was more often broken for love or lust than joined in for the same. Perhaps sheep had a better go of that sort of thing, as they had less property and political entanglement to complicate it all.

Gaston was asleep. I regarded the head in my lap and smiled. Love was a far more precious thing when it was not expected.

I studied the sails, which were rather like strange square clouds rippling and glowing in the moonlight. The wind had died down a little, and dropped in temperature enough so that I was torn as to whether to sleep on deck or not. If it picked back up, it would be just cool enough that a thin blanket, which we did not possess, would have been nice for sleeping this high up on the quarterdeck. If the wind died completely it would be quite pleasant, but we would not be sailing toward our goal. I supposed I should always put the ship first.

The Bard was watching Tom intently, and it had nothing to do with lust. This was the stare of a master expecting his apprentice to notice a thing. Tom was lost in his own reverie and oblivious. Dickey was eyeing Tom as well, his face also filled with annoyance, as he had seen what I had: the lower sails were luffing a bit. The man at the whipstaff stuck his head up to check on us, looking for orders.

With a sigh of annoyance, the Bard told the man to do as he thought best to stay with what wind there was. Then he ignored Tom, who finally turned to take a notice of things. Instead, the Bard addressed me.

"There will be fog at dawn."

This had occurred several times, and I was always thankful we were in open ocean when it did. Sailing through fog caused me a great deal of consternation, especially the one time it had been thick enough I could not see the bow from the stern. Of course, it always burned off quickly once the sun rose; but still, it was more dangerous than sailing on a moonless night.

I did not relish waking in its shroud, but I also did not wish to expend the effort to go and check the door to the cabin to see if we could enter yet. Gaston's slumber seemed to be exerting a pull upon me, and I decided to join him. I moved to lie beside him, and curled about his back. I soon drifted to sleep, even over the sound of the Bard chiding Tom about never mastering sailing if he was not constantly aware of the wind.

I woke to a muffled grey morning. There was just enough light to make out the Bard kneeling next to us, tapping insistently on my shoulder. His eyes were searching the fog bank.

"What?" I whispered.

He waved me to silence. Gaston and I sat up and peered about with him.

I could not see the bow in the fog. I could hear men snoring and the omnipresent rushing of water past our hull and the creaks of a ship at sea. The fog echoed the sounds back upon us, so that it sounded as if there were ships all around.

I could not fathom what the Bard was in a tizzy about, but I knew what concerned my person; and I stood and relieved myself over the rail. Gaston did likewise, and we continued to listen and look around us. The wind was very low and barely moved our sails. We were drifting through the fog more than sailing. I reckoned that would all change soon, as it was becoming lighter every second.

A sharp voice cried out the number of bells, in Spanish, somewhere off our port stern. The bells being rung cut through the fog as well as the voice had, and I glanced frantically about. Every man on our quarterdeck was now awake and staring in wonder toward the sound.

The Bard hissed and motioned the men who could see him to silence. Men scurried forward to carry the order.

"Striker," the Bard hissed at me.

Gaston caught me before I could run. "Muskets. Your pants."

I swore silently and fastened my breeches, as I ran down the stairs and around to the cabins. I stopped at Cudro's door on the way. I threw it open and nudged his hamock until I received a sleepy grunt and a bleary glare. I whispered, "There is a fog. We are atop a Spaniard." His eyes shot wide as my words sank home.

I took the last step to the aft cabin and dove into it. Striker and Pete were curled naked together in their hammock. We had torn the bunk out weeks ago to make more room. I was tempted to upend them, but that would not have kept them quiet. I grabbed Striker's shoulder and whispered in his ear the same words I had given Cudro. He frowned at me, and I left him and opened the windows to peer out. Pete climbed out, and joined me. There was a huge dark shadow out in the grey.

We swore quietly in unison and dove for the muskets. Striker was already out the door at a run. Pete and I retrieved all of the weapons in the cabin. He donned his weapons and I mine, and then we picked up our matelots'. Belfry dove into the room.

"Striker needs his pants," he hissed. This set Pete to quiet laughter.

We found Striker on the quarterdeck, whispering orders that were passed along as quietly as possible. He was still naked, and looked far more relieved to see his weapons than his breeches.

In short order, every musket we had was along the rails and hanging in the rigging. The Spaniard's bulk was visible to all now, and I wondered that she had not seen us yet. She was huge; and I felt fear at her presence, much as I did at the whales, though of course she was far larger. She seemed to be hanging steadily off our port stern at a distance of maybe fourscore feet. Our positions had changed very little relative to one another since we heard her bells. She did seem to be coming alongside slowly, though, and had most probably been creeping up on us all night once the wind died. In another hour or so, she would have passed us completely in the fog, and we would have been none the wiser. But now the sun was rising, and with it the wind, and between the two, the fog hiding us from one another would be gone.

The Bard, Cudro and Striker huddled with their heads together on the quarterdeck. Pete stood with Gaston and me on the rail, with our muskets on the ship. We could not see movement on her yet, and she was beginning to pick up a little speed. The Bard had our sails trimmed so that we were, too; and so we quickly matched her, so that she stayed just a little behind us. If we fell back beside her and she saw us, we were dead, as she would be able to broadside us. That would, of course, be if her cannon were loaded and run out before we could get clear of her.

Striker joined us.

"We're going to take her," he whispered, and went on to explain the plan of attack. Gaston and I had a specific function to perform. Then he was gone to spread the word.

Those of us who would board passed our loaded muskets off to men who would shoot as they could. Gaston signaled Belfry, and told him to collect all the wounded in one place as he was able.

"You should stay," I told Gaston. "You are our only surgeon."

Gaston shook his head. "If I stay, then you stay; and that would be foolish, as we will need every man we have to take this monster; and as you heard our captain, there is a thing which we can do easily. If we do not take her, the men will not need a surgeon, as they will need a priest."

I could see the logic behind it; and I nodded and kissed him on the lips. He grabbed my head and pulled my mouth to his for a true kiss that left me warm.

"Be careful," he admonished once we parted.

Bemused, I nodded again.

"I should return to England then," I teased.

"See that you do. You would do well to leave now."

"I still cannot swim."

The Bard was at the whipstaff, and the *Mayflower* slid toward the behemoth until Cudro, Pete, and several others were in range for grapples. The first and last thing the Spanish sailors in the forecastle heard was the whine of the hooks being spun for throwing. Gaston and Julio killed both sailors with thrown knives. The hooks went over the galleon's gunwale at the same time, and we began to swarm up them before the *Mayflower* was even made fast.

For those of us first on board, the galleon seemed a crewless ghost ship. There was still so much fog we could not see the length of her. I gasped at the sight of the deck, as this vessel was every bit as large as the one we took before. Striker led eight of us in a run for the quarterdeck and the captain's cabin, even as someone sounded the alarm and bellowed in Spanish for all hands on deck. Cudro was to lead another group of men to block the hatches leading up from below.

Gaston and I found the captain asleep, without his pants. My matelot, a scary sight for any well-bred Spaniard who had just been roused from slumber by an alarm, clapped his hand over the man's mouth and put a pistol to his privates. Once we had his somewhat calm attention, I explained in my best Castilian that we were there to rob him, and if all cooperated we would leave them alive and well.

He gathered his wits about him, and when Gaston removed his hand he asked smugly, "That is all fine and well, but what do you English dogs intend to do with the four galleons sailing right behind us? Are there a fleet of you?"

I had no ready answer for that, as obviously it had not been considered. The Captain seemed amused at my momentary consternation; and I smiled at him and said the first thing that came to mind.

"We will have to see if they can sink one of their own ships, because we have a galleon now."

His eyes widened slightly, but he kept his composure. We prepared to lead him out and he sputtered, "At least allow me to dress."

In his nightshirt he was wearing at least as much cloth as either of us. We looked at one another, and Gaston shook his head. "Non."

Once up top, the Spanish captain looked about him in wonder at the fog; and then he looked aft, where obviously no ships could be seen in the mist. He went as white as his shirt. I told Striker what the man had said, and he had me ask the captain a series of questions concerning this ship's armaments, the number of men aboard, the names of the other ships following, and where the rest of the Galleon fleet was, as it was a great deal larger than five ships. The captain raised his chin proudly and refused to answer.

Pete swept the man's feet out from under him and pinned him down, and Striker smashed one of the Captain's fingers with the brass pommel of a pistol. I watched the other officers. One younger man sputtered with fear.

"Same questions," I said pleasantly.

He glanced about him, and recoiled from the admonishing looks from his peers.

I slashed the one with the sternest expression above the knee with my rapier. The scared one started talking.

We were aboard the *Madonna Hermosa* and she mounted thirty-eight cannon and was manned by two hundred and thirty-four men. She was due to pick up an additional complement of marines in Havana. She was being immediately followed by four other galleons, but they had let themselves separate in the fog to avoid accidents. So it was possible they were not as near as the captain had believed. The rest of ships of the Galleons were behind them. The most important thing from our perspective was that the *Madonna* was carrying the interesting combination of cocoa, silver, and emeralds. There had been no hesitation in his recitation of this to indicate he was holding much of anything back. I conferred with Gaston and Striker, and we all agreed that he appeared to be forthright with us.

I asked the man the amount of silver and emeralds. He said one chest of emeralds and three of silver. We instructed the captain to have them brought above. His compliance was gained by the breaking of two more fingers. He finally shouted orders into the hatch Cudro was guarding, and shortly thereafter the chests began to arrive on deck. The first small one was indeed filled with gems, though most were of an inferior quality.

As the next chest was being negotiated up through the hatch, Cudro, Pete, Striker, Gaston, and myself pulled aside and quickly conferred.

"I say we take the booty and run," I said.

Striker was laughing quietly. He looked about. The fog was clearing every minute. There was no telling when the other Spanish ships would show.

"I concur," Striker said. "We haven't lost a man and we have enough to make this voyage worthwhile."

"I think the men will be pleased. Better have them scuttle their cannon," Cudro said.

The order was given to move the chests to the *Mayflower* as we received them. The *Madonna's* captain lost the rest of his fingers in getting the cannon scuttled. I felt he was quite stubborn for no good reason. Meanwhile, we took everything the officers possessed. Soon, we had the gems and the first chest of pieces of eight upon the *Mayflower*, and our men were hanging on the sides to watch as the galleon's ordinance began to be shoved out their gun ports one by one.

This all happened far more slowly than we were comfortable with.

Only a few of the cannon had been scuttled, and we had not taken possession of the second heavy chest of silver by the time the fog burned away and we sat upon open ocean. We could see two other galleons. They were not close, but even before realizing the *Madonna* had a ship beside her, they had been maneuvering to close their formation. Thankfully the *Mayflower* was tucked in beside the larger vessel, in order for the chests be hoisted over. Our vessel was not visible unless they were on the galleon's starboard. Unfortunately, one of the other galleons was, and shortly saw us. She put on a great deal of sail and made for us. We demanded the second chest, and the Spaniards below, realizing we must have reason for our sudden haste, began to dawdle. If we began shooting the ones visible, we would have to kill them all and wade in blood, ours and theirs, to reach the remaining silver. We decided to take what we had and run, and we abandoned the galleon as quickly as we had boarded her.

The Bard turned us west, and we ran before the wind, until we actually passed the other galleons on a long arc and came around behind them: to begin to beat our way across the western Caribbean, towards Jamaica and Hispaniola.

There was a great deal of rejoicing and laughter, and all hailed our brilliant bit of luck. Though we had not gotten it all, what we had taken was a hefty sum indeed. There was one remaining keg of beer, and we opened it that night, as soon as we were sure we were well round the Spanish. It was not nearly enough to make the lot of us drunk, but one would not have known it from the party that ensued. The musicians played, and there was dancing and revelry throughout the night.

As Gaston had never been much of one for that sort of thing, and Pete and Striker were, we retired early to the cabin to peruse the books we had taken from the galleon's officers. We doubted any other would want them, but technically we could not claim them until the booty was shared out. We could read them, however. Unfortunately all were religious tracts or awful romantic novels, and not the salacious type either. We set them aside and regarded one another.

"Despite the books it was an auspicious thing," Gaston said.

"Thank God you are practicing witchcraft. If you had not conjured that fog, who knows what would have befallen us."

We laughed, yet I noted it did little to ease his tension.

"What is wrong?"

"It was too easy."

I nodded. I had heard that from several others, including Striker. There was yelling on deck, and I grinned. "Perhaps something disastrous will occur tonight to set things right. I am sure young Tom could provoke a duel or two." I remembered I had not told him of my new plan. I quickly related my thoughts from last night.

He chuckled. "You should leave match-making to Pete."

"Non, I am as talented as any man, and I have meddled in the affairs of many."

"To what success?" he grinned.

"A few duels..." I regarded him curiously as he laid his head on the small table we had made out of the bunk.

"You think too much, and so do I. Make it all go away," he murmured.

We retired to our hammock, and I endeavored to do so. As always, I only wished I could give him the release I achieved; but he seemed relaxed when we finished, and he smiled lazily at me. I cuddled next to him, and we listened to the sounds of the party continuing overhead.

"If we see another ship in the morning I think most of us will be without our pants," I said.

Low laughter rumbled through his chest. "I think Striker set a fine example for us all this morning. I have met no other captain who would put his ship before even his dignity."

"Dignity is worthless if you are dead, but I concur." I chuckled. "I know of few men who would run out to command their troops naked as the day they were born, though it is not as if he has anything to be ashamed of in that area."

"Nor would you," he said.

At first I winced, as I had not meant to imply that he did; but as I saw the gaze he had upon me, I realized he meant something else entirely.

"Truly?"

He nodded and gazed at the ceiling with a mischievous smile. "I have noted that you are better endowed than Striker, both flaccid and aroused."

I had noted the same, but was not one to hold court on the matter. "And this pleases you?"

"You are mine. You are better. It pleases me."

"So in your competitive Gallic heart this matter holds merit and nowhere else?"

He laughed. "It seems well-formed."

"It thanks you." I considered pressing him further, but I knew it truly could not carry much other interest with him. I was pleased he had said as much as he had, and that he looked on it with pride.

"It gives me pause," he whispered, and immediately flushed.

The possible interpretations of this gave me pause, and I found my head cocked like a dog's before I realized it.

"In what way?"

He sank even further into the hammock, if that were possible, and sighed. "I did not wish to discuss it."

"Then we shall not. I will be filled with curiosity and unable to sleep, but I shall endure." I kissed him on the temple and made as if to roll over.

Gaston caught my shoulder and snorted derisively. I settled down on my elbow and his eyes returned to the ceiling as he sighed again. "The size gives me pause if we were...If I was to allow you to..."

My heart lurched for a moment with excitement, and I thought of whales and Spanish galleons and all manner of terrifying things to keep myself from becoming aroused at the mere thought that he had harbored a thought on that matter.

"Good Lord," I whispered, "you have been thinking on a great number of things, have you not?"

He nodded and studied the far wall. "Over the years, I have noticed that many find pleasure in being the recipient."

"It can be extremely pleasurable unto itself."

"This is a thing you wish, non?" He was still not looking at me.

"Oui, but I will not ask it of you. If we never engage in that, then I will..."

"Endure," he said.

I grabbed his chin and turned his head to face me. "In truth, as I believe I have mentioned, I would rather you were aroused and buggered me."

His eyes narrowed, and he pulled my hand off his chin and kissed my fingers. "So would I." He frowned. "Other than... it being proof of my... desire, would you find it pleasurable?"

I mirrored his furrowed brow. "Oui..." I found myself flushing. Now I did not wish to discuss the subject. "Beyond the feelings it engendered in my heart and mind, I found it physically pleasurable when... done gently. And beyond that...." I sighed. That was not wholly the truth.

I stopped talking and started thinking. I decided it was safe to go poking about in the shadows.

"I did enjoy it," I stated with more conviction. "Or rather, I wished to enjoy it and I felt...that it could have been immensely pleasurable if I had been with someone else. Because there were aspects of it that seem to be knotted up with the matter of it providing proof and the like... But yet separate as well. I resented both of them for it, or rather, I resented Shane for the manner in which he did it and Alonso because he would have it no other way. I was not allowed to mount either of them."

I gazed into Gaston's green eyes and tried to put the indescribable into words. "It is immensely pleasurable to me, both physically and in spirit. One must surrender in ways that are difficult for me, and upon doing so I found great peace for a moment. Even if all of these other thoughts were running amuck in my mind before and after, and even if it started and ended in pain, I achieved some kind of peace with myself when it occurred. There is this need to expel it. This feeling of being impaled. And then there is this knowledge that one must accept it and endure and in doing so it gets easier and the peace comes and... By God, it is the most spiritual sensation I have ever experienced. And then the pleasure comes. That is the thing that a man can give me, and a woman cannot."

Gaton nodded and I felt he did understand.

I kept exploring. "And I... I resented Shane and Alonso, because they would never understand what they had wrought on me and I had felt this thing, and I could not share it with the one who brought me to it, and I was very alone. I wanted to surrender to them. I wanted it to be an act of love. But it could not be. It was a thing of lust and left me feeling dirty and confused. It belittled it."

He rubbed my back, but I did not let him pull me down to him yet. I took several ragged breaths. "Of course that was the least of my concerns, and I distracted myself from it all admirably. In looking back, I did myself poor service in that. As always, I asked so little, and expected less, and called it more." I wiped threatened tears away with annoyance, and tried to compose myself.

"Someday I will be honored to take you there," he whispered. "Whether it proves anything or not."

"It will prove I love you," I said with surprise. "It proved I loved them. Why should such a simple thing be so confusing?"

I was heartened by the discussion, though, as I had discovered another thing and it had not ripped my soul asunder to do so. I smiled at him.

"I see now that the act itself was not the cause of the reciprocal self-loathing I engaged in before; it is separate and merely tarnished by all of that. Perhaps some day I will polish it with you, and hold it to the light and cherish it for what it is."

"Storming the gates of Heaven," he said.

I finally remembered my own words and the night on *North Wind* when we had watched the men in the bow make love.

"I have... I suppose there have been a few times I have engaged in that as it is meant to be. Some of my lovemaking with Alonso, in which I was the recipient, was of that nature, and a powerful and wonderful thing. It is hindsight and a greater understanding of myself that makes me question it now. But at the time, it was quite wonderful and the best I could imagine. And some of the lovers I have taken... the act reached that level of intensity. But it has been a rare thing and I.... I almost feel I have misled you in a sense, in that the beauty I wanted you to see is not common. But you know that, do you not?"

He shook his head. "Oui, you did not mislead me. You gave me much to think about that night, as you always do."

"That is truly the most reciprocal aspect of our relationship." I grinned and slipped into his embrace. In time, I let myself sleep with his fingers playing through my hair.

I woke to the sound of the door clattering open and the feel of Gaston tensing beneath me. I grabbed a pistol from the netting with my left hand as my right was under Gaston. The lamp had guttered, and the room was dark except for the reflected moonlight from the waves through the windows. There were several people, and I sighed with annoyance, as I assumed it was Pete and Striker staggering in drunk. Then I remembered that was impossible, given the meager amount of beer. I guessed someone had been hoarding a bottle or two of rum.

Then Belfry spoke. "There must be a lamp. Ah, here it is." The lamp surged to life as he turned up the wick, and we blinked at Belfry, Dickey, and Tom, who were soon blinking at us. When Belfry raised his hands, I realized we had pistols trained on them. When Dickey averted his gaze, I realized we were naked.

"What the Devil are you doing?" I yelled. I replaced the pistol in the netting and returned to glaring at them.

"We thought this cabin was empty," Belfry sputtered. "We needed privacy." He looked alarmed at his own words and added quickly, "For a discussion." His eyes flicked to the ceiling. "Um, you are naked."

"Of course I am. I am in my hammock, in my cabin, and it is night."

Dickey chuckled and said, "Our apologies. We will leave."

"Nay, nay, you are here. We are awake and now I am curious." I looked at Gaston and shrugged. "Are you curious?"

"Non, merely awake," he rasped.

"Hand me that water bottle, would you?" I said. "And what is this about?"

"Will you dress?" Belfry asked.

"Nay," I snapped.

Gaston grabbed my face with both hands and turned me to look at him. "I would like my clothes." He was more bemused than angry.

I sighed, and a minute later Gaston and I were dressed and we all crowded about the table.

"Now what is this about?" I reiterated.

"They wish to chastise me," Tom said. He sounded and looked far drunker than the keg of beer would have allowed; and I surmised he had been into a hidden stash, if no one else had. Dickey and Belfry appeared quite sober.

"You are being quite the little tart," Dickey said firmly.

I sighed and understood. So something had come to a head, so to speak.

"Has anyone threatened a duel as of yet?" I asked. They all regarded me with surprise. "Perhaps you should finish lecturing him," I sighed.

"He is being flirtatious," Dickey said. "He has no intention of bedding the man."

"I was not," Tom said. "They had some rum. I agreed to dance."

"Who?" I asked.

"Jackson."

"Which one is Jackson?"

"You have seen him," Belfry said. "He's tall, a musketeer, very muscular with dark hair."

Gaston laughed. I regarded Belfry quizzically. "As we have been at sea for a month with the same men on a small ship, I am sure I have seen him, but you will have to do better than that."

"Aye," Dickey said, "You have only eliminated fifteen of over eighty men. Jackson is one of Hasting's men."

I swore.

"What does that matter?" Tom asked.

I could not tell him my suspicions because if I did it would be all over the ship. "It has nothing to do with who you choose to associate with. It may have a great deal with who chooses to associate with you." I could see Hastings putting one of his men up to seducing Tom, just to anger Cudro into doing something stupid.

Tom leaned on the table and smirked. "I am not taking a matelot. I have no need of one. So I will not add to the political turmoil on this vessel."

"You do not have to take a matelot to add to the turmoil," I said. "You are actually causing more trouble by not taking one. If you are with one man, then there is less for speculation and no one can be using you as a tool to provoke others."

He rolled his eyes, and I knew he was too drunk to engage in this discussion. Dickey and Belfry were frowning at me, though.

"What do you mean?" Dickey asked. "I have been concerned that he will get himself abused because someone will not realize he is merely flirting."

"I am concerned that he will be used as a pawn to provoke a duel that will change the balance of power on this ship," I said. "And even if that were not an issue, he is an attractive man, and there are lonely men who wish to be with him; and that can cause duels if he favors one over another, even without commitment, actually especially without commitment. This is a serious matter that someone, including Tom, could lose his life over. For example, if he were abused, he would be expected to duel to defend his honor." I winced inwardly as I said it. "Is he capable of such a thing, or would you feel the need to step forward in his place?"

I could see that Dickey now grasped the situation. Belfry appeared horrified. Even Tom seemed to have listened. He was frowning.

"Truly?" he asked.

"Yes. Matelotage is a very serious matter, and trifling with men's affections in these parts carries far more weight than dallying with maidens, though I have known many a court situation where the gravity would be equal to this. Young English ladies in the country are seldom armed, and other young gentleman who may feel the need to compete for them are, thankfully, seldom competent at dueling. The man worth the most pounds per year always wins anyway. Here, the man you spurn may kill you, or another man may kill him. Toying with them is not a game. Here you must get married or not dally at all. And I do realize how that goes against your nature, but by your own account you do not favor men."

"I have mused upon a possible solution," I added. "Aye, I do waste my time thinking of your social status, and meddling is a recreation of mine. You may wish to consider pairing with someone in name only. For example, if Dickey and you were to declare yourselves as matelots and act it to some degree, then that would alleviate the other tensions for as long as Dickey sailed with us."

"Nay," Dickey said.

I sighed. "I am not asking you to bugger one another; and believe me, it would make neither of you appear less manly amongst the Brethren."

Dickey's eyes flicked from me to Gaston and back. "It is a serious issue; and if I am to engage in such a thing, it will be sincerely and with someone I am willing to die for."

I was, of course, not the only one surprised at this. Dickey looked at Belfry and Tom and gave an apologetic shrug.

"You are my friends, but…. Please take no offense." He stood. "With your leave," he said formally, and left us.

Tom was quite flummoxed, but Belfry seemed more concerned than fazed.

"Well, then," Belfry said. "Perhaps we should find our beds as well."

"May I sleep here?" Tom asked. He was still staring at the door.

"If you do not mind sleeping upon the floor," I said.

Tom shook his head. He did not move.

"Well, then," Belfry said. "I will go to our cabin then."

We wished him a good night, or rather morning, and watched him go. Tom had not moved.

"Are you well?" I asked. He shook his head.

"He has always cared for me," he said dully. "I cannot believe I have angered him so greatly that he will no longer care for me."

Gaston and I exchanged a look.

"Tom," I said kindly. "It is late, or early, and we are all tired, as I am sure Dickey is. Let us sleep on it, and perhaps you two can speak in the sober light of day and reach an understanding."

Tom shook his head, and slid off the chair to crawl into a corner and sleep. In my own way, I was as baffled by the outcome as Tom. I looked to Gaston, and he shrugged and turned down the lamp. We returned to our hammock and cuddled together. I lay awake and watched the reflected moonlight glint off the ceiling. I was beginning to feel I knew nothing of people and all of my suppositions concerning others might be suspect. For all I knew, Hastings was our staunchest ally.

We woke to Pete and Striker snoring loudly in their hammock and Tom curled uncomfortably in the corner. We took our time with our rudimentary morning toilet, and went out into the sun. Men were strewn everywhere, as if they had been thrown by a giant hand. All of them were snoring or drooling and apparently alive. I harbored a suspicion that there had been several heretofore-unknown caches of alcohol.

We found the Bard at the whipstaff. He appeared half dead. I pried his hand from it. "Go lie down."

"Where's Tom?" he asked.

"Dead to the world in our cabin," I said. He raised an eyebrow. "I do not feel I have the liberty to speak of the reason for it. He was drunk; ours was a safe place for him to sleep without complication."

He frowned but shrugged. "I can't sleep without someone to relieve me."

"Are we on a proper course?"

"Aye, but we are beating." He showed me the heading we were on and the one we needed for Hispaniola. I understood that, and as Gaston paid close attention as well, I knew we were at least capable of staying on course.

"Will we need to tack right away?" I asked.

He shook his head.

"Then rouse Belfry, and we will manage."

He frowned at me and then at Gaston, and shrugged. "We're in open ocean and the weather is fine. I don't suppose you can wreck her."

"Never assume, but we will do our utmost not to." I took the staff and he went to his cabin. I felt the pull of the rudder and tested my control a little. The ship felt as though it were a living thing, much like a horse that I was controlling more by her good nature than any degree of power I could exercise.

Gaston was grinning at me. "You finally have the helm. Are you proud of yourself?"

"Oui, I am. I like this. For the moment. I will become quite frustrated when it comes time to tell the crew to adjust the sails for the tack, as I know the words but I am sure I will misuse them, and they will stare at me as if I am daft."

Gaston looked about and grinned. "There are crewmen to adjust the sails?"

"That may be a problem then."

My matelot walked the deck and found a number of somewhat-coherent crewmen; and they were prepared to tack when it came time, as long as they could sleep again afterwards.

Whilst he was at this, Dickey emerged from their cabin and joined me. "May I ask you a question?"

"As long as it is not the name of that sail yonder."

"That is the main topgallant," he said.

I sighed.

He grinned and pointed at each sail on the main mast from top to bottom. "Topgallant, main, course."

"All right, then, you may question me once you find food for us."

He chuckled and went in search of food. He returned after Gaston had found my sailors. Dickey handed us fruit and cold roast beef. We ate happily and I nodded at him.

"Ask away."

"Is love something one finds or is it something one builds?"

We choked on our food for a moment, and I laughed. "Good Lord, man, men have spent their lives pondering that question!"

"In your experience."

I thought on my experience and regarded my one true example. "Both. You find the kernel of it, and then it grows with a great deal of nurturing."

Gaston nodded his agreement.

Dickey regarded the horizon thoughtfully. "I wish to find or grow love."

I swallowed a lump of meat I was not finished chewing, so that my mouth would be free to say nothing.

"It will cost in ways you never consider, and it will be worth any price," Gaston said.

I was touched by his answer, and I nodded thoughtful agreement. Then I turned my attention back to Dickey. "Where do you intend to seek it?"

He appeared uncomfortable. "I have always thought it would be found in one place, and yet I have learned that this is not always the case. So I will seek it where I find myself and where it finds me."

"So you are allowing that you may find love with a man?"

"Aye," he nodded and flushed.

"I have recently encountered several arguments for love between men being superior to love between man and woman, though I have seen couples of both persuasions who have achieved happiness or at least contentment."

"I have seen more happy pairs of matelots than I have seen happy married couples in England," Dickey said.

I sighed. "So have I. Something often seems to go sour in marriage; and it becomes a burden and not a thing the participants take delight in. It is a social obligation."

He nodded. "My parents loathe one another, and they will make each other miserable until one of them shall die; and I think still the misery will continue. Tom's parents seem to have some affection for each other, at least from what we have witnessed, but still they lead very separate lives, her with her garden meetings and social circles and him with his business. Of our own age, the couples who seemed very much in love during the courtship quickly tired of one another once the knot had been tied. The more in love the harder they fell. Yet none of that seems to hold true here. I talk to man after man who has been with his matelot for years on end, and they still care for one another and share all things."

"I honestly do not know if that is a nature of men being with men or of the life we lead in the West Indies," I said. "Though sharing all aspects of one's life with another does seem to play a part. May I ask you something?" He appeared curious but nodded his assent. "What are your feelings toward Tom?"

He frowned and would not meet my eyes. "Nothing has ever occurred."

"I am not suggesting it has," I said quickly. "I am merely curious." Though less curious now that he had defended their behavior first and not offered the common answers: he is my friend, brother, what have you. So he had entertained thoughts on the matter.

"He does not love me," Dickey said.

"Ah," I said sympathetically. "That is unfortunate, as you have so much history together."

"Aye, history," he snorted. "The older we got, the more he pursued the ladies, and the more incidents I had to help him escape. I am truly tired of it."

"Then that answers my question; and I believe we have reached a point where it would be advantageous to tack, as the wind seems to have played out a bit."

Thankfully, Dickey and one of the sailors told me what to do at the helm, and Dickey and Gaston directed the other men in bringing us around and setting the yards and the like, as we switched from close-hauled to starboard to close-hailed to port in order to continue working our way up the prevailing northeasterly wind. Our course would eventually take us between Cuba and Jamaica, and into the Windward Passage to reach Tortuga on the northern shore of western Hispaniola. At the moment, we were presumably south of the Cayman Islands we had careened on, and west of Jamaica.

During this maneuver, Belfry appeared; and seeing all was well, kept silent and went in search of a cup of chocolate. The cook was not available, and Belfry found himself manning the cookfire to heat water. Dickey and Gaston continued to help with the sails; and so the morning proceeded with those of us who were conscious doing what was necessary to keep the ship afloat until the rest recovered sufficiently to function. The decks were not swabbed and stoned until afternoon, and I hoped the wood had not taken the heat badly in the interim.

Striker appeared during my seventh tack, and was quite amused as I did my part to bring her around smartly.

"You may have missed your calling," he said.

"I had a calling?" I asked.

"Perhaps. What do you know of emeralds?"

"Bloody Hell," I said. "I can judge them a little but not rate them, as I have seen a good deal of jewelry containing them but not fashioned it or bought it. What are your concerns?"

"How and when to divide them. They are not all equal in value. We did find several smaller boxes inside the chest containing the best of the lot, and I feel them to be worth a fortune if we could find a buyer for them. I do not think we can sell them in the New World and receive anything near their value, though. And I do not think anyone on Tortuga or even Port Royal can give us half their value in a lump sum. And if we hand them out to the men, the tavern keeps will underrate them to such a degree the men will be robbed while drunk. Not that I can prevent that with any of them, anyway. Obviously the matter will go to a vote; but I wanted another opinion as to the best course of action so that we may convince them of it," he said quietly.

"All very valid concerns, and I see the dilemma clearly. Let us think on it. Am I to understand that the booty has never been comprised of gems before?"

He nodded.

"Is there any amongst us who knows more of gems than I?"

"I will ask about," he said, and went to do so.

While he was at that, a sailor in the rigging shouted a sighting. Striker was soon on the quarterdeck again. I could barely see a speck on the horizon.

"She's alone," he said, "or appears to be, unless she's traveling with another vessel well to windward. And she's northbound and reaching. I can't make her colors. Let us get a bit closer."

We were close-hauled to starboard again, and the mystery ship was off our starboard bow. I could not turn into the wind to bring us closer, and a tack would take us the other way. I supposed I could turn to parallel her course so that we were also reaching northbound, but I was hesitant.

"Let us wake the Bard," I suggested.

Striker regarded me quizzically, and then apparently realized I was not normally at the helm.

"What a good idea." He bounded down the stairs to knock on the Bard's cabin door.

The Bard took one look at the situation through sleep-bleary eyes, and told me to turn and parallel her course. Then he started yelling for a new trim of the sails. Once this was accomplished and we were running sideways to the wind to match the other ship's speed, he began to angle us slowly toward her by degrees. It would be a while before we closed, but we would reach her by evening, unless she ran from us. The only way she could gain speed to do so would be to turn with the wind, and that would just bring her closer. The Bard said a good man at the helm could escape us, though.

The other ship was a two-masted brigantine with a square-rigged foremast and a fore-and-aft-rigged main. She was low and fast-looking, with the longer lines of the *North Wind* or the *Josephine*, with no forecastle to speak of and a low aft-castle, probably comprising only a quarterdeck above cabins set partially below the main deck. The Bard said she had a shallow draft; but she seemed to be holding course quite steadily – without listing to leeward, even with a strong wind on her beam – and from that, he surmised she probably had a goodly keel, much as the *North Wind* had possessed. Striker estimated her at one hundred and fifty tons. This was meaningless to me until Striker said the *Mayflower* was a two hundred ton vessel and the *North Wind* had been around a hundred tons.

By the time we were close enough to see her flying English colors, all of our men were on deck and watching. There was a little disappointment in this, as a lone ship would have been easy prey. However, her being one of ours was cause for celebration as well. No one recognized her as sailing from Port Royal, though, and none of the French who knew ships, which Gaston did not, knew her from Tortuga. We came on to her anyway, to hail and give greeting, and at least find out who she was. To insure there was no confusion, Striker ordered the Union Jack added to our plain Jolie Rouge on the mastheads.

Soon we noted that she was not slowing to meet us, and she had a number of men aloft. The Bard said she would run and prepared accordingly. The rest of us speculated as to why she would do such a thing, and threw the rusty cannon overboard to lighten us for the chase.

The Bard was ready; and when the brig turned slightly toward us to run on a broad reach, he did the unthinkable and tacked back to starboard, so that we were running toward her distant wake. The brig's captain saw his chance, or so he thought, and he turned full toward our old course to run with the wind. The Bard laughed and brought us around to starboard to do the same, so that for a while we had our stern to her. Then we were running with her and a bit ahead, and closing the angle nicely.

"I would suggest relieving ourselves of any other cannon we are not particularly fond of, whether they be rusty or not," the Bard called to Striker.

Our captain shrugged. "That will leave us well down."

"This will not be a battle of cannon," the Bard scoffed.

The men began to heave the remainder of our cannon overboard. I laughed and commented to Gaston, "I hope the brig is watching, so that she can witness how friendly we are, to throw our cannon over just to greet her."

He found this amusing.

The brig did not take our reduction in armaments as a sign of peace, and ran scared yet again. She turned away from us on a broad reach, so that she still had the wind; and she widened the distance between us. Once again the Bard was amused and ready. We took the wind on the beam and cut across her wake, so that now we were fully windward of her, even though the distance between the ships was growing. We even overshot her by a bit. Then our Master of Sail turned us to run with the wind down upon her. The brig could lay about all she wanted and not escape us. All she could hope to do was outrun us. Apparently she had the ability to do so, as she proved to be faster than the *Mayflower*. Then we realized all we could hope to do was not lose her, until something changed to allow us to get within range of our muskets at least.

Striker took a reading off the afternoon sun, and those of us on the quarterdeck looked at the chart. We were on a latitude with the Caymans, and heading due west into them and a setting sun. Striker and the Bard conferred. We could not blunder through a small chain of islands at full sail in the dark. Neither could the brig. She would either slow and fight, or she would change course to swing north around them. If she continued to run, and we lost her in the dark, we could presumably find her in the morning – unless she did something truly drastic in the night, such as drop anchor and let us sail by. The Bard did not think her master that clever, as he had been quite predictable so far.

"In the name of contrariness," I said, "we could let her go and sail on with what we have, a bird in hand and all."

Several sets of eyes glared at me.

"There is a principle at stake here," Striker stated, quite emphatically.

"I want that ship," The Bard said with equal conviction. "The bastard at her helm cannot sail her, and she deserves better."

"And she could be transporting manure," I said with amusement.

They shrugged in unison.

I saw no reason to argue. We were not terribly low on provisions, and we did want another ship. The men were incredibly enthusiastic about the chase, as the taking of the galleon had been a bit anticlimactic for them. I was weary, and found my matelot on the quarterdeck, and we napped in companionable silence.

Gaston gently shook me awake at dusk. I looked about and saw the brig between us and the setting sun.

"She decided to fight," Gaston said. "She is flying Spanish colors now."

"Truly?"

In my limited understanding of naval engagements, once two ships decide to fight, they endeavor to outmaneuver one another in order to best bring their primary armament, their cannon, to bear. Being buccaneers, and no longer having cannon, this would not be a concern. We had a good seventy musket, and they could be aimed in any direction with great alacrity. The Bard only needed to maneuver to keep us away from the brig's guns for a single run at her. And we were still to windward.

The brig's captain was apparently convinced we would run alongside her for a broadside. Of course, like a true buccaneer, the Bard set us directly to the brig's stern. I readied weapons; but Gaston and I were as far from the impending action as we could be, and Cudro had an abundance of men champing at the bit to board.

"There will be wounded, and I will need your help," Gaston said.

I looked to the weapon-wielding mob at the bow wistfully. I had not realized being the matelot of a surgeon might entail being a surgeon's assistant. I was not afraid of rent flesh, as long as it was not my own; it was the oft-screaming men who bore it that would disturb me.

Our forecastle was well over the brigantine's quarterdeck, and our men cleared most of the resistance with musket fire well in advance of boarding. Then they jumped down to swarm over the hapless prey. The brig had not been manned with marines, and she had maybe thirty men. She was ours within minutes. Very few of the Spaniards lived, and we did not lose a man though we had four wounded, only one of which was critical.

Two of the wounded had glass in their feet, a thing I sympathized with greatly. The other man had a cutlass slash to his arm. As even more proof that we were very much in the eye of the Fates of late, the worst wound had been delivered to Dickey, who had insisted on boarding. Pete carried him back to us. We were already tending the arm gash. Gaston took one look at the hole in Dickey's chest, and told me to bind the arm wound tightly until he could return to it. We got the other men up along the rail, and someone found a bottle of rum for them on the brig. They drank and chatted through pain-gritted teeth. We labored to save Dickey's life.

The shot had entered Dickey's chest and lodged in his ribs. Dickey was thankfully unconscious when Pete arrived with him. Gaston dug the lead ball out easily enough by bending two of the back ribs, but then he grew concerned about the lung. Blood frothed every time Dickey breathed, and it trickled out of him in a steady stream between those breaths. Gaston broke two of Dickey's front ribs, and I held them aside while my matelot explored the wound from the new angle. He pronounced the lung grazed and probably bruised. There was little to be done, but it might not be fatal. Gaston pushed the ribs back into place and sewed the holes closed.

We covered him with a blanket, and left Tom to hold his hand, pray, and watch his breathing for any sign of change. Gaston took the rum bottle from the other three wounded men and finished it off, much to their chagrin. Then we patched them up. They had all witnessed the work on Dickey, and they were respectful and cooperative patients, other than complaining about the rum.

When we finished, Gaston checked on Dickey, and I sat on the steps to the quarterdeck. Striker saw me there, and strode up with a wide grin that quickly disappeared when he saw our wounded friend.

"How is he?"

I shrugged. "He is not bleeding as he was before. Whether he will live is anyone's wager."

"Cudro said he made a good account of himself, until a man hiding down a hatch shot him."

"That is usually the way of such things. Wounds are rarely well-received or expected. How is the brig?"

"She's a beauty. Not a Barbados sloop, but a fine craft nonetheless. The Bard is quite pleased."

"And was she loaded with manure?"

"Nay, wool, cotton, and leather. And salted mutton." Striker shook his head and grimaced.

"Who the Devil has sheep in the tropics?"

Their records list several Terra Firma ports. She was heading to Havana to sell her goods on an unofficial basis."

"So more Spanish smugglers?"

"Aye."

"So now what, Captain? I know you want the ship, but is she not a prize now owned by all?"

"Now there will be a truly inspired division of the booty." Striker grinned. "I will need you and your matelot's assistance in the matter."

I was not alarmed, as I was curious and thought the Gods seemed to be smiling upon us.

Tortuga

August
1667

VII

Twenty-Four

Wherein We Venture to Tortuga

The brigantine was named *Maria*. Cudro, as was his duty as quartermaster, took command of her to sail to Tortuga. The Bard sent his best man to pilot her; and he would have sent Tom as well, but the young man refused to leave Dickey's side. The rest of the buccaneers were left to decide for themselves upon which ship they chose to sail to Tortuga. As Gaston needed to stay with Dickey, we would remain on the *Mayflower*. Unfortunately, this left us in a bit of a predicament, as the five people with the most interest in the brig, namely Striker, Pete, the Bard, Gaston and myself, were not on her. Cudro and his men, and Hastings and his cronies, were.

I stood on the quarterdeck and watched men transfer their gear with alarm. I noted my concerns to the Bard.

"Perhaps we should send Julio, Davey, Liam and Otter to protect our interests," I said. "But in the possible event of Cudro or Hastings deciding to strike out on their own, I would not wish to lose good friends."

"You truly trust Cudro so little?" The Bard asked.

"Aye, nay, I do not know. Hastings I do not trust. Cudro, I simply dislike."

"Why?"

"He once used my matelot poorly; but they have since reached a state of truce, and Cudro vows he had reason for his ire."

Striker joined us and I relayed my concerns to him. He regarded me as if I were daft.

"We will see them on Tortuga. The booty stays aboard this ship."

I had not thought of that. In all the excitement of getting a new ship, I had forgotten the silver and emeralds. Then I recalled he had mentioned a plan of some sort.

"What is this plan you have?"

"We will go below and discuss it once they are sailing safely alongside," Striker said.

"On a leash of greed, or at the very least, need," I said.

We moved Dickey into the steerage cabin Cudro had occupied and placed him on the floor. Dickey lying flat upon a surface was in better keeping with his health and breathing, and certainly less painful with his mangled ribs, than bending him up in a hammock. Tom moved in with him.

Soon both vessels were on our original course, beating our way up to pass north of Jamaica and into the Windward Passage. Gaston and I retired to the aft cabin with bowls of mutton stew. Pete and Striker were already there. After leaving Belfry at the helm, the Bard joined us.

"Are we all in agreement as to wanting that brig?" Striker asked.

"I am curious," I said. "What is the usual course of events upon capturing a prize? I know the Admiralty Court if we sail back to Port Royal. But what does that entail?"

The four of them frowned at me, and Striker shook his head. "Lord, Will, I keep thinking you have been amongst us far longer."

"As do I, as I feel I have been upon the sea forever, yet it has only been a mere four interminable months." I grinned.

"And not all of that has been at sea," the Bard said. "We should not even count you a sailor."

"He is not a sailor, he is a fliebuster," Gaston said.

"And a boucanier," I added.

"The course of things is that a prize is sailed into Port Royal and surrendered to the Admiralty Court as being salvaged from the Spaniards. They are given an amount of time to sail in and claim her. Then she is put up for auction. The proceeds of which are split between the men of the ship that took her, after the court takes a percentage for the Crown of course. Now, the captain or the quartermaster who took her could be the only bidders, and thus they merely buy out the other men's shares and give the Crown its share."

"Surely you jest," I said.

They laughed.

"So, if the *Mayflower* had not been the only ship Bradley and all of you survivors arrived on, it would have been subject to this?"

The Bard and Striker nodded.

"And, I gather, so would this brig if we sailed into Port Royal. What of Tortuga?"

"They will not ask," Gaston said. "We will be selling cargo and spending money."

"That is decent and considerate of them," I said. "So where does that leave the ownership of both vessels?"

"The *Mayflower* belongs to the men who shed blood to take her; however, she is nominally considered to be Bradley's, as he was captain at the time," the Bard said. "The brig belongs to all of the men of the *Mayflower* for this voyage. If we were to continue to sail with her and the *Mayflower* together, she would be manned by whoever wished it and have an elected captain. We would do well not to sail into Port Royal for a bit, yet; or if we did, it would behoove us to do so with a mostly French crew and the ability to claim we bought her or the like."

"But... Some of us wish to own her," I said.

There were nods all around.

"How is that accomplished? Do we buy out the other men's interest?"

"Precisely," Striker said with a grin. "The same as if she were up for auction, except there will only be one set of bidders and the Crown gets none of it."

I thought of all the treasure on this voyage that the Crown would see none of. "What will Modyford, or for that matter Morgan and Bradley, think when eventually we return with two ships, no cargo, and wealthy buccaneers?"

"That we cheated the Crown," Striker said.

I chuckled. "And how do you intend to address that matter?"

"We will give them a bit of something and lie about the true amounts," Striker said.

"So we will bribe them."

"Aye. Do you take issue with it?"

"Me, bribery? Never. I have always said the fastest way to a man's heart is a well-greased palm."

They laughed.

"Aye, but I will not go that far to appease them," Striker said.

"I meant money, you dog." I grinned. "So you intend that we should buy the other men out of the brig. How will we go about that? You mentioned our cooperation earlier."

"How much did you spend on provisions?" Striker asked.

I nodded as I saw his plan. "We have receipts for one hundred and seventy pounds; you have a like amount for sails and other items for this ship – which means we are already due at least three hundred pounds from the booty in recompense, in addition to our shares. The brig is worth what?"

"Four hundred pounds or so."

"Truly, only that?"

They all nodded.

I shrugged. "So we get the men to agree on a price, and then we use the receipts and our shares against it, and we have a ship and they still have all their shares. And then, of course, Bradley gets the *Mayflower* returned to him. Am I correct?"

"You possess a keen intellect for grasping a situation," Striker said.

"In addition to that, I say we take the largest of the emeralds for bribing Modyford. As we have discussed, we can't sell them for their value. In the end, when he sells them in England he will probably recoup far more than the ten percent due the Crown. But if we cannot get their true value they may as well be rocks to us anyway. And he will be happy in that he will not have to share them with the Crown."

"Aye, I can see that. What of the cargo on the brig? Sell it and divide it? And what of the rest of the emeralds? I believe you were going to attempt to locate a man amongst us who knows more of gems than I. But then I believe you were distracted by the appearance of the brig."

Striker nodded. "I remembered to ask about a little as we gave chase, but no one came forth. I believe we are on your own."

"Well, at the very least we should set about sorting them."

"During the day, on deck, so that none accuse us of pocketing any."

I shrugged. "They will be easier to sort in the light of day."

I looked about the table and my eyes fell upon the Bard. "Not to be rudely inquisitive, but were you planning on being an owner, or did you simply wish to sail this new ship?"

He shrugged. "I have no money invested in this voyage, as you two do to put against her value. I do have an extra share as Master of Sail. I do have a goodly amount tucked away in Port Royal. It will depend on whether the four of you wish to have an extra partner or no. And, though I know you will harbor misgivings, I know Cudro is also interested in her."

We all sat in thought.

"DoNa'LikeVotin'," Pete said. He looked at all of our quizzical expressions and shrugged. "EveryManHavin'ASayBeFair. ButAGroup O'MenBeAsDumbAsSheep. SixMen Captain MasterO'Sail Quartermaster Surgeon." He had counted off the four positions on his fingers; and now he looked at me and then his hands, where he had two more fingers cocked, and he sighed. "An'WhatEverItIsWillAn'MeBe. IfThereBeSixO'Us An'ItBeArShip ThenNoElections WeGiveTheMenASayWhenWeWant WeDoNotLikeAMan ThenWeDoNotSailWith'Im. Control LikeChessPieces WeBeTheImportantOnes TheyBePawns."

I agreed with him, and I found that vexing. There was still a little of Rucker's voice left within me saying that democracy was the best form of government. Unfortunately, my years of experience since his idealized tutelage had taught me all too well that not all men are educated enough to make their own decisions, much less decisions for others. Additionally, most men are sheep, even here where they are well-armed. As long as men were free to come and go and no one was forced under anyone's rule, I felt a benevolent monarchy served the best interests of any group. An oligarchy was a little more troublesome, but I was sure we could manage it. We needed men, and if men were to want to serve with us, they must be treated well and fairly. Therefore their interests were protected by ours. And they would be well-armed pawns, and not easy to force to anything truly against their will.

We would be six wolves, or rather four wolves and two centaurs, with as many sheep as we could pack on the brig. And some of those sheep would undoubtedly be wolves in wool suits. What Pete proposed was no different from what we had now, except for it involving less uncertainty and need for currying favor.

"I concur," I added to the general nodding of heads.

I met Gaston's eyes and knew we both wished to discuss the matter in private, though he had publicly agreed to Pete's proposal, just as I had. I gathered it stirred thoughts in him similar to mine. It made for other interesting issues, as well.

"Pete and I get titles, though."

"Aye," The Bard agreed. "You can be the purser."

There was laughter all around.

I sighed. "If I am correct, that would make me in charge of victualing."

"And cargo, and booty, and the selling of same, and the sharing of same," Striker said.

"All right, then, I can see where that would be useful. And Pete?"

"Strictly speaking," the Bard said, "he is not an able seaman; and I cannot see him as bo'sun. He is also not a gunner or a carpenter. In the Navy he could be a lieutenant, even the first lieutenant, essentially the first officer on a merchant ship."

"FirstMatelot," Pete laughed.

"Hold," I said. "Pete, please take no offense, as I mean you none. At this time, if something were to happen to Striker, what would occur? Prior to this meeting."

"If it is a matter of command on land or during battle, then Cudro is still quartermaster and the command passes to him," Striker said. "If we were about to go into combat or something arose prior to Tortuga, the first thing we would do is hold an election to choose a new quartermaster for this vessel. If we are at sea and it not be a matter of battle, then the Bard takes command until an election is held."

That was as I had remembered from the articles. "If Pete were first officer, he would supercede that, correct?"

They nodded.

"Pete, what would you do if something were to happen to Striker? After you have done everything in your power to preserve any life he had left, meted out revenge on any who dared harm him, and railed against God?"

Everyone was quiet as my words sank home. Striker looked to Pete. "He is right; you cannot be next to command if something should happen to me, because you will get the men killed out of anger or grief."

Pete nodded soberly. "ItBeTrue."

Striker was regarding Gaston and me. "If I had my druthers, I would choose Gaston as my second in command; but the men will not follow him, and he's our surgeon."

"Thank you," Gaston said sincerely.

Striker nodded and pointed to me. "You, however, would have the support and advice of every man at this table; and even if you know little, you learn fast and react well. So I feel you should be the first officer."

Gaston, the Bard, and even Pete were nodding in agreement. Having been raised a wolf, I knew I would sleep well at night in the bowers of this scenario. I would be in control if the person I chose to place my trust in was taken from me, or rather us. I did not truly want to be responsible, as I knew what that entailed; but knowing I would have a say in my own destiny and the destiny of others in a crisis was reassuring to me.

"I will accept." I chided Striker with a grin, "However, you had best keep your head about your shoulders, as I do not wish to command."

"You will have duties," Striker said.

The Bard chuckled, "The same that he has already assumed."

"That echoes my thoughts exactly," Striker said. "You are already acting as first officer."

"It is his breeding," Gaston said, and grinned.

"Lord Will," Striker chuckled. "Are you sure you would rather not be captain?"

"Just because a thing is prevalent in a man's nature does not make him enamored of it. And I feel it is less in the breeding than in the training."

"IBePurser?" Pete asked.

"Nay," Striker and the Bard said in unison.

Pete's head slumped down upon his arm on the table, and he worried at a knot in the wood with his thumb nail. "LikedItBetterWhenYouBe Quartermaster. ThisBeDull."

Striker grimaced and tousled his hair. "I am sorry, Petey, I truly am."

"NayIBeAnArse." He sat up and shook his head. "YaWaitedALongTime."

"It will be more to your liking this winter," Striker said. "We will sail with Morgan and raid on land, and you and I will be in the thick of it as always."

This seemed to cheer Pete a little.

Later that night, Gaston and I stood at the aft railing, with our chins upon our arms and our eyes upon our wake. "I did not come to the West Indies to command ships or buccaneers," I said.

"I did not wish to become a surgeon for the same."

"Then what the Devil are we doing?"

"I always wanted friends. I feel I have treated the few who have tried to befriend me poorly. Now we have friends who need us to do these things. I feel they would do much for us, so why should we deny them?"

"Oui, oui," I sighed. "That is reasoning I guess I have oft followed, not always to good result. I did not intend to become an assassin in Florence, or a thief in Paris, or a duelist in Geneva. I have a habit of falling in with people who seem fond of me and whose opinion I value and... In that regard I am not a leader at all. I find ways of facilitating other's needs. I find myself going with the herd, assessing its needs and then insuring they are met."

"Perhaps that is what centaurs do," he said somewhat wistfully.

"Are we maturing and accepting the yoke of responsibility?"

He sighed, a long pronounced sound, and I was sure he had expelled every iota of breath in his body. "Oui."

"Then what the Devil are we doing?"

He chuckled.

The next day, we counted silver and sorted emeralds. Julio and a man named Krahe proved to have fine eyes for gems. We removed all the stones from the chest, and came to see that they were not all cut. They quickly became two piles, faceted and not. Then we separated the cut ones according to perceivable value, based upon the related factors of their size, color, clarity and how flawed they were. I quickly realized just how much I had learned about gems in the courts. We soon had little piles spread along the deck. They ranged from the truly fine stones of the largest size, least flaws, deepest color, and greatest clarity, to the small, pale, flawed, and cloudy gems.

This done, we assessed the uncut rocks. I had heard many times that the cutting and shaping of gems was an art and a stone could be found or made in the process. Some stones were flawed inside and easily shattered; and a deficient jeweler could ruin a good stone quite easily. So even though some of the hunks we regarded might have yielded gems of impressive size, it was unlikely they could be cut of a piece to form only one gem. And, of course, uncut they held more potential than value. The Spanish had jewelers in the New World; we did not.

The silver was easier. Striker and others had long since ascertained that we had exactly thirty-five thousand two hundred and eighty-seven pieces of eight. All eyes were now on the gems. I explained my concerns in assessing value for the larger uncut hunks to Striker, in front of all the men aboard the *Mayflower*. I ended with, "If a man were to take these to England, they would have more value to him than someone attempting to sell them here."

"And who would do that?" someone asked.

"Modyford," I snapped.

Striker explained that we had to bribe the governor with something, and the uncut emeralds looked to be our best bet because we could not get full value for them. The men seemed to understand this, and any grumbling ceased. It was agreed by those present that Modyford could have the largest of the uncut hunks. Of course, this would need to go to a vote amongst all the men when we divided the treasure; but for now, the matter was resolved.

I had been thinking on how best to tackle the problem of value during the entire sorting. I could not tell how much the gems were worth in Port Royal, or any place in Christendom. I had initially been baffled as to how to assign value. Then I had come upon the idea of keeping their value relative to one another and not assigning a monetary amount. So I had set about puzzling out a ranking system, wherein a certain number of lower value stones would equal one from the next rank up, and so on. Then I determined the total number of shares we required, eighty-four, and divided the stones into eighty-four equal piles based upon their ranking. Of course, the best stones were worth more than a share; and so I judged them at two shares apiece, and figured they could go to matelots or men like the Bard or Cudro, who received more than a single share.

When this was accomplished, it was getting on to late afternoon, and we discovered we did not have eighty-four sacks to put them in. Striker looked upon the piles and quickly called a halt to the ships; and we roped them together, and distributed the shares then and there.

First came a great deal of discussion and voting concerning the brig. Striker had cleverly counted out the amount we would receive for the expenses and such, and was able to show them how much would not be distributed to them if we did not buy the brig from them. This swayed many men.

When all was said and done, the brig belonged to Striker and Gaston in exchange for the receipts and all of our shares of the silver, the emeralds, and the cargo. Even without the emeralds, I guessed we bought the *Maria* for over six hundred pounds. We managed to keep Pete's and my shares from the matter; and thus, as pairs of matelots, we came out with some money beyond the ship. We had already discussed ways in which the Bard and Cudro could be allowed to buy their way into the endeavor later. Striker had pulled Cudro aside as soon as the boats were lashed and explained the matter to him; thus he aided us greatly in swinging the votes.

Every man received about one hundred and five pounds in silver. After this was parceled out, everyone except Striker and Gaston drew lots and chose a pile of emeralds. Tom chose for Dickey. I drew a low number and happily picked a pile I had been eyeing.

Once it was all done, I stumbled to our cabin to lie down, as I felt as exhausted as if I had been in battle all day. My bemused matelot found me just as I had drifted off, and I was almost annoyed with him.

He pulled the emeralds from my pocket and arrayed them on my chest. They ranged from a small faceted sliver to a large rectangular gem with few facets and several flaws. All possessed excellent color and vibrancy, though.

"Do these have special value?" he asked.

"They match your eyes." I showed him one by one. "This is the color of your eyes in sunlight, this in candlelight, this, when you are angry, this is sad, this is in moonlight, and this is when you are in the shade and calm."

He doffed his weapons and crawled into the hammock next to me. "Which do you prefer?"

I held up the darkest green. It was roughly the size and shape of my thumbnail. "This, as it is what I see when we make love."

He studied the stone. "My eyes are truly this green?" he asked. I nodded. He shrugged and regarded me. "I suppose. I am oft amazed at how blue your eyes are. You rival the sky in sunlight."

I smiled, as I had not realized he considered such things.

"If we ever find sapphires, you can show me," I said.

He shrugged. "I know little of gems, such as their names and types. I do know that no gem I have seen matches the color of your eyes." He scooped up the emeralds and returned them to a small cloth bag. "We will have to hide my eyes somewhere, as I would not want to sell them now."

I chuckled. "Non, they are quite precious." Then I sighed, as somehow the laughter had drained me again.

He regarded me curiously and touched my forehead. "Are you well?"

"Oui, I am greatly tired, though. Sorting the stones was a most engaging labor. I truly did not realize how much time passed. I do not think I have eaten or drunk all day, and then there were the hours of arguing with the stakes being very high indeed. I feel wrung out, and I know I shall be seeing stones in my sleep."

"Poor Will, and here I am showing them to you again."

"I did not mind."

He left and returned with water, fruit and a little hot roast beef. I wolfed the food down and drank until my belly sloshed. He sat in a chair next to me and watched, more the physician than my lover.

"Do not look so serious," I chided. "I am fine."

"I was thinking that you have only been here four months. You have not seasoned yet. We must keep you well clear of swamps and bogs, and I want you to remain in the ocean breezes as much as possible." He shrugged. "So I will not be showing you the Haiti while we are on Île de la Tortue, even though it is just across the channel."

"I am sure we will return there and you can share it with me someday."

He nodded distractedly. "I do not know if you will see it as I did. I do not know what I would share of it." He frowned.

"I do not think you would see Florence as I did, though I am sure you would appreciate it, especially the art. I am sure I will see something of beauty on the Haiti."

"I know. But it is not a place of beauty but of healing for me. In that, it was very private. I would share that with you; but it is not so much the place, but what it means to me."

"Thank you," I whispered. I thought on things he had said of his time on the Haiti before we sailed. "It appears we will be seeing your Doucette after all."

He sighed and shrugged.

"Do you feel he will be happy to see you?"

"I imagine so," Gaston shrugged. "I imagine he will be delighted, especially when I return with a patient. But there is always my concern that I have abused our friendship, such as it was, one too many times; and that he will not welcome me with open arms. Even if that is the case, I am sure he will welcome Dickey, and his hospital will provide the best place for Dickey to recuperate. And I am sure he will give me my money if I ask."

"So he is still holding the money your father sent for you?" I asked.

"Oui, I made loan of it to him to run the hospital. He had barely dipped into it, when last I asked of it; and he returns what he can when he is well paid."

I sighed. "I feel as if I will be meeting your father in some way. Which gives me confusing emotions, as your father is someone I think I wish to kill." I paused and considered him. "When last you talked of this, you said they likewise shared a connection in your heart."

Gaston nodded thoughtfully. "Oui, I have expended great thought on the matter. I believe I am enamored with living in defiance of my father. And Doucette, in acting like my father, attracted my ire as if he were the original target of it. I have been a disappointment to both."

"I understand. In a way I had two fathers myself; and I disappointed both, in that their designs for me were at cross purposes to one another. Will I be an added disappointment to Doucette?"

"I do not know. He was the one I first lied to about my inability to function. He always wanted to set one of the whores upon me, to prove my health in that regard. I wanted none of that. They were always such sad and ugly women that even if my manhood had been interested, I would have never allowed myself. He has very definite notions about men and sexuality. He is thoroughly of the mind that men never truly favor other men, as it is not within the nature of the design and function of our sexual organs. He said men only lie with other men to fulfill a need of the mind when women are not available. It is an act of desperation and proof of what marvelous and adaptive creatures we are."

I raised an eyebrow. "Well, that has not been my experience of the matter."

"Truly?" he teased and joined me in the hammock, coming astride me and then lying atop me so that I was fully covered by him. "Nor mine."

My manhood informed me it had not exerted itself at all during the day and would very much like to do so now.

"Non, wait," Gaston said. "I forgot. You are tired. I am sorry." Grinning, he began to push himself off me. I pulled him to me with such force that I nearly winded us both. I slid my hands down his ribs and waist until I could clutch his buttocks and grind him against me. His eyes widened a little, and he quickly kissed me with a fervor approaching passion.

Tortuga proved to be a lush, green, mountainous hump; and I could see why it was referred to as the Turtle or Turtle Island in

every language except English. The small island was separated by a
two-league-wide channel from the rocky coast of the Haiti. The port,
Cayonne, was a deep and good-sized bay, well guarded by a fort on a
rocky peak in its mouth. A mountain rose several hundred feet above
the town.

There were three ships at the wharfs and one anchored in the
bay. We were pleased to see that one of them was Peirrot's ship, the
Josephine. We anchored our ships near her, and leaving Cudro and the
Bard in command of the respective vessels, the rest of our cabal went
ashore in the longboat. A small crowd had gathered for our landing,
and we were quickly greeted by a representative of Governor D'Oregon.
Gaston translated for Striker, and we soon had a number of merchants
happy to bid on the brigantine's cargo. Gaston had been correct. They
were happy to see us and would be all too happy to take our men's
money.

My matelot inquired of his friend Doucette and the hospital, and was
assured all was well. Striker rowed out to the brig in another longboat
with the merchants. He no longer needed us, as Cudro would translate
for him once they were aboard. We returned to the *Mayflower* to retrieve
Dickey and our gear.

Dickey was doing well, in that he was not dead and he had woken
two days after the injury. His pain had been great, and Gaston had
begun giving him laudanum; and this had left him in a stupor. Tom
was always at this side, except when he had been called to duty on
deck; and then Gaston had watched over the injured man. Dickey once
fevered for over a day, and Gaston was gravely concerned; but that
abated, and Dickey's color and breathing improved. We were not pleased
about the necessity of moving him, but Gaston was sure his friend's
hospital and care were best for Dickey. Tom came with us.

Cayonne did not appear much like Port Royal, except for the nature
and dress of its denizens; and there were differences even there. It was
a little place hemmed in by hills, whereas Port Royal was surrounded
by water. There were the same types of buildings: shops, a blacksmith,
sailmakers, taverns, brothels, houses, warehouses and the like, all
jumbled together. However, where Port Royal looked as if someone had
taken an English shire and set it on sand, Cayonne appeared more like
seaside villages I had seen near Florence and along the south of France.
The buildings were designed lengthwise, so that they were one room in
depth, with balconies and windows or walls of slatted doors that could
be opened to allow the breezes through. And where in Port Royal the
townspeople dressed as they would in England, here the merchants
and others were sometimes difficult to discern from the buccaneers.
The whole exuded a naturalness and comfort that Port Royal lacked.
Cayonne and its inhabitants were not clinging to the pretense that they
were somewhere else.

Doucette's hospital was in a large house next to the Catholic church.
Gaston told me his friend worked with the Jesuits to help the needy and

they were all close friends. I was not pleased at this. I had a distrust of anything Catholic and especially the Jesuit, as like any educated man, I had been raised to fear the Inquisition. Gaston assured me priests were easy to shoot, as they were seldom armed; and thus in the West Indies, all but the Spanish ones were quite docile. I found this amusing.

We entered the courtyard, and Gaston led us into a dormitory of sorts. Two of the ten beds were occupied with ailing men. Tom and Gaston set the stretcher across two other cots. I happily relieved myself of all of our gear and set it upon another. A boy hurried to meet us, followed by a young priest in a Jesuit's cassock. Gaston told them his name and asked them to bring Doucette. The priest appeared confused, and earnestly asked Gaston a number of questions about Dickey. The boy's eyes widened with surprise, though, and he scurried away.

A minute later, a man entered with the boy and a young woman in tow. Gaston had not described Dominic Doucette, and I had pictured a kindly older gentleman. Instead I found us confronted with a virile man, who appeared possibly only a decade older than I, with odd, long, thick white hair worn in a ponytail, and a handsome countenance despite a heavy brow and nose. His pale blue eyes missed nothing, though he seemed to spare Tom and myself little attention. To my surprise, he ignored Gaston as well, and bent over Dickey. Without even a greeting, Gaston told of the wound and what he had done for the man. Doucette nodded thoughtfully and raised the bandages to examine him.

As they were thus engaged, I took a moment to study the young woman. Once she had caught my eye, it was hard to pull my gaze away. She was a lovely, lithesome girl with long, mahogany hair and fair skin. Seen from the left, she was beautiful, with finely sculpted features. Yet the right side of her face was marred by an ugly scar that had split her cheek in two and ran from her temple to the corner of her mouth, which was now permanently puckered in a smirk. Her deep green eyes flicked from mine, and I realized I was staring. I forced my eyes away and murmured an apology.

Gaston and Doucette were still discussing Dickey as they eased him off the stretcher and onto one of the beds. So I approached the young lady and addressed her in French.

"I did not mean to discomfort you. Allow me to present myself, I am called Will." I bowed.

She flushed a little and curtsied awkwardly.

"Madam," there was evident pride in the title, "Yvette Doucette. I know what I look like."

I winced inwardly at the shame in her words. "You are quite lovely from all angles save one."

She regarded me quizzically, and then she smiled. "Thank you."

I cocked my head toward Doucette and queried, "Your husband, perhaps?"

She nodded proudly. I responded with a respectful nod of my own. That was interesting. Gaston had not mentioned a wife.

"I am Gaston's matelot," I said and indicated him.

"Gaston?" Her eyes widened for a moment, and then she smiled and regarded him with new interest. "So that is Gabriel? We have not met. I arrived after he left."

I blinked at my matelot stupidly. Gabriel? I felt unusually stupid. Of course Gaston was not his given name. It might not even be his surname. Many of the buccaneers had a habit of taking on whatever name suited them or others; I had.

"Oui," I muttered for her benefit.

She was frowning. "He is so lucky. You cannot tell."

"What?"

"That he is scarred. Monsieur Doucette says he would not have been able to save me, if it were not for what he learned from treating Gabriel. He has said I am less scarred about my body, but I feel Gabriel is far luckier. He has no marks one can see."

I noticed she was wearing long lace sleeves. I also noticed Gaston and Doucette were no longer talking, and they were now looking to us. Doucette studied me with a dismayed frown very similar to the one Gaston wore while perusing Madam Doucette.

Monsieur Doucette sprang to his feet and stepped to the girl's side.

"This is my wife, Yvette. My dear, this is Gabriel."

"Gaston," Gaston said firmly and then nodded toward me. "That is my matelot, Will. Will, Doucette."

The dismay returned to Doucette's eyes as he regarded me. Then he smiled pleasantly and it was gone, though it was replaced by a hint of resignation.

"Pleased to meet you, I am sure." He bowed.

I returned it. "Likewise. And this is our friend, Tom..." I struggled to remember his surname. "Eaton."

Tom frowned as he did not speak a word of French, but at mention of his name after seeing an obvious introduction, he demonstrated a sufficient understanding of the situation to bow correctly.

"I hope you will all be staying," Doucette said.

Gaston nodded. "For a while."

"Excellent. We have several guest rooms upstairs." He turned to lead us.

I began to gather our gear. I explained where we were to go to Tom. He asked if he could stay with Dickey, and Gaston relayed this to Doucette, who nodded amicably. So Gaston and I followed Doucette and his wife through the courtyard, up the stairs, and along a wide balcony, to a room with a series of slatted doors for a wall and a wide window on the other side. There was a bed, desk, chair and to my amazement, a tub.

Madam Doucette noticed my delight. "I can have the boys bring water."

"Please."

She called down to the first boy and told him to fetch others and then water. Doucette was leaning on the wall, regarding Gaston, who was doffing his weapons. The physician approached my matelot and I thought that perhaps they would finally embrace; but instead, Doucette swiped at the mask about Gaston's eyes and asked, "Why do you persist in doing that?"

Gaston flinched and glared at him. "I like it and it bothers you."

Madam Doucette and I exchanged a glance and then looked elsewhere. And here I had wondered why Gaston had painted himself with the mask that morning, as he had not done so in weeks.

"I would like Yvette to see your scars," Doucette said. "I have told her much about them."

"Doucette," Madam Doucette chided softly.

Gaston heaved a resigned sigh. Doucette did not flinch from his gaze or retract his words. Gaston removed his tunic. Now I was annoyed, but I said nothing.

Madam Doucette gasped. "They are worse than mine. I am sorry."

Gaston regarded her quizzically. She began to unlace her bodice. I frowned. The boy staggered in with a large pail of water, followed by two equally burdened Negro boys. They filled the tub and the first boy announced he would bring the kettle up. I nodded acknowledgement as no one else seemed prone to.

Madam Doucette doffed her blouse; and I found myself staring at what would have been two lovely breasts if they had not been marred with long puckered scars.

"Yvette was slashed with a knife," Doucette was saying. "Thirty-three times. All fairly deep wounds, but not mortal in the usual sense; though I faced blood loss and the concerns of infection, as I did with you." He began to drone on about the treatments he had employed. Madam Doucette looked uncomfortable.

I could see Gaston struggling with his composure. I could see his hand beginning to clench and unclench. Near that hand, I noted something else that was quite shocking. There was a telltale bulge in the front of his breeches. Gaston had an erection.

I was both overjoyed and depressed.

I stepped into the midst of them and faced Doucette, with Gaston safely behind me.

"That is enough."

I was peripherally aware of Madam Doucette quickly dressing and the boy returning with the kettle. Doucette occupied the center of my attention, though. He seemed quite flummoxed that I had dared intercede, though he was not angry. His mouth opened and closed several times before he spoke.

"Why do you take issue with...?"

"Surely you dissemble," I said calmly. "Are you blind or just insensitive?"

Doucette recoiled and looked from Gaston to his wife and back again. "I meant no..."

Gaston's arm snaked around me, and I was forced to fight my own onslaught of anxiety as he pressed against me from behind. I could feel the thing I had seen; and I heard him gasp in my ear, as he must have felt it too. I wondered if he had been aware.

"You will have to excuse Will," Gaston said tightly. "He is very protective."

"I am sorry," Doucette said.

"I do not mind showing the lady that someone is more scarred than she," Gaston said. "But..."

"Non, say no more. You are correct," Doucette said. "I have been beastly." Madam Doucette hurried from the room with a small sound. With a last apologetic look to us, Doucette ran after her, pleading her name.

Gaston released me and I closed the wall of doors. Once we had privacy, I regarded him. The bulge was still there.

"Perhaps you should enjoy that while you have it," I said gently.

He shook his head and turned his back to me. "Non, it is vile."

This was quite alarming to hear. "Why is it so?"

"It is wrong."

"Oui, but why?" I moved so that I could at least see him in profile and sat on the bed. The telltale bulge was gone. He had effectively dismissed it. The very idea of that was akin to blasphemy to me, and I was disappointed.

"I am not supposed to have one in response to her. She is my friend's wife and a fellow victim and a lady and... she is not you."

His words were very sweet in content, but his agitation and mounting anger belied them. "Your reaction to her could be considered the sincerest flattery for her as your friend's wife, and for her beauty as a lady. And as for the other, you are a man, and your member obviously favors women, as most men's do. There is nothing wrong with that."

He turned to face me. His breathing had grown shallow and his eyes were filled with tears. What alarmed me the most was the spasmodic clenching of his fists.

"I dissemble," he spat. "Do not excuse my behavior until you know the depth of its depravity. It was not because she was a woman. I have seen a number of naked women, and that has not occurred."

I held up my hands in supplication. If I had thought it would calm him I would have left and let the conversation lie; but I knew we would see this through. I chose to ignore his references to depravity for the moment.

"Perhaps it has occurred now because you have been stimulated in other ways of late and your manhood has begun to wake. And... Have the other naked women been in close proximity to you, and comfortable in your nakedness? Those factors could have profound impact on your perception of the situation."

His eyes were hard. "That is not why."

"Then tell me."

"She resembled my sister. Not truly in face, but in hair and color and... body." He choked on the last word and looked away.

"Oh," I said stupidly as many things leapt into my thoughts. It would explain a great deal. It made several pieces of the puzzle slide into alignment; and I doubted my conclusive leap was on faith alone, but more on logic in light of the evidence presented.

"You would not be the first man attracted in that way to one's own kin. There have been numerous plays. All tragedies, as you well know... ." I winced at my last choice of words and he turned to me again.

"Say it," he snarled. "I cannot. Say it!"

I understood what he wanted now. "It is likely..."

I took another deep breath and rushed into it. "It is likely you bedded your sister, and that was the event that drove your father to act toward you as he did with such rage and malice."

He took a long, shuddering breath and nodded. "When I realized I had become aroused, I... It was as if a door opened for just a moment, and I saw... My sister was my angel, lying in that bed all in white."

I waited, as he seemed lost in reverie. When the tension left his shoulders I said quietly, "Gaston, it is good that you know this now. You can forgive yourself and..."

His eyes snapped to mine, and they glittered with anger – and something else.

"Non!"

I sat very still and forced myself not to look away, or even blink, until his eyes flicked from mine.

"There was more," he whispered. "I cannot see it." He regarded his slowly opening and closing hand as if he could see a thing I could not. "Blood."

I recalled every reference, no matter how slender, he had ever made concerning his sister, family, or that event. He had said his sister was dead. I was faced with a dilemma. Should I prompt him and possibly bring the last thing to light so that we could be done with the mystery once and for all? Or should I let him be? I wanted done with it.

"You said your sister died. How? Did your father...?"

"Non!" he hissed; and he was upon me, driving me back onto the bed with his fingers clawing at my mouth to close it. I did not resist. I lay quiet beneath him.

"Non, non, non," he moaned as he collapsed on my chest. I was not sure if I had an answer to my last supposition, or not. After a while, I wrapped my arms around him, and he quieted somewhat.

I pulled his fingers off my lips. They would be bruised later.

"We should use that tub," I said gently. I rubbed his back a bit, and eased him over to my side. He lay where I left him, with his eyes closed. I pressed a kiss on his temple and went to check the tub. It was fine.

His eyes were open when I returned to the bed, and he asked calmly. "Why would I do such a thing? I remember all the visits I made home, and that did not occur during any of them. If the supposition is true, then it was only that once."

"I do not know. Perhaps it did not occur and we are leaping to unwarranted conclusions." I did not believe this, even as I said it; and I could tell from his eyes he did not, either.

He shook his head. "It was her."

I nodded. "And there is more to it. I do not want you to think on it now, though. I want you to bathe, and I will trim your hair and shave you, and then perhaps you can nap for a time. That seems to set you to rights."

"I am sorry," he whispered.

I gave him a grim smile and pulled him to standing. "Do not be sorry. Do not apologize to me for things you cannot help. Though I would appreciate some contrition over things you can."

"What would you have me apologize for?" he asked earnestly as he doffed his breeches.

I could not help but look at his flaccid member and wonder a great many things. I looked away and shrugged as I led him to the tub.

"I cannot think of anything at the moment, but I am sure something will occur to me."

He sat in the warm water, and I took up a sponge to bathe him. My hand shook, and we saw it.

"Do I frighten you?" he asked.

I found myself studying my hand, watching to see if it would succumb to the tremors again.

"It is not you, precisely," I murmured. "The demon that possesses you manifests in rage and sorrow. My demon shows itself in fear and shame and sometimes melancholy. Yours just calls to mine, that is all."

"Can you blame me for nothing?" he asked.

"You blame yourself for everything already; why should I add to it?"

He sighed and leaned forward at my urging, so that I could wash his back. "What do you fear when it grips you?"

"I cannot answer that. What are you angry at when the rage grips you?"

"I see. Everything and myself."

"The fear is omnipresent, so much so that I feel I fear the fear itself. I can chase about and name things that cause it to twitch."

"Have you always possessed it, or been possessed by it? Or did it develop when...?"

"Shane brought me to it. Before that, I was merely different and haunted by the knowledge that I was never quite as I should be in anyone's eyes."

We were silent as I finished bathing and shaving him. As I trimmed his hair, he spoke.

"Will, you must not let me abuse you so," he said.

"But you do not."

He frowned. "Will, the rain is the fault of no man, yet you are not so stupid that you would stand in it if you could seek shelter. When I storm, you need to seek shelter from me."

"You asked me to never leave you; and I fear, truly and rationally, what would occur if you are left to your own designs or the mercy of others. I cannot abandon you when you need me most."

He craned his head back so he could regard me. "Then fend me off and strike me, as you did on the galleon. Believe me, I will thank you for relieving me of my consciousness when I am in that state."

"We both know I only succeeded in that endeavor because of Pete's involvement. If it had just been you and me it would have been an even match; non, not even that. I have seen you fight. You are far better than I, unless we are at each other with rapiers. I could not have struck you down by myself. If I become your enemy when you are in that state, then our demons will battle and we both may not survive."

Our eyes held for a time, until he realized the correctness of my argument; and his head sagged back on the tub in resignation. I sat back upon my heels in relief.

I continued with his hair. He began to sob bitterly.

"I am an abomination."

"Non." I held him.

"I have harmed the only people who have ever loved me."

"I do not think that makes you an abomination. You have not done these things with malice."

"How do you know?"

I had often had these arguments with myself. I knew there was no winning them. All one could do was drown them in some fashion until they passed.

"I love you, and I want you to sleep now. If you love me, you will rest." It was unfair but necessary.

He nodded meekly, and I hauled him out of the tub and dried him. I put him to bed and stroked his hair until he slept. Then I sat in the tepid water and cried.

I wondered what more the Gods wanted of us.

Twenty-Five

Wherein We Journey Through Darkest Night

We woke to a light rapping on the door. I was surprised I had dozed.

"Sirs, dinner will be served soon, and the guests are arrived," the boy said.

"Hold, hold." I had wanted something; and as I staggered to the door, I remembered. I handed him a small coin. "Please fetch me some hot water for the basin, not the tub. And a bottle of wine. And what guests?"

"The Fathers."

"Fathers? Priests?"

He nodded.

"Bring wine."

He scampered off.

"I hate priests," I said. "You cannot trust them. One errant thought at dinner under the guise of intellectual discourse, and then five years later you write a paper the Church dislikes, and suddenly those words uttered under the effects of wine and cheese are brought back to haunt you by an inquisitor. That happened to an acquaintance of mine in Vienna. He escaped with his life intact only by agreeing never to publish again."

Gaston pushed himself up to sit against the headboard. He appeared calm and a little bleary. I wanted to ask how he felt, but that would indicate there might be reason for him to feel poorly. Though I was sure he had not forgotten that afternoon, I did not want to do anything to make him dwell upon it. I crossed to the bed and embraced him.

"Wine?" he queried with a grin. "Do you need fortification before dinner in order to dine with priests, or do you feel I need to be inebriated lest I fly into a rage and butcher everyone at the table?"

"I so dearly love you," I whispered.

"Will, please do not ever stop."

"I will do my utmost not to, though you may do your utmost to convince me otherwise."

He kissed my lips gently. "Tonight, after you argue with priests, please make it all go away."

I chuckled. "I will do my utmost to thoroughly distract you."

Our kiss was interrupted by the boy's return. He had brought one of the Negro boys with him again; and they had a bottle, kettle, ewer, basin and towels. They set them all upon the desk. I thanked them and they left with happy smiles.

"Will you assist me in shaving?" I asked and uncorked the wine for a long drink.

"If you trust me with a blade at your throat," he said, only partly in jest.

"I would bare my throat for you any time," I chided gently and sat in the chair. I lie my head back and closed my eyes. He made quick work of shaving me and trimming my hair. I thought on it, as I could not speak while we were thus engaged, and found that I did trust him. Even at his darkest, I did not believe he would kill me. There was a distinct possibility he might injure me, but I did not think he would set about to take my life with malicious intent. Perhaps I was a fool, but I knew I could not live without these foolish notions; so I shoved all others aside.

We finished the wine and donned our spare clothes and favorite weapons, and looked a little less rakehell than usual. At least we appeared fairly clean and well-kempt, despite looking like buccaneers with little attire and many swords and pistols.

I did not question our arming ourselves for dinner at a friend's house. As we would be dining with priests, I found our armament comforting. I was also not surprised that Gaston reapplied the mask. I briefly considered having him paint one on me.

Thinking of his defiant behavior with Doucette reminded me of another thing. "Your name is Gabriel?" I asked.

He froze and then sighed. "Oui. Please do not call me that. It is my name no longer. Though your pronunciation is sufficiently different to..."

"Ah, I am sorry, Gah-bree-el."

"I do not like to hear that upon your lips." He frowned.

"Then I will not say it ever again. May I ask, though, is that your given name or your surname?"

"Given."

"And Doucette has used it...?"

He shook his head. "It is complicated. I knew not what else to allow him to call me, and he began to do so when I was healing. I chose to allow the familiarity to continue. I do not wish to discuss it."

"May I ask if you were named after the angel?"

"Oui," he shrugged. "But it is no matter." His look hovered betwixt imploring me to change the subject and demanding I do.

"I understand," I said sincerely. "I am sorry. I just felt the fool when they spoke of you and I did not know who they spoke of. We have never discussed your name." I shrugged apologetically. "So you view even that aspect of your life before the Line as truly dead?"

He nodded. "It is only here that I am in limbo betwixt the two."

I sighed at my stupidity yet again. "I will endeavor to anchor you to your real life here and distract you." I embraced him, and he relaxed a little. "But first indulge me a moment longer," I teased. "Why are you called Gaston?"

"That appellation was given me by a Dutchman I met on the Haiti," he sighed with a small smile. "Gaston was a name he used for Frenchmen. I think it was a mispronunciation of Gascon, and he meant it as a joke, since people from Gascony are purported to be loud braggarts."

I chuckled. "And you are anything but."

He shrugged. "The name stuck, as many names like it do amongst the Brethren. I am happy with it in that regard. It means nothing."

"It means much to me. I can not conceive of calling you anything but. It is now the name of the object of my deepest desire and greatest wonder." I nuzzled his neck.

He rolled his eyes, only to grin a moment later and kiss me deeply. I was reluctant to leave the room. Unfortunately, my stomach had needs.

Everyone was already in the dining room, but they had not been served as of yet. Doucette sat at the head of the table and watched us critically. Madam Doucette regarded us curiously from the other end. There were three priests of varying ages sitting along one side. I smiled amiably and Doucette introduced us to Fathers Pierre, Paul, and Mark. The young priest we had seen in the hospital was not among them. I noted that Tom was not among us either.

"Excuse me, our friend Tom...?"

"He speaks no French, and I believe he tried to tell me he wished to remain with your wounded friend. So I took him dinner and some books," Madam Doucette said. "He seemed content. Is that acceptable?" She appeared concerned.

"Oui, oui, I was merely curious," I assured her with a smile.

We sat opposite the priests, with Gaston to Doucette's right. A young Negress served soup. I realized we would be having a dinner of courses. This seemed in keeping with the fine pewter, white-washed walls, and delicately-carved table.

"So, Will, you are English, non?" Father Pierre asked after he finished saying grace. He seemed to be the oldest.

"Oui, I am."

"Your French is excellent, and you possess exemplary table

manners."

"For an Englishman?" I teased.

He frowned momentarily, and then smiled. "For a fliebuster."

"Ah, well, thank you. I never managed to impress my mother or my governess; yet I have never been asked to leave a table. At lease not for my table manners," I corrected quickly. Gaston chuckled beside me.

"What were you asked to leave a table for?" Doucette asked with mischievous curiosity.

"In the matter of one of the instances I cannot discuss the particulars as there is a lady present; and in the others, I believe I offended my host in some fashion, generally with the discussion of politics, religion, or some other matter that many thought I should leave well enough alone."

"She is not a la..." Father Mark, the youngest, said – and trailed off quickly with a jerk, as someone had kicked him. Father Paul, I assumed. He was next to Father Mark and appeared alarmed. Father Mark looked far more annoyed than repentant.

Everyone was quiet. Madam Doucette studied her plate. Doucette was exchanging a grave look with Father Pierre. Their heads came together, and they whispered to one another.

"Father Mark," Father Pierre said quietly when they finished, "we will speak after dinner."

The young priest appeared resigned to this, and he returned to eating with the stiff composure of someone who knows all eyes are upon him. I wondered if anything else would be said at the moment. I was appalled. Madam Doucette was still, and flushing slightly. She would not raise her eyes.

"Father Mark, is it?" I said with a jovial demeanor. "Let me explain a little to you of manners. First, if you are at a table with any woman in her own house, she is a lady. If she is your host's wife, she is a lady. And if a gentleman in your presence, who you might assume is able to acquit himself better than you in combat, says she is a lady, she is a lady. Now, I would suggest you apologize."

Father Mark frowned. "Are you threatening me, sir?"

"Oui, I believe I am. Are you feeling threatened? If not, perhaps I should renew my efforts."

"Will, you cannot threaten a priest," Father Pierre said with bemusement.

"I beg to differ," I said with an affable smile. "As long as I am willing to accept the consequences of my actions, I can threaten whomever I choose. Let me rephrase that, as there is a variable involved. I can attempt to threaten whomever I choose. The perception of whether or not they are threatened lies with the individual I mount the attempt with."

"But he is a priest," Father Pierre said. "But I forget; you are a Protestant of some variety, are you not?"

I did think before I spoke. I knew I would never be able to travel in a

Papist country again. "Non, I am an atheist."

Father Pierre blanched. The other two priests regarded me with shock. Madam Doucette's expression was one of awe; but whether this was from wonder or horror, I could not discern. Doucette and my matelot were fighting losing battles against the expression of their amusement.

I continued. "So, Father, are you implying his faith renders him incapable of fear and therefore he cannot perceive himself as being threatened? Or are you implying that the Church should prove a larger threat by far to anyone who attempts to threaten their priests?"

"Neither," Father Pierre sputtered. "He is a man of God and should be accorded respect. Apparently such a thing does not matter much to you, though."

"Non, it does not, and that is partly due to my observation that the men of God never seem to have a great deal of respect for God's other children. And if this is suitable to God, I have very little use for Him. What right does God grant Father Mark, there, to cast aspersions upon his hostess?"

"She is a whore," Father Mark said.

"I am a married lady!" Madam Doucette shrieked, and hit Father Mark full in the face with her soup, pewter bowl and all. Whilst he squalled and fell back onto the floor, she stood and looked about wildly. Her gaze settled on her husband.

Doucette was clapping and cheering. "That is my girl! Now you feel better, non?"

She thought on it, and grinned sheepishly with a nod.

I looked to Gaston, and he appeared as surprised as I. Father Paul was trying to assist Father Mark in wiping soup from his face. Father Pierre stood with a great deal of dignity.

Doucette looked up at him and smiled affably. "I do not think that reprimand will be in order now, Father, as Madam Doucette has finally decided to speak her own mind on the matter."

"I see that," Father Pierre said with a trace of masked amusement. "I think we will take our leave."

Doucette obligingly walked them to the door.

Gaston leaned to me during the confusion and hissed, "Damn you, Will, we have not even made it through the soup and already you have threatened a priest and driven them from the house! Are you in such a hurry to return to our room?"

I laughed. "You said you wished for me to distract you; I merely endeavored to start as soon as possible."

Madam Doucette was giggling behind her hands. I met her green eyes over her steepled fingers.

"May I assume that Father Mark has been an ongoing matter of concern?" I asked.

She nodded. "Monsieur Doucette is always telling me that I should speak my mind and that I have a right to do so. That I do not have to take insults from any man any longer. It is hard for me. It was before; and now, after," her eyes flicked away. "It is harder still."

I wondered who had slashed her thirty-three times, and knew I would never ask. Her profession had come as no surprise to me, considering what Gaston had once said of Doucette's clientele. I assumed a member of her prior clientele had scarred her, but perhaps there was another story.

"Allow us to toast your victory this evening, then," I said, and raised my glass. Gaston followed suit.

Doucette yelled, "Wait, me too," and hurried to join us, after pausing to kiss Madam Doucette on the cheek. We toasted her; and then Doucette politely ordered the next course from the serving girl who was trying to clean up the mess.

Then his eyes found me. "You thought I would let a man insult my wife, non?"

I sighed and shrugged apologetically. "I am sorry. I did not understand the situation, and furthermore, it was not my place. I make a great habit of rushing in where angels fear to tread, so to speak."

He chuckled and appeared thoughtful. "You are a gentleman."

"Thank you. Not every man I encounter shares your good opinion of me, and many times I would not warrant it."

He studied me with a small, knowing smile; then his eyes shifted to Gaston, and then away from both of us to contemplate his glass.

"So what manner of troubles have you caused elsewhere?" he asked.

I was happy to oblige him, and proceeded to regale them with the details of both our voyages, neglecting of course Gaston's bout of madness and the witchcraft charges. Thus the remainder of the evening passed pleasantly enough.

Madam Doucette finally retired, and Gaston and Doucette went to check on Dickey. I was left to wander about with a lamp. To my delight, I discovered a library, and set about perusing the titles. Most were medical volumes, but there were also a number of historical and philosophical works.

I was deeply engrossed in a tome when I sensed movement in the doorway. I turned to find Doucette regarding me. He shrugged. "Gabriel has gone up to... your room."

"Ah, I should follow along then."

He glanced at the book I held. "I assume you are educated in Latin and possibly Greek."

"Latin, oui, Greek, non. And having lived for a time in Florence, I possess greater prowess in the more common spoken form of Latin than I do in the classical variety, though I can muddle through as long as I am not asked to translate ancient kings speaking of future accomplishments. According to my tutor, I tend to lose track of my tenses and become somewhat lost in time in those instances."

He smiled. "When I first saw you, I thought you were one of the common barbarian horde; and I wondered at that, as I could not see him associating with an uneducated man in any fashion. Are you of noble birth as well?"

"For whatever value that may have, oui." I replaced the book and joined him near the door.

"What do you know of him?" he asked.

I smiled and shook my head. "A great many things that I do not feel at liberty to discuss with anyone, including you. And as you most certainly feel the same concerning me, that leaves us both at a loss. Though I am sure there are a number of things we know that would serve the other well in... caring for him, perhaps."

"You know how he arrived here?"

"I know the incident that left him scarred occurred immediately before he left France, and that one of his father's men placed him on the ship in your care. And that you tended him until you reached this island and his body was healed. Then he left you and lived on the Haiti for a time."

He nodded. "Do you know how the incident, as you call it, occurred?"

"Do you?"

He smiled. "Does he still not remember, or will you not tell me?"

I took the time to consider my answer, and let him see me in thought.

"He remembers more and more, and I will not discuss that with you."

"I suppose that is your prerogative... as his matelot."

There was a mocking quality to his words, and I did not care for it. Though I could not precisely name it as contempt, it bore close relation to it. I recalled Gaston's words when he first told me of the man before me.

"You do not approve of matelotage?"

He waved my words aside. "I understand it, and I have no approval to give or withhold on the matter. I merely did not think he would become involved in it. He has always expressed such disdain for it and the men who engage in it."

I found that interesting, but did not allow my thoughts to show: especially as he was watching for my reaction. I wondered at his game.

"He did not expect to meet me."

Doucette smirked for a moment. "Non, I suppose he did not." He sighed and settled himself more comfortably against the wall. "When they brought Yvette to me, and I began to heal her, I thought, now here is a girl for Gabriel; and I refrained from expressing my own feelings toward her, in the hopes that he would return. Eventually I came to think he never would, and I married her because she is a precious girl and deserves a home of her own."

"Of course she does." I pushed my annoyance aside and let myself contemplate what a disaster and possible tragedy that would have been for all involved. How could Doucette not have realized that? The same way he had not realized what an imposition his pride in his handiwork was with both of them.

"Tell me," Doucette said. "If he were to meet a proper girl he would be attracted to, would you release him?"

"Release him? You make it sound as if I have entrapped him in some fashion." His words bothered me more than I cared to admit; and I thought of the dismay I had felt upon seeing his erection that afternoon.

"In a way, you have, though I do not think it with malice."

"How kind of you."

He shrugged. "It is a matter of convenience for all of you. You fancy yourselves in love because all men form close ties; but you know that it is not as it is with a man and a woman."

"I do know that; intimately, in fact. It is not the same, and I rather favor one over the other. I am not with Gaston out of convenience or a lack of alternatives. I wish to be with him."

He shook his head with consternation. "And you have been with women?"

"Oui, a number of them."

"And still you feel you prefer men?"

"Oui."

"Is that because you wish to be a woman?"

I was taken aback by the thought of it. "Non. Non, not at all."

"Perhaps you secretly harbor a desire to be a woman. Perhaps you are not even aware of it."

"If it is a thing of which I am totally unaware, then I would have to admit the possibility of it, simply because I cannot deny the existence of something I, by definition, cannot know. However, I do not think that to be the case. I do not feel I am in any way a feminine man."

"Are you attracted to Gabriel because he possesses feminine qualities?"

"Non, quite the contrary. I am attracted to Gaston because of his manly qualities and demeanor, though on occasion he does behave in a manner some may define as feminine."

"What about him attracts you?"

I chuckled with bemusement. I found it difficult to believe I was engaged in the discussion. "It would be easier to ask what I am not attracted to in his person."

"And what would that be?"

"Well, in truth, his madness. He is not overly fond of it, either. We would both like to overcome it and rid ourselves of it."

He snorted dismissively. "Madness, what does that really mean, Will? There is nothing medically wrong with him. I can attest that no damage was done to his head. Oui, he is easily angered; all severely wounded people are for a time. And like any intelligent man with a fine creative mind, he is prone to periods of fantasy and intense introspection. Such things are often attributed to madness by those unfamiliar with it. I feel it is a thing he has been told and he has come to believe the words of others."

I was incredulous and did not bother to hide it. Gaston had truly hid it from him well.

"I suppose," I said carefully, "I must be unfamiliar with your definitions of madness, and sadly am forced to rely upon my own. I love him and I cannot be so charitable."

"What does he do?" Doucette asked arrogantly.

"I do not feel I should continue this conversation tonight. If you will excuse me."

Gaston appeared in the doorway behind Doucette; and I surmised he had been listening. Doucette turned to regard him with surprise.

"I thought you went up," he said.

Gaston shrugged. "I did. Will was not there."

"We were just talking about you," Doucette said. "Will is of the opinion you are mad."

"I have been listening, and I am." Gaston's gaze was level and reproachful.

"According to whom?" Doucette scoffed. "The uneducated and superstitious?"

Gaston shook his head with annoyance. "I know I am mad, by my definition. I experience acute emotional states in which I am unable to maintain rational control of my actions or faculties. You can call it what you will. I call it dangerous and debilitating. At those times, I become a threat to my friends, and I am at the mercy of my enemies. There is often accompanying memory loss and intense feelings of confusion. I can be driven into these states by specific circumstances; some I have catalogued, others I have not. Most, if not all, of these triggering events appear to be related to my being flogged and presumably the events leading up to it."

There was an awkward period of silence. Doucette finally broke it.

"I need to think on this. Would you be willing to discuss the details with me in the morning?"

"Of course." Gaston shrugged.

Doucette appeared more thoughtful than arrogant as he began to leave us. Gaston stopped him with a light touch on his arm.

"Will knows far more about me than you," Gaston said. "Do not be dismissive of him."

"I meant no offense," Doucette said, but it was obvious he wished to say something else. He left us instead.

"How much did you hear?" I asked, and grimaced as I recalled the topics of conversation.

"All. I came down as soon as I did not find you. He was watching you for awhile before you saw him. I did not mean to spy upon you, but upon him, as I wished to see what he would say outside of my presence." He led me up to our room.

"Are you surprised?"

He shook his head. "His goading you concerning Madam Doucette was interesting. And I do not mean that in a pleasing way. The rest I expected." He closed the door behind us, and I set the lamp on the desk.

"I was curious as to his game," I said, "else I would not have spoken with him at all."

"Do not vex yourself over it," Gaston said. "He is at best an absent-minded chess player. He can discern a short series of moves and rarely sees the longer consequences."

"As I do not."

"Non, you perceive many things about those around you on occasion. He understands bodies but not minds," Gaston said thoughtfully. "I had not realized that, until seeing him this time."

"I worry for Madam Doucette," I said. "She is as wounded as either of us in many ways, and she has had the good fortune of coming into the graces of a benefactor, and he does seem to care for her and wish her well. Yet based on what we have witnessed, I wonder that he does not cause her more grief. When he said he wished to hold her in anticipation of your return, all I could imagine is what a tragedy that might have been."

"I thought on that, too," he said sadly and removed his weapons. "Without you... Unprepared as I would have been without you in my life, since you have wrought great changes upon me... I would have visited irreparable harm upon her, and even myself, especially in light of what I... we know now about..."

I had doffed my weapons while he talked, and I embraced him. "You did not wish to think about that. I am to distract you."

He smiled. "You are doing a poor job, despite the threat to the priest."

"Ah, so you did not find the rest of my conversation with him distracting?"

"Oui, I did." He grinned. "Especially the part where he insisted that possibly you secretly wished to be a woman." He pounced on me playfully, and we fell back upon the bed.

"It is truly strange," I chuckled. "He is not the first man to cast that aspersion at my person on account of my favoring men. It is as if they can conceive of the matter in no other fashion. Men and women are the components of all things sexual, as they feel God intended, and therefore if one favors men, one must be a woman. I would suppose the same is true if a woman favors women. They would suppose she secretly wished to be a man. I would rather imagine that a woman who favors women simply wants nothing to do with men."

He was sitting astride my lap, and he crossed his arms and frowned down at me. I raised a questioning eyebrow.

"And I possess female qualities?" he asked with little humor.

I rolled my eyes and then decided the matter should be discussed. "You behave quite passively on occasion, especially in regards to matters of a sexual nature. In my thinking that is a feminine characteristic. I am not making complaint. And I understand why."

He uncrossed his arms and ran his hands up my ribs to my shoulders and out my arms. He tugged at my shirt and sat back so I could partially sit to pull it over my head. Then he doffed his shirt. His fingers returned to my ribcage. With both hands moving in tandem, he played along the edge and then traced the arcs of my ribs and breastbone. Then they strayed to my nipples. I gasped at the sudden pleasure, and he lingered to toy with them until he had me arching for more. At which point he leaned down to tongue and suckle my left nipple and I moaned contentedly. He stopped and I opened my eyes to find him studying me.

With a curious frown he took my right hand and pulled my arm across my body, so that he could roll off me to lie at my side. I turned my head to regard him curiously. I remembered an abbreviated version of the same events when we first toured the *Mayflower*.

"I did that to her," he sighed. He did not seem in any way vexed or angry, or possessed of any emotion, really.

"Oh," I said. Even as I grappled with how disconcerting that may have been for him, my nipples and cock were curious as to whether that meant he would not do that again. "Did she enjoy it?"

He nodded. "Yet there is still something else, Will. Something more I dare not let myself see again. I am not ready."

"Then do not force yourself."

"I think I shall continue to be the woman in our relationship."

I groaned and rolled onto my elbow to glare at him. "Now you are falling prey to their reasoning. That is not what I intended. And I have known a number of exceedingly aggressive women."

"I jest."

I rolled on top of him, and he regarded me with amusement; yet fear haunted his eyes.

"Make it all go away," he whispered.

I retrieved the salve he liked from our bags, and began to kiss and caress him with ever increasing passion. Always in the back of my mind was the thought that perhaps, now that it had been awakened, his manhood would rise to my ministrations. It did not.

When I had touched everything I could reach while he was upon his back, I began to see to myself and slid against him. He stopped me with hands on my hips and bade me with gentle pushes to lift off of him. I complied reluctantly and he rolled onto his belly. He clutched at the bed clothes, hugging them under him, and spread his legs enough to make his offer very clear. My heart stumbled in its racing.

With trembling fingers, I rubbed the salve onto the small of his back and his buttocks. His breathing was very shallow; and curiously, I could see the strain of his trying to relax. I ran my thumb over his entry, and he twitched at the new sensation. I was so overcome with lust it was difficult to think clearly; but there was a persistent thought that I could not hurt him. If I hurt him now, it would be a thousandfold more difficult to induce him to let me do it again; and after sampling this new pleasure my desire would be a thousandfold greater. I had to progress slowly and carefully, despite my aching cock and the blood pounding in my ears.

"Will," he whispered.

With fingers still teasing him, I leaned closer to listen.

"Do it," he said. "It is all right. I want this."

"I know," I breathed in his ear. "But have patience. I do not wish to hurt you."

He shook his head. "It is all right. I want it to hurt."

I took a deep breath to refute him; and then I realized what he said. He would have been kinder to hit me with a bucket of ice water, as the surprise would have been less. I was off him and at the window, before the anger hit in a great wave of red that nearly left me blind. How could he? How could he say such a thing? I was possessed of an urge to hurt him, but not in that way.

"Will?" he hissed. He said my name several times, and I finally turned to look at him. I was afraid he would come to me, and I did not know what I would do. He was regarding me over the small dune of the bedclothes with frightened and curious eyes.

"What is it?"

"That you owe me an apology for," I growled.

"What is... What did I do?"

"How dare you? I will not be the instrument of your self-castigation and guilt!"

His eyes widened in surprise, and then he frowned in consternation; and I was forced to admit that perhaps he had not realized. For some reason, this only made me angrier, though I thought that was not possible. As a result, I felt compelled to explain.

"I love you. I would never hurt you. Ever. For you to ask me, especially..." The words left me, and I was only able to flounder in my rage and pain. I sank down the wall with a groan of frustration.

"I did not.... That was not my..." He sighed heavily.

I looked to him. He had rolled onto his side and clutched the bedclothes to him, so that he was wrapped about the ball of them at his belly.

"Perhaps it was," he whispered so softly I had to strain to hear him.

"I wanted," he continued, "you to make it go away. You always do. You eclipse all in that fashion at times. This thing... This knowledge, it haunts my mind. It is everywhere. I am terrified of it. I wanted... Tonight it was not enough. Even your touch could not take my mind from it. I wanted more... sensation. I wanted pain. And I suppose it is as you said. I feel I deserve the pain. And I think I wished for the other thing you talked of once, for the feeling of submission. I wanted to belong to you. I want to be... Will, I feel you are the only chance for redemption I possess."

My anger could barely hold in the face of his truth. I clung to the anger anyway. I could not give up on it so easily. The anger felt good. It felt powerful. It drove the fear into the shadows. He could not hurt me if I was in the clutches of anger greater than his madness.

I did not question my reasoning. I let the rage tear through me. I roared with frustration and pounced upon the bed, startling him into casting about for a weapon, his eyes narrowed with the need to fight.

"I thought you wanted me to hurt you," I said in English, with a voice I barely recognized as my own.

His eyes blazed with defiance for a moment; and then it left him. All the tension left him. He nodded almost imperceptibly, and he slumped back onto his side clutching the bedclothes. He closed his eyes.

I crouched over him, trembling with an overabundance of emotion. He had surrendered. I could indeed do whatever I wished. I gazed upon his ravaged body, and another piece of the puzzle clicked into place. He had done this before. When faced with his father's rage, he had simply submitted. He had not fought. I had wondered at that, as I could not believe he would have been so easily taken and strung up for the beating with so little other damage. I had assumed he had been struck on the head in some fashion to render him unconscious. But no, he had surrendered.

If he could force himself to stand in harm's way, then he could force himself to do other things as well. I was still angry enough not to fear him; and now I understood that, too. This was the only way. We had to be free of this thing hanging in his mind. If I sympathized with him and felt his pain I could not help him. I had to be strong.

I pushed him on his back and sat astride him.

"Look at me," I said in English. His eyes opened obediently. "This ends tonight."

He recoiled and started to reach for me, only to stop himself.

"Not us," I spat. "This thing, this incident, the event that haunts you. We will drag it into the light and beat it to death."

I leaned forward with hands braced on either side of his shoulders, and held his eyes with my own. "Let us start at the beginning. Why did you go home? You were living at the monastery, correct?"

He nodded.

"It was near Christmas? Did you always go home at Christmas?"

"Non."

"Then why this time?"

"I do not..." he said in French.

"Aye, you do. Think. Remember."

He frowned, but it was at his memories and not me.

"There was a letter," he said in English. He nodded to himself and continued in my language, "She wrote me. She asked me to come home. She was ill. She was always sickly, but she had contracted consumption. There were flecks of blood on the parchment. She jested that she could have signed her name with it. She was weak, though. They did not give her long, and she wanted to see me before she passed. I did not believe it. She had always recovered before. Yet I went."

He closed his eyes and battled the remembered pain; I battled the urge to hold him.

"What happened when you got home?" I asked as coldly as I could manage.

"I saw her. She was so frail. Like a bird. She could not lift her head from the pillows. They had her propped up, with her hair spread all about. They had been bleeding her, again and again, and the cuts on her arm were the only color she had. Even her eyes and hair were pale and drained. Her skin was so thin you could see the vessels, and it was as white as the bedclothes. She was in such pain. She said sometimes every breath was agony, and so they gave her laudanum.

"She was happy to see me," he nodded. "They would not let me stay long. I promised her I would sneak in and see her later. There was a secret door in the wall of her bedchamber.

"My father had returned from hunting, and we ate together that evening. It was one of the few times I ever shared his table. He asked me a great many things about the monastery, and it was a pleasant conversation. I told him I wished to become a monk. I was afraid he would be angry, but he was not. We even discussed whether or not I had inherited my mother's madness, and I told him I feared I had. He broached it gently, but he explained that he did not want me to inherit from him; and if I would be happy as a monk, that would be the best for all. I agreed and said I would sign papers to that effect. He had married again after my mother's death, and his new wife gave him three children. Two were healthy boys. So he had an heir. I asked if I could gain some form of stipend to help the monastery, and he agreed to a handsome sum. I was very pleased with the outcome of that meeting."

He frowned. "I felt at peace. Then I returned to my sister. The nurses were sleeping in the anteroom, and we were alone. I joined her in the bed, as we had done as children. We talked about death and how ready she felt she was, and how she was tired of the lingering pain. And yet she was sad that she had never had a chance to live. I told her of what I had seen since last we had been together. She told me of the books she had read."

"She had a coughing spasm of such severity I thought I should call the nurse, but she told me where the laudanum was instead; and I gave her some, and tried some myself, as she said it made pain of the heart recede as well. Then she asked me...."

He lay silent beneath me with his eyes tightly closed, though it did little to keep the tears from leaking from them. Mine were the same even though they were open. The anger had deserted me, but as I knew what he would say next, I pressed on despite the sick feeling in my gut.

"What did she ask?"

He shook his head. I grasped his shoulders and shook him firmly but gently. His eyes opened.

"She... did not wish to die a virgin."

I caressed his cheek. "And you could deny her nothing."

"She was the only one who ever loved me, Will, the only one who ever understood. And I had been sent away and we had been separated after... my mother's death. She had been left alone, getting sicker and sicker, while I had been fighting my way in and out of all those schools."

"So you lay with her."

He nodded. "I knew it was wrong."

"But you meant well. And then she died?" I asked.

He shuddered and clutched at me.

"How did she die?" I asked.

"Even you cannot love me..." he whispered.

I knew. "You gave her peace, did you not?"

He was sobbing, and alternately pounding on me feebly and clutching at me. "I had never... It was easy. The knife slipped right in. And she smiled. She smiled and said thank you. And then she left me. She was gone. I felt her soul depart. There was blood. I did not think she had that much blood left in her. And I held her, and she got cold. And then... And then they found me in the morning. And... And... Will. Non. Do not make me remember any more."

I knew what happened next. We both did. I held him and let him cry.

"I still love you," I murmured in French. "You were a good brother. You did nothing wrong. I am sure that if she realized the pain it would cause you, she would not have asked what she did of you. I hope I have the strength to do what you did, if the need ever arose with someone I love as much as you did her." Of course, there was only one person I had ever loved that much, and I was holding him.

He let me calm him. Eventually he slept from exhaustion. I did not sleep for quite a while. When finally I drifted off, I dreamt of waking to find him dead in my arms in a spreading pool of blood. I woke abruptly, and spent the rest of the night sitting with my back to the headboards and his head in my lap.

He found me thus when he awoke. He regarded me with sleepy yet curious eyes, until memory of the night's events returned; and he became sad.

"Have you slept at all?"

"I dreamt poorly," I whispered.

He sat beside me and took my hand. Neither of us spoke for a time. Distantly we could hear the house stirring below.

"I feel as if we have completed some fearsome journey," I said.

"Oui," he said. "And I feel peace, but it is not the peace I expected."

"You would not wish for death, would you?" I asked.

He regarded me somberly, and finally shook his head. "I do not want to die, not now. What would be the gain in it? I did then."

I gave a bemused snort. "Much as I feel about Shane, I suppose. Why kill him now if I did not then? Not that our tragedies are equal in any way or similar, yet..."

His fingers covered my lips. "Our tragedies were similar in that we were hurt. That is all that matters."

I thought on it, and knew I did not wish to think on it further; nor did we have to, for now. I smiled. I rubbed his hair and eased over him to leave the bed.

"We should be up. I feel we need to breathe in the breeze and see sunlight and... relieve ourselves and eat, and..."

"Not dwell on anything of merit," he supplied.

"Just so. There is much to be harvested from last night, but not now, not on a full bladder and empty stomach, and me with no sleep."

He smiled and joined me in dressing and gathering our gear. We found the boy and inquired of food. He led us to the dining room, and shortly the Negress provided us with a sumptuous meal of bacon and eggs – and to my amazement, toast with butter and jam. I marveled on this last, and took great delight in savoring leavened wheat, as I had not tasted its like in a good eight months.

Our host and hostess had not yet appeared, and we ate alone. I was relieved in this, as I was beginning to feel positively cheerful; and I did not relish discussing matters of Gaston's mental state with Doucette or having to negotiate any manner of social relations with anyone at all other than my matelot.

"How do you feel?" I asked.

"Relieved." He paused and considered his bacon. "In that I now know, not in that...." He sighed. "I am not free of it, Will. It lurks and threatens to overwhelm me, and I know not if I should attempt to ignore it or immerse myself in it until I drown or learn to swim. Yet at the moment I feel too tired to mount the effort of the latter or manage the former."

"Then you shall do neither and we will go and... see Cayonne. You can show me the sights. And we can inquire as to how things go with our wolves and the others. And in all make a busy day of it."

"I was to speak with Doucette this morning," he stated with hopeful curiosity, as if asking that I should produce an escape from that as well.

"Leave him a note." I threw my last crust of toast at him and he dodged it with amusement.

We found Dickey awake and Tom feeding him little bits of egg and toast. Dickey still appeared wan and weak, but he seemed to be on the mend. We sat with them for a spell and discussed Tortuga. Dickey soon drifted to sleep under the effects of the laudanum.

To my dismay, Doucette found us there and joined in the conversation at hand. Then as Dickey was asleep and Tom's attention was starting to wane, he suggested we continue the conversation over his late breaking of the fast; and thus we were drawn back into the house. I listened with interest as Gaston and Doucette discussed local politics and news from France and the like. Doucette was obviously well-informed on these matters.

"How often do you receive news here?" I asked.

Doucette shrugged. "It is the storm season, so we will not see any ships for several months now. I would assume the same is true of you

English. When ships are sailing from France, I receive mail on almost all of them. I have a great many correspondents. In the season of the hurricanes, I make the most of my time in replying to the more lengthy discourses and working on my manuscripts and sending them off."

"So you write for publication?"

He shrugged. "The occasional missive or paper. They are on the back shelf in the library, near the desk, if you wish to peruse them. As most are medical, or deal with local observations on flora and fauna, I do not know if they will interest you."

"Possibly, if we are here long enough to provide me the time," I said.

"Or for you to become bored," he said.

Gaston regarded him sharply, and I wondered if Doucette had meant his words as self-deprecation of his own work or a slight jab at me. It made me realize once again how uneasy I was in his presence, and how little trust I felt for him. Despite the fine conversation, I felt we should be going.

"We were going to inquire of the ship and such," I reminded Gaston; and he turned a disapproving look upon me, until he paused to consider my intent and understood my meaning. At which point, he appeared apologetic.

"Will is correct," he told Doucette. "We should be going. So if you will excuse us. Perhaps we can continue the discussion at dinner."

"I thought we were to discuss your... madness," Doucette said.

I cursed silently, and Gaston met my eyes with a resigned sigh. "That discussion may be better reserved for another day," Gaston told him.

Doucette appeared disappointed. "Truly? May I ask why?"

Gaston was slow to answer. "My control ebbs and flows, and at this time I am not possessed of any confidence in my command of my emotions and faculties."

"Perhaps this is the best time to discuss these things, then," Doucette said.

I winced at the irony. I could not refute him. I had reasoned thus the night before, which was of course what had brought us so far.

"I gave a great deal of thought to your words," Doucette continued. "Both from last night and from before, and to the words of others on the matter." He studied Gaston intently, and my matelot ignored him and perused his cup with equal resolve.

"And what conclusions have you reached?" Gaston asked, with resignation tinged with annoyance.

"That I am lacking in empiric evidence. I wish to discuss the matter with you and hear your observations and to conduct some tests."

"Tests?" I asked.

"Oui," Doucette smiled. "For example," he stood and left the room.

"Tell him no and let us leave," I implored.

Gaston sighed and nodded. "He is as stubborn as you."

"I am not sure if that is good or bad for either of us, as I do not know your true feelings on the matter," I said lightly.

"I am inured to it," Gaston smiled.

"Then I am thankful for that," I chuckled.

Doucette returned. He was holding a horse whip. At first I merely recognized the object; and then my mind recalled the significance, and my heart skipped a beat. I considered yelling, "Do not look," or something equally ridiculous, but I have found that always causes the undesired action.

The coiled whip hit the table with a thump, and Gaston's eyes widened for a moment. I was not sure what his reaction would be, and I sat very still and waited. He pulled his eyes from it and closed them, while clutching at the table and swallowing hard. His breathing sped up, and he paled. I judged that he might become ill and lose his meal.

"Interesting," Doucette said. "So you do react to the mere sight of one. I would not have thought your reaction would be so pronounced."

I stood and snatched the whip off the table and flung it to the corner.

"You bastard!" I snarled. "You heartless monster!"

Doucette stepped back with surprise. "I was curious. It has not harmed him."

"Do you wave knives in front of your wife?"

He shrugged and shook his head. "She has no reaction to knives."

"So you did?"

"People often react strongly when they have experienced trauma. When this occurs, they need to be desensitized to the object or situation. The mind is quite capable of conquering and soothing the body's remembered fears. If Gaston sees enough whips, he will separate the act from the object, and they will have no hold over him."

"Presumably, but it is not a thing he need do now." I needed to get Gaston away from him and someplace where he could calm down. I was not sure if going to our room was wise, as it would involve staying in this house.

I turned to regard my matelot, and found him standing with his eyes full of murder and a knife in his hand.

"Damn," I said. I was on the wrong side of the table.

Doucette was regarding him curiously. "Now do you recall the event when you...?"

He stopped talking when I hit him square in the chest and sent him sprawling into the wall. Then I was around the table and between them.

There was recognition in Gaston's eyes when they met mine, and I was greatly relieved. I discovered I felt no fear of him in a direct sense. I was deeply afraid of what he would do to Doucette or himself, however.

"What do you wish to do?" I asked, pleased at the calmness of my tone.

"I want to kill him."

"That will solve nothing."

"He will never trouble me again."

I was confused. All of the physical symptoms of his madness were there, but he seemed very lucid.

"Put the knife down, please, and we will discuss this."

"Move," he snarled. "I will not suffer him anymore. He hurt me. I cannot bear it again." The last was as much of a wail as his broken voice could manage. I could see him slipping farther from my grasp. I seized upon whatever I could.

"How did he hurt you?"

"You know what he did."

"That is not your father."

He peered around me, and the sight of Doucette seemed to give him pause.

"Non. Non. He is the other one," he growled. "He is worse. That one is a cold-hearted bastard who thinks only of himself and no other. All things with him are matters of intellect. He is incapable of love. He is an automaton of medicine. He thinks he is smart. He thinks he is the master of reasoning. He is a fool. I do not owe him anything. I do not owe him my life."

"I am a fool?" Doucette roared from beside me. For the second time that morning, my heart was clutched painfully by fear. I whipped my head round to regard him. He was angry and ready to fight. My condemnation of his mental acumen died in my throat, as I saw movement out of the corner of my eye. I whirled back and thrust myself between them again, in time to catch Gaston. We rolled to the floor, knocking Doucette ahead of us.

I was not sure if my matelot had turned his frustrations to me, or if he merely wanted me out of his path. He seemed intent on pinning me to the floor and not on reaching Doucette at the moment, though. Much to my panic he succeeded, getting astride me and applying his formidable strength against my own. Then he abruptly stopped with horror in his eyes.

"Non, non, non," he sobbed and his hands went to my side. I looked down, and was thankful I was already lying upon the floor. The knife was protruding from my flesh, or rather the hilt was. The length of the blade was obviously inside me. I could feel it now as a dull aching wrongness. He pulled the blade free, and I gasped.

I was thankful I possessed a true grasp of why this particular thing horrified him, beyond the obvious I would have assumed a mere day before.

"I will not die," I whispered.

He would not look at me.

"Gaston!"

His eyes flicked to mine. The rage was gone, and there was only a scared little boy trying to staunch the flow of blood with his hands.

"It will be all right. You must.... Doucette must do surgery."

His eyes hardened, and I felt despair welling in my breast.

"Gaston."

"He will not touch you," he snarled.

"Then you will have to do it."

His emotions swung back to fear. "I do not..."

"If you do not, I will die."

His eyes hardened again: but with resolve this time, and not fear. He picked me up off the floor and carried me to the hospital rooms to lay me upon a surgical table. The pain radiated through me in ever-increasing waves as he tore my shirt away. Each threatened to swamp my consciousness.

"Gaston," I clutched at his hand. He squeezed back.

"Leave him. I will..." Doucette said from the doorway.

Gaston snarled in response.

"You are behaving like an animal," Doucette said. "Get control of yourself."

I pulled the pistol still at my belt and aimed at Doucette with a shaky hand. "Get out!"

Doucette stepped aside, and several men I did not recognize took his place. They were moving very quickly. I fired, and missed. Then they were upon us. Two held me down, and three more jumped atop Gaston. I could see little of that, as I had my own battle to contend with, though it was not much of one as I was nearly helpless. They quickly restrained me and Father Mark loomed over me, to gleefully shove a stick in my mouth.

"Take him where we discussed," I heard Doucette order. "I have to try and save this one."

I roared around the stick and then the pain hit anew as Doucette probed the wound. Blackness took me. I dearly wished to smite the Gods.

Twenty-Six

Wherein I Rescue My Matelot

There was pain and I knew I was not dead. As always when waking thusly wounded, I am not sure whether I should rejoice or not, as the pain often seems not worth surviving. This was one of those times. I moaned and hoped someone would relieve my suffering in some fashion.

"Will?"

At first I could not recognize the voice, as it was not the one I wished to hear. Then it came to me: Tom. I opened my eyes and saw ceiling. I turned my head toward the sound, and found Tom sitting nearby at the foot of Dickey's cot. He appeared concerned. I supposed that was as it should be. I had been stabbed, had I not? There was much I needed to remember. I attempted to move and found I could not. I was bound to the bed. Then all returned to me and the anger burned the pain away.

"Damn it, what the Devil?" I gasped as I tugged at the ropes binding my wrists.

"They said you should not move about," Tom said. "How...?"

"Where is Gaston?" I asked.

"I am told he is well... considering," Tom shrugged.

"Considering what?" I snarled. "Where is he? And release me, damn you."

"Nay. Will, you should not become riled. It cannot be good for you. Lie still." He grimaced with disapproval and concern.

I looked to Dickey, where he reclined against bunched pillows at the head of his cot. He looked no less troubled than his friend.

"Dickey, how long have...?"

"You've been lying there for two days. I believe you have been drugged for the pain and such, and... Mister Doucette was concerned that you would become agitated upon waking, which you have," he sighed.

"They rushed us and took Gaston away and..."

"They say he stabbed you," Tom interjected. "That he went mad and stabbed you."

"Doucette set it upon him and Gaston wished to kill him. I interceded. It was an accident that I was wounded."

This seemed to have some effect on Dickey's thoughts, but little on Tom, as the blond boy frowned. "I will tell them you need more laudanum," he said and stood.

"I do not! I need to know where my matelot is!"

Tom left the room and I turned to Dickey and hissed, "Has anyone from the ship been here?"

"Nay," he shook his head. "Well, not that I have seen them. Tom may have spoken to them, but I must tell you Mister Doucette spoke to him at length, and now Tom is quite convinced that what has occurred is in Gaston's and your best interest."

"Oh, damn. They must be told. I need to speak to Striker and Pete. Will you help me?"

"Hush," he said.

"To the Devil..."

"They are coming," he hissed quickly.

Through the haze of pain and anger, I realized he was watching someone approach from the direction Tom had departed.

I whirled my head about and saw Doucette. He sat on the cot next to mine and leaned over to examine my bandages.

"You must be calm, Will. Healing does not come to those who are agitated," he said in French. "You narrowly missed having a perforated bowl. Your pancreas was badly sliced. I believe it will heal in time. But only if you let it."

"Where is Gaston?" I asked in English.

"I understand your question, but I do not have a command of English."

"Then answer the damn question," I snarled in French. "And release me."

"He is well," he smiled kindly. "I am treating him, just as I am treating you. Until I am sure neither of you will behave in a deranged manner, you are not going anywhere."

"Was he wounded? Did your damn men hurt him?"

"Non, non," he shook his head regretfully at my supposed misapprehension of the matter. "I am treating him for his madness, now that I begin to understand its severity. I should have done this years ago, and I feel guilt that I have served him so poorly. But I did not know..." He shrugged helplessly and appeared sincerely contrite.

"How are you treating him?" Memories of the asylum in Florence returned and my gut churned.

"He must come to terms with what occurred. If images or thoughts of the flogging induce his madness, then he must be helped to become less sensitive to them."

I did not like the sound of that. Panic clawed at me. Dickey could not understand what the bastard said, and Tom had not returned, not that he would have understood either – or aided me, apparently. And Doucette appeared so reasonable. I was the one raving.

"You have no right to treat him," I said as calmly as I could manage. "If he is not himself, it is my concern. It is the way of the coast."

He snorted derisively. "Damn fool boucaniers. As if I care about their laws. This is a French colony governed by French law. In your case, my holding you here could be questioned," he acceded. "But you are a foreign privateer and wounded. Until you stop raving and agree to return to your ship I am honor-bound to keep you from causing trouble in Cayonne. As for Gabriel, I am the only one who can make those decisions."

"What do you mean?"

"He has been judged to be incompetent and remanded to my custody."

"In two days? You have a court here...?"

"Non, years ago, by his father."

"Non. You were paid to care for him but..."

"Non. After that. I began to correspond with his father upon arriving here. I wished to understand what was to be done with him. His father, though he has never imparted the details of what occurred, wishes for Gabriel to be cared for. He also does not wish for him to inherit. So he had Gabriel declared unfit and then remanded to my custody by a French court.

"Gaston never mentioned..."

"He does not know. I thought it would trouble him, and truly, there was no reason for him to know."

My horror was boundless, and I knew Doucette read it for what it was. To my further surprise, he did not gloat. He appeared sad.

"I am sorry, Will. You must understand; this is for the best."

I struggled to think. "Hold, you say you did not realize he is mad, but you accepted his care when he was pronounced unfit? Did that not seem..?"

"I thought his father distraught, and... politically motivated. I was well aware that something had passed between them. And," he shrugged ruefully. "I have always thought it a matter of the inheritance. Apparently there was some trouble with Gabriel's mother, and the father is convinced she was mad, too. Though I think it likely he wished for an excuse to have the marriage annulled so he could marry another. I know of physicians that have been called in to advise on such matters. It is a... problem, if you will, of the wealthy. I believe your King Henry caused no end of trouble over the matter."

"You are wrong."

"How do you know? What has he told you?"

"Go to the Devil."

"Come now, Will. It will aid him if I know all there is to know."

"I will see you in Hell."

He nodded sadly. "Your devotion is misplaced in this instance. Rest and we will speak again. I will send someone with laudanum. You need to sleep, and even if the pain does not keep you from it, I can well see your thoughts will."

He left, and I pulled at my bonds until my wound ached nearly enough to send me under the waves of consciousness.

"Will?"

I looked around. I had forgotten Dickey.

"You must help. He intends... Oh, Lord..." I was struck speechless by the entirety of what he intended. He would endeavor to use me against Gaston.

"The priest comes," he hissed.

I implored Dickey with my eyes and he nodded ever so subtly. The spark of hope ignited in my chest.

Dickey slowly rolled over and dug under his cot.

A throat cleared and I looked up to find Father Paul looking down at me kindly. He had a bowl, spoon, and stick, presumably to pry my mouth open with if necessary.

"Please do not make this difficult, Will. Doucette says you are quite distraught."

"Sit down and be quiet," Dickey said firmly.

Father Paul's eyes went wide, and he sat on the cot and set the bowl and other items aside before raising his hands. I looked to Dickey, and found him holding a pistol.

"Now, release Will," Dickey said.

Father Paul had understood the pistol well enough, but he did not speak English.

"Release me," I snarled in French. "Thank you," I breathed to Dickey as the priest untied my left wrist.

Dickey swallowed. "It is the least I can do. You are my friends, and something is amiss here. Even if I didn't understand what he said, I understood. He is holding you against your will, and Gaston as well. I don't know how much more I can do, though, it still hurts to breathe."

The priest was eyeing both of us as he finished untying me.

"Can you walk?" I asked Dickey.

He nodded. "Can you?" He was not being facetious.

"I will not know until I try." I smiled weakly.

"Tell him to sit down," Dickey instructed.

I relayed the command, and the priest sat.

"What do you feel we should do with him?" I asked.

"Do you wish to kill him?" Dickey asked carefully. He did not appear to like that idea.

"Nay." And I truly did not, and not just because of the trouble it might cause. "Let us render him unconscious or restrain him, or both. If we start killing priests in a Papist colony, we are done for. And I feel he is not to blame."

Dickey nodded.

I slowly pulled myself up to sitting and got my legs off the bed. The room spun for a moment. The pain pounded in my temples.

"My son, this is a foolish thing," Father Paul admonished quietly.

"Non, non, you are the fool involved in foolish things," I breathed. "Lie down."

He lay on the cot I had occupied, and I carefully tied his hands as mine had been. Then I stuffed a wad of sheet from the next cot into his mouth, and wound the excess around his head so that he could not dislodge it, with one last fold over his eyes so he would not be staring at us.

After all that exertion, I felt the need to nap; and it did not bode well for the endeavor. I forced myself to keep my mind on the tasks at hand.

"Do you have all your weapons?"

Dickey nodded. He had pulled himself to standing and appeared as unsteady as I felt.

"Do you know where mine are?"

He shook his head and handed me the pistol he had brandished at the priest. Then he knelt gingerly next to his cot and began to pull out the rest of his gear from beneath it.

"We cannot fight, Will," he gasped.

"I well know it. I wish for you to go to the ship and fetch our friends. They can fight."

He regarded me with grateful eyes and then regarded the door with trepidation. "I do not know where the ship is."

"On the water," I smiled wanly. "Downhill. I believe that will be to the right."

He grinned back. "I think I shall find it, then. What shall you do?"

"Sneak about and locate my matelot."

"Can you stand?"

I thought he had already asked me that; and then I realized I had not truly done it yet. I stood slowly and found it no worse than sitting. I nodded.

"Do not do anything foolish until we... or rather, our friends return," he panted as he stood again. He handed me his rapier.

"Dirks, please. I do not feel I can wield that."

He passed me his dirks. "Me, neither." He smiled and donned his repaired tunic slowly. "If I am forced to duel betwixt here and the ship, I am a dead man," he gasped through the fabric.

"I do not think that will be necessary, though Doucette had men who attacked us. If we are lucky, they will not be about or not recognize you." And there was one other. "I am concerned you will encounter Tom."

He finished pulling his tunic down. "Do not be. He will not stop me."
There was great assurance in his words.

"Then God speed and thank you."

"Be careful," he whispered and walked slowly to the door.

I was startled to look about and find two other men in the room.
Both ailed, though, such that they did not seem cognizant of me. I
walked slowly to the door leading to the surgery and the house and
considered my options. The pistol seemed ready. I unsheathed one
of the dirks. I did not wish to shoot anyone. The noise would draw
too much attention. I was in no shape to battle even a fat priest with
a knife, though. It would be best if I were not seen at all. Even if the
viewer did not know I should not be about, they would still question my
walking around clad only in breeches with a bandage wrapped around
my middle.

Thus I listened carefully at the doorway, before slipping through
and into the interior courtyard. It appeared to be late afternoon, and the
shadows were long. I was relieved when I heard talking and saw a gaggle
of women and boys about the cookhouse at the back of the space.
Thankfully, Madam Doucette, the Negress, the boys, both white and
black, and several other servants were clustered about the cookhouse
partaking of something hot and delectable. Madam Doucette declared
loudly that the cook had outdone herself. I silently commended the
woman myself for distracting the lot of them.

I made my way along a wall, cursing the design of the house. If it
had been a large English manor, I would have been able to traverse its
length via interior corridors well blocked from sight. Here, all was open
to the sky, breeze, and prying eyes.

Once I reached an auspicious corner for hiding, I leaned on the
wall and considered the architecture from a different perspective.
Where could they have put Gaston, if he were in this building at all?
There was no cellar. The lower rooms were all used up by the medical
facilities and dining room and Doucette's study. I doubted he would be
in the bedrooms upstairs, but I supposed they could have him trussed
or drugged. These rooms would be damnably difficult to search, as
the lot of them opened onto a balcony that was easily visible from the
cookhouse.

I peered out cautiously and found the room we had used. Its
shutters were open. Most of the upper rooms were open, except for one.
To reach it, I would have to crawl up the stairs and along the inner edge
of the balcony.

I crept to the closer stairs. I would be mounting them in the open.
Once at the top, I could drop from sight again. I listened; there was
still a great deal of conversation at the cookhouse. I peeked out; no one
was looking this way. I stepped out and started up the stairs. It was
not easy, and I made slow work of it; but I heard nothing untoward as
I went. When I reached the top, I collapsed, not entirely due to a need
to conceal myself. I knelt there against the wall and caught my breath

until the world stopped spinning.

There was a creak and I glanced over and saw a skirt.

"Will?" It was Madam Doucette.

I stayed down and lured her in. She did as expected, and knelt beside me with a gentle hand on my back. I set the pistol down and grabbed her arm with my right hand. I put the point of the dirk under her chin with my left. Fear suffused her features and she screwed her eyes closed and panted. Then I saw the scar again and I gasped.

"Oh, God, I am sorry. I am sorry. Truly, I mean you no harm, and I do not wish to be cruel, but I must find Gaston and I cannot allow you to stop me. Do you understand?"

"Oui. Do not hurt me, please. I beg you."

"Will you call out?"

"Non."

I took the dirk away but maintained my grip upon her, such as I was able in my condition. She covered her mouth to hold in the sobs.

"Mistress?" someone asked from the bottom of the stairs. Her eyes shot wide with renewed fear.

"Please, I beg you," I whispered. "Help me. I just wish to take him and go. Please. You will never see us again."

"Mistress?" This time I recognized the voice as being the boy's.

"What is it, Jean?" she asked. Her back was to the stairs, thankfully.

"Is something amiss?"

"Non, non, I just... I am helping... Will... fetch something from his room."

She made a fine go of sounding normal, but my eyes narrowed at her choice of words. She shook her head subtly.

"Isn't he wounded?" Jean asked.

"Oui, and a bit drugged, but we shall manage. I need to speak with him, anyway. Go eat some more pie."

I heard him on the stairs. "But..."

Madam Doucette frowned and her voice hardened. "Must you question everything? I am capable of caring for myself on occasion," she snapped.

"Oui, madam," Jean sighed and scuffed his feet off across the courtyard.

She pressed her fingers to her lips again in regret.

"I am sorry," I whispered. "You can apologize to him later. For me as well."

"He was here when I arrived; he is... fond of me. I am his first infatuation."

"Then he will forgive you," I smiled. "You will help me?"

"Oui, though I am sure you will see that you need not be so concerned."

"Have you seen Gaston... since...?"

"Non, Doucette said it was best if only he saw him. Gabr... Gaston is... mad, non?

"Oui."

She seemed relieved I understood this. "The doctor is afraid he will try to hurt someone else. He is in the end room, here."

I had been correct; it was the one with the shutters closed. I nodded, and she helped me slowly regain my feet. I wished to tell her the truth of it all, but I did not want to risk her cooperation until I saw the state Gaston was in. It occurred to me that he might be in such a state that I could not handle him alone. I hoped Pete and Striker would arrive soon.

There was a lock on the door, and she fumbled with a keyring. None of the keys worked. It was a poor little hasp upon the door, designed to keep the curious out and little else. If I had my health I could easily kick the door open. I shoved a sheathed dirk behind it and pried. She helped me and two of the nails popped loose. We opened the door.

I did not know what to expect. My heart was in my throat. And then I saw him, and a roar started deep in my chest. I clamped my hand over my mouth before I could release it. I was distantly aware of Madam Doucette collapsing to the floor next to me with a sob.

Gaston was gagged and strapped in a heavy chair so that he could not move, not even his head from side to side. He was naked. That was not what I wished to scream about; nay, I wanted to tell the Gods about all the whips hanging about the room so that if he opened his eyes he could not avoid them. Thankfully his eyes were tightly closed. His breathing was ragged and he had clawed the wood of the chair so that his nails were cracked and bleeding.

I staggered to him. He flinched as I neared him.

"Gaston, my love," I murmured. He made a pitiful sound. "I love you," I murmured over and over again. I unfastened the gag and he sucked in a great lungful of air, as a drowning man does when at last he finds the surface again. His eyes snapped open. They were wild, but lit with recognition upon seeing me. In turn I recognized the demon of his madness in their depths.

I crawled atop him as best I could, so that I eclipsed all else he could see. Then I worked on the strap restraining his head. I kept murmuring to him.

"There will be no more. You are safe now. I love you." His eyes did not leave mine. They were filled with fear and horror and not rage, yet.

"Close your eyes," I whispered. He did as I bade, and I was able to turn my head to release his arms. He immediately clawed at my shoulders.

When I looked back at him, I started with renewed horror. The skin about his eyes was dark, and I had thought it his usual mask; but nay, it was bruised. Yet it did not look as if he had been struck in the face. Only his eyelids were purple and puffy.

"What did they do?" I asked and gingerly touched the area.

"I used the little hooks on that table there to hold his eyelids open," Doucette said.

Gaston snarled at the sound of his voice and buried his head in my shoulder.

Several things flashed through my mind. I needed to kill Doucette. My back was to the door. Worse yet, it was behind me on my left. The pistol was in Gaston's lap, so that it could be gripped with my right, not my left. Gaston was still strapped to the chair. Everyone in the house would hear the shot. I did not know what Madam Doucette was doing. I did not know if Doucette had a weapon on me. I did not know if he once again had half dozen men behind him.

Then the yelling began. It was Madam Doucette.

"You monster!" I heard flesh hitting flesh before I could turn. "You are inhuman!" she punched him again. "A pig! A dog! A rabid thing! You disgust me! I hate you!" She punctuated every statement with another blow, and he regarded her with amazement and defended himself. She was doing little damage.

I noted Doucette had a pistol.

"Keep your eyes closed," I told Gaston and pried his fingers off my shoulder.

He kept them closed, but he did not stop clutching at me; and I could not get my arms free to bring the pistol up.

"Gaston! I must shoot someone," I hissed.

Oblivious to us, Madam Doucette changed tactics, backing away to yell. "You monster! You said you were helping him as you helped me! You are so damn stupid! How did you think you would get away with this? Did you think they would forgive you? Did you think I would forgive you if I knew? They will kill you! And you deserve it! You bastard!"

Gaston stopped grabbing at me and clapped his hands over his face. I threw myself back, and fell off him and out of the chair. I landed hard and spots danced before my eyes. I tried to focus. Doucette was regarding his wife with wonder and confusion. I got the pistol up and fired. The ball caught him high in the right shoulder. I had nearly missed.

Yvette screamed and dropped to her knees.

Doucette's face contorted in surprise and shock, and he dropped his pistol.

Jean arrived and threw himself upon Yvette to protect her.

I realized I did not have powder and shot to reload. I scrabbled at the straps on Gaston's legs while Doucette slumped to the floor.

Then Pete was in the doorway, and it was like looking upon the face of God. I was overcome with relief and salvation for a moment. He grinned at me.

I turned my back on the rest of the room and dealt solely with my matelot again. Gaston had doubled over, and I returned to murmuring things for him as I worked on the final straps. Then another set of hands worked with me, steadier hands.

"Will?" Striker hissed from beside us as he helped ease Gaston out of the chair.

I met his worried eyes and shook my head. "I must get him out of here."

"Where?"

"Somewhere quiet."

Someone was roaring in French and I looked up, startled. It was Gaston's former captain, Peirrot. The man had Doucette off his feet and pressed against the wall.

Right behind them, it seemed as if the entirety of Cayonne was trying to fit inside the tiny room, and they were all angry. There were so many people that someone stumbled on us and had to catch themselves on the chair above my head.

I scuttled backwards for the safety of the corner. Every movement was agony. Gaston was a ball in my lap, and he twitched with every sound. He had some limb of his against my wound.

Then there were hands upon us. Pete picked Gaston up in his arms and lifted him from me. And then Striker and Liam had me on my feet between them. Cudro bellowed and smacked people and drove a path to the door. As we turned to go through, I saw Otter bringing a terrified Madam Doucette with us with Jean as rearguard.

Unfortunately, the balcony along the way was worse than the room. We pressed on. I was in agony; the only thing keeping me conscious was fear. I was afraid that at any moment Gaston would realize I did not hold him, and turn into a feral creature of rage and terrible power.

Cudro led Pete the length of the balcony, to the stairs, down them to the courtyard and across it to the street. We still did not stop. Consciousness began to desert me. Again and again I would slip into velvety darkness, only to have it torn asunder by another lightning bolt of pain, movement, and sound.

Pete stopped and dropped Gaston. We stopped, and thankfully the darkness stayed at bay. Gaston was crouched and snarling. It was as I had feared. I tugged free and threw myself before him. Once again his eyes lit with recognition at the sight of me. The anger did not fade, though. He came and embraced me protectively while casting about.

"Gaston," I whispered. "My love, you are safe. I am wounded. The ship, we must reach the ship. Let them get us there."

He pulled back and examined my bandage with deft fingers. It was red in the middle, where it had been clean before. I had torn the stitches in all the movement. His eyes were wide with horror, and I guessed that much of it was remembered.

"Gaston, help me to the ship. Follow Pete."

He searched my eyes, and I smiled as best I could. His fingers had returned to clutching, but I could see the rage hovering about him.

"All will be well. We are escaping. You will care for me. Be my legs. Let me guide us."

Clarity bloomed in his gaze, and he nodded.

"We are one." He helped me to my feet and got his arm around my back.

Liam approached us diffidently with a blanket. I realized Gaston was still naked. He let me wrap it about his shoulders; and then, with me leaning on him, we made our slow way down the street with the others arrayed about us. We now appeared to be over twenty men strong.

Gaston's eyes darted about and he started at every sound. His breathing was fast and ragged. But he handled me carefully as we made our way to the wharf, and into and out of a longboat to reach the *Mayflower*. Once safely inside our cabin, he sat me on a chair and tried to push the others out.

"I need to know..." Striker was saying.

"Ask Madam Doucette," I said, "and let us be for a time, please."

He nodded.

"Thank you," I remembered to call as the door started to close again.

Striker shook his head with a small smile; and then he was gone, and there was a door between us and the world, and we were safe. I hoped they would sort it out without us. I leaned on the table.

Gaston had his medicine chest open and was quickly going through various things. When he came to me to cut the soiled bandage away, I touched his cheek. His eyes met mine.

"How are we?" I asked.

He considered this, and finally shook his head jerkily and concentrated on cutting the bandage. Once he had it clear, he examined the wound and apparently decided it did not need more suturing. He applied a clean bandage. He seemed concerned at the puffiness of my belly.

"Are you hungry?" he asked.

I thought on it. "Non, thirsty."

He found a corked bottle and bade me sip only a little. I found I could not hold the weight of it and bring it to my lips steadily. He helped me. I saw his bloody nails again.

"You will lie on the hammock now and stay still," he admonished as I finished.

"In a moment. First let us see to your hands."

He examined his broken nails with concern, and allowed me to help him clean and bandage them. He became agitated while we did this, and I saw anger flash with the pain in his eyes as I trimmed the broken sections.

Once that was complete, he searched about and found a coil of rope we used to string the hammocks.

"Bind me." His eyes had gone hard, and his voice was a growl.

I faced him without fear and shook my head. "You will not hurt me."

He gave a derisive snort, and his eyes went to the wound.

"You did not intend that. It was an accident. I merely got in your path, when I should not have, I might add."

"Non." He looked away, and his breathing quickened. Dozens of things flitted across his face.

"Oui, all will be well, my love. I forgive you."

He shook his head with more agitation. "Non, you do not understand." He sounded as he had while bandaging me. "The horse... the horse is running wild. You are all that holds me to this world. You must... hobble me while you sleep. I cannot trust myself." His eyes found mine again and hardened. "You cannot trust me."

I held my ground in his gaze, but I understood.

"Do you wish to dress first?" I asked. "Or relieve yourself?"

He gave a little gasp of surprise and did both things. I was thankful we had spare clothing aboard. I wondered if we would ever see the things we left at Doucette's again.

Once he was dressed and empty, he turned his back to me and presented his arms behind him. I bound him securely above his damaged wrists, with enough slack in the rope to not hurt his shoulders.

"Can you join me in the hammock thus?" I asked.

He nodded quickly with a shuddering breath. When he turned to face me, I saw the tears. I gingerly brushed them away and he kissed my fingers and then moved closer to kiss my cheek.

"Do not let me go, Will."

"Never, my love." I held him.

We later reached the hammock and slept, or at least I did, with him quiescent in my arms.

I woke to his hiss of my name, and found him wild-eyed and angry and glaring at someone. I rolled back enough to look over my shoulder, and found Pete sitting in the chair watching us. It was night, and the lamp hanging from the beam swung just a little.

"HowAreYa?" Pete asked.

I thought. "I am in pain, and thirsty, and hungry." I gave Gaston a questioning look.

He calmed a bit and snorted. "I am stiff, and hungry. Will may have broth."

Pete nodded sagely and scratched his head.

I grinned at him. "Gaston is not well, but we will live."

He sighed. "WeBeenWorried. FeltGuilt. WeSpentTheLastNights PissDrunk. Didna'KnowYaTwoBeInTrouble."

"We know," I sighed. "I intend to beat Tom senseless when I see him."

"Two...?" Gaston whispered. "Will, when did I... when were you stabbed?"

"In the morning, two days ago." I looked to Pete for confirmation. He nodded.

Gaston shook his head. "I do not remember... He must have drugged me for some of it."

"He kept me drugged. And I did not wake, until perhaps a half hour before I found you. If Dickey had not helped me, I might be there still."

"Aye, OnAccountA'YarFriendsBein'RightIdiots."

"Nay, nay," I sighed. "You came as soon as you knew. I was damn pleased to see you."

Pete snorted. "WeRanThereAfterDickeySayThereBeTrouble. WeDidNa' Give'ImTimeTaSayWhatSort. JustThatYouBeWoundedAn'Gaston BeCaptive. WeGotThereAn'WanderedAboutUntilWeHeardTheScreamin' An'TheShot."

Gaston sighed. "What shot? What happened? All I remember is you saving me and then I realized someone other than you held me."

"An'IDroppedYaRightQuick. YaGrowled."

"I am sorry, Pete," Gaston said.

The Golden One shook his head and shrugged. "IWoulda'If'nItWereMe."

"I shot Doucette. In the shoulder." I looked to Pete. "He was not dead when we left, but Peirrot was there and had him against the wall. Or was I suffering delusions?"

"HeNa'BeDead," Pete snorted, and then grinned. "PeirrotBeat'ImGood Though. ThereBeABigFightInOurWake."

Gaston's eyes had gone hard again. "He will not live to an old age."

Pete nodded. "HeBeYours. ButYa'Canna'Kill'ImWhileWeBeHere. FrenchiesLove'Im. StrikerCanTellYa'More. HeDoneTalkedTa'TheBastard. AnTheMayor. AnPriests." He shook his head with a derisive snort and frowned seriously. "WeNa'SayTheWholeOfItThough. AllO'ThemWantTa KnowWhatIt'sAbout. ButThoseThatKnowStayedQuiet."

My matelot sagged into my shoulder with relief. "Thank you, Pete."

Pete patted his shoulder. "IGoGet...Broth." He smirked.

"Tell me everything," Gaston said when he was gone.

"May I release you first?"

"Non."

"You seem quite reasonable, though a little more taciturn than usual."

He shook his head, and his eyes were sad. "While you slept... I thought I could kill you with my teeth. I thought to crawl over you and free myself with the dirks you left on the floor, as I did when the galleon sank. Then I would escape to the Haiti and recover myself. And then I thought of the horrible things I have done and I wished to die. I thought I could fool you into complacency during the voyage home and throw myself overboard at night. But I am bound and I... clung to that. I wished for you to bind me because I love you. Because you love me. And I know that is a thing of sanity. But then my mind drifts away again, and my thoughts travel some new ugly path. And I pull at my bonds and then I remember that I wished for them. And so on."

I embraced him as tightly as I could manage. "I will not release you."

"When I look in your eyes I know what is real. You are a beacon, and I am lost without you."

"I will be whatever you need me to be, my love. When Doucette told me..."

His eyes narrowed. "What?"

I told him all that Doucette said. Gaston became distraught, and his breathing quickened. I saw the madness light his eyes again. He snarled curses at Doucette and his father for a time, and was thus engaged when Striker entered.

I waved Striker to sit. Then as best I could in the hammock, I took Gaston's face in my hands. "Look at me."

He recoiled with terror. I released him and waited. His eyes were on mine, though.

"I love you," I murmured.

"He made me look," he whispered in French. "He touched me with them."

I cursed my stupidity. "That will not happen again. You are safe here. Come here and let me hold you." He snuggled against me again, burrowing his face in my shoulder.

With a little urging, Gaston rolled with me so that I could lay on my back and regard Striker. He had set two items on the table. One was a small money box with a crest upon it. The other was a leather satchel.

"We have your weapons and bags from the house as well," Striker said.

I smiled. "I was wondering if we would see them again. What are these?"

"Gaston's." He patted the box. "He is a wealthy man. Apparently, Gaston's father has been sending money for his upkeep every year. That bastard Doucette was honest enough to keep it for him. That and money that Gaston was sent here with. Of course, Doucette was receiving a stipend from the father as well, for caring for his son." Striker looked as if he had a great many questions, but he did not ask them.

"How much?" I asked.

"Five hundred Francs a year." He frowned. "To Doucette. He sent Gaston a thousand a year. This chest is full of Florins."

"Holy..."

"I do not want his money," Gaston spat.

"Well, my love, I do not want my title, but you have persuaded me to hold on to the possibility of it while it may be of use. We will do the same with your father's money."

Striker chuckled.

I took my eyes off the chest and regarded him. "So Doucette just gave it to you?"

He shook his head. "Nay, his wife did. Doucette wished to meet with you, or rather Gaston. He wishes to apologize and explain himself. I told him I thought that unwise. So did his wife, partly because of concerns that you might hurt him further, and partly because he is doing poorly in the aftermath of the wound and the beating. He has a great headache, apparently. His words were slurred as if he was drunk when I spoke to him."

"They probably have him drugged." I shrugged.

Gaston frowned. "Or a severe wound to the head."

I shrugged again. "What is in the satchel?"

"She said you may find that of more import," Striker said. "There are apparently French legal papers in here, and a number of letters from Gaston's father."

I sagged deeper into the hammock with a great sigh of relief. Gaston peered across my chest at the satchel with great interest.

"May I ask?" Striker asked diffidently.

"Tell him," Gaston said.

I was not sure how much he meant, so I decided to stick to the particulars. "Gaston's father had him declared unfit to inherit and insane, and remanded him to Doucette's care. Gaston did not know."

Striker swore. Then he peered at us curiously. "May I assume Gaston's father is as noble as yours?"

"You may. They are cut from much the same cloth, after a fashion," I smiled.

"My father scarred me," Gaston said.

I was surprised at his admission. Striker merely nodded and looked at the chest. "It would seem he suffers guilt over it."

"He should not," Gaston said sadly. "I did much to anger him."

"But not..." I sighed as he gave me a baleful look.

He buried his face in my shoulder again. I looked back to Striker. "I understand we cannot kill Doucette. So when do we leave?"

"Nay, he is well loved here and... he has deflected all blame from Gaston; still, many are angry that someone would shoot him in his home. And we have not been willing to explain why to the common crowd. We will leave with the wind at sunrise, unless you have other concerns."

I did not, but I was not sure of Gaston. "We will talk. So we will sail to Port Royal?"

He shrugged. "Not both ships. We want to keep the *Virgin Queen* out of sight until after I have a chance to deliver those emeralds." I raised an eyebrow at the name and he grinned. "The Bard named the brig after Queen Elizabeth. I think it fine, as she was the patroness of the great hero Drake. Yet the Bard said it had a thing to do with her being Shakespeare's patroness, but I know not what he was prattling on about, as he was drunk."

I chuckled. "It has to do with his name." I explained about Francis Bacon.

Striker shook his head. "That clarifies a great deal. So, we wish to sail the *Virgin Queen* west up the coast of Jamaica and careen her there. There are some suitable beaches. I'll deliver the *Mayflower* back to Bradley."

I nodded. "I have no complaints, but we will talk."

Gaston was silent.

Pete arrived with a bowl of something I guessed was broth, and a plate of meat and cheese, and a bottle of wine. My stomach growled at the smell of it. They left us, and I regarded Gaston.

"Untie me," he said quietly. "For now, while you are awake. I would read those letters and feed myself." He wormed around so I could reach his bonds and release him. He rolled back around and embraced me, once his arms were free. I returned it, despite the growing pain in my side from all of the moving about.

"You will have to help me sit," I murmured when at last we acceded that we could not squeeze each other into ourselves through the strength of our arms alone.

He frowned. "I would rather you lay still."

"I would rather I pissed and shat."

With a sigh, he aided me in easing out of the hammock and relieving myself. I was surprised I needed help with the last, but I was far weaker than I had assumed while reclined. He finally sat me in a chair, and I sipped broth and water under his watchful eye. Meanwhile, I watched with longing as he consumed the cheese and meat.

He asked several times if I wished for laudanum, and I refused. I wished to be clear of thought until we were well away from Tortuga.

Once finished with our repast, we opened the chest and regarded its contents for a gold-dazzled time. He was indeed a wealthy man. Once this had seeped through his mind, he closed the lid with a snap, and I regarded the unicorn rampant coat of arms of the House of Sable on its lid. There were wolves in the Dorshire and Marsdale arms. It had much to do with my thinking of the nobility as wolves as a child. I thought the unicorn appropriate for Gaston. I knew not of its applicability to his ancestors.

"Sable," I mused. "Saw-blu. Sand. As Say-bull, it is an animal in English, or the color black."

He frowned as he sorted the packets in the satchel.

"I am ever the animal," he snorted and opened a document to read it.

I puzzled at that. "What was your given name?"

He smoothed the page flat and turned it toward me. I read where he pointed. "Gabriel Dennis Michel David de Sable." It did not explain his animal reference.

"It is not the name I was raised with," he said. "Father stripped me of that." At my curious look he added, "I was Comte de Montren. They called me Renard in school."

"Ah, oui, I can see them calling you a fox."

"And now I am a sable," he sighed distractedly.

"Non, you are a centaur, names are meaningless." I fingered the carved shield on the chest and recalled again the achievements in arms held by my ancestors. "I gather the de Sables were noble."

"These are my great-grandfather's arms. I wonder why my father chose to send it. Perhaps it was lying about, or perhaps he wished for me to remember the rest of my ancestry. I possess nobility of all lines," he sighed wistfully. "My mother was the daughter of a Vicomte, and her mother, the daughter of a Marquis. My great-grandfather was the Comte de Sable. My grandfather impressed the king in a war and was granted the title of Marquis de Tervent, which my father now holds."

Pride had blossomed in his eyes as he spoke. I thought it likely he valued his nobility far more than I.

"Your father may have stripped you of title, but he can not take the blood from your veins. Cannot a Frenchman be noble by birth without a title?"

"Oui... though..." He shook his head and smiled. "It is no matter. I am Gaston the Ghoul, and a centaur and matelot to Lord Will the Fool."

I laughed, as pleased with his jest as I was relieved that he would make it. "What other accolades might one need?" I teased lightly.

He regarded me warmly. "I can think of none at the moment."

"You will always be gentilhomme to me."

"I feel I will always be so in my heart," he said thoughtfully. "Raised by and with wolves as I was, I know not how to conceive of myself as a commoner."

I nodded solemnly and perused the rest of the document bearing his birth name. It was the one Doucette had spoken of. It granted him guardianship of Gaston. It was signed and sealed by the magistrate, and then again by the Marquis de Tervent, who I now knew to be Gaston's father.

"We must remedy this, somehow," I said. "Or you must never set foot on French soil again. I would have Theodore read it, but I would have to translate it for him. Still, we may parse something of interest from it."

He nodded and shrugged. "I will not return to French soil, except to kill Doucette."

"And then this will be but a small matter on your list of concerns." I smiled.

He fingered a single folded sheet before opening it quickly and reading. He passed it to me. It was from Madame Doucette. She wished us well, and apologized sincerely for all that had occurred. Someday I wished to thank her again, but as the next time I saw her we would likely be about to kill her husband, I doubted she would judge me sincere, or kind.

He took up another packet. It appeared to be a letter, and it was addressed to Doucette.

"This is my father's hand," he said with reverence. There were eight of them. He handed the first to me. "Read them, please."

"Aloud?"

"Non, read it and tell me if I wish to."

I did not argue that I could not know that. As my eyes flowed over the rough script, I tried to envision the man who had put pen to page. All I could conceive was an older version of my matelot, and I wondered as to the accuracy of that image. Perhaps Gaston favored his mother. Either way, the letters banished the monster I had conjured when first I learned the identity of the man who had so marred my love.

His father's tone was quite formal to Doucette. He did not know the physician, and occasionally it was apparent he did not wish to know the man. He was thankful someone was watching after his son, and he sent money to insure Gaston's well-being and as payment for Doucette's continued services as guardian. He never addressed the incident directly, or the events related to it, but he expressed great regret and sorrow concerning them. He endeavored time and again to explain that Gaston was mad, and it was a condition as inherited as the title should have been. He did not wish for Gaston to be treated or mistreated in any way. Reading the letters, it was hard to believe the man had beaten his own son within an inch of his life.

I passed each to Gaston as I finished it, and he too read them. We did not discuss their contents. He began to weep by the third letter. When we finished them, he sat quietly and watched the lamp. I watched him.

"I shall write him," he said softly.

"To what end? I am not passing judgment; I am merely curious."

His eyes and tone hardened. "To tell him of Doucette's... betrayal. To tell him I resent being remanded into anyone's custody and I do not want his damn title." The surge of anger passed. "To tell him I forgive him."

I had known he forgave the man, but the breadth of that forgiveness was very clear to me at the moment. "That is noble, and I admire you for it."

He studied me. "I think of what you have told me of your past, and I would not forgive the one who harmed you; yet you can see why I do not blame my father, oui?"

"Oui, I can." I had not thought in terms of meting out forgiveness for my own suffering. I could not conceive of it. I mulled it over. Shane would never receive my forgiveness, as what he had done had been perpetrated with malice; and though I had been party to it, I had not provoked him. And then there was my father.

"I cannot forgive," I sighed.

"Not even yourself?"

I looked at him sharply and found him smiling kindly. I sighed again, and shook my head as I understood his intent.

"I do not know. I still believe you can and should."

"Will, I committed incest and fratricide," he whispered.

I sighed. "Oui, but you did not do it with malice. I do not believe your sister felt sinned against. She was on her death bed, so you did not take her from the world so much as hasten her going. And as she was dying, there would be no issue, no mad, sickly or otherwise enfeebled offspring." I winced at my poor choice of words. He was mad, and his sister had been sickly, and under that argument against incest, one could wonder at the relation of his parents. "You harmed no one and were in turn harmed."

A thin, reluctant smile twitched at his lips. "Will, can I truly do no wrong in your eyes?"

"I would duel Saint Peter for your honor. Yet since neither of us profess to believe the gates of Heaven follow the final night, it is not cause for concern." I cupped his cheek and held his gaze steady. "Forgive yourself."

He captured my hand and kissed my palm. Then he shook his head.

"I do not know how. I think of all the things I have done." He touched my bandages.

"That was an accident."

His eyes slowly returned to mine; and once there, they seemed to gaze into my soul. He found something to his liking in the depths or shallows of my being, and he gave me the ghost of a smile.

"Oui, it was. I never wish to hurt you." He shook his head, but not before I saw panic shadow his eyes.

"What?"

"You cannot trust me when I am mad, Will," he said sadly.

I sighed. He had been doing well for a time there, despite the letters.

"We have paper. Would you write him tonight? We could leave it for someone to post before we sail."

He took a steadying breath and nodded slowly. "I would tell him of you, and that if he must remand me to someone's custody it should be yours."

"If he must, and if he will, I would rather it be me than any other. Though I would rather it not be a necessity at all."

He retrieved paper and pen and began to write, passing the pages off to me as he completed them. The letter was terse and concise. He told his father he had only recently remembered the events of that night, that he forgave him, that he had severed ties to Doucette after the man had tortured him in the name of treatment in disregard of the father's wishes, and that he was with me. Unlike my euphemistic words to my father, Gaston made the depth and nature of our relationship very clear, and he named me by title. Then he told his father how to reach him, in that letters could be sent to Peirrot's French agent here in Cayonne, or to Theodore in Port Royal. He signed it simply, Gabriel.

I dusted and folded the pages, and he addressed the packet. The only seal we had was mine, and so he used that.

Once this task was completed, he ventured from the cabin to give it to someone to take ashore. As he trusted himself on this, I did not worry. Still, I was relieved when he returned a few minutes later.

"Striker said they would have it rowed to the *Josephine*," he said. "I am sure Peirrot will post it for me."

"Now what?"

He packed the other letters away, and stowed the satchel and chest under our hammock next to the medicine chest.

"I am tired," he said when he sat at the table with me again.

"Then sleep. I will watch over you."

"More than sleep can cure, Will. I need to be alone, but I do not wish it. When I have been gripped to this degree before, I have retreated to the woods to clear my mind and find my soul."

He had slipped away to the Haiti. "Then let us go."

He was startled, and then he released a great sigh of relief. "You would go with me?"

"Oui. Try and stop me."

"Non. I would not, but you cannot go where I would in your condition; and perhaps I should not, as it is French territory. And..." He regarded me sadly.

"Do you feel I would hinder the process?"

He nodded. "I must be... human while about you."

I tried to fend off the panic. I was terrified of letting him out of my sight. "Could you retreat in the woods of Jamaica? Perhaps we can go somewhere there, and you could wander about alone as the need grips you, and I could stay by and be there for you."

He considered the table and thought on it, for several excruciating minutes. Then he met my eyes again and smiled.

"Oui. Let us do that."

It was my turn to sigh with relief. "Sleep now. You did not sleep while I did and..."

"You should..."

"I will. But I wish to think for a time, myself."

His eyes narrowed, but he shook it off and smiled anew. "I love you."

"And I you."

He stood and kissed me gently. Then he climbed into the hammock. He dropped into slumber far sooner than I would have thought possible.

I sat and watched him sleep. I could hear the water lapping the hull and the murmur of quiet conversations on the quarterdeck overhead. My side ached dully, but I was loathe to take any laudanum, and Gaston had suggested I drink nothing but good water for a time. I was weary, so that sitting was a difficulty. Yet I watched him sleep and mused on love.

Yvette's short missive had been dated. In about a fortnight, it would be one year since the day I watched Alonso sleep that last time. Irony gripped me. Here I was watching my lover sleep, whilst contemplating the immortal mysteries, whilst on the threshold of escaping a city I was no longer welcome in, and being given traveling money by a whore after fighting a man. There were many differences to be sure, but I found the similarities I discovered in my reverie amusing.

I would watch Gaston grow old and fat. I could not conceive that I would ever be forced to watch him marry. And yet, I was shackled by a sense of responsibility that eclipsed all other brushes I had experienced with such confinement of my whimsy. I wondered what Alonso would think of my acceding to this version of maturity. The Devil with title and family; I now gazed upon a man I would live and die for and, perhaps more importantly, spend my days caring for.

This was the love I had wondered at. This was the stuff of poetry, play, and myth. It was equally transcendent and harrowing. There was no condition that could be placed upon it. It was enduring and conquering. And I had never felt its like before.

Or had I?

I had loved Shane with no condition or boundary. I had been incapable of throwing up walls to protect myself.

The thought was troubling. Yet, like any comparison of this night to that one a year ago, comparing my love of Gaston to my love of Shane was truly more a matter of justification than realization. There was one very crucial difference between the two.

Gaston loved me. Shane never did.

And, of course, Shane was an utter bastard who did not deserve to live; and though my matelot was not an angel, he was worthy of love in ways Shane would never achieve.

And Gaston loved me. Me, above all others. I had never stood so very high.

I eased out of the chair, and gingerly crawled into the hammock.

He shifted and woke at my presence. "You sleep now?"

"Oui."

"Where is the rope?"

I sighed. I had forgotten. "On the floor."

He leaned out and scooped it up. I stopped him as he began to present his back to me.

"Lie as we usually do," I instructed.

He curled beside me, his face admonishing. "Will..."

I put fingers to his lips. He sighed but said nothing. I bound his left wrist to mine.

"This arrangement will do little to protect you," he warned.

"Will it anchor you?"

He nodded sincerely.

"Then it is enough. You will not hurt me."

He shifted until he was more comfortable and kissed my temple. "You are my fool."

"I surely am." I smiled.

I felt the Gods smiling, or perhaps smirking. I was too tired to tell.

End - Volume One

Continued in

Matelots: Raised By Wolves, Volume Two

and

Wolves: Raised By Wolves, Volume Three

Bibliography

The following titles do not represent the entirety of my studies; but they were the most useful, and the ones I would recommend for anyone interested in doing their own reading about the buccaneers and this period of history. To that end, they are ranked in order of usefulness to my research.

Exquemelin, Alexander O., *The Buccaneers of America* (translated by Alexis Brown, 1969), Dover Publications, Inc., 2000. Original publication, Amsterdam, 1678.

Haring, C.H., *The Buccaneers of the West Indies in The XVII Century,* New York: E.P. Hutton, 1910.

Burney, James, *History of the Buccaneers of America,* London: Unit Library, Limited, 1902. First edition, London, 1816.

Burg, B.R., *Sodomy And The Perception of Evil: English Sea Rovers in The Seventeenth- Century Caribbean,* New York: New York University Press, 1983.

Pawson, Michael & David Buisserat, *Port Royal Jamaica,* Jamaica: The University of the West Indies Press, 1974.

Buisserat, David, *Historic Jamaica From The Air,* Jamaica: Ian Randle Publishers, 1996. First edition, 1969.

Marx, Robert F., *Pirate Port: The Story of the Sunken City of Port Royal,* New York: The World Publishing Company, 1967.

Briggs, Peter, *Buccaneer Harbor: The Fabulous History of Port Royal, Jamaica,* New York: Simon And Schuster, 1970.

Dunn, Richard S., *Sugar and Slaves: The Rise of the Planter Class in the English West Indies, 1624-1713,* New York: W.W.Norton & Company, Inc., 1972.

Apestegui, Cruz, *Pirates of the Caribbean: Buccaneers, Privateers, Freebooters and Filibusters 1493-1720,* London: Conway Maritime Press, 2002.

Marrin, Albert, *Terror of the Spanish Main: Sir Henry Morgan and His Buccaneers,* New York: Dutton Children's Books, 1999.

Pyle, Howard, *Howard Pyle's Book of Pirates,* New York: Harper & Row, Publishers, 1921.

Cordingly, David, *Under The Black Flag,* New York: Random House, 1995.

Kongstam, Angus, *The History of Pirates,* Canada: The Lyons Press, 1999.

About the Cover

The illustration used on the cover of this book is a detail of Howard Pyle's *Attack on a Galleon*. The piece was painted in 1907, as part of a series of paintings and illustrations for Howard Pyle's Book of Pirates. The original painting now resides in the Delaware Art Museum.

Howard Pyle is regarded by many as the father of American illustration. There are numerous books and web sites devoted to his work and legacy, so I will not waste words here saying what many others can tell you. I do have this to say, though. Pyle seems to be one of the few illustrators who have ever read Exquemelin or Burney (see bibliography). In his art and writing, he accurately depicts what we know of the buccaneers in terms of dress and tactics. He essentially represents buccaneers, circa 1630-1680, and not romanticized notions from later centuries about "pirates" from the Golden Age of Piracy, 1680-1720. The first time I saw this piece, I knew it had to be the cover of this book.

For more information, please visit
www.alienperspective.com

Printed in the United States
122387LV00003B/52/A